Joy Dettman was born in country Victoria and spent her early years in towns on either side of the Murray River. She is an award-winning writer of short stories, the complete collection of which, *Diamonds in the Mud*, was published in 2007, as well as the highly acclaimed novels *Mallawindy*, *Jacaranda Blue*, *Goose Girl*, *Yesterday's Dust*, *The Seventh Day*, *Henry's Daughter* and *One Sunday*.

Also by Joy Dettman

Mallawindy
Jacaranda Blue
Goose Girl
Yesterday's Dust
The Seventh Day
Henry's Daughter
One Sunday
Diamonds in the Mud

Joy Dettman

PEARL IN A CAGE

MACMILLAN
Pan Macmillan Australia

First published 2009 in Macmillan by Pan Macmillan Australia Pty Limited
1 Market Street, Sydney

Copyright © Joy Dettman 2009

The moral right of the author has been asserted.

All rights reserved. No part of this book may be reproduced or transmitted by any person or entity (including Google, Amazon or similar organisations), in any form or by any means, electronic or mechanical, including photocopying, recording, scanning or by any information storage and retrieval system, without prior permission in writing from the publisher.

National Library of Australia
Cataloguing-in-Publication data:

Dettman, Joy.
Pearl in a cage / Joy Dettman.

9781405039574 (pbk.)

A823.3

The characters and events in this book are fictitious and any resemblance to real persons, living or dead, is purely coincidental.

Typeset in 11.5/13.5 pt Times by Midland Typesetters, Australia
Printed by McPherson's Printing Group

Papers used by Pan Macmillan Australia Pty Ltd are natural, recyclable products made from wood grown in sustainable forests. The manufacturing processes conform to the environmental regulations of the country of origin.

Dedicated to my Mum. She's dancing the Charleston in high heels, singing 'Ramona' – out of tune. She's sweeping up stardust to powder her nose, playing hide and go seek with the moon.

To Don, who read the first draft of Pearl in a Cage *as the pages came hot from my printer, and to Kay Readdy, insightful friend and trusted early reader, I offer my heartfelt thank you.*

BOOK ONE

THE MIDWIFE

Until that December morning Gertrude Foote had found little good to say for Vern Hooper's new motor car. It was noisy, it stunk to high hell, and she'd ridden more comfortably on a camel's back. That morning, she blessed its noise and ran indoors. If he'd come on horseback, he would have caught her head down in a dish of water, rinsing the dye out of her hair. There were things folk needed to know and a lot more they didn't, and that she dyed her hair was one of the latter.

There was little vanity in Gertrude. The dyeing of her hair wasn't about vanity; it was a means of keeping old age at bay, that's all, and so far it seemed to be working.

She had a lot of hair; it took a lot of rinsing, more than could be done in one dish of water, but with no time now to do more, she grabbed a towel and got it wrapped on turban fashion. She emptied that telltale rinsing water around the roots of her climbing rose, propped the tin dish upside down on her tank stand and before the car came puttering and spluttering into her yard, she was waiting for him behind her chicken-wire gate. It wasn't much of a gate — tall enough to keep her chooks away from the house and garden, though offering minimal protection should that motor car turn feral. But he got the thing stopped and she opened her gate.

'You put my chooks off the lay for a week every time you bring that thing down here,' she said. 'What's wrong with your horse?'

'He's out at the farm and I'm in here.'

Vern Hooper unfolded his lanky frame from behind the steering wheel. There was a good six foot five of him to unfold, plus a thatch of wiry steel grey hair to offer a few extra inches. Apart from his eyes, lost years ago in the creases of a farmer's permanent squint, his features were of a size to suit his build — big nose, big ears, long jaw. By no stretch of the imagination could Vern be called a good-looking man.

'Cecelia Morrison just dropped dead,' he said. 'Ogden wants you, Trude.'

'I've got an alibi,' she said, and was rewarded with a grin. There was something about Vern's grin, sort of shy, a little lopsided, something about it that made his face look just about right to Gertrude.

'Guilty by intent?' he said.

'Could be too. What happened to her, Vern?'

'Something very sudden.'

'I'm halfway through washing my hair . . .'

'Finish it,' he said. 'I've got nothing better to do.'

Christmas was over, the New Year not yet born, and as far as Vern was concerned, those few days between the two just wasted time. Six years ago he'd wed a widow with a modern sawmill and a nice house in town. She was no farmer's wife. He'd put a manager in on his farm and moved into town to learn what he could about her sawmill.

There was money in Woody Creek timber; there always had been, though it was hard fought for until a few years back. Three big modern mills, to the north, west and east of the town, had changed all that. Six days a week folk lived with the constant shrieking howl of the big saws, the constant stream of bullockies hauling logs in from the bush, of drays hauling cut timber up to the railway yards.

There was a shocked, lost feeling to the town when the mills shut down over Christmas, a lonely, waiting feeling, which Vern shared. His wife didn't enjoy having him underfoot. His housekeeper didn't enjoy him poking around in her kitchen. He'd been roaming, looking for something to do, and now that something had happened.

He followed Gertrude into her house, which was only a house by reputation. Rough-built fifty years ago, it was a two-roomed hut, its front door opening onto a clutter of kitchen table, chairs, stove, cane couch, washstand, dresser, big old Coolgardie safe and no room to swing a cat — if she'd had one to swing.

'What time did it happen, Vern?'

'Your daughter found her around ten . . . in the dunny.'

'No.'

'Fact.'

'No.'

'As true as I'm standing here. She told Ogden she hadn't sighted her mother-in-law since breakfast and thought she must have been lying down. She said she went down to the dunny and there she was, skirt up, bloomers down.'

'Oh my God! What a place to breathe your last breath . . .'

'Yeah, but as Moe Kelly said when he saw her sitting there, it's sort of poetic justice.'

Maybe it was. Cecelia Morrison was an overweight, overbearing bugger of a city dame who'd suffered from a severe case of delusions of grandeur. She and her stationmaster son, Norman, had moved up to Woody Creek eight years ago, and two years after that, Amber, Gertrude's only daughter, had wed Norman.

'Amber must have got a shock.'

'She's running the show. Norman, being Norman, is . . . being Norman,' Vern said, and no more needed to be said.

That marriage had been a recipe for disaster, even without a live-in mother-in-law. Gertrude had tried to talk some sense into that girl, but trying to stop Amber from doing anything she'd set her mind on doing was like bullfighting with a handkerchief for a cape.

A heavy brown curtain hung at a gap midway down the western wall of the kitchen. Gertrude lifted it and disappeared into her second room, as long, near as narrow, more cluttered than its mate and offering less light. The head of her double bed was against the southern wall, her dressing table squeezed in beside it. She had two unmatched wardrobes set along the western wall, and crates, trunks, boxes, piles of newspapers and sundry filling the northern end. It was an unholy mess she kept promising herself she'd clean up one fine day, but she had a fifteen-acre property to run and on fine days she was busy — and on the other days she was just as busy. For the past twenty-odd years she'd delivered most babes born in Woody Creek, then stitched them up a few years later, set the limbs of a few. Always someone at her door wanting something, always more pressing things to be done than housework. Anyway, her mess was familiar and as long as she moved nothing around, she could put her hands quickly on whatever she needed.

She removed her turban, tossed the stained towel over the foot of her bed, found a comb amid the general clutter on her dressing table and proceeded to do what she could with two foot of copper-brown hair. Without fail, she gave her hair a hot olive oil treatment once the dye was rinsed out. No time for that this morning. Maybe tonight.

A centre part and she combed it over her ears, pinned it so it would stay there, then plaited what was left, coiled it and reached for a pair of ivory pins, bought in Japan thirty years ago. They held the plait in place, the pins crossed like a pair of knitting needles, which didn't sit well with her working trousers and boots, but folk were accustomed to the way she dressed — or most of them were.

She peered into a mottled looking glass, shrugged, then as a concession to her daughter, or her daughter's dead mother-in-law, she swapped her faded shirt for another, swapped her working boots for light Indian sandals, then returned to the kitchen.

A tall woman, she hadn't put on more than a pound in the past thirty years. Height and slimness ran in the Hooper family. Gertrude and Vern were cousins, or half-cousins. There was something of the Hooper line in the strong bone structure of her face, though she'd avoided the large features. Her mother had sworn that one of her forefathers was a Spanish pirate who'd captured his wife from Tahiti. There could have been some fact in that tale; Gertrude had the dark eyes and olive complexion; they gave lie to her fifty-four years, most of which she'd spent out of doors working like a navvy.

Vern watched her walk to the bottom end of the kitchen where she leaned down and spoke to someone he hadn't known was there.

'I have to go into town for a while, love. We'll get you comfortable before I go.'

Vern squinted to gain a better view. Still seeing nothing, he walked down to where a ten- or twelve-year-old darkie was lying on a mattress against the back wall, half-hidden by a chest of drawers.

'You're at it again, you flamin' halfwit!' he said.

'I brought her in the day before Christmas and didn't give her a snowflake's chance in hell, but you're coming good, aren't you, love?'

The kid didn't look too good to Vern — she looked to be made of matchsticks, and one had snapped. There was a splint on her left leg.

'She's not one of old Wadi's,' he said.

'I doubt it. He's got two new women out there with him now.'

'Where's he got them?'

'About eight mile out. They're in that old trapper's hut. Mini, the one who came in looking for me, is one of the mission girls.'

'Why didn't she go to them?'

'Wadi done like mission,' Gertrude said, doing a fair impression of Mini's accent.

Old Wadi, a half-breed black who had inherited the worst of both races, had been hanging around Woody Creek's perimeter for years, helping himself to what he needed at the time, be it mutton, beef or girls from the mission.

'You'll get folks' backs up again, encouraging him into town.'

'I'm not in town, and when did you know me to give a tinker's curse what the good folk of Woody Creek have to say about me?'

'Not often.' He grinned.

He watched her carry that kid out to the lavatory and back in, watched her wash a pair of narrow little hands not a lot darker than her own.

'She's light-skinned,' he said as she placed the girl back on her mattress.

'She's damn near white. Those mission folk need their backsides kicked for leaving kids like that out there,' Gertrude said, cutting bread, spreading it with treacle and dripping, filling a mug with goat's milk then stirring in a heaped spoonful of sugar. 'I counted six kids and they all looked half-starved.'

She offered the bread and milk to the girl. 'You drink the lot now. You eat every crumb.'

Wood poked into the firebox, its door closed with a slam, the flue closed, kettle moved to the hob, and she reached for a black wide-brimmed felt hat she'd owned ten years or more, not a feminine hat, and well worn.

'If we're going, we'd better get going,' she said.

It wasn't the first time she'd ridden in Vern's car, though she still didn't trust it. It stank of petroleum, and the knowledge that she was sitting on a tank full of stuff likely to explode didn't instil her with confidence. It saved the saddling of her horse, and that's about all she'd say for motoring, except that it got her the two miles into town in the time it would have taken her to bring Nugget down from his paddock.

Amber was in the kitchen with Ernie Ogden, the local constable, a stocky, freckle-faced bloke in his late forties, a likable bloke who Gertrude had known long enough, had had dealings enough with, to call by name. Norman and Moe Kelly, the undertaker, were in the parlour, a wall away from where the mound of poor old Cecelia Morrison lay on her bed, covered by a sheet Gertrude had no desire to lift. She'd spent the past four years dodging that woman when she could.

Ogden lifted the sheet. 'Constipation can bring on a stroke,' he said. 'I've seen them go like that before.'

'A normal-sized heart in that sized body can't be expected to keep on pumping, Ernie.'

'She was sixty — so your daughter says. She must have had Norman young,' Ogden said.

'He's not forty yet.'

'Is that right! I would have thought he was my age. So, what do we write down?'

'Heart stroke,' she said. 'Cover both options.'

A doctor may have made a more accurate diagnosis. If they were prepared to put him up for the night, they could bring one in on the train. In an emergency, if the emergency wasn't too acute, they took the injured party down to Willama, thirty-nine miles of rutted road away. There were three doctors and a hospital down there. Gertrude handled the minor emergencies.

'It is not an option, Mr Kelly!'

Norman was a wall away but there was no mistaking his voice. He didn't sound like Woody Creek, didn't sound like a stationmaster either; he might have made a good parson. Gertrude flipped the sheet back into place while Ogden opened the door. He wasn't above eavesdropping. Nor was Gertrude. They stood side by side listening.

Cecelia's demise had traumatised her son; the place in which she'd chosen to do it had embarrassed him; the weight of responsibilities fallen to his rounded shoulders confused him.

His mother had not encouraged him to make decisions. He'd grown to adulthood doing what she'd told him he should do. Moe Kelly was now telling him what he should do, but it was not what his mother would have wanted him to do. This much he knew.

The shock of seeing her so seated, the stress of the past hour, the brandy Amber had poured for him, had drained his strength — and drained it straight into his bladder. Desperate to urinate, but unable to consider returning to the place from which they had so recently removed his mother, Norman's mind was in turmoil.

'All I'm saying, Mr Morrison, is we'll peak at around a hundred today and tomorrow will be hotter. We have to bring a bit of logic to this.'

Moe Kelly's voice was nasal — too many years of taking sawdust up the nose. It was hard to tell if he was male or female by his voice. He had the height of a woman, hair a woman might have killed for, a deep auburn, thick and wavy, but the muscle and sinew of a man. He could saw and hammer from dawn to dusk, then take his wife out to a ball and dance her off her feet.

'As you are aware, Mr Kelly, there is no train until Monday evening.'

'Forget your trains for a minute, Mr Morrison. What I'm trying to tell you decently here is that a woman of your mother's size can't wait until tomorrow, let alone Monday.'

Norman grasped the mantelpiece for support as his blood drained down to his ankles, threatening to release his bladder on the way. He'd been an unattractive child who had grown into an ugly man. Now in his fortieth year, the family curse of fat settling on him, his face was being absorbed, his small features forced into its centre. When he'd possessed hair, when he'd stood shoulders straight, head high, he'd brushed the six foot marker, but his hair was gone, his shoulders, permanently rounded; they had rounded more since seeing his mother slumped against the lavatory wall. He was much smaller now. He felt smaller than Moe.

'You must understand, Mr Kelly, Mother's relatives are spread far and wide. Her senior sister lives on a vast property in central New South Wales, her senior brother resides in Portsea. There is another in western Victoria. The Reverend Duckworth's parish is, I believe, a good hour from the city.'

'Duckworth?' Moe asked.

'Mother was a Duckworth. Her brother, the youngest of the family, will wish to read the service.'

Moe released a nasal sigh. 'Then what I'd suggest, Mr Morrison, is that you get in contact with your Reverend Duckworth and you explain to him that we've got none of the city's fancy storage facilities up here. He'll no doubt advise you to move things along.'

'It will be done on Tuesday, with dignity, Mr Kelly,' Norman said. 'With dignity.'

'It's your funeral,' Moe said, and he took off out the front door mouthing 'Duckworth'.

Norman made a beeline for the back door, along the verandah and out to a tall wooden gate in his eastern side fence, which gave him access to the railway yard and to the station's tin-shed lavatory. He ran the last fifty yards.

Gertrude and Ogden watched him go. Cecelia's bedroom window looked east.

'He's not going to make her wait until Tuesday, is he?' Ogden said.

'It won't be done with much dignity if he does,' Gertrude said.

They closed the door on their way out. Ernie returned to the kitchen to have another word with Amber, while Gertrude had a look around Cecelia's parlour — while she wasn't in it.

There was a display of peacock feathers used to screen the fireplace. Beautiful things set in a large blue-green vase. It, and the feathers, matched the heavy window drapes. It was a fancy room, or the furniture was fancy, designed for better than a railway house — as was Cecelia. The house, built by the railway department to a proven design, looked like a thousand others. Passage leading from front door to rear, giving access to six rooms: the main bedroom, bathroom and kitchen on the west side; the parlour, Cecelia's bedroom and the nursery on the east side. It had verandahs front and back. Gertrude coveted its verandahs, but she wouldn't have given a brass farthing for the kitchen. It was a good size, but with the stove always burning and windows on both north and west walls, it was hellishly hot during the summer months.

Ogden left via the rear door. Gertrude waved goodbye then took his place in the kitchen where Amber stood at the north window, looking for Norman.

'How are you feeling, darlin'?' Gertrude said.

'How should I be feeling?' Amber replied. She was in the eighth month of her third pregnancy. Her firstborn, a girl, named for old Cecelia, was near school age; her last born, a son, Clarence, had died at birth.

'Vern said you found her.'

'I didn't know she was dead. I thought she'd passed out,' Amber said, placing bread on the table, a wedge of cheese, a little butter melting in a butter dish. She glanced again through the window.

'I tried to rouse her, then yelled for Norman. He knew she was dead. He went red. He went white. He started shaking like a jelly. I had to run over and get Ogden.' She set two cups on the table.

Gertrude, eager for crumbs, sat down to listen. Amber was more talkative than usual, or for once had something to talk about. Her eyes were brighter, her face more animated. She wasn't mourning her mother-in-law.

There were few in town who would, which may have been why Norman was determined to bring his relatives up here. There was nothing more lonely than a funeral no one attended.

'He's been over to the station lavatory,' Amber said, taking down an extra cup, pouring three cups of tea. In the past four years Gertrude could count on one hand the times she'd been offered tea in Norman's house.

He was surprised to see her in his kitchen. He stood in the doorway eyeing her — or eyeing his mother's chair, which she'd had the temerity to sit on.

She nodded her greeting while searching for words she might say. Gertrude wasn't often lost for something to say. 'A sad time for you, Norman.'

He nodded.

Accustomed to seeing him wearing spectacles, she stared at a face that looked unclothed — his eyes caught with their pants down. They were the big sad eyes of a bloodhound, one who had misplaced his mistress and couldn't sniff out her trail. Gertrude felt what might have been a wash of pity for her son-in-law. He was chinless, jawless, his cheeks melting into jowls; his snub nose, set too close to his upper lip, looked lost in the bulk of his face. About the only positive thing Gertrude had ever had to say about Norman Morrison was he didn't look like his beak-nosed mother — though she'd had more character in her face.

She glanced at Amber, and for the umpteen-dozenth time wondered what that girl had ever seen in him. Amber had been cut from a fine fabric, which may not wear well but was too pretty to pass by without a second glance. She'd never reached her mother's height, had never reached higher than five foot five. She had the build of her father's family, had taken after them in colouring too. She had their curly hair, blonde once, still blonde where the sun bleached it, but darkening at the root.

'Are you eating today, Norman?' Amber called.

He'd disappeared into the bathroom, a small room a wall away from the kitchen. They could hear him in there, but he didn't reply.

'Where's the little one?' Gertrude never used her granddaughter's given name. She called her little one, Sissy, pet, darlin', anything bar Cecelia. Loathed that name — or the woman who had previously worn it had given her an allergy to it.

'She's over the road with Maisy. I can't have her here while...' Amber nodded across the passage to Cecelia's room.

Maisy, Amber's friend since kindergarten, had wed George Macdonald, a mill owner twice her age. She'd given him a baby a year and he'd given her everything that opened and shut. At times, Gertrude blamed Maisy for introducing Amber to Norman. At times, Maisy blamed herself for the same thing.

'Did Moe say when he'd be moving her?' Gertrude asked.

The dead usually spent a night in Moe Kelly's cellar, which would be degrees cooler than this house.

'It took four of them to get her out of the lav and up here. It'll take more to get her down Moe's cellar steps,' Amber said. She sat opposite her mother. 'Eat,' she said. 'I've cut the bread. Someone may as well eat it. Norman!' she yelled.

Gertrude helped herself to a slice. She baked her own bread. It was of a more solid construction than the baker's loaves, filled up more space in the belly, but she never said no to a slice of the baker's bread.

'How many rooms have they got over at the hotel, Mum?'

'Six or more, and they've got those sleep-outs the family use in summer,' Gertrude replied, mouth full.

'I don't know where he thinks we're going to fit everyone.'

'He's not expecting all of them to come up here, is he?'

'They'd travel a week to watch a Duckworth dog fight,' Amber said.

'The town won't see anyone go short of a —' Gertrude closed her mouth as Norman returned to the doorway.

13

'Have you seen my spectacles, Amber?'

'You took them off before you tried to lift her,' she said. He flinched, requiring no reminder of that awful moment. 'Did you look on the shelf down there?'

He glanced in the direction of *down there*, but didn't want to go there, so he stood on in the doorway, lost, lonely, his eyes indecently exposed.

'How many of your folk are likely to make the trip?' Gertrude said.

'Two have passed,' he said.

'Three now,' Amber said. 'Which leaves twelve. Three unmarried. Nine couples, not counting his cousins — and there's umpteen of them.'

'Where did your mum fit in?'

He turned to run, aware that he and his mother had never fitted anywhere, then the meaning of Gertrude's question became apparent. His jowls trembled as he lifted his chin. 'She was the eighth born,' he said. 'The middle man, and not one lost in childhood.'

He flinched again, his eyes daring a glance at the bulge beneath Amber's apron, then he was away, down the gravelled path to the lavatory near hidden by shrubbery at the bottom of the garden. His world a blur without his spectacles, his bladder could not force him back to that place; his need to see could.

Gertrude was eating a second slice of baker's bread when Moe Kelly, Ogden, Vern and George Macdonald arrived to move Cecelia to Moe's cellar. It took time — time enough for the dishes to be washed, the table cleared, time enough for Maisy to bring Sissy home screaming blue murder. Sissy hadn't appreciated her forced removal from her mother.

Gertrude left them to it and walked out front, hoping to catch Vern on his way home. Her main concern when she'd driven in this morning had been for Amber, but her daughter was sitting in the parlour now, relating her morning to her friend. Gertrude's afternoon would be better spent in giving her hair a hot olive oil treatment then a damn good wash. Every hair on her head felt as if it was trying to crawl away.

THE RELATIVES

Cecelia Morrison died on a stinking hot Friday, and, as Moe Kelly had warned, Saturday was worse. He and the local ice man spent much of the morning carrying block after block of ice down to the cellar, packing them under her and around her. Something had to be done.

Then, around noon, a north wind gathering up dust from distant deserts hit the town, turning the sky red, the sun glowering through it like the eye of evil. Moe had nothing against a bit of heat, though he could do without the dust. Stripped to the waist, sweat running, he was in his work shed preparing timber for Cecelia Morrison's coffin.

He was a fine hand with wood. He could knock together a utilitarian cupboard or craft a fancy table, and he was known for his rocking chairs. He could turn out a good-looking coffin too when he put his mind to it, though he didn't appreciate his labour going underground.

The sun was thinking of setting, the coffin taking shape, when Horrie Bull, the publican, and one of the wood cutters carried Horrie's best customer into Moe's shed feet first. Old Willy Duffy, father of Betty, living on borrowed time and donated grog for the past fifteen years, had succumbed with an empty glass in his hand. Fate was putting the boot into Cecelia Morrison née Duckworth. Died in a dunny, wrapped in a canvas shroud, packed in ice, and now sharing her quarters with a man who'd been a stranger to soap and water since birth.

Moe didn't waste a lot of time on old Willy. He dropped him into a pine box and hammered the lid down, aware he was donating that box, just as the grave diggers would be donating their labour to dig that thieving old coot's hole. The Duffy family was not known for the paying of bills.

They got Willy in the ground at eight on Sunday morning, dust swirling, more dogs than mourners in attendance, and by ten Moe was back in his shed, screwing fancy handles onto a fancy coffin he'd make Norman Morrison pay for dearly.

A busy day that dusty Sunday jammed in between Christmas and New Year of 1923. At the hotel, Horrie Bull and his wife were running around like chooks with their heads cut off, preparing rooms. At Vern Hooper's house, the housekeeper was airing beds while the telegram boy spent his day running backwards and forwards between post office and Norman's house. He didn't have far to go. The buildings were separated by a paling fence.

Amber had aired Cecelia's vacated room and made up her bed with clean sheets. It wasn't as if she'd died in it. She changed the sheets in the nursery, cooked cakes and biscuits, tidied her cupboards, swept and polished the floors, dusted the furniture again while Sissy followed in her wake demanding attention.

'Norman! Will you get her out from under my feet for five minutes? I've got things to do.'

As had Norman. He was up to his elbows in paper, matching names to available beds. To date he had thirty-three replies to the affirmative and only twenty-six beds.

'Come, Cecelia,' he said. The girl didn't come. 'Look at your book, Cecelia,' he said. She didn't look at her book. 'We will have to accept the Bryants' offer, Amber,' he said.

'What's wrong with the Bryants?'

'Distance from town.'

He chose a clean page and began again.

Bryant: Bess and John. Wilber and Millicent.
Hooper: Olive and Frederick, Louise and Martin. Bernice and Victoria.
White: Viv, Grace and Lorris.

The list grew longer while the temperature rose. At three he received a telegram from his Box Hill cousins. All three were coming, thankfully without their wives. Not that Norman had anything against their wives. Finding beds enough was the major concern.

At four o'clock, Paul Jenner, one of the out-of-town farmers, rode into town to get Gertrude. His wife had gone into labour two weeks before her time. It was her first, and could take all night in coming. There was no gain in telling him that though, not when his wife was screaming in pain. Gertrude fed her chooks early, milked her goats, set milk, water and biscuits within reach of little Elsie, saddled her horse, tied a wet handkerchief over her nose and mouth bandit fashion, and by five she was on her way to Jenner's, a good three miles out along Cemetery Road. Two hours before dawn, while wind near picked up and shook that house, she delivered a poor wee boy with a withered foot.

'The blood supply has been cut off by the cord,' she said. 'It's stopped its growth.'

'It'll be getting through now though, won't it?' the new father said.

Maybe it would.

'It could do just that, love,' Gertrude said, knowing she was giving false hope, but knowing too that at such times she had nothing else to offer. 'The doctors in Melbourne might be able to do something — if it doesn't improve by itself. Those chaps can do some remarkable things nowadays.'

She stayed with them until there was light enough for her horse to see where he was going. He took her home, where she got his saddle off, got her boots off, then fell face down across her bed. Near midday, she awakened, her goats unmilked, her chooks unfed, her garden unwatered.

Two o'clock: Woody Creek frying beneath a blazing sun and a crow fell dead from the currajong tree growing in the railway station yard. The kids playing beneath the tree tried feeding it water, and when they couldn't raise it from the dead, they dug a grave with sticks and had their own funeral service.

At three, a bunch of older boys playing on the stacked timber behind Macdonald's mill found a snake with two heads, both ready to strike. They killed it then carried it around town, displaying it at front doors for a penny. Some paid. They got a better look than the ones who didn't. Moe paid up, grateful for that snake. It had cleared the kids away from his cellar window. A dead body sleeping on melting ice couldn't compete with a two-headed snake.

Seven fifteen: the sun setting behind Charlie White's grocery shop; Moe Kelly sitting at his kitchen table totalling up the cost of fancy handles, timber, labour and ice; Norman pacing his station platform perusing his latest list, the two-headed snake hung out to stink and dry on the railway yard's fence, little Cecelia asleep in her parents' bed, and the train announced its coming with three elongated hoots.

Amber removed her apron, slid her arms into a loose-fitting smock, forced her feet into shoes, combed her sweat-soaked curls, then walked out the side gate and the fifty-odd yards to the station in time to see the first Duckworth step down to the platform.

They kept on stepping down, from the first and the second-class carriages. Aunt Louise, Cousin Ottie, Aunty Milly and Uncle Wilber, Uncle Charles the parson, his wife Jane and son Reginald, Uncle someone, Aunty Bessie . . . A babble of Duckworths. A scream of them. A smack of air kisses, of roving greedy eyes measuring girths on those unseen since the last wedding, the last funeral. They were too much. They were too many.

The in-laws were leaner, less vocal. They stepped to the side, stepped back, found walls to get their backs against. Amber got her back to a wall, got her hands protectively across her stomach.

Horrie Bull, armed with the hotel's trolley, came up the platform, fearing his next few days but mentally totalling up the money. His first approach was to the in-laws, who in turn approached their partners, but Duckworths had a way of discounting others when surrounded by their own.

Conversations unfinished on the train must be finished, sisters unseen in twelve months must be told twelve months of news. Now. Not later.

'Just make sure I'm at the same hotel as Louise, I said.'

'Tell them we need a room adjacent to the bathroom,' Louise said.

They didn't know what they were in for — nor did Woody Creek.

The sheer bulk of Duckworths overwhelmed Norman's little station; for ten minutes, the sorting out of them, the finding of and identifying of luggage, overwhelmed Norman. But he was a methodical man when armed with his lists. He sorted his relatives. He separated them. The three male cousins, late inclusions, initially allocated to the hotel, were scratched out and reallocated to Maisy and George Macdonald; Louise and husband reallocated to the hotel. Vern and Joanne Hooper had a large house — they took two couples, plus two female cousins. Lonnie and Nancy Bryant, who owned land four miles west of town, had plenty of spare, if worn, bedrooms. Norman allocated them two pairs, plus his unwed Portsea uncle. Charlie and Jean White took two singles. Parson Charles and wife Jane had been allocated Cecelia's vacated bed; their unwed son, Reginald, was to have bedded down in the nursery — until Norman sighted Aunty Lizzie, his maiden aunt, who had taken it into her head this morning to make the trip without her maiden sister. He scratched out *Reginald*, wrote in *Lizzie*, then scribbled *parlour couch* beside Reginald's name. He was young. He could tolerate the discomfort.

Horrie Bull took the rest. He and his trolley led them via a diagonal short cut, down a narrow path between tall dry grass, around a peppercorn tree and over a road to his hotel. Vern's youngest daughter, Margaret, led the Hoopers' guests down the same track, then continued on to Vern's house, while Vern loaded five into his car and delivered them out to the Bryants' farm.

By eight o'clock, the town had absorbed, or been absorbed by, Norman's relatives. By nine, they were fed; by eleven, all bar the three Box Hill cousins were in their beds. The cousins were playing poker in George Macdonald's kitchen and telling tales out of school — about Norman.

Nancy Bryant, three months past her sixtieth birthday, had washed the last of her guests' dishes and reset her dining room for the onslaught of breakfast. She was emptying the dishwater onto her herb garden when she heard what sounded like an infant's cry. Surely a night bird, though no bird she'd heard before in the near forty years she'd lived on this land. A feral cat perhaps. Unconvinced, she walked deeper into the yard.

A country night is dark when the moon is hiding. Unable to see a foot in front of her, she returned to her enclosed porch for the lantern Lonnie had left burning there for his guests' convenience.

Chains rattled. The dogs were disturbed by that late light and by the scent of strangers, and as Nancy walked by their shed, old Boss-dog asked his low question.

'Go to bed,' she said, eager to go to her own.

And she heard it again, louder this time, or louder because she was nearer. She'd borne seven children, was grandmother to twelve; she could recognise a baby's cry when she heard it.

She walked to the house fence where she swung her lantern, signalling to whoever was out there. 'Hello,' she called. 'Hello out there?'

No reply, and if she kept this up she'd disturb her guests, who had been sufficiently disturbed tonight when one of them had wanted a bath and been offered a small basin of precious tank water. She and Lonnie had done their best to make them comfortable but would be pleased to see their backs come morning. Family was one thing; they'd put up with what they got. Guests were something else.

She yawned, turned back to the house and took two steps towards her bed. And there it was again, that tremulous wail of the newborn. There was someone out there, and she'd find them too — or old Boss-dog would.

The lantern lighting its small circle, she walked across to the shed where five dogs were chained each night. Boss-dog was her mate, fifteen if he was a day, a kelpie/border collie cross and no smarter dog ever whelped. Folk laughed when she told them he understood every word she said. Well, let them laugh. She knew what she knew.

'Where's the baby?' she said. 'Go find the baby.' She released him from the chain and the old dog, unaccustomed to attention at midnight, wriggled for more. 'Where's the baby? Go find the baby.'

The grandkids played hide and seek with him. He knew the game, and if his eyesight wasn't as good as it used to be, his hearing not so sharp, there was nothing wrong with his scenting ability. He laughed at her, got in the last lick, then ran to the house-fence gate.

There was a time when he would have been up and over the gate without breaking his stride. Tonight he allowed her to open it. Then he was off, scouting the north paddock. She followed with her lantern, her eyes not much use outside its circle of light, her ears compensating.

There were sheep in the far corner of the paddock. She heard a few sheepish complaints. Seconds later Boss-dog reported in.

'It's out there somewhere, boy. Go find the baby.' He circled, seeking direction. She had none to give. 'Go.' She waved her arm in the general direction of the railway line and he took off again into the night.

Try following a black dog across a paddock on a moonless night, she thought. It couldn't be done.

And she heard it again, not much more than a weary protest, but a baby's protest and close by. Boss-dog heard it — and found it. He was calling her with his 'over here' yelp and she ran, her lantern lighting her feet, ran to the boundary fence.

He was on the other side, in the scrubby gully beside the built-up railway line. She placed the lantern down and climbed between the wires. Her face at dog level was an opportunity too good to miss. Boss-dog stole a kiss then ran laughing back to his find.

It wasn't a baby. He'd found a woman lying face down. A black-clad, black-headed woman.

'Are you all right, dear?' She patted her shoulder, shook it. 'Are you hurt, dear?'

There was no response, or none from the woman.

'God in heaven,' she gasped as a newborn grunted at her elbow. It was entangled in the woman's clothing.

'Lonnie,' she screamed. 'Lonnie!'

The house was too far away and Lonnie's hearing worse than Boss-dog's.

'Go home,' she said. 'Get Lonnie. Lonnie. Home, boy. Go wake Lonnie.'

Boss-dog took off across the paddock to do her bidding.

One dog barking will set off the rest. The Bryants had five. Their chorus raised Lonnie and four of the five relatives.

Until their dying days, those four would relate the tale of their night spent as guests of Lonnie and Nancy Bryant. The beds were old, the facilities archaic, the food heavy, the water rationed, and when Bessie found her way out of the rabbit warren of passages to ask if someone could please shut those dogs up, she found her hostess cutting an infant's cord, with a kitchen knife — on the kitchen table.

'Good God, woman!'

Until her dying day, Bessie Watson, née Duckworth, would tell how she'd thought that woman had been getting a head start on her guests' breakfasts.

One of the male in-laws helped Lonnie carry the woman across two paddocks and lift her into the rear of the Bryants' fancy gig. He assisted Nancy up to the seat, the baby held in her arms. All four relatives watched the lantern strapped to one of the cart's shafts, then watched that meagre light fade off into the dark, while the dogs, aware their masters had left them in charge, took charge, determined to rid the property of the scent of stranger. Duckworths were loud, but not as loud as five barking dogs.

'It's bedlam,' Bessie yelled. 'How are we supposed to sleep?'

'How far out are we?' Milly wailed.

'Miles.'

Only four miles, or four and a bit, and once out on the road it didn't take long to get to town. The Bryants crossed over the bridge, considered turning left and down the forest road to Gertrude; considered waking Vern Hooper, who might drive that woman down to Willama; instead, they headed into town to rouse the constable.

Ernie Ogden had great faith in Gertrude's doctoring skills. He fetched his bike, lit his lantern, then rode before them through a mile of strung-out town and out along that dark bush road, not for the first time wishing Gertrude lived a bit closer in.

No dog to give warning of their approach, she was sleeping soundly when Ernie knocked on her wall.

She came towards his light, white-gowned, her long hair hanging. No need to ask who wanted her. Lonnie was behind Ogden, the woman in his arms, Nancy behind him, hugging a towel-wrapped infant to her breast.

No room to put anything, anyone, down in Gertrude's kitchen. She moved her lamp to the dresser, flung a blanket over the table, then Lonnie eased the woman down, the old table five and a half foot in length, was just long enough.

'Who is she?'

'Nancy found her in the gully beside the railway line —'

'Boss-dog found her.'

'We thought she could have been one of Monk's mission girls. He's got a couple of them working out there.'

'She looks more Italian to me. Jenner's got a couple of families of them out at his place,' Ernie said.

'How's she going to get from his place out to ours?' Lonnie said.

'She wouldn't have, not wearing that shoe,' Gertrude said. The stranger's right foot was shod, her left wasn't. She removed the shoe, looked at its two-inch heel. 'City,' she said. 'Light that lamp for me, Ernie.'

Ernie lit it, set it on the washstand, placed his hurricane lantern on the stove hob and turned the wick high. Strange tall shadows playing on wall and ceiling, three shadows standing still, Gertrude's ever moving.

23

'No way of knowing how much blood she lost?' Two shadows shook their head. 'No one else around? How far from the road? She's no tobacco grower's wife,' she said. The coat now off, a blood-soaked gold frock was exposed; a fancy thing, its yoke encrusted with beadwork. 'She's dressed for travelling.'

'Lost a lot of blood by the look of it,' Ernie said.

'Births are bloody,' Gertrude said, bundling the coat and pitching it through her open doorway. The men followed it outside as Gertrude reached for her scissors to cut the frock away.

'Girl or boy?' she asked, nodding towards the baby, now lying on her cane couch grunting.

'Girl,' Nancy said. 'It's such a pity to cut that frock, Mrs Foote. Blood will usually wash out.'

They got it off intact. It followed the coat out the door. They bathed the woman, removed her stockings, bound her gashed knee. Apart from a few scrapes, it appeared to be the woman's only injury. They clad her in one of Gertrude's nightgowns, then called the men in to lift her onto the couch.

Gertrude turned to the baby. She was a fragile little mite, but determined enough to make herself heard. By two, she was sleeping in a makeshift crib, the kettle had boiled and Nancy was pouring tea. They sat then, four sets of eyes watching that stranger, waiting for her to come around and tell them who she was.

'She must have seen our light and tried to cut across the railway line towards it,' Lonnie said. 'The line's built up high at the spot.'

'What is a woman in her condition doing walking around in the dark?' Ogden said.

'Fell off the train?' Gertrude said.

'No one opens the doors of a moving train.'

Then they heard her breathing stop, or heard her sigh out a breath and not bother to draw another.

'No! Don't you go doing that!'

But she'd done it. She was gone and nothing Gertrude could do about it. She walked outside and Nancy wept.

THE STRANGER

The Bryants went home to their guests, Ernie went home to get an hour or two of sleep. Gertrude walked. She'd slept well before they'd come knocking and there was no sleep left in her.

The wind had dropped sometime during the night. She hadn't noticed when. The sky to the east was growing lighter. Dawn wasn't far away, and maybe a better dawn.

She glanced at the bloody towels, blanket and stained clothing piled against her outside wall. If she was going to get that blood out, she'd need to get them soaking. She gathered the load, carried it across to her shed-cum-washhouse, where she dumped the lot into a single wooden wash trough.

A rainwater tank on her west wall supplied the water, though rain hadn't supplied what was in it. Through the summer months she and her horse spent many an evening hauling water from creek to tank — and they'd be at it again by nightfall. It took eight buckets of water to half-fill that wash trough, which was as much as she could do in the dark.

Little Elsie was still asleep in her corner. If she'd been aware of what had taken place in this room tonight, she'd made not a murmur. A shy and frightened little girl, it was unlikely she'd have murmured no matter what she'd seen.

Wood in the stove, kettle filled, and Gertrude walked out into the first light to cut greens for her hens and goats, to beat the birds to two buckets of apricots. Each year she made a few dozen pots of apricot jam.

She had four goats milking. It all took time. She fed her chooks, collected her eggs, and by seven was back at the trough, wringing out her washing for the clothes line.

There was a bulge in one of the coat's pockets. She reached in and withdrew a small purse, a pretty, hand-embroidered thing, six inches by four, the type of purse a woman might like to take out with her in the evening. Using the flat of her palms, she pressed excess water from it, then carefully opened it, seeking something that might identify the woman. There was little to find. A wet ten-shilling note, a few coins, a handkerchief and a soggy piece of brownish cardboard, which threatened to disintegrate when she tried to straighten it. She was using newspaper to press moisture from it when Ernie Ogden came back, Moe Kelly and his funeral van behind him.

Moe took the stranger away. Ernie stayed on to drink a mug of tea and to study the stranger's purse and its contents. The cardboard was still damp, but once flattened, it proved to be an old luggage label. *Destination* was printed clear, printed black, but where that destination might have been wasn't clear. The ink used was red and had bled. They could make out a definite *T* and maybe what could have been an *R* or a *P*, then a clear *V* and a very definite *Wood* followed by a *C*, which had to be Woody Creek.

'The T and V could be a name.'

'Tom Vevers,' Ernie said.

'Could be.'

'I'll have a word with him.' He spread the handkerchief on the table. It was a white lace-bordered thing with a blue *JC* embroidered in one corner.

'She didn't leave us much to go on,' Gertrude said.

'She could be one of Jenner's Italians. I'll get out there when the hour's a bit more reasonable.'

'You know his infant was born with a crippled foot?'

'I heard. Damn unfair. He went right through that war, you know.'

'Damn unfair.' Gertrude turned again to the handkerchief. 'At least we've got her initials.'

'I wouldn't place too much store in initials on a hanky, Trude. Folk find, borrow, lend, steal hankies.'

'It looks like her — fits with what she was wearing. Dainty, pretty, city things. And look at that shoe.'

'Not the sort most would choose to go walking across the countryside in.'

'It screams of city store to me,' Gertrude said. 'Everything about that woman screams city store and money to spend in it. The frock she was wearing — the beadwork alone on it must have taken someone hours, days, to do. And I probably ruined it by washing it. Crepe has got a bad habit of shrinking when it contacts water.'

'She was dressed for travelling, you thought.'

'I'd stake my life on it. Any chance that she came in on the train last night?'

'Squizzy Taylor could have come in on last night's train toting two shotguns and not a soul would have noticed him amongst your son-in-law's lot,' Ogden said, standing up and draining the last drips from his mug. 'And as much as I might like to, I can't sit around here all day.'

The babe was stirring. He watched Gertrude lift her from the makeshift crib, feel the makeshift napkin. 'I'll get her off your hands as soon as I can.'

'She's doing no harm, Ernie. She's not doing a lot of anything, the poor wee mite.'

The land around Woody Creek being flat as a tack made it good bike-riding country. Within minutes Ernie was back in town and approaching a group of strangers leaning against the pub wall, looking for something to look at and hard pressed to find it. He skidded his wheels to a halt beside them.

'Morning,' he said.

They were a middle-aged to elderly lot, all males, bar one, and she sucking as heavily on a cigarette as they. He leaned his bike against a verandah post and took out his own packet, lit one.

'You wouldn't have a youngish woman in your group, would you, thirty-odd, long black hair?' he asked, blowing smoke with the crowd. A bunch of heads shook in unison. 'Any passengers you might have seen on the train who'd fit that description . . . dark complexion, wearing a black overcoat?'

They were Duckworths, or wed to Duckworths; they'd seen nothing but other Duckworths. Ogden took two quick drags on his smoke, killed it, then pushed off towards the station to ask about unclaimed luggage, or any passenger last night who might have fitted the woman's description.

Norman had his mother's funeral on his mind. He was no help.

Nor was Melbourne when the post office chap got a phone call through to an uninterested sergeant, who showed less interest still when Ogden described the stranger now sleeping in a pine box in Moe's cellar. No wedding ring, had an Italian look about her, died maybe of blood loss after giving birth beside a railway line. It didn't sound like a priority to the city sergeant.

'I'm thinking of getting her onto the train this afternoon,' Ogden said. 'I need someone down there to know she'll be coming.'

The chap didn't want her coming, or not until he'd taken a look at who he might have had reported missing. He told Ogden to give him a call back around midday, then left him holding the telephone listening to a few hundred miles of dead wires swishing. The post office chap hung it up and Ernie Ogden went home for breakfast, where he related his night's work to more interested ears.

Duckworths talked. He'd say that for them. The bunch staying with Vern got together with the bunch from the hotel, and before he'd downed his second cup of tea, a flat-faced girl of twenty-odd and a chap of fifty-odd were at his door.

'Mum spoke to that woman you're describing at one of the stations,' the young Duckworth said. 'Mum said to me that she wasn't game to take her coat off for fear someone would steal her brooch. She had the most gorgeous brooch.'

'A black coat?'

'They all wear black — she was one of those dagoes, Mum said.'

He forgot about his tea growing cold. Two foreign-looking women wearing black overcoats in yesterday's heat wasn't likely. He hadn't found a brooch — though maybe the reason he hadn't found the brooch was the reason the woman had been found beside the railway line four miles from town.

'Did you notice if she was travelling alone?' he asked.

'I couldn't say. I went into the canteen to get Mum a cup of tea. Mum might know. I'm not sure where she's staying.'

'She actually spoke to her, you say?'

'Just passed the time of day. She was very taken by that brooch. It had a ruby in it as big as a hen's eye, she said.'

'I appreciate you coming around,' he said.

They left, he followed them out, followed them back across the railway lines where he found Vern hiding from his batch of Duckworths in Miller's boot shop, trying on boots he didn't need.

'Caught you,' Ogden said.

'Your jail is looking better by the hour,' Vern said, putting his own boot back on.

Two minutes later they were heading out towards the Bryants', Ernie now on the scent of a brooch.

Vern knew that road well, had known it since infancy. His land was out on this road, his father's land, his grandfather's. He'd ridden a horse to and from school for a couple of years, knew every paddock, every tree. It was good land out this way, bone dry right now but the creek was close by. Vern's grandfather had come with the first wave of hardy souls who had settled this area. He'd claimed his fair share of that creek, as had old man Monk, who had also got a good chunk of forest, which he'd harvested. He'd set up the first sawmill, an old pit mill. The modern mills put him out of business.

Lonnie Bryant was out with his dogs, but they found Nancy in, and she more than eager to show them where she'd found the stranger. They spent half an hour searching the area, looking for the brooch. They found blood, found the second shoe, midway between the railway line and where the woman had ended up, which could have suggested she'd been pushed from the train by whoever now had her brooch.

Near ten, they left Nancy with her Duckworth guests, and Vern, in no hurry to join his own, turned again down the bush road to Gertrude's property, where they found her attempting to interest the infant in sucking boiled water from a teat better suited to a motherless goat than a newborn infant.

'You didn't find a brooch pinned to that coat last night?' Ogden said, placing the second shoe beside its mate, still on the hearth.

'If it was on it, it's still on it.'

Her hands full, Gertrude pointed with her elbow to a cane laundry basket and her night's washing, already bone dry and removed from the line ten minutes ago. The sun was sucking moisture from wherever it could suck it today.

A domesticated man, Ernie folded the towels and blanket, turned the gold crepe frock right side out, shook it, then offered it to Vern.

'Someone paid big money for that,' Vern said. He knew the cost of women's clothes. He had a wife who liked spending money, and two daughters from previous marriages, still schoolgirls but with very definite opinions on what they wore.

'I almost cut it off her,' Gertrude admitted, offering the teat again to an uninterested mouth. 'It's beautifully made. You could wear it inside out.'

'Someone will be looking for her,' Ogden said, patting the coat down, feeling for the brooch he couldn't see. He shook it, willing that brooch to fly free. It didn't. It wasn't caught up in the lining either, nor in the pockets.

'Nice-looking coat too,' Vern said. 'Beautiful fabric. It wasn't made in Australia.'

'It smelled like wool when it was wet.'

'A wool mix,' Vern said. He knew his wools.

'Everything that woman had on her back reeks of money,' Gertrude said. 'And she's been up here before too, or someone she knew has been up here.' She slid the now dry luggage label across the table.

'A few years back, though. It's one of the old labels,' Vern said, turning it over. He did a lot of train travelling with his wife.

'Any chance she's connected to Norman's folk?' Gertrude said.

'Not from what they say,' Ernie said.

'One of the young Duckworth's lady loves?' Vern suggested. 'Decided to follow him up and surprise him in front of his family?' Ogden nodded, considering the theory, while Vern looked at the handkerchief, the ten-shilling note. 'The sum of a woman's life,' he said. 'It's not much, is it?'

'And this mite — who won't be long behind her mother if I can't get her sucking.'

'It's too small to live,' Vern said.

'Not all infants are ten-pound Hoopers,' Gertrude said.

'What's it weigh in at?'

'A smidgen under five pound. You might see if Jean and Charlie have got any decent feeding bottles up there. She's gagging every time I get this one in.'

'I'd be gagging too,' Vern said. 'I take it you won't be going in for the funeral?'

They were burying Cecelia Morrison at eleven thirty, then having a luncheon wake at the town hall, which would save the billeting families the hassle of feeding their guests lunch.

'What I had to say to that woman I said to her in life,' Gertrude said.

HOT GOSSIP

The six men who hauled Cecelia Morrison's coffin up and out of Moe's cellar had a lot more to say about her, but the less said about what they said or how they got that coffin up those narrow steps the better. How they were going to lower it into a six-foot hole with dignity, Moe didn't know. The woman must have weighed twenty-three stone and her coffin didn't weigh a lot less.

He'd used his best timber and done a champion job on it — and a dozen at the church told him so. He'd get orders out of this funeral, for fancy tables and cabinets. A bit of advertising of his craftsmanship never went astray.

Cecelia had a good turnout. The Duckworths filled the front pews, but the locals were well represented — a few there to get a closer look at Norman's relatives, and a lot of elderly men who never missed a chance to see someone younger beat them in the race to the graveyard.

Norman had requested the choir, a blend of Woody Creek's old and young voices. Some days they got it just right.

Charles Duckworth was a parson. He and the local C of E minister combined their talents in a service lasting an hour, but noon on a midsummer day was no time for a funeral, be it short or long. The church was small, badly ventilated, and today full of perspiration and supposition.

Ernie Ogden had seven sons, ranging in age from three to fifteen, who'd heard more than they should have heard. Moe Kelly had three near grown sons and a girl of twelve, who'd seen more than they should have seen. One kid guarding a secret is one too many. Half a dozen kids, not too concerned about getting their facts right when they pass on that secret, leads to a general buzz of misinformation.

'They say that one of the stationmaster's relatives was murdered last night, one of the ones who stayed out with Nancy and Lonnie Bryant.'

'No.'

'It wasn't a Duckworth. It was some foreign woman who came up with one of the men.' Whispering then.

'A baby?'

'Shush! And that's what I heard. I don't know how much truth there is in it.'

A handful of the hardiest women and fifteen-odd men followed Moe Kelly's funeral van the block and a half to the cemetery. They heard the grunts, heard that coffin drop down; they scattered hot dirt, then hurried back to the town hall, a red-brick utilitarian barn of a building with multiple doors. It offered space for folk to spread, offered lavatories — little better than tin sheds, but readily accessed through a side door.

The lavatories were abuzz today, and not all of it due to blowflies.

'They reckon she was with one of the chaps staying at the Macdonalds'.'

'Is it a fact that she had a baby?'

'It's fact, all right. It's down at Nurse Foote's place. I was in Charlie White's when Vern Hooper came in wanting to buy a titty bottle with the smallest teat they had.'

Suicide was suggested. An unmarried woman left in the lurch might have thrown herself off that train.

'Someone told me she was one of Jenner's dagoes.'

'Some of those dagoes import wives from Italy, you know. Imagine what one of them might do if his bride turned up in the family way.'

'Slit her throat as quick as look at you.'

'I heard she died of snake bite.'

'Did you see that snake those kids got down behind Macdonald's mill. I never saw anything like it in all my life.'

'The devil's work. I couldn't look at it.'

Hot sandwiches went down well with hot gossip, and there was nothing wrong with warm sausage rolls. The tea was too strong or too weak. The cream melted in the cakes. The jelly on the trifle reverted to its liquid state, but it all went down. A few remembered why they were there, though most conversations commenced and ended with the unknown dead woman. Very few strangers found their way to Woody Creek, and when they did, the locals always managed to connect them up to someone before they left. That dead woman was the first to arrive and die before any proven connection could be made.

Ogden lunched at the wake and he listened. He spoke to the woman who had admired the brooch. She wanted to be helpful but there was little she could tell him.

'She could hardly string two words together,' Aunt Olive said. 'Very hard to understand. I said what a terrible day it was for travelling and she said something that sounded like, always summer. I admired her brooch and I think she said it was her mother's. And that's about all that was said.'

He spoke to another dozen but learned nothing more, so he went home for a second lunch.

At two, he placed his second call to the city and got a pommy on a bad line. All Ogden got out of him was how folk moved around during the festive season, and how long it could take before that woman was reported missing — if a report ever came in. Women died in childbirth every day. It was one of the hazards of married life. Unwed woman died every day in attempting to abort the results of their low life. Ogden was pleased he hadn't been born a woman.

He wasn't too pleased about putting that coffin on the train on a day when the thermometer on his shaded verandah showed a hundred and nine, so he walked around to talk to Moe Kelly.

'I don't feel right about loading her into the goods van, Moe, subjecting her to six hours of roasting in a pine box and maybe no one to pick her up when she gets there. We'll bury her in the morning. I'll get young McPherson in to photograph her, and when she's claimed — if she's claimed — her folk can move her where they want her. The community box will pay.'

John McPherson, a shy, lean and lanky lad who looked younger than his seventeen years, had an interest in photography, which his parents encouraged. He'd photographed a few babies, a few brides, his parents and neighbours, but never the dead. Until that day, he had never looked upon the face of the dead.

His mother helped carry his equipment down the steep steps to Moe's cellar, where he set up his tripod and weighty camera while Moe and Ogden moved the open coffin over to where they might take full advantage of the light coming in through a high window and they propped the top end of that cruel pine box on a block of melting ice. Much had melted during the last days and the cellar's clay floor hadn't absorbed it well. It was greasy underfoot. John McPherson watched his step as he stretched out the leather concertina section of his camera, lined up on the coffin, then disappeared beneath a black sheet. There was a blinding flash and it was done.

His mother wanted to get away, but John took a step nearer to the coffin. It was too sad. A pretty woman's final photograph shouldn't be in a cheap dress in a cheap box in a greasy cellar.

'Can you . . . do something with her hair, Mum?'

She couldn't, but Moe Kelly removed the pins and settled it around her shoulders. John moved his equipment closer, close enough to capture her face in near profile.

'Can you move some of her hair over that grazing, Mr Kelly?'

The hair was moved, then, overcome by sadness, John hid again beneath his black sheet to clear his eyesight before capturing the final photograph of a beautiful stranger he'd caught sleeping.

They buried her at eight in the morning on the first day of January, 1924. Vern Hooper was there, Gertrude, Constable Ogden, the local parson, Moe Kelly, John McPherson and his mother, and the grave diggers, who stood back, studying their blisters.

What was there to say about a nameless woman no one had yet missed, when you didn't know if she was Catholic, Muslim, Jew or Callithumpian? What could you do but go to the good book and find something to say? The parson chose a brief passage. Then she was gone.

It wasn't the type of funeral any one of those mourners might have wished for themselves. No one wanted to hang around. The parson and the McPhersons left together. Vern, Ernie and Gertrude followed them to a big old gum tree growing on the far side of the cemetery gates. Ernie's bike leaned against it, Gertrude's horse was tethered to one of its low-hanging branches, Vern's car was parked in its shade.

'What's happening with the infant?' Vern asked.

Ernie was more interested in his bike's back tyre. It had a slow puncture or a leaking valve.

'I spooned some water into her before I left, but there's so little of her. She's weakening,' Gertrude said.

'We've got nursing mothers in town. There'll be one amongst them who'll take her in until we can see if any of her folk are found,' Ernie said, applying a bit of spit to his valve, which didn't seem to be leaking.

No problem at all in finding a nursing mother in Woody Creek; the begetting of kids was the main activity after sundown. Finding one willing to take on an extra baby was the problem. Ogden had already asked a few chaps if their wives might be willing. He'd found no takers. Kids came, wanted or not, and their folk welcomed them, but it took a special type of person to put the same time and effort into a stranger's infant.

'Paul Jenner's wife is a kindly sort of girl,' Vern said.

'She's got enough to deal with right now,' Gertrude said.

'Could you see your way clear to getting the babe down to Willama?' Ogden asked Vern.

'I'd have Joanne down there if I thought the car would make it. These temperatures would have her kettle boiling before I hit the ten-mile post.'

'What's wrong with her?' Gertrude said.

'The usual, aggravated by too many folk treating her house like a hotel.'

It was Joanne's house, built for her by her first husband. Vern had done the wrong thing by offering to put up the Duckworths.

'There's still a few hanging around, I see,' Ogden said.

'Not at my place,' Vern said with feeling.

Ogden mounted his bike and pushed off; Gertrude freed the rein, swung up to the saddle and was away. Vern stood on alone, watched her ride.

He may have been the wealthiest man in the district. There wasn't much in life he couldn't have if he wanted it — apart from what he'd wanted since his eighteenth birthday and maybe even before that: Gertrude. He'd told her she was marrying him that day. She'd put up no argument, though their folk had. They'd been deadset against cousin marrying cousin. He'd argued that they were only half-cousins and half-cousins didn't count as blood; he and Gertrude had shared a grandfather who'd gone through four wives. Vern hadn't won that argument — or Gertrude.

As he watched her turn to the right at the town hall corner, he sighed anew for the interference of dogmatic old men, and for the rare race of sons he and Gertrude might have bred. She'd wed a city man, and left him in India a few years later, but by the time she'd left him, Vern had been wedded to an Englishwoman with five hundred pounds a year but slim hips. It had taken him a while to get her with child, and he should have known better than to do it. Hooper infants had a bad habit of killing their mothers. A Willama doctor had saved his daughter but couldn't save Vern's wife.

He'd been made a fool of in his second attempt at wedded bliss. She'd popped his second daughter seven months after the wedding, and in the time it had taken him to get a saddle on his horse. She might have given him half a dozen more — had he believed her first was his own. He hadn't, so she hadn't. He hadn't touched her in eight years, hadn't planned to touch her in another eighty, but she'd come to grief beneath the hooves of a stallion she shouldn't have been riding, and he hadn't mourned her.

Joanne, his current wife, had given him a son, and for that son Vern loved her, which had nothing to do with the way he felt about Gertrude. Young love is unrelated to older love. What he felt for Gertrude hadn't altered since he was an eighteen-year-old boy, and if he lived another forty years, it wouldn't alter. He loved her. He wanted her. And he couldn't have her.

A couple of times, between wives, he'd come close to getting his heart's desire. Amber had been the fly in the ointment each time. Gertrude put her first in everything. After a time, a man grows tired of coming in second place.

Vern sighed, and folded himself into his car, but sat on looking down the wide dustbowl the locals called Cemetery Road.

Woody Creek was spreading south along Cemetery Road, the younger folk preferring to see ghosts walking in the night than floodwaters creeping. If things kept going the way they'd been going since the war, that cemetery would end up in the centre of town.

Lack of transport had a lot to do with the town's growth. Most born in Woody Creek stayed on to wed, which may have led to a bit of inbreeding but it kept money earned in the town working for the town. The rains had been coming when they were supposed to come; the farmers were doing well, which meant the businesses were doing well. Not that Woody Creek relied on her surrounding farmers to keep her afloat. Timber had got this town growing. The railways' order for sleepers was up each year. Timber was used in the mines. They built wharves from red gum, bridges, used it for fencing, and burned what was left over.

Vern was making money hand over fist, as were his mill workers, tree fellers and the bullockies who dragged those logs into the mill. A lot of folk lived well off timber. The big steam-driven mills could cut more in a day than the old pit mill could do in a month.

Uncountable tons of timber were freighted to Melbourne each year, yet barely a dent had been made in that forest. There was wood enough around this town to keep those mill saws screaming for a hundred years.

EXPECTATIONS

A forest doesn't evolve unless it finds the right conditions. It doesn't ask for much, other than space in which to spread. It will stand up to years of drought — if that drought is balanced by a decent flood every once in a while. The creek, twisting through the forest like a stirred-up snake, could be relied on to strike more or less regularly. Crops were lost beneath its floodwaters, stock drowned, families washed from their homes, but that forest drank her fill and gave birth to saplings.

Gertrude was eyeing a healthy clump of the things growing beside her boundary gate as she dragged it shut, looped a circle of rusting wire around a leaning gatepost — and for the umpteenth time promised her gate a new gatepost — and the gatepost a new gate. She'd been making similar promises for a year or two now, but hadn't got around to keeping them. She promised that clump of saplings an axe — and that was a promise she'd need to keep before the things started pushing over what was left of her fence. Everywhere she looked this morning she saw something that needed doing.

Her father had wrestled these fifteen acres from the forest, fenced them, then spent the remainder of his life fighting an ongoing war against red gum saplings hell bent on reclaiming his land. Had he followed his father's wishes and wed a neighbour's daughter, he might have ended up with more. An independent man, Gertrude's father, he'd learned to live without money — as had his daughter. In this old world, some are written down to do it easy but most are born to do it hard.

Amber had chosen a harder row to hoe when she'd wed Norman Morrison. She'd had a few nice boys come calling, then ended up with the worst of the lot — which Gertrude blamed on the last flood. The Morrisons had offered Amber a bed for the duration, and after three weeks in that railway house then coming home to floors covered in mud and green slime . . .

They'd been shovelling side by side for an hour or more, scraping up that stinking mud and pitching it out the door, Gertrude pleased to be home, pleased she'd had no floor coverings to lose, when Amber had let out a howl of the damned, pitched her shovel out the door, then followed it.

'To hell with it,' she'd said. 'I'm marrying him.'

'Who?'

'Who do you think!'

'Wally Dobson?'

'Norman!'

'Norman Morrison! You don't suddenly decide to marry someone like Norman Morrison just because you're sick of shovelling mud. Now pick that shovel up and get me some water. We'll sweep the rest of it out.'

'I deserve something better than this.'

'Then you don't marry a man like Norman Morrison, you fool of a girl. You don't love him.'

'Who are you to give advice on love? You left my father before I even knew him.'

'He went missing.'

'So you say.'

'I wasn't much older than you are now, I had you in my belly, I was stuck in India and he was gone, and if I'd stayed there I would have starved. And he didn't worry too much about you starving either, my girl. Now get me a couple of buckets of water and the old straw broom.'

'People don't live like this.'

'No. There's a lot who live worse.'

'And plenty who live better.'

'Yes, well, I can tell you now, you'd be a damn sight more comfortable riding a wet log downstream with a chook perched on one end and a goat on the other than in tying yourself up with those Morrisons. I didn't raise you to be a fool, so don't you go acting like a fool and ruining your life.'

Should have kept her mouth shut. Amber had wed him anyway.

Not that there was a lot wrong with Norman — or maybe there was nothing in the man to be wrong with him. He was lacking — lacking in self, or he'd had it drained out of him by his battleaxe of a mother. At times Gertrude made the effort to attempt some sort of communication with him, but it was like talking to a trained cockatoo — one trained by a parson. He could parrot plenty of big words, but when he'd finished what it was he had to say, you were left feeling that he'd said nothing at all — or nothing that made any sense. About the best Gertrude could say for her son-in-law was that he must have taken after his dead father, because old Cecelia hadn't had a lot of trouble in making herself clear.

For a time after the birth of Amber's daughter, Gertrude had tried to get along with Cecelia Morrison, aware that she'd need to if she wanted to play a part in her granddaughter's life. She'd delivered that crumpled little mite, had loved her at first sight. Every Friday she'd visited Norman's house, welcome or not. But old Cecelia had jumped Gertrude's claim, and she wasn't the type of woman to share her possessions. For six months Gertrude had persisted — while biting her tongue to a rag. Then one day she'd stopped biting it, and that was the end of that.

Things would be different with the next one. Gertrude may not have had anything specific against Norman, but she couldn't say the same for his mother. Her feelings towards Cecelia Morrison had been very specific.

The saddle off, she set it in a crook of her walnut tree, sent her horse on his way and glanced towards her chook pens. She'd have eggs waiting to be collected, but she had that baby and Elsie waiting inside. The eggs could wait a little longer.

Not a sound coming from the house. She opened the door, expecting to see Elsie lying where she'd left her. She wasn't there.

Old Wadi's been here, she thought. She'd near come to blows with him the day she'd carried Elsie away from his camp.

'Elsie?'

'She bin cryin', missus,' the girl replied from the bedroom.

Gertrude lifted the curtain, walking from bright light into dark. No window in her bedroom, but a wide wooden hatch. She lifted it, propped it wide, and as the light streamed in she saw the girl holding the new titty bottle.

'You've got her sucking? You good girl,' she said. 'You clever girl.' Elsie stood on one leg, her hip adding balance against the bed. 'How did you get in here, love?'

'Slided,' the girl said.

Gertrude checked the level of water in the bottle. It had gone down. She fetched a chair from the kitchen, got Elsie seated, and without disturbing that teat. 'Let her suck for as long as she will, darlin'. It's thirsty weather.'

A large stone bottle of water lived in the Coolgardie safe all summer long. Gertrude filled two enamel mugs and carried them to the bedroom where she handed one to Elsie. No thank you was voiced, but those big brown eyes thanked her.

'You like that baby?'

'I gettin' one sometime.'

'Some long, long time,' Gertrude said.

She went about her morning feeling a weight lifted. She'd ridden into that poor woman's funeral feeling sick at heart that she'd missed something, that her carelessness had allowed the woman to die. She'd been concerned that the babe might follow her mother. But she was sucking, and if she'd suck on sugared water she'd suck on goat's milk.

Eggs made up the bulk of Gertrude's income. Charlie White at the grocery store and Mrs Crone from the café-cum-restaurant took the bulk of them. A few buyers came to her door for eggs and vegetables in season. A few bought her goat's milk. The McPherson family, who lived near the bridge, were regular buyers, and had been since young John's birth. They swore by her goat's milk.

Mid-morning, she scalded a little, diluted it with boiled water, added a pinch of sugar, sat Elsie on the cane couch and handed her the baby and bottle. They got an inch of milk into that shrunken little belly, and two hours later she took an inch more.

Gertrude lost that day, but it was a hopeful, satisfying day — or it was until Ogden's oldest boy came riding down her track just after seven.

'Who wants me now?' she greeted him.

'It's the stationmaster's wife, Mrs Foote. He said it's her time.'

'It can't be,' she said, then bit her tongue. No use arguing due dates with a fifteen-year-old boy. 'I wonder if you could fetch my horse up for me, love, while I grab what I need. He's in the bottom paddock behind the orchard.'

It had to be a false alarm. She hoped it was a false alarm, or that babe could come backside first and Amber didn't need that. Nor did Gertrude, not after losing the last one. It was too hard on the heart, too hurtful to the soul, when a grandmother delivered her own dead grandson.

She hadn't planned to deliver this one. Vern had promised to take Amber down to Willama before it was due. There was a nurse down there who ran a house where expectant mothers could stay close to the hospital. That had been the plan. Amber had never been one to stick to plans.

She changed the babe's sheeting napkin and considered how long she might be gone, considered leaving Elsie in charge. But she couldn't. Having got the taste for goat's milk, that wee stomach was demanding it every couple of hours. If things went bad in town, Gertrude could be in there all night. She'd have to take them in with her, drop them off with Ogden and his wife, which she couldn't do on horseback.

'I'll take the cart, love,' she told the boy. 'I might get you to give me a lift with a few things before you go.'

He carried Elsie's mattress out; she carried Elsie, then went back for the baby. She filled a jam jar with scalded milk, almost forgot the titty bottle, placed them with other bits and pieces into her basket, her every action reminding her of nights long ago, of lifting Amber from her warm bed and carrying her into a stranger's house. Too many of those nights, and that little girl knowing too much too early. No choice back then, as Gertrude had no choice right now. Life might have been a whole lot easier for Amber had her grandparents made old bones. They hadn't. Life was what it was; life was all there was, and folk had to do the best they could with what they were handed.

The door slammed shut and Gertrude stood checking her mental list. Out to the cart then, where she used the spokes of the big old metal-rimmed wheel as a ladder. Her seat was a backless bench — her cart no fancy rig. With a click of her tongue, a flick of the rein, she encouraged her horse to pull. He was an all black gelding she'd named Nugget, and he preferred carrying her to pulling her cart, but she got his head turned for town.

Norman was waiting at his front gate. She tied the reins to a cartwheel, which made an effective brake, then, Elsie and the baby looking comfortable enough on their mattress, she went inside to take a quick look at Amber.

Maisy was with her, and one of Norman's aunts, and it was no false alarm. Her waters had broken and that baby was in a hurry to get out. He came headfirst an hour later, a good size for an eight-month baby.

'He's got the Hoopers' long limbs, darlin',' she said.

He didn't offer the newborn's wail, which was of no immediate concern though it became a slight concern when Gertrude's usual tricks failed to raise it. She took him out to the kitchen table, away from Amber's eyes. There was a handful of Norman's relatives out there. Seventy-five per cent had left town after the funeral; Amber's batch had stayed on. Gertrude cleared them from the kitchen before clearing the babe's airways. She slapped his little feet, expecting him to protest her treatment, needing him to protest.

'What's wrong?' Amber called from the bedroom. Gertrude didn't reply. She didn't know what was wrong.

Maisy came to the kitchen door to see, and found Gertrude breathing her own breath into her grandson's mouth. She'd birthed ten of her own; she didn't ask what was wrong. She knew.

'Get me a couple of basins, Maisy. Quick. Hot water in one, cold in the other.'

Knew her voice sounded too urgent but there was urgency now. She only had so much time to get him breathing and she didn't want to think about how much of that time she'd already used up.

A stoneware basin and one of enamel were placed on the table. She dipped tiny feet into the cold water, then into the hot, attempting to shock him into gasping that first breath. She sat his tiny backside in each basin.

'Mum! Mum!'

Shook him. Blew in his face. Tried the water again. The hot was cooling. And Amber was howling.

'Go to her, Maisy.'

Maisy didn't argue. She went. Only Norman standing at the door now, his eyes afraid. Gertrude looked at his eyes but couldn't hold them. She turned to the bold-faced clock on the mantelpiece eager to tell her how much time had passed since the birth. Too much. Way too much.

This was her grandson, her flesh, her blood. Here was the little boy she'd lost to the crazy sod she'd wed. Here was one of the Hooper line. He had the brow, the hands, and he was dead. And her girl was crying for him and Gertrude wanted to cry for him.

No time for that now. She wasn't the grandmother tonight, only the failed midwife.

'Get your family around to the hotel, Norman,' she said, hating him at that moment, cursing him for loving her pretty, moody girl and for giving her grandsons she couldn't make live.

'Norman,' Maisy yelled. 'Norman! You're needed in here!'

He left the doorway. His parson uncle took his place there.

'It will be better for all concerned if you move your family over to the hotel for the night,' Gertrude said. 'She'll need . . .' Amber was screaming. God knows what she'd need.

The parson left the doorway and Gertrude wrapped the tiny boy, kissed his little dead face, then carried him to the bedroom where Norman and Maisy were attempting to hold Amber down on the bed.

'He didn't breathe, my darlin'. I couldn't make him breathe.'

Amber snatched him, crushed him to her breast. 'Useless backward old fool,' she screamed. 'Get out! Get out!'

Her anger was ugly. It had always been ugly. She needed a punching bag tonight and Gertrude had always been a convenient punching bag, always swinging back for more punishment. She left the room, walked out to the front verandah, out to the gate.

Her horse heard her. He muttered his disapproval. She'd forgotten him, forgotten she'd left Elsie and that baby out there at the mercy of biting mosquitoes.

'God help me,' she said and she went to them.

They were sleeping, or silent. She walked to her horse to lean a while against him, her chin lifting, her eyes staring hard at a starry sky, and each star blurring, growing tails. Wiped her eyes, wiped them again, clearing the blur. Her tears weren't going to help anyone tonight. A couple of deep breaths might.

Heard the side gate slam, didn't know if someone was coming or going until she heard a male voice praying, then two male voices — Norman and his uncle, or perhaps the cousin. Prayers could give comfort to some. She doubted they'd comfort her girl.

Who could have imagined this night? She'd seen it all so very differently. What more could she have done? What would Archie have done?

Amber was right in calling her a backward old fool. She was untrained in the modern ways of healing — just a grandmother with an enquiring mind and a desire to fix what was broken. All she knew she'd learnt from Archie, on Archie. She'd lanced her first boil one night when his hands were shaking too hard to hold the knife. He'd talked her through the stitching up of his own head. Just a girl then, a fool of a girl thrown into situations she couldn't control, but learning from them.

'A brat will birth itself if given half a chance,' he'd said. He was right. She'd seen it happen many times. He'd been right about most things medical, but she'd known more about life, about people, and she knew now that she had to get that baby over to Ogden before its little belly started making demands. She was easing it from Elsie's protecting arm when Amber screamed and Maisy came at a run through the front door.

'They've taken it away from her, Mrs Foote.'

Gertrude pushed the stranger's infant at Maisy. 'Take her over to your place, love. I didn't know this was going to happen. Take her and run. I'll come by later,' she said.

God works in mysterious ways, his wonders to perform . . . or perhaps the devil had his own tricks up his sleeve that night. It's inconceivable how tiny lungs, how immature vocal cords, can raise the racket they do; surprising too, just how far a baby's wail will carry in the night. Such helpless beings, all they have is their wail and God gave this baby a beauty.

Amber howled a reply, believing her child, like Lazarus, had been raised from the dead. And Gertrude ran, passing the parson in the gateway. Punching bag or not, she was needed in there.

'Bring him back. Make him bring my baby back.'

'Shush, darlin'. Your baby couldn't live. Shush now my darlin' girl.'

Screaming, fighting the hands holding her. 'Liars, all of you. I heard him.'

'It's that dead woman's baby, darlin'. A little girl.'

Charles, the parson, carried the stranger's baby into Norman's house. He put it into Amber's reaching arms.

And the world calmed.

A CRUMBLING HOUSE

Norman's daughter, named for her paternal grandmother, was a Duckworth in the making. Still three months short of her fifth birthday, young Cecelia Louise was loud and chunky. She made Maisy Macdonald's twin sons look like midgets. The past week spent over the road in a house so filled with Macdonald children, her own demands had gone unheard. She was home now.

Her grandmother, who had gone missing, was still missing. The other one, the Granny one who wore trousers, was there, but worse than that, there was a baby stuck to her mother's chest. Young Cecelia Louise was not pleased with the alteration to her lifestyle.

'Why did her come here for?' she demanded, fists on her hips, in perfect mimicry of her missing grandmother.

The *her*, aimed at Gertrude, was intentionally misunderstood. 'She's a tiny wee girl who has no mummy, so your mummy is taking care of her.'

'I don' want dat fing and you too here. I want my granmuver here!'

Amber passed the infant to her mother and reached out to her daughter, but Cecelia Louise had lived through a wretched week and she wanted her mother to know about it. She threw herself to the floor where she lay on her back screaming and kicking herself around and around in circles.

Norman, drawn from his mother's room by the noise, stood in the doorway, watching a fine display of spleen and wondering what freak chance of good luck prevented his daughter's head hitting the leg of the bed or dressing table. His mother had made herself responsible for her granddaughter's training. He'd had little to do with the girl, and had no idea of how he might interrupt her outrageous display.

'Pick her up and put her on the bed,' Amber directed.

Norman approached tentatively, reached for and caught a solid ankle, which halted his daughter's foot-stamping circles but increased the intensity of her scream. He released her.

'When are they removing . . . it?' he asked.

Amber was buttoning her gown. The infant's belly not yet full, her meal put away, she added her tremulous wail to Cecelia's.

'They're waiting until the weather cools down,' Gertrude said. Vern and his wife had agreed to deliver the infant to the city, though no one yet had claimed her.

'And while he waits for the cool change, bedlam reigns in my house, Mother Foote.'

'I'm keeping her alive, Norman,' Amber said.

Out of her mind with grief on the night her son died, she may have convinced herself the child was her own. She'd changed a lot of napkins since.

'Does the world require one more fatherless brat?' he said, clearing the doorway as Gertrude vacated the room, taking a portion of the noise with her, but leaving behind the whirling, screaming dervish.

'Lift her onto the bed,' Amber said again. 'She'll hurt herself down there.'

'What in God's name is wrong with the girl?'

He did as he was bid. He grasped his daughter's wrists, heaved her to her feet and set her on the bed. She slid off to the floor. He caught her, lifted her a second time, with similar results. On his third attempt, he hauled her screaming down the passage and into the nursery where he sat her on her bed and held her there.

'Your mother is indisposed, Cecelia. You will remain here until you calm.'

49

She had other ideas. She kicked him low in the stomach and was off the bed and out the door before he got in breath enough to moan to the ceiling. 'My house is crumbling, Mother. My house is crumbling.'

The cool change arrived in the early morning of the eighth day of January, the temperature plummeting to a pleasant seventy-eight degrees. Norman, freed from house and noise, was walking his station platform, enjoying the breeze, when Vern came across the lines.

'Morning, Norm.'

Norman offered a tight smile. 'Pleasant to feel a breath of air at last, Mr Hooper.'

Only since his relatives had used Hooper's house as a hotel had he been on speaking terms with Vern.

'We'll be heading down to the big smoke this afternoon,' Vern said.

Joanne saw her Melbourne doctor three or four times a year. There were doctors in Willama, an hour away by car on a good day, but the best doctors were in Melbourne and Joanne Hooper could afford the best.

Vern took his cigarettes from his pocket, slid one into his mouth and offered the tin. Norman, as had his mother, had long craved the acceptance of Woody Creek's upper-crust. She'd gone to her grave without that acceptance. Now here was Vern Hooper, not the conventional upper-crust but certainly one of the town's leading citizens, standing on the railway platform offering his cigarettes and seemingly in no hurry to leave. Norman wasn't a smoker. His mother had not approved of the habit. But she wasn't watching, and he was growing accustomed to not having her watch his every move, so he took a cigarette, accepted a light and puffed blue smoke into the morning air.

'I was talking to your mother-in-law yesterday. She says Amber has done well by the infant.'

'It appears so,' Norman replied.

They made hard conversation until their cigarettes burned down, until Norman's head, unaccustomed to the nicotine rush, felt light. He was relieved when Vern flicked his butt onto the train lines. He aped the action.

'It won't upset her — parting with the babe?' Vern said.

'She has done her Christian duty to a motherless child, Mr Hooper.'

'Vern's the name,' Vern said, turning to go, then turning back. 'I dare say Amber will fix up something for us to feed it during the trip?'

'It shall be done . . . Vern.'

'Righto then. See you at three, Norm,' he said, and he crossed back over the lines.

Norman smiled. Some smiles open up a face, shine behind the eyes and invite the world to approach. Not Norman's. His smile sucked his mouth in, taking his small nose with it; it inflated his sagging cheeks, forcing his jowls into many. Thankfully he didn't do it often, though today, content with his world, the smile lingered a while.

Eight years ago he'd taken up residence in Woody Creek. For almost six of those years he'd been wed to a local girl; however, until his mother's death, until the influx of his relatives, the loss of his son and the taking in of the stranger's brat, he had been ignored by the community — unless they wanted to buy a train ticket. This past week no one had ignored him. The local minister had called by twice, and on the second occasion he had brought his wife along to sit with Amber. Several women of consequence had come to his door to enquire after Amber or to view the brat. Nancy Bryant had popped in twice, and on the second occasion she'd brought a tiny jacket she'd made for the infant. It was odd how that nameless sucking, soiling scrap of yowling humanity had crept into the psyche of this town.

Then yesterday. Again Norman's jowls became many as his features disappeared in a smile. Yesterday, George Macdonald, husband of Maisy, who had billeted Norman's three male Box Hill cousins, having learned from them that Norman had been an inveterate penny poker player as a boy, invited him to join his poker group.

'A few of us get together on Friday nights, and seeing as I heard you were a bit of a card sharp in your youth, Norm, I thought you might like to come over,' he'd said.

Baptised Norman, he had always been Norman, except to his school-wagging, Box Hill cousins. They'd called him Norm. Until yesterday, George Macdonald had called him Norman — or nothing. The shortened version of his name had a friendly ring to it, a country-town ring.

The infant was feeding when he popped over to the house to inform Amber of Vern Hooper's arrangements, its tiny hand grasping at the milk-giving breast. It was barely human, though looking a little more so now than when it had arrived. He stepped nearer. Odd, he thought, how they are born with an instinct to feed and little else, each one much the same as the next. A strangely moving sight, that of a mother with a child at her breast — of course, they were not mother and child.

He coughed, announcing his presence. Amber lifted her head.

'The Hoopers will be travelling today. Vern suggested you might prepare a feeding for the journey.'

Amber nodded. She was seated on a rocking chair, near the window.

'Are you in a draught there, my dear?'

'It's a relief to feel cool,' she said.

'Indeed it is.'

He loved her dearly when she was happy, which was not a common state. She looked both happy and well this morning. He walked to the window where he reached around the chair to close the lower sash just a little. Close to her, the scent of new life was strong. He stood looking down at the milk-white breast, the tiny mouth fastened to it, and he felt moved to reach out a finger and touch the shell of pink ear. And the infant turned from the breast to his touch.

'My word,' he said. 'It senses touch.'

'I'm trying to feed her, Norman. She takes long enough without you disturbing her.'

'Yes,' he said. 'Yes, indeed you are, my dear. Are those eyes blue perhaps?'

'They'll go brown. Her mother's were brown.'

'No doubt,' he said, lingering close to his wife. 'Cecelia was born with hair as I recall . . .'

'All three were born with hair, Norman, and two of them are dead.'

'Yes,' he said, stepping away. 'Yes, my dear.'

'You may as well know now that I'm not going through that again.'

'And you will not,' he said. 'You will not.'

The train was due in at three. It gave fair warning of its approach, then shunted around for twenty minutes while the flatbed carriages loaded high with bleeding red timber were connected. With the Hooper house only a sedate two minutes' walk from the station, Norman had not expected Vern and his family to sit cooling their heels in his waiting room, but by two fifty-five, he was looking for them.

Their housekeeper crept up on him. 'Morning, Mr Morrison,' she said. 'Mr Hooper said to tell you he's so sorry to inconvenience you and your wife, but Mrs Hooper just took a bad turn. They won't be travelling today after all.'

An inconvenience, certainly, though he made the correct mutterings, then watched the woman go on her way before hurrying across the station yard to inform Amber of the new arrangements.

The babe, packed into a large shopping basket, was on the kitchen table, Cecelia lying on the floor beneath the table, sucking sugared water from a titty bottle and Amber nowhere to be seen. He claimed the bottle. The ensuing scream brought Amber running.

'Hooper's wife has taken a bad turn. They are not going,' he yelled, the bottle held out of Cecelia's clawing reach.

'Then let her have it, Norman!'

The train hooted up near Charlie White's crossing. He had to go. He looked at the clawing girl, at Amber, at the titty bottle. Certainly Cecelia was missing his mother — as was he — but was that good reason to encourage errant behaviour?

53

She'd been weaned late from the breast, and after the death of their first son, Amber had clung to her living child, who'd returned willingly to the breast and remained there until Amber was again with child. They'd weaned her to a titty bottle, and very recently to cup. The reintroduction of that bottle into the house had raised memories of old habits, which must not be allowed to continue. The child was nearing school age. He took the bottle with him to the station.

Then, on Wednesday evening, he caught Amber putting that lump of a girl to bed with a bottle full of milk.

'This will not do,' he said.

'Give it to her, Norman. I'm tired.'

'You make a rod for your back.'

'Give it to her, I said.'

'I have spoken, Mrs Morrison. You will heed what I say!'

'Go to hell, Norman,' she said. She fought him for the bottle, the girl, out of her bed, stamping, screaming for it.

'Is it your intention to send her to the classroom with a nipple in her mouth, Mrs Morrison?'

His voice, raised by necessity, added to the noise. He had to go, but had nowhere to go. He escaped, with the titty bottle, out the front door, and when they pursued him, he went the few steps further to his front gate, then out the gate. The town hall was directly opposite his house. Lights were showing over there tonight.

'For God's sake, Norman. Give it to her. I can't take any more.'

Nor could he. His daughter's scream was horrendous. For a moment he considered taking the easy road, the quiet road. If that girl been less Duckworth, he may have wavered, but he had memories of a great lump of a boy, head and shoulders above his classmates, running home from the terror of school to the comfort of his mother's breast. A cowering shudder travelling from head to bowel, Norman stepped onto South Road, aware that his daughter, though she may not know it, was screaming out to be saved from herself, aware too that he must do the saving. He popped the teat, wasted the milk to the dust, then, bottle and teat in his trouser pocket, he crossed over the road towards the lights.

'A lovely night, Mr Morrison,' Jean White, wife of the grocer, said.

'Very pleasant, Mrs White,' he replied, or pleasant now he had placed some distance between himself and the noise — so pleasant, he followed Jean and Charlie White down the side of the town hall and into a rear meeting room where the Parents and Citizens' Association members met each month. He was a parent. He was a citizen. He took a chair in the back row, then, head down, closed his eyes and thanked God for a town hall just over the road — or he thanked God until Tom Palmer nominated him for the vacant position of chairman.

Norman's jowls lifted, his nostrils flared; he stared, not expecting the nomination to be seconded. Jean White seconded it, and minutes later, Norman found himself duly elected and sitting up front with the secretary.

At ten fifty-five, he called the meeting to a close and crept home, afraid of his reception there, but more pleased with himself than he'd felt in twenty years. The house was silent. He crept around to the rear verandah, felt out his mother's cane chair and eased himself down to it, eager to relive his night of glory.

He had never attended town meetings when his mother was alive. She had made her presence felt at most, though was never nominated for office. In the eight years he'd been in Woody Creek, he had never volunteered his services to the town. Always embarrassed by his abbreviated education, cut short at sixteen; however, comparatively speaking, that made him an educated man in this town. The timber industry demanded brawn not brain.

He drew a breath, released it; wished he had a cigarette and smoke to release. Two had been offered tonight. He'd accepted both and the sweet scent of tobacco clung to his clothing as the sweet scent of acceptance clung to his soul. Such a heady brew, and previously untasted by Norman.

Much had changed since his mother's death. He had never spoken to the Bryants until they'd offered to take in a few of his relatives. Lonnie Bryant was a wealthy man, his family one of the oldest in the district. Norman had had little to do with the Hoopers or the Whites before his mother's death. Now Nancy

55

Bryant visited his house, Jean White always passed the time of day, Vern Hooper had offered his cigarettes and his given name.

Norman's financial situation had also received a shake-up. As his mother's only beneficiary, he'd inherited her all, which he'd believed would be a meagre fifty pounds a year from his grandfather's estate. But she'd had four hundred pounds invested in a government loan, paying interest of four and a half per cent, which would net an extra eighteen pounds a year. She'd had seven hundred pounds in a bank account, at a miserly interest, but even that earned fourteen pounds per annum — and not one penny, not one brass farthing, had she paid into the running of his house. His stationmaster's wage was poor. There had been times when, if not for careful management and his mother-in-law's free supply of eggs and garden produce, he may have struggled to supply some basic need.

'Not one farthing,' he muttered to the night. 'And not once did I question her financial situation.'

Cecilia Morrison had not encouraged questions.

However, her miserly hoardings, when added to his stationmaster's income, made him a man of means — and a worthy chairman of the Parents and Citizens' Association.

The Hooper family put off their city trip until Vern's daughters were due to return to boarding school and university in early February. Norman hid the titty bottle in his ticket office. Cecelia's behaviour continued to deteriorate. The babe continued to thrive. Gertrude's horse spent long hours tied in the shade of the currajong tree in the station yard, and Norman spent long nights standing beside his mother's vacated bed, studying his wife's sleeping face.

He slept alone now. His movement in their shared bed, his snoring, even his breathing, disturbed Amber — though not so Cecelia's breathing. She had been removed from the nursery to share that second double bed. He found himself studying the small replica of his mother, and at times wondering how his fine-featured wife had produced such a child.

The stranger's infant now slept in the nursery. He studied it at night, touched a shell ear with an index finger, much as he might have touched a stray kitten dumped in his backyard. And each time his finger dared to touch, that seeking mouth turned to him.

He could not recall Cecelia ever turning to his touch, could not recall having touched her at this early age. He recalled little of his first months of fatherhood, the child having come too soon after the wedding, his bride withdrawn from him for too long. Had Cecelia's ears been so small? Had her features been so . . . so near human, her eyes so wide and watchful?

Perhaps too much was made of blood and blood lines, he thought. Take Vern Hooper. That man had been desperate for a son, and he'd ended up with a gangling, lop-eared, sickly boy whose birth had made an invalid of his mother. Take George Macdonald, he thought. He, after a veritable production line of washed-out girls, had produced a pair of uncontrollable, near albino male brats who could do no wrong in their parents' eyes and little right in others'.

On an evening in late January, his house sleeping, Norman walked the rooms watching the peace of his family. Cecelia looked a mote more vulnerable in sleep. His index finger extended, he touched her well-fed cheek, expecting her to turn to his touch. She whined, slapped as at a mosquito, and Norman backed quickly away — away to the nursery where he stood looking over the cot's bars, listening to a gentle hiccup.

The child fed four-hourly now. She had settled into a routine and he appreciated her unfailing adherence to it. She sucked, she soiled, she slept. His finger reached to touch a perfect ear and, as she turned to his touch, he felt . . . an empathy towards the fatherless being.

His own father had died of his heart before Norman's birth, leaving mother and babe to the collective charity of the Duckworth family. No relative had come forward to claim this mite.

'Your ears are transparent shells,' he said.

The child hiccuped again and her tiny mouth opened in what he chose to believe was a smile.

RECOGNITION

Young John McPherson's full-length photograph of the stranger in her pine coffin, sent via mail to the Melbourne police, was printed in the Saturday edition of a popular Melbourne newspaper, on page four, beneath the headline: 'DO YOU RECOGNISE THIS WOMAN?'

Her mother, had she been alive, would not have recognised that dead face. The eyes were closed, the eye sockets twin dark smudges of shadow, the face greyed with grazing and her long hair pulled back like a Quaker's wife. She was clad in a cheap black funeral gown, run up by Moe Kelly's wife on her sewing machine.

Had they thought to dress her in the beaded, gold crepe frock, a Melbourne hotel maid may have recognised it. She'd sponged and pressed that frock twice. She might have heard the husband call her Jules.

The hotel manager, had he seen the photograph, may have recognised her as half of the couple who'd spent a week at his establishment during the police strike. He could have looked up the name of that couple, made the identification; however, he did not, on principal, purchase that particular newspaper, which claimed to sell eighty thousand copies daily. When he found time to read, he read the *Herald*.

A jeweller in a third-floor workroom near the corner of Collins and Elizabeth streets saw the photograph. At first glance, he was certain she was half of the couple from whom he'd purchased a diamond ring and two gold bracelets. But only two days ago, the husband had returned alone, this time with a garnet necklace and earrings. He'd said his wife had borne him a fine strong son.

On guard against buying stolen property, the jeweller always got a name and address from the seller. On the first occasion, the chap had identified himself as Albert John Forest. On the second he'd been Alfred Forester, though on both occasions he had given a similar Hawthorn address. The jeweller remembered the couple well, not for any outstanding feature, but for the brooch the woman had worn. The chap would have sold it. His wife, a foreigner, had been adamant that it was not for sale.

The jeweller's first response was to contact the police, though since the police strike he had little respect for the swine. He'd spent thirty hours behind a locked door, expecting his to be the next door to fall to that rioting mob. He went about his business, though all morning he kept returning to stare at the newspaper photograph. It is odd how at first glance, something, someone, can hit a chord in the mind, how the mind can be so certain, but the more we look, the more we consider, the more we question our first judgment. By noon, the jeweller, now uncertain, decided it was safer not to become involved.

Albert, or Alfred, Forest or Forester recognised the woman in the photograph and wondered if the police had that brooch. He read the few lines beneath the photograph and found no mention of a brooch, but a brief mention of the brat. It was a female and currently being cared for by a stationmaster and his wife. He read of the farmer's wife who had found the woman, of the midwife who couldn't save her, of the constable, the photographer. One of them would have that brooch.

'Some you win and some you lose,' he said, ripping that page from the newspaper, folding it once, twice, three times before sliding it between the pages of *Great Expectations* — not that he had any great expectations, not right now, but a month or two could see him right. The book tossed into a wooden trunk, he picked up another and glanced at the cover before tossing it after its mate. Three more followed it. He needed to shed weight, and shed it today.

Her jewellery box, a fancy thing, the lid inlaid with mother-of-pearl, was empty apart from a few trinkets. He slid a ring onto his smallest finger. It could be worth a bob or two. He scooped up a necklet and matching earbobs. The pearls were small, the gold had little value. He dangled one of the earbobs a while, watching it spin. A thing like that makes you wonder how it was made, he thought, then, with a shrug, he dropped the earrings and necklet into his pocket. The jewellery box could have been worth money. But not today. He was in a hurry. He reached for a handful of photographs, saw the brooch in one. She was wearing it as a hat ornament. He claimed that one — he could use it as proof of ownership. There was no doubting that it was the same brooch.

'A great pity,' he said. 'It was worth a lot more than a few bob.'

The remainder of the photographs dropped into the jewellery box, he closed it and upended his own small travelling case onto the bed. Quite an accumulation. That was what happened when a man stood still too long: he accumulated. He enjoyed a good novel when he had nothing better to do. He'd accumulated seven. Weighty things, books. One after the other he tossed them into the trunk. He packed a few items of clothing, glanced at a notebook, read a word or two, smiled, then tucked it into the jewellery box with the photographs.

For an hour, Albert — or Alfred — selected and rejected as he sorted through the accretion of his months of stagnation. Then the case was closed; the lid of the trunk closed, locked and the small key slid into his wallet. One last glance around the room for forgotten items and he walked downstairs to pay his bill and order a cab.

It took him and his luggage to an address in Hawthorn where a maid let him in.

His sister was in the small sitting room, watering her indoor plants. She didn't turn to his greeting.

'Tell the old man I'm leaving my trunk with him for a month or two,' he said. 'Or has he croaked?'

She poured a little water and moved on to the next plant, wiping a spill from the windowsill with her finger. She wasn't wearing black, which no doubt meant their father was still with the living.

The cabbie carried the locked trunk inside and through to the lumber room where they pushed it into a corner.

'Give me two minutes,' he said. 'I'll go back in with you.' And he returned to the sitting room.

His sister wasn't there. He stood a moment looking at the greenery, smelling the scent of damp earth, then he reached for a pot and upended it, smiling as the dirt scattered.

Of the eighty thousand copies of the *Sun News–Pictorial* printed on the last Saturday in January 1924, most would meet their end in lighting fires, polishing shoes, cleaning windows, wrapping meat and wiping backsides, though one copy survived intact for sixty years. Young John McPherson wasn't proud of his first published photograph. His mother was. She placed her copy in the bottom drawer of the writing desk.

John was rightly proud of the close-up shot he'd taken of the dead woman's face, though too embarrassed to show what he had captured. She appeared to be sleeping. He convinced himself that she had been sleeping, and in the dead of night made an enlargement, which he later placed with the newspaper in the desk drawer.

Norman read the article. By Monday he was expecting Ogden at his door to inform him the family had been found, that they'd be arriving to take the child away. No one came, and on the Wednesday, it was Norman who approached Ogden.

'You have surely had some response, Constable?'

'There's always some response, Mr Morrison, though we've heard nothing which you might call a positive response.'

'You will keep me informed?'

'As soon as I hear something, you'll be the first to know.'

Schoolchildren returned to the classrooms. Cecelia was old enough to go with them, though Amber did not agree. Norman didn't argue. He waited for the infant to be claimed, becoming stressed with the waiting and by his own thoughts.

Then Vern Hooper came to his door. He and his family would be travelling down to the city on Saturday.

The time had come. And far better if it had come sooner.

On the Friday night, Norman walked the house, walked it late while his family slept. His family. For most of his life he'd lived on the perimeter of the families of others, always craving his own family, his own home.

Late when he walked out to his front verandah to light a cigarette, it took two matches before he got it burning. And he sighted an answering glow from Ogden's verandah. A reflex action perhaps; certainly there was little conscious thought behind it. He found himself over the road, at Ogden's fence.

'I am more and more convinced, Constable, that it is God's plan for my wife and I to raise that child.'

'A very worthy thought, Mr Morrison, but there are a few legalities involved in the doing of it.'

'It was . . . was more or less found on my doorstep, and on the night our own infant died. I believe God sent it to us.'

'Is that your wife's view of things, Mr Morrison?'

'It is my wife who has kept it alive, Mr Ogden.'

'And that's a fact,' Ernie Ogden replied.

'Does the good book not tell us that it is every man's Christian duty to provide for the more vulnerable in our society?'

'The parson says so.' Ernie wasn't a big church man.

'What is . . . what do you see as the . . . the major difficulty?'

'Paperwork, Mr Morrison. And city folk wanting to stick their noses into places they know nothing about — in the main.'

'A nameless child has no future.'

'That's true enough too. There's little doubt the babe will end up in one of their orphanages, and some of them I've seen I wouldn't wish on one of Duffy's dogs. It's just the legalities of the thing, Mr Morrison. There's no doubt in my mind that she'd have a better future with you and your wife.'

No doubt at all, Ernie thought, so why make it difficult with legalities? He had that dead woman in the cemetery and Morrison's dead babe there. He had an infant very much alive and a living mother with milk in her breasts. The stationmaster's income was assured. He lived in a well-kept house in the centre of town — his own infants kept dying. Maybe it was God's plan.

'If we had a few more days to think about it,' he said. 'There was one chap in the city who claimed to be the husband, though he seemed more interested in any jewellery she might have been wearing than in the infant.'

'The Hoopers are travelling tomorrow.'

'The best decisions aren't best made fast, Mr Morrison. Come through and sit down. I'll fetch another glass.'

Norman accepted a glass of ale. He was not a drinker, but he sat with his neighbour looking out over the sleeping town, while a cool breeze coming in soft from the south stirred the shirt on his back.

'I dare say that when it's all boiled down, a bit of tidying up of bookwork could circumvent the legalities — so to speak. As long as you're certain; as long as your wife is certain, Mr Morrison. I mean, she'll be the one doing most of the raising.'

And thus J.C., a woman of good family, was forgotten — though not quite forgotten. While ordering a large and ornate tombstone for his mother's grave, Norman was moved to order a second stone for the mother of his shell-eared daughter. It was small, cheap, grey, with the minimum of words: *J.C. LEFT THIS LIFE 31-12-23*.

AN UNTIDY LIFE

Norman named the infant Jennifer Carolyn, for the initials on the handkerchief, and through the remainder of that long hot summer, Amber kept her clean, comfortable and well fed. Gertrude visited once or twice a week, ate lunch with her family on Fridays.

All seemed well until the tombstones were erected and on a Sunday afternoon in early March the little family walked out to the cemetery with flowers to place on old Cecelia's grave. Her stone, of white granite, had three angels perched on it, at each side and on top. It looked very fine indeed, was one of the finest stones in the cemetery. She would have been pleased with it, and with her name cut deep.

No mention of the stillborn boy they'd buried with her in that grave.

'It's as if I'd never carried him,' Amber said. 'It is as if you expect me to forget him. You had no right to put him in with her anyway.'

She was expected to forget him, as Norman hoped others would forget him. Jennifer Carolyn had been registered in his place.

'It was considered . . . considered expedient at the time, my dear.'

'You should have opened up his brother's grave.'

'Charles suggested —'

'To hell with Charles, and all of your Duckworth relatives. He was our son and I carried him, and I'll never put her in his place.'

'He will never be forgotten by us —'

'Then why didn't you put his name on your mother's stone!'

'We did not name him, Amber.'

She walked away from his ornate stone, left him there with the children, the pram pointed in the wrong direction. He manoeuvred the thing around, set its wheels back on the gravelled path and pointed it towards home. He lifted the stocky Cecelia to her feet, pointed her in the direction of her mother.

'Walk,' he said. 'Amber! Will you come back and get this child? Amber?'

She waited and took the bawling girl's hand. Norman pushed the pram home.

The subject of tombstone and name on tombstone was not raised over dinner. He hoped it was buried. She got the children settled while he read the paper. All seemed well.

But all was not well.

'You and your Reverend Charles Duckworth didn't give me time to name him, did you? You let that praying old swine rip him from my arms —'

'Enough, Mrs Morrison. You are upsetting yourself.'

'I was upset when you wanted to name my daughter for your mother, when you wanted to name my boy Clarence Arthur. Why didn't you name this one for your family?'

'Jennifer?' He glanced towards the nursery. 'She is not . . . is not of the . . . line.'

'Lucky Jennifer,' Amber said, swiping his newspaper from the table.

He picked it up, sorted the pages. She went to bed, with Cecelia.

He went to her later, kissed her, hoping to make the peace. 'Your place is in my bed. This has continued too long.'

'I told you I wasn't going through that again, and I meant it.'

He sighed and his lower regions sighed. No doubt her mood would pass. He hoped it would be soon. It was not natural for a man of his years to be denied the comfort of his wife. His sleep was disturbed.

She disturbed it again before dawn. He heard her in the kitchen and, when he crept out, caught her pouring a glass of brandy. He reached for it. She was a determined girl. The table between them, she drank it down like water.

'You will turn the babe into a tippler,' he said.

'I can't sleep.'

'Nor I. Come to my bed. Perhaps we can comfort each other.'

'Go to hell,' she said. And she poured more brandy.

'You must not, Mrs Morrison. It is not fitting for a woman to drink hard spirits!'

'It's your fault that he died anyway,' she said. 'If you hadn't brought every relative you own up here then expected me to run around after them, I would have carried him to term. They killed him, and you let them do it, then you let that cold-blooded old parson bury him in with her. Did you even ask me what I wanted?'

'You were in no fit state!'

'Then you should have waited until I was in a fit state. Did you ask me if I wanted to raise Jennifer?'

'You screamed for her, my dear, dear Amber.'

'I was out of my mind. You could have stopped me.'

'You are difficult to stop.'

She'd emptied the glass and was reaching again for the bottle.

'No more. What you put into your mouth makes its way to the child.'

'The child,' she said. 'As if I give a damn about the child. She's not mine. I feel nothing for her, Norman.'

He claimed the bottle. 'What is one expected to feel for an incontinent infant?'

'You tell me. You tell me what I'm supposed to feel. I spend my life trying to feel what I'm supposed to feel, and I feel nothing.'

'Surely love for a child grows, as it does between man and wife?'

She laughed then, tried to get by him, but he caught her arm, pulled her to him, desperate to hold her, to prove his love for her in the only way he knew how. She stamped on his bare foot and got away, opened the back door and went out to the verandah.

'Come to bed,' he said.

'Do you know what I really feel, Norman? I feel sick in the stomach every time you touch me. I can't stand you or your bed, and if you don't know that by now, then you're more fool than you look — and that's saying a mouthful.'

'Mrs Morrison!'

But she was gone, in her nightgown, gone out the back door, down the verandah and out the side gate.

He did not pursue her. This business of the tombstone had upset her. Perhaps placing the dead infant in with his grandmother had been poorly done, though a practical solution at the time. Three funerals in five days, the heat excessive, the earth bone dry, and that boy had not gone to term, had not breathed, had not been baptised. It was Charles who had suggested he be placed with his grandmother. Moe Kelly had seconded the motion and the grave diggers had applauded with blistered hands — earth newly broken being more easily removed.

And at the time, Norman had not been himself. Still traumatised by his mother's passing, and now his so-wanted son's, he had left the arrangements to Charles. Later, as things had evolved, he had come to believe it was God's will that his son be forgotten and Jennifer Carolyn raised in his place. However, for Amber's peace of mind, a name, if not a date would be added to his mother's stone. Archibald Gerald perhaps, for her father. She had been fond of her father.

He raised the subject the following night when she poured her glass of brandy early. He poured himself a small drink — only to empty the bottle.

'I have been thinking we should name him for your father, my dear.'

'Don't try to crawl around me, Norman. I meant what I said last night.'

Two more days, the brandy not replaced, he found her pouring cooking sherry. He claimed the bottle, emptied it onto a shrub growing beside his back verandah.

For three days his meals were flung at him, his bed remained cold, and tiny Jennifer, rarely heard, now screamed for the breast.

'We will make other arrangements for her,' he said. 'I will take her to Melbourne at the weekend, deliver her to the authorities and confess my guilt. Until then, she must be fed, Amber.'

'And what will people think of me then?' she snapped.

'It is of no consequence what people think of you, or of me. We must have peace in this house.'

'I have to live in this filthy town!'

'Then tell me, tell me, please, what it is you want me to do, my dear, dear Amber, and I will do it, only feed that child.'

She knew what she wanted him to do: to get out of her life, or to give her the money to get out of his. Couldn't say it. She bared her breast and fed the baby.

Exhaustion tumbled Amber into sleep each night and nightmares flung her back into wakefulness. Each was different, but each the same. Her son's cry led her into dark forests, through graveyards where she wandered between gaping holes searching for him. She found him too, and in terrible places — in the creek, hung from a hook in the butcher's shop, floating face down in the green sludge of her mother-in-law's grave. She found him in cartons of groceries, under the bridge. Always dead.

Maisy saw her despair. She took both children to her house each afternoon while Amber slept, her nightmares fewer by daylight. Gertrude spent too many of her days in town caring for her grandchildren while watching weariness strip the little flesh from Amber's fine bones. But on many a day when Maisy couldn't come, when Gertrude stayed at home, Norman came from work to find his wife locked in her room and the two children screaming.

'Amber. The children need you. Amber!'

His voice dragged her from dream. She'd found her son in her mother's old trunks, underneath the verandah, found him crumbling, but had placed him to her breast. And woke heart racing, her arms empty.

Opened the door, saw him, the living baby screaming in his awkward arms, Cecelia bellowing at his knees. Put the infant to suck, and its sucking made the emptiness within her grow. Its sucking opened gaping hollows in her heart.

Nothing inside her now.

Empty now.

Hollows have a way of filling with whatever the wind blows in. Amber's hollows filled with a rage she had to contain. She was an inferno of unreleased rage. It glowed in the dark, lit her way when she walked in the night. Lit up the darkest corners of her mind, showing her what she should not see, showing her the beast she'd wed for his railway house and for his mother's fine bone china tea set. Showing her the beast's child, ugly, clumsy.

And showing her the infant's finer bones, her well-defined features, her big blue eyes. Loved her beauty. Loved that tiny nose, that little chin. Hated her own daughter's flat, fat face, her thick Duckworth feet, her coarse dark hair.

Hate and love became confused. Had to hate the child of that stranger and love her own. Must love her own. She'd carried her. Did love her. Did. Did. Hadn't she rejoiced at the moment of her birth?

Ruby she'd thought to name her, Ruby Rose, a pretty name for a pretty child. Ruby and Amber, she'd thought, mother and daughter. And I will be the perfect mother to my perfect child. I will make a perfect home. I will cleanse myself in my child.

His mother had scoffed at her choice of name. For two weeks her beautiful baby had remained nameless, and at the end of those two weeks there was no beautiful Ruby Rose, only Cecelia Louise, flat-faced, hook-nosed, infant replica of the old Cecelia.

Hated the sight of her.

Had to love her.

How could anyone love that pig-eyed, sullen, wilful, screaming, resentful . . .

Resentful of Jennifer.

69

And why shouldn't she resent Jennifer? Amber resented her beauty.

And she smelled wrong.

Cecelia smelled right.

In the dark, Cecelia smelled beautiful. Smelled like home.

Home?

Wanted to go home.

Where was home?

Not her mother's hut. She hadn't been down there since she'd left the place. Norman's house was home, his mother's fine furniture, her velvet rug big enough to near cover the parlour floor, her peacock feathers in their expensive vase, her heavy drapes.

This house was home.

Not Norman. Couldn't stand him. Couldn't stand the smell of him. Always hovering over her. Always watching, trying to touch her. Couldn't stand the thought of his thick hands on her.

Cecelia had his hands. She had his feet. But in the dark, in bed, when she couldn't see her, when she held her close, she could feel love for her.

Did love her. Not him. Loathed him.

'You are my wife, Mrs Morrison. You swore your vows before God —'

'Take your God and shove him, Norman. And take that baby with you.'

In an era when God sat assuredly in heaven, when man, made in God's image, sat a few degrees to his left, when wives loved, honoured and obeyed their husbands — whether they did or not — Amber was severely out of step.

She had been raised by an independent woman to believe that man's reward was gained on earth by hard labour, that Sundays could be better occupied in digging post holes than in praying. In a good woman of sound mind, wrongful attitudes can be forgivable.

Amber's mind was not sound.

It happened in mid-March. She'd nursed Jennifer at ten at night, then crawled back into Cecelia's bed where she'd slept soundly until dawn. She'd dozed thereafter, waiting for

Jennifer's call, but for the first time the baby had taken it into her head to sleep through the night. Amber's breasts were full. Perhaps the low neck of her gown released a leaking breast, or dreaming again of her crumbling son, had she bared her breast so he might suck. The how of it was of no concern, just the awakening to bright light and to the pure and perfect peace of her own girl's mouth at her breast, and to the sweet relief of a full breast emptying, and the blissful relief as love for her girl filled the gaping hollows within her soul.

'Mummy's precious girl,' she whispered as she kissed the sweet-smelling hair, buried her nose in the scent of it. 'You're Mummy's own very precious girl, aren't you? Take it all, my beautiful,' she said. 'Empty me.'

THE BIRTHDAY

Cecelia celebrated her fifth birthday on 26 March. Gertrude rode in on the Friday for a birthday lunch and was relieved to see her daughter looking more relaxed.

Norman appeared less stressed and quite expansive — for Norman. He asked after Gertrude's health. She told him she was well. He suggested there could be a thunderstorm before the day was through. She said her tank and garden could use the rain, that she'd spent half of this summer bringing water up from the creek. He suggested she pay the water carrier to fill her tank. She told him the water carrier cost money and with the creek just over the road she preferred to take what she needed free of cost. That was the limit of their conversation.

Amber had bought Cecelia a frilly pink dress for her birthday. That girl wasn't the right shape to wear frills, but if you can't say something nice, then you're better off keeping your mouth shut. Gertrude kept her mouth shut. She kissed her granddaughter, wished her happy birthday, then offered a brown paper-wrapped parcel. It contained a rag doll she'd spent a week of nights in making, and one of those nights in stitching in a full head of black woollen hair. She'd made a frock, underwear, had knitted stockings, constructed shoes from a piece of black satin. She watched it unwrapped, eager for Sissy's reaction.

There was little reward for her labour. Within minutes of the unwrapping, the doll's face wore a chocolate icing-sugar scar, and one shoe, plus the foot, had been chewed to pulp. Gertrude said not a word. If it meant biting her tongue to a rag, she would play a part in the lives of her granddaughters.

Maisy and her four-year-old twin sons arrived at two. The doll's bloomers came off while its sex was determined.

'Kids will be kids.' Maisy laughed.

Kids would be kids. Gertrude picked up the bloomers, placed them with the frock on the table, and sat a while longer catching up on local gossip. Maisy knew everyone and most of their business. At three, mercifully, she guided her pair of monsters towards the front door. Amber walked out with her, and Sissy, still dragging the now naked doll around by its hair, went out to the back verandah where Jennifer was sleeping in her pram, a mosquito net keeping the insects at bay.

Gertrude was washing the dishes when she heard the baby scream. She went to the back door and saw Sissy untangling her head from the netting. There was no question as to why Jenny screamed; there were pinch marks on the cheek, the skin broken by fingernails.

'You mustn't hurt Jenny.'

'Did not,' Cecelia denied.

'I can see the mark of your fingernails. You mustn't do things like that, Sissy.'

'Did — not — do — noffink,' Sissy said.

'You're fibbing to Granny —'

The doll missed her head by inches. It landed in the lavender bush as Sissy flung herself to the floor to scream.

Amber came. She knew who was at fault. 'What did you do to her?'

'She pinched the baby.'

'And you hit her?'

'I did no such thing. She knows that I saw her being a naughty girl. That's all that's wrong with her.'

'And you threw her doll away.'

'As if I would, Amber. She threw it at me — and she doesn't need comforting either,' Gertrude added as Amber picked up that hulking great girl. 'Look what she did to this little one's face.'

73

'She was only trying to make her smile,' Amber said. 'You're always coming up here, fussing over her, putting her before your own granddaughter.'

'That's not true and you know it. It's the first time I've been near her all day,' Gertrude defended. She placed the quietened baby back into her pram and retrieved the doll. 'Come with Granny and we'll dress your dolly in her pretty clothes again.'

Cecelia, straddling her mother's hip, was exactly where she wanted to be. She snatched the doll and pitched it further.

'She needs curbing, Amber. Her behaviour is getting out of hand.'

'Save your meddling for your darkies,' Amber said. 'It's not needed here. Neither are you.'

Gertrude stepped back, just a reflex step, then another, not so reflex. She'd left her basket in the hall. She collected it on the way out.

Her horse was waiting for her out front, her good and patient Nugget. She placed an arm over his neck and leaned for a moment, feeling the need of that contact. She felt picked up and shaken to her roots, her heart dancing at a hundred miles an hour.

Amber had always had her father's fair colouring, his curly hair, his fine-built frame, but never his eyes. She'd seen them today, had seen him looking back at her, and those eyes could still send tremors from the base of Gertrude's skull running down her spine. She looked at the hand stroking her horse's neck, expecting to see it trembling. It wasn't. Her shaking was internal.

She'd learnt to keep most of her feelings inside, to keep herself to herself. Self was the best place to keep some things if you didn't want them turning into common town gossip.

She glanced at the house, placed the basket on a fencepost, then, foot in the stirrup, she mounted, set the basket before her, flicked the rein and started for home.

And she had troubles there too, brought on by her meddling.

Did she meddle? Maybe she offered advice too readily, but it got to be a habit. And when a man's wife or child was sick, he wanted someone to tell him what to do. Most in town trusted her to meddle. Some even paid her to do it.

Shouldn't have told her that Sissy needed curbing. Maybe shouldn't have agreed to falsify that birth registration. Shouldn't have taken little Elsie from Wadi's camp — or should have sent her home to him a month ago. Should have done a lot of things and shouldn't have done a lot more. But you can only do what you think is right at the time, and sending that girl back to Wadi to starve wasn't right.

Not that he was starving at the moment. Three of her young goats had gone missing in recent weeks. She knew he'd taken them, knew why he'd taken them. Three times he'd come for Elsie. She'd hidden. Gertrude kept her milkers tethered now, in the orchard paddock behind her house. That thieving old coot knew better than to venture too near. She'd pulled the rifle on him the last time he'd come creeping around, and got off a shot too, just to show him she knew how it was done.

It was a mistake becoming attached to those kids. She'd done it before. Two years back she'd brought in an eight-year-old boy with a chest infection and got him well. Wadi had come to her door demanding him and the boy had gone willingly. Six months later he was dead. She'd sworn that day she'd never do it again, but she'd gone and done it again. Couldn't stop herself . . . from meddling.

A planter of seed, Gertrude, a gardener. She loved the watering, the tending, the watching of a spindly plant grow sturdy. Three months ago she'd planted a silent matchstick child down the bottom end of her kitchen; she'd poured in goat's milk, plied her with fresh eggs and sugar, tended her and watched her grow from that silent matchstick child into a pretty, smiling girl.

Watched her little belly rounding out too, and for a time had convinced herself good eating was responsible. It had little to do with eating, and was no shock at all to Elsie. She liked babies, knew where babies came from, and saw nothing wrong with having one of her own. Gertrude had put her age at ten or twelve when she'd brought her in, and God only knew how she'd got into that state. Elsie wouldn't say.

Ernie Ogden knew she was in the family way. Last week he'd arranged with Vern to take her out to the mission. They'd come by late one morning but Elsie had seen them coming and she'd taken off. All day she'd been gone, Gertrude and the men convinced she'd gone back to Wadi. She'd come home at nightfall.

It had to be done. Vern was coming down tomorrow, planning to catch her eating lunch — and Gertrude not looking forward to tricking that little girl.

She glanced at Vern's house as she rode by. Joanne Hooper was seated in the shade of the verandah, her boy at her side. She nodded a bare acknowledgment to Gertrude's wave. Like old Cecelia Morrison, Joanne had never made the transition to country. City born, city educated, city clad, she'd moved to Woody Creek with her first husband during the war years. He'd been worth a fortune, but hadn't lived to spend it. Everyone had expected Joanne to sell up and make a beeline back to the city when he was killed, but she'd wed Vern instead. She was a nice enough woman — though not nice enough for Vern.

Their boy was a worry to Gertrude. No doubt they fed him well, but he looked like a half-starved, elongated gnome, all ears, eyes and mouth. He clung to his mother — or she clung to him. Vern barely got a look-in.

Gertrude rode on, not eager to get home today, knowing that Elsie would be waiting at the gate for her, waiting with a smile. She wouldn't be smiling tomorrow — and Gertrude would be feeling like Judas Iscariot.

It was nice to be welcomed home, nice to have the gate opened and closed behind her, nice too knowing that her stove was burning, her kettle boiling, her goats not tangled up in their tethering ropes and no chooks in the garden. But she had to go. She'd get proper schooling at the mission, and if she didn't, then her baby would. The decision had been made and Gertrude had to stick to it. She had a daughter in town and two granddaughters. They were her family, her future. She had to put her mind to making that relationship work.

'Home again, me darlin'.' Gertrude greeting that smiling face as she handed down her basket.

Elsie had a way of hop-skipping when she was happy. Gertrude followed her down the track, knowing that she couldn't go playing tricks on that trusting little girl, that she had to be told that Vern was coming tomorrow.

They got the saddle off, got Nugget back into his paddock. They gave the chooks fresh water, collected ten more eggs, and it seemed like the right time.

'Vern will be coming by to take you out to the mission, darlin'.'

Didn't say when and Elsie didn't ask. Her smile vanished, and, fifteen minutes later, she vanished.

Gertrude milked her goats, moved their tethers, filled up their water trough, had a look in the shed for Elsie, looked underneath the tank stand, overgrown by her climbing rose. There were too many places to hide on her acres.

'Elsie.'

That girl's approach to problem-solving differed from Gertrude's. She'd put off what she didn't want to do today in the hope that it might be forgotten by tomorrow. And if it wasn't forgotten tomorrow, then maybe she could put it off again. She knew too that Vern didn't like driving after dark. Two minutes after Gertrude lit the lamp, she crept inside, head down, crept to the bottom end of the kitchen, to her mattress, where she sat cross-legged, looking at the floor.

'You have to go, darlin'. My house isn't big enough for you and me and a baby.'

'Baby only a little feller, missus.'

'Babies grow into big fellers. The mission has got plenty of room for babies.'

Elsie measured the kitchen with her eyes, stood and moved her mattress closer to the corner, hard in against the wall. She glanced at Gertrude, wanting her to see how easily the space problem could be overcome.

'I'll go out there with you and tell the lady all about your baby. There'll be lots of girls out there for you to talk to, lots of babies to play with,' Gertrude said, unwrapping half a dozen sausages she'd bought in town.

Elsie liked sausages. Gertrude watched her watch them, knowing she'd come to see them placed into the hot fat. She loved watching sausages squirm as they fried.

She wasn't wrong.

'They like alive ones, missus,' Elsie said, creeping to her side.

'The butcher makes them in his sausage machine,' Gertrude said, stabbing one with a fork, turning it.

'They like fat worm. Wriggle-wriggle, missus. How's him make them sausages?'

'With a bit of meat, a bit of this and a bit more of that.' She turned two then caught that girl's eye. 'How did you make that baby, Elsie?'

Elsie looked left, right, anywhere but at her inquisitor. 'You fryin' some 'taters too, missus?'

'A man hurt you when he made that baby. Where did that man come from, Elsie?'

No reply.

'You tell me who hurt you and I'll fry you some potatoes.'

So it was blackmail. She'd tried all else — and it didn't work anyway.

Elsie stood head down, studying her narrow feet. Her hands were as narrow. She was a tiny girl, five foot nothing and fine. Gertrude had cut her lice-riddled hair near to the scalp on the day she'd brought her in from the camp. It was a mass of black curls now — a pretty, sad-eyed kid with the sweetest nature. And what hope did she have? The mission folk would take that baby and try to turn Elsie back into a twelve year old. Time couldn't be turned back. What had happened to her had happened and she liked babies.

They'd teach her to read and write. She was young enough to learn, capable of learning — capable of learning a lot of things if she could see the sense in the learning. Milk she could drink. She'd learnt to milk a goat. Bread she could eat. She could get that bread started in the mornings. She could sew on a button. Buttons kept her frocks done up, but what use was reading and writing to a kid who'd spent most of her life barely surviving? It had taken Gertrude a month to get a pencil into her hand, another to teach her that E made the sound for Elsie. A teacher might have done better — would maybe do better at the mission.

'You're a good girl, Elsie, and a big help to me. I'm going to miss you so very, very much.'

'I stay in shed, missus. Plenty room in shed.'

'God save me from your eyes, darlin',' she said, then to save herself she turned to her sack of potatoes, selected a big one, gave it a brush off, a quick wash, a wipe, then sliced it into the pan. She wasn't a fussy cook and never had been. Her meals weren't fancy. The potato sizzling, fat spitting, her fork busy turning sausages and potatoes while Elsie took knives and forks from the dresser drawer, placed plates on the hob.

'Grab me a couple of eggs, love.' No sooner said and they were in her hand.

Potatoes and sausages moved to the side of the pan, two eggs broken into the fat and she stood flipping fat over the yolks, turning them blue.

No wasted effort in Gertrude's house, nor extra washing up. Two meals served from a frying pan, hot fat poured into the dripping bowl, the pan wiped out with newspaper, the paper burned, the pan hung on its bent nail beside her stove, ready to cook the next meal, and Gertrude sat and picked up her knife and fork.

Elsie stood opposite, looking down at her piled plate. 'Wadi,' she said.

'You want to go back to Wadi?' Hot potato in her mouth.

'Wadi hurted me. He put baby, missus.'

Had to spit that potato or swallow it. She swallowed and it burned all the way down. She rose, her chair legs squealing, as Elsie shrank back, back to the washstand.

They were a different race, folk said, they had different attitudes. You can't put a white head on a pair of black shoulders, folk said. And Gertrude knew it. She knew it. But it didn't make the way they lived right, and that little girl wasn't black anyway, and whether she was black or white, it didn't give that jabbering bastard of a man the right to rape a twelve-year-old girl.

She walked to the door to suck some night air down her burning throat. Had to say something. Had to find something to say.

'Thank you for telling me.' Too stilted, too cold. 'You're a good girl for telling me, darlin'.'

'Lucy runned, missus. She say we not go to mission, missus. He get us from mission. We going our daddy. Wadi comed and getted me. He don't like runnin'. He done . . .'

She showed her leg, her broken leg, and Gertrude's stomach, shaking since she'd left town, decided to reject that hot potato, and Sissy's birthday cake too. She ran into the yard and vomited. She wasn't the vomiting type, but she held on to her fence tonight and vomited her heart out.

Washed her face, washed her hands at the tank, stood leaning there, staring through her fence at the dark hump of her walnut tree, her mind circling from Amber to Elsie, from Wadi to Archie, from India to Argentina.

Didn't hear those bare feet behind her, didn't know Elsie was there until she felt her breath on her arm.

'No use both of our meals getting cold, love. Go inside and eat.'

'Them in oven, missus.'

Gertrude lifted her eyes to the sky, pleading with them not to let her down. She was a healer, not a howler.

That timid bird-like hand barely touching, that was what did it. Touch is what the human spirit craves and no one ever touched her. She wailed like a punished child, turned and grasped that girl to her, holding her hard against her and howling, for her, for Amber, for the doll she'd spent so much love in sewing, and for tiny Jenny too, who might have been better off placed in a children's home, or raised down here, fed on goat's milk, this little girl loving her. She'd made a mistake. She'd made a terrible, terrible mistake. She'd signed her name as witness to the birth of that little girl, registered as the child of Norman and Amber Morrison. She'd done the wrong thing by that poor dead woman and by her baby.

'I goin' tamorra, missus. You stop cryin' now. Plenty room at mission, missus. Wadi won' get me. I goin' tamorra, missus, aw'right.'

'You're not going anywhere,' Gertrude said, kissing that worried face. 'We've got room enough. Baby's only a little feller.'

'You stoppin' cry now, missus.'

'You say Mrs Foote and I'll stop,' she said, kissing her again.

'Foot sound like walkin' on it, missus.'

'You're right,' she said. 'And I'm tired of being walked all over. You call me anything you want to call me, darlin'.'

'Mum sound good, missus.'

'Mum sounds beautiful to me.'

GROWING FAMILIES

Jennifer was five months old the day Amber left her sitting in her highchair while she got the sheets on to boil. That was the day Cecelia discovered that if she placed her shiny new shoes against the seat of the chair and applied enough pressure, the chair tilted, and if she applied a little more pressure . . .

Amber heard the crash and, seconds later, the scream. She ran to the house where she found Cecelia looking down at the chair and the bellowing baby.

'She fallded.'

'How?'

'She fallded, I said!'

The chair, chosen for Cecelia, was sturdy and stable. Amber had strapped Jennifer into it so she couldn't fall. The straps released, she looked at a growing bump on the baby brow. She looked at her arms, her legs, while Jennifer screamed. Nothing appeared to be broken. Amber sat and put her to the breast, and in time Jennifer sucked.

'I want some titty too,' Sissy demanded, slapping her mother.

'In bed,' Amber said. 'Now be good, or Mummy will sleep in Daddy's bed.'

Babies bounce. They bruise easily. She told Norman Jenny had rolled from the bed while she was changing her napkin. She repeated those words to Maisy. Gertrude didn't see the bump. She was no longer welcome in her daughter's house.

Jenny was almost seven months old and still bald the day Elsie gave birth to a son with black hair two inches long. The new mother laughed at him and set Gertrude laughing. During the following months there was much laughter in those two cluttered rooms.

No laughter in Norman's house and no love. He slept alone while his wife slept in his daughter's bed, the door closed against him. He was a man of forty years, a man with carnal desires he could not admit to, or not consciously. At night, his subconscious shocked him. He feared he was possessed by demons. Wicked, sinful dreams invaded his sleep, dreams of one of the Duffy girls. And he awakening in such a state of arousal he ran from the house to the chill of the backyard.

His dreams began infiltrating his waking hours. He saw that Duffy girl walk by his house, pursued by three dogs, and Lord, God almighty, what was happening to him?

'Our Father, who art in heaven, hallowed be thy name . . .'

He found himself aroused by the sound of Amber's bathwater running down the pipe and into the garden. He was aroused by the sight of her forearm reaching for a loaf of bread, by the breast she bared occasionally to the infant.

'Lead us not into temptation. Deliver us from evil.'

He found himself walking the station platform by day, planning his night ahead, arguing his case mentally, rehearsing his arguments over and over until he was word perfect, but come nightfall he lacked the inner fortitude to put his case before his wife. He was afraid of her. Only in the dead of night did he dare to creep into Cecelia's bedroom, to stand beside that bed breathing in the scent of his wife's pale hair, gazing on an arm bared in sleep — and to fantasise the lifting up of her, the carrying of her to his own bed, the locking of his door, and the taking . . .

Then the most incredible of all dreams awakened him one cold and frosty dawn. Half-asleep, he flew from his demon bed to walk the passage on chilled bare feet, to stand outside Cecelia's bedroom door long enough for his feet to turn to ice, then to slowly, quietly, turn the knob and ease that door open. And his eyes could not believe what they saw. The sight of that flattened nipple as it popped from his daughter's mouth shocked his heart from its natural rhythm. Like a trapped vulture, it lurched in his breast while his arousal grew to that of a crazed bull.

Certain his heart was about to explode, as had his father's, he lost all reason, and while Cecelia watched in milk-drooling, open-mouthed silence, he dragged Amber from the blankets, carried her out one door, in through another. And he turned the key.

She fought him, but in silence. She slid from his bed, but he caught her gown and tumbled her to the floor rug where he finally subdued her.

He was a shipwrecked, salt-caked sailor washed by a wave into safe harbour. His landing was rocky, but he clung there while the crashing waves rocked him. Not until the tide went out did he look down at where he'd landed. In the struggle, her gown, a low-necked cotton thing, had been ripped from neck to hem and her breasts, twin mounds of naked perfection, stared up at him.

Norman's lovemaking had ever been a thing of the dark, of the bed, silent, due to his mother's presence in the house, and well blanketed. It was an animal need he was not proud of, which he had only requested on Saturday nights — pleaded for some Saturday nights, bribed for — but bribe or plea, he had always treated Amber with the greatest of respect, completing his task with alacrity, following it with a brief apology then turning his back.

This morning, though relief had come fast, he did not apologise or withdraw. He was out of breath, on the floor, and a man of his size did not rise from the floor as gracefully as a dolphin from the ocean. And he was stark naked and uncertain of how he'd got that way. His heartbeat, however, had regulated, and now beat in his breast like a victory drum.

'Let me up, you brutal swine,' Amber hissed.

'I am not done,' he said, staring down at the peaked nipple so recently in that girl's mouth. He felt moved to suck there, but resisted temptation, easing himself up so he might better view his naked woman. Supporting himself on one hand, he allowed his other to explore those twin breasts, to brush the nipples.

Certainly he had fondled her breasts in the night, but to watch his hand's exploration —

'She's having a seizure. Let me go to her.'

She? He turned his head to the noise on the other side of the door, of which, to that moment, he had been unaware.

'Let you go to her and have a repetition of your deviant behaviour, Mrs Morrison? I think not.'

His fingers brushed an erect nipple and within her he stirred, but he quelled the urge and allowed his hand to play.

'The girl will be sent to a boarding school.' Kissed one breast, then the other. 'Where her conduct will be curbed — and your own, my dear Mrs Morrison.'

'I'll take her and leave you.'

She fought him, and he watched her fight, her breasts finding a life of their own, falling to the side, rising towards him, arousing him wildly. He moved within her as she strove to get a grip on his hair. He had little enough left, and what he had was shorn regularly. She attempted to remove his ear and may have succeeded. No matter. He had two. She raked his face with her nails, and he moved deeper, determined to reach the girl within, the laughing girl he had seen at church and loved.

'Boarding school. I will see to it . . . today.' Like the recitation of a joyous poem. 'Your place is . . . beside me . . . my dear, my beautiful Amber . . . to love . . . to honour . . . to obey.'

'I loathe the sight of you.'

'Then I suggest . . . you close your eyes . . . my so precious . . . my very dear Mrs Morrison.'

She cursed him, his mother, his family, but Norman was beyond hearing. The kicking, the screaming outside his locked door, slid far away. He took his time with her, took his fill of her, and when the last of his need drained from him, he rose like a dugong from the ocean floor and fell to his bed, sucking air.

The key scratching in the lock opened his eyes. He turned to view her one final time but she'd clad herself in his morning gown.

'You're not sending her away, Norman. She's all I've got.'

You have me, he thought, but with little energy for other than thought, he did not reply.

'I'll send her to school here,' she said. 'I'll go down and speak to Miss Rose today.'

She spoke to her. Cecelia spent one morning in the junior classroom. A senior girl walked her home at noon, with a note from the infants' mistress suggesting Cecelia was not yet ready to take her place at school, that perhaps they should try her again after the Christmas holidays.

The following week was difficult, but remarkable in many respects for Norman. Over that period of seven days, he made love to his wife on nine occasions, and on three of those occasions during daylight hours.

Cecelia was rabid. Jennifer was miserable. The breast denied to one was denied to the other. Jennifer turned to her thumb for sucking comfort. Cecelia slapped and pinched, taking comfort where she could.

She hadn't appreciated her morning at school. All she'd learnt there, and from the Macdonald girls, was that the headmaster had a strap and that naughty children who couldn't behave themselves got whacked around their legs with that strap.

She learned much more at home. She pushed Jenny off the verandah and Amber told Norman she'd fallen off. Cecelia tried something new. She whacked Jenny around the legs with the string shopping bag and kept on whacking until Amber took the string bag away and hung it high, then told Norman it must have been some sort of rash, that she must have had a reaction to something in the garden.

'I can't watch her every minute, Norman.'

Cecelia raked Jenny's cheek with her fingernails.

'She scratched herself on the rose bush,' Amber lied.

Cecelia, now approaching her sixth birthday, though not overly burdened by intellect, was bright enough to realise she was a protected species and thus could upgrade her attacks with impunity — as long as Norman wasn't around. Norman had keys. He could lock her out of his bedroom and lock her mother in, and on the one occasion when he'd caught Cecelia slapping Jenny, he'd locked her in her own room.

The key to her door went missing on her birthday. She'd given herself a secret birthday present — tossed the key into the lavatory pan then belted Jenny across the face and dared her father to find that key. He had another one. It didn't fit her door but he carried her kicking into the nursery and locked her in there. And when he let her out, he'd taken the key out of the lock and put it up high so she couldn't get it.

She had to watch out for him. She became expert on Norman's comings and goings. She learned to tell the time, knew when the clock hands said twelve o'clock and it was lunchtime. She learned to smile at him, just like Amber smiled when visitors came, learned to play nicely with Jenny, drew pictures for her, built castles from wooden ABC blocks . . . until the clock's hands said one o'clock and he walked out that side gate and back to his station. Then she could throw those blocks, jab Jenny in the leg with the point of the pencil and watch that baby mouth opening in shocked surprise, even before the scream came out.

She swung an empty lemonade bottle at that bald head one windy afternoon, and was surprised at the results. Jenny fell over. She didn't bawl and didn't get up.

At twenty-two months, Jennifer had less meat on her bones than a day-old lamb and less hair on her head than a newborn mouse, which made the inch-long split in her scalp look worse than it was. Amber picked her up and ran with her to Norman. He didn't see the scalp wound, only the left eye socket filled with blood. He carried her over the road to the constable's house, while Amber comforted Cecelia, who hadn't realised that a little hit with a lemonade bottle would cause so much fuss.

Ernie Ogden's wife had seven boys. She'd seen her share of blood. She mopped out the eye socket, looked at the gash, told Norman it would need a few stitches, told him to press the pad to the wound, then she yelled for her oldest boy to ride down and fetch Gertrude.

Norman carried Jenny home, her tiny arms clinging to his neck. Perhaps the seed of love had lain dormant in his heart since her baby mouth had first turned to his touch. He realised how deeply its roots had become entrenched that day when he held her down on the kitchen table. He could feel the pain in his own bowel as Gertrude placed each stitch into baby flesh. His spectacles fogged for her, and when it was done he scooped her back into his arms.

'Forgive me,' he said. 'Forgive your daddy.'

He had not asked the question of Amber, the how, the where, and thus had not received the lie. She attempted to take Jenny from his arms; he didn't release her, but walked with her up and down the passage while she sobbed the last of her pain into his shoulder.

Gertrude asked the question. She was packing her equipment into her cane basket. Norman came to the door to hear Amber's reply.

'She fell over. She never walks if she can run,' Amber said.

Jenny heard that lie. She lifted her head from her father's shoulder and, her big teary eyes looking into his, she removed her sucking thumb from her mouth and pointed it at Cecelia. 'Sissywidabotta, Duddy,' she said.

'I did not do noffink to you.' Jenny's speech, still unintelligible to an adult, was crystal clear to Cecelia, who had watched the entire bloody operation with morbid interest. 'You're telling big fat liars.'

'What did she say, love?' Gertrude asked.

'Noffink.' Cecelia backed away to her mother.

'Can you show Daddy what happened to your sore head?' Gertrude encouraged.

Eyeing the stranger who had hurt her, Jenny slid the long way down to the floor, took Norman's hand and led him out to the back verandah where, with two hands, she picked up the lemonade bottle.

'Sissywidabotta,' she repeated.

'She's telling liars,' Cecelia yelled, but Norman had the bottle, Jenny's sucking thumb was accusing her again and two sets of eyes were believing that thumb.

'I did never do noffink like that,' Cecelia screamed. She knew that the fastest way to change the subject was to throw a tantrum. By necessity, all conversation ceased when she screamed.

'I know you didn't do it,' Amber soothed, on her knees beside her. 'No one thinks you did it, sweetheart.'

'A baby doesn't know how to lie,' Gertrude said.

'She doesn't know what she's saying either, and I don't know what she's saying. As if Cecelia would hit her with a bottle.'

Jenny stood watching her sister's performance, her thumb returned to her mouth, the other hand feeling her stitches, while Norman placed the offending bottle with others of its ilk beneath the verandah. She ran to him. He picked her up, but a glance at Amber and he set Jenny back on her feet.

He is afraid of her, Gertrude thought, and a wave of compassion washed through her. She'd never liked the man, had once likened him to a bloodhound. He had the bulk, the hangdog eyes, even the jowls of a bloodhound — but one whipped into submission as a pup, trained to fetch and carry for an old bitch. He was of a size to be dangerous, but off his mother's leash he belonged to no one. Not to Amber, that was obvious. Not to that screaming brat of a girl kicking herself in circles on the verandah. Maybe little Jenny could claim him. Someone had to claim him or he was a lost man.

It's hard — no, it's near impossible — to see the wrong in those we love, she thought, and when we do see it, we do our best to ignore it. Through the years she'd ignored the worst of Amber. There were times she'd told herself that Norman deserved what he got, that he should have known better. He was ten years older than Amber and city raised; he should have known better. Fifty, a hundred times, she'd blamed him for ruining her daughter's life. Today Gertrude allowed herself to admit that her own girl was the despoiler. She was ruining Cecelia's life, and unless she was stopped, she'd ruin Jenny's. There was something sadly wrong with Amber, something missing in that girl. Always as pretty as a picture, but there was hard, non-giving glass in front of that picture now and God only knew what behind it.

'Get up from there. You'll get splinters in your bottom,' Gertrude said. Cecelia raised the volume. 'You need to get her to school, Norm?'

'She'll go when she's ready to go,' Amber replied.

'She's more than ready to go. She needs to be spending her days with kids her own age, not abusing babies,' Gertrude said. And she needs a few of those kids to give her back a dose of her own medicine. 'She's supposed to be reading and writing, adding her sums, not splitting babies' heads with lemonade bottles.'

'She didn't hit her, I said, and don't think you can start coming up here again, tossing around your advice on child raising. I spent more nights in other people's beds than I did in my own — and so did you, you unprincipled old trollop.'

'Turning your attack on me, my girl, won't convince anyone that a lemonade bottle didn't make that gash. And lifting that girl up like that won't do your back any good either. You're pregnant again, aren't you?'

'If I am, you won't be getting anywhere near it.'

'Vern's boy is in boarding school,' Norman said.

'His useless mother spends her life trotting to theatres in the city, that's why he's at boarding school,' Amber said.

'She's not trotting anywhere right now. She's in the Alfred hospital with a growth. They're operating next week,' Gertrude said.

'Oooh, cross your fingers, Mum. You might get another chance at him,' Amber said, hauling her load indoors.

Gertrude turned to Jenny, standing quietly at her side. The side of her scalp was swollen, the flesh raw, four spiky black stitches standing tall. It would leave a scar, but her hair would eventually grow through to hide it. Tiny wee ears, dear little nose, wide, watchful eyes. Even in the state Gertrude had seen the stranger, it was obvious she'd been a beautiful woman. This mite had her fine features and her Mediterranean complexion, not her eye colouring though. That woman's eyes had been brown.

There'll be bigger problems than split scalps in this house before those two girls are much older, she thought as she reached down to kiss the tiny mite who leaned into her leg like so much thistledown.

'Keep those stitches dry for a week, Norm,' she said. 'Dab them with a bit of iodine twice a day. I'll come in on Friday and take them out.'

DESERTION

Trouble came in cycles when it came to Woody Creek. Months could pass and not a call made on Gertrude's time, then some star moved out of line and they were back at her door again, day or night. She delivered another Duffy on the night following Jenny's accident, delivered it in a shed not fit for dogs, but plenty of the flea-riddled mongrels wandering in and out. Clarry Dobson's wife went into labour that same night. She wanted a girl and ended up with another boy. On the Tuesday, one of the tree fellers came to get her. Big Henry King, a champion wood cutter, who could fell a tree faster drunk than most could do it sober must have been sober. His axe had slipped, sliced through his boot and damn near split his big toe in two. Big Henry's foot hadn't seen water in a year or two and his house had seen less. The Kings were a cut above the Duffy family — they didn't own flea-riddled dogs, though Henry's wife may have made up the shortfall. Gertrude refused to go inside so Henry hopped outside and sat on the crate he used as a kitchen chair. She washed his foot while he cursed her. It seemed that he'd missed the bone. She flushed the wound with saltwater then stitched where she could while he called her everything but a lady. By the time she'd reached the stage of dousing it with iodine, he was threatening to come after her one night with his axe, but she bound it tightly and told him to stay off it for a day or two, unless he wanted to lose his toe. She didn't tell him to keep it dry. Unless it rained, there was not much chance of him getting it wet.

'I'll pop in on Friday and see how it's going. Keep it up higher than your heart and it will give you less pain,' she said. He was walking up to the hotel for a painkiller before she was on her horse.

Then that same day, Joanne Hooper died on the operating table.

Vern brought her home on the Wednesday night and they buried her on Thursday, the service held at the little Methodist church, which was hard pushed to hold twenty-five, including the pastor. They packed in fifty that day and fifty more stood outside. They were there for Vern. Few in town had been on more than nodding acquaintance with Joanne.

Gertrude didn't go to the wake. She went to Norman's house, intending to take out Jenny's stitches. Amber was pale. She'd spent the day vomiting.

'When are you due, darlin'?' Gertrude said.

'None of your business,' Amber said.

'I'll take Jenny down with me for a few days. Get some rest.'

Jenny would forget her first ride on Gertrude's horse. She didn't enjoy it and was pleased to be lifted down to Elsie's arms. She enjoyed Joey, a fat little boy, the colour of creamy coffee, who toddled behind her all day. She didn't cry for her mother, and when on the following Friday she was lifted down from the pony cart at Norman's gate, she clung to her grandmother.

'Ina-cart,' she said. 'Go ina-cart now.'

Norman did not argue when Gertrude took Jenny home for one more week. He had plans for that week. Cecelia was to commence school.

Miss Rose, the infants' mistress, was a pixie of a woman, four foot ten, her features pointed, her auburn hair cut in a sharp fringe and chiselled bob. She'd believed in fairytales at nineteen, had planned to marry her Prince Charming and raise a family of pixie children, but her fiancé had gone off to fight a war and he hadn't returned. As a nineteen-year-old girl, she'd vowed never to wed but to spend her life in some worthwhile cause. Too small and gentle-natured to nurse, teaching had been her second choice.

She didn't look like a teacher, didn't dress as a teacher; she clothed herself in filmy greens, pretty pinks, plums, in beads, gold buckles and foolish hats. She was wearing one such foolish hat on the morning Norman delivered a screaming Cecelia to her classroom. The hat flew west as she stooped to speak to the child. Norman retrieved it.

'She'll settle down quite quickly when you leave, Mr Morrison,' Miss Rose assured him.

During her seven years of teaching, Miss Rose had known many difficult days, had handled many difficult children, but that Monday eclipsed all others. She'd dodged a flying slate, calmed a bitten infant, bathed a scratched face, tolerated an hour of screaming, and all before noon, when she called for reinforcements.

Woody Creek's school was a little taller than the average house but looked much the same as many residences. It consisted of three large rooms, each one opening onto a wide west-facing verandah. There was a cloakroom down the southern end of the building, partially open to the elements, and a narrow washroom at the northern end. The headmaster, John Curry, taught the senior children in a large room at the southern end. He wasn't a big man, but he kept a firm control. Miss Rose ran down that verandah fifteen minutes before the lunch hour, Cecelia's scream pursuing her.

'Please,' she said.

No more need be said. Her normally alabaster complexion was rosy red, her auburn hair, where never a tendril stepped out of line, was awry.

Like Galahad to the rescue, the headmaster led the way back to the junior room where he found the girl lying on the floor between two rows of desks, the other children grouped together near the door, watching the show. Some were amused, some chewed on hair, chewed on fingers. All were interested when he hauled Cecelia to her feet, carried her screaming out to the yard and dumped her beside the flagpole.

She ran the two blocks home, screaming all the way. Norman returned a relatively tame child. She remained relatively tame until he was out of sight, when the school day continued as it had begun.

'Miss Rose, she pulled Irene's hair nearly out by its roots.'

'Miss Rose, she dug her fingernails nearly through my neck.'

Mr Curry spoke to Norman at the station. He suggested the girl may be unteachable. He mentioned her lack of respect for mistress, students and for himself. He suggested an educator in the city who was seemingly having some success in teaching the unteachable. Norman listened with great respect. He didn't mention that his daughter had no respect for him, nor did he agree that the girl was unteachable. He nodded, and Mr Curry went on his way convinced the problem had been overcome.

The stationmaster continued walking his daughter to school and the teachers gave up attempting to get rid of her.

'Do unto others as you will have others do unto you, Cecelia,' Miss Rose said. 'A badly trained dog bites, Cecelia. Are you a badly trained dog or a child?'

She bit Irene Palmer at playtime. Bit Ray King later. Threw missiles.

'Miss Rose, Sissy Morrison pulled Valma's pants down and some boys were looking.'

'Miss Rose, she's sitting on Sophie and pulling her hair out by the roots.'

Previous hair-pulling had gained the offender a full day of wearing a long hay-band wig, be the offender male of female. It was uncomfortable and reputedly full of head lice. No child chose to wear it more than once. The wig, offered to Cecelia on her second day at school, had ended up the in lavatory pan.

Cecelia grew taller during the months of Amber's pregnancy. Her face, all broad chin and brow, was as flat as a freckled dinner plate, with as much character. Norman purchased a large rubber protective sheet when her bed-wetting became a regular occurrence. He paid Clarry Dobson's unmarried sister to handle the laundry, while Amber kept to her bed, or kept to it during daylight hours. She walked on moonlit nights, walked for hours.

In the care of her grandmother and fed well on goat's milk, eggs and garden greens, little Jenny grew in height, confidence and vocabulary. And her hair grew through, not dark as expected, not straight like the stranger's, but tight, springy coils of gold.

'She's one of God's angels, sent to us for a purpose,' Nancy Bryant said.

She visited with Gertrude now, or with Jenny. She brought tiny hand-knitted sweaters and her grandson's outgrown garments for Joey. She praised Elsie's biscuits, praised her chubby brown-eyed son, and in time Elsie stopped running when she saw Nancy's smart green gig coming down the track.

During the seventh month of Amber's pregnancy, Charles, the parson, wrote suggesting Amber spend the final months with him and his wife in Melbourne. They were now living in central Melbourne, just around the corner from a fine lying-in hospital. Amber wanted to go, but Melbourne was a six-hour train journey away and that trip in her delicate condition could put the unborn child at risk.

In early March, Norman placed a phone call to the Willama hospital, explaining his wife's situation and asking advice. One of the doctors agreed to make the trip to Woody Creek to assess the situation. He arrived at the designated time and, to Norman, looked little more than a callow youth, a youth who drove a sporty car. Norman paced the passage for an hour visualising what that youth may be doing to his wife.

He was at the door when it opened.

'The pregnancy appears to be progressing well,' the youth reported. 'However, given your wife's history, all care must be taken. We have a well-equipped hospital in Willama, experienced doctors. I would suggest the child be born there, and the final weeks of your wife's confinement be spent in Willama, close to medical assistance.'

There was a boarding house a few blocks from the hospital, run by a nurse and her husband. The youth offered to take care of all arrangements.

'Should there be any difficulty in arranging transportation, the hospital now has a reliable vehicle, which for a small fee . . .'

The youth's fee was not small. Norman paid it, then the sports car went on its way and Amber found new energy to argue for Melbourne. Her infant was not expected until late April.

'What's the difference between sitting in a comfortable first-class carriage for six hours to sitting on your mother's couch, Norman?'

'The doctor suggests —'

'To hell with what he suggests. I didn't want him up here in the first place.'

Norman did not relent. A room was booked for her in Willama, from 19 April. Vern agreed to transport her there. Maisy agreed to travel with her.

So March passed. Cecelia had her seventh birthday. Norman bought her a book. She didn't like books. It ended its life in the lavatory pan.

And April came, a delightful month of warm days and cool evenings. Perhaps Amber walked too far on the evening of the sixth day of April. She awoke on the seventh day in pain.

Born to breed, Amber never suffered long in expelling her babies. Within two hours of the first twinge, she was pushing the head out. Gertrude, again waiting to deliver her grandchild, prayed to God, to Jesus and his mother, to anyone who might be up there, to please, please take care of this baby, to please allow it to be born alive, to let it breathe.

She thanked God when the little sports car pulled up out front and the boy driver stepped over the gate and inside. Willingly she gave way to him and got her back to the wall, held her breath until the baby was delivered, held it until she saw her granddaughter draw her own first breath, until she heard her cry, then Gertrude ran from the room to cry.

The delivery fast and easy, the babe pronounced healthy and of a good size, the doctor took morning tea in Norman's kitchen, took one more glance at mother and child, accepted his fee and departed, leaving Amber beaming and holding her living baby girl.

'Leonora April,' she said, accepting her mother's kiss, allowing her to kiss her granddaughter.

'A beautiful name for a beautiful baby, darlin'.'

'She is beautiful, isn't she? She's got a dimple in her chin.'

'She's the living, breathing image of you when you were first born.'

'Thank God for that much,' Amber said, and she laughed.

Norman came to listen, to watch her laughter. It had been too long. He wasn't aware of why she laughed. Gertrude knew. She sat with Amber for an hour that morning, watching happiness exude from her girl's every pore, laughing with her, drinking tea beside her bed, and praising the wonder of that little girl.

So much happiness in Norman's house that day and that night. Jenny left in Elsie's care, Cecelia with Maisy. Gertrude slept in her granddaughter's bed, and the joy of being awakened by that newborn cry, the ecstasy of watching her at the breast.

For two days there was happiness in Norman's house. For two days tiny Leonora April sucked, cried, soiled. Then her cry weakened and she stopped sucking.

Vern and Gertrude drove mother and babe to the hospital, where on the fourth day tiny Leonora April died.

Amber screaming then, screaming, smashing, hitting out at that young doctor who had told her her baby was healthy, slapping at white-clad nurses and cursing, cursing God and her mother, Norman and his mother.

They calmed her with their potions and told Norman he should take her home. She refused to go home, so they moved her to the boarding house room booked for two weeks from the nineteenth. It was close to the hospital and to that young doctor's care. Far better she stay there until the babe was buried. Far better the house be cleared of baby things before she returned.

Cecelia would ever remember the few brief days of Leonora April, her wail, her napkins. She'd remember that coffin too and Leonora lying in it, dressed in a gown of satin and lace and looking like a china doll in a box. She'd remember one of the church ladies lifting her to kiss her baby sister goodbye. She'd kissed her cheek, expecting it to feel like the face of her china doll. It was more like kissing cold bread dough.

She'd remember Amber's face on the day Vern Hooper brought her home from Willama. It had the look of white bread dough. Leonora's eyes had been closed. Amber's were open, but they may as well have been closed. She couldn't see where she was going. Didn't know where she was. Gertrude led her by her hand. She put her into the bed.

And Cecelia wanted to be seen. She hit the blind-eyed stranger, yelled at her until those eyes saw her, until those arms opened, then she threw herself into them, hugging her, holding her forever. Never, never would she forget the blissful relief of being back in Mummy's arms.

Later, there was the long train journey with Norman and Amber, the chuga-chuga-chug of the train and no talking. Then Uncle Charles and Aunty Jane meeting them at a station that wasn't anything like Norman's station. And Cousin Reginald driving a green car that took them to a house made of bricks, and Aunty Jane taking them to a bedroom with only one bed in it where she was going to sleep with her mother.

Then no more Norman or Jenny or Leonora April. No more keys and no more school either. She'd won the war! She wasn't sure how she'd done it, but she'd won!

AN AGREEABLE CHILD

On the Sunday following his trip to the city, Norman made the long walk down to Gertrude's property and that evening he carried Jenny home. Perhaps it was the wrong thing to do, but his house was empty and he didn't know how to live in an empty house. It took some time to become accustomed to single parenthood, but Jenny was an agreeable child, content with little — which was as well. He had little to give. She accompanied him to the station each day, where she sat content for hours, colouring newspapers with her crayons, building towers from boxes and chuckling when they fell down.

He had never taken a comb to a child's hair. Now he found he must. Her hair, her colouring, had surprised him, and each morning when he brushed her wilful curls he was surprised anew. He had taken into his house the infant of a woman of foreign appearance, dark of eye and hair. He had expected a dark-headed child, but somewhere in Jennifer's genealogy lurked an antecedent with sapphire blue eyes and ringlets of gold. She was a beautiful thing, a gem chanced upon.

To love and be loved in return is every man's right. Norman was unlovable. Surely he had loved his wife, though by the second week of her absence, he was not missing her. She had accused him of putting a stranger's child before his own had he dared to show an interest in that golden mite. Now he sat at night, her fairy weight on his lap. He found himself spinning foolish rhymes so he might hear her chuckle.

There was an old man from Willama, who wore only half a pyjama . . .

And the near unbearable pleasure of her lisping conversation at the meal table.

'I don like dat meat, Duddy.'

'Why don't you like that meat?'

''Cause dat's fwom baah lambs, Duddy.'

She liked sausages. She loved potatoes, fried, mashed or roasted. They cooked their meal together, Jenny sitting on the table while Norman made his preparations. Within a month of Amber's leaving, Norman's life had become . . . easy. His house had become a home. Newspapers piled up in corners. Clearing a table of condiments between meals was time poorly spent. A parlour was a fine place to toss laundry brought in from the clothes line, and a very fine place to play hidey.

Norman was a man of many faults. He knew each one. His mother first, then Amber, had listed them often. As a husband and father he had struggled, but he'd had no example to follow. His own father had died before his birth, so each step taken down that convoluted road of marriage and fatherhood had found him negotiating unknown terrain. His mother had considered infants to be incontinent, godless little animals, until trained to be otherwise. She had stated many times that it was the woman's responsibility to train them, as she had trained him — trained him with her disappointment, her disapproval, her denial. With those tools at her easy disposal, she could have trained a rampaging rhinoceros to sit up and beg for a Bible.

Norman's first book had been a Bible. From infancy, he had been carried to church each Sunday. From infancy, he had prayed with his mother every night. At her knee he had learnt that those of the Church of England faith were God's chosen people, that Catholics were thieves and liars, Jews must be punished forever for the murder of Jesus Christ, and that the remainder of mankind, Chinese, blacks and others, were so far removed from God that Norman could ignore their existence in the sure and certain knowledge that once he got to heaven he'd be free of them — and perhaps free of the Catholics and the Jews. However, even as a callow lump of a boy, Norman had visualised a segregated heaven, much like the cemetery where each Sunday he'd been taken to visit his father. All religions were catered for in that cemetery, though well separated. Norman had enjoyed his cemetery visits. He had ongoing memories of his father's solid headstone.

He had no ongoing memories of home, or school. He and his mother, left near destitute by the death of his father, had become the collective responsibility of *the family*. For the first sixteen years of his life, Norman and his mother hopped from Duckworth to Duckworth, from grandparent to uncle, uncle to aunt, an endless circle of train journeys through city and country, to beach and to mallee, the billeting relative seemingly happier when loading that well-travelled luggage back onto the train than when unloading it.

Had he not been a reader, Norman's disjointed education may have suffered for his many moves. His religious training had been ongoing. Uncle Charles, the parson, friend and mentor, father figure of his childhood, had primed him to follow his lead into the ministry. Then he'd wed and bred his own son to follow him, Cousin Reginald. Norman was twelve when first introduced to the screaming Reginald. He'd taken an instant dislike to the squalling infant who'd ousted him from his uncle's affection.

In hindsight, there were few Duckworths he had not disliked. Uncle Ollie owned a hardware store in Collingwood, and behind his counter, as a twelve-year-old, Norman had learnt to add and subtract with lightning speed. He'd feared Uncle Ollie, who had been determined to get his pound of flesh out of Norman if not from his sister.

The maiden aunts, Lizzie and Bertha, Norman had adored. They'd shared their small topsy-turvy dwelling in Coburg with five silky terriers. He'd learnt much in that house, had been allowed to iron his own linen, to stitch on a button. The aunts had taught him to crochet colourful woollen squares, which they then stitched together to form warm blankets for the dogs. He'd spent a few fine months in Coburg. His mother had spent those same months in her room. She'd developed an allergic reaction to dogs, though only indoor dogs.

His Bendigo uncle had owned umpteen border collies. His mother enjoyed Bendigo and had carried Norman there annually. He'd learnt to ride a horse in Bendigo, to dig a post hole, hammer a nail, use a saw. In Portsea, Norman had learnt to shave with a cutthroat razor — perhaps his bachelor uncle had hoped his hand might slip.

His varied education, his variety of lifestyles, had given Norman good survival skills but denied him the ability to sustain long-term relationships. Six weeks at his grandparents' house during the Christmas season had been long term. Then Grandfather Duckworth died and Grandmother moved in with Uncle Charles and Aunt Jane, which meant there was no room at that inn for Norman and his mother. Then the Bendigo uncle sold his property and bought land in central New South Wales — of course visitors would be very welcome, but sadly the school was fifteen miles away.

At fifteen, Norman and his mother spent five months at Box Hill, in the house of the Duckworth black sheep, Uncle Bertie. He drank. Forever more, mother and son would remember those months as eternal — intolerably eternal for Cecelia, but those same five months with his three rowdy cousins had been the best of Norman's life. They'd taught him to play poker and to wag. Had he known it was to be his last year of schooling, he may have played less poker, wagged less. His examination results that year convinced Charles and the relatives collectively that he was not ministerial material, and thus further expenditure on his education was not warranted.

An uncle by marriage, a bigwig in the railways, secured for him a position at a suburban station, which spelled the end of the Morrisons' nomadic lifestyle. The family collectively found them a pleasant flat. They furnished it, bits and pieces donated from each house. Someone donated a framed photograph of his father, dusty but intact. The family, collectively, agreed to pay the rent until Norman's earning capacity was such that he might support his mother, then mother and son were moved in. No doubt a collective sigh of relief was expelled that day.

Not so by Norman's mother. She was accustomed to better than a small second-floor flat. For sixteen years she'd lived as a guest in one house or another, where sisters swept floors or paid domestics to do it. She had never shopped for groceries, knew nothing about cuts of meat or the soiling of her hands in peeling filthy potatoes. She was distressed. She wanted to go . . . home.

The two survived in embryonic squalor until Norman's earlier domestic training at the hands of his maiden aunts came to the fore. He bought a broom. He swept the kitchen floor. There was little to sweep. He washed and ironed his work shirt, fried bacon and eggs, progressed to chops and potatoes.

During the second month, he began to revel in his release from relative-hopping, to rejoice in awakening each morning in the same bed, in that same small room, knowing immediately where he was because his father hung on the wall to the right of his bed. He celebrated his leaving of that flat each work-day morning, his arrival home to it each night, delighting in the ritual of placing his own key in his own front door.

If not for his mother, Norman's solid reliability, his methodical habits, may have carried him far in the railway department. By the age of twenty-eight he was employed in one of the city offices. His wage now adequate, he paid the rent and careful shopping allowed him and his mother to live well enough. Then he met Sarah, a girl employed by the railways for her typewriting skills. In time he made the mistake of bringing her home.

His mother had not been fond of the common people. At their first meeting, she labelled Sarah common. 'If you have so little respect for me and for your dead father's name to attach yourself to the daughter of a common butcher, then it is time for me to die,' she'd said, and she'd taken to her bed to do it.

After a month or two, the family became concerned for their sister's wellbeing. Given another month, the railway bigwig found a vacant position in Woody Creek, a three-bedroom house supplied. The application was made. Norman got the job.

The town surprised him, as did the residence. It shared a fence with the post office. The station was sixty-odd yards from the back door, the police station a similar distance from his front door, and the C of E church not much further away.

His mother was not impressed, but she had room to move, and by that stage of her life she had required considerable space to move in. Also, Norman would now be spending his working days within earshot.

'Norman!'

'Norman!'

'Norman!'

On their first Sunday in Woody Creek, he walked her to church where they were introduced to the congregation. He'd heard Amber's laughter, then sighted her, and who would not have sighted that pretty, laughing girl. Twice more he sighted her at church before Maisy and George Macdonald made the introductions.

His mother, always intrusive, asked what her father did.

'He's a doctor,' Amber said.

Some time passed before the Morrisons became aware that Amber had barely known her father, that she lived in a two-roomed hut two miles from town, that her mother wore trousers and was rumoured to be on with Vern Hooper, but by then Norman was obsessed and determined to wed her.

For two years he had pursued her doggedly, had defied his mother for love of Amber. And he had won her. But what had he won?

She confused him, confounded him, and since his mother's death she had threatened time and time again to leave him and take Cecelia with her, her threat initially chilling his very soul. Now? Now, when she had perhaps left him, he was . . .

'Happy,' he said. 'Are we happy, Jenny-wren?'

She nodded adamantly.

'How happy are we?'

'Dat big,' she replied, her tiny arms spread wide.

'My word we are,' he said. 'What shall we cook for dinner tonight?'

'Gwanny eggs.'

'And where do Granny's eggs come from?'

'Fwom da chook.'

'My word they do.'

Amber had not penned a line in the weeks she'd been away. Charles wrote regularly of appointments, of doctors, of the weather. June came in bitterly cold, according to Charles. Jenny and Norman were not feeling the cold.

In late June, Charles wrote again, this time of an English doctor, a specialist in the problems of the female, who would be visiting Melbourne through July and with whom an appointment had been secured for Amber.

> *... on Thursday 21 July. I suggest your wife and daughter spend the first half of the month with you, then return to us ...*

Norman scanned the rest, then fetched his equipment to reply.

> *My dear Charles,*
>   *Rather than suffer the long journey home, only to return for the July appointment, I suggest my wife remain in your care.*
>   *Please find cheque enclosed.*
> *Sincerely, Norman.*

Charles was appreciative of the cheque. He replied the following week, expressing a genuine concern for his nephew's situation. He agreed that Amber's visit might be extended, but added:

> *... I cannot but stress the importance of a child's early education, nephew. Your aunt also wishes me to convey her concerns regarding Cecelia's interrupted schooling ...*

Cecelia's interrupted education concerned Norman. He wrote two replies but shredded both. That night he lay in bed mentally planning a trip to the city so he might bring his daughter home. Come morning, he placed that plan on ice. He would make the trip in July with Jenny. He would be at his wife's side at her specialist appointment, and if she was pronounced well, then he would bring both wife and daughter home.

Or would he?

For the first time in years, he was not awakening each morning with an acid stomach. The last time he could recall eating a fried egg for breakfast had been at his Box Hill cousins' home, but Jenny loved eggs so he fried eggs.

The tranquillity of his breakfast table, the laughter at night while they cooked and ate their evening meal, and later, Jenny sleeping on his lap while he read his newspaper amid the dishes. Had any man ever known such perfect peace?

In late July, he received a letter from the specialist suggesting there was much still unknown regarding the incompatibility of husband and wife, suggesting that for his wife's mental well-being Norman might in future consider the use of a prophylactic during intercourse. He enclosed the address of a city establishment where Norman might procure such items. He also enclosed his bill.

Charles wrote suggesting Amber's recovery was something of a miracle, that her visit might now be safely brought to a close.

Norman didn't reply, though he knew he must make some move to retrieve his family. But surely if Amber was well enough to attend the theatre with Reginald, as Charles had stated in his letter, then certainly she was well enough to get herself and daughter home. When she was ready. Far better the decision to return be made by her than to force her home unready.

'Far better, Jenny-wren.'

'Far better, Duddy-wen,' she agreed.

'*Copy cat from Ballarat, stole a hat and wore it back,*' he chanted.

'*Copy fwog, sat on a log,*' she said and she laughed, and he laughed and kissed her curly head. Was there ever such an exquisite child? Was a man ever as happy as he?

He wrote a cheque to the doctor, then a second, with a brief note, to the supplier of medical equipment in Richmond. He wrote a third to a large city store, enclosing with this one an order form found in a recent catalogue. He'd never owned a bicycle. His mother had considered them both ungainly and dangerous. Frequently now he found himself looking back to those halcyon days of boyhood, those five months of laughter in Box Hill.

Never had Norman enjoyed Woody Creek winters. They were frosty, foggy and bitterly cold, but surely winter did not come that year? Surely July could not be at its end? A package arrived for him one Wednesday, a not so small square package. His bike arrived on the first Friday in August, and what a glorious month August was turning out to be.

With no train to meet on Sunday, Norman mounted his shiny red bike early, Jenny tied into a child's seat the bicycle company had fixed over the rear wheel. He hadn't ridden in twenty years but, as with poker, he had not forgotten how.

They rode to the bridge that first Sunday, Jenny chuckling when they hit a rut and all but came to grief, her eyes wide with wonder when they stopped to stare at two spoonbills, at a family of musk ducks at play. Norman had made a study of Woody Creek's bird life. For half an hour they watched birds come and go, her little hands applauding their flight.

Near midday he lifted her back into her seat, tied her in, then pedalled off down the forest road to Gertrude's house, arriving pink-faced, bright-eyed and windblown. An enjoyable morning, filled with chuckles and learning, and when he lifted her down from the bicycle, her tiny arms clung a while.

The unlovable who chance on love in odd places find it a soul-cleansing elixir. She was not of his blood, his line, but somehow of him, this magical, miraculous being.

They ventured into the forest again the following Sunday and played guessing games when they heard the staccato sound of a hammer echoing through the trees. They found Vern Hooper's car parked in the shade of the walnut tree beside a pile of sappy red timber. Norman leaned his bike against the fence, then, hand in hand, they crept up on the hammerers at the rear of Gertrude's house.

'Booo!' they cried in unison, laughed when Gertrude dropped the beam she'd been supporting. She and Vern were constructing a lean-to.

'Amber?' Gertrude asked.

'From all reports, very well, Mother Foote. It seems that my cousin is now squiring her around to theatres.'

'When are they coming home?'

'I imagine it will not be long. Reginald followed his father into the ministry. It seems that he will shortly be heading for the tropics, no doubt to save some black souls,' Norman said. Charles had written:

> *Your wife has been taking full advantage of her time in the city, however, I would now suggest the time has come to bring the visit to a close. Reginald is leaving for Port Moresby and will be away for six months. As you will be aware, nephew, my wife and I have many commitments . . .*

'You'll be going down to bring them home?'

He sighed, looked at the construction. Certainly he had considered making the trip. 'The timing,' he said. 'Work commitments . . .'

And, more importantly, his house, which would require a severe going-over. However, that was a problem for another day. The construction they were adding to the rear of Gertrude's kitchen appeared more problematical. He studied the existing roof, the work already done on the new construction, attempting to make some sense of what they were doing, but finding little. They appeared to be flinging together a shelter, not a room. He watched Vern measuring timber for a rafter.

'Might I suggest you cut it a mote longer, Vern, if you intend joining it to the existing rafter. Leakage,' he said.

'We're not joining her in.'

Vern was a farmer. He knew how to fling up a shed in a hurry. He started the cut as Norman knocked on existing wood.

'You're thinking of cutting a doorway,' Gertrude said.

'Simple enough, I believe, Mother Foote. Your construction could . . . would then become a part of the house.'

Vern eyed him. He'd planned to have the shed up by nightfall and to have Elsie and Joey installed in it. He stopped cutting and followed Gertrude and Norman inside to take a look at her kitchen's rear wall.

'If we could do it without damaging my roof it would be a damn sight more convenient, Vern,' Gertrude said.

Not for Vern. He had his own agenda, but he called a smoko and they walked out to look at the pile of raw timber, at the second-hand corrugated iron he'd purchased at an auction. There was more than enough.

He eyed Norman, who was lifting one end of a four-by-two and sighting down it, as his Bendigo uncle had taught him to sight down new beams, seeking out the bow. His Bendigo uncle had taught him the rudiments of measuring, sawing, the basics of hammering. During one of his stays in Bendigo, he and his uncle had built a lean-to onto the milking shed, built it so it didn't leak.

Norman dusted his hands and removed his jacket, aware that he should leave Vern to it, but also aware that with a little time and labour, a useful addition might be constructed.

'Perhaps I might . . .' He removed a pencil from the pocket of his jacket and sketched the existing building on green timber. 'With a little effort, the new rafters could be fixed with half-joins and bolts to the existing rafters.'

'I didn't buy bolts.'

Norman looked at Vern, nodded, then continued. 'The new roofing could then be slid in beneath the old, which will prevent any leakage. The doorway would be cut between existing wall supports . . . and a solid crossbeam . . . there. If I make myself clear, Mother Foote.'

'Gertrude,' she said. 'Trude, Gert. You've known me long enough, Norm.'

'Yes,' he said. 'The floor —'

'Floor?' Vern said. He hadn't been planning to floor it.

'Could be supported by those four-by-twos. Placed on edge. The kitchen floor, as I recall is . . . as low?'

'Lower in places,' Gertrude said.

Vern straightened his back and lit a second cigarette. He could see a day's work turning into ten, could see Gertrude's imagination had been captured — and see her bed growing further out of reach.

110

They found bolts enough in the station shed. They found a near new ladder there, then, armed with Norman's box of tools, the two men drove again to Gertrude's land where they looked at the kitchen roof and decided to wait until next weekend before pulling any nails out. A few clouds had blown in.

The corner posts were in and solid. They could get the walls up, get the floor supports down. The floorboards would wait for next weekend. They worked all afternoon, worked until rain started falling; at six they sat down to one of Elsie's bacon and egg pies and a mound of fried potatoes. Stayed late, stayed until Jenny fell asleep on Norman's lap. They drove home at ten, in Vern's car, the bicycle tied to the trunk.

Norman carried Jenny to her cot unwashed, then fell to his own bed, where he slept like the dead until his station lad came knocking at his door. Grit in his bed when he awakened, more in Jenny's. Grit in her hair when he brushed it.

'What a fine pair we are,' he said. 'But what a fine day we had, Jenny-wren.'

The letter came that afternoon.

Dear Nephew,
Your presence in Melbourne would be appreciated . . .

Dear Charles,
I have important commitments this weekend. Please find enclosed a cheque . . .

THE RETURN

She gave no warning of her intention. When she stepped from the train, for an instant he saw a stranger — two strangers. Cecelia had grown in breadth, and her hair, a functional bob when he'd left her with Charles, was longer and frightfully frizzed. Amber was clad in a smart brown hat and a beige suit he had not previously sighted.

'You look very smart, my dear,' he greeted her. 'And you, Cecelia,' he lied.

'The wind's blowing my hair everywhere, Mummy,' Cecelia said.

'It was a better day in Melbourne,' Amber said, evading his kiss. 'Our case came up in the goods van.'

'I will . . . see to it,' he said, glancing towards Jenny, busy reading the pictures in his newspaper. Perhaps she didn't recognise the strangers. Perhaps they didn't recognise her with hair. Amber didn't greet her.

Sissy recognised her. She stood hands on her hips, staring. 'She's got curly hair too, Mummy. Who curled her hair?'

Too familiar, that nasal whine. Memory rushed him and acid rose in his throat. He flinched from it, glanced quickly towards his house and swallowed bile, aware that his rooms, so comfortable for man and child, would be judged unfit for human habitation by Amber.

'You gave no warning of your arrival, my dear. I had planned...' Planned to pay Miss Dobson for a few hours of cleaning.

'Were you expecting a drum roll?'

'A word. One word, perhaps.'

She had no words for him. She was walking away from him. He turned to the train. He had commitments.

'The house,' he said, 'is . . . untidy.'

'He who expects nothing is never disappointed,' she tossed over her shoulder.

He shuddered, got that train on its way west, swallowed more bile, shuddered again as he watched the train disappear over Charlie's crossing, aware he should have snatched his exquisite child and gone with it.

Too late now.

The station lad came with Amber's case. 'Do you want me to take it over to the house, Mr Morrison?'

Norman shook his head. He took the case, then reached out a hand to Jenny, who scrambled to her feet.

'Shall we run the gauntlet together, my fair, pretty maid?' he said. 'Or shall we . . . run?'

'Wide on da bike, Duddy.'

'Would that we could, my Jenny-wren,' he said. 'Would that we could.'

Amber met them on the verandah, an unwashed pot in her hand. 'There's filth everywhere —'

'Three months —'

'You've lived like pigs.'

'We have managed —'

'You disgust me!'

'That, my dear, is no longer newsworthy.'

He placed the case on the verandah and returned to his station, Jenny toddling happily by his side. She was enough. She and his station would be enough.

They didn't go home for lunch. Norman sent his lad across to the bakery to purchase a large beef pastie, which the three shared at noon. At two, he saw Amber and Cecelia walking across the railway lines. He didn't see them return. Hoped they'd vacated his filthy house — moved into one of the hotel rooms — gone home to Gertrude. No. No. He did not wish that on his mother-in-law.

At five that evening, he braved his back door. And smelled something cooking. Led by his nose, he entered a kitchen no longer his own. She'd been scrubbing. She served four meals from her scoured pots. He did the wrong thing by swapping Jennifer's meat for his potato and gravy, but balanced his sin quickly with a comment on Cecelia's hair.

'Mummy bought curling tongs you make hot on the gas stove.'

'My word,' he said.

'We haven't got any gas here.'

'No,' he said.

He attempted to wash the dishes, but Amber wanted him gone from her kitchen. He went into the parlour, as yet his own. He got Jenny into her nightgown and sat with her on his lap until she slept.

Cecelia refused to walk down to the lavatory in the dark. Amber offered a chamber-pot. Cecelia wanted a proper lavatory like in Melbourne. It had begun! Norman escaped to his railway station for a cigarette and a cup of tea. He returned at nine thirty and went with alacrity to his bed, his door closed.

But she opened it and slid in beside him.

'Weary after your big day, no doubt,' he said.

'There's nothing to do but sit on the train,' she said.

In the dark, she sounded like his Amber. Her hand on his chest felt like her hand. He held it a moment, expecting her to remove it, to turn her back. She didn't. He took it to his lips, kissed it.

Love exists in the heart. When old love dies, memory of it lingers long in the mind, and in lower regions. Norman's memory stirred. The touch of her limbs in that bed, the scent of her skin, her hair, the feel of that chaste cotton gown — and the mental image of what was beneath that gown. He sighed, a hopeless shuddering sigh, and he rose up from his pillow to claim her mouth. She did not spurn him, did not draw away.

Along with the bicycle, he had on the specialist's advice secured for himself a supply of prophylactics, by mail order in a plain brown-paper wrapper. There would be no more dead infants. He'd unwrapped the items and hidden them in the corner of his underwear drawer, which was now not as tidy as it had been then. The rattle of his search was somewhat cooling to the blood. He was not surprised when she moved to her own side of the bed. He slid from his side, removed the drawer, emptied it to the floor. And his hand found what it sought, but while he was preparing himself, she left his bed, left his room, his door slammed behind her.

He followed her to Cecelia's bedroom. 'The specialist advised —'

'Go to hell,' she said.

He went to the hell of his now empty bed and for the first time in months it felt empty. He was a man with needs and she had raised those needs.

He did not sleep well, but rose as usual, brushed and dressed Jenny, chose not to fry an egg, ate toast, fed Jenny toast, then took her to work with him. Again, they shared a beef pastie for lunch. Again, they returned to the house after five, but it was no longer their own. Their parlour had been turned around, each item of furniture moved, all dust removed, and the peacock feathers missing. Norman searched for them; he'd tickled Jenny's nose with those feathers.

They ate as well-mannered visitors in Amber's kitchen that evening. Norman put Jennifer early into her cot, which had not yet received its share of Amber's cleaning, then soon after he went to his own bed, where, with more hope than expectation, he placed one of his prophylactics in a folded handkerchief beneath his pillow. She did not come to his bed that night, and the following day his room was stripped. No doubt the contents of his handkerchief went with his sheets into the copper.

That evening, in the brief minutes while he bathed and shaved, Jennifer was attacked ... by the rose bush.

'You should have cut it back in July,' Amber said.

'Perhaps you might consider cutting that girl's fingernails back, Mrs Morrison.'

'We're in the house for two days and you're already blaming her for everything that happens to your Jenny-wren. I told you, she did it on the rose bush.'

'She did it on the rose bush.' Sissy repeated her mother's lie.

'You are turning my child into a monster, Mrs Morrison — in body and deed.'

'She's your child. What did you expect her to turn into, Norman?'

He went to his bed at eight. He was sleeping when she came to his room. The night was dark, the room black as pitch, but he required no eyes to see that she was stark naked. The woman was mad. She had as much as named him monster, and now this. She had never been an eager partner to his nocturnal habits, had never made the initial approach, had more often than not spurned his advances. Tonight, she made an attack on his person.

What man, denied his natural release for near on twelve months, will not respond to a willing woman — in body. Certainly his manhood responded to her touch, but his mind was repelled. He removed her from his person. He held her wrists, held her at a distance.

'I believe we need time to become reacquainted, Mrs Morrison,' he said. 'And we have been advised to use . . . protection.'

'Getting all you need from your Jenny-wren,' she said.

He sprang from the bed like a virgin violated, snatched up his pillow and backed away from her, the pillow shielding his untrustworthy lower regions.

'You have gone mad, Mrs Morrison. Remove yourself from my room.'

Her reply may have been better received in a brothel, a well-insulated brothel. He ran from her to the nursery, to the narrow bed next to Jennifer's cot. No sheets on that bed, but two blankets. He slid between them and lay watching that closed door, fearful it might open.

Norman's prophylactics — two packets of twelve with two missing — would perish in time, but his house was clean, his mother's furniture gleamed, the scent of beeswax polish permeated his parlour, phenol flavoured his meals and, miraculously, his shaving mirror, where previously he had squinted to see, now offered a clear reflection.

He cut his losses, took Jenny to work with him, and left his wife to her cleaning.

Amber's days were long. There is only so much dirt one can erase from a house. The dirt she pursued was internal. She sought it in dark wardrobes, beneath beds, on tiny nightgowns. Smelled them before dropping them into the boiling copper, stood for an hour one day her poking stick holding a tiny gown beneath boiling suds, convinced that the filth she pursued was on that nameless stray he'd brought into her house. She found traces of it everywhere. It clung like a scum to the chairs, the table, the walls.

She found it on Cecelia.

'I told you to stay away from her,' she snarled as she scrubbed her girl in the bath, scrubbed her red while Cecelia screamed. Hating that bloated white body, that fat, flat face, wanting to push her down in the water, hold her down, but loving her too, loving the smell of her.

A ewe identifies her lamb by its scent. In the darkest cellar on the blackest night, Amber could have identified the scent of Cecelia; by September she could no longer breathe unless Cecelia was near. Kept her from school. Kept her from play.

Cecelia had spent three months at her mother's side, had sat beside her at her uncle's table, slept beside her, shopped with her, visited elderly aunts and uncles with her. At Amber's side, she'd been the centre of attention, a Duckworth through and through, they said. She'd been appreciated in Melbourne. In Woody Creek there were no aunties and uncles, no Cousin Reggie, only her mother — and Jenny, who stank of evil.

'You stink of evil. You stay away from me or you'll make me stink too, Mummy said.'

'What's ebil, Sissy?'

Sissy wasn't too certain. '*Deliver us from evil,*' she said. 'From church.'

She hoped Cousin Reggie would soon deliver her and her mother from evil. She wanted to go back to where there was gas so she could have curls, where there was a proper lavatory with water in it instead of stink.

Her grandmother was evil too and Maisy wasn't much better. Both women came to the house sometimes but they didn't come inside.

Nancy Bryant knocked on Norman's door on a Friday when Sissy was almost missing being at school. She opened the door. Amber didn't invite her visitor inside. She took the offered jar of cream, took the doll Nancy's granddaughter no longer wanted.

'Hasn't she turned into the prettiest little pet you ever did see, and wasn't that hair a surprise?' Nancy said.

Cecelia preened for an instant, smiled.

'It's like spun gold,' Nancy said.

Gold was yellow. Cecelia's hair was the darkest of browns. She stopped smiling and Amber closed the door.

Poor, plain, pudgy Cecelia, years behind her age group at school and falling further behind each day Amber kept her at home. Poor lumpy Cecelia, head and shoulders taller than most in her grade and two or three stone heavier. She'd eaten well in Melbourne. That's what Duckworths did. Even Aunty Jane, a slim in-law, had assisted with the weight increase. She'd made toffee on her stove so Cecelia would be good while Amber went to the theatre with Cousin Reggie.

By October there was an unbridgeable gulch between the two halves of Norman's family, which neither side attempted to cross.

To a large degree, Norman lived as he had prior to Amber's return. On Sundays, he rose early, packed a picnic lunch and off he rode on his bicycle, Jenny strapped on behind.

Sissy sat with her mother in the parlour, listening to strange stories about evil people. She wanted to ride on that bike. She wanted to have a picnic lunch.

'Jenny drawed a bum, Daddy.'

'I drawed a apwicot.'

'She's showing you the wrong way round, Daddy. She had it the other way when she drawed it . . . and she said . . . and she said it was Granny's bum, doing number —'

'Enough!' Norman howled. 'It is a very fine apricot, Jennifer.'

'It's a bum,' Sissy yelled. 'She said it's Granny's bum doing —'

'Go to your room.'

'Bum. Bum. Bum.'

Norman manhandled her into the nursery where she spent an hour screaming and causing what havoc she could. She remembered his locked doors. She didn't like his locked doors.

He took Jenny riding on a Sunday in late October and when they returned, Cecelia was waiting alone at the gate. And he threw a lifeline across the gulch.

'Perhaps you might like to go for a short ride, my dear.'

She liked, but not a short one. They rode for half an hour, but when they returned, Jenny was waiting at the gate, weeping. She was not a crying child. He saw immediately the cause of her tears. Her tiny leg was red from thigh to knee. He carried her indoors.

'You will keep your hands off this child,' he warned Amber.

'What about you, Duddy?' Amber said. 'Do you keep your hands off her, Duddy?'

There were no more bicycle rides. He had two daughters and a wife who had lost her reason.

'Shall we walk down to the bridge to visit the birds?' he offered.

Sissy's thighs rubbed when she walked. She wanted to ride. Norman had something to offer and she wanted it, wanted all of it.

November was worse than October. On Friday, Gertrude's trading day, she'd delivered Joey to the station to play a while with his only friend and was on her way back to collect him when Maisy, who had been watching out for her, called as she crossed over the road.

'She says she's got a growth in her womb, Mrs Foote, and he's not doing anything about it. I'm worried sick about her.'

'I can't get near her, love. She won't open the door to me.'

'Someone has to do something.'

Gertrude left Joey to play a while longer and followed Maisy to Norman's front door. They knocked, Maisy called at the bedroom window.

'I'm not leaving, Amber. I want to talk to you.'

Amber opened the door, saw her mother and tried to close it, but Maisy was a heavy girl. Gertrude followed her inside.

She saw the growth, recognised it for what it was, and without a word turned and strode across to the station.

'You fool of a man!' she said.

Norman knew he was a fool, but this afternoon he required some clarification. His jowls shook as they lifted in question.

'She can't go through that again.'

Then he knew. 'Your fears are baseless —'

'She's expecting. The doctor told you she couldn't go through that again.'

'There may be no cause for concern —'

'Of course there's cause for concern. She's half out of her mind now.'

'My meaning . . .' He coughed, turned to the children, then he lowered his voice. 'She has been home since late August, Mother F — Gertrude,' he said, watching her face closely, hoping to see understanding dawn in her eyes. It did not. He looked away to his house and to Maisy, now heading across the station yard. 'August,' he repeated. 'It is now November. As you see, there may be no cause for concern.' Again he coughed. 'The incompatibility factor will not apply . . . in this case . . . if I am . . . at fault.'

And he saw light begin to dawn. 'You're saying . . .'

'I am saying that no more need be said on the subject — and will not be said by me . . .' He turned to the children, squatting on the platform, building a long train from ABC blocks, and he smiled at their lisping conversation.

'Altogether far too much is made of blood. See what treasure we find when we discount it, Gertrude.'

PAPER PETALS

December came, and Miss Rose received an offer of marriage from John McPherson, now a twenty-year-old, sweet and gentle boy. Of course she couldn't wed him. She was years his senior. A tempting offer though, and made more so when Cecelia Morrison was returned to her classroom.

It came to a head on a Friday two weeks before the annual school concert. Miss Rose heard a bellow, saw Ray King spring from his seat and back away from Cecelia. In size he was a fair match for the girl, but he was a stutterer, a silent lump of a lad who, when upset, could not get out a word of accusation.

Others spoke for him. 'Sissy Morrison stabbed him in the leg with her pencil, Miss Rose.'

The pencil was sharp. It had gone deep.

'You will not be in the concert, Cecelia.'

'I am so in the concert.'

'Badly behaved children do not wear flower costumes.'

At two, the costume ladies arrived: Miss Blunt, spindly, bespectacled spinster daughter of the town draper, seamstress of renown; and her assistant, Mrs Fulton, large, motherly wife of Robert Fulton, proprietor of the feed and grain store. They had nothing in common other than their ability to make magic with their hands. Give them wire, mosquito net and tinsel and they handed back a pair of fairy's wings; give them a few rolls of crepe paper and they could turn a group of dusty children into dancing flowers.

When Cecelia realised Miss Rose intended standing by her threat, she did what she usually did — screamed blue murder, stamped her feet, and her bladder released its load. She was a big girl with a large bladder. They left her screaming in the classroom and moved into the utility room next door where one by one the children were fitted.

At three thirty, when the bell rang to end the school day and the costumes were packed away, one remained, large, very pink, its skirt a series of paper petals. Miss Blunt had minimal experience with urine-soaked children. Mrs Fulton was a mother of nine. She approached the girl, the pink frock over her arm. Sissy eyed it and kicked in its direction.

'It's a pity you won't be in the concert,' Mrs Fulton said. 'You have such a strong voice. We need strong voices on stage, don't we, Miss Rose?'

Sissy sniffed hope. She wanted to be a flower on the stage. She wanted to wear that pink costume too. She wriggled up to her bottom, glanced at Miss Rose who may not be the boss of the concert.

'Does she know the flower song, Miss Rose?'

'I know everything,' Sissy said. Wanted to try on that costume. It looked just like a flower. 'I won't . . . do things,' she said.

'What things won't you do, Cecelia?' Miss Rose said.

'Stab him again.'

'Or pull the girls' hair, or scratch, or misbehave with the twins.'

Sissy eyed that pink. 'I won't.'

They tried it on her. There was a lot of her and the frock made more of it. She wouldn't be missed on stage. They walked her to the utility room to admire herself in the mirror. She was docile. She allowed them to tie on her flower hat.

'My word, don't you look gorgeous,' Mrs Fulton said.

Poor Sissy Morrison. She'd never look gorgeous, but that lolly pink costume and a little psychological blackmail allowed Miss Rose to gain a modicum of control. On Mrs Fulton's advice, for the week preceding the concert, the flower frock hung in the classroom beside the blackboard, a pair of scissors dangling on a length of string beside it.

'Each time you misbehave, Cecelia, each time you refuse to do what I ask when I ask, I will cut off one of your frock's petals with my very sharp scissors.'

Of course Sissy tested the threat. Three times she tested it. And watched the petals fall.

If not for the annual school concert, Sissy Morrison may never have learnt to use a pencil for its intended purpose.

If not for the annual school concert, Amber Morrison may not have gone stark raving mad.

The venue for all entertainment was the Woody Creek town hall. Balls were held there, dances, meetings, wakes, parties and concerts. All were well attended.

Sissy wanted her mother to see her on stage in her beautiful costume. Amber was six months pregnant. She never left the house. But she was losing that girl to the other side, and Sissy was all she had. On the night of the concert, she laced on her corset, laced it tight. Couldn't do up the waistband of her beige suit skirt but the jacket covered the gap. She walked with Norman to the hall, sat at his side, in silence through the early items, sat stiff as a board, eyes forward — until the dance of the flowers, when she rose to her feet.

Cecelia's costume was a cruel farce and Norman was in on the joke. Amber wanted to snatch her girl from the stage, hide her away. Wanted to rip the wand from the dancing fairy's hand and with it make her daughter beautiful, wanted —

Had to get out. They'd blocked her in. A couple behind asked her to sit. Norman asked her to sit, but Amber stood staring at the stray seated on Norman's lap, and she could see her future, see that pretty little golden bitch on that stage, a dainty flower, a dancing fairy —

Couldn't breathe for the stench of her. Raised her hands to snatch her, throw her, but Norman moved, then others moved. They let her out, and while the audience applauded, while children took their bows, Amber ran from the hall.

'What's wrong with that woman?'

'It's the first time I've seen her out in months.'

'Someone told me she had a growth.'

'Joanne Hooper died of a growth.'

'It can't be serious. Her husband's not going out with her.'

The concert continued without Amber.

She didn't go home. She walked through the memorial park, a narrow area between the town hall and Maisy's house. It went through to a back street where homes had been built facing the sports oval. She crossed the road, walked diagonally across the oval to the cemetery fence, then along it to the road. The large cemetery gates were locked, the smaller gate was never locked.

She entered the place of the dead, a dark place tonight, but she knew the way to her dead children, her beautiful children, who would have danced on stage in fairy wings, who would have sung sweet songs. She lost time with them.

The concert ended at ten thirty. Norman took the girls home, Sissy happier than he'd seen her in years. He got them into bed, then walked the midnight streets searching for his wife. He walked for an hour but didn't find her.

She was not a well woman, but with a living child in her arms, he was convinced she would again be his happy, laughing wife. He had not fathered her child and thus was convinced it would be born alive. He would raise it. Perhaps a son this time. Every man needs a son.

Amber returned at dawn. She slept through the day but rose when he put Cecelia into bed. She slept through the following day, and that night he moved Cecelia into the small bed in Jennifer's room.

Christmas came and went unheralded in Norman's house. Dust fell and remained where it fell, the house and Cecelia neglected while Amber slept by day and walked by night.

Maisy found Sissy's infestation. She had eight daughters and had fought many a good fight against head lice. Eradication began with a pair of scissors. Sissy's rat-tail hair fell in clumps to the floor. The process continued. A thorough wetting with a combination of kerosene and olive oil was followed by a combing with her small-toothed comb. The head then wrapped in brown paper and a towel was left an hour, so any living louse might suffocate. A good wash with a strong soap, a little vinegar added to the final rinsing water, and if anything had lived through that, Maisy would get them when she repeated her treatment the following week. Cecelia lived through it and tolerated it well enough. It was attention. She craved attention.

She had the Duckworth, dead straight hair. Maisy had cut her a long fringe; it covered much of the Duckworth brow. She'd given her an ear-length bob. Sissy liked it, liked standing in front of the mirror combing it. It was her mother's fault for laughing. Nancy Bryant's fault too, for meeting them in the newspaper shop on that Saturday morning in February and talking about Jenny's hair and not even noticing Sissy's haircut.

It was Norman's fault too. If he hadn't left the scissors on the little verandah table when he'd cut something from the newspaper, Sissy wouldn't have known where to find them. And it was Miss Rose's fault, because those scissors reminded Sissy of the ones she'd used to cut those pink paper petals.

Norman was at the station sending his train on its way, the girls left playing on the verandah, where Sissy found the scissors and decided to play hairdressers. Jenny accepted her haircut as she accepted most of Sissy's games. A fair percentage of her hair had fallen before Amber opened the back door.

She was nightgown clad, soiled nightgown clad, her own hair uncombed in days, unwashed in more, her belly big with child. She stood in the doorway, staring at the small springs of gold littering the verandah.

Sissy offered the scissors. 'Her head was itchy like my head, Mummy.'

Amber ignored her. She stood looking at Jenny who sat amid her fallen curls like a shorn angel.

'Daddy said my hair will grow again, Mummy.'

Sissy blamed her haircut for her mother's neglect. It had to be her haircut. A month away from her eighth birthday, her mind filled with much that should not have been there, but lacking in much that should, Sissy floundered. Her world was not as it had been and she didn't like it. Then her mother, who had only cuddled and kissed and whispered secrets, pushed her. Sissy landed hard and the scissors slid.

Amber watched their slide and felt her last control sliding with them, over the edge, over the edge and gone. Saw that lump of a girl scrambling backwards away from her, saw the stray sitting, staring.

There was relief in the release of rage. There was bliss in that first connection, that sharp *whack!* of celebration. It sent that pretty little bitch spinning. Amber's foot joined the party, but her balance was not good enough. Almost went down. Saved herself though, against the wall, got hold of an arm and swung that pretty little bitch. Grabbed what was left of her hair, smashed her face into the floor. Kill it. Get rid of the thing. And the noise.

'Shut up. Shut up, I said. Shut up!'

Mr Foster, the new postmaster, was making a pot of tea when he heard the noise. He went to his semi-enclosed verandah, glanced over the fence and saw too much. He ran.

Mr Foster couldn't run — he had a club foot and a twisted spine; he used a walking stick — but he ran anyway, through to the post office, out the door, across the few feet to Norman's front gate, and around to the back of the house in time to see his neighbour hammering a senseless infant's head into the floor, the other girl pulling at her own hair, screaming.

Mr Foster used his walking stick, and not for its intended purpose. He hit that woman, if woman she was; he snatched up the infant and, at a limping run, returned the way he'd come.

He was a city man of thirty-odd, unwed and unlikely to wed. He'd been in town over a month and not a soul, not his neighbour, nor his neighbour's wife, had welcomed him there. And surely he had done the wrong thing. A man could not walk into a neighbour's house, attack his wife, snatch his child.

He looked towards the constable's residence, was limping across the road with his senseless bundle, when he saw Jean White walk from the grocery store. He'd had dealings with her across their respective counters. He turned, went to her, pushed the baby into her arms.

'The woman next door has gone mad,' he said.

'Oh my God,' Jean moaned and ran into the store with the baby. 'Charlie! Charlie. For God's sake, get Norman.' She laid Jenny on the counter where she looked at the mutilated hair, the bleeding mouth, the nose pouring blood. 'Get Norman. Get the constable, Charlie. I think she's killed her.'

She hadn't killed her. Jenny stirred when Norman came to gather her into his arms, to weep on her; then Jenny cried because he was crying. Jean White was wiping her own tears when Ernie Ogden and his wife came at a run. Jenny clung to Norman, hiding her face against his shirt, wiping blood to his shirt. Wouldn't let them look at her face until Charlie tried bribery. He offered two fat humbugs from the large jar on his counter, and when she wouldn't take them, he opened her hand and placed the humbugs into it.

Three is the age when the fog of infancy begins to lift, when the world starts filtering through, when images imprint the blank pages of the mind so vividly they remain forever. Amber's attack may be overprinted in the coming years, but Jenny would never forget her first haircut. Eighty years from that day, seated in a Melbourne salon, her hair attacked by a megalomaniac wielding scissors, Jenny would lift her left palm to her nose, certain a trace of aniseed remained. Forever more she'd associate those black and white striped sweets with a bad haircut.

AMBER'S ESCAPE

They hid Jenny and her injuries at Gertrude's house, two miles from town, surrounded by forest. Few visitors ventured down there and most who did only came to buy her produce. Maisy took Cecelia.

A decision had to be made on what to do about Amber. Mr Foster had diagnosed madness; Jean White agreed with him.

For some time, Norman had known his wife was not herself, but surely she should be given time — time for the infant to be born. Once it was in her arms, she would miraculously revert to the pretty, happy girl he had wed.

'She must be very close to term,' Gertrude said. She didn't want her daughter committed and that's what Ernie Ogden was suggesting. 'If Norman is agreeable, as long as we keep the children out of the house . . .'

No one was sure when that babe might come. Amber had been in the city through May, June, July and most of August.

Ogden tried to speak to her. She locked herself in her room. His wife had more luck. Amber showed her a fine tea set, showed her a vase, reputedly a gift from Queen Victoria. Mary Ogden asked when the baby was due. Amber told her she had a growth in the womb.

There are varying degrees of madness, which make its diagnosis difficult for layman and expert alike. How do you draw the line between common run-of-the-mill child abuse and a murderous mania? How can you state for a fact that what looks like paranoia isn't green-eyed jealousy? How can you pick a blatant bare-faced liar from some poor demented soul who has lost her grasp on reality? You can't.

'She's as mad as a rabbit,' Mary said. 'And whether she is or not, any woman who'd do what she did to that little girl deserves putting away, Ernie.'

'Yeah, but try putting yourself in her shoes for a tick, love,' Ogden said. 'She's lost three and she's having another one that's not her husband's. She's got nowhere to go. She's got to stay in that house and face him every day knowing that he knows. Do you reckon you'd be feeling as sane as you ought to be?'

'I wouldn't have got myself into her state in the first place, and I wouldn't go taking it out on a three-year-old baby if I had.'

'I'm not justifying what she did to that little girl. All I'm saying is that any woman, given her situation, can't be blamed for going a bit funny.'

Madness wasn't a bit funny, nor were some of the places they put those diagnosed as mad. He'd sent two Woody Creek residents to asylums in the fifteen years he'd been in town. He'd put one of the Duffy boys away after he'd tried every other means of stopping him from climbing over the back fence of the convent and exposing himself to the holy sisters. He'd put George Macdonald's retarded mother away after the third time she'd lit a fire on her bedroom floor — to keep the wild animals out of her room. The curtain had caught on fire on the last occasion; she might have burnt the family in their beds if her grandsons — maybe the animals she'd sought to keep out — hadn't smelt smoke.

'She seems calm enough now, Norm,' he said. 'That doctor chap said he'd get up here to take a look at her as soon as the garage gets his car back on the road.'

The doctor didn't come for a week, and on Thursday night, or the early hours of Friday morning, Norman heard Amber walk through the house and out the back door. He waited for her to return, and when she didn't, he went looking for her.

The moon was full and, with not a cloud in the sky, he saw her clearly. She was down near the oleander tree. He approached on slippered feet, saw she was using a shovel and appeared to be digging a hole. He believed she was sleepwalking, acting out a nightmare. He spoke her name gently as he reached to take the shovel.

And she turned it on him.

The blade was not dull. Had he not ducked, raised his shoulder at the last moment, he may have lost his head. The blow disabled his arm; he heard the grinding of bone as he fought her for the shovel, saw the blood painting his nightshirt black. Only when he gained the shovel did he feel the pain of his injury, only then did his good hand rise to explore. The blade had cut deep. He backed away — and felt something soft, something giving, beneath the sole of his slipper.

Then he heard the grunt. The weak protest of life.

'What have you done?' he howled, falling to his knees in the dirt, finding the warmth of flesh there. 'Woman, what have you done?'

One arm useless, he slid his right hand beneath the curve of a tiny spine, the round fruit of its head, lifted it awkwardly to his lap, its birth membrane trailing in the dirt. 'We will raise it. We will raise it.'

She was gone. The back door slammed. He tried to rise, but required a hand to push himself up from his knees. No hand to push with; one arm hung useless in the dirt, the other held the newborn. Unable to rise, he lifted his face to the moon and howled like an injured beast.

The town awoke to a different morning; to Vern Hooper's car parked in front of Norman's house, to Vern and the constable standing out there with him. Vern's car lights were unreliable, they were waiting for daylight before they hit the road.

The birds knew better than to warble their song that morning. They sat silently in the trees, peering down at the scene as Mr Foster peered silently through his bedroom window. Three men blowing smoke at the dark eastern sky, willing it to begin its change, while the grass growing alongside Norman's front fence lapped faster of the evening's little dew. The sun was coming to steal it away.

First that glint of gold over the trees. Then that flush of palest pink.

'Righto,' Vern said. 'Hop in the front, Norm. You'll get an easier ride.'

Norman's shoulder had been beyond Gertrude. They'd roused her from her bed; she'd padded and bound it tightly, had told them it needed more stitching than she could do, told them his collarbone seemed to be broken.

More was broken than his collarbone. Norman was broken.

The baby was dead, its nose, its mouth, full of dirt. Whether it had choked on dirt or was born dead, Gertrude couldn't — or wouldn't — say. In her heart she knew it had fought for life. Norman knew he had heard that life.

Nothing to be done now. They'd given it into Moe Kelly's hands.

'No good for you or your wife will be achieved by opening up that can of worms, Mr Morrison,' Ogden said. 'No one can say for certain what happened out there.'

Amber was ready to go. She wanted to go. She'd packed her case, bathed and clothed herself in her city suit, found her city hat, set it on wet hair. She put on her jacket, its pocket heavy with coins and she held that pocket so the coins would make no noise when she walked out to the car.

Ernie carried her case. He sat her in the rear seat and sat beside her. Norman and Vern sat up front. And so they drove off into the sunrise, Willama thirty-nine long and silent miles away.

The grave diggers opened up the grave of the babe's siblings, and at sun-up on the following day, another tiny coffin was added to the hole. Moe Kelly and the grave diggers covered up Amber's adultery.

Earth once disturbed can't be disguised; and how do you explain a missing stationmaster?

'They say he's at the hospital. I know his oldest girl is staying with Maisy.'

'As if she hasn't got enough of her own.'

'That's what I said to her.'

'Someone told me a while back that his wife had a growth in the womb.'

'That was Vern Hooper's wife, but it wasn't in her womb. She didn't have one. They say her innards were riddled with it.'

Norman came home and it was learnt that he'd broken his collarbone, that he had fourteen stitches in his left shoulder.

Then young Patty Kelly, Moe's daughter, let it slip that her father had buried another Morrison baby. Rumour-mongers don't need to be good at arithmetic. They have eight fingers and only require one thumb when counting nine months in reverse.

'Late May or June. She was in Melbourne most of May and all of June.'

'How can you remember that?'

'She had that last baby, the girl that died, in the April, had a breakdown and they took her down to some city doctor in early May. I remember clearly. It was the week of Barbara's wedding.'

'I heard she went mad and hit him with the wood axe.'

'Some men deserve operating on with a wood axe. That's the third one she's lost.'

'The fourth one.'

'Third or fourth, he must be some sort of animal in the bedroom.'

'You'd never think so to look at him, would you?'

The young Willama doctor was having similar thoughts. He'd had several dealings with Norman Morrison and he did not appear to be an unsympathetic man.

'Your oldest girl is not yet eight, you have a three year old, Mrs Morrison, and you've lost four infants?'

'Yes.'

'Did you carry them full term?'

'Yes.'

She felt cleansed by the antiseptic smell of the hospital. She could breathe deeply of air filled with new possibilities. She made no complaints, made no demands, said not a bad word against her husband, who had said more than a few about her, as had the constable who'd brought her in.

She had little to say, perhaps too little. She ate little, but was she deranged? Not in the young doctor's opinion. He was impressed by her loyalty to a husband who had seemingly kept her pregnant since her wedding night. He didn't know of the three year old with two black eyes, a mouth split by baby teeth and wallboards, a face, an arm, a tiny body black and blue. He didn't know the dead infant was not her husband's, or that she'd attempted to bury it alive beneath the oleander tree, or that she'd chosen that site in advance. The earth was always damp beneath the oleander tree, kept that way by the run-off from the washhouse troughs.

The young doctor didn't know much.

One of the women sharing Amber's eight-bed ward knew a little more. She didn't sleep well and, aware her ward mate crept around in the night, she placed her new red purse under her pillow.

On the sixth morning of Amber's stay in hospital, a nursing sister noted that Amber was not in her bed at six. At eight thirty, another checked the women's bathrooms. At nine forty-five, the young doctor was searching the verandahs and grounds for his patient.

That's when the owner of the red purse noticed it wasn't where she'd left it.

'She's pinched it,' she wailed. 'I knew I couldn't trust her as far as I could kick her.'

Then an elderly woman limped down to ask one of the nurses if she'd removed a tobacco tin from the pocket of her dressing gown. There was no tobacco in it. Her husband had given it to her with five shillings in it, just in case she needed to buy something.

A girl down the bottom end of the eight-bed ward started searching for the gold crucifix she'd hung over her bed. A woman in a two-bed ward across the passage was missing a ten-shilling note and her wedding ring the sisters had told her to remove in case her fingers swelled up. Someone had lost money from the pocket of her jacket.

The sisters were buried beneath an avalanche of losses — a lot of it was snow but there was solid rock in there too.

And no sign of Amber Morrison.

A train passed through Willama between seven thirty and eight o'clock each weekday morning. By the time the search for her had begun, Amber was well on her way to freedom.

SIMILARITIES

Sissy knew her mother had gone mad and gone missing. The Macdonald kids told her so. They were supposed to be kind to her. That's what Maisy said, but Macdonald kids didn't play fair. Sissy gave Jessie one little slap and the rest of them ganged up on her, the big ones holding her down while Jessie paid her back ten times over. They cut her fingernails back to nothing just because she'd accidentally scratched Dawn. They locked her in a spider-infested shed. Eight against one wasn't fair. And if the twins tried to help her, the girls locked them in separate rooms until the two boys almost went mad.

'I want to go home,' she told Maisy.

'Your father is sick,' Maisy said.

Everyone was sick, her mother, her father and Jenny. Sissy was sick too, sick of Maisy's house and Maisy's kids and Maisy's kids' father. She escaped one night while they were eating dinner. She said she was going to the lav and instead went home.

Norman was more lost than sick. He was a constant itch, an ache, a throbbing anguish. He was trussed up like a turkey for roasting, the strapping around chest and shoulders creating the itch, aggravating the ache. With only one hand with which to grip, he couldn't get a grip on himself. He couldn't tie his shoelaces. Clothing himself was a struggle, bathing an impossibility. He was a mountain climber attempting to find a handhold on a glass mountain. By day, he gained an inch or two. At nightfall, he slid back down. Bed was an agony. He woke weary to begin again, to light the stove, feed it with oversized lumps of wood he couldn't cut. Feeding himself was too much effort. He walked to the station unfed, his shoelaces dragging through the dust.

Didn't want to deal with his wailing daughter. Couldn't deal with her. Told her to go back to Maisy, then cringed from her when she ran bellowing into her bedroom.

One of the church ladies had brought him a bowl of soup and a slice of cake. He'd been fighting one-handed to heat the soup when Cecelia arrived. He spilled it into two bowls, halved the cake, called her to the kitchen.

She emptied her bowl, ate her cake and his, drank the little milk remaining in his jug. Now he had no milk for his tea. And he wanted a cup of tea. Wanted to place his head on the table and howl.

'You must return to your Aunty Maisy. As you see, I cannot care for myself, Cecelia.'

'I'm not going back there, I said.'

No energy to fight her. He went to bed without his cup of tea. She went to her own.

He had managed alone before — when he'd had two hands. He had spent three months in this house with Jennifer. A different time. A different child. He had been a younger man. His shoulder hadn't throbbed, itched, ached, screamed when he rolled onto it in the night. The wound wasn't healing. Vern was driving him to Willama in the morning, leaving early.

He smelled urine when he rose at seven. He couldn't handle a wet bed this morning. He left her sleeping in urine, closed her door, fought with his clothing for half an hour then scuffed across to the station, tripping over his shoelaces. His station lad tied them, then made him a cup of tea. At nine, Norman left him in charge and drove off to Willama with Vern.

A long and painful day, and Cecelia waiting for him, surly because he'd gone missing for most of the day. He'd bought sliced ham in Willama and a loaf of bread, a tin of powdered milk. He mixed a little and placed the rest up high. They ate the ham with chunks of fresh bread. Difficult to cut a fine slice with one hand. She demanded more ham. He had no more. He mixed more milk. She drank it.

'I am going to my bed, Cecelia. Go back to your Aunt Maisy.'

He walked to his room. She followed him.

'I'm not going there, I said.'

He propped against his bed, looked at his shoes, aware he must untie the laces but lacking the desire to begin. 'Then go to your own bed.'

'I'm not sleeping there either. It's wet.'

'Then you may sleep on the floor,' he said, forcing one shoe off by applying pressure to the heel with his other.

She stood watching him struggle, then went to her bed. One side was almost dry, though not by morning. A whiff of ammonia can raise the senseless from a faint. The pervasive stink of stale urine roused Norman from his cave of itching, aching self-pity.

He found clean sheets, filled a bucket with warm soapy water, then offered Sissy instruction on how she might remove the saturated sheets, wash down the mattress protector, dry it thoroughly with an old towel, then remake her bed. She looked at him as if he were mad.

He went to work. She went to school, uncombed, unclean.

The church ladies delivered a pot of stew that afternoon. He poured it into a pot and placed it on the stove. He'd renewed his supply of fresh milk, and that night he fought her for it, one-handed, then stood guard in front of his ice chest while she stamped her feet and screamed.

'I will pour you a glass of milk when your bed has been stripped and your mattress protector washed, Cecelia. As you can see, I have but one good arm.'

She went to her room, kicked the bucket of water, spilled it on her floor, went for a slide on slippery linoleum, landed hard and remained on her back to howl. He didn't attempt to lift her. He closed the door on her noise and returned to the kitchen, closed that door also, then stood staring a large potato in the eye. It took some considerable time to peel it one-handed, but by nine his potato, well boiled, was mashed and keeping hot on the hob, the donated stew shrinking as it simmered. Cecelia was silent. He crept to her room and found it empty. She was in the nursery, in the narrow bed, fast asleep. It had no rubberised protector. He could not leave her there.

He shook her shoulder. 'Your meal is ready, Cecelia.'

'You woke me up!'

'You are in the wrong bed. Up, my dear.'

'I hate you! Get away!'

'One wet bed is more than sufficient.'

'I'm sleeping in here, I said.'

'You did, and very definitely.'

He took her upper arm, then, dodging the worst of her blows, manually removed her and most of the blankets from the bed, deposited her in her own room, found the key to the nursery door, fought her away from the door, then locked it against her.

She was weary, as was he. He stepped over her on his way to the front door, which he closed behind him. There was a bench seat down the eastern end of his verandah and a packet of cigarettes on the parlour windowsill. Two left in it. He slipped one out, got it into his mouth and, with practice, learned the best means of striking a match without setting fire to his sling. He sucked the first cigarette down to a butt, then lit the second from the first, hoping to borrow energy enough to continue the battle.

She grabbed his leg as he stepped over her on his way back to the kitchen, almost overbalancing him, but he saved himself, freed his leg and continued.

His stew was drying out, his potatoes required heating. He breathed deeply, left both pots on the hob, and prepared a second bucket of soapy water, added a dash of phenol, found the soggy cloth, plopped it into the bucket.

'Shall we work together on this, Cecelia? My one good hand is at your disposal.'

'You go to hell.' Her mother's words.

Epic battles are recorded in history books. Men who achieve great feats are hailed worldwide as heroes. Norman was nobody's hero, but he fought the epic battle of the wet bed and at ten forty-five that night he won. They washed the mattress protector together, they dried it, got clean sheets roughly spread; and at eleven ten, they sat down to a sloppy mush of potatoes— he'd added too much boiling water — and a very tasty stew. They ate bread later, neat enough slices. She held the loaf while he sawed.

The following morning, she tied his shoelaces, or knotted them.

'Train a child up in the way he should go and when he is old he will not depart from it,' the Bible advised. The reverse also applied: *'Raise a child in the manner of a wild animal and God help the trainer when the child grows large enough to bite.'* His sin, his most grievous sin. From her birth, he had taken the easy road with Cecelia. He could blame none other than himself now that the road had turned rocky.

He was a man of books, accustomed to written instructions, but with no instruction booklet to guide him in the taming of his child, he turned to the past, to his own boyhood — not to his mother's child-training methods, but to his months spent with his aunts Lizzie and Bertha and their many dogs. They'd owned five, all near human, and each one knowing its place in the pack hierarchy; puppies trained to know their place, good behaviour rewarded, poor behaviour receiving the aunts' turned backs. During the weeks of Norman's incapacitation, he applied his aunts' rules of puppy-training to his daughter, and though she may never heel nor sit, beg or roll over on command, her snapping and howling decreased significantly. Her bed-wetting persisted, until he found the dusty commode in the washhouse, placed there when his mother had outgrown its narrow confines.

Sissy's rewards were great when for a week her sheets were dry, her chamber-pot emptied. His arm grown stronger, he pumped up his bicycle tyres and away they went, west, out to mushroom country where they collected a billy full, which they fried in butter and ate on toast. They rode east to where the city men were stringing their electricity wires so Woody Creek might shine more brightly at night. In May, they rode south out along Cemetery Road and spread their blanket on damp grass, picnicking on hot chocolate from a flask, on ham and cheese sandwiches.

The frosts of winter, the wet or foggy days, interrupted Norman's training. They couldn't ride through a pea soup fog and she punished him for it. He purchased a dozen unbleached calico sheets. Urine and frost bleached them white before the daffodils started opening their trumpets to a weak sun.

They found a field of daffodils out near the Three Pines siding, where together they explored the old mill workings. He attempted to make their Sunday rambles instructive. She was a child who required, demanded, instant gratification, but that day he discovered her interest.

'*Beside the lake, beneath the trees, Fluttering and dancing in the breeze,*' Norman quoted as they surveyed the daffodils.

'Miss Rose knows that one,' Sissy offered.

Encouraged, he recited more. '*Continuous as the stars that shine And twinkle on the milky way, They stretch'd in never-ending line Along the margin of a bay . . .*'

'All right,' she said.

Given time, man can move mountains, or tunnel through them, or fly over them. Given time, a bad haircut grows out, bruises fade clean away and some memories fade with them, or go deep underground. Given time, those city workmen erected enough poles, strung enough wires, and electricity came to Woody Creek.

There was a celebration at the town hall for the turning on of the lights and Vern Hooper was ready for it. He was the first in town to buy an electric refrigerator, though not the first to buy a wireless.

'So, what do you say, Trude?'

He had a fine house and he wanted someone to share it. She chose to misunderstand his proposal.

'It's all very fine. If our folk could see all this, they wouldn't believe it.'

Jenny couldn't believe it. She was attempting to see inside that wireless. There was a man inside it singing.

'How did . . . how did he get inside?' she asked.

'Electricity,' Vern said.

'Where did it get from?'

'It comes in those wires, girlie. Comes all the way from the city.'

'Can I see it come?'

'No one can. It's just there. All around us, they say.'

'Like fairies?'

'Something like that,' he said. 'Some sort of magic.'

'Is that man inside that thing like . . . like a fairy man?'

'From what I can tell, it's a box full of valves, girlie.'

Jenny knew about gnomes and dwarves and elves. Now she knew valves, which were wireless men that sang, who she couldn't see because they were magic. Lots of things were magic. Granny was. She could make things on her sewing machine and make jumpers with wool.

Vern's Margaret was making a jumper for her brother. She'd said so when Granny asked. She talked funny because she went to school on the train, not to Sissy's school. Jenny liked listening to Margaret talk. She liked Vern's house too. It was a magic house with thousands of flowers and short grass she could play on, and pictures of lots and lots of people hanging on his walls. She liked photographs of people.

'Why did you have just one, Granny?'

'One what, darlin'?'

'Picture.'

'Have I got one?'

'Your big boy and girl — with the fly-hitter thing.'

'Where have I got it, my darlin' girl?'

'You know. Wiff your thing for hitting flies.'

Gertrude's wedding photograph hung on a hook near her bedroom doorway, in the place it had been so proudly hung by her parents thirty-odd years ago. It shared its bent nail with her fly swatter.

'That's Archie Foote. That's your grandpa,' Gertrude said.

'Why is Itchy-foot my grandpa and not Vern?'

'Damn good question, girlie,' Vern said. 'I'm thinking to fix that, though.'

'Itchy-foot was your mummy's daddy, like I'm your mummy's mummy.'

'And Margaret's daddy too?'

'I wouldn't put it past the weasel-faced cur —'

'Shush with that in front of her, Vern,' Gertrude warned.

They left soon after. Vern's daughters were on the verandah, dressed in their Sunday best even though it wasn't Sunday. Jenny waved to them. Gertrude gave Margaret a second glance, then a third, as she walked by.

Lorna, Vern's firstborn, had inherited the Hooper height and more of it than Gertrude, which, when combined with her mother's looks, was not good. Margaret was a plump and fluffy girl who might have stretched to five foot three. There was no saying who had fathered her — other than it hadn't been Vern. She had her mother's platinum blonde hair, but with more curl. There was a lot of her mother in her, and more so since she'd grown into her woman's shape, but there'd always been someone else lurking behind Margaret's face. Out of the mouths of babes, Gertrude thought. Strange how even a child's eye sought out similarities, made its own comparisons — a leftover perhaps from when we swung in the trees, when the ancestors needed to judge fast who was family and who was foe.

'Will Mummy's daddy come home sometime, Granny?'

'No, darlin'.'

'Will Mummy come home when I come home?'

'I don't know, darlin'.'

Would she turn up at that station one day? Would Norman take her back if she came home?

'Do I have to live in . . . in her house . . . when she comes, Granny?'

What did babies know? How much did they remember? Gertrude didn't want to send her home, but Norman wanted her home and he was her father — for all intents and purposes.

'You've got a good daddy and a big sister in there, and you've got me down here. And you remember, darlin', that no matter what else changes in your little life, I'm going to be right here for you.'

'Even when I'm very, very big?'
'My word I will. Even when you're as big as me.'
'Even when I'm big as Vern's Lorna.'
'Don't go wishing that on yourself, me darlin'.'
Poor Lorna, she had the dimensions of a totem pole.

LOST AND FOUND

Jenny returned home in the spring of 1927 and Elsie missed her. Two small children played more contentedly than one. Joey was three years old, his birth registered in some city office. Gertrude said Elsie's birth may have been recorded at the mission, but Elsie didn't want to go there to find it. She had a sister, Lucy, who was older, who may have known her birthday but like their daddy, she'd gone.

Elsie now shared Joey's birthday, on 17 July. She may have been sixteen. She was no more. A pretty, dark-eyed girl with a mop of tight black ringlets hugging her head like an astrakhan cap, her hands fine and birdlike, but unafraid of work.

She'd taken Joey with her to the shed while she got the copper burning.

He missed his playmate and wanted Elsie to play. He liked hiding underneath the big old wooden wash trough. She called into many odd places before pouncing on him. He came out laughing, something grasped in his hand.

'What you got there, Joey?'

His hand hidden behind his back, he wanted to continue the game. She tickled him until he gave up his find. Then no more laughter.

'Where'd you find that?' She could see gold through the crust of red dirt. She cleared a little soil from it between her hands. 'Where'd that come from, Joey boy?'

'Dat mine,' he said.

'That's Mum's, more like it.'

Gertrude was down at her boundary with wire and pliers, attempting to encourage another year or two from her gate. She stopped twisting wire, dropped her pliers.

'It's that brooch!' she said, taking it, rubbing it with her thumb. 'It's that woman's brooch. Where did you find it?'

Joey had pointed in under the wash trough when Elsie had asked the same question. She knew little of what had gone on the night of Jenny's birth. She remembered waking to Gertrude's house filled with strangers and movement and light when there should have been no light. Remembered the baby crying. If she'd heard talk of the brooch, she'd forgotten. She stood close, watched Gertrude tap and blow soil from it, rub it against the leg of her trousers.

'It must have been on that coat. It must have fallen down behind the trough when I tossed everything in to soak that night. Or it's been on the floor and I've kicked it under the trough.'

Gertrude couldn't believe it was found, couldn't believe what she held in her hand either. Those diamonds looked real and some of them were big. And the ruby set dead centre was as big as a hen's eye. It was a beautiful thing. She considered riding into the town with it there and then, but her boundary gate was falling apart, so Elsie took the brooch back to the house and placed it in a bowl on the mantelpiece where it remained until Friday.

Ogden and his wife had never seen anything like it. The brooch was a good inch and a half in length, an elongated oval with fancy goldwork around the edges and rows of red and white stones circling out from a central ruby. No wonder at all that it had caught the eye of Norman's relative.

'She was on that train all right,' Ogden said. 'She was coming up here for some reason, though why she'd walked four miles from town, I don't know.'

'Folk fall from trains. I read of a case a while back where someone opened a train door thinking they were coming into a station. It's easy enough to lose your balance when you're carrying.'

'No unclaimed luggage was ever turned in.'

'If this had been found when we found her, someone would have recognised it,' Gertrude said.

'I've got the name — somewhere — of the chap who reckoned she could have been his absconding wife, back when that newspaper story came out.'

Mary returned to her kitchen and Ogden and Gertrude walked down the verandah to his office. A half-grown boy was in there reading. Ogden evicted him, closed the door behind him.

'A man doesn't put a lot of thought into how he's going to house and feed his kids when he has seven,' he said. 'He doesn't consider the boots they'll wear out, the space they'll take up.'

'They come in small packages, Ernie.'

He opened drawers, rifled through them and slammed them shut. What he sought was somewhere, but near four years had passed since that night and a lot of junk could pile up in four years. Things changed. His oldest boy, fifteen then, was now going on nineteen and working in Melbourne. His youngest, three at the time and taking up little space, was seven and making his presence felt.

He tried his desk drawers. 'Hallelujah,' he said, withdrawing a large manila envelope which he upended onto his counter. The embroidered purse was in there and six or eight sheets of paper. Gertrude reached for the purse to look again at the few items found on the woman, while Ogden scanned the papers until he found what he was looking for.

'That's him. *Albert Forester. No fixed address. Enquired after identifying jewellery.*'

He offered the paper and she glanced at it, expecting more but only finding those few words.

'He didn't describe the brooch?'

Ogden scratched at his neck. 'From what I recall, he didn't specify what jewellery. The chap who spoke to him reckoned he was out for what he could get. They tried to get an address out of him, some place where he might be contacted, but he told them he'd been travelling, attempting to find his wife, that he'd contact them again when he found accommodation.'

'He knew there was a baby?'

'It was in the newspaper at the time. That's what convinced the chaps who spoke to him that he was a fraud. The fellow I spoke to said that Mr Albert Forester showed as much interest in the infant as a louse might show in vinegar. He was after jewellery. A man with a missing wife doesn't ask about her jewellery first and the offspring later.'

'Would it be worth getting John McPherson to photograph the brooch and get it in the papers?'

Ernie was pinning the brooch to the stranger's handkerchief. 'Start advertising this,' he said, 'and you'll have Albert Forester and every other louse in Melbourne up here claiming it — and claiming that little girl too.'

Gertrude didn't want anyone claiming that little girl. It had been hard enough losing her back to Norman. She watched brooch and handkerchief placed into the purse, watched Ogden fold the sheet of writing paper, fold it small enough and slide it in beside the handkerchief, place the purse into the manila envelope and the envelope into the drawer.

'As far as I'm concerned, Trude, the purse, and what it contains, belongs to that little girl and to no one else. Case closed,' he said and he closed the drawer.

A week after the brooch was found, Squizzy Taylor, a notorious Melbourne gangster, was gunned down in a Carlton house and Mrs Ogden's firstborn son lodging in the same street — and the woman he lodged with knew the woman who had been caught up in the gangsters' vendetta.

'What if he'd been walking by when it happened, Ernie? What if he was dying in hospital and we couldn't even get a train down to him until tomorrow? I tell you, I can't stand having him all the way down there, never knowing where he is or what he's doing.'

In November they found out what he was doing. He was gambling. He won ten quid on Trivalve in the Melbourne Cup, and while his mother bewailed his gambling ways, he sent a telegram to his seventeen-year-old brother to be on Saturday's train. He'd got him a job. And then there were five, and Ogden's fifteen year old itching to go with his brothers.

Vern's offspring were at school and university in Melbourne. He saw them two or three times a year. In December of 1927, he travelled down by train and brought them home in his new car, his daughters in the rear seat, his son at his side. His daughters were not willing passengers. They preferred Melbourne. His son was carsick.

There was little entertainment in Woody Creek. He took his family to the school concert where his daughters sat in silence through two hours of boredom while Noah built his ark and filled it. Ogden's nine year old played Noah, in a long black coat and cottonwool beard. Cecelia was one of the giraffes, and tall enough. The highlight of the night was the Macdonald twins who played front and backside of a donkey.

Norman was there with Jennifer. Life had been easier before he'd brought her home. Cecelia resented competing for his time. His arm still ached if he lay on it, but it was strong again. He no longer expected Amber to step down from each Melbourne train, though the sight of a slim pale stranger alighting could still set his heart lurching like a frog in a pool of sludge.

Each Friday, Gertrude delivered her jams and eggs, her fruit and vegetables to Norman's kitchen and stayed on to iron a few things, cook a meal and bake a batch of oatmeal biscuits. From time to time, the church ladies brought around some offerings; occasionally Maisy delivered a cake. They managed. They ate a lot of sausages and potatoes. The house grew in untidiness — the kitchen floor was more often than not sticky with spills, book covers and newspapers frequently stuck to the kitchen table, pencils were occasionally washed up with the knives and forks, but they managed.

Sissy made slow progress with her reading, her mind at times a locked door to Norman, her uncomprehending stare defeating. He blamed himself, blamed his lack of early involvement with that daughter.

There had been no such lack of involvement with Jenny. At times he feared he may be straining her young mind, but she enquired so he replied.

During the evening meal, and in the hour following it, his kitchen became a schoolroom. This had been his habit prior to Jenny's return home and Norman was a creature of habit. As the months passed, he'd become aware that his instruction, prepared for his nine year old, was being more readily absorbed by his four year old, who could, in the blink of an eye, reduce his convoluted information down to the central core and occasionally slip it in some back door to her sister's mind.

To those who have no use for it, learning to read is a trial. To the seekers of answers, reading is only a code waiting to be broken and the keys to that code all around.

Jenny was such a seeker.

Maisy was a mother to Norman's girls. She had ten of her own and barely noticed the two extras. They played in the park beside her house, in her backyard. She fed them if they were there at mealtimes, kept her eye on them when they ran back across the road to the station, or told her older girls to keep an eye on them.

Jessie, her youngest daughter, was Sissy's age and an average scholar. Her twin sons were fourteen months Jessie's junior. There was little more than a year between any two of Maisy's brood.

They were playing school in the backyard on a hot January morning midway through the long school holidays, when each child, admit it or not, was beginning to look forward to the daily routine of school.

The twins were eager to return to the battleground of the schoolyard; they had no use for books — they couldn't read — which didn't mean that their sisters could make fools of them by getting a four year old to read their Christmas book.

'Show-off,' they chanted. 'Show-off.'

'If you won't play properly, then you can't play,' Maureen, the senior Macdonald daughter said.

Sissy didn't like playing school, or Jenny. She added her voice to the chant. 'Evil show-off. Evil show-off.'

The Macdonald girls walked away when the twins started picking plums and throwing them. Sissy, once the girls were

149

out of sight, picked up fallen lemons and threw them. Lemons hurt when they connected. Jenny would have run to Norman if the twins had let her out the gate. They held it shut. She knew another way, between two broken fence palings. She scuttled through, but they saw her in the park and chased her with sticks, so she went the other way, ran all the way up the road and down the lane behind the police station, then down the road towards Charlie's railway crossing. From there she could run down the railway lines to Norman. Except they were waiting at Charlie's crossing and they had more lemons.

She ran out towards the slaughteryards, then across someone's paddock to the railway lines, aware that she wasn't allowed to be down here by herself, but Sissy and the twins weren't allowed to be chasing her and throwing things at her either.

'I'm telling Daddy on you,' Sissy yelled.

Jenny pretended she couldn't hear her, as Norman had advised; she continued walking down the centre of the lines.

'I'm telling Daddy you went over Charlie's road. I'm going back to tell him right now, you evil show-off.'

Jenny walked until Sissy stopped yelling, and when she turned around to see if she was coming, she couldn't see her, but she saw something else, something she'd never seen before. Those train lines looked exactly like a giant had ruled them on the ground with his grey lead pencil, like he'd marked Woody Creek exactly in half!

They'd been placed down when the town was little more than hotel and general store. Desperate to get from A to B, railway surveyors gave no thought to the settlement's possible expansion, but laid the lines parallel to the only street, then, for convenience, placed the station a stone's throw from the hotel. No one had expected the town to grow as it had. This was farming country, wheat and wool country. But the railways had offered ready transport to the city and there was a forest surrounding the settlement, a forest begging to be harvested.

Old man Monk had owned a hundred acres of forest. He'd set up the first pit mill. Others had followed. Timber-getting required many labourers, labourers required wives, wives had kids, required or not, and kids required education.

The town fathers ran out of space in the main street, north of the line, and when the more substantial structures came, they set them south of the line. The two banks were in South Street, the town hall, post office, police station, Norman's house, George Macdonald's house. The hotel, café, butcher, newsagent, boot shop and bakery were in North Street, Blunt's drapery on the eastern corner of North Street, Fulton's feed and grain store on the corner of South Street, Blunt's crossing between them. Charlie and Jean White's grocery store sat on the western corner of South Street, and on the other side of his crossing the Methodist church claimed the North Street corner.

And Jenny could see the lot. She could see the hotel roof, the station roof, the tall bank's roof, Blunt's red roof, and those lines running straight down between them.

If she looked the other way, she could see five dusty sheep and two cows staring at her from behind the slaughteryard fence. Knew why they were waiting there too, and it made her feel very sad for them, so she looked north towards the creek and the trees because Granny lived down in those trees. That made her sad too, because living at Granny's house was good. No one threw lemons there.

You had to think of something happy if you felt sad, Elsie said, so she thought of Vern's valve fairies and, like magic, she saw a stone, which was very interesting indeed because it was brown with black stripes.

Something blue twinkled at her eye and it was just a little way ahead. She looked behind at the roofs then ran to find the blue. It was only broken glass. From a distance though, it had looked like magic.

She didn't mean to walk further, except there were flowers growing down beside the lines, like purple paper flowers. She picked a stem, but there were more of them, just a little way ahead.

Saw a blue-tongue lizard sunning himself, too sleepy to move until she tickled him with a flower. Then he moved and, chuckling, she followed. Followed butterflies that danced in the sky like fairies. Saw an eagle, way up high, gliding like an aeroplane. She ran a while with him, her arms outstretched, 'Vroom. Vroom. Vroom.'

Chased a grasshopper, tracked a family of ants that must have lived underneath the lines. Squatted for a long time waiting, watching two ants carrying a caterpillar home for their dinner.

It might have been her dinnertime. She stood and looked back to see the roofs. And they were gone. They weren't the other way either, and she could see where the train lines stopped, or disappeared through a ripply wet window. Whichever way she looked they'd disappeared. Then across a paddock she saw something that was truly magical. The trees were flying in the sky, and there was water, lots and lots of water, which must have been magic water because even the creek didn't have much water in it. She ran towards that ripply window, determined to find out where those train lines had gone to.

Jenny's story may have ended on that Saturday in January of 1928, and ended barely a mile from where it had begun, if Vern Hooper hadn't decided to take his boy out to the farm that day. If he hadn't given up attempting to interest him in the land, he might have stayed out there until sundown. Instead, they'd eaten a bite of lunch with the manager and his wife then left for home.

Jimmy was staring out the car window at dry farmland when he saw her. He pointed a finger.

'More emus?' Vern asked. Jimmy liked emus.

'A little girl, sir.'

'I'm not one of your flaming schoolmasters. Call me Dad or Pop.'

Jimmy didn't know his father well enough to be on such familiar terms. He'd been sent away to school because his mother was sick. She'd died, and his sisters said he was sickly, which meant he was going to die soon, which meant he had to spend school holidays at a guesthouse near the ocean. His sisters liked that guesthouse. He didn't care where he was as long as it wasn't at school.

Vern stopped the car and looked to where his boy pointed. There was no mistaking who it was. That hair stood out like gold in sun-dried clay.

'Run over to the fence and ask where she thinks she's going.'

Jimmy, a shy, gangling, lop-eared boy, was obedient. 'Dad says, where do you think you're going?'

'Magic land,' she said.

She didn't know Jimmy but she knew Vern. She let him lift her over the fence.

'You're as red as a beetroot,' he said. 'Were you looking for your granny's house?'

'I can't live there any more,' she said.

He removed his hessian waterbag from a bull-wire hook fixed to his car's grille and let her drink her fill, then trickled a good dose over her curls, over her sunburned shoulders.

'Why not?'

'Sissy said.' She wiped trickling water with her forearm. 'About the prince's pills, Sissy said.'

'What prince's pills?' Vern had no qualms when it came to digging information out of kids.

'Granny got the prince's pills off the trollops,' she said with a shrug. 'So I can't live there now.'

It took a second or two to decipher her words, then Vern laughed, he roared, wiped tears from his eyes, held his stomach and groaned with laughter, and for a time was incapable of driving. He was still chuckling when he pulled the car into the shade of a peppercorn tree out the front of Crone's café and sent Jimmy in to buy three big ice-cream cones.

He'd expected to find a search party out looking for that girl, or at least to bump into Norman searching the streets for her. Just a normal Saturday afternoon in Woody Creek — or not so normal. His boy was talking.

Vern demolished his ice-cream in three bites, while the kids leaned against the horse trough, licking and discussing magic, his boy having more to say in three minutes than Vern had heard out of him in three weeks.

'Did you come through that place with all the trees flying up in the sky?'

'That's a mirage,' Jimmy said.

They licked.

'My daddy has got a big mirror in his bedroom and . . . and when you turn the sides you see a hundred, hundred faces — forever faces.'

'Mirage, I said. Not a mirror. It's sort of a reflection,' he said, tonguing the last of his ice-cream down, flattening it, crunching on his cone.

She watched him crunch, tried pushing with her tongue as he had, but found her finger more efficient. She licked it clean, then took a bite of cone.

'I saw a emu running very, very fast. I bet he could get in the mirror . . . mirages.'

'Nothing can,' Jimmy said.

'Why?'

'Because they're not there. They disappear before you get there.'

'Like fairies disappear.'

Fairies to little kids were like Santa Claus. Jimmy knew all about him and them, but he wasn't the boy to go opening the eyes of kids half his size. 'A bit,' he said.

'How do you know everything?'

'From school.'

'When I'm five, I can go to school, Daddy said.' She bit, crunched. 'Can you read yet?'

'Yeah.'

'That's good,' she said. 'Do you go to school with Sissy?'

'There's no girls,' he said.

'Where?'

He waved a hand, wanting the subject away from school. 'My mother died,' he said.

'My mother got sick and went a long, long way away, Daddy said.'

'Did she die?'

'Just gone.' Little hands lifted, empty hands.

'My mother went to the hospital to get operated on and she . . . she stayed there.'

'Didn't she get a grave with angels?'

'She's got a grave with a stone and my name on it, and . . . and my father's.'

'My grandma has got three angels and only her name. Cecelia Louise Morrison and Duckworth too.'

'Duckworth?'

'Sissy said she should have ducks on it, not angels. When I get dead, I want angels, with big flying wings.'

THE PROPOSAL

'It must have taken that kid an hour to get out to where she was,' Vern said. 'She was damn near to Bryants'.'

'My God. What's he thinking of?'

'He thought she was with her sister at Macdonalds'. That woman has got too many of her own to take care of without taking care of his.'

Gertrude was seated on a packing case stool, squirting milk into a bucket she held gripped between her knees. 'He's struggling.'

'He's like a tightrope walker balancing on red-hot wire,' Vern said. 'A man alone wasn't meant to raise kids. It's not the way nature intended.'

'I told him I'd raise her but he wanted her home.'

Flies swarmed around the goat and Gertrude, taking advantage of her busy hands. She flicked at them with her elbow, shook them from her face.

'I heard something today I haven't heard in a while. The little one told me she's not allowed to live down here because Sissy said you got the prince's pills off the trollops. Three guesses as to where that came from.'

'I've heard it put worse.' Milk squirted, flies buzzed and bit. She flicked at them. 'Amber was a sweet-natured little girl until he came up here and filled her head with his lies. It's like that man carried some infection around with him, Vern, some spoiling disease, and she caught it. She was never the same girl after that.'

'Did you get back any word from the city?'

'No. God know what she's living on — if she's living.'

'Do you reckon he's dead yet?'

'Archie? He'll never die. I've told you that before — or not while I'm alive.' She moved to the next goat and her fingers worked again. 'I've had the feeling lately that she could be with him.'

He lit a smoke and puffed a while. He hadn't come down here to talk about Amber or Archie Foote. He had a proposition to put to her, but wanted to get the right reply. He eyed her, sucked on his cigarette, watched her send one goat on its way and start on the next before he broached the subject.

'You could have some say in the raising of those girls if you lived in town.'

'Live in that hot box? With Norman?'

'With me, you flamin' idiot. I've been thinking about bringing Jimmy home, letting him go to school up here for a few years. He was getting on well today with your granddaughter. It could be the making of him, having those girls close by.'

'Where did you leave him?'

'In the backyard, following ants, both of them. My housekeeper said she'd keep an eye out.'

'You could have brought them down with you.'

'Jimmy's always pleased to get rid of me.' He stood puffing smoke, listening to the rhythm of the milk squirting into the bucket. 'We look to see ourselves grown better in our kids, hope to see ourselves somewhere in them. Every last one of mine ended up ninety-nine per cent their mother.'

'They've got your height — or two of them have.'

'That girl needs height like she needs a hole in her head. Where's she going to find a husband?'

'She'll meet someone.'

'I sent her to that university to meet someone and what did I get for my money? A know-all bugger of a girl with her mother's superior outlook and a face you could crack eggs on.'

'You're a cruel man, Vern Hooper.'

'I'm an honest man — and if you're honest back, you'll agree with me. She's as ugly as sin.'

'She'll grow into herself.'

'She's already grown out of her flamin' self.' He dropped his smoke and ground it into the dirt. 'So how about it? Moving in with me? We'll take a trip to Willama, you come back with a ring on your finger and who's going to ask if we're wed or not?'

'A few years back, I might have dropped my milk bucket and knocked you over running for the car. Things have changed in the last years, Vern. Your girls aren't going to take kindly to having me move in.'

'They know I'm not a man to live alone, and if they don't by now they ought to. They won't come home. I told them a while back they could toss a coin to see which one of them got to stay home and look after their brother and you'd think I'd suggested they earn their living on the street. How does a man like me end up with a pair of girls who think they're above living with him?'

'He educates them.'

She sent her last goat on its way, passed the bucket over the fence, then climbed between the wires. He led the way back to the house.

Apart from Elsie's lean-to and a couple of chook pens, every building, every gate and most of the fences on her patch of land had been built by Gertrude's father. He hadn't been a tidy builder but he'd built strong.

'You said you'd marry me forty years ago.'

'You were better looking then.'

'So were you — but I'm willing to cut my losses.'

'Take that milk into Elsie for me, will you? I'll feed my chooks.'

Her father had built her shed, a big one, or built three tall solid walls and roof, then knocked together two massive doors to fill a fourteen-foot gap. Gertrude couldn't remember them being closed in her lifetime. Ten or fifteen years back, she'd given those doors a second life as walls for her cockerel pen. She made good money from her cockerels at Christmas time.

Her father had planted the orchard — and cared for his trees better than she. She hadn't pruned them in . . . not since the year

Amber wed. There was only so much time in a day, and a damn sight less on a winter's day.

Good sense told her she ought to move in with Vern. They could never marry. She'd walked out on Archie Foote over thirty years ago, and when she'd tried to divorce him, he'd come back and ruined everything. She hadn't tried a second time, maybe a case of leaving sleeping dogs lie.

Her granddaughters needed her in town and she knew it. Norman needed her in town. But Elsie and Joey needed her down here too. If Vern's offer had included taking them with her, she would have gone in a minute. He never said a word against them, but there was no way he'd have them living in his house.

It was Vern who had suggested the lean-to. He'd paid for the roofing iron, donated the timber — his plan to get Elsie and Joey out of her kitchen. Then along came Norman and ruined his plan, for which she'd been grateful. They'd constructed a worthy addition to her house, big enough for bed, wardrobe and chest of drawers, which had cleared a lot of space in her kitchen and bedroom.

She scooped wheat from bag to basin, tossed it to her chooks, then turned to look at her house and Vern leaning in the doorway. His head near brushed the top of her doorframe. He always ducked it low when he entered, more habit than necessity.

She didn't join him, not immediately, but stood, her back to her chicken-wire gate, attempting to see the house through his eyes. It wasn't much of a house, but a pretty sight right now. A pink climbing rose had forgotten its place. It clambered up her western bedroom wall and over most of the roof, adding colour and insulation.

Vern's house, by comparison, was palatial. He had rooms leading off rooms, verandahs leading into rooms, lawns and garden he paid Wally Lewis to keep weed free and a hedge of the finest roses in all of the land. She loved his roses. Maybe she could get used to a bit of luxury.

How would he feel though, when they came knocking on his door in the middle of the night, wanting her to bring the babies?

He was accustomed to it. Since he'd bought his first car, a lot had come knocking on his door.

Did she want to live in town, start wearing skirts instead of trousers? Vern didn't like her trousers. He'd bought her the most beautiful blouse back before Amber had got involved with Norman. She hadn't worn it since Amber's wedding. Not that she had anything against pretty things; she loved pretty things — not a lot of use owning them if you had no place to wear them, though.

She glanced over her paddocks, her land, her safety. She'd sworn once that she'd never leave it; swore too that she'd never again join her life up to any man's.

Vern wasn't just any man. Vern was Vern and she loved him like a brother — though not always like a brother. Kissing cousins, she and Vern. We should have wed back when we were kids, she thought. Should have lived on his farm and raised a dozen sons. Should have. Could have. She'd been born to farm, born to breed.

Healing wasn't in her blood. She was a midwife by default — or her fault for marrying a half-mad quack with itchy feet, who, depending on his mood when he woke in the morning, might set her up in a mud hut with a mob of missionaries intent on healing the hordes of Africa, or install her in a cabin on a luxury liner while he doctored the rich. She'd spent the best part of eight years following him around the world, and had nothing good to say about those years, other than what little she'd learnt of healing, she'd learnt from him — or on him.

She'd manhandled a black baby into the world one night when Archie had ridden off for supplies and stayed away for three weeks. The father of the babe had paid her with a scrawny chicken. She'd wrung its skinny neck and fried it for her dinner, picked its bones for breakfast then made soup out of them that night.

She'd done her first stitching of flesh on Archie when he'd come home bleeding like a stuck pig from a two-inch gash over his left ear. A mob of Spaniards had done their best to make her a widow at twenty-one, and in hindsight she would have been better off had they been successful. She'd stitched him up and they'd moved on.

He was an opium addict, had been an addict when she'd wed him, though she hadn't known it at the time. He'd told her he had weak lungs, that the crate of medicine he'd carried to Africa was vital to his survival. Maybe it was; laudanum was a potent mixture of opium and alcohol. She hadn't known what it was back then. She hadn't known much back then. She'd cried for him the first time she'd seen him crazed by his need for his medicine. And when the madness left him, when he'd promised to use no more, she'd believed him. In Germany, in Japan, she'd believed him. Argentina, when he'd used his drugs on her and aborted her baby boy and almost killed her in the doing of it, she stopped believing.

'All fixed, Tru,' he'd said. 'All fixed.'

She'd tried to leave him in Argentina. He'd told her she'd never leave him, that she was necessary to him. He hadn't needed her; he'd needed the money his family paid him to stay out of Australia, and would continue to pay him while she was at his side. They wouldn't let her starve, he'd said, though she'd done her fair share of starving.

For near on eight years he'd collected that quarterly payment. It had followed them to India, to his opium paradise, to her heated-up hell. The trains were purgatory. They'd spent days on them, travelling native class, hard seats, chickens squawking, livestock bleating. The stink, the heat — she'd passed out and known why. Archie, too sick and sorry for himself, hadn't noticed he'd planted another baby inside her.

There'd been nothing much left of Gertrude by then, other than hope for her baby, other than determination that he wouldn't find it, other than the knowledge that she had to get away from him before he found out about this baby and murdered it too.

He'd got his money, got his opium, and she'd watched him and waited, able to read him now like her father could read the weather in the morning sky. She was almost four months along with Amber the day her stars had slipped into alignment. She'd got away.

Until her dying day, she'd never forget that coming home. The smell of the town. The scent of wet gum leaves. The goats, the grass, the orchard just bursting into bud. And the sounds of home, the cackle of chooks, warble of magpies. And her mother's scream. And her arms, and her tears, and her father holding her, and the smell of his pipe tobacco. Safe. Safe. Home.

She'd been back for a week when Mick Boyle's son went down with scarlet fever. Two weeks later, half of the kids in town started dropping like flies. She hadn't known much, but the little she'd known was fifty years more advanced than what old Granny McPherson, the then midwife, knew of treating the disease. She'd worked with her for weeks, and about all she could recall of that time was the relief of being home and of her baby fluttering around inside her.

Granny McPherson brought Amber into the world, a pale, bald little mite, but with all of her bits and pieces in the right places. She hadn't looked like Archie, not at birth. Maybe as a three year old she'd shown a fleeting resemblance to Archie's sister, but she'd outgrown that. She'd never missed having a father, or she hadn't while her grandparents had lived. They'd adored her and she'd adored them. Lost them too early. One after the other they'd gone, he first, and less than a year later she'd followed him.

Just Gertrude and her darlin' girl then, living too far from town, scratching for every penny. And old Granny McPherson growing too old to deliver a difficult baby. Gertrude was young enough, strong enough. She hadn't wanted the job, but they'd kept on coming to her door.

How many times had she lifted Amber from a warm bed then set her down on a strange cold couch? One too many. Amber had grown old enough to resent it. She'd grown old enough to resent any calls on her mother's time, Vern included.

After the death of his first wife, he'd asked Gertrude to wed. She was thirty-nine at the time, young enough to have half a dozen sons. They'd had a daughter each. They'd wanted a few sons.

Fools, both of them. She should have moved out to his farm back then and lived in sin, but her own and Vern's upbringing wouldn't allow that. She'd heard nothing from Archie in thirteen years. Vern was convinced that he was dead. She wasn't, so they'd set the wheels of divorce in motion. The solicitor sent the papers to Archie, care of his father, and six weeks later the sod turned up on her doorstep.

That was the end of her marriage plans — and her relationship with Amber. She blamed Archie Foote for ruining the bond she'd had with her girl. He'd rip a rare flower from its stem and crush it beneath his boot, for no reason other than he could.

And he wasn't a good place for her mind to go wandering near nightfall. The sun and hard labour scared him away. Come nightfall and every memory of him was like a pit of quicksand, waiting to suck her down.

'How old is she now, Trude?'

Gertrude turned her eyes from the past to Vern. He was still standing in the doorway, smoking again, maybe watching her face remembering. He could read her well, as she could read him.

'She was thirty-two this year.'

'The little one, Jennifer,' he clarified.

'Jenny? She's not long gone four.'

'She was talking away to Jimmy like a little old woman today — discussing tombstones.'

'That's Norman's doing. He speaks to those girls as he might to his parson uncle.'

'So, how about it — moving into town and having some say in her raising?'

Maybe he glimpsed the thought of refusal, which wasn't what he'd come out here for.

'Come down to Willama with me when I go to pick up the Abbot boy. We'll stick a ring on your finger.'

'I've still got one somewhere, Vern. I've been thinking about it, but we're past making the change.'

'Speak for yourself,' he said. 'They're letting him out on Monday morning. We could go down on Sunday night.'

She sighed. And why shouldn't she go with him? Maybe she didn't want to move in with him, but there was no good reason why a couple of their age couldn't spend time together.

163

'I wouldn't mind doing some shopping down there . . .'

'We'll make it an overnight shopping trip. Give you plenty of time for shopping,' he said, happy now, that grin splitting his face and shaping it up just fine.

Something about that man's grin had a softening effect on her heart, something about it — about him — made her smile.

'I haven't got that much to spend,' she said.

OLD LOVERS

She took care with her dressing on Sunday evening. She wore the blue silk blouse Vern had given her, then a cool change blew through, dropping the temperature down enough to make her know she'd need a cardigan. She tried on a worn green thing she'd had for years and it was an insult to the blouse, so she changed her trousers for the skirt she'd made for Amber's wedding, then reached for the stranger's lightweight black coat, not expecting it to fit, but over that silk blouse it fitted well enough.

It was a beautifully cut thing, lightweight but woollen or a wool mixture. There'd been a time when she'd owned fancy clothes, when Archie had chosen to spend his money on her back. Most of what she wore these days started its life on her treadle sewing machine but she recognised class when she saw it.

'You're a fine-looking woman when you take trouble with yourself,' Vern said.

'You'll have to keep reminding me to sit with my knees together,' she said, straightening her skirt as she settled into the passenger seat.

'I'm a truthful man, Trude. I can't say that that's what I've got in mind.'

'You're a terrible man. I ought to change my mind about going.'

'But you won't.'

She didn't. The evening drive was pleasant, the meal that night was too much, but nice anyway. He'd booked a room at a small hotel, a double room. She told him he was past it, told him she'd forgotten how it was done, but he had one thing on his mind and, when all was said and done, neither one of them was past it.

They ate a good breakfast in the dining room and were waiting at shop doors for them to open. She bought four yards of hard-wearing grey fabric and two of a pretty floral for Elsie. She bought a pair of shoes for Joey. Vern wanted to buy her a pair with heels three inches tall, and got niggly when she wouldn't try them on.

'You're moving in with me,' he argued. 'You won't need to walk in them.'

'I didn't say I was moving in with you, and even if I do, I won't be getting around in skirts and high-heeled shoes. If you want to waste your money, buy me a bag of wheat for my chooks.'

'Bugger your chooks,' he said. 'You're my wife. I want to buy you nice things.'

'I'm not doing anything in a hurry so it's no use pushing me. Let me come to my own decision in my own time.'

At ten they picked up the Abbot boy; by midday they were back in Woody Creek and Gertrude pleased to be there and back in her trousers and comfortable shirts.

She told Elsie that night that she might be moving into town with Vern and asked her how she'd feel about staying out here alone with Joey.

'For how long, Mum?' Elsie said.

'I don't know, love. It's just a maybe.'

Elsie and Joey in bed, Gertrude, weary in body but not in mind, wasn't ready to sleep. She poured a mug of tea, put the lamp out and pulled a chair up to her open door, needing time in the dark to sort out her mind. There was a moon shining bright tonight, enough to see by. She sat looking out over her land, sipping scalding tea and attempting to dissect the past twenty-four hours.

Old mopoke calling, a plover replying, her mind slipping back to other nights, other doorways in other lands, waiting for Archie to come home.

He'd had the looks of a saint and the soul of a devil. She'd been wed around three months, had been on the boat to Africa when she'd gone to her cabin to get a jacket and caught him and a friend there in what might be called a compromising situation. To a nineteen-year-old country girl who hadn't known about such things, she'd seen no more than two naked men. Embarrassed, she'd closed the door and run.

A year on and she'd known more — known a lot more. She'd pitched a bucket of water at him, as she might at a rutting dog. Archie hadn't been happy. He hadn't marked her face but he'd damn near crippled her.

No one knew the full truth of her years with Archie. Her mother wouldn't have understood what she was talking about. Her father wouldn't have wanted to know that she knew of such things, and maybe she hadn't wanted Vern to know how much she knew.

Her biggest mistake had been made in keeping what Archie was from Amber. She'd raised her to believe her father was a clever doctor who travelled the world healing sick children. And it wasn't a lie. He had been a clever doctor when he'd used his skill in healing. She'd told Amber he'd disappeared in India so she'd had to come home to Granny and Grandpa. That wasn't a lie. He'd gone missing all right, as had the sixteen-year-old son of a British army officer, who, with a dozen of his cronies, had gone looking for him; she hadn't waited around to see if they'd found him either.

Thirteen years of not thinking about him, then he'd turned up at her door, better looking in his forties than he'd been in his twenties, and dressed like a toff. She'd greeted him in boots and trousers, and he'd laughed in her face. She'd stopped his laughter. She'd loaded up her father's rifle and pointed it, told him there were easier ways of getting shut of him than the divorce courts, and there was plenty of room on her land to bury vermin too, then she'd let off a shot at his shoes and laughed at him when he'd danced.

He'd gone, though not far enough. He was a nephew of Mrs Monk, out at Three Pines. He'd gone out there, and on the following Sunday, he'd ridden in with Max Monk, a chap of Vern's age, neighbour and friend of Vern's since boyhood. She could hardly pull a gun on him. And Amber was at home. She'd seen that wedding photograph. She'd known who he was. Thirteen, at the stage of crossing over from girl to woman; he couldn't have chosen a worse time to show up.

'That mongrel would charm the bloomers off a nun and have the choirboys' off for seconds,' she told the night.

They hadn't stayed long that Sunday. She'd made it clear to Monk that she didn't want Archie on her land, and he hadn't come back. But, unbeknown to her, he'd gone to the school and taken Amber from the playground, bought her fancy shoes from Miller's store, a white Sunday-go-meeting frock from Blunt's. She hadn't brought them home, not then. She'd hidden them somewhere.

Gertrude may never have found out she'd been meeting her father if not for Amber's first verbal attack.

'You had boyfriends all the time you were married to my father,' she'd said. 'You took me away from my father because he loved me. I'm going to live with him in Melbourne, and his house has got more rooms than Monk's house.'

She'd raised her girl to believe her father was a good man. How could she turn around and tell her he was the devil incarnate who had so violated his family's trust they'd paid him to stay out of the country? She couldn't. How could she stop a thirteen-year-old girl from hankering after her handsome doctor father? She'd tried.

He'd hung around town for a month, then disappeared, still owing Richard Blunt for Amber's frock. Gertrude paid for it. Amber had worn it until it turned to rags. Bad months those, and the bad became worse. Amber blamed her because her father had gone, blamed Vern too. Angry months.

'She'll get over it faster if you stay away for a while, Vern,' Gertrude had said — which had got Vern's nose out of joint, and when it was out of joint he'd damn near cut it off to spite his face.

Lorna was two or three years old at that time. He'd employed Rita Jones, the eighteen-year-old daughter of one of Monk's labourers, to nursemaid her. Rita must have been doing a bit more for him than she was paid to do, because the next thing Gertrude knew, Vern had wed her, on the quiet. The marriage lasted nine years, and during those nine years, Gertrude had rarely set eyes on Vern or his wife.

He'd come for her the day Rita died. There was nothing she could do. Nothing anyone could do. A crazed stallion had trampled her, smashed in the side of her head. She was dead within hours. She went to the funeral, heard later that he'd taken his girls down to a city boarding school, then a week or so after Rita's funeral, he rode down to Gertrude's and tossed a wedding ring at her.

'Put that on your finger, or I'll hold you down and hammer the thing home.'

'It's been a week, Vern!'

'Eight days,' he'd said. 'Put it on.'

'I won't be a party to it. Six months is the least you can wait.'

'Six months less eight days,' he said.

He'd still been a farming man then, and living alone in their grandfather's old timber house. Amber was in her twenties, working as a pastry cook at the hotel and spending her weekends in town with Maisy and George Macdonald, so Gertrude started spending her Saturday nights out at Vern's farm. Happy months those, maybe the best of her life. She was in her late forties, but certain she'd have time to bear a son or two, and every month praying they'd got one started. Too happy, too involved with each other, they hadn't noticed the Morrisons, hadn't noticed Norman pursuing Amber.

Amber brought him down to meet her one Saturday afternoon. Gertrude had been rushing around getting things done so she could ride out to Vern, but she'd put off her chores, made a cup of tea and done her best to talk to Norman. They'd left for town at five, and by five thirty she'd saddled her horse and ridden off.

They were bird-watching on the bridge when she'd crossed over. 'A pleasant night for a ride, Mrs Foote,' Norman said. She'd agreed it was and continued on her way.

Amber was waiting for her on Sunday evening.

'You've got the principles of a trollop,' she said. 'If the Morrisons find out that you're on with Vern Hooper, and his wife hardly cold in her grave, they'll have nothing more to do with me.'

Which, in hindsight, might have been a good thing.

'Give her a month, Vern,' she'd said.

'That girl has been dictating my life and yours for too long, Trude. Pack your bags and leave her to her Morrisons.'

That's what she should have done — should have moved in with him when the creek flooded that year. He'd wanted her to. She had two foot of water running through her house, ninety per cent of her land underwater. Her chooks took to the trees, Amber moved in with the Morrisons and Gertrude and her goats had moved in with the McPhersons — which had put a bee up Vern's nose. He was a man who liked to get his own way, and when he didn't, he took it hard. He hadn't come near her for a month and she'd been too busy to concern herself with a grown man's sulking.

Joanne Nicholas was widowed around the same time as Vern. Her husband had got himself caught up in one of the belts that drove the big mill saws. He'd died badly, and Joanne hadn't taken well to widowhood. How Vern had become involved with her, Gertrude didn't know, but he had, and within two months they were wed. Then Amber wed Norman and, to rub salt into a weeping wound, Joanne became pregnant. She was over forty, too old to be having her first child, even if its father had been a midget — which Vern was not. By seven months, she was at bursting point.

'If you don't want to lose her, you'll get her down to the city doctors,' Gertrude had told Vern. He'd taken her advice.

Amber gave birth to Cecelia in March. Six weeks later, in a city hospital, Vern's son was cut early from Joanne. She'd never got over that operation.

'I had the height, the hips,' Gertrude told an owl as he whispered by. 'I had the strength to give him a dozen sons.'

Should have defied their grandfather, run off and wed at

eighteen. Should have. Too late now. She had a good life down here. She loved her accidental grandson, loved Elsie.

What other reason did she have to stay down here? A life of hard labour, that's all. And for how much longer could she keep it up? Ten years? Fifteen? And what happens when I'm too old to labour?

Joey will be old enough, she argued.

She could have a good life with Vern. They'd grown together. They laughed at the same humour. In so many ways they were two of a kind.

He's pig-headed, she argued. He doesn't sulk often but, by God, when he does, he takes his time getting over it.

He's an honourable man, honest to a fault. I trust him.

You swore once that you'd never trust your life to another man.

I'm only fifty-nine. I'm young enough to need a man. And Norman needs help with those girls. And Jimmy might grow on me.

And Joey? Your dreams for Joey?

She sighed for lack of an answer and for all of her sons unborn, sighed for the daughter she'd dreamed for, and the dead grandsons she'd brought into the world and watched die. She sighed for Cecelia, the only blood she had to continue her line, then sighed more deeply because the only line that girl would ever continue would be the Duckworth line.

The dregs of her mug flung in the face of the night, she stood and reached for her water ladle, dipped out half a mug of water, dipped her finger into the salt pig she kept on her dresser and walked outside to clean her teeth, as she did each night. Rubbing, spitting salt, rinsing and spitting — and thinking how nice it might be to turn on a tap when she wanted to brush her teeth.

Not so nice sharing the bathroom with Vern's daughters. She could never find more than two words to say to either of them.

But they'd stay in Melbourne.

She rinsed her mouth, gargled, spat and looked up at the moon. It was throwing its weight around tonight, splashing her house and yard with its softening light. Her world looked a picture by moonlight.

She reached up to withdraw the Japanese pins from her plait. Only two of those pins left. Archie had bought her a half dozen. Lost, broken — all but these two. She took more care with the two than she had of the six, placed them each night on the top shelf of her washstand. Her hair was as heavy as it had ever been, and as dark — thanks to the bottle of dye Jean White swapped for a few dozen eggs. Gertrude took pride in her hair, and in her figure. Maybe her waist wasn't as slim as it had been at nineteen, her breasts not so firm, but she wasn't in bad shape for a woman nudging sixty.

So proud to lose her waist when Amber was inside her, every day looking at herself, searching for evidence that her baby was growing. But damn pleased too to get her body back when Amber was born. She'd tried on every frock she'd owned, every skirt. Not that they'd been a lot of use around this place. Wire fences ripped sleeves, thorns grasped at hems. Amber was six weeks old the day she'd gone hunting in one of the trunks she'd brought home from India, seeking something serviceable. She'd found a pair of Archie's trousers. They'd fitted her well around the backside though she was longer in the leg than he. She'd had to let the hems down.

Her mother had been aghast. She'd told her she was not stepping outside the door dressed like a hoyden. She'd called Gertrude's father. He'd taken one look at Archie's trousers and laughed. He'd had a laugh on him worth listening to, a laugh that could make her mother laugh. In time she'd got used to seeing her daughter in trousers.

Three pairs of his trousers she'd brought home with her, four or five of his shirts, a jacket, two pairs of his shoes. She'd left that sod nothing when she'd packed up their room in India, not his clothing, not his books. She'd had an hour to pack and she'd done it in less.

It had taken her parents longer to realise she wasn't going back to handsome Archie. They'd thought she'd walked out on the match of the century, had visualised their Gertie at the side of her handsome doctor husband.

'He can give you the world, darlin',' her father had said when Archie came asking for her hand.

He'd given her the world all right — or all of its filth and degradation.

She shook her head, attempting to clear that sod from her mind. 'Bed,' she said.

Her bedroom hatch, closed all afternoon to keep the sun out, now kept the moonlight out. She heaved it wide, propped it, pleased by the breath of cool air coming in off the walnut tree.

She'd slept in huts that had no hatch, slept in shelters without walls, slept on trains and in bug-riddled beds in filthy hotels — and in a few that were fine. She'd sailed on tramp steamers and on ships of the line, had travelled up rivers in native dugouts, had seen more of the world during the years she'd spent with Archie Foote than most in Woody Creek would see in ten lifetimes. He'd had no fear, would try anything, go anywhere. He could make himself known in a dozen tongues.

She'd feared — had always feared — what she couldn't control. Needed to know she was in control of her own small space in this wide, wide world. Amber had been the largest part of her world. Couldn't control her, not once she'd grown. Had feared for her. Feared for her still. Not a day went by when she didn't think about her, wonder what she was doing, how she was living, if she was living.

And she couldn't talk about her to Vern. On a few occasions lately when she'd brought up Amber's name, he'd made his feelings very clear on that subject. Not that she blamed him. She'd always put her girl before him.

Maybe it's time to start putting him first, she thought. Elsie and Joey will do all right down here, and it's not as if I'll be far away. I can come home whenever I feel like it.

How often will I feel like it? Once a week? Twice a day?

I'll have a refrigerator at Vern's, electric light.

'To show up all of my wrinkles,' she told the moon.

Didn't know if she wanted to live with him; maybe thought she ought to want to live with him. And those girls in town — they needed her. Norman needed her in town.

'What do I need?' she said.

Her head out through the hatch opening, she searched the sky, seeking the stars' guidance. The moon was shining so bright, she couldn't see how the stars might be aligned.

'I'd be running back here every night,' she whispered to the man in the moon. 'I'd be back here every morning and most afternoons. And who needs electricity when they can have your old light for free?'

DISCOVERY

'Independent bugger of a woman,' Vern muttered. Ten or fifteen times a day he found himself repeating those words. And she was an independent bugger of a woman and he was staying away from her. She was also staying away from him — and he didn't want her to stay away. He wanted her hammering on his door, pleading for a second, or maybe a fourth, chance. He considered hanging his hat up to Nelly Dobson, who did a bit of the heavier cleaning for him. He took pleasure in imagining Gertrude's face when word got back to her.

'Independent bugger of a woman. You always were and you ever will be. A man needs an independent bugger of a woman like he needs a hole in the head,' he said, but before the words were out of his mouth he knew he spoke a lie. He needed her like he needed sugar in his morning cup of tea. A man won't die if he doesn't get that heaped spoonful of sugar stirred into his cup, but without it, every day starts off sour. He needed her in his bed. And he probably wouldn't die of that either, though he maybe wouldn't want to live as long. He needed her to tell him what he ought to do about Jimmy, needed her to hear what he was thinking about doing.

He should have got that boy back into school in February, but he had too much on his mind to worry about schooling a boy who didn't want to be schooled — and who didn't need it anyway. The drought was on his mind, and his hungry sheep. And the creek bordering his acres was down to a trickle, and Max Monk, his neighbour, worse off than he. Monk had more stock, more staff, was dependent on his land for his living — and he enjoyed the high life. Vern had his mill. He could afford to buy feed for his stock.

Then, as if he didn't have enough on his mind, his farm manager went and broke his wrist and was less than useless.

'Independent bugger of a woman. Useless little bookworm bugger of a boy.'

He dragged Jimmy away from his book, forced him into the car and out to the farm. Couldn't get him outside. He wanted to sit in the manager's parlour reading out-of-date newspapers. He dragged him from the newspapers, showed him how to spread a few bags of wheat for the sheep. He walked him down to the creek where he found two of the woolly-brained buggers stuck in the mud. He went in, up to his knees, and hauled one out while Jimmy stood in the shade hunting flies from his eyes and howling over an old ewe, stuck to her neck and barely worth saving.

'Get back up to the house if you don't like seeing what life's about, boy.'

Thigh deep, up to his armpits in greasy, grey mud, and something stabbed him on his wedding ring finger. He considered it a sign from Jesus telling him he wasn't meant to wed that independent bugger of a woman, or maybe that he was meant to hang up his hat to Nelly Dobson — which would save him a bit on her wages. He got the ewe out, saw her up on her feet, then walked down to where the creek had a bit of sand to walk out on, where he washed the mud off.

Three days he kept that boy out there, and by the time he got him home, he was mozzie-bitten, fly-bitten, had sore eyes from the dust and was more than willing to return to his schoolmasters. Vern paid John Dean's oldest boy to give his manager a hand and he took off for the city to get rid of his son. He was staying at his half-brother's house when his wedding finger started giving him pain. Maybe he should have stayed down there, but he took the train home and was halfway back when he noticed the swelling. By the following day, his hand was up like a rubber balloon. He put it down to a city spider bite. His housekeeper didn't. She told him to get down to Gertrude.

'That independent bugger of a woman,' he said. 'I wouldn't go near her if I was dying.'

By late afternoon, he felt like dying. He didn't go to Gertrude. He drove down to Willama and drove home with a bottle of blood-cleaning potion and sulphur pills, and his hand throbbing and near useless.

The pills worked on his belly, not his hand. He was as sick as a dog, couldn't keep a thing down. His housekeeper noticed the red streaks creeping up towards his elbow.

'I've seen a man lose his leg, then his life with blood poisoning,' she said. 'You get yourself back to those doctors, Mr Hooper.'

He didn't want to lose his arm — or his life. He got himself out to the car, got it started, but knew he'd never drive the distance. There are times when a man has to swallow his pride. His went down like burning bile, but he drove to Gertrude.

'You fool, to neglect something like that,' she yelled. 'Get down to Willama. I can't deal with this.'

He'd sat on her cane couch and doubted he'd ever leave it. She was holding his hand and it felt good. 'They'll cut it off,' he said.

'How did it start?'

'Something bit me in the city. What's it matter?'

'It matters. Where did the swelling start, you fool of a man?'

'My ring finger. It was Christ warning me off women.'

'Then it's a pity it didn't bite you years ago.'

'Who are you to talk?'

'I only did it once.'

She was holding his arm now and her hands were cool. She studied each finger.

'I love you,' he said. 'I love your hands.'

'I love yours too. What did you get up to in the city?'

'None of your business.'

'If you want to keep that hand, it is. How did you do that?'

She'd found the stretched scar of something newly healed on the pad of his ring finger, half an inch from where it joined the palm.

'A man can't recall his every scar, and I'm too crook to care.'

'Then start caring, Vern. Can you drive if I go with you?'

'I could fly if you were with me, Trude.'

'You're running a fever and it's no joking matter. This is bad. We've got to get you down there.'

'They're not cutting it off. Do something.'

His finger was purple, his hand was getting to be that way, and he'd kept nothing other than his pride down since yesterday morning. He wasn't a passing out sort of bloke, but he was about to do it. He lay back on her couch, his head resting on one end, his knees hanging over the other.

'It's more likely that cut has had some infection in it and healed over, than to be the bite of something. I've told you a hundred times that farm cuts need looking after.'

'Stop nagging me and do something.'

'Remember you said that, my lad.'

She poured boiling water into a small bucket, stirred in a few tablespoons of salt, added a dash of lysol, placed a clean towel over a kitchen chair, the chair beside the couch, the bucket on the floor, dipped her lancing tools into the bucket, added cold water enough to drop its temperature down from boiling to steaming point, then she took Vern's wrist and plunged the hand in and out of that water, and while he was yelling about the heat of it, she punctured the balloon of his wedding finger, right over the stretched scar. Hand back into the bucket, then her lancing tool went back into the same hole, opening it deeper, wider.

'Keep your hand in that bucket for as long as you can stand it,' she said.

He couldn't stand it, so she took his wrist and plunged the hand in again.

By the sixth or eighth plunge, the water in the bucket had lost a degree or ten and when she told him to leave his hand in the water, he did as he was told.

She made up a poultice of bread and boracic acid, crushed garlic and enough honey to bind the mess into a paste, then she plastered it over the wound and bound it there with sheeting.

She emptied the last of her brandy into a glass, sweetened it with honey, soured it with the juice of a lemon, crushed two aspirins into it, added a dash of boiling water.

'Drink it.'

'I can't keep anything down.'

'You'll keep this down. Drink it.'

'I'm not a drinking man.'

'Stop arguing, Vern, and do as you're told for once in your life!'

He drank it, and when it stayed down, she saddled her horse and rode into town for salt, metho, aspirins and a bottle of rum, known to heat the blood faster than brandy.

Gertrude's treatment was never pretty and usually painful, and the more she learned about healing, the more she knew how little she knew. She treated infections with heat and salt. She'd seen it work in the old days, and she'd make it work on Vern. She loved that pig-headed fool of a man; she may not have wanted to live with him, but she didn't want to live without him.

Every two hours, on the hour, she prepared that scalding bath for his hand, and that night, she helped him to her bed then offered a larger dose of her rum and honey brew. She told him to sip it, but he emptied the glass and it went to his head.

'Get in with me, Trude.' It was the first time he'd been invited into that bed.

'You'd be lucky to raise a finger tonight, my lad.'

'Hop in, and we'll find out.'

'There's two kids a wall away. Go to sleep.'

'I tried to get them further away and the bugger foiled me. *One kiss, my bonny sweetheart . . .*'

'You're drunk,' she whispered, but she leaned down and kissed his lips.

'That's not a kiss. That's an insult.'

'I need two good hands to hold me, darlin',' she said, escaping his one good hand. 'When you've got two, I won't insult you.'

'Promise?'

'Cross my heart and hope to die.'

'You'll marry me?'

179

'A weekend in Willama. Now go to sleep.'

He was snoring peacefully when she bedded down on the couch, a hard bed, but she'd slept on worse.

Three nights he spent in her bed, and for three days he spent a good percentage of his daylight hours with his hand in that bucket of steaming saltwater. On the second day the poison stopped creeping up his arm, and by the second evening the swelling in his hand started centring where it had begun, in his wedding finger. On the third morning, the wound exploded, and what came out of the hole she'd dug had to be witnessed to be believed. He didn't believe it, but he started mixing his own saltwater.

He drove home on the fourth morning, promising to follow her instructions to the letter. It took a week for the infection to ooze away, and when it did, and that hand, though peeling, was back to its dinner-plate dimensions, he held her, kissed her and told her she was an independent bugger of a woman and he'd never loved another and how about that trip to Willama.

In March, she left Elsie in charge and kept her promise. They planned another trip in April, but Lorna brought Jimmy home in April.

'You'll have to stay home to care for him,' Vern said. 'I'm run off my feet right now.'

Lorna had engagements in the city. She was involved with a bunch from the university, intent on changing the world.

Through May and June, Jimmy remained in Woody Creek, and what was a man supposed to do with a nine-year-old boy who didn't like sheep and ran from the dogs when Vern took him out to the farm? And what the hell could he do with a boy who couldn't stand the noise of the mill when Vern took him there, who came home worrying that his nose or his lungs were full of sawdust, who wandered around half of the night afraid he was suffocating?

Vern hired a maid to help his housekeeper and he started leaving the boy home in their care, until he came home one afternoon to find Jimmy washing dishes in the kitchen wearing the maid's apron. The boy seemed happy enough, but he had too much of his mother in him already without putting on a woman's apron.

In July, Vern took him back to his schoolmasters. In September, Lorna and Margaret brought him home. They stayed two nights, then he was on his own.

Whatever Vern might have felt for Norman Morrison, respect had never come in high on that list, but with that boy like a millstone around his neck, he found himself drawn more often to the station to have a smoke with Norman while Jimmy sat around drawing or looking at books with a four-and-a-half-year-old girl.

'I was running amok at his age,' Vern said.

'Children are not always what their parents hope they'll be, Vern,' Norman said.

In October, he had a smoke with Norman and ended up inviting him and the girls around to share his Sunday evening meal. Jimmy and Cecelia were of similar age. If his boy wanted to play with girls, then Vern might at least supply him with one his own age. Norman accepted the invitation, and Vern went on his way to the post office, Jimmy left to play.

Wished he could take that invitation back when he picked up his mail and saw a letter wearing an English stamp and postmark. Didn't want to open it. Took it home and sat looking at it for ten minutes before he found the nerve to see what was inside it.

'Christ save me from that,' he said.

Henry Langdon was Vern's first wife's younger brother. Vern had met him a week before their wedding, then spent the next three months trying to get rid of him. England was half a world away. Folk who made the trip felt obligated to get their money's worth before making that trip home. Langdon had made the trip a second time to see his sister's grave and to meet his motherless niece. Now he wanted to repeat the exercise, and he was bringing his wife with him.

Vern pitched the letter, and damn near got his housekeeper who'd come in to see what he wanted. He wanted his flamin' youth back; that's what he wanted. Twenty-four when he'd wed

181

Lorna Langdon, who had looked much like her daughter and been seven years Vern's senior. If the truth be told, he'd wed her for her five hundred pounds a year — and because Gertrude had gone sailing around the bloody world with Archie bloody Foote.

'Visitors,' he explained to his housekeeper, picking up the letter. 'Visitors you can't get rid of.' He pitched the letter at his table, watched it slide down the polished surface. 'And we've got more on Sunday evening. The Morrisons. Sorry,' he said. 'I don't know what his kids eat.'

They were good eaters. Maybe they weren't accustomed to much. The older girl's table manners made Jimmy look like a young gent. Little Goldilocks used her fork as a spoon. A silent meal, just the scrape of knife and fork. Vern had other things on his mind, namely Henry Langdon. He had nothing in common with him. And not much in common with Norman. He looked at Jimmy and Cecelia and knew that all they'd ever have in common was their age. He wouldn't be repeating this exercise.

Then Jimmy disappeared and didn't return. Cecelia took to roaming his house, picking up things she shouldn't have been touching, while Goldilocks sat on the floor as close to the wireless as she could get, watching for the little men to fly out. Vern had picked up a station playing decent music. Listening to it gave him a reason for silence. Between songs, he and Norman managed a few words to say about Melbourne, a few to say about the weather, then Vern went looking for Jimmy and found him reading in his room.

'We've got guests, lad. Get yourself out to the sitting room and do the right thing by those girls.'

The boy was obedient, Vern would say that much. He followed his father back and sat beside Jenny, near the wireless.

Jessie Macdonald had already told her that there were no little men in wirelesses and no racing horses either. She'd said there were records inside, though she hadn't known how the horse racing her father listened to got inside.

'Are records inside that, Jimmy?'

'No. They play them on transmitters that turn them into air waves, and inside the wirelesses they've got valves and things that catch the waves and turn them back into . . . into music.'

'Even racing horses can make . . . make the waves?'

'Everything can.'

'What does . . . what do the valves look like?'

He pointed to the electric light globe. 'A bit like that globe, but they just make . . . like red spots instead of light.'

'You have a bright boy,' Norman said.

'He's bright enough,' Vern said. 'Bright enough to get out of going to school. I don't know what I'm going to do with him. Don't know what I'm going to do with any of them. And I've got a pair of mad pommy relatives coming over to spend Christmas with me and I don't know what I'm going to do about them either.'

Whichever way you looked at it, 1928 had been a bad year for Vern, first with Gertrude refusing to move in, then his lanky daughter developing her communist leanings, and his other fool of a girl stuck to Lorna's elbow, following wherever she led and without the brains to know into what she was being led. He wanted those girls out of that city — or wanted Lorna out of it before she got herself and her sister into trouble. He'd never concerned himself greatly with Margaret, who had about as much Hooper blood in her as that little goldie one — now attempting to get her head inside the back of his wireless — had Morrison blood.

That thought sent a jolt through Vern. It shook up a decent dose of guilt from deep down inside him. Norman showed no preferential treatment with those girls — and if he did, his leaning was towards the little one. The reverse applied with Vern. He'd always treated Margaret as a ring-in, had more or less ignored her. Not that she'd missed out on anything. He'd spent as much on her schooling as he had on Lorna's and more on her clothing. It was just money, though. He'd spent no love on that girl, wasted none of his dreams on her — blamed her for her bloody mother's trickery and nine years of hell, that's what he'd done.

He sat watching Norman while some tenor filled the small sitting room with his voice and that little girl sat enraptured, head up, hands clasped, knees folded, Norman watching her, pride enough shining out of that man's hangdog eyes to light the room — until his other girl whinged to go home. She washed the pride away.

Maybe the night wasn't a total waste of time. Maybe Vern learned something about himself. Gertrude spent a lot of time calling him a pig-headed man, telling him Margaret was a better daughter to him than Lorna would ever be. And maybe she was. She was the one who had knitted his elongated sweater — the first he'd ever had in his life that fitted. And he hadn't mentioned her in his will. Not that he'd left much to Lorna — she'd get her mother's money and maybe a bit from the Langdons. They weren't breeders; Lorna was the last of that blood line. Most of what Vern owned would go to his boy, his hope for the future. Not a lot of hope there. If he could get him back to school, he might turn him into a parson.

Norman left at nine thirty. Jimmy went to bed, and Vern wandered and scratched his head, knowing there was no way out of that Langdon visit. By the time his letter got to them, they'd be on the boat.

'Just when you think things can't get a whole heap worse, they surprise you,' he muttered. 'However . . .' and he went to Joanne's library, to Joanne's — or her first husband's — desk. Her writing paper was still in the drawer, her pen and ink. He didn't do much writing.

Dear Lorna,

I just got word from your Uncle Henry. He's on his way. I'll need you to find out the details of when his boat gets in, and to be down there to meet him when it does. He's bringing his wife with him this time so I'll need you up here. Of course, I realise it might interfere with your social, or socialistic, life, but going by the last times he came out here, he'll stay for months, and I can't take more than half an hour of him, so you'll need to give your landlady notice that you'll be moving out. It's no use me paying rent on your rooms if you're not using them. You can get something else when you go back, or move in with my brother at Balwyn . . .

The Langdons arrived in early December. Leticia Langdon had an accent you could cut with a knife and she never shut up, and she looked like something the cat might drag in on a wet morning. Vern started cutting lunch with them on the second day of their visit. He started cutting breakfast. By the third week he was cutting dinner, and by the fourth Jimmy had developed a sudden interest in farming. They spent days out there, then days and nights. Vern taught him to drive the new tractor, taught him to swim, and that kid started getting a bit of colour in his face, though he still ran from the dogs — who enjoyed the game.

The Langdons stayed through January, then February came and maybe they'd got the hint. They were packing up to leave.

'As far as I see it, lad,' Vern said to Jimmy, 'you've got yourself two choices here. You go back with your sisters to the city when they take the visitors back, you stay with your masters, you stop playing sick and you learn to be a city man; or you start going to school up here and you learn to like sawdust and flies.'

'Righto,' Jimmy said.

'You want to go back to your schoolmasters?'

'I want to stay with you.'

They shook hands on the deal, Hooper hand meeting Hooper hand. There was no doubting who that boy belonged to, not with those oversized hands and their double-jointed thumbs.

PROBLEM CHILDREN

Miss Rose had forty-seven children in her classroom that year, forty-seven children seated in four rows — her kindergarten group, her largest group, on her left; grades one and two in the centre rows. Then there was her upper second grade, created this year and situated on her right. These were her problem children, old enough to have moved down the verandah to Mr Curry's room, but not sufficiently advanced to manage there. So Mr Curry said. He didn't want them.

Then, a week after school went back, Vern Hooper delivered his son to her classroom, a great gangling boy, all legs, arms, head and ears. He was the height of a twelve year old.

'Mr Curry?' she said, her eyebrows disappearing beneath her auburn fringe.

'We saw him. He suggested he might do better with you for a time,' Vern said, and he left, closing the door behind him.

Her upper second grade consisted of three desks capable of seating six children. Ray King and Cecelia Morrison sat alone, not by choice but by choice of their mutual victims. Ray was a giant for his age, a docile, stuttering, barefoot boy, his hair clipped to the scalp and with a smell about him that suggested an unfamiliarity with soap and water. His father, district wood-chopping champion, also known for his ability to drink any man under the table, and his mother, an evil-mouthed, long-haired and lousy hag, survived in a shack opposite Macdonald's mill. Miss Rose pitied Ray. She kept her distance, but did what she could for him, which was little enough.

Vern Hooper's son was decked out in his private school uniform and toting an armful of his old school's books. She couldn't inflict Ray on him.

She glanced at Cecelia, still prone to occasional hair-pulling, which wouldn't present a problem. The Hooper boy had little more hair than Ray. Cecelia was clean.

'Do you know Cecelia, Jim?' she said.

He flinched. A few children flinched for him, but Cecelia lifted her elbow and moved to the right of the two-seater desk. Jim placed his books down then sat on the edge.

The Macdonald twins were seated in the front row of upper second grade. The first day school went back, Miss Rose had attempted to separate them, had placed one alone in the front desk, one at the rear with Ray, but they'd made her own and Ray's life a misery by mimicking his stutter in unison. How they did it, she did not know, but two voices speaking in unison was less unnerving when they came from the same desk. They were small for their years and of unfortunate appearance, toad-like, their most commanding features their violet-grey eyes — cruel eyes, if a child's eyes could be cruel. Both boys were capable of learning when they wished to learn, which wasn't often enough to learn much of anything. They enjoyed singing and had a natural ability with rhyme. They chased Ray home from school four nights out of five, chanting their cruel rhymes.

'*R-r-ray King is l-lousy,*
His m-m-other is a f-frowsy.
He smells like a dog,
'Cause his f-f-father likes the grog.'

Could she blame them? Ray's hands and neck had years of dirt ingrained into them, and no doubt as much where she couldn't see. He was old enough to keep himself clean. Certainly he brought much of the tormenting down upon himself.

He gained some relief from the twins' torments that day. They turned their joint attack on Jim Hooper.

'*Lanky poofter, drongo Jim,*
Dropped his brain in the rubbish bin,

*Scared to get dirty getting it out,
Or his sister will give him a punch in the snout.*'

No one, other than their sisters, was safe from those wicked little boys, not the Catholic sisters or the few children who attended their school behind a tall green corrugated-iron fence. The twins walked by that fence twice a day, dragging sticks along it. They went cat-hunting on moonlit nights, bagging their catch then dropping them yowling over the convent fence.

The second Morrison child, delivered to the classroom this year, came in for her own share of verbal abuse. Miss Rose had kept her distance from Jennifer, fearing a second Morrison screamer. As yet, the scream had not come. A dainty child, she sat in the kindergarten row, her long hair pulled back tight in man-made, lopsided plaits, her frock, man-bought, too dark, too large, too long, her shoes too heavy for tiny legs.

Until Jim Hooper joined her group, Miss Rose had watched Jennifer standing on the verandah waiting to walk home with the Macdonald girls. She walked home with Jim now, the twins behind them, chanting.

'*Old J.C. she went off to have a pee,
Squatted down behind a tree,
Dropped her pants and found Jenny . . .*'

Expected trouble rarely came. The weeks passed and Miss Rose was barely aware the Hooper boy was in her classroom. And he should not have been there. His handwriting would put a sixth grader's to shame, he was reading in advance of a sixth grader, and his spelling put her own to shame. The little Morrison girl was another surprise — a pleasant surprise in a very small package.

A tangle of days, that school year, an interweaving of heat and rain, fire and frost, schoolyard fights, skinned knees and tears. There were bad, bad days when she planned to get out of town, and good days when everything went right and she decided to stay a while longer.

Then there was spring, that perfect time between the frost and heat, between fog and dust, when Woody Creek became green and the scent of Vern Hooper's hedge of roses fought down the stink of sawdust. She planned the school concert in spring, chose the songs, sketched the costumes, met with Mrs Fulton and Miss Blunt to see what could and could not be done.

Jimmy refused to be measured for a costume. Sissy didn't want to wear an onion costume, but Miss Rose had learnt how to deal with Cecelia Morrison.

'That's your choice, Cecelia. You may sit in the audience this year.'

'I want to be something else.' The twins, Sissy's only friends, had major roles in the concert. Jenny had a major role, and Sissy wanted one. 'I just said I don't want to wear a stupid onion costume.'

'We need one more onion, but if you don't want to be on stage this year, then you may leave. Good afternoon, Cecelia.'

'I want to be in the twins' song, I said.'

'As you are aware, the princess has already been chosen. Good afternoon, Cecelia.'

Her replies sounded somewhat bored, starting high, ending low. There was a definite rhythm to her Cecelia Morrison voice. It never altered. Always cool, calm, slow and controlled. At times, she believed she was making progress with her. At other times, she walked out to the verandah to breathe a while and to count the days to December. Thereafter, Cecelia would be Mr Curry's responsibility. Only fifty-three more school days.

'I'll be a stupid onion then!'

'Wonderful. Line up with the other onions. Flower fairies, over here, please, in a row.'

Australia went to the polls in October and Scullin was voted into the top job, then, before the month ended, the New York Stock Exchange experienced record declines in stock prices. It was reported in the Melbourne newspapers, but the running of the Melbourne Cup made bigger headlines. Australians liked their race meetings.

When Joanne was alive, Vern had taken her down to Melbourne every year for Cup week. He tried to talk Gertrude into going with him. She wouldn't go and there was no joy to be had in going down to the Cup alone. He had a flutter. He put a fiver on Nightmarch's nose, and won a wad — all thanks to Jimmy's night-marching.

Two nights out of three, that kid walked. Vern listened for him, woke to find him opening the front door, or standing outside Vern's door, and, on a few occasions, attempting to get into Vern's double bed. Another man might have invited him in. Vern wasn't that man. He marched him back to his own bed.

He wasn't the man to sit enthralled through school concerts either, watching group after group of kids in fancy clothes singing off-key. Gertrude wanted to go this year. Jenny was singing.

'You wouldn't come down to the Cup with me,' he said.

'You pig-headed two year old,' she said. 'Jimmy wants you to go.'

'You take him then — and stay in town overnight.'

He had his housekeeper make up one of the back rooms for her — he planned on doing his own marching in the night. He was shaving when he heard the train pull in. He was sluicing his face when he heard it pull out. And five minutes later, Margaret and Lorna walked in, unannounced, unexpected, Margaret's hair looking a mite singed.

'And there goes my night,' he said.

They'd taken rooms at a guesthouse in Brighton, which had gone up in smoke while they were sleeping. Margaret escaped in her nightdress. Lorna escaped through a window, fully clad, case in hand. They'd had two choices: Vern's half-brother out at Balwyn, who Lorna considered a halfwit and his sixteen-year-old son a congenital moron; or Woody Creek. Margaret quite liked her uncle and cousin, but her need for clothing had weighted the scales in favour of home. She'd arrived wearing Lorna's severe grey suit, the skirt pulling across her buttocks, dragging in the dust, the jacket barely covering her breasts.

Three hours later when Gertrude rode into town, the concert seemed the lesser of two evils to Vern. The horse left to eat what he could find in Vern's backyard, he walked with Gertrude and his son across the lines to the hall.

The punishment began with a maypole dance, the pole threatening to topple. It was followed by Victoria Bull's tap dance. She did it well enough. The ringmaster was popular. Each time he doffed his hat between the opening and closing of the curtains, the audience applauded, so Vern applauded, though he had no idea whose kid he was applauding.

He recognised the big rubber ball rolling across the stage. He'd given Jimmy five bob from his Cup winnings and he'd spent half of it on a big colourful ball, more suitable for a girl than a boy. He heard Jimmy laugh as one of the Macdonald twins, clad in a green frog suit, hopped across the stage chasing the ball. The princess wandered on. It was one of the younger Macdonald girls. To Vern they all looked the same, undergrown and washed out. She spent some time searching for her ball, while off to the side three seniors sang the sorry tale of the prince turned into a frog by a wicked witch. The frog hopped around the stage holding the ball, hopped over to the princess to offer it. The princess thanked him profusely, gave him a mock kiss. The frog croaked, made a point of wiping his mouth, then fell theatrically to the floor, frog-kicking as the lights went out. It wasn't a blackout, though they'd had a few in town. The stage lit up seconds later, the twin in the frog suit having swapped places with the other one, clad as a prince. It was well done and worth the watching and rightfully received a thunder of applause.

'Who is he?' Vern asked as the ringmaster doffed his hat.
'Ray King.'
'That stuttering lump of Big Henry's?'
'Shush,' Gertrude said.

Few in the audience recognised Big Henry King's son. Miss Rose had taken it upon herself to send him down to the creek with a bar of soap, a towel and strict instructions to soap himself all over, from head to toe, as he'd be wearing Richard Blunt's trousers and waistcoat and Moe Kelly's old top hat on his head. Cleaned up, he looked a different boy; dressed up, he was a class act. And he followed her directions to the letter, doffing his hat as he drew those curtains back to display twelve onions, clad in green crepe-paper tunics, brown bulbs on their heads.

'Jenny's in this one,' Jimmy said.

'Where?'

The onions were circling, jeering at something in their midst.

'Shush.'

The onions stepped aside to reveal a large flower hat and, hiding beneath it, Jenny clad in purple and pink. Then the surprise of the night. That little girl opened her mouth.

'I'm a lonely little petunia in an onion patch . . .'

Her voice was strong and sweet. Heads lifted, feet stilled their shuffling as the petunia wiped at mock tears.

'Boo hoo, boo hoo, the air's so strong it takes my breath away,' she sang, the onions crowding her, leaning in, making a cage of their arms over her head.

Vern was almost enjoying himself, and Jimmy showing more enthusiasm than usual, sitting forward while the little petunia sang as she fought her way between the onions, weaving in and out, attempting to escape their patch.

'I'm a lonely little petunia in an onion patch, Oh won't somebody transplant me.'

Sissy did her best. She stuck out a foot. Jenny, her hands clasped in plea, her little face lifted towards the heavens, didn't see it. She tripped and went sprawling. Anyone with good eyesight had seen what happened. There was a communal gasp, a communal breath held, then a hum of indignation as Sissy Morrison smiled.

Norman, watching from the fifth row, had been expecting some form of retaliation. All week it had been threatening. He rose from his seat as the petunia scrambled to her feet and Miss Rose left the piano to brush pink and purple petals straight, to set the large flower hat straight, to reorganise her circle of onions. Back at the piano, she played the introduction to the final chorus, but Jenny didn't sing. She stood looking down at a dragging petal, trying to tuck it back where it belonged. It wouldn't stay there. It dangled down past her knee.

'Children,' Miss Rose urged. Again she played the introduction.

There was a hush of expectancy, a second of silence after the final note while Jenny wiped an honest tear from her eye. She opened her mouth, though not to sing.

'You spoil everything, Sissy,' she said.

'You spoiled it. You made Mummy go away because you smell evil,' Sissy said, and went in for the kill.

Like a mouse evading a predator, Jenny ran for cover. Ray King looked big enough.

Ray knew he should have pulled the curtain, but the item wasn't over and he'd been told only to pull the curtain after Miss Rose had played the last note. Then it was too late to think about pulling it.

Sissy had grabbed a handful of pink and purple petals, which reminded her of the pink petals in her first concert costume, before her mother went mad and ran away, before everything bad. Crepe paper is only paper. It can be shaped, stitched and gathered, but each row of machine-stitching leaves behind a series of tiny holes, which makes a fine ripping line. Sissy came away with a handful of petals.

The ringmaster was supposed to stand in the wings during each item. He wasn't supposed to move until it was time to close the curtain. Miss Rose had said so. Ray loved Miss Rose and he wanted to please her. The ringmaster was definitely not supposed to defrock nasty bitches. But Ray King knew all about nasty bitches. His mother was one, and his father told her so six times a week and twice on Sunday, and next to his mother, Sissy Morrison was the nastiest bitch he'd ever come across.

Had he known that green onion tunic would peel off, like skin from a banana, he may not have done it, but she should have had the sense not to pull away. She knew what she was wearing underneath that tunic. He didn't — or he hadn't. Her rolls of green-tinged fat shocked him, as did her baggy white bloomers. He stood mouth open, big brown eyes afraid, stood frozen, clutching a handful of green crepe paper while Sissy screamed and released her bladder.

The headmaster ruined the climax. He drew the curtain. The audience heard the slap. Two sharp slaps.

Norman heard them, heard the familiar bellow. He'd left his seat and was approaching the stage door when he saw Cecelia's white bloomers disappearing into the night. He took two steps to follow her, glanced at Miss Rose and her helpers mopping the stage, chasing drips; saw Jenny sobbing against the ringmaster, his arms protectively around her.

Until a few moments ago, Norman had been unaware of the role Jennifer was to play in the concert. Cecelia was the dominant presence in his house; Cecelia's voice, her needs, were paramount. Until a few moments ago, Jenny had never argued with her sister. She, as he, had made allowances, had accepted.

He walked onto the stage, around the mopping women, to do his own mopping up. He wiped her teary eyes, wiped her nose.

'You make me proud, Jenny-wren.'

Ernie Ogden was at the concert. His youngest boys were performing; his two eldest still lodging in Carlton, but his wife was on cloud nine. He'd put in for a transfer and they'd heard today that he'd got it.

'The town won't be the same without you,' Vern said.

'I doubt I'll be the same without the town, but the wife is deadset on educating the younger boys. We'll be going to a nice little place, a farming and orchard community, close enough into Melbourne for the other boys to live at home.'

'Who'll be replacing you, Ernie?' Gertrude asked.

'A younger bloke, they say. He should be up here between Christmas and New Year. If you can hang on for a tick, there's something I'll leave in your keeping, Trude.'

He was across the road and back in minutes and handing her a manila envelope. She remembered it, didn't want the responsibility of it, tried to hand it back.

'There'll come a time when that little girl will want to own something that belonged to her mother. She's got a better chance of getting it if it's in your hands.'

'If it's up to Norman, she'll never find out, Ernie.'

'Time's a strange thing. It alters what was into what is — and whether she ever finds out or not, it belongs to her. Give it to her for her twenty-first.'

Gertrude folded the top of the envelope down and forced it into her handbag. Vern was waiting, Jimmy was waiting.

'I hope all goes well for you and Mary,' she said.

'It will go well enough. I'll keep my ear to the ground on your daughter's whereabouts. Sooner or later you run into every coot you've ever known in that city.'

'Vern was saying it's getting to the stage where you can't see the forest for the trees down there these days — or the streets for the traffic.'

'We'll see a lot of changes, no doubt. Did you ever hear anything back from your father-in-law regarding your daughter?'

'I got a note from his solicitor. The old chap died early in '24. His daughter is still living at the house, but she hasn't seen hide nor hair of Amber — nor have any of Norman's family, not that I would have expected her to go to them.'

'The hardest part is the not knowing, I dare say.'

'It gets easier. Others fill up the spaces,' she admitted.

CASH SALES ONLY

If ancient man hadn't invented the wheel, would he have taken to the skies sooner? The war had opened the eyes and minds of man to what he might do if he lifted his feet off the ground; the twenties showed a glimpse of mankind's magnificent future, of world travel, not in the slow boats of the ocean but in great airships of the sky. By 1929, those airships were offering the luxury of ocean liners combined with the speed of an aeroplane — to those with enough money to pay. There were photographs in the newspapers of fine dining rooms, of tastefully furnished lounges where the rich and famous could party all night high above the problems of the world — or those of them fool enough to risk their money and lives to a great bladder of gas, which, like a balloon, could be blown wherever the wind chose to blow it. A few had been blown off course in storms. The gas holding those things up had a bad habit of exploding and frying its crew; still, there was no shortage of rich folk willing to take the gamble. Fear had gone on holiday during the twenties.

Aeroplanes stuck with the old wheel. They took off on them, landed on them, and while they were up there had a far better chance of getting their passengers intact from A to B than did those airships, but their size placed a limit on carrying capacity. An aeroplane was a fine thing for carrying mail from place to place or riding in in an emergency, though those who rode in them never claimed to have had a comfortable trip. The future of aviation seemed to be in the airships, which admittedly needed improvements. Millions of pounds had been invested in them.

Not that air travel in any form was a reality yet in Woody Creek; acceptance of cars had been slow. A bullock wagon or a horse and dray had a better chance of traversing most of the roads around Woody Creek where a good rain could turn tyre-ripping ruts into muddy bogs. There were no two ways about it: geography held Woody Creek back, distance between one place and the next. Geography dictated their lives — but saved their lives too. Kids in the cities died by the hundreds of polio; thousands more were crippled for life by that disease. Woody Creek had two mild cases of it in ten years.

Distance cushioned the town from the stock market crash. Even the ripples created by it petered out before they got there. City newspapers wrote about it, as they wrote about exploding airships, but if fools wanted to gamble with riding gas-filled balloons or with stock market shares, they had to accept the consequences. The bulk of Woody Creek's breadwinners, employed in the timber-getting industry, wouldn't have recognised a stock market share if it landed face-up on their kitchen table.

Joanne Hooper's first husband had left her a few shares, which she'd left to Vern. He'd never taken a great interest in the things, though he glanced at them during that gap between Christmas and New Year. He might have lost a few hundred quid, but only if he sold. He didn't know how to sell them, so he didn't.

Then the twenties ended. Ernie Ogden's furniture and kids were loaded onto the train, and in mid-January of 1930, Constable Denham's furniture was unloaded and moved into Ernie's house. That was when the depression ripples started crashing into Woody Creek.

George Macdonald, Vern Hooper and Charlie White ran Woody Creek, and very few interfered with the way they ran it. They were the three richest men in town. George and Vern owned farms run by managers, owned sawmills and nice-looking houses. Charlie, the grocer, more or less owned the business centre of town — or owned the buildings that housed the business. Each week he collected rent from Blunt's drapery, Crone's café, Miller's boot shop, Fulton's feed and grain store and Abbot's saddlery. Ten years back, he'd built three identical houses on a block south of his store, then moved with his wife, Jean, and daughter, Hilda, into the middle house, so he could keep an eye on the two he rented out. He'd never had a problem in getting his rents on time. Folk paid up, he put the money in the bank, and when he had enough to spare he bought a few shares. He was losing sleep over the money he'd lost on paper.

Vern, George and Charlie didn't mix socially; they rarely agreed on any given subject, were hard pushed to raise a nod when they passed in the street, but standing shoulder to shoulder, fighting for the same cause, they made a formidable trio. They'd agreed to give the new copper a day to get settled in, then they went together to welcome him to town. They didn't stay long.

Denham was in his early thirties, a big, red-faced, heavy-featured man with a red-eyed wife dressed like a Quaker. The trio was not invited inside.

'He's too bloody young,' George said.

'His wife looked as if she had a burr in her bloomers,' Charlie said.

'He won't last a year,' Vern said.

'Curtains pulled at this time of day. He didn't want us looking in,' Charlie said.

'City,' Vern said.

'Where were his kids?' George said.

'He's got three. They came over to the shop this morning looking for headache medicine. There'll be more headaches than hers in this town before long,' Charlie said.

School went back in late January. Denham's son, who looked much like his father, was dressed like a parson's son; his sisters walked off clad in starched white pinafores. Those kids made their presence felt at school before their father started making his own felt around town. They expected toilet paper in the lavs. Woody Creek kids were lucky to find a bit of newspaper. Woody Creek kids came home from school dusty, always had, always would. The new copper's kids came home dustier than most and usually howling. Denham's first complaint was to the school.

The trio heard about it.

'If he's going to live here, his kids will have to learn to fit in,' George said.

Charlie nodded, but Vern looked off into the distance. His boy still wasn't fitting in. There were days when he came home dusty and tear-stained — and he carried his own toilet paper.

Horrie Bull, the publican, was the first man in town to call Denham an officious city bastard — to his face. He and his wife had bought that pub before the war, and they'd run it well, run it the way country folk liked their pub run, and Ernie Ogden hadn't interfered with how they'd run it either.

'You've been warned, Mr Bull,' Denham said.

'If you hang around here long enough, lad, you'll learn that up here a man's thirst isn't dictated by a clock,' Horrie told him, friendly like. Horrie was a fat and happy, friendly man. You couldn't rile him if you tried, and a few had tried. He was a slow-moving, slow-talking, reasoning man. 'A chap who's working twelve hours straight sawing up wood needs to wash the sawdust from his throat,' he explained.

'Six o'clock is closing time, Mr Bull.'

'You're making a big mistake, lad. You start out on the wrong foot up here and you'll be limping in no time flat.'

'Is that a threat, Mr Bull?'

'Bullshit to your threats. I'm just doing my best to explain to you how things work up here —'

'Six o'clock, and if you don't comply, I'll have your licence.'

'Get off my premises, you officious city bastard —'

Denham charged him with abusive language, which would mean his licence. Mrs Bull marched him, hat in hand, to Denham's door. They weren't invited in. Horrie apologised on the verandah and the pub started closing its doors at six, which had a few more calling the new copper an officious city bastard — or worse.

Vern and George were not drinkers and never had been. Charlie wasn't a big drinker, but that pub closing its doors at six upset his daily routine. For years he'd been accustomed to closing his shop door sometime before six, walking around to the hotel, having two slow beers and catching up with the town news while Jean went home to cook his dinner. A leisurely walk the few blocks home gained him his daily exercise and put him in a relaxed frame of mind to enjoy his dinner at seven on the dot. Now he had to miss out on his two beers, or close early and drink fast. A beer drunk fast didn't taste the same, and what was he supposed to do while waiting for his dinner to cook — other than argue with his bludging son-in-law?

Charlie was neither fat nor thin, neither tall nor short, he had no outstanding feature other than a head of silver white hair and bike rider's legs, all sinew and overdeveloped calf, which he didn't mind showing off in long shorts when he rode around town making the deliveries. He'd wed the best-looking girl in town thirty years ago and still considered her the best-looking girl in town, and she told him regularly that he was still the best-looking feller in town. They had a good thing going, Charlie and Jean White — or they'd had a good thing going until Denham moved in.

Charlie and Jean had the one offspring. Hilda had turned up nine months after the wedding and ruined their love life for more than a year, so Charlie made certain it didn't happen again — for which he was now truly grateful. Hilda had picked up with a returned man who'd lost his right hand during the war and had an aversion to getting the other one dirty. Instead of the bride moving out after the wedding, Alfred Timms, the bludging groom, moved in — and he wouldn't put on an apron and get in behind the shop counter.

'Stop your arguing, Charlie, and come out here and set the table,' Jean called.

'Tell him to set the table,' Charlie said. 'It only takes one hand to pick up a plate.'

'Stop picking on that boy.'

'Boy? He's thirty bloody years old!'

'And stop using that language in my house!'

'I'll use what I like in my own bloody house.'

Charlie worked all day with Jean. He slept beside her every night and there was never a harsh word between them. Every night now she took his son-in-law's part between six and seven. And whose fault was that?

Bloody Denham's fault, that's whose fault.

Things got worse for the Denham kids.

> *'Nancy boy Denham, your mother sucks lemons.*
> *Your father's got his thumb shoved halfway up his . . .'*

Three days out of five, one of Denham's kids ran home howling; three weeks out of four, Denham was down at the school, which didn't improve life for his kids, so he went a step further. He knocked on George and Maisy's door and had the audacity to suggest they get their boys under control.

The twins could do no wrong in George's eyes, and he wasn't known for pulling his punches. A lot of words were said, a lot of threats spoken, on both sides, and George's boys listening in to every word.

They didn't sleep well on nights of the full moon, though it no longer troubled them. Their bedroom window opened onto the western verandah and they'd developed the habit of climbing out, climbing over the fence to the memorial park, then wandering the town getting up to what mischief they could.

There was a full moon two nights after Denham knocked on their father's door. Around midnight, broken bricks started raining down on the roof of the police station-cum-residence. Denham's wife, pregnant again, panicked, his kids screamed, but before he could get his trousers on, the noise stopped.

The next night, same time, same scenario. His wife and kids might have been screaming, but Denham had his trousers on and his boots. He was hiding in the shadows on the far side of the road, crouched beneath a tree overhanging the post office fence. And he sighted the little buggers, recognised them and gave chase. It was no contest. He was a young and fit man. He grabbed one and hauled him kicking back to his lockup where he locked him in.

The twins had a separation complex. Since birth they'd slept side by side. They had twin beds now, but a bare two foot of

201

floor separated them. Bernie climbed back into his bedroom, but he couldn't lie down, couldn't sit still. He jiggled for half an hour then returned the way he'd come.

When Denham came at daybreak to unlock the cell door, he found a twin asleep against it, as close as he could get to his brother. He let out the one who was in, then followed the little buggers home, watched them climb the park fence and climb in through their window. Their parents would be none the wiser if they weren't told, so he knocked on their door and told them where their sons had spent the night and why.

'You've got no right locking up nine-year-old kids,' George said. 'Those boys aren't old enough to know right from wrong.'

'Then you'd better teach them fast, Mr Macdonald, because if you don't, I'll do it for you,' Denham warned.

He didn't know who he was dictating to. George was a nuggety little Neanderthal with more hair in his jutting eyebrows than he had on his head. He had a comical look about him until you saw his eyes. Fifty years of living in the shade of verandah brows had washed out their little colour. They were not the sort of eyes a man could look into without feeling cold knives running up and down his spine.

Denham felt the knives. He turned to a front window where he saw a dozen or more of George's pale purple eyes peering at him from beneath a lifted lace curtain.

'You've been warned, Mr Macdonald. You get control of those boys.'

'I'll get control of you, you city bastard. There's a law against locking up under-age boys,' George said. 'I'll get you kicked out of the force for this.'

Maisy placed the phone call to a Willama solicitor who George spent fifteen minutes yelling at.

'I want that bastard charged with the illegal locking up of a minor,' George roared. 'I want that officious bastard and his sour-mouthed wife and prissy-mouthed kids out of my town.'

George wasn't into prissy-mouthed kids. He'd started breeding late, but had ended up with ten and barely a clean mouth amongst the lot of them.

At fourteen, he'd inherited his grandparents' land and his retarded mother. For a time he'd considered leaving home, but someone had to see to his mother, so he'd stayed on and worked, and in time he turned a hundred acres of weed and disrepair into a productive farm. He'd borrowed on his farm to set up his first bush mill, and a few years later he'd had more money than he'd known what to do with, which should have made him a bit more attractive to the opposite sex, but hadn't. He'd craved family, had dreamed grand dreams of starting his own dynasty, but any prospective mate not scared off by his looks took one look at his mother and ran. He'd been waiting for a haircut when he read an article about the male bowerbird, which built a fancy bower, decorated it with anything blue, then sat back and waited for the females to come.

George bought land in the centre of town and paid a builder to make him a fancy bower — six bedrooms, a man-sized kitchen and a fancy sitting room with blue curtains — if the females had come calling, his mother scattered them with the broom he'd bought so she might sweep his floors. She'd been no trouble out at the farm. In town she was big trouble.

He'd employed young Maisy Roberts to keep an eye on her. Maisy was a girl of sixteen raised by a mean-hearted aunt who had taught her how to cook and clean and dodge broomsticks. She had no trouble dodging his mother's. Six months down the track, his house clean enough, a hearty meal on the table each night, his mother under control, George asked Maisy if she'd be interested in making things a bit more permanent. She told him she wasn't planning on leaving the job, and what did he mean by more permanent?

She was barely seventeen when they'd wed. George was pushing forty. She was still seventeen when their first daughter was born. She gave him seven more, at twelve-month intervals, before his persistence paid off with twin sons. Give a man a son after eight daughters and he thinks that boy is Jesus Christ. Give him two and he's got Jesus Christ and God Almighty beneath the same roof. George believed the sun rose and set in his boys' pale purple eyes.

Few in town agreed with him. Those little swine had been running wild since they'd learnt to crawl, and Denham's roof wasn't the only one in town stoned on nights of the full moon. They didn't stop at roof-stoning either. Shop windows were whitewashed, Miss Blunt's underwear stolen from her clothes line and pegged on the railway yard fence. They'd mutilated Vern's rose bushes, renamed his son Rosie, called his daughters Wattle and Ironbark — though all bar the mutilation of his roses, Vern considered to be character-strengthening. His kids were all a little light-on in the character department.

Joey had been in school for three days before the twins renamed him 'Darkie'. Gertrude wasn't too concerned about it, nor was Joey. He liked going to school with Jenny. He knew Jimmy too. In late February, Gertrude was standing at the school gate, seeing Joey safely indoors, when the headmaster approached her.

'I suggest you keep the boy home for a month or two,' he said.

'Miss Rose says he's doing well.'

'We'll reassess the situation in a month or two,' he said and he walked back to his classroom.

She entered the school ground, and was stepping up to the verandah when Miss Rose walked Joey from her room.

'What's going on?' Gertrude said.

'I'm so sorry, but we've had a complaint, Mrs Foote.'

'You said he was doing well?'

'It's not . . .' She patted Joey's cheek. 'I'm afraid I'm not at liberty to say more.'

There were a few in town who looked at that little boy sideways. Gertrude sifted names as she took Joey's hand and walked him back to the cart, lifted him to the seat and continued into town. She'd sort it out, but not in front of him.

She'd brought in two baskets of eggs, one for Charlie White, one for Mrs Crone. She was lifting the heavier of the two down when she met Ernie Ogden's replacement.

'Lovely morning,' she said.

'Is that black with you?' Denham said.

204

'Run into Charlie, love,' Gertrude said, knowing now who had been complaining at the school. 'I'll only be a minute.'

Joey tried to run into Charlie, but Denham blocked his pathway.

'Back in the cart,' he said. 'I can't dictate how you choose to live your life, lady, but decent folk don't have to dodge around blacks when they come in to do their shopping.'

'You've got your head shoved so far up your own backside, you can't see which way you're headed,' Gertrude said, taking Joey's hand, determined to walk him around that sod. Denham caught the handle of her basket and six dozen eggs rained down, smashed, splattered down. She stood looking at the waste of eggs meant to pay for a bottle of hair dye, for a packet of tea, baking powder.

Joey didn't know what was going on. He was supposed to be at school. He was supposed to go into Charlie's but that man didn't want him to. He scampered back up to the cart and sat cowering there.

'Bullying women and babies won't make you stand taller in this town, you thoughtless mongrel.'

'Any more of that and I'll slap a charge of abusive language on you, lady.'

She nodded, looked at that little boy who didn't have an ounce of fear in him, and his big eyes were afraid. She looked at those eggs leaking their goodness into hard-packed clay, then she stooped, picked up an unbroken egg, reached for another. Maybe his self-satisfied smirk brought it on, or Joey's eyes; she wasn't sure, but something raised in her a desire to hit back. She did it fast, slapped both hands down on his shoulders, wasted two perfectly good eggs on that mongrel of a man and considered them well spent.

'Add common assault to that charge, you overgrown cur.'

Rich yolk dribbling, eggshell clinging to his shoulders, his smirk wiped away by surprise, she returned to her cart.

The confrontation took place in front of Charlie and Jean White. They were standing in their doorway. Denham turned to them.

'You're witnesses,' he said.

'He's deaf and I'm short-sighted,' Jean said.

Old Betty Duffy, on her way into town to buy a bit of flour and tobacco, claimed the less-broken eggs. Her pack of half-starved dogs picnicked on the rest, then watered Charlie's verandah posts in appreciation.

Denham was just marking out his territory. A man, like a new dog on the block, needs to erase the scent of the last dog with his own stink, but something had to be done about him before he stank up the whole town.

MAKING IT THROUGH

In March of 1930, there were three big sawmills and one bush mill working at full production in Woody Creek, each of them employing eight to fifteen labourers; then there were the bullockies who hauled the logs in from the bush, and the chaps with horse teams, and the chaps who felled the trees. The big steam engines that kept the saws spinning needed servicing by men who knew what they were doing. Horses needed to be shod. Harnesses needed repairs. Cut timber had to be loaded onto railway trucks. What happened to it thereafter was of little concern to the mill men as long as the money kept rolling back into Woody Creek.

But the timber industry was a chain, one link relying on the other.

Snap!

And the chain started falling apart.

A city man had no use for timber unless he wanted to build something: a house, a bridge, a fence. In 1929, houses had been springing up like mushrooms — on borrowed money. In 1930, the building industry dropped dead. The government had been spending up big on public works, spending borrowed money. Australia, reliant on her wool and wheat exports, now at rock-bottom prices, couldn't maintain her balance of payments. Government spending had to stop so public works stopped, throwing more out of work. The country was in debt for millions, which few had known until the crash. Unemployment had been a problem for years, but a problem denied. No more denial. 'FIFTY PER CENT OF CHILDREN ATTENDING SCHOOLS IN THE COLLINGWOOD AREA HAVE UNEMPLOYED FATHERS' the newspapers howled.

Woody Creek, isolated, insulated from the greater world's woes, sat back and watched for a time — until Mick Boyle gave his fifteen workers two days' notice that he was closing his mill, getting out before he lost the shirt off his back. He'd chosen the wrong time to update his mill machinery, updated with the bank's money. He got out of it with his house, a couple of horses and a dray.

Tom Palmer had been Boyle's mill boss for years. He had five kids to feed and a house he'd borrowed money to build. He knocked on Vern's door. Tom was a good worker, a reliable and decent family man.

'I'm stockpiling timber no one wants to buy, Tom, and I can't keep it up indefinitely. Come and see me again when things pick up.'

A man could manage on short rations for a month or two. Things would pick up. The government would do something. They had to.

But the government did nothing. Government machinery had not been set up to supply assistance to the needy. That was what the churches were for, and the smaller charitable organisations. They tried, but charities, set up to offer temporary relief to the needy, were put under pressure as destitution spread. The banks added to the misery. They failed to understand that you could put a stone through a mangle and still not squeeze blood out of it. The banks were owed thousands so they squeezed. Thousands were evicted from the homes they could no longer pay for, throwing more human souls onto the streets. There was real suffering in the cities. Folk were starving in the cities.

Then George Macdonald closed his bush mill. Eight men lost their jobs, and there was talk of Vern Hooper cutting down to a three-day week. And Max Monk, owner of Three Pines, a big property eight or so miles from town, sacked a chap and his wife who had been working out there for years.

'They say he's up to his ears in debt.'

The rumour-mongers were at it again, circulating disaster, though few believed them until Monk sacked his two farm labourers, and one of them with him for twenty years. He was home with his wife now from Monday to Sunday, home, jobless and unpaid in two months.

'The bank is selling him up.'

'Max Monk? Bullshit.'

Three generations of the Monk family had owned Three Pines, and for those three generations Vern's family had been Monk's nearest neighbours. They shared a fence, shared the creek, though the Hooper land was around half the size of their neighbours', and their house less than half the size. Vern's manager now occupied the old Hooper house and he cared for that land as if it were his own. For six months of the year, Monk's house stood vacant while Max, his wife and daughter spent up big on their grand tours.

'They reckon he's been owned by the bank for years.'

'He owes Robert Fulton a fortune, I know that much.'

'There's a lot more than Monk owes Fulton. His wife was telling mine that they're feeling the pinch.'

'If Monk goes under, he'll take a few down with him. Charlie White was saying yesterday that Monk hasn't paid a brass razoo off his bill in six months.'

'It's the greed of those big bastards that caused this.'

Norman Morrison's job was secure. He'd taken a legislated wage cut. The government was finally doing something. Salaries across the board were reduced, but balanced by a drop in the cost of living. Norman watched his pennies but he managed.

The Church of England had started up a relief committee, so the Methodist church ladies started their own. Who knew for how long the bad times might last. Lorna and Margaret Hooper were good Methodists but drew the line at going door to door collecting old clothes and shoes for the needy.

Vern had wanted those girls home from the city; now he had them at home he wondered why he'd wanted them there. With little going on at his mill, he spent more time out at his farm.

He was walking down by his section of the creek when he saw his neighbour walking in his garden. Old man Monk had built his house so it overlooked the creek. His son's wife had designed the garden leading down to the water. It was overgrown, neglected now, but as a boy Vern had envied it. Flowers weren't encouraged on Hooper land. Vern's grandfather had needed every square inch of his land, and his stock had got the best of it, the house relegated to the driest corner, a few feet back from the road, its only garden, then and now, a stand of shading blue gum trees and an old rose bush neglect couldn't kill. Vern had taken two or three cuttings from it, given that rose a second life in town, and every year it repaid him a thousandfold.

He took his time in approaching his neighbour that morning, in climbing the bordering fence. He waited until Max was sitting on the grassy bank, tossing sticks into slow-running water. He'd spent a lot of his boyhood envying Max.

They said their good mornings.

'I've been hearing a lot of talk in town, Max. Any truth in what I'm hearing?' Vern was not a man to beat around the bush.

'According to the bank, I don't own the shoes I'm standing in — sitting in, Vern.'

'You've got a lot of stock out there.'

'The bank's got a lot of stock.'

'That bad, is it?'

'They won't get everything.'

'How's your wife taking it?'

'She's on a boat, halfway home with what she can carry. Our girl and her husband went ahead last month with a bit more. I'll be joining them after the auction.'

'How soon?'

'Ask the bank.'

Max never was much of a farmer. His grandfather had been the farmer, and to a lesser degree, his father — who had made the mistake of hitching himself up to Eliza Foote, aunt of Archie bloody Foote. That was when the rot had set in. She'd watered down old man Monk's blood. They'd only raised the one son, then made the mistake of educating him in England where he'd wed a pom who hated Australia. She'd given him a daughter who, like her mother, wasn't fond of country life.

'Have you got a smoke on you?' Max said.

Vern didn't move without his cigarettes. He offered his pack and eased himself down to his backside to sit a while and watch that creek. There was something soothing about watching water flow down that same course it had been travelling for thousands of years, something eternal about flowing water. A man's blood might flow as strong and eternal if he made the right alliances. Vern had been guilty of watering down the Hooper blood with bad marriages. It was his grandfather's fault, though. If he hadn't been so deadset against cousin wedding cousin, the Hooper blood would have stayed strong.

'Do you hear anything of your mad cousin these days?'

No need to mention names. Max only had one mad cousin.

'The last time I set eyes on Archie was a few months before his old man died. He came up here wanting me to invest money in one of his get-rich-quick schemes.' He blew smoke at the trees. 'I gave him fifty quid to get rid of him, and considered it well spent.'

'Is he still living?'

'They say not. They tracked him as far as Egypt after his old man died. The old bloke went soft on him during his last years of life and left him a few hundred quid. The family reckon Archie's dead or he would have been back for his money — which I wouldn't mind getting my hands on right now.'

'What's it going to take to get the bank off your back?'

'Too much — though I might raise it — if I had reason to raise it. My wife hates the place and I couldn't pay my daughter enough to spend a weekend here — and she's barren.' He pitched a stick into the water. 'It's over, Vern. As poor old Ned said when they stuck the noose around his neck, such is life.'

'Your grandfather would roll over in his grave.'

'Could be that he will.'

Max stood and pitched his cigarette butt towards the creek, picked up a small branch and pitched it further, watched it get itself turned around and head off downstream.

'Life as our old folk knew it is finished, Vern. This depression has been rushing towards us for a while and we've sat back watching it come. It will sort out the men from the boys.'

Robert Fulton's feed and grain store spent more days with its door closed than open. He owed, and was owed, thousands. There were whispers that Paul Jenner, out Cemetery Road, was ready to walk off his land.

It was a disease, a creeping, crawling contagious plague, which by the end of 1930 had a grip on the throat of Woody Creek and was squeezing the life out of it.

Fulton's doors remained closed after Christmas. He owed Charlie three months' rent on the shop and more on the house he lived in. A good family the Fultons, with a bunch of well-mannered, well-behaved kids. They'd been Charlie and Jean White's neighbours for twenty years. Jean wouldn't have let Charlie evict them had he wanted to.

Richard Blunt had been standing behind the drapery store counter for forty years, his wife, then his daughter, sitting in the back room stitching fine garments, altering trousers, taking up hems for those who could afford to pay. Not many in town could afford to pay for fine clothes now, but the Blunts, frugal folk, owned a big old house opposite the school. They took the infants' mistress in as a lodger. Her job was secure. She paid her rent to Richard and he paid his to Charlie.

Old man Miller and his wife from the boot shop were feeling the pinch. Boots still wore out but folk weren't replacing them. Crone's café-cum-restaurant did all right. No one expected old mother Crone to give anyone credit.

George Macdonald kept his big mill saws screaming a week longer than Vern's and their howl was a wild thing's call for its mate. Then the howl died, and the town fell silent. And the town grew still. And the mill men grew still. They leaned against verandah posts watching their kids' clothes turn to rags, listening to their women too proud to beg, but not too proud to send those rag-tail kids up to ask Charlie for a pound of flour on tick, please, to ask the baker if he might have a loaf of stale bread, please.

'You ask him nicely now, say please. And wash your face before you go.'

The butcher had a sign up on his door: *Cash sales only*. A lot of kids couldn't read.

'Mum said please can she have half a pound of sausage meat, please, and she promises she'll pay you as soon as things get betterer, please.'

The Duffy family were the first to apply for susso, though they weren't on their own for long. The government, struggling to supply some form of relief to the starving, the homeless, were not doing much of a job of it, and that bloody pig-faced officious bastard of a Denham wasn't making it easier for those in need to ask for help.

Don Roberts and his family were starving, but he was too proud to go to the police station to register for relief, to sign that statutory declaration stating that he was a useless bastard who couldn't keep food in the mouths of his kids. Then the saddlery closed its doors. The Abbots went on susso.

'You've got to do something,' Lenny Abbot said. 'Something's got to be done.'

George and Vern did what they could. Every couple of weeks, one mill or the other was started up. They cut up stockpiled timber for firewood. A bit of money in one family helped a lot of families in this town.

Kids were dying of starvation in the cities. Proud folk were being buried by the coppers, laid side by side with strangers in communal graves. If a man couldn't afford to eat, he sure as hell couldn't raise the few quid necessary for a funeral.

Vern had been down there looking for buyers for his stockpiled wood. No one was buying, and when he walked some of the streets, he knew why. The city shops were open and women were still shopping in their fur coats, but out in the back streets, he saw it, he smelled the destitution. He stood and watched hundreds — men, women and their kids — queuing up for a tin mug of weak soup. Winter was coming. How were they going to survive through winter? He stood out front of some place handing out clothes, handing out old army coats dyed black, preparing the homeless for a long, cold winter. He came home depressed to sit in Gertrude's kitchen, pouring out what he'd seen.

'How can a country turn bad so fast? What the hell were we doing? Why didn't we see it coming, Trude?'

'How is she living through this, Vern?' She, Amber, that girl Gertrude had lived for, dreamed for. 'Is she queuing up with the hundreds?'

'All I know is she had a good husband prepared to feed her, and two kids she left motherless. All I know is, whatever she's doing, she's thinking of herself, not you.'

'She was a good kid until that sod came up here and filled her head with his lies.'

'Oh, I meant to tell you a while back, Monk reckons he's dead.'

'Archie?'

'So he said. Lost in Egypt somewhere.'

'I'll believe it when I see it.'

'He was saying that they tracked him there when his old man died. He was left money in the will. He would have been back for it if he was alive.'

'I won't believe he's dead until I see his name on a tombstone — and I mightn't even then, Vern.'

The depression had little effect on Gertrude's way of life. Eggs were her money; she had no less of them now than she'd had before. She had her goats, her garden. She made her jams in season, stored her apples and potatoes in her shed. Nothing changed at Gertrude's house.

The town still called on her, and the calls still came in cycles. Fewer babies were born in Woody Creek but she delivered more. Husbands who could previously afford to get their wives down to the hospital for the birth now came knocking on her door. She went when she was called. She gave what she had to give.

On a Friday afternoon, she pulled her cart into the shade beside the town hall where she set about unloading a box of apples, a few dozen spare eggs and a couple of pumpkins. The ladies relief committee handed out her donations to those in need — and to a few who weren't yet in real need but held out their hands anyway.

Denham was there, sticking his nose in where it wasn't wanted.

'Let me help you there, Mrs Foote,' he said, attempted to take the crate of apples.

She pushed by him, got him in the shoulder with the crate, made no acknowledgment of him. She hadn't spoken to him since the day of the broken eggs and didn't plan to speak to him. Maybe there was a bit of the Hoopers' grudge-holding blood running in her veins, but it had taken him to point out to Joey that his skin made him different to the other kids'. Joey knew now, and no longer wanted to go to school, no longer wanted to drive into town with her. She'd never forgive Denham for that. She hated him for that.

He was the cause of her first disagreement with Vern's daughters. The Denham family went to the Methodist church and Vern's daughters considered the constable's sourpuss wife to be one of the few civil women in town. She received regular invitations to afternoon tea. Gertrude walked in on them one Friday, and the three eyed her trousered outfit as they might have eyed a man from Mars clad in a kilt. Bell-ringing bum-sitters Lorna and Margaret, ringing their little brass bell for Vern's housekeeper to fetch them hot water for their teapot, treating her as the paid help. She'd been with Joanne in Melbourne, had come up here with her, and when Joanne died, she'd stayed on to look after Vern. She was Gertrude's age, a decent, caring woman who deserved better than two bum-sitting girls ordering her about.

'Get off your backside and fetch your own water,' Gertrude said. She hadn't been to the house since.

She wouldn't have driven out to Monk's auction with Vern had she known those girls would be going. Nancy and Lonnie Bryant were out there so she left Vern with his family and made a beeline for the Bryants' gig.

Carts, drays, motor cars were all looking for space in the shade; a lot of folk from town had come out on Mick Boyle's dray. He'd gone into the carrying business, be it people or goods he wasn't fussy. Property owners from further out were there, a few city agents had come in on the train. You could always recognise a city man. Monk's better furniture and his few good paintings had been sent down to the city to big auction houses. The rest was set out on wide verandahs. Gertrude was in the market for buckets, dishes and a single bed for Joey, if she could get one for her price. Monk had a few old iron beds, a few bundles of bedding.

Lonnie wanted the disc plough and Monk's forge. He missed out on the plough but got the forge. Lorna wanted two crates of books. Vern's bid was the only one. Margaret wanted a music box, as did Horrie Bull's wife. Margaret missed out. Gertrude bid on a mess of buckets and tin dishes. She got them, along with a bundle of shovels and spades she hadn't realised were part of the same lot. She made a bid on the second bed, but Horrie, feeling guilty about getting the music box, told her he had two better beds rotting in his shed and she could have both for the price of the carrying. He'd get Mick Boyle to bring them down.

They auctioned the property late in the afternoon. The crowd had cleared, only the diehards remained. Vern wasn't interested in more land. He'd only hung around to see what it made and to get an idea of what his own land was worth. He'd had no intention of putting in a bid — or not until the auctioneer was about to knock it down to a bloke wearing a suit and for a pittance. He upped the bid, determined that land wasn't going to some city bank manager for a song. The agent went over him, so just to be ornery, Vern went up again. Gertrude elbowed him this time and told him not to be a fool. He moved away from her, and it was on. Eight times the agent came back at him, but he must have had a limit, must have reached it. The property was knocked down to Vern.

'You're a pig-headed fool of a man, Vern Hooper. What do you need with more land at this time of your life?' Gertrude said. 'You should be hanging on to your money. Who knows how long this will last?'

'Land lasts,' he said, doing his best to hide his shell shock. He'd expected the coot to make one last bid. 'Grandpop would have approved. He kicked himself until his dying day that he hadn't spent up big during the last depression. And he always resented Monk having a finer house anyway. Now he owns it.'

'He's dead, you fool.'

'Well, he can haunt it at night.'

Margaret and Jimmy were impressed with the house they now owned. They spent half an hour roaming their father's new acquisition, climbing down to Monk's cave of a root cellar. Lorna was more impressed when a few months later Vern bought a house in Balwyn. It was next door to his half-brother's house and he got it for a song. Certain that it was her father's intention for her and Margaret to live in that house, chaperoned by their uncle next door, Lorna was not pleased when Vern left the previous owners in as caretakers.

He'd been a young bloke during the depression of the nineties. He couldn't remember much about it, other than listening to his grandfather lamenting the fact that he'd sat on his money instead of buying while prices were low. Joanne had left Vern a small fortune, which he considered to be safer in land than in the banks right now. He had five hundred a year still coming in from his first wife, money sitting in banks bringing in little interest. Property was easier to keep track of. It was there. You could walk on it, pick up handfuls of it. He bought old lady Wilson's house when she moved down to Willama to live with her daughter. He bought the paddock next door to his mill. He went property mad while his mill lay idle one week out of two.

'Stop it, Vern,' Gertrude said. 'People are talking about you.'

When a man has work and money enough to live on, there is little envy. When a man starts flashing his money around while others can't find coin enough for a beer, that's when envy grows and memories of worthy deeds grow short. When you sit all day watching your wife unpicking the seams of her best dress then stitching it back together, its unfaded inside now on the outside, what else can you do but envy that pair of stuck-up Hooper bitches walking out to do their shopping in fancy city suits. Envy of his neighbour can eat into a man's heart.

Vern paid his skeleton crew of mill workers to cut a few railway truckloads of firewood he freighted down to Melbourne marked *For Relief*. The railways carried it free if marked *For Relief*. The Methodist mission handed it out to those in the greatest need.

'There's folk in town who could use a load of wood,' people said. 'And he sends it down to bloody strangers in Melbourne.'

Lonnie and Nancy Bryant's city son and his family had moved back home. Horrie Bull had his sister and her husband living in one of the pub's sleep-outs. Melbourne's population decreased during the worst years of the depression as those who could, fled from its destitution to rural areas. Twelve squeezed into houses hard pushed to hold six. Sheds in backyards were made habitable.

'The city's no place to be if you can't find work,' they said.

'There's wood for the taking up here. A kid can drag his billy-cart down to the bridge and pick up a load in five minutes.'

'A man can trap a rabbit, toss a line in the creek, fire his shotgun into a flock of galahs and bring down enough for a stew ... and there's nothing wrong with parrot stew either, if you can find an onion.'

'You need to live in that city to know what it's like down there. It's all right for them with money. They're still trotting off to their theatres, still driving their fancy cars and turning their eyes away so they don't see their starving neighbours.'

No one starved in Woody Creek. But a split had opened up in the fabric of the town, separating those who had from those who had not, drawing a heavy line between complaining bludger and silent battler.

The strong men, the proud, could still make a few bob felling trees, splitting logs with metal wedge and axe, hand-cutting sleepers for the railways. They could cut foot blocks to freight down to those who could afford to buy wood in Melbourne. The strong men and the proud worked from daylight to dark, determined to keep their families off relief.

Big Henry King, father of stuttering Ray, champion drinker and wood cutter, was one of the biggest, the strongest of men, proud of his strength too — until the forest turned on him one day and felled him. Gum tree branches can be snappy bastards; they'll kill you when you're least expecting it. That branch didn't do the decent thing by Big Henry; it didn't kill him outright. Vern drove Gertrude and Constable Denham out to the accident site. Gertrude sat beside Vern. Denham sat in the rear seat. They spoke only to Vern. But the three worked together to get Henry out of the bush, to get him down to the hospital.

'You couldn't kill that big bastard with a ton of bricks,' the drinkers said that night in the pub's back room. 'He'll pull through all right,' they said.

Big Henry spent three months in hospital and returned to Woody Creek a cripple with the use of one arm. He was a strong man. He might have lived that way for years, but a month of his wife's derision was enough. He told his boy to bring him a basin of water and his razor, that he wanted to clean himself up for Sunday. He didn't waste the water, and he didn't see Sunday. His one good arm was strong enough to do what it had to do.

He was Woody Creek's first suicide, though no one saw it as such, and not a soul blamed him. The timber men made him a red gum coffin and gave him a send-off the likes of which hadn't been seen in many a year. He ended up two rows down from J.C., the stranger who had come to Woody Creek and remained. Ten days later, they opened up his grave and put his nasty bitch of a wife in with him. No one believed she'd died of a broken heart. That woman had never had a heart to break.

Then Ray, that hulking great stuttering boy with his big brown innocent lamb's eyes, disappeared.

For a week the men had something to do. For a week they felt like men again. They combed the forest calling to Ray; they dragged the creek for his body. They didn't find him. Eventually they gave up looking, and a few more men gave up being men and went on susso. What gain was there in fighting it? The life they'd known was gone and Big Henry lucky to be out of it.

Ray King's disappearance was big news at school. The Macdonald twins swore they'd caught a fish at the weekend and when they were taking it off the hook it said, 'L-l-leave m-m-me al-l-lone.'

Robert Fulton, father of nine, feed and grain store proprietor for twenty years, not built to cut wood or trap rabbits, took his rifle out to Three Pines Road one morning. They found him at nightfall, a bullet through his head. Some said he must have fallen on his gun. Some called it suicide. His wife called it cowardice.

'You had no right,' she howled in Moe Kelly's cellar. 'How do you expect me to feed those kids now?'

She fed them. Gertrude gave her a young milking goat and taught her oldest boy how to milk it. Jean White gave Emma, her fourteen year old, a job in the shop. Miss Blunt passed on a few sewing jobs — Mrs Fulton was a fine seamstress.

Tom Palmer, mill boss at Mick Boyle's mill for fifteen years, paying off his own house for ten of those years and still managing to put a bit away, had been doing what he could to keep up his house payments. He'd tried sleeper-cutting but he never was an axe man. He sewed wheat bags for cockies, allowed his oldest girl, Irene, who looked sixteen but wasn't yet fourteen, to take maid work with Hooper. And Christ how he hated watching his girl walk off to work each morning, hated knowing she was running around after two grown women capable of running around after themselves; hated it, but had to swallow it and keep it down.

'If a man can keep a roof over his head, he can keep the wolf from his door,' Tom said. 'It won't last forever. It can't last forever.'

He took a job as a shearer's cook, which meant leaving his own roof for three months, but Geoff, his oldest boy, was fifteen. He put him in charge, told the rest of his kids to help their mother, and off he went. They brought him home two weeks later, his leg broken, and that was the end of that.

Or maybe it wasn't.

'You still need a cook, I take it,' Wilma Palmer said. 'I'm used to cooking for a crowd. My boy and I will cook for your shearers.'

Her husband was in the hospital. She was in the early stages of pregnancy, but she and Joss, her twelve year old, travelled with the shearers for those months, her younger children left in the sole care of their big brother, until Tom came home on crutches. She was six months gone with that baby when the shearing season ended, when the boss shearer took her to the train and told her his blokes were planning to kidnap her next year, that they'd never eaten so good, so she'd better be on the lookout. They'd passed the hat around for Wilma and her baby, and she and Joss returned home with more money than they'd seen in one place before.

Wilma and Tom Palmer would make it through. When a man and his wife are prepared to do what it takes, they'll always make it through. Pumpkins and potatoes now grew where flowers had once bloomed. Chooks stalked their proud front yard and a cow lived in their backyard, the younger Palmer kids picking grass for her on their way home from school each day. That cow kept milk in their bellies.

ARRIVALS AND DEPARTURES

In December of 1931, George Macdonald went to a farm auction and bought a new Chevrolet truck. He didn't know how to drive it but considered it past time he did. The previous owner delivered it, offered George a few pointers on driving, then lifted his bike down from the tray and rode away.

The following morning, George got it started up. He found a forward gear, the thing let out a howl and took off towards the railway station.

'Whoa, you bastard. Whoa!'

George jumped for his life before it hit the currajong tree, or tried to climb it.

Denham wandered down to stick his nose in. 'Are you licensed to drive, Mr Macdonald?'

'Shove your licence up your . . .' A cigarette administered with a shaking hand got his mouth closed.

The tree was well grown. It had shed a few pods, was still trembling, as was George. The earth was trembling, or maybe it was the train coming in.

The accident drew a crowd. The train driver and fireman walked over to take a look, the bank manager and Charlie White walked down together, then Norman came and a few of the male passengers wandered over. One was a rusty-headed, freckle-faced, underfed lad with sixpence in his pocket and a sugar bag containing his worldly possessions over his shoulder. He'd spent the last twelve months on a cousin's farm, fifty-odd miles further west, where they were surviving on boiled wheat, treacle and a rabbit if anyone could catch one. He was hungry, he was homesick, and George Macdonald, now walking in circles around his truck, sounded like Collingwood on a bad night. The youth made a beeline towards that glorious sound.

The twins were there. The youth thought he might be seeing double; starvation did that to you. Then he saw the damage to that beautiful truck and it damn near broke his heart.

'Made a mess of it,' he said to Denham, who was studying the bumper bar curled halfway around the tree trunk.

Denham eyed him but said nothing.

'Beautiful pieces of machinery, these,' the kid said, taking the makings from his pocket, rolling a smoke like he'd been rolling smokes for twenty years. He looked fifteen, looked like someone had taken hold of an unshorn twelve year old and stretched him long. He was taller than Denham. George came up to his elbow.

'Where are you from?' Denham said.

'Round and about,' the kid said.

'City?' Denham said. A city man could always pick another. They spoke faster. They had a different way of moving.

'Was,' the youth said.

'Where have you been?' The train had come in from the west.

'Fighting the bunnies for a blade of grass.'

Smoking was contagious. Norman offered his pack to the train driver and fireman. George lit another, then Denham lit up.

'I could get her off that tree,' the kid said to George, who looked more worried than the rest of the crowd so no doubt owned the truck.

'What are you? Fifteen?'

'Eighteen. Me and my old man used to drive a truck like this one for Maples, carting furniture. Back when folk could afford to buy furniture.'

The twins had climbed up to the cabin. George dragged them out, told them to piss off, watched them go as far as the fallen fence where a dozen or more kids were standing. They'd never seen a truck try to climb a tree.

'I've got sixpence says I can move her,' the kid said, squatting at one of the front wheels lifted off the ground, walking around to the other. It was on the ground.

'Then put your money where your mouth is, boy,' George said.

The kid looked around, walked off to help himself to stacked timber no one wanted to buy, aging, greying, in the railway yards. The men stood back, watching him jam two thick boards beneath the front wheel. Then, with a grin, he climbed up to the driver's seat. He got her started on the second attempt, stuck her in gear, stuck his head out the window.

'It wouldn't do any harm if a few of you pushed . . .'

He let out the clutch, they pushed, the tree shuddered, chucked down a few more pods, metal screamed, and the truck pulled away.

'Keep the bastard going while she's going,' George bellowed.

'Where do you want it?' the kid yelled.

'Over the road.'

George ran ahead, hunting kids out of the way, as, expertly, his truck was driven out through the railway yard gate. A minute later it was back in the place where it belonged.

'You're a bloody godsend. What's your name?' George said as the kid swung down to the ground.

'Harry Hall.'

The entertainment over, the train hooting, passengers headed back to continue their journey.

Harry reached for his sugar bag. 'You owe me sixpence,' he said.

George found two bob and flicked it at him. 'Who taught you to drive?'

'Had to learn when my old man's sight went on him.'

George watched the kid put his two bob in his tobacco tin, watched him roll another slim smoke and strike a match like a bloke who'd been lighting up for forty years.

'You're going home then, are you?'

'Going somewhere,' Harry said around his fag. He got it burning, then, with a wave of his hand, walked off towards the train.

George watched him cross the road. 'Do you reckon you could show me how to control that bastard? I'd pay you.'

The kid turned. 'I'd drive that truck for nothing,' he said. 'Though I'm not averse to taking your money.'

It wasn't a good day for George. Maisy had picked up a letter from the post office posted at that same post office. John Curry, the headmaster, had considered saving the postage stamp, and handing it to George, then escaping before he opened it. The envelope contained the twins' exam results and a letter stating that Curry would not have the disruptive swine back in 1932. He had offered the name of a good school outside of Melbourne, which, to use George's own translation, guaranteed to turn obstreperous little bastards into something better.

Denham spent his life harassing those boys. Maisy couldn't control them. She'd been pleading with him for twelve months to send them away to school, though suggesting they be split up, sent to schools well separated. George considered his options, considered separation — until he learned that he got a discount on the fees for two. He paid twelve months in advance and in January of 1932 he delivered them.

'It's for your own good,' he said. 'I would have given my back teeth for the opportunity I'm giving you.' They looked sick and he felt sick. 'If someone had sent me away to school when I was twelve year old, I would have kissed their feet.'

'We're eleven.'

'Then I would have licked their feet before I kissed them. Now get in there and learn something.'

They stood staring at him, green-capped, slack-jawed, wet-eyed, looking for all the world like a pair of stranded frogs, their bellies full of stinging ants. He walked away. It was for their own good. Denham was threatening to have them locked up as juvenile delinquents.

The town breathed easier. Curry breathed easier.

Sissy Morrison didn't breathe easier. Back in first grade, girls had learnt to give her a wide berth. They gave her a wider berth now. The twins were her only friends. She'd walked to school with them, walked home with them, tormented Jenny with them, talked about interesting things with them. She had no one now. She came straight home from school each day, came home to an empty house, and nothing to do there other than to eat what she could find, and if she couldn't find anything worth eating, she stoked up the stove and made toffee — and ate the lot before her father and Jenny came home.

Gertrude filled the biscuit tins on Fridays. Sissy ate them by the handful on Saturdays. Jenny played with friends on weekends; Sissy ate. She was close to her thirteenth birthday, her face was an eruption, her shape that of a bag of wheat. Sissy was a misery.

Then Jimmy Hooper happened, Jimmy the gangling, big-eared loner. If a child chose to walk a while at his side, Jimmy walked. During her first years at school, Jenny had walked by his side. She walked with little girls now. Simon Denham had hung around Jimmy until he'd found other friends. Ray King had watched ants with him until he'd gone missing. Joss Palmer had discussed tractors with him before he'd left school.

Jim was working that year from ninth-grade leaflets posted up from the city and posted back when they were done. He worked without supervision in the utility room, which he was forced to vacate when Miss Rose required it for her group.

Sissy sat in the fifth grade row of desks, at the rear. She was taller than John Curry, and heavier. He kept her at a distance, attempted to ignore her. When he could not, he sent her from the room. Sissy was always pleased to go.

He sent her from the room on Miss Rose's music afternoon, which meant Jimmy had vacated the utility room and taken his books out to an old desk on the verandah. The day was hot, the desk in the only patch of shade. Sissy shared his shade, staring at him as he leafed through a book and took notes on what he found. Then she saw a photograph of the Sydney Harbour Bridge. They'd been building that bridge since before her mother left. She looked at it over his shoulder.

'We're driving up to see it opened, Pops said.'

'Who?'

'Just me and Pops.'
'Way up there?'
'He says so.'

It happened over a week or two. Cecelia was desperate. Jimmy was available. It was an odd relationship, more dog and master than friendship, but mutually beneficial. Jenny walked to school with Dora Palmer. Sissy now walked over the railway line and knocked on Hooper's door. Jimmy walked with her.

DISTANT PLACES

Gertrude didn't receive a lot of mail. She wouldn't have gone by the post office if Vern hadn't told her he'd send her a postcard from Sydney. There was no postcard but Mr Foster handed her an official-looking envelope. She turned it over and saw a Melbourne solicitor's name and address on the back and her heart started pounding. Knew it was about Amber. And feared the worst. And Vern wasn't home. Not wanting to be alone when she read it, she walked over to the station.

'It's from a solicitor,' she said.

Norman paled as he watched her open the envelope and too slowly remove a sheet of heavy paper, scan it, frown over it.

'It's not about her,' she said. 'Thank God.' She offered the single page. 'He's dead. Her father. Thank God.'

Norman read the few typewritten words. 'Egypt?'

'He . . . he did a lot of travelling.'

'Eight years ago?'

'Is that what it says?' She claimed the page and read the words again, able to take in more on the second reading, not that there was a lot to take in, only that she was his beneficiary. 'They'll be going by the will he made before we left for Africa.'

Amber had told him much about his mother-in-law, though nothing of her travels. 'You have seen Africa?'

'Not much of it.'

'My word,' he said. 'My word.'

He made her a cup of tea, offered his station biscuits, while she spoke a while of Africa, mentioned Spain, Japan, Indian trains, then the letter was read again, read aloud, studied — each word of it, each full stop, the signature.

'It makes no mention of what his estate might be worth,' Norman said.

'A two-bob watch and a bill for its repair, knowing Archie. He wasn't the type to die before his last penny was spent.'

'It suggests you send your marriage lines . . .'

'Damn fools,' she said. 'They address the letter to me, I receive the thing, and now they want me to prove I'm who my name says I am. I doubt I've still got them, and doubt it's worth the trouble of looking.' She folded the page into its envelope. 'Have you heard anything from Vern?'

'Only that they have arrived safely and that the car went well.'

Vern had bought himself another new car, a Hudson this time, big, solid, reliable and needing a long trip to run it in. Sydney was far enough. Jimmy rarely asked for anything. He'd asked if they could take Cecelia. Vern told him that the girl couldn't travel up there without another female along, so Jimmy asked Margaret if she'd go, and yes she would. Then Lorna, who was not fond of car travel, condescended to accompany them. What had started out in Vern's mind as a father and son trip, a chance to spend some time with that boy, had been waylaid by woman. And an uglier bunch of mismatched human souls would be hard to find, but a bloke down the far end of the newly opened bridge wanted to take their picture.

Vern stood back and lit a smoke while the three girls and Jimmy were photographed. As pre-teenagers, his daughters had looked as good as they ever would. They were in their twenties now, more than old enough to be wed and giving him grandchildren, but the likelihood of either of them doing it was nil minus ten.

Lorna had the Hoopers' dark colouring and too much of their height. She could look him in the eye without raising her chin, and she had a chin you could hang a coat on, her mother's acerbic tongue and hawk nose — which was still growing. Only a father might consider that girl less than ugly. There was no denying Vern was her father, but by the living Christ, there were times Vern might have liked to deny it. Along with her general ugliness, she had an ugly nature. She couldn't stand Sissy Morrison. Not that Vern blamed her for that, but a woman of her years could have made a better attempt to hide it.

Margaret had taken the girl under her wing, and by the seventh day of that trip from hell, anyone not in the know might have considered those two much of an age. Margaret had never looked her years; she'd rarely had the chance to be a child, having spent her life stuck to Lorna's elbow. She had her mother's pretty silver blonde hair but more of it. It was eye-catching. Her features were small, sharp, like her mother's, other than her eyes, which were a watery blue and too large for their sockets. She'd had the look of a pinch-faced, traumatised rat when she'd arrived home after the fire. She still had a rodent look about her, but one that was having a damn good time in a cheese larder and she didn't look as bad with Sissy walking at her side. If he could prise her away from her lamppost sister, she may have a chance of catching herself a man.

Lorna was a lost cause. She walked like a man, dressed like a man, apart from her too long skirts. She knew the latest cricket score, knew how many runs Bradman had made before they got him out, and how they'd got him out. She followed the Melbourne football teams, knew the names of the top players.

Jimmy barely knew a cricket ball from a football. Vern had bought him a cricket bat and stumps, had bowled a few balls at him. Jimmy dodged them. Vern had bought him an expensive football, taken him out on the road in front of the house to have a few kicks. He'd stood off at a distance, arms by his sides, waiting for the ball to fall on his head. He liked driving that car, though. He'd driven it a good third of the way to Sydney. He seemed to be enjoying himself too, and tolerating the crowds better with that girl and Margaret at his side.

They were away for ten days in all and a lot can happen in ten days. The solicitor's letter had set Gertrude to searching for her marriage lines. She'd upended her house, found a lot of other things she'd misplaced or forgotten, but not what she was looking for. She had a feeling she'd burnt them, or maybe she'd just felt like doing it. They were gone anyway, unless Amber had taken them. She'd have to ask Norman to have a look through her things. Not that it was worth the trouble, not that she would have given that letter a second thought, if Norman hadn't convinced her that there had to be some money or personal effects involved or the solicitor wouldn't have bothered writing. It was something to think about, something to dream about, and when Vern came home, a reason to ride in and get him to place a call to the solicitor's office — place it three times before she got connected to the right chap.

She identified herself, told him she'd received his letter, that her marriage lines seemed to have disappeared. 'What I need to know is whether it's worth my effort finding them.'

He wouldn't tell her how much was involved, but he told her there were some personal items and that it would be to her financial gain. He said, if she couldn't find proof of her marriage to Dr Archibald Gerald Foote, she would require two letters of identification, from a minister of religion, doctor, solicitor or constable stating they had known her for a period of years. She didn't hear how many years. A flock of corellas chose to fly over at that time, a flock big enough to block out the sun. A distant voice on a telephone couldn't compete with that screeching.

'To hell with it,' she said and put the phone down.

In June, a second letter arrived from the solicitor. Gertrude didn't get around to replying to that one. He wrote again in August, and to shut him up she told him she was looking into getting her letters of identification. There were no more letters, or not until January of the following year when Mr Foster handed her two. One was from that ratbag solicitor. She recognised his envelope. No pleasant memories were attached to the name of Archie Foote and the last thing she wanted to see was a crate of his personal items.

The second letter was in a small white envelope, also with a Melbourne postmark, and the handwriting on it looked like a woman's. It could have been Amber's handwriting. She worried it for a time, then ripped her way in and stepped back to the post office wall to read it.

Dear Mrs Foote,

It wasn't from Amber. Relief, disappointment, then a wave of fear passed through her bowel. It was about Amber.

> *I am writing to you as one mother to another. Ernie feels that you may be better off not knowing the following, but I know I'd want to know, even if the news was bad.*
>
> *Ernie has seen your daughter. A woman calling herself Amber Johnson was arrested six or eight month ago for taking to a chap with a carving knife. He ended up with a few stitches. She might have been released if she hadn't attacked one of the jailers. A few days ago, Ernie found out they'd transferred her to an asylum for the criminally insane which is somewhere out west of Melbourne. As soon as he heard the name, Amber, and what she'd done, he thought it could have been your daughter, knowing of that business with your son-in-law. He took it upon himself to make the trip out to the asylum to see her for himself.*
>
> *He says she's sadly changed. The life she has been leading can be hard on a woman, though I'll say no more about that, which is the reason why Ernie decided not to write to you. He says that you, her husband and girls are better off keeping the memory of who she was, but as I said before, if it was one of my boys gone off the rails, I'd want to know.*
>
> *They are all doing well. Billy's job in the bank was safe. Robert was out of work for a time but he is now working in a menswear shop in Box Hill. The others are still in school.*
>
> *As I said to Ernie, if they can't get jobs, then it's no use them leaving school.*
>
> *I hope you are keeping well, and I am truly sorry to be the bearer of bad news, but I haven't been able to rest easy since I found out.*
>
> *My best regards to yourself and family,*
> *Mary Ogden*

Gertrude looked at the railway station, took two steps towards it, then turned. Norman wouldn't want to know about this, and his girls were better off not knowing. Maybe she'd have been better off not knowing.

But Amber was alive. Wherever she was, she was alive and being cared for.

I have to get down there. Vern will lend me the money. Or maybe he won't — not if it's going to get me involved with Amber again. Archie must have left something of value or the solicitor wouldn't bother writing. Maybe he struck it rich then died before he could spend it.

She'd been baptised Church of England, but rarely graced the church, and the ministers came and went. The Catholic priest had been around for years. He knew her. He'd write me a letter, she thought. And I've got Ernie's address. I'll get one from him.

She started across the road, wanting to get home and write to Ernie and Mary, then she glanced again towards the station. Like it or not, Norman had to know. He was Amber's husband.

He was in his office, sorting through a pile of paper. She didn't beat around the bush.

'She's alive, Norm. Ernie Ogden has seen her. It's not good news.'

She offered her letter. He turned to his papers.

'I'm going down to see her. I can't know where she is and not see her.'

'No doubt you feel duty-bound, Gertrude . . . as I feel duty-bound to protect my daughters.'

233

LOST AND FOUND

Elsie had been eleven or twelve years old when Gertrude brought her home. She was ten years older now, old enough to keep things running while Gertrude was away.

'Snib that door before you go to bed. Charlie's son-in-law will pick up the eggs on Fridays, and if Mrs Crone wants anything, she knows where to come. If you go easy on the kerosene it should last until I get back. If you run out of anything, tell Charlie's son-in-law when he comes down for the eggs.'

She didn't know how long she'd be gone, didn't know what she'd find when she got down there, or if she'd be able to find anything at all. The city, the world, had changed since a nineteen-year-old girl had moved in with her in-laws back in 1889. Too much to take in, too much to learn back then, and most of what she'd learnt swiftly forgotten. She'd forgotten a weekend spent at Box Hill until she'd read that name in Mary Ogden's letter.

In 1897, when she'd worked her passage home from India on a boatfull of diphtheria, she'd come ashore in Melbourne, but seen nothing of the city. She'd ridden with her trunks from the docks to the railway station, where she'd sat until it was time to board the train home.

Ernie and Mary Ogden had offered her a bed for as long as she needed to stay, which she'd accepted, until Vern said he'd make the trip with her. He knew every inch of that city, knew that Mitcham was miles out the eastern side of Melbourne and the asylum miles out the other side.

'We'll do less travelling if we stay in a city hotel,' he said.

He had his own agenda. He booked them in as Mr and Mrs Hooper.

They went out to the asylum on their second day in the city and were led into a room housing a skeleton, empty-eyed, sores circling her mouth. Vern didn't recognise her, or not until she spat at her mother. He took off like a cobra leaving a mongoose party. Gertrude wasn't far behind him. It shook them up. An hour later the smell of that place was still clinging to their nostrils. The image of those staring, soulless-eyed women with their grasping, hopeless hands stayed with them longer.

'It's an offence,' she said.

'Walk away from her, Trude.'

'It's an offence. It's an offence to mankind.'

'Walk away.'

'I gave that girl life, Vern. I can't walk away.'

'Christ,' he said and shuddered. 'Christ.'

They were in for a second shock the following day. Vern had rung through from Woody Creek and made an appointment with the solicitor. They saw him on Wednesday at ten, when Gertrude handed over her letters of identification. There was money due to her. Archie's father had left him five hundred pounds, which had been sitting in the solicitor's account since 1924.

'There are costs involved,' the solicitor said.

'And quite a bit of interest,' Vern said.

There are bad shocks, then shocks of the other kind. One can't cancel out the other, but it can take the edge off it. Gertrude walked the city streets that day feeling rich for the first time in her life, feeling rich and sad, homesick and hot, headachy and lost, and not too sure if she was nineteen or sixty.

'I'm out of balance, out of time, out of place, Vern. Hang on to me, will you? I don't know if I'm feeling faint or if my feet are off the ground.'

'Your hat's out of its time,' he said, drawing her into a city store and sitting her down while he chose a new hat, black, with a cheeky red feather; a merry widow's hat he named it. He asked the saleswoman to put her old hat in the box, and Gertrude felt ridiculous, but she walked at his side, her feather bobbing.

He told her she needed a pair of shoes to match her hat and he wanted to buy her a pair.

'Stop wasting your money.'

'I'm doing my bit for the retail traders — and I've been wanting to dress you for years.'

'I thought it was more the other way around.'

'That too.'

She let him buy the shoes. Maybe she was enjoying herself. He bought her a black suit with fitted jacket and straight-cut skirt that sat halfway up her calf, so he bought fine stockings too.

'If you're going to flash your legs you may as well do it with a bit of pride,' he said.

They were loaded down and halfway back to their hotel when he sighted a black and white striped blouse in the window of a fancy-looking shop. He wanted it.

'Stop throwing your money away. That thing is more costly than my suit.'

'A good-looking woman ought to dress in good-looking clothes.'

'It's a long time since I qualified.'

'Then I'm seeing you in hindsight,' he said. 'And in my hindsight, you make a lot of the present company look like a donkey's backside.'

'Where am I going to wear something like that at home?'

'You've got so intent on denying who you were, you've forgotten who you are.'

'If I'd gone out to Monk's place that day clad in rags, the sod wouldn't have looked at me, would he?'

'If you'd listened to me when I told you he was a twisted little bastard, you wouldn't have looked at him,' he said, and he went into the shop and bought the blouse.

She told him she was paying him back just as soon as she got her money. He told her she was marrying him and could work off her debt. They argued when she refused to wear her new outfit out to a meal with Ernie Ogden and his family, so she wore the whole new rig the next day, to a doctor's appointment.

They were seeing the chap who had treated Amber when she was in Melbourne after the birth of Leonora April. He had her records. Gertrude didn't tell him the entire truth, only that her daughter had lost another child, had a nervous breakdown, left her husband and children and had been missing for six years — and where they'd found her and the condition they'd found her in.

He suggested a colleague, one who specialised in problems of the nervous system, and he placed a phone call to him while they sat in his office. The phones in Melbourne surprised Gertrude. Business folk seemed to use them as folk at home used their back fences. He spoke for five minutes, explained that the couple was down from the country, that the problem was urgent. Gertrude heard her name mentioned twice. The chap he spoke to agreed to make time for them at five that afternoon.

More trams, more walking in high heels, but Vern found the place, and they were too early — then sat late and he grew impatient and left her sitting.

'Mrs Foote.' The doctor greeted her, eyeing her hat appreciatively. 'Not a common name,' he said.

'I'm the only one I know.'

'I know another. My sister is also a Mrs Foote — a Mrs Frederick Foote. A relative of yours perhaps.'

'Could be.' She'd known a Freddy Foote, a younger cousin of Archie's.

'Frederick is a pharmacist,' the doctor said. 'He was the son of a Doctor Gerald Foote, cousin of Miss Virginia Foote.'

He led her into his fancy office, seated her, seemed more interested in finding a common connection than in why she was there — or maybe he thought he was relaxing her. She wasn't feeling relaxed. Her shoes were crippling her, so she gave him the connection in the hope he'd move on.

'Virginia Foote was my sister-in-law. I knew her as a girl of fourteen.'

He pointed a finger and smiled. 'Which makes you the family scallywag's missing wife? Archie's wife.'

'We separated before my daughter was born.'

'My word,' he said. 'So, we are here to discuss Archie's daughter. What age would she be, Mrs Foote?'

'Thirty-seven.'

'You were obviously a child bride,' he said.

Cheeky sod, she thought, but sent a silent thank you to Vern for her suit and fancy shirt and hat.

It was six thirty before she got out of that office, and Vern nowhere to be seen. She walked out to the gate, hoping he hadn't gone off somewhere and forgotten where he'd left her, but he was holding up a lamppost, sucking on a cigarette.

'I've been visiting with a long-lost cousin,' she reported as they walked down to the tram stop. 'I probably said too much but he was a disarming sort of chap.'

She'd poured out Amber's life, other than her attack on Jenny and her attempt to bury her last baby alive. He'd known of Archie's addiction, had known more about him than she. Archie had become the skeleton in the Foote closet, and a well-documented skeleton.

She was still relating her tale when they walked into the hotel room, and she couldn't get those shoes off her feet fast enough, get those stockings rolled down.

'Anything else coming off?'

'Sit down. I'm talking,' she said. 'He told me how Archie died, Vern. He and two of his ne'er-do-well friends got themselves involved in selling stolen artefacts in Egypt. He died in prison, Vern. He's buried in a unnamed grave, and it may not be very Christian of me, but you don't know the relief I'm feeling tonight. The hearing of it from one of the family.'

She talked for an hour, talked through dinner, too wound up to eat, but sipping on wine, and her face colouring up with it.

'He and half a dozen others were caught going over the wall and they shot him. You'd think I'd care. You'd think that somewhere deep down inside me, I'd feel pity for him, and all I'm doing is rejoicing.'

'Me too,' he said. 'Now you can marry me.'

'You've had three wives. Quit while you're ahead. I trust

that chap, Vern,' she said. 'I told him everything. He's treated Archie's sister. She's been in and out of hospitals for most of her life, thanks to her bastard of a brother. He'll do something for Amber. I know he will. It's like I was led to him, like Archie's money led me to him. Maybe he's hanging around out there somewhere until he makes restitution. There's something bigger than us, guiding our way. There's some reason why I was sent to that particular chap. I'll have to go out to that asylum again though, let her know what's happening.'

'For Christ's sake, woman. Give it up. She's not capable of taking anything in! She's a spitting, clawing, raving lunatic —'

'She'll take it in. She's as mad as hell because life didn't turn out the way she planned it to go. She's her father all over again. I've seen him worse; and seen worse than that asylum too.'

'You walked away from him.'

'I hated him.'

'And she hates you.'

'I know you don't understand, but I have to try, Vern.'

'You'll be going by yourself then,' he said.

'I'd never find the place. You don't have to go near it. Just get me somewhere close and I'll go in alone.'

She was his wife in bed, maybe the only place she'd ever be his wife. He tried to talk her into marrying that night. She talked him into taking her back out to the asylum.

He went as far as the gate and watched her walk off, clad for comfort in her sandals and the skirt and blouse she'd worn to Amber's wedding. He sat under a tree and lit a cigarette. He didn't expect she'd be in there long.

The attendants kept Gertrude waiting for half an hour, and when they let her in to see Amber, she knew why they'd kept her waiting. Her daughter was in a cage of a room, her hands strapped to the arms of a chair, and in no mood for visitors. With no other weapon available, she used what she had, her saliva.

The woman attendant stood at the closed door making it obvious that she didn't need the interference of visitors, but today Gertrude was prepared and that long greasy hair, that rag of a dress, the spite and spittle wasn't as shocking.

'You're putting on a damn fine show, but I've got no time for it today. Vern is waiting for me.'

Amber spat again. Her aim was off.

'Your father is dead. He died trying to get out of a place much like this, though maybe worse. They locked him up for stealing.'

She dodged to the side, almost evading a good aim, but not quite. She took a handkerchief from her pocket, wiped her skirt.

'Do you want to die caged up like a spitting wild animal, the way your father died?'

'I wish you dead.'

'I knew you were in there somewhere.'

'I hate you, you lying old trollop.'

'You hate me seeing you like this, I know that much. And I hate seeing you like this. I've got a doctor coming out here sometime next week. His sister is married to your father's cousin. He knew your father, knew your grandfather, he knows your aunty, and he's prepared to help me get you out of this hellhole.'

The woman who'd brought her to the room didn't like that. 'Are we ready?' she said.

'A minute more.' She turned again to Amber. 'I've done as much as I can. It's up to you to decide if you want to get out — or to die in a cage.'

She stepped back as Amber spat.

The woman opened the door and Gertrude turned to her. 'How long is it since her hair has been washed?'

The woman shrugged.

She's just an outsider, Gertrude thought, paid a pittance to do a terrible job. She feels nothing for her charges, doesn't care if their hair hangs in greasy clumps, doesn't smell the stink of this place. She's here for the money. Folk will do terrible things in order to eat.

Gertrude was halfway out the door when she remembered the photograph she'd been carrying in her handbag since she'd boarded the train in Woody Creek. She turned back.

'Cecelia has grown into a big girl. She'll be as tall as me before she's done.' She removed an envelope and slid the photograph free. 'Vern took her up to see the new Harbour Bridge when it opened,' she said, holding the photograph up, at a distance.

It was Cecelia's prized possession, a four by six inch print of Lorna and Jim posed behind Margaret and Cecelia, the arch of the bridge behind them. She'd given it to Gertrude to show to her mother. Norman had tried to keep the facts from the girls and from the town, but most knew Amber had been found — found sick in hospital.

Maybe, just maybe, she saw a glint of interest in Amber's eyes. She held the photograph a little closer, ready to save it from spittle.

'She wanted to come down with me to see you —'

'Get out,' Amber screamed, and Gertrude left.

Sixteen days in all Gertrude spent away from her land. The shine can wear off a city in less time. A hotel room can grow small, a forty-year love affair stressed by proximity, and a smart black suit and fancy hat grow commonplace. In sixteen days, feet can become accustomed to walking in high-heeled shoes — accustomed, though not happy in them.

The first doctor had brought in a surgeon and a specialist of the mind who ran his own clinic. On the fifteenth day, Gertrude sat in the surgeon's office at Norman's side. He was Amber's husband. She'd be paying the bills but it was up to Norman to make the final decision on what was to be done.

Two men sat on the other side of the desk. The specialist, an Englishman, was in his forties, a balding, bombastic chap suffering a permanent case of sunburn to the face. The surgeon might have been fifty, a smaller man. He opened the conversation.

'The fact that gonorrhoea is not so prevalent amongst women as amongst men is the salvation of the human race,' he said. 'In almost every case found in the female patient, the disease so mutilates the reproductive organs that conception and childbirth are impossible.'

Norman's mind was with his girls, taken in once more by the good folk of Woody Creek. He was wishing he was with them, or at the hotel with Vern listening to the cricket match. He did not want to be subjected to this. Did he want her cured? He would not take her back — with or without her diseased uterus. The thought of her repelled him. He sat, hands almost folded in prayer, index fingers tapping his lips, holding what was within him in, while the doctor continued the lecture on topics unfit for general discussion. He harped on the female functions and Norman, seated at his mother-in-law's side, bowed his head, hoping to hide his flush. It was a relief to him when the Englishman spoke.

'The patient has a hysterical mania, which is a state in which the ideas control both body and mind, Mr Morrison, thus producing morbid changes and functions. The mania appears to be increased during the menstrual cycles. I would suggest the patient has also an inherited instability of the nervous system. This, aggravated by the loss of her four infant children . . .'

The specialist of the mind continued but Norman heard nothing beyond *inherited instability*. Those two words jammed in his mind and his thoughts returned to Cecelia, who had begged, demanded, screamed to accompany him to the city to see her mother.

He had achieved much with her during the past year. The influence of the Macdonald boys removed, the womanly influence of Margaret Hooper, Sissy's friendship with Jim, had steadied the girl. She'd slimmed down a little, had taken an interest in her appearance, could peel a potato, iron a frock.

There was no closeness between his daughters. Their personalities so diametrically opposed, it was unlikely that a closeness would ever grow. Jennifer was a gentle, silent child, eager to please. Cecelia had a dominant personality. In any group, Jennifer was standing silently within the inner circle, Cecelia demanding on the outer. She had the size and desire to push her way to the centre, but when she did, the group quickly reformed, leaving her again on the outer.

He pitied her. His early years had been spent standing outside the circle. But that had changed. An organiser, Norman, a methodical man, on every committee, he had found his way to the inner circle in Woody Creek — since his wife had left home.

He did not want to be here. He had argued against making the trip. He had not seen his wife, did not wish to, would not see her.

Did he want her out of that place?

The doctor was still speaking. Norman heard nothing, or heard nothing until he heard the one word he did not wish to hear.

'. . . home.'

It penetrated.

'Home?' he repeated, aghast.

'Indeed, Mr Morrison. In two such similar cases, I have achieved quite remarkable results and returned formerly demented women to their homes and families where they continue to lead useful lives.'

Norman stood too quickly. This was not why he was here. His chair fell to the floor. He picked it up, stood it on its legs, his own legs trembling with the need to run. But he could not run. He had come here to make a decision and one must be made.

Always decisions. He did not make them lightly.

'I have . . .'

I have heard enough. I have done enough.

'I want . . .'

I want to run. I want to return to the place of peace I have found.

Like a hamster surrounded by killer dogs, his eyes darted from door to doctor, Gertrude to door, from the doctors to the medical forms Gertrude had brought him here to sign.

'If she's left in that place untreated, she'll be dead in six months,' Gertrude said. 'She's sick, she's angry, but she's not mad. She shouldn't be in that place.'

'I don't . . . I don't . . .' His eyes pleaded with her to release him.

'I don't know either,' Gertrude said. 'All I know is that I'm paying these two men to tell me what can be done. If the operation is as safe as they say, if there's one chance in a hundred of it getting her out of that place, then you have to sign those papers and give her that chance.'

'Take . . .'

Take this cup away from me and from my children, Mother Foote.

'She's thirty-seven years old, Norman.'

And I am not yet fifty, but today I feel . . . I feel that my life is ending.

The red-faced specialist of the mind was offering his pen. Gertrude took it. She offered it to Norman. It was a very fine pen. He could not refuse it. He studied it a moment, glanced at Gertrude, at the doctors, then sighed.

Knew he was signing away his life, and the lives of his girls. He knew it, but he signed. *N.J. Morrison. N.J. Morrison.*

BOOK TWO

COMMUNICATIONS

Each fish, each frog in the creek will create its own ripples. Amber Morrison's ripples, always more problematical than most, began washing against Woody Creek in March of 1933.

Gertrude was never seen in a bank, then two Fridays in a row she was seen walking out of the National Bank, and on the second occasion she was clutching what looked like a chequebook.

'What does she need with a chequebook?'

It was rare for her to receive a letter. Each Friday now she queued for her mail and usually received something — and replied by return mail.

> *7 April 1933*
> *Dr J.T. Waters,*
> *Please find enclosed cheque in payment of your accounts to date, with my appreciation.*
> *Yours faithfully, Gertrude Foote*

> *15 April 1933*
> *Dr W. Rouse,*
> *Please find enclosed cheque in payment of your account, with my appreciation.*
> *Yours faithfully, Gertrude Foote*

There were whispers regarding Amber's finding, of her major surgery, spoken of behind hands with the occasional whispers of *growth in her female organs*. There were whispers too of a *private sanatorium*, which, to many rumour-mongers, spelled consumption.

'Does anyone know how they found her?'

'Someone said Ernie Ogden found her.'

'Maisy would know then. Her second girl has just got herself engaged to Ernie Ogden's oldest boy.'

'If she knows, she's not saying anything.'

Mr Foster, Woody Creek postmaster and, for a short period, neighbour of Amber Morrison, felt the ripples. He knew the address to which Gertrude addressed her letters, but few spoke to Mr Foster. Most took their mail and got out of his pokey little office.

Ripples usually die a natural death, but those created by Amber Morrison continued to widen. Charles Duckworth, who for the past six years had been hard pressed to post off the obligatory Christmas card to Norman, now sat to put pen to paper.

7 May 1933

My dear Nephew,

It is with a heavy heart that I put pen to paper this day. It has been brought to my attention by my good wife that, during her charitable work amongst the unfortunate, she came upon the woman who was your wife. My further enquiries ascertained that she was admitted to the institution with your full knowledge.

I sympathise with your situation, and might add that I would expect no less from you. Certainly the deserving amongst these wretched women should be treated with all care. However, I stress, and in the strongest terms, nephew, that under no circumstances should you involve yourself again with that woman, nor consider allowing her to come within a hundred miles of your impressionable daughters, nor should you waste more of your limited funds on the rehabilitation of a woman who, to quote her treating physician, has neither conscience nor remorse.

Trust that these harsh words have been written with only your best interests and the interests of your daughters at heart.
Your loving uncle, Charles Duckworth

1 June 1933
Dear Doctor J.T. Waters,
   Please find enclosed cheque for April and May accounts.
Yours sincerely, G. Foote

23 June 1933
My dear Nephew,
   In my capacity as a minister of God, I have taken it upon myself to attend the clinic where the woman is being held, and this day spoke at length to the treating physician, who is convinced that a cure for many forms of madness and immoderate behaviour can be effected by the use of electrical current applied to the brain, which he believes can readjust the thought processes of his patients and in some cases erase all previous memories. The treatment is experimental, and considered to be without merit by his colleagues, however, when the woman was brought into the room and introduced to me, she greeted me civilly, as she might a stranger.
   My fear, nephew, is that he will indeed be successful, and that you will consider it your Christian duty to take that woman back into your home.
   Thus, though it pains myself and my good wife, we feel it is our duty now to inform you that seven years ago, whilst that woman was a guest at the manse, and during a period when she was considered to be sane, her deeds were such which cannot, will not, be forgiven by myself and my wife — nor should they be forgiven by you.
   Your cousin, an inexperienced and impressionable young minister, who sought only to bring comfort to a bereaved cousin, became hypnotised by her wiles and was led by her from his chosen path in life. To this day your cousin remains

in Port Moresby, consorting with natives and leading the life of a drunken waster. I do not write these words lightly. Do not read them lightly.
With my best regards, your uncle, Charles Duckworth

30 June 1933
Doctor J.T. Waters
Dear Sir,

Thank you for your report of the seventeenth. I am relieved to hear of Mrs Morrison's continuing improvement and congratulate you. You state in your letter that she is eager to see her daughter. She should be made aware that she has two daughters, sir, both as eager to see their mother, however, at this time, it would not be in their best interests to reopen old wounds. If in time her recovery is proven, I will re-evaluate the situation.

Further to your letter: I am prepared to offer Mrs Morrison a reference stating that prior to her illness she was an excellent pastry cook with good housekeeping skills, certainly sufficient to secure for her a position in some large establishment. Her monetary independence can only be beneficial to her continued recovery.
Your faithfully, N.J. Morrison

6 July 1933
Doctor J.T. Waters,
   Please find enclosed cheque.
G. Foote

18 July 1933
Doctor J.T. Walters,
Dear Sir,

Further to our last correspondence, accommodation has been secured for Mrs Morrison at a respectable rooming house in Richmond. Details below. Until such time as she is well enough to find employment, I will cover the cost of her lodgings.

> *As to suitable clothing, the Reverend Duckworth and his wife have offered to secure for her an adequate wardrobe, which will be delivered to your establishment prior to her release.*
> *Yours faithfully, N.J. Morrison*

1 August 1933
Dear Doctor J.T. Walters,
   Please find cheque for July's account, with my gratitude.
Yours sincerely, Gertrude Foote

5 August 1933
Dear Norman,
   There's nothing I can say except I'm sorry . . .

There was more, much more, two pages more, though Norman read no more. Had he recognised the handwriting on the envelope, he would not have broken the seal. He felt disgust, revulsion at the handling of the paper, and quickly lifted the stove's central hotplate, thrusting pages and envelope into the embers. Only when it flared did he think of Gertrude, who may well have been pleased to read it. She had paid for her daughter's cure in a private sanatorium and clinic at no small cost, but had heard not a word from her.

Maisy was in touch. Her engaged daughter, who travelled each month to the city to spend time with her fiancé, had visited Amber in Richmond. She was not immediately recognised, but seven years is a long time in the life of a young woman. Maureen Macdonald had grown from a shapeless thirteen into a womanly twenty. Maureen reported that Amber looked like hell, but seemed well.

Then in late August, Maisy came to the station with pages of familiar handwriting, addressed to *My darling daughters*.

'I've read it, Norman. There's nothing in it that they shouldn't see.'

'No,' he said.

'They'd love to —'

Norman stepped back, lifting a hand to keep her and that defiled thing at bay.

'Sissy is fourteen,' Maisy said.

He did not need to be told his daughter's age, nor did he require any further disruption to her life. She had been eight when Amber left and remembered her well. He had not been able to keep her mother's rise from the dead from her, nor from Jennifer, though he had tried. Jennifer had no memory of the woman, but was enchanted by the idea of 'mother'.

'I understand how you feel,' Maisy said. 'And I won't go against your decision. But I'm telling you now, Norman, if they find out when they're older that she wrote to them and you wouldn't let them read the letter, they'll hold it against you for life.'

'So be it,' he said.

She turned to leave, but changed her mind.

'Someone has probably told you I was born, as they say, on the wrong side of the blanket. My mother got herself into trouble when she was sixteen. Her aunty raised me to believe my mother didn't give a damn about me. I didn't know she wrote until I started working for George and he came home from the post office one day with a birthday card addressed to me, a ten-shilling note in it. She'd sent me a card and money every year, and I'd never seen card nor money. She died the year Maureen was born. I never got to see her. My aunty died a few years later and everyone thought I was terrible because I didn't go to her funeral.' She placed the folded page on the station windowsill. 'At least think about it,' she said and she left.

A gust of wind blew the thing to his platform. He could not leave it there. He retrieved it and took it into his office, where with fingertips he opened its folds.

My darling daughters,

It has been so long since I've seen you. I've been very sick but now I'm feeling well again and the one thing that could make me feel better still would be a letter from my darling girls . . .

The letter moved him. He offered the page that night after dinner, and later, the table wiped down well, he offered each of his girls a sheet of paper and a pen.

Few children remained in the schoolroom after their fourteenth birthday. Cecelia did not do well there, had no desire to be there, but her reading was barely adequate and her handwriting was not. Perhaps some good could come from this.

He sat with his girls, watched the pens dip into the well, overseeing each word written.

Dear Mummy,
We are well up here. I hope you are well down there . . .

Then Sissy's desire to write waned. He suggested she tell her mother of her picnic at Hoopers' farm.

I went out to Hoopers' farm on Sunday and Jimmy drove all the way there. I made some toffee to take and put peanuts in it.

She looked at him for inspiration. He suggested a mention of school.

I'm old enough to leave school now but Dad won't let me.

He suggested she begin again, and to delete mention of school. She refused to begin again, managed two more lines, and finished with, *Love from Cecelia XXX.*

Jenny's pen continued to drink at the well. Her handwriting was large as yet, but well formed.

My dearest Mummy,
I wish I could remember you. Granny says I can't because I was only about the size of a skun rabbit when you first got sick, so in case you can't remember me either, I will put in a photo that Mr Mcpherson took at the concert last year. I'm the fairy in the middle with the magic wand. I had to touch all of the little flowers' heads and wake them up so they could dance. Anyway, I asked Daddy if I ever looked like a skun rabbit and he said that I was as bald as a newborn mouse when I was born, which was really very funny because we were having

dinner at Granny's, and afterwards, when Joey and I went out to play in the shed, what should we find but six baby mice underneath some old wheat bags!!! They were about as big as my pointer finger and pink, so I took one inside and opened my hand to show to Daddy, and I said is that what I looked like when I got born? Exactly, he said . . .

She ran out of paper before she ran out of words. *Lots of love, Jenny* was squeezed into the bottom corner.

He addressed the envelope, included the snapshot taken at the concert of a fine-boned, slim-necked, slim-limbed fairy child with wings and wand and the crown of a princess perched on a mass of crinkling curls.

A shy child, his Jenny-wren, with a voice that charmed the town at the school concerts. She was his pride, his delight. Cecelia, though vastly improved, still had her moments. The walk to and from Gertrude's property for their Sunday meal with her assisted in keeping the Duckworths' curse of fat at bay. Cecelia was a solid girl, but hopefully, having passed her fourteenth birthday, had reached her adult height — which was not a lot less than Norman's and made her occasional tantrums difficult to control.

So August ended and September arrived with its glorious cloud-free days. The girls looked for a reply to their communications but received none, due perhaps to Charles, who had found a position for Amber in a large city laundry, ironing. The wage was minimal, as was her rent at the boarding house. In the past she had been efficient with the iron; perhaps in time she might become self-sufficient, Norman thought.

Then on a Friday morning in September, three passengers stepped down from the train: the Hooper women from the first-class carriage and a stranger from second class. He didn't recognise the second-class traveller, a grey-clad, pinch-faced woman, her long straw-grey hair drawn back hard from her face, a grey beret covering much of it. He took the Hooper women's tickets, reached for the stranger's —

'Hello, Norman.'

He dropped the ticket and turned quickly away, walked past his staring station lad and on trembling legs went about his business. She remained, watching him, waiting for him, a cheap hessian shopping bag weighing heavily on her arm. It was her only luggage.

The train, unconcerned that his world had been turned on its ear, puffed off to continue its journey, while Norman stood watching it go, praying that when he turned around she would be gone. Not to be. She was approaching. He could not evade her, but stepped for protection behind the station trolley.

'Did you throw out my clothes, Norman?'

'This will not do,' he said.

'All I want from you is my clothes — if you've still got them.'

'You were . . .' clothed by Charles Duckworth and his wife.

He glanced at a grey tweed skirt made for a larger woman, at a grey cardigan that had seen better days, at heavy shoes. *Vengeance is mine* . . . Charles and Jane had taken their cruel revenge.

'You jeopardise your position, madam. It was not easily found.'

Found by Charles, guaranteed to steam the starch from her backbone, to wear her ladylike hands down to the bone . . .

'I don't work on Fridays.'

'I have . . . I agreed to cover the cost of your room until you . . .'

'Have you thrown my clothes out, Norman?'

'Yes,' he said. 'No. I will . . . will have them delivered to your mother.'

'I'll be at Maisy's.'

He turned, walked west towards his house, turned back. 'You will not come near the house.'

'Whatever you say.' And she was gone.

He walked to his side gate on legs unstable as straws. This had not been expected. This he could not deal with. Not on such a day. Better she had come in winter, in bitter weather; or in summer when the red winds tossed their dust over the town. Not today, not on such a glorious day.

255

He stood watching her cross the road, watching her open Maisy's gate. The specialist of the mind might well claim to have effected a miraculous cure with his electricity, to have turned a diseased gutter trull into a productive laundress. He did not know the half of it — or knew only the half he had been told. But perhaps she had come for her clothing and would be gone tomorrow. It was not in his nature to discard anything of use. Her clothing was as she had left it, crowding his wardrobe, his drawers. He would gain needed space — and be rid of the last of her.

He drew a breath, lifted his jowls, watched her greeted on Maisy's verandah, watched several Macdonald girls pour from the house, their colour absorbing her grey. She would not receive that same greeting from many. Woody Creek did not look kindly on absconding wives and mothers.

Maisy's door closed and, with no more to see, Norman entered his own yard, diverting down to the washhouse for an empty carton. He had a stack of them and chose one of the largest. She had a position to return to, and certainly, with work not easy to find, she would not be fool enough to put that position in jeopardy. Certainly it was her intent to leave tomorrow. There was no train on Sunday.

And if she did not?

Norman shuddered and went inside to attack a task he'd delayed too long — the packing up of his dead wife's belongings for . . . for charity. She was dead to him. He would be charitable and today all memory of her would be gone from his house — before his girls came in from school. They must not learn she was in town.

But of course they would learn. She was over the road with their Aunty Maisy and half a dozen of her big-mouthed daughters. And if the Macdonalds might be silenced, his station lad had seen her. The Hooper women had recognised her. He cringed and his trembling hands, filled with her light underwear, burned. He dropped the load to his bed and stepped back. His girls must be told, and by him. He would supervise a brief visit . . . tonight. They would deliver her clothing and . . .

He could see no further. He stood staring into the looking glass, attempting to see further. Saw his reflection staring back, saw the hand reaching for the scar on his shoulder, aching again, aching since he had seen her. A mental ache perhaps, but none the less severe. He looked towards his mother's travelling case, placed many years ago on top of the wardrobe, and as he reached high to lift it down, the box containing Amber's wedding gown fell, the dust of fifteen years showering him. It stung his eyes and his tears flowed — only to cleanse his eyes of dust, and his nose. He sniffed, shook away the blur, then, jowls trembling, his pudgy hands trembling, he flung drawers open, flung clothing into the case, flung it hard and harder, filling, overflowing the case he could barely see.

They came home separately, his girls, Jenny first. She heard him in the bedroom and came in. An experienced and efficient packer of cases, Norman, but not today. Items had scattered to the bed, the floor. The box containing her wedding dress upended, a froth of satin spilled out.

Jenny squatted beside the box, feeling the satin. 'Is that Mummy's wedding dress?'

He nodded, claimed the box, fixed the lid on, and she picked up a brown felt hat.

'I almost remember that, Daddy.'

Better she did not remember. He claimed it too. The girls would be told, but together. He would speak the necessary words once. He sniffed. Norman was not a sniffer.

Five minutes later a banging door, a school case hitting the passage floor heralded Cecelia's entrance. A kitchen cupboard opening, slamming. He sighed, left his packing and, with a hand on Jenny's shoulder, guided her out to the kitchen, where he sat. They looked at him. He was not normally in the house at this time. Cecelia had cut one slice of bread and was working on the second.

'Your mother is in town overnight. She has come for her belongings.'

'Where?' Two voices as one.

'With your Aunt Maisy. After dinner we —'

They were gone, bread and jam forgotten on the table. They were out the front door and running, Jenny ahead, but not far ahead. He watched them to Maisy's verandah, sighed for the fine day lost, for the spring sunshine he had been enjoying, then returned to the packing up of his wife, who was not the woman they had run to see. His pretty, laughing Amber was dead and would remain dead.

It took two trips across the road to be rid of her clothing. On his first trip, he carried his mother's case and the large flat box containing the wedding gown, sealed tightly now with strong twine. On his second trip, he carried a large carton loaded high with shoes, hats, overcoat and jacket, old ballgown and sundry.

He had remained unsighted when he'd placed the case and box on the verandah, but on the second occasion, the oldest Macdonald girl saw him coming. She held the front door wide.

Maisy's kitchen was a babble. She came from it and directed him to a small room at the rear.

'She is leaving tomorrow,' he said, more statement than question.

'I said she could stay for the weekend, Norman.'

'Her position . . .'

'She said she doesn't work on Mondays.'

'Nor on Fridays, so it appears. Tell the girls they are required at home,' he said, and he walked back to the verandah to wait.

They did not leave willingly, but on the third telling, they left.

He saw her on the Saturday, walking with Maisy. He recognised the striped frock, saw her hair; it had lost much of its brightness but refound its curl; her mother or Maisy had been at it with their scissors. From a distance, she looked . . . looked more herself.

The girls visited with her for an hour on Saturday evening, but he filled their Sunday, walking them early to Gertrude's to take the midday meal with her, walking them home in the late afternoon, and for once Cecelia led the way, eager to visit again with her mother.

He expected Amber would leave on the Tuesday train. He looked for her to come. She did not. He looked for her on Thursday. She did not leave, and each evening at six o'clock, he was knocking on Maisy's door to retrieve his daughters.

Gertrude came to the station on Friday. He offered tea, but she'd taken tea with Maisy and her daughter.

'She seems well,' Gertrude said. 'She's very quiet, probably embarrassed that I saw her at that place. She's on tablets — Maisy was saying that they're some sort of blood-strengthening pill. She looks anaemic, thin as a rake, but she seems better than she's been in years, Norman.'

'Seems,' he said. 'The weather in Melbourne sometimes seems fine in the morning, Mother Foote — Gertrude,' he corrected quickly. Years had passed since that old name had slipped out. He must not go back. He would not go back. 'I have seen it change in the blink of an eye.'

'I'm feeling hopeful, Norm.'

'Hope can . . . can at times shield the mind from reality,' he said.

'Without it, what have we got?'

MIRACLES

The month continued to excel itself, each day brighter, warmer, than the last. Norman had no complaints with September — or perhaps one. Amber had taken root in Maisy's rear bedroom. But he had never seen his girls happier or more sisterly. They sat at night at the dinner table relaying every word spoken by this miracle, their mother, always missing, always sick, now healed and returned to them — almost returned to them.

'When is she coming home, Dad?'

'Your Aunt Maisy has a spare room, Cecelia. We do not.'

On the Wednesday of the second week, Cecelia arrived home with her dark hair a nest of rag sausages.

'Good Lord,' he said. 'What have you done to yourself?'

'Mum did it,' Sissy said.

'So it will be curly like mine,' Jenny said. She'd stood for an hour in Maisy's bathroom watching the operation. Sissy had a lot of hair.

'The end most assuredly does not justify the means. Do you hope to sleep in those things?'

'I have to.'

Usually difficult to rouse in the mornings, Cecelia rose and left the house before he had the stove burning. He was serving the porridge when she returned, her hair now a mass of corkscrew curls. The specialist of the mind had not promised to perform miracles, only stated that his patient might lead a useful life. He had made no mention of his patient performing miracles.

'I see you have invited a movie star to share our porridge, Jennifer,' Norman said.

He was not known for his humour. His breakfast table was not normally a place of laughter, but that morning his girls laughed at him, then with him, and perhaps for the first time he knew the true meaning of *Home, sweet home*. Then, miracle of miracles, Cecelia went willingly to school — if only to display her bobbing curls, which he had to admit were an improvement. They lent shape to her face, balanced her height, did something to disguise her heavy chin.

A week more that woman remained at Maisy's and each evening of that week time was stolen from Norman's after-dinner lessons by his daughter's need for rag curls; however, Maisy had assured him the visit would soon be brought to a close. It was common knowledge that her second daughter was marrying Ernie Ogden's oldest son on the final Saturday in September and that the Macdonalds would require every bed they could get. Maisy and George might round up three cousins between them, but the Ogdens could multiply that three by itself, double the total and still insult as many again who had not been invited.

Cecelia was old enough to show an interest in wedding gowns and wedding plans, Jennifer perhaps not. Her after-school visits to her mother shortened, and on the Saturday prior to the wedding, she spent the morning at the station and the afternoon with her friends.

She had three best friends: Dora Palmer and Gloria Bull, who were already ten, and Nelly Abbot, who wouldn't turn ten until February. Jenny and Nelly sat together at school and Mr Curry confused their names. They were of similar size and colouring. He didn't confuse Dora and Gloria who also sat together. Dora was long and dark, Gloria round and dark.

Jenny had realised early that her friends had mothers and fathers and she only had Norman at home. Since she'd first asked the question, she'd been told that her mother had become very sick and had to go away. Jimmy Hooper's mother had gone to a city hospital to be made well and she'd died. Jenny's mother had gone to a city hospital and been made well, though it had taken a very long time. She liked the idea of having a mother, even if she couldn't live at home, which Norman said was due to a lack of beds. Which wasn't the real reason, because Gloria's father and mother were fat and they slept in the same bed in the same bedroom, as did Dora's mother and father, who were thin. Amber was thin, Norman was a bit fat, but they would have fitted in one bed. They didn't want to fit, that was the reason why Amber lived at Maisy's. They didn't even want to talk, because Norman, who had always played poker on Friday nights with George Macdonald, had stopped going over there to play.

It was confusing. It was worrying too, but today she wasn't even going to think about spare beds and mothers and Norman's poker, because she and Dora and Nelly were playing mothers in Gloria's playhouse shed, which was out the back of the hotel and the best place to play because Gloria had no little sisters or brothers wanting to play, and no big ones to spy on their play — her older sister went to high school in the city. She had the best dress-up things too. Gloria's mother had given her a box of hats and bags and scarfs, things people left behind in the hotel rooms, and on that Saturday afternoon she brought out a huge bunch of paper flowers, grown too dusty to leave in the dining room. The Bulls were preparing for an influx of wedding guests on Friday night.

It was the flowers that suggested their game that day, and Nelly's grandmother, who had died two weeks ago. The friends clad themselves in hats and stray gloves, tied scarfs at their throats, chose purse or handbag, then, armed with their paper flowers, they walked sedately across the railway lines, across the park and sports oval, to the hole in the cemetery fence, where they climbed through and made their way to Nelly's grandmother's grave, still a red hump in the earth with only a wooden cross.

'We're going to get her a stone when things get better,' Nelly said, playing the game. 'Stones cost a lot of money, you know.'

'My word they do,' Dora said.

They gave the hump four flowers, poking their wires deep into the dirt, then they walked off to visit Jenny's grandmother Duckworth, who was lucky because she'd died in the olden days when people had plenty of money. Her stone was tall and white and had three fat angels climbing on it — except today the Macdonald twins, either bored with the wedding plans or their visitor, were climbing on it and drawing rude body parts on the angels.

'We're telling on you,' Nelly said, forgetting she was a grown-up lady.

'Get lost kid's-stuff,' they said.

The twins had learnt nothing of importance during their time away at school, other than how to catch a train into the city and where to get a free meal when they got hungry. The principal had threatened to send them home if they repeated the exercise, and as they'd wanted to go home, they'd repeated it twice. Their end-of-year exam results, which arrived home before the twins, included the words *incorrigible, young rogues*, and concluded with *expelled*.

Mr Curry refused to take them back. He suggested a good reform school. George told him what he could do with his good reform school, then gave up, as he'd given up attempting to drive his truck. Harry Hall could park that thing on a sixpenny bit if required.

The twins, thirteen last May but still waiting for their growth spurt, weren't the size of average thirteen-year-old boys. Dora, waiting for her growth spurt to stop, was close to them in height and not scared of them. She had two big brothers, who were a foot taller than her and who'd get those twins if they ever hurt her.

'We're going straight over to tell Mr Denham what you're doing,' she said.

The twins dodged Denham when they could, but he wasn't in sight so they continued their drawing. One drew a giant sausage on the top angel's round belly. The other one gave it a smiley face. The girls may not have understood its meaning, but had seen similar rude drawings quickly washed away or painted over. They walked off to continue their game.

Dora's grandmother's grave had a shiny black stone. They gave her four flowers, then shared the last of their dusty collection between a mother and her five children who had died of

263

diphtheria thirty years ago and a lonely grey stone that had no name, only *J.C. LEFT THIS LIFE 31-12-23*.

'She's your mother,' one twin yelled.

'Yours was Snow White, you dwarves,' Dora yelled back, then, their borrowed hats held down, the girls ran for a hole in the wire fence because the twins got upset when anyone called them dwarves.

They chased them, chanting one of their stupid rhymes.

'Old J.C., she went off to have a pee,
Squatted down behind a tree,
Dropped her pants and found Jenny,
Old J.C., now stinks out the cemetery,
Since many long years ago —'

'We're going straight to Mr Denham and telling him that you said dirty things to us, as well as drawing dirty things on Jenny's angels,' Dora said, safe on the other side of the fence. 'He'll make you scrub them like he made you scrub Charlie White's windows.'

'On a ladder,' Nelly yelled, 'because you're dwarves.' She had three big brothers and wasn't scared of the twins one little bit.

They ran then, handbags flapping, hats in hand, scarfs flying, across the oval, over the road and down through the memorial park, the twins yelling after them.

'Ask your father why your mother went mad if you don't believe us.'

The girls were safe in the park. The Macdonalds' house windows overlooked the park fence and one of the Macdonald girls was always looking out. The twins were scared of their sisters.

Dora knew there was some secret about Jenny, who had her birthday on the same day J.C. had died. She'd heard her mother and father talking about Jenny, and about her mother, who no one had expected would ever come home. She hadn't heard enough to know what the secret was, only enough for her father to tell her that she must never mention anything she might overhear in the house. She eyed the twins, who could be old enough to know the secret.

Jenny wanted to go back to the playhouse. She walked away from the group to sit on the swing and watch things.

A swagman, an old one, walked across the road wearing a long black coat. He had a Father Christmas beard and walked with a stick, though he didn't use it like Mr Foster used his walking stick. She thought he'd walk past, but he didn't. He was going to cut through the park. She swung a little and closed her eyes. She liked swinging with her eyes closed. It was a bit like flying. She thought he would have gone past, but he'd stopped and he was looking at her. Then he looked down and reached for something in the grass.

'Yours,' he said, offering something on a chain.

She wasn't supposed to talk to strangers. She'd been told to stay far away from those swagmen. Lots of them passed through Woody Creek now, young ones and old ones. She shook her head.

'It's not mine,' he said. 'Perhaps it fell from your handbag, madam.'

Then he smiled and tossed what he'd found, and with a reflex catch it was in her hand, and he was walking on his way towards the sports oval. It was the most perfect, precious thing she'd ever seen in her life! She stopped her swinging and slid from the seat.

'What did he give you?'

Little girls are all-seeing. They clustered around her, eyeing the pretty thing, a pearl trapped in a tiny cage of gold.

'He found it. Just down there,' Jenny said.

'He should have given it to Mr Denham.'

Jenny nodded. That's what you had to do if you found things that didn't belong to you. She didn't want to give it to Mr Denham. It was so beautiful, but someone must have lost it.

Old J.C., she went off to have a pee,
Squatted down behind a tree . . .

MRS MORRISON

Maisy came to the station on the Wednesday prior to the wedding. Had Norman known why she was there he would not have greeted her with a smile.

'Could you see your way clear to take her for the weekend?' she said.

'We have no spare beds.'

'Sissy said Jenny could sleep with her and Amber could have Jenny's room.'

'I believe her mother has offered her a bed.'

'You know as well as me that she won't go near that place. I'm sorry to do this to you, but it's happened. I didn't invite her, Norman, and I didn't think she'd stay this long. Not that I mind having her. She's doing most of the cooking and cleaning for me. If it was anyone other than the Ogdens, I'd find room somewhere, but I can't have her there with Mary and Ernie. They know everything. It would be too uncomfortable for her and for them.'

'She will be at the wedding?'

'Lord, no! That's another thing I feel bad about. She's been my best friend for thirty years and I can't even invite her to my daughter's wedding. It's a terrible mess all around.'

Did he feel a mere hiss, a whisper of pity — pity for his wife, the whore — or perhaps for his neighbour, his girls' surrogate mother? He could not have managed without her these past years. Now she was asking something of him.

'No,' he said.

'It would only be for the weekend.'

'I'll pay for her accommodation at the hotel.'

'It will be full of the Ogdens and their relatives on Friday night. I wouldn't ask you, but I've already asked Jean White and . . . and she's as bad as the Ogdens. Just Friday and maybe the hotel can take her on Saturday and Sunday. She'll clean the house up for you.'

His house did not require her cleaning. He did not require her to touch one grain of his dust.

Maisy wouldn't leave; the station lad was listening.

'If I tell her to stay out of your way, she will, Norman. You wouldn't need to see her. George isn't putting off his poker night. Come over straight from the station.'

He had missed his Friday-night poker. He looked towards the house denied him this September, and Maisy, seeing him waver, pressed her advantage.

He capitulated. 'Friday night,' he said.

He stayed well clear of his house that Friday, stayed clear of it until ten minutes before six, until the smell of her beef and onion stew began wafting across the station yard. He followed it home, where he found his girls setting the table for four. The woman spoke to him. He acknowledged her with a nod. At six, she served the meal, then placed the fourth meal into the oven and left the room. Norman ate hurriedly, collected his pouch of small change he put aside for poker nights, then he left the house.

She kept to her room on Saturday morning. He and his girls left at ten thirty for the wedding and didn't return until the train, loaded with wedding guests and the honeymooners, had gone on its way. Mary and Ernie Ogden were not on it. They and their four youngest would return to Melbourne on Tuesday's train.

'All I'm saying, Norman, is it would cause less talk in town if she was to stay where she is for the weekend,' Maisy said. 'I'm sorry.'

He roused his girls early on Sunday morning and by nine thirty they were on their way to spend the day with Gertrude.

On their return, in the late afternoon, they found the woman up a ladder cleaning windows that had not seen a cleaning cloth in seven years.

Her egg and bacon pie that night was a work of art. He watched her cut it, serve it.

'Take your meal with us, Mrs Morrison,' he said.

'I don't want to overstep —'

'The girls will appreciate your company.'

On Monday night, the girls gone to their shared bed, Norman was seated on his front verandah smoking a final cigarette when Amber returned from her evening walk. She did not immediately enter the house. Perhaps the lack of light lent her confidence to raise what was in her mind.

'You need a housekeeper, Norman. I need . . . need a home.'

He expelled smoke, considered several replies but could not find an apt one, or perhaps found it but couldn't speak it.

'I've stayed out of your way,' she said. 'It's worked out all right, hasn't it?'

She had stayed out of his way. His house was clean, his laundry flapping on the clothes line in the morning, ironed and put away by evening. His girls were happy.

'Could I stay a few days more, a week — and if it doesn't work out, I'll go. I'll just be the housekeeper, Norman.'

'The girls will soon become disenchanted with their shared bed, Mrs Morrison.'

'If they do, I'll go.'

'Decisions are best slept on,' he said.

Norman did not make decisions lightly. He slept two nights on this one, then, while the girls were at school on the Wednesday, he spoke to Amber of a week's trial, then perhaps a week-by-week business arrangement. 'You will be paid a small wage, from which I shall deduct board and lodgings —'

'You don't have to pay me, Norman.'

'If the arrangement continues past the week, you will receive a wage, Mrs Morrison. I have drawn up an agreement, which we shall each sign.'

Perhaps she glanced at his agreement before signing. He retained the original and offered her the carbon copy. Perhaps she read what she'd signed, or burned it. It stated that he would make no demands on her, over and above her housekeeping duties; that he would accept no interference from her in the handling of his daughters; that he would require the kitchen between seven and eight from Monday to Thursday, at which time she would absent herself; that after the deduction of bed and keep, he would, each Friday, pay her seven shillings and sixpence.

So the last of Jenny's belongings were moved into Cecelia's bedroom, and Norman's moved into the nursery, a wall away from the girls. His housekeeper was given the front bedroom, somewhat separated from his little family.

He was ever watchful. He did not trust her. She was subdued, had come to his house armed with two bottles of her blood-strengthening tablets, which she kept in her room. He did not venture there. At times, while he tutored his girls between seven and eight she came to the kitchen to wash a tablet down, then stood on at the door listening to his lesson. Occasionally, he caught her staring at him, and twice she'd attempted to apologise.

'I'm sorry, Norman.'

'We are all sorry for many things, Mrs Morrison. Our aim perhaps should be to do nothing more that may in the future require apology.'

Trust may grow in time, but, like damaged nerve endings once crushed, trust is slow in making a recovery. During daylight hours, when he listened to his daughters' laughter, when he saw their smiling faces, their well-ironed frocks, he sometimes felt the first feeble tingle of trust's growth, but as night came down around his house and he lay in his narrow bed, that feeble tingle became an ache. His shoulder would not allow him to trust.

Jean White shared his shoulder's distrust.

'She's as fake as a two-sided penny,' she said to Charlie midway through October.

'What's she done to you?'

'Coming in here giving me the leftovers of her fake hospital manners, that's what she's done — and looking at my hair roots while she's doing it. Have you noticed how she won't look you in the eye?'

'You wouldn't either if you'd done what she's done.'

'It's more than a guilty conscience. There's something in her eyes that she doesn't want you to see. She's like a snake, hiding her venom until she's ready to strike.'

'When have you seen a snake getting ready to strike?'

'I don't have to. I know what one would look like.'

'Gertrude says she's better.'

'That's something else too. Gertrude hasn't been to Norman's since Amber moved back home.'

'How do you know?'

'Because I watch her, that's how. She drops her eggs off here, then takes a basket down to the station.'

'How do you know she doesn't go in through his side gate?'

'Because she always went in through the front gate, that's how I know.'

'You're getting to be a gossip in your old age, Jeanny.'

'Only to you, Charlie, and you don't count.'

A smart businesswoman, Jean White, not a hard woman, but one not easy to take down. She knew everyone in town, knew who was in work and who wasn't, knew who she could trust to pay their bill when things picked up, and who'd take what they could get and run. She trusted Norman, couldn't say that she liked him, but trust was enough at times.

'You mark my words, Charlie. She'll turn. A leopard can't change its spots.'

DAFFODIL YELLOW

Someone had once told Sissy that a person's life was measured in seven-year segments, and at the end of each segment there was a change, until you reached seventy, the three score years and ten written about in the Bible. In her case, it had been proven. For the first seven years of Sissy's life, her mother had made her world the way it was supposed to be. Those years were followed by a seven-year drought of life without her mother. Now she had returned and the only drawback was the sharing of her bed and bedroom with Jenny, a price Sissy was willing to pay.

Life continued to improve, even at school. She liked being on stage in the school concerts, but for the past two years had only been in the choir. Ian Abbot had a good voice — he always sang alone on stage, as did Jenny. Nelly, Ian's sister, was wearing the fairy princess costume this year, and for the first part of that item she'd have the stage to herself. Johnny Dobson did magic tricks, Gloria Bull tap-danced. Then, out of the blue, Miss Rose turned to Sissy and asked her if she'd like to do a recitation this year, which meant she'd have the stage to herself.

'I'll do the daffodils one,' Sissy said quickly. She already knew the first verse of it from back in the days of bike-riding with her father — and he knew it right through.

'It will mean memorising it, Cecelia,' Miss Rose said.

'I know,' Sissy said. 'I can.'

Jenny's life didn't fit any seven-year plan. She didn't mind having her mother at home, apart from losing her bedroom. She liked being able to say 'my mother' like Nelly and Gloria and Dora could say 'my mother'.

Amber cleaned like a mother, washed and ironed, but didn't do much shopping, didn't go to church. She put Sissy's hair in rags two or three nights a week — which made sharing that bed even worse, because Sissy couldn't find a comfortable place to put her head on rag-curl nights.

Amber cooked like a mother. She made treacle puddings with custard that didn't even have one lump in it. She made individual meat pies; her mashed potatoes were as smooth as cream, her beans were green instead of grey, and her cabbage, shredded so fine then fried fast in a pan with flavours, was delicious. Norman had cut his cabbage into chunks which he'd boiled up until the chunks softened, which meant the bits that weren't chunks turned to grey slime.

But Dora's mother could cook too, and she could talk and laugh while she was cooking. She could threaten to slap backsides but rarely did it, and if she did, she ended up kissing whoever she'd slapped. She had so many kids she sometimes forgot Jenny wasn't one of them and kissed her too.

Jenny's mother never slapped, laughed or kissed. She was like the plaster Mary that Mrs Crone had standing on a table in the corner of her café, with a sign propped against it: *Please do not touch.* Amber's sign was invisible but Jenny could read it. She didn't touch.

Sissy wasn't much of a reader. She leaned against Amber in the kitchen, sat beside her in the parlour and leaned her head on Amber's shoulder; then in November, she led her by the hand down to Blunt's shop where they stayed for half an hour.

Mr Curry's students were encouraged to participate in the concert, though not coerced, and not supplied with costumes. The fitting of a shapeless child presented few difficulties, as did the stripping off and cladding of small children by the costume ladies. This was not the case with the older children. They were asked to present themselves at the hall in suitable clothing.

At the Friday practice, Johnny Dobson did his magic act and told Miss Rose his mother had made him a magician's cape from one of her old black skirts and was making him a cardboard hat to wear. Ian Abbot said he was borrowing his big brother's long trousers for the night.

Sissy recited the first verse of 'Daffodils', was prompted through the second, then she told Miss Rose she'd be wearing a daffodil yellow dress which her mother was paying Miss Blunt to make.

'We bought some crepe paper too, yellow and orange, and Miss Blunt is making us a bunch of daffodils. Some of them my mother is going to pin in my hair, and some I'll just hold, and we're going to —'

'I'm sure you will look delightful, Cecelia,' Miss Rose said. 'Now, can we run through the third verse, please.'

'Can I read it today?'

'You may read it today, but I want you word perfect next Friday.'

Gloria Bull practised her dance. She'd wear her sister's outgrown dancing costume.

'Jennifer?'

Jenny sang 'Sweet Little Alice Blue Gown', and when asked what she might be wearing on the night, she shook her head.

'Do you have something blue?' Miss Rose asked.

Perhaps she did. Perhaps Amber was paying Miss Blunt to make her a dress. She looked at Sissy. 'Have I got —'

'You've got that one,' Sissy said. Jenny's school frock was navy blue.

Thus began the torment of William Wordsworth's 'I Wandered Lonely As A Cloud', which forever more in Norman's house would become 'Daffodils'. Sissy practised on the verandah, in bed, between seven and eight from Monday to Thursday, and she couldn't get past the second verse.

'*The waves beside them danced, but they . . .*' Norman encouraged. 'Give me the next line, Cecelia.'

'I'm tired of it, I said.'

'I too am tired of it. *The waves beside them danced, but they . . .*'

'I'll read it, I said.'

'You chose to learn the poem. *The waves beside them danced, but they Outdid the sparkling waves in glee . . .*'

'It doesn't even rhyme!'

'That is not your concern.'

'Well, it's stupid.'

'Many critics would not agree with you. Recite with me: *The waves beside them danced, but they . . .*'

'I told you I was tired!'

'Do not raise your voice to me! *The waves beside . . .*'

At the Friday practice, Sissy could make it through verses one and two, then her mind went blank.

'The stupid thing doesn't rhyme. It throws me out of rhythm every time,' she argued. 'It's plain stupid.'

'You chose the poem. You have until Wednesday afternoon to decide if it's stupid or not, Cecelia. Who is next?' Miss Rose said.

The last of the children gone by four thirty, Miss Rose went to the costume cupboard seeking something blue. She'd decided today that her 'Sweet Little Alice Blue Gown' must be clad in blue. Plenty of pinks in that cupboard, a purple and gold cape; she considered it. She also considered a frilled yellow, but she wanted blue. She thought of the relief bin at the town hall, though anything worth wearing that ended up in that bin didn't remain long in it. And Jenny's father, who clad his girls plainly but well, may consider a relief bin frock an insult.

Had he been an approachable man, she may have approached him. He was not, so she picked up her purse and hurried down to Cox's newspaper shop, catching him just as he was about to close his door.

'Crepe paper,' she said. 'Blue.'

He offered a choice of three. Only one fitted her mental image of 'Sweet Little Alice Blue Gown'.

'Three rolls should be adequate, thank you, Mr Cox.'

Miss Rose lodged with the Blunt family, and that evening greeted Miss Blunt at the front door with an apology, the crepe paper and a plea. 'Please, could you see your way clear, my dear Julia?'

Miss Blunt had already made two frocks for the Morrisons, Cecelia's yellow and Amber's olive green. She'd spent hours making a bunch of daffodils — and received little appreciation for her labour. But by seven that night, Miss Rose's scissors were snipping blue paper and Miss Blunt's sewing machine gathering while in Norman's kitchen, the torment of Wordsworth's poem continued.

'*For oft, when on my couch I lie.* Continue, Cecelia. *For oft, when on my couch I lie . . .*'

Sissy stared vacantly, her hair a mass of white rag sausages.

'*In vacant or in pensive mood.* We have been over this, over and over it. Repeat those lines with me.'

'I'll read it. She let me read it at practice.'

'You agreed to learn the poem.'

'I've learned enough. I'll do the first two verses.'

'The poem has four verses. *For oft, when on my couch I lie . . .*'

On Wednesday afternoon, Sissy told Miss Rose she was only doing the first two verses.

In all of the years Miss Rose had been dealing with that girl, neither her method nor tone had altered. 'Thank you, Cecelia. That will be all.'

'I'm doing just two?'

'No. You will be assisting the ladies in the dressing room. Good afternoon.'

Sissy didn't want to assist the ladies in the dressing room. She wanted to stand on that stage alone, in her daffodil yellow dress with her daffodils pinned in her hair over her left ear, her hair curled in rows and pinned back at one side. Amber had already tried it that way, with the flowers and the dress.

'All right then. I'll know those rotten two verses by Saturday.'

'You were told to know them by today. That will be all.'

'I'm not helping dress kids!'

'That is your choice. Good afternoon, Cecelia.'

Dismissed for the third time, Sissy stood open-mouthed, blood flooding her brow, her cheeks, her heavy chin.

'Well . . . well, you go to hell then, and you can take your stupid poem with you too, and your stupid school as well, and your stupid haircut. If you didn't know it, that style went out of fashion ten years ago,' she said, and she ran for the sanctuary of her mother.

Norman saw her run across the station yard. He heard doors slam, watched something yellow fly from his back door. He gave her five minutes by the station clock, then followed her home where he found the unworn yellow frock lying in the dust and several paper daffodils blooming on his lavender bush. He picked up the frock, shook it, plucked the flowers from the shrub and went inside.

She was in the kitchen, head on the table, Amber behind her, patting, soothing, kissing. He placed the frock down, the daffodils on it. Cecelia lifted her head long enough to swipe the frock and daffodils to the floor. He picked them up, placed them again on the table.

'I will deal with this, Mrs Morrison.'

She moved away but didn't leave the kitchen.

'Explain your infantile behaviour, Cecelia.'

'She said I'm not in the concert,' Sissy yelled, and the frock flew, narrowly missing the stove. Her chair fell as she stood, then an enamel dish Amber had been about to use for her treacle pudding flew, hit the stove, clattered to the floor.

'Go to your room.'

Sissy ran to Amber. Norman turned his back, picked up the chair, the chipped bowl, the frock, the daffodils, one from the stove, slightly singed. He drew two deep and calming breaths, then turned back to the battle.

'Remove yourself from that girl, Mrs Morrison.'

She tried, but Cecelia clung.

'Cecelia! You will obey me. Release your mother and hang up your frock.'

'You can go to hell too,' she howled. 'If she said Jenny couldn't be in it, you'd go down there and tell her off, wouldn't you?'

Norman had never told anyone off in his life. He took his daughter's arm. Sissy shook him off and ran to her bedroom.

'That woman has always hated her, Norman.'

'That woman has attempted to train her in good habits of self-control, Mrs Morrison, and Cecelia is too old for these displays of infantile spleen.'

Amber was looking at the yellow frock. He claimed it and walked across the passage to his daughter's room, where again he took her arm and attempted to lead her to the wardrobe — and got an elbow in the ribs for his trouble.

'She's disappointed, Norman. Leave her to me.'

'Your interference, madam, is not helping matters. Go to your room.'

'You're on the school committee. She's right. You'd be down there fast enough if it was —' Caught her mouth in time, almost in time.

'You are employed to care for the house. Care for it.'

'She's my daughter —'

'Which you chose to forget for some considerable time.'

'Don't you come at me with that.'

He turned, walked away. But the years, those aching years he'd put into that girl. He stepped from foot to foot in the passage, every nerve ending urging him to go. And he must not. His housekeeper must go. The key to his room was in his underwear drawer. He retrieved it and returned to Cecelia's room. She was a heavy girl. It was no small task to manhandle her from that room, fight her into his own, close the door and hold it while inserting the key, but he got the door locked.

Panting, heart racing, he turned to Amber. 'Your services are no longer required, Mrs Morrison. You will leave my house tonight.'

'You've always leaned to that other one —'

'Pack your bags, madam.'

'You think I don't know why?'

'Pack your bags.'

'If I go, I'll take Cecelia with me.'

'And train her in the ways of a whore?'

'You bastard.'

'If I am so, then it is you who have made me so, madam. Out.'

His spectacles lopsided, the bridge wire twisted in the scuffle, he faced her in the passage, his lips a small tight split in the sagging pink cushion of his face.

She went to her room and closed the door. He walked out to the verandah where he stood attempting to adjust his spectacles while waiting for his heart rhythm to steady. Oddly enough, his shoulder, which required little excuse to ache, had tolerated the unaccustomed exercise well. He flexed it, drew a deep steadying breath, set his spectacles back on his nose and returned to his station.

BLUE ANGER

She watched the side gate close, then walked to the locked door and stood listening to Cecelia's injured bull bellow. She knocked, but was ignored, or not heard. Walked around to the window, but the curtains were drawn. Attempted to open a window that had never opened, not when they'd furnished that room as a nursery fourteen years ago. She tapped gently on it, wanting her girl to pull back the curtain. Cecelia screamed, and Amber turned towards his station. He was watching her. He wanted her gone.

This was her house. She'd wed him for this house, and for his mother's furniture, her bone china tea set. And wanted to run from him on her wedding night . . .

She'd tried that. What else was out there? Worse than him, that was what else. Choices had to be made, the bad measured against the worse.

They'd taken her memories in that place where she'd been; this house had brought them back. Her hand on a familiar bowl, and she remembered using the bowl. A tablecloth spread, and she remembered embroidering it.

She walked around the house and inside via the front door, where she stood a moment staring at the hall table. Loved the grain of that timber, and the vase she'd always set on it, a delicate thing Norman's mother had sworn was a gift from Queen Victoria to some Duckworth long since dead. She walked into the parlour where she squatted before the crystal cabinet, her finger tracing the rim of gold decorating a dainty cup. Eight dainty cups, saucers and plates, a tiny milk jug, a delicate sugar bowl, the large cake plate. All there, all perfect. Didn't want to leave them, or leave her big-as-an-ox baby, her plain-as-mud baby, but her baby.

'Take a pill,' she said. 'Take a pill, slow down and think.'

They'd given her two bottles when she'd left that place, a hundred in each. She took what she needed, and who knew better than she what she needed.

He had at one time kept the key to that door on top of the kitchen dresser. She felt for it, but didn't find it. Even if she had, she couldn't let her girl out. He wanted her gone from this house. She had overstepped her boundaries. She didn't like boundaries.

'Cook him some dinner,' she said. 'A broth of oleander flowers, a stew of its twigs. A tea sweetened with pills?'

She smiled and looked at the pill on her palm. Too precious to waste on the beast and his stray. She washed it down, then stood on at the window, looking out but only seeing in.

'Make a start,' she said. 'Let him see you have made a start.'

Back in the bedroom, she climbed onto a chair and got his mother's case down from its place on top of her wardrobe. Underwear in, hat on the open lid, shoes on the bed. He'd see it when he came in. He wouldn't see her. He'd think she'd gone to Maisy's, gone to her mother's, gone to the hotel. He'd believe what he wanted to believe. Always had. Hadn't changed since the day she'd met him.

Not a brutal man, though. She'd known brutal men. Remembered that too. Remembered everything now.

Outside then, out as far as the front verandah. The bench seat had been bought since she'd left. His packet of cigarettes and matches were on the parlour windowsill. She didn't like smoking, had never enjoyed the habit, but the burning of a cigarette used time. She needed to use time, so she lit one and watched it turn to ash; lit another.

The side gate gave her fair warning. It squealed on heavy hinges and she was out the front gate. It didn't squeal. She walked right, down past the post office, its door closed, past the bank, taller than its neighbours, down past Charlie White's shop. Her eyes shielded from the cut of a low-hanging sun, she failed to see, or chose not to acknowledge, Jean, who glanced out before closing the old green doors. The corner forced a decision. West, out towards the slaughteryards, the sun in her eyes, or north and over the railway crossing. More people to the north, more eyes to stare, but she couldn't stand the glare. She turned.

A walker passed by. She offered a nod in reply to his 'Good evening'. No words in her for the outsiders. Plenty within.

Knew every inch of this town, every house, every vacant block, every pair of eyes staring from behind lifted curtains. Turned west again, the setting sun now fallen behind towering trees growing alongside the creek. She followed the creek along a track that ran through the bottom of Dobson's land then through McPherson's. She'd walked this way with her father. Always thought of him in this place. Loved him, loved him, loved him — and hated that old bitch. Wanted that old bitch dead.

Wanted her father's money. Nearly five hundred pounds, Maisy said. Five hundred pounds! That money should have been hers, not that old trollop's who had dragged her from her father's house and back to a hut to rot.

Glanced towards the forest, darkening now. What if she walked down there and asked the old bitch for half of what she'd got? What had she ever given her?

'Nothing.'

Wanted to watch her grow old, crippled, crawling, begging.

Matches rattling in her pocket. She laughed.

'Burn the old bitch in her bed,' she said.

Saw him behind her then, a lanky beanpole of a boy she'd seen at Maisy's house. He worked for George.

'A nice evening, Mrs Morrison,' he said.

She nodded and walked on, followed the creek down to the bridge.

And the bastards with their eyes were there too. Two of them, sitting in her place underneath the bridge, an old one with a long white beard and a younger one, boiling a billy.

She had to go.

Climbed up the bank and out to the road. Go where? She had nothing. Nothing. Nothing. No one. No one. No one.

Threw his matches at a tree and watched them scatter, then turned towards the town.

Lights showing at the McPhersons' windows, dog barking. She walked past, walked past George Macdonald's mill. Turned to the left before Vern Hooper's block. Couldn't face him. He knew where she'd been. They all knew. His daughters knew.

Walked by Henry King's derelict hut. Someone was living in it. Walked the diagonal across the road, across a vacant paddock, taking the route she'd walked on her way to school, cutting the distance where she could with diagonals. Retraced her childhood steps to the school gate, unchanged in thirty years, as the school was unchanged. She'd run down that same verandah, played in that same schoolyard. Happy here, her and Maisy, Sylvia and Julia. Wanted to open that gate and go back to twelve again, before the breasts, before the womb, before . . .

'Everything.'

Julia was lucky. She'd lived opposite the school gate. Maisy was almost as lucky — her aunty had lived near the Kings. Sylvia wasn't so lucky. She'd lived four miles out, had ridden in on horseback. She'd got lucky later, got married and went to live in Sydney.

She turned to Julia's house, as unchanged as the school — except for the woman watering the garden. It wasn't Julia. Recognised the haircut. 'Bitch,' she said.

How long had she been teaching up here? Amber was already wed, already thick with Cecelia, when the infants' mistress had come new to town. She'd looked like a girl. She still looked like a girl. Never had a man to age her, that's why. Hated her for her independence, her lack of need of a man to pay her bills.

The hose left to run, the teacher came to the gate. 'It's Mrs Morrison, isn't it? What a lovely evening for a walk,' she said.

A chimp stretches his lips in a grimace when angry or afraid. Amber offered a similar stretching of her lips as she turned to walk on. Then she changed her mind. She crossed the road.

'Cecelia is distraught,' she said.

'I'm sorry to hear that, but I'm afraid we ran out of time, Mrs Morrison.'

'She reads it well.'

Miss Rose picked up the hose, directed it on a fern. 'A reading is not a recitation, Mrs Morrison. I did explain to Cecelia that she must memorise it. She was given time.'

Then Julia Blunt popped her head out. 'I was sure I recognised your voice, Amber. One moment, dear.'

Always smaller than her classmates, now bespectacled, her shoulders narrowed by labour over the sewing machine, Miss Blunt returned displaying a froth of blue, the three rolls of crepe paper transformed into an old-world gown, its ankle-length skirt stiff with layer upon layer of paper frills.

Amber could recognise beauty when she saw it. She knew who'd be wearing it.

'We're all so proud of your little songbird's voice. You are in for a delightful surprise, my dear.'

'Her father paid you to make that?'

Amber's question was innocent but her tone accused. Like puppets attached to the same string, the women shook their heads while two mouths shaped the same lie.

'The costume fund.'

Their visitor stretched her lips in the chimp's grimace and walked on.

'She is not the girl I once knew,' Miss Blunt said.

'One hears such terrible rumours,' Miss Rose said.

SAND IN THE DESERT

Miss Rose came by Norman's house on the Thursday evening with the costume, but overhearing more than she wished to hear, she chose not to announce her presence and hurried away.

There were no dressing rooms at the town hall, only the meeting room on one side, the supper room on the other and an open area beside the stage. Windows were uncurtained and thus offered no privacy, which was the prime reason costumes were not provided for the senior students. However, she had supplied a costume for Jennifer. Thus she must get it to the Morrison house prior to the concert.

On Friday at five, John McPherson arrived to transport the last of the props and costumes to the hall, and while he and the costume women carried their loads indoors, Miss Rose ran across the road with the blue, arriving at the Morrisons' gate in time to see the husband removing his wife from the house, while from indoors came a scream she knew too well. Again the infants' mistress turned tail. She'd dress Jennifer in the lavatory.

Time slipped into a different gear between six and seven thirty. Always chaotic, that last hour, the rounding up of infants, the late arrivals, the tying of fast bows, the finding of shoes, and she loved every minute of it.

As did John McPherson, who for the past three years had been setting his camera up in the stage wings to trap the best of the concert magic.

He trapped Jenny in her Alice Blue Gown and matching bonnet, trapped those eyes still wide with surprise, trapped her shy smile, and in his darkroom well after midnight, when he watched the photograph develop, he knew he had come of age. Only a boy in 1923, his camera new the evening he was called on to aim his lens at a dead woman in a pine coffin. He had wept when he'd developed those prints, wept because the best photograph he'd ever taken was of a beautiful dead woman. At twenty-seven, his camera now an old and familiar friend; he'd captured living beauty.

He made a second print, which he personally delivered to the *Willama Gazette* office on Monday morning, with a brief covering story. And they printed it, on the front page of the Wednesday edition, beneath large capitals: 'WOODY CREEK'S SMALL SONGBIRD'. And below it:

Jennifer Morrison, ten-year-old daughter of Woody Creek stationmaster Mr Norman Morrison, stole the show on Saturday evening with her delightful rendition of 'Sweet Little Alice Blue Gown'.

No mention of Amber, who had not yet left Norman's house; his one attempt to remove her having raised the demon in his daughter. Bedlam. Bedlam and worse. He'd walked Jennifer over the road in the dead of night and roused Maisy. 'For a few days,' he said. 'Cecelia is . . . is crazed.'

During her menses, that girl had always been at her most difficult. He had secured a booklet instructing him how best to deal with a developing woman. It suggested she should be protected from chills and spicy foods, which could put extra strain upon delicate organs already congested. It suggested the menstruating female should receive tender care, be kept away from parties, dancing and other stimulation. However, her menses this month, having coincided with her disappointment at not taking part in the concert, when added to his ongoing attempt to evict her mother, had caused an over-stimulation. She'd attacked him about the head and shoulders with the heavy end of the hair broom, thrown her meal at him, refused to attend to her hygiene — and wet her shared bed. Her behaviour such that he'd spent the night of the concert at his station and, had a goods train filled with cattle gone by, he might have hitched a ride with them to a city slaughteryard.

Sissy was calm on Monday, slept for most of the day, then on Monday evening he saw that woman offering her a glass of water and a pill. Norman may have been a fool who too often in life had taken the easy road, but he was not an utter fool. He'd demanded his housekeeper produce the pill bottle, which was not immediately forthcoming. He'd threatened to search her bedroom, while she'd argued of blood loss, of Cecelia's need for the blood-strengthening pill. Few would have doubted her argument. He'd doubted and begun with her underwear drawer, emptied it to the floor, flung her clothing after it, emptied a toiletries case to the bed, showering the coverlet with powder.

In time she'd produced the things, and they were, as he had feared, an opiate.

Amber had never feared him. He'd given her no cause to fear him. That night, she'd had cause. He'd left her to clean up the mess and taken her bottle with him.

She'd pleaded later, begged, made promises. He'd offered one pill. She'd asked for two, which he'd given and watched swallowed.

Tuesday was hell, until Amber bribed Cecelia into a semi-calm with a brown paper-wrapped parcel from Blunt's.

Wednesday began well. Then that newspaper arrived. The day ended badly.

Thursday! Norman came from the station at six, afraid to enter the house. And he found Cecelia bathed, calm and clad in a flouncing floral, highly unsuitable for a girl of her years and shape — however he did not voice his opinion.

Jenny's Alice Blue Gown, hurriedly removed in the parlour after the concert, left unhung on the couch, unsighted during the days she'd spent with Maisy, was gone when she arrived home on Thursday evening, no doubt collected by one of the costume ladies and hanging safe in the school cupboard. She thought no more of it until Miss Rose asked her to please return the frock to school on Monday.

She searched Sissy's wardrobe, searched Norman's, wasn't game to search Amber's.

'Daddy, do you know what happened to my Alice Blue Gown? Miss Rose wants it back.'

He didn't know. He too had been searching . . . for Wednesday's *Gazette*. He lifted a finger to his lips and glanced towards the parlour. Amber and Sissy were in there, turning the pages of a catalogue.

At Maisy's house, Jenny had her own bed in Jessie's room. Now she was back to sharing a bed and Sissy could kick like a mule. Then, on the Saturday morning when Jenny went down to the lavatory, when she had a quick look to see if Sissy had thrown Norman's newspaper into the pan, she saw something frilly. It was no longer blue, but it was crepe paper, a crepe paper frill. It didn't bear closer identification but she took a deep breath outside, held her nose and went back for a second look. It was her Alice Blue Gown.

She knew Sissy threw things in that pan when she got in one of her bad moods. She'd thrown books in it, thrown Jenny's kitten poem in — and told her she'd done it too. The newspaper was probably down there.

Didn't want to start Sissy up again now that she'd stopped, like Norman didn't want to start her up, but that dress was the most beautiful thing she'd ever seen. She'd felt special in it, had sung better in it, and Miss Rose wanted it back on Monday.

'I'm telling Miss Rose you threw that costume down the lav, Sissy.'

'I didn't touch your stupid dress.'

'You did so. I saw it.'

'Who looks in lavatory pans?'

'Who knows that you throw things in lavatory pans?'

'Don't you accuse me.'

'You did it because I was in the concert and you weren't.'

'As if I care, you evil little stray.'

'You were jealous that everyone couldn't see your daffodil dress.'

'I don't even like yellow, and as if I'd ever be jealous of you.'

As if she would. She had everything. She had three new dresses now, the yellow, the pretty frilly floral and a green and beige print. And she'd even got her own way about leaving school. She had no reason for jealousy.

Jenny was jealous of those three dresses. She loved pretty things and Norman only ever bought plain dark-coloured dresses. Having a mother had changed everything. It had changed Norman. It even changed Christmas.

They always had Christmas dinner with Gertrude and Joey and Elsie, but because Amber wouldn't go, Sissy wouldn't go, so Norman didn't go.

It was the worst Christmas ever. Amber roasted a leg of lamb and Jenny could smell it roasting for hours, then Amber stood at the table slicing into it with her fine-bladed carving knife, and she must have forgotten Jenny didn't eat lambs because she gave her two fat slices. Norman removed them to his plate. He swapped the lamb for some of his vegetables, which tasted of lamb. And the Christmas pudding wasn't the same as Granny's and had no threepences in it, and there was no Joey to giggle with, no funny presents. It was like Christmas didn't come that year. It was like Norman wasn't Norman that year and Sissy wasn't Sissy. She didn't look like Sissy in her frilly floral, with her hair a mass of waves, and lipstick even, and new shoes.

Norman said that sisters must love each other, but sisterly love wasn't easy in a shared bed. And those three pretty dresses hanging in the wardrobe didn't make it easier, or the costume in the lavatory.

The Bible said to love your mother and father. Loving her father had always been easy. She loved his big, soft, puppy-dog eyes, his chubby face, his voice, which could make the most boring story sound a bit interesting. Until Amber came home, Jenny had found no fault in Norman, and with only his example to follow, she'd patterned her behaviour on his. She walked away from unpleasantness, did unto others as she would have them do unto her, forgave Sissy her trespasses — or most of them. Until Amber came home, Jenny had been well on her way to becoming a female Norman, a pacifist, ill equipped to handle the more unpleasant aspects of life.

There are significant moments in every life, moments when had we walked a different path, turned a different corner, caught a different train, we may have found an alternative future. If Miss Rose had chosen a different song, if that froth of blue frills hadn't seemingly materialised five minutes before Jenny had to walk on stage that night, if she had never heard of Cinderella and fairy godmothers, if she hadn't glanced into the lavatory pan . . .

Life happens. Perspectives alter. Age wearies and disappointments weigh heavily.

Jenny's tenth birthday should have been a disappointment. She'd thought Amber might give her a pretty dress. She didn't. Norman gave her a present that felt like a book and turned out to be a Bible; a very nice Bible with a white leather cover, but nonetheless a Bible and there were already three of them in the house, and the words in one were the same as in another. She'd thought Granny might come to the house, but she didn't. She'd given Norman her present: a pretty dressing gown, which Jenny thought might have been a dress until she got it unwrapped. Joey gave her a baby yabby in a jam jar, which she was only allowed to keep until after lunch, then she had to take it down to the creek and let it go. Then something happened which made it the best birthday she'd ever had.

Mr Denham called her over to his fence. She'd given him the pendant the old swagman had found in the park and told him she'd found it, because kids weren't allowed to take things from strangers or even talk to them.

'Finders keepers,' Constable Denham said.

'I didn't . . .'

Couldn't tell him now that the old swaggie with the Father Christmas beard had found it; anyway, he was long gone. That was what swagmen did. They walked into town, then walked out, and no one knew where they came from or who they were. Some stayed a day or two under the bridge, some camped in the shed beside the sports oval, but Denham didn't allow any to become comfortable.

'You did the right thing by handing it in, Jennifer,' he said and he dropped it into her hand.

She ran back across the road with her treasure, and it was hers. An old swagman wouldn't want it. She ran inside with it, into the kitchen, where they crowded around her, admiring her treasure.

Norman said it was very old and made of real gold, that the pearl within its ball of gold would be a real pearl, made by an oyster in the ocean. Then he claimed it, to put away until she was old enough to appreciate it.

Sissy was already old enough to appreciate it. She wanted to wear it to the pictures on Saturday night. She stamped her feet for it, so Norman told her she could stay home from the pictures. Margaret and Jimmy Hooper were calling for her; she couldn't even scream or they'd hear her. She vented her frustration in bed that night, by sprawling over three-quarters of it.

'Move over, Sissy.'

'Go to hell,' Sissy hissed and kicked.

'I'm sick, sick, sick of sleeping with you. Get over your own side or I'm calling Daddy.'

Sissy kicked again, Jenny retaliated with her heel. Sissy belted her with her forearm, so Jenny grabbed a handful of her hair.

Norman's room was a wall away. He opened their door. 'This is not fitting behaviour for young ladies. Apologise to each other.'

'She started it.'

'You started it. You kicked me because you weren't allowed to wear my necklace to the pictures.'

'It's not your necklace —'

'It will be claimed,' Norman said.

'Mr Denham said it would have been already, and finders keepers,' Jenny said.

'You probably pinched it from someone anyway,' Sissy said.

'Then why did I hand it in?'

'Apologise, Cecelia. Apologise to each other.'

They apologised, but didn't mean it. He went back to bed. Sissy wanted the last hit. It wasn't much of a hit, but tonight

Jenny wasn't going to let her win. Even a dyed-in-the-wool pacifist will take up arms to fight for what she believes is a just cause. That Alice Blue Gown was such a cause, and probably the *Gazette* with her photograph in it; six inches of bed was a just cause too, and that pendant she wasn't allowed to wear until she was old — and everything.

Norman came again. He rolled a blanket into a long sausage and placed it down the centre of the bed. 'Your mother will leave tomorrow. I have had enough of this hoyden behaviour.'

Sissy didn't like that threat. She moved over to her own side of the bed.

Vern Hooper gave Norman respite from decision. He invited Sissy to accompany his family to the beach for a fortnight. Amber didn't want Sissy to go. Norman, always pleased to be rid of that daughter, gave her a five-pound note and told her to behave herself. She left with the Hoopers on the Thursday train, and Jenny had that entire bed to herself for fourteen days.

And she had her mother to herself.

On Friday evening, Norman took up his coin pouch and walked across the road to play poker. By seven thirty, Amber was sitting in the parlour, working on her embroidery, Jenny sitting half a room away, turning the pages of a city catalogue and attempting to think of a way to start a conversation with her mother. If Sissy was home, she would have been sitting beside Amber, showing her things in that catalogue.

Maisy said that Amber was shy with Jenny because she'd left a baby and come home to a big girl. Maisy said that Sissy and Amber had been close before Amber had become unwell. Maisy said that if people made the first move with Amber, she met them halfway. Tonight Jenny was determined to make that first move.

It took a while, but she finally found a page of shoes, some with heels that looked about four inches high; she took the open catalogue to the couch and sat. It was a long couch. She didn't touch Amber, who, so busy with her embroidery, didn't notice Jenny had moved. She sat flipping the pages, like Sissy flipped pages, and when she got back to the shoes, she took a deep breath and said: 'Have you seen people walking in shoes like those, Mummy?'

Amber glanced at the page, then made another stitch. Jenny sat watching that needle diving in and out, in and out, the silk thread following it until the silk grew too short and Amber had to place her embroidery down to rethread the needle. She was aiming that thread at the eye when Jenny reached out a finger to touch, not her mother, but a near-completed silk rose.

'It's like magic,' she said. 'That rose looks as if it would even smell like a rose.'

Amber's hand was shaking. She snipped a little from the thread, moistened it between her lips and lined it up again. This time the thread went through the eye.

'I could thread the next one for you —'

And Amber struck, like a single-fanged snake.

A cat has springs in its legs. In the blink of an eye, a cat can place six feet between itself and danger, then land facing the enemy. Jenny was unaware of how she'd covered the distance between couch and passage, was not immediately aware of the needle stitching her frock to her thigh, or not until she pulled on the dangling maroon thread and pulled the needle out.

The shock of the attack masked the pain, but that needle now on the hall table, her leg stung. She rubbed it, eyes wide with disbelief, mouth open. Her mother wasn't even looking at her, or looking for her needle. She'd found another and was threading it with the same maroon silk.

Jenny lifted her skirt, looked at the bead of blood, wiped it with her finger.

'You're . . . you're a mirage.'

Amber ignored her.

'You're like . . . like mirage water in the desert that looks so real people die of thirst trying to get to it. And they . . . they just . . . end up drinking sand.'

'Bedtime,' Amber said.

Maisy's twins said Amber had gone mad, hadn't got sick. Maisy's twins said . . . But Amber was getting to her feet so Jenny ran. Out the front door, out the gate and down to the post office.

Didn't know why she'd run that way, except there was a light at the window, and the post office door was recessed and dark, a good place to hide and keep watch from. She knew she should have gone to Maisy, but then Norman would have had to leave his game, and it was probably her own fault anyway. She should have stayed away from her, stayed in the kitchen, gone to bed. Granny knew about Amber's invisible *Do not touch* sign. She didn't try to get near her.

She peeped around the recess. Amber wasn't coming, and even if she did come out that gate, Mr Foster was in his office. She could hear a thump, thump, thump, almost like her heartbeat, then his thumping would stop but her heartbeat didn't.

The bottom half of the post office window had been painted so no one could see in, but if she stood on tiptoe she could see a bit through the top window. Keeping close to the wall, she crept down to see what he was thumping.

Mr Foster was a twisted little gnome man, not often seen on the street. Behind the counter, or limping off to the Methodist church, he was always dressed in the same brown suit or maybe he had two suits cut from the same bolt of cloth. The kids at school made fun of him. They copied the way he walked. He wasn't walking tonight, and he wasn't wearing his brown suit either, just a shirt and waistcoat, with gold bracelet-like armbands to make his shirtsleeves short enough. People were more interesting when they didn't know they were being watched, and even more interesting when you could see one small part of that person. She could only see his head, shoulders and arms tonight and he didn't look twisted. And he had a moustache. Had he always had a moustache? He was thumping envelopes with his rubber stamp. Around Christmas and New Year, his pigeonholes were always full of mail.

Shouldn't be spying. It was bad manners to spy on people. She turned again to Maisy's house, hoping Norman would lose all of his threepences fast and come home early. Most Fridays he didn't get home until midnight.

She walked back to the doorstep, felt with her hand for where a dog might have been, then sat. She shouldn't have leaned back, because that door rattled, and when she took her back away from it, it rattled again. Up then, fast. He was coming. He wore a funny brown boot with a six-inch sole and heel that made him clunk when he walked. Always and forever she'd known that sound. Always and forever she'd known that he wasn't dangerous, even if a lot of the kids at school said he was.

She was standing, her back at his verandah post, when he opened the door. 'I'm sorry I disturbed you, Mr Foster.'

'Shouldn't you be in bed, lass?'

'Daddy's playing cards at the Macdonalds'.'

He didn't ask what her mother was doing. She thought he'd ask. And his open door was letting too much light out and it was shining right on her. She moved to the shadows of a tree growing over the fence between Norman's yard and Mr Foster's, and perhaps he saw her peering at her father's house.

'What time are you expecting your father home?'

'Sometimes he comes early.'

The lights were on at the police station. There was a street-light out front of the town hall; it lit the road, lit a pale circle to Norman's gate. And they saw that gate open, saw Amber step out, glance up and down the street.

'Jennifer. Jennifer, I want you inside now,' she called.

Jenny didn't move.

Amber saw her neighbour and approached. Jenny broke cover and ran back to the post office step.

'Good evening, Mrs Morrison,' the postmaster said.

'Get home,' Amber said.

'I'm staying here,' Jenny said, stepping up and into the post office. The little postmaster followed her and stood like a sentry guarding the door.

'Get out of my way, you perversion of nature,' Amber snarled.

'There are perversions, Mrs Morrison, then there are corruptions, and given our history, perhaps we should not stoop to name-calling in front of the child.'

'You like them young, do you? Or just take what you can get, you twisted ape.'

'Twisted ape I may well be, Mrs Morrison, but I was never so wise as my three cousins. When I see evil, when I hear evil, I speak loudly of it.'

He turned to the child who stood behind him, big eyes brimming. 'The constable is still showing a light. Will you walk with me across the road, Jennifer?'

'I want to just stay here with you,' she said.

An unmarried man of his appearance needed to step lightly. He chose not to that night. He closed the door on his neighbour, locked it against her, then took his little visitor down to his sitting room where he poured lemonade and offered fancy biscuits. And he had a wireless. Jenny visited with him until ten thirty, when he walked her home, and waited at the open door until she had ascertained that her mother was sleeping. Once Amber had swallowed her pills, she wouldn't move until morning.

RIPPLES IN THE CREEK

If Mr Foster had one friend in town, it was Jean White. A busy woman, she was, like Norman, on every committee, but still found time most mornings to pop her head into the post office to pass the time of day. He waited for her on the Saturday morning, desperate for her advice on what he ought to do concerning his evening visitors. He was standing at his door at ten fifteen when the Fulton girl ran bawling from the grocery store, dodged Mick Boyle's horse and dray, then ran into the constable's yard. Seconds later, Denham ran ahead of her back to the grocery store. Something was amiss.

Something was very amiss. Jean White was dead, dead behind the counter where, for the past thirty years, she'd spent most of her days. Dead, and nothing anyone could do about it. And Charlie, sitting on the floor, cradling her in his arms and howling.

The Fulton girl ran home bawling. She told Alfred, Jean's son-in-law, who came running, his wife behind him, to find Charlie refusing to release his first love, his only love, and old Charlie White howling was a sight to behold.

Denham closed the store that morning and the town went into shock. Jean White had been in her mid-fifties. She'd never had a day's illness.

Not a soul complained when those twin green doors remained closed on Monday morning; if folk needed sugar, they borrowed from a neighbour. Most in town expected those doors to stay shut until after the funeral.

A big funeral, half the town was there. Half the town saw tough old Charlie looking ten years older than his age and still bawling like a baby, holding on to his hysterical daughter, while Alfred attempted to hold both of them up with his one arm.

A few expected those twin green doors to open on Tuesday. They didn't, and folk who had lent their neighbours a cup of sugar had now run low on it. Tea canisters were empty, and how were you supposed to feed your kids when you had no flour? During these bad times, fried dough filled a lot of kids' bellies. Those on susso were feeling the pinch. They lived from hand to mouth.

Norman was out of butter, and he had a crate of it melting at the station, along with other grocery store stock. He and his station lad walked around the growing pile until more came in on Wednesday, when Norman took it upon himself to knock on Charlie's door, express his concern for the family, and also for the perishables.

Alfred contacted Mick Boyle. He delivered the stock from station to storeroom, and Alfred made the mistake of leaving the front doors open — and was near knocked down in the rush. He knew nothing about groceries. He hadn't paid for a pound of butter since he'd wed, had no idea of the price of a packet of tea. Susso coupons meant nothing to him. He didn't know where his in-laws kept their change drawer.

'If one of you can go and get the Fulton girl, we might be able to serve you,' Alfred said.

Someone got Emma Fulton, who didn't know where Charlie hid his change drawer, but knew the price of things, so they started writing dockets, which began an even greater rush in through those doors. Charlie wasn't known for his charity. Word that he was giving tick got around fast.

Around two that afternoon, Hilda noticed people walking by with full shopping bags. She told Charlie, who told her that the one-armed mug of a man she'd married could burn the bloody place down for all he cared. He could still see Jean lying on the floor behind the counter frothing at the mouth, could still feel the life draining out of her. Stroke, they'd diagnosed, massive stroke, vein burst in the brain, they said. He didn't care what they said. She was gone and he was never again setting foot inside that bloody shop.

'You've got responsibilities to the community, Dad,' Hilda said.

'Bugger the community,' Charlie said and he turned again to stare at the passage wall, watching for shadows. Ten, fifteen, twenty times an hour he saw Jean's shadow walk by to the kitchen, hurry into the bedroom. He knew she was gone, but here, in her house, he kept catching glimpses of her. He could hear her too, not that she said much that would have importance to most, but to him, her voice was a melody.

> 'Charlie, how much did you put on that baking powder?
> What do you feel like for dinner, Charlie?
> Charlie is me darlin', me darlin', me darlin' . . .'

She was out there somewhere, clinging on like hell to the life they'd shared, and maybe waiting for him to come. And he wanted to go to her.

On the Friday evening, while Charlie sat watching shadows, twenty-odd kids were swimming down at the bend behind Clarry Dobson's place. Nelly Abbot was there with her big brothers. The day had been hot and the evening wasn't cooling down. The older kids skylarked, dunking, diving, swinging out over the water on a rope; the younger kids stayed out of their way when they could, and yelled when they couldn't.

Nelly was small for her years but could swim like a fish. She was last seen waiting her turn to swing on the rope. No one noticed whether she'd had her turn or not. No one noticed she was missing until the light was almost gone. The crowd at the creek had thinned out. Her brothers thought she'd walked home with someone. One of the girls said she'd seen her running off into the bush. No lavatory down at the creek but plenty of trees. She'd probably come back, the girl said, though she couldn't say for sure.

'Nelly! You'd better not still be down here, because we're going home,' her brother yelled. They had been told to get home before dark.

The Abbots lived on the north side of the lines, a couple of houses west of the hotel. The boys were home in minutes and Nelly wasn't there.

'Who was she with?' Grace Abbot asked, not too concerned. 'What were you thinking of, letting her walk off by herself?' Ten minutes later and still no sign of Nelly, she was becoming concerned. She walked out to the street. 'Nelly! Nelly!' Kids coming from many directions. Nobody had seen Nelly — not after she'd run off into the bush.

Panic then. 'Get the constable. Go and get your father.'

A dozen men were raised quickly from their parlours, a dozen lanterns lit, a dozen more joined them before they got to the creek.

A pretty sight: lights glowing all along the curve of that creek, lights reflecting in the dark water, though there wasn't much that could be seen by lantern light. Too many clumps of reeds took on the shape of a missing child. And logs too, logs creating ripples as the creek flowed around them.

A hundred searchers, men and women, were down there by ten, shining flashlights into the forest alongside the creek, and that eternal calling, calling.

'Nelly! Nelly!'

Two dozen or more searched through the night, and were thankful for the dawn — and afraid of it, afraid they'd see that red bathing costume.

'She wanted red,' Grace Abbot said. 'It was brand new this year. She could swim like a fish. She could swim when she was two years old. I tell you she wouldn't have drowned.'

The boats were put in the creek at dawn. They concentrated their search downstream from the bend, following its twisted way, following it down one side then pulling hard back up on the other side, prodding around every snag, searching every reed bank. No sign of Nelly.

They looked further afield. A middle-aged swagman had passed through town two days ago. He could have been holed up in that patch of the bush, waiting his chance. The Willama police were in town. Gertrude saw their car drive by, no doubt heading out to Wadi's camp. There were a couple of strangers known to be staying out there with him and his women, living black.

At sundown on that Saturday, Gertrude's tank dry, she harnessed Nugget up to her water carrier — a forty-four-gallon water drum her father had fixed up with a set of wheels and shafts. Joey went with her. Water-getting was an easier task with two, one to pump, the other to stand out on that log keeping the end of the hose in clear water.

They were backing Nugget up to their log when they saw what was beneath it, saw that hair, blonde, long, curling like Jenny's curled.

'Go home, Joey! Run home, darlin', and stay there.'

Joey was staring at what Gertrude had seen. He thought it was Jenny, but it had no face, only blood and flies. Gertrude blocked his view with her body and took his shoulders, turned him away.

'Go home, darlin'. It's that little girl they're searching for. You be a good boy for me now and run home to Elsie. I have to ride in and tell the constable.'

He ran. Gertrude unhitched her pony from the barrel, mounted him bareback, and rode into town.

There were men down near the bridge.

'The constable,' she called, and two or three pointed across the creek. She saw him, helping a group pull a boat out of the water. Over the bridge she rode, down the slope, between the trees. Denham watched her approach.

'She's found,' she said, glancing around for the father, hoping to God that he wasn't in earshot. 'Down near my place.'

'You're upstream,' Denham said.

'She didn't drown.'

She slid from her horse and walked with that pig-faced man back through the trees, spilling out what she'd seen to a man she hadn't spoken to in three years. Some things were bigger than personal feuds.

Her horse had taken himself off for a drink. The garage chap's truck was parked on the far side of the bridge. She drove with him and Denham out along her road, led them down her well-worn track to the creek, pointed to the log behind her water barrel. Didn't want to go nearer. Gertrude had delivered that little girl. She'd delivered the Abbots' first daughter and seen her buried when she'd died of appendicitis. Wanted to go home and hide her head for the shame of all mankind. Didn't want to think of those poor Abbots. Suffering wasn't fairly apportioned in this cruel old world. Some got none of it. Others got the lot.

She was crossing her stretch of road when the first of the walkers came around the curve before her land. Didn't want to speak to them. Didn't want to see Len Abbot amongst them, but he was there. And he didn't need to see what she'd seen.

She walked down to meet them. 'She's been found, Lenny. You go home to your wife now.'

He tried to push by her, but she took his arm and others took his arms. Not a big man, Lenny Abbot, not a young man who could start over. He'd run the town's saddlery; a clever man with leather.

'Take him home, lads,' she said. 'Tomorrow will be time enough to see his little girl. Get him away from here.'

Stood guarding her road and water track until young Mick Boyle and Horrie Bull came to take her place. She went home then, went home where she had no water to waste in washing this terrible day from her. She wasted what was in her bucket, took her washbasin to her room and flung her clothes off, soaped her face, soaped the sweat of what she'd seen from her, got herself clean and into fresh clothes before she spoke to those scared-eyed kids.

'I need you to hold me for a minute, darlin's. Just hold me.'

Elsie served a meal at seven. Gertrude couldn't eat. She put her plate in the oven and took her chair outside, needing to sit in the dark with her thoughts. Strange thoughts darting around her mind tonight: Denham, her horse, Lenny Abbot, Charlie. And Vern too. And where was he when she needed him? Hoped her horse would find his own way home. He knew the way, if someone hadn't taken charge of him. John McPherson might.

He'd been down at the bridge. He could have put him in his paddock. She'd get him in the morning.

A swarm of men over the road now, cars parked alongside her section. Moe Kelly's van was there, and the Willama police car. This was murder, the brutal, terrible murder of a child. This was too big for Woody Creek.

Water. All she had was in her kettle, and what was left in her stone bottle. Her barrel was down at the creek, with her hand pump. Didn't want to go back there, get the water-carrier to fill her tank. Tomorrow's worry.

She sat until the last car drove away, sat slapping mosquitoes. Too dark to see them, too sick at heart to feel their bite — sick at the sickness of mankind. Couldn't get the image of the curly head out of her mind. Couldn't get that first fear that it was Jenny out of her mind — or that dreadful, that terrible, appalling relief that it wasn't.

God help that poor Abbot family. God give them strength.

Elsie and Joey came out to the dark to kiss her goodnight, her beautiful, gentle kids. She held them, kissed their faces.

'You should eat something, Mum.'

'I will, darlin'.'

Maybe she would.

It must have been after nine o'clock when she heard the rattle of someone coming down her track. That got her to her feet. Whoever it was showing a weak light. Couldn't remember if she'd closed her gate or not. Didn't want anyone on her land tonight.

She walked to her chicken-wire gate, then went inside for her rifle. Too many strangers wandering around town these days, and no trust left in her. Couldn't see much, only the swinging light. Relying more on her ears than her sight, she recognised her water barrel, recognised that sloshing sound of a full barrel.

'Who's there?' she called into the dark.

'It's Harry Hall, Mrs Foote.'

She knew his name, had seen him around town this last year or two, had seen him driving George Macdonald around in that truck; but he wasn't of this town, and a terrible murder had been done here, and no man of this town could have done such a thing to that little girl. She knew too that Harry Hall had been living in a hut down behind McPherson's land, fifty or sixty yards from the swimming bend, and whether he'd brought water or not, she didn't want him on her land.

'I appreciate your thought,' she said, dismissing him.

'Can I pump it up to your tank for you, Mrs Foote?'

'I'll manage from here, lad. Thank you.'

Maybe he saw her gun. She could see the shape of him now, but not his face, not his eyes. You needed to see folk's eyes. She stood at a distance, the rifle under her arm. She knew how to use it.

'You'd better be getting off home.'

She felt her full age tonight, her bones hadn't appreciated that mad barebacked ride. One day she'd grow old, and tonight she wanted him off her land before he saw how damn old she was.

'I know where you're coming from, Mrs Foote,' he said. 'I don't blame you. There's a few more in town feeling the same way tonight.' He was carrying a lantern and he lifted it, lit a bit more of himself. 'It will be all right tomorrow. George knows where I was last night.'

'I'll know too then, lad, but I don't know tonight.'

'Of course you don't. I did the wrong thing coming down in the dark. I'll leave you to it then . . . or you can stand there and hold the gun on me while I pump this lot up to your tank.'

'It's loaded,' she said.

'Righto,' he said, and he went about backing the horse up to the tank.

There was a lot of length in him. She stood watching him pump, relieved to know she had water, that she wouldn't need to go down there in the morning. He got the barrel emptied and started leading her horse and barrel back up the track.

'Where are you going?'

'One of these will last you five minutes this weather,' he said.

'One is more than I had. I appreciate your thought —'

'It's as much for me as for you, Mrs Foote. I'm not going home tonight — or not until a few of the hotheads pass out. I may as well be doing something useful.'

'Where were you last night, lad?'

'Having dinner with George and family. We were eating when Denham came knocking. He knows where I was, Mrs Foote. It's just a few with a bit too much in their tanks, that's all. They turned my hut inside out. Might have turned me inside out if I'd been in it.' He stood a while, the horse blowing raspberries. 'I wouldn't lie to you, Mrs Foote. My word is gold. It always has been.'

Her dad used to say that. A man's word is his gold. Maybe she'd said it a time or two herself. He was walking away; her horse seemed to trust him — and he didn't trust everyone. She let him go and took her rifle inside.

She held the hose while he pumped up the second barrel of water and didn't argue when he went back for a third. She was waiting for him in the yard when he returned, waiting with her own lantern to unharness her horse, give him a rub down and a bucket of oats for his labour, and surely that boy deserved no less.

'I've got a meal in there. It could be a bit dried out, but you're welcome to it, lad.'

'I've never yet said no to a free meal, Mrs Foote.'

He washed up at her tank and, like Vern, ducked his head as he came through the door. Like Vern he didn't need to, though had his hair not been flattened by sweat, he might have. In the better light of her kitchen, he looked like a half-starved kid stretched out to breaking point, and one who didn't waste his pennys on haircuts.

She made tea, working quietly. She lifted the plate from her cooling oven, lifted the lid covering it, offered him a knife and fork, then stood watching him eat.

Just a snub-nosed boy, and not a good-looking boy, not by anyone's standards. His hair was a rusty red and he had a plague of freckles. His hands were near as fine as Elsie's, though twice as long. He looked fifteen, but had the world-wise, world-weary way about him of a man three times his age — and the table manners of a duke. Someone had trained that boy.

Joey slept on a single bed down the bottom end of the kitchen. He woke and lay watching Gertrude's late-night visitor but didn't move from his bed. If Elsie was awake, she stayed behind her curtain.

The clock on her mantelpiece told her the time was eleven thirty. It would be near enough to right. She poured him a second cup of tea, then found a brown paper bag and placed a dozen eggs in it.

'I dare say you can use them.'

'They'll feed me for a week, Mrs Foote. Thanks.'

Near twelve when he left, the kerosene in his lantern's bowl topped up, that light shining brighter as he walked up the track.

Monday was a busy day. They were clearing the lunch dishes when three city detectives and Denham arrived at Gertrude's door. Denham introduced her as the town nurse. She was no nurse, but while the truth was being stretched she introduced Elsie as her daughter. The city men, accustomed to foreigners, didn't look twice at Elsie's darker than normal complexion. They wanted to know what she'd seen. Elsie had seen no one, whether she had or not.

Bullockies travelled that road; each day a truck or two drove by; wood cutters walked and rode out from town; swagmen wandered by, and more than a few came to Gertrude's door wanting a bit of boiling water for a cup of tea — a common swagman ploy, offering a billy containing a bare pinch of tea leaves, hoping the woman of the house would add a pinch more and maybe a pinch of sugar. A few had walked away with a treacle sandwich, a few eggs, the tail end of a loaf of bread.

It was common conjecture that Nelly had been killed by one of those wandering men who camped alongside that creek, who Joey sometimes spoke to when he set his few rabbit traps.

He was setting his traps when the city men came. They wanted to speak to him. Gertrude walked them across her goat paddock to the road, where she stood listening for the sound of metal hammering metal. Those traps had long pegs that required securing in the earth. She couldn't hear him hammering and her heartbeat started its own thumpity-thump. She'd seen that little girl's mutilated face. She hadn't wanted Joey going off alone today. But he was a big strong boy for his years, and nobody's fool, and he'd wanted to get a rabbit, and no boy needs to have an old woman's fear planted in his heart.

The older policeman told her while they walked the track alongside the creek that the killer had used a slim-bladed knife, that they'd counted thirty stab wounds to the upper body and throat and eight or ten slash wounds to the face.

'Joey!'

A nine year old wouldn't stand a hope against a madman with a knife, no matter how big and brave he was —

He came from between two trees. It took willpower to stop her hands reaching for him. Instead, she introduced him as her big grandson, and her beautiful grandson dropped his last trap and offered his hand. They shook it, all three of those city men shook it. The hand wasn't offered to Denham. Joey showed the men a wheat bag he'd pulled from the reeds, and maybe the mark of that bag being dragged along the track that followed the creek. There was blood on the bag. The men took it with them when they left.

LIFE GOES ON

Woody Creek had a few minor roads leading out from town but none that would loosely qualify as main roads. If you took the road alongside the railway line and followed it east for fifteen miles, you hit the road to Melbourne. A left-hand turn away from Melbourne took you northeast, and twenty-odd miles further on you came to Willama, a good-sized inland town.

Eighty-odd years ago, old man Monk had claimed land out the other side of town and named his property Three Pines, for the three big Murray pines growing alongside his gate. Two of those trees were dead and Monk's property annexed now to Hooper's land, but the road leading out there had retained the name. Three Pines Road started at the hotel corner, curved down past Hoopers', past Macdonald's mill, around McPherson's bend, over the bridge and out to the better farming land in the district. Bryants were out that way, Don Davis, Hooper and a dozen more.

There was the stock route road, which cut a diagonal out to the Aboriginal mission and continued on into the back end of Willama — a more direct route if you had hooves. Then there was Cemetery Road, which started on the town hall corner, went out past the showground and cemetery, out past Duffy's acre, past a handful of dirt farms and eventually on to some place.

The forest road, Gertrude's road, forked off from the Three Pines Road a few hundred yards east of the bridge, promptly disappearing into the wall of trees that followed the creek, twisting and turning like a snake with a chronic bellyache. That road led out to where most of the logging was done. The bush beyond Gertrude's land was honeycombed by timber tracks.

Charlie White, determined to die and go to where Jean was, had pumped up his bike tyres and pushed off that sunny afternoon, planning to take one of those tracks. They all led to the creek. His aim was to ride until he was too tired to ride any longer, then end his ride in the creek, clinging to his bike, the weight of which should hold him down. He couldn't live without Jean, couldn't grow old without her at his side.

'Think about that poor Abbot family,' his daughter said.

And he'd tried to think about them, but ended up feeling more sorry for himself. Jean's death was yesterday's news, sidelined now by murder.

'Life goes on, Charlie,' his son-in-law said. 'People die, and those left behind just have to make the best of it.'

His bloody son-in-law giving him advice. His bloody son-in-law not taking a scrap of notice of him when he told him to let the shop rot. His bloody son-in-law, who had refused to get in behind that counter these past six years, now suddenly taking a liking to Charlie's white aprons.

So let him have those aprons. Let him have that shop. Charlie wanted to die. For years folk had been telling him he rode that bike like a madman, that he'd come to grief one day. Today was that day.

As he made his right-hand turn off Three Pines Road, Harry Hall, transporting a load of railway sleepers, was making a left-hand turn out of the forest road. They hit head-on and Charlie and his bike took wing.

If there was a thought in Charlie's mind, it was of Jean, waiting out there somewhere to catch him as he flew by. Another man would have died. Another man would have flown headfirst into a tree and knocked his brains out. Fate is a bastard. Charlie landed on his scrawny backside between two trees and slid into a blackberry bush.

Harry expected to find a dead man. He jumped from the truck and ran in the direction he'd seen Charlie fly — and was greeted by accusation.

'You can't do anything properly, can you, you useless yard of pump water?'

Harry untangled him from the blackberry brambles. He got him into the truck, tossed his buckled bike on the back, turned the truck around and drove down to Gertrude, who stopped collecting her eggs and helped get Charlie indoors.

Most of his injuries had been caused by thorns. He'd twisted his ankle, ripped the backside out of his riding shorts, but she could find no broken bones. She bound his ankle, removed a few thorns with her needle, dotted his scratches with iodine, then made him a cup of tea while Harry delivered his load to the station yard, delivered Charlie's bike to the local garage, delivered the news to Charlie's daughter that her father could be a bit late home tonight, then drove again down Gertrude's track.

Charlie was talking, talking and blubbering, Gertrude sitting at his side, holding his hand. Harry sat outside talking to Joey, until Charlie was all talked out. Then he drove him home.

Elsie saw Harry Hall up at the boundary gate mid-week. 'That kid is up to something, Mum,' she said.

Then on the Friday, Joey saw that elongated form back at the gate.

'Go up and see what he wants, Joey,' Elsie said.

'Stay away from him, love,' Gertrude said.

On the Sunday morning, when Gertrude went out early to milk her goats, George Macdonald's truck was backed up to her gate.

'What's he up to?' Elsie said.

There was a good hundred and fifty yards between Gertrude's house and her western boundary, and that gate shielded by a clump of saplings she hadn't got onto cutting down.

'Maybe he's got his eye on one of us,' she said.

She left Elsie giggling and walked up to see what that boy was doing. He was rolling a post off the truck's tray. She watched it drop down, then saw him struggling to drag a rough construction off the tray and not speaking kindly to it while he struggled. His back to her, she crept close before announcing her presence.

'What are you up to, Harry?'

'Oh, you're about already, Mrs Foote. I thought I might get it done while you had a bit of a sleep-in and you'd think the elves had been busy in the night.'

He'd made her a gate from timber off-cuts.

'Whatever possessed you?' she said.

'I couldn't get the flaming thing open when I brought Charlie down here. I thought I'd have to lift the old coot over it and carry him down.'

'There's a knack to it,' she said.

'Face it, Mrs Foote. It's knackered.'

She laughed. It was well and truly knackered, and had been so these past ten years. She'd been meaning to do something about it. She had the money; it was just a case of finding the time. And now he'd done it. And he'd cut her two new gateposts, thicker through than he.

'They're beauties,' she said, rolled one with her foot. 'They'll see me out, love.'

'You're only a chicken, Mrs Foote. I might need a bit of a hand getting them in, though. I think I gave myself a hernia getting them on the truck.'

She lent him a hand. It took longer to get the old gateposts out than it might take to get the new posts in, but they got them out with crowbar and shovel, making the post holes deeper, wider, as they worked. Elsie brought up mugs of tea and toasted egg sandwiches for breakfast. She stayed to watch that first gatepost dropped in, stayed on to watch the dirt rammed down with the back end of the crowbar.

He'd spent his own money on hinges and a latch for the gate, and Gertrude wasn't standing for that.

'I'm paying you for those and for your time, Harry.'

'You'll insult me, Mrs Foote.'

'You'll insult me if you won't let me pay.'

'Righto. Then I'm paying you for my breakfast.'

'I'm paying for those hinges and latch, lad.'

'Righto. Then I'm paying for dinner the other night — and for those eggs.'

Like a pair of two year olds arguing, but working like a pair of men while they argued, and Joey laughing at both of them and Elsie laughing too — and making a joke later.

'Are we going to add lunch onto his bill, Mum?'

They ate greens and corned beef at two, ate a fresh baked loaf of bread between them, then at five that afternoon, they lifted and hung the gate, all four testing its swing, its latch.

'You came down here and measured up for that,' Elsie accused. 'We saw you.'

'I saw you too,' he said and grinned.

Pale blue eyes, stubby red lashes, but something about the way those eyes looked at Elsie. Maybe Gertrude hadn't been too far wrong when she'd said that boy had his eye on one of them.

He ate with them that night then stayed on for a hand of cards. He was telling them how he'd asked Moe Kelly about gate-building when Vern drove in.

'You've got a new gate while I've been gone,' he said.

They laughed and introduced their gate builder.

Vern had travelled home with his family and their guest, but apart from time spent on the train, he'd seen little of them. He'd dropped them off at a rough little weatherboard house bought, sight unseen, at Frankston, where he'd left them to fend for themselves, hoping a bit of discomfort might give them an inkling of what this depression was about, hoping it might be character-building. His character already well built, Vern holed up in a city hotel for those same two weeks, where he'd spent his days talking up Woody Creek timber to whomever he could.

'I've got orders, promises of orders. With a bit of luck I should have the mill back in full production a month from now.'

Irene Palmer, Hooper's maid, took the news of Vern's city trip home to her mother.

'Go around and see him, Tom,' Mrs Palmer said. 'He said he'd keep you in mind when he started hiring again. First in, best dressed.'

Vern took on Tom Palmer, and told him to keep his eye out for four more good men. Word got around fast in Woody Creek. Twenty turned up for those four jobs. Vern took on six.

Then Walter Davies, a Willama mill man from way back, came to town and took a room at the hotel. On his third night in town, he knocked on George Macdonald's door. Some men were down and out; some were down but climbing.

'I've been poking around out at your bush mill, mate. I lost the shirt off my back in '31, but I'd like to have a go at getting that old mill back into business. I'm in touch with a timber yard in Melbourne I used to supply. They're willing to put the money up, take a chance on me. If you're willing to take the same chance, you've got my guarantee that you won't lose on the deal.'

That mill had been rusting, rotting, for five years.

'Go for your life,' George said.

Six more men got work with Davies. It could be a month or more before they started cutting, but until they could, George would fill the timber yard's orders. He took on a couple of extra men.

A few kids returned to school wearing new shoes, a few had a new frock or shorts. Nelly wasn't with them. An inseparable foursome of little girls had become a threesome, and threesomes are uncomfortable when a school desk only holds two. But Nancy Bryant's daughter had come home from Sydney, and Nancy's granddaughter rode her bike into school each day. Mr Curry sat her with Gloria. He sat Jenny with Dora, and not once did he confuse their names.

The city police came and went, and came again, until one day they came no more. Nelly's oldest brother left town. He should have watched his little sister. Ian, the second boy, refused to return to school. Grace Abbot had a nervous breakdown and spent three weeks away at a city hospital, but life went on.

Charlie White hadn't developed a taste for living, but as the alternative meant dying, and he'd found he had no taste for that either, he reclaimed his grocer's aprons and took back his shop.

There was little pleasure in living without Jean, but he took what pleasure he could in baiting his son-in-law.

'You gave old Betty Duffy credit! Any bloody fool in town knows not to give a Duffy credit, you one-handed mug of a man!'

At eight o'clock on the third Monday in February of 1935, the town lifted its collective head and turned to the near forgotten howls of George's and Vern's competing mill hooters. They kept it up for half an hour, neither one prepared to allow the other the final hoot, and women who had once complained of the noise walked out of doors to listen to the fine music, and men who hadn't got lucky with work got up from the breakfast table, stopped milking cows, feeding chooks, to walk down to the corner, hands rubbing unshaven faces, tongues licking dry lips, hope in their eyes, though shading that hope with hands gone soft from lack of labour.

'Unemployment is falling in the cities, falling slow but steady.'

'The building trade is getting things moving.'

'That Davies bloke from Willama has got some big orders they say.'

'I wonder when Mick Boyle will start up.'

'Old Mick is past it and young Mick never was a mill man's bootlace.'

OF MUTUAL NEED

By May, Harry Hall had a permanent invitation to Sunday night tea at Gertrude's house, sharing what they had. They ate a few rabbits. Joey liked trapping, and you had to taste Elsie's rabbit curry to know what a curry was.

Gertrude had little time or aptitude for cooking. These days she rarely peeled a potato. She'd decided she had no aptitude for teaching either, during her first years with Elsie. Hours she'd spent with her, trying to interest her in writing her name and learning her ABC. Then Amber had disappeared and Gertrude had invited Norman and his girls to share their Christmas meal. She hadn't made a Christmas pudding in years, but she'd dug out her old recipe book and, her finger following directions, she and Elsie had rounded up the ingredients. That was the day Elsie saw some sense in knowing how to read. She'd taken a fancy to that recipe book, learning quickly to see the difference between a cup of sugar and a teaspoon of salt. Once Joey was old enough to take an interest in pencil and book, Elsie progressed along with him.

With card-playing, Elsie had never required a good reason for doing it. She and Joey both might have been born with a pack of cards in their hands. Mention a game and they'd drop what they were doing to play. They were playing five hundred on a Sunday night in June when rain started pouring down and hissing onto the stove. Harry smiled when the women rose from the game to place saucepans in strategic places, which stopped the hissing but began the song of the drips.

'Better than some of that music you hear on the wireless,' Harry said.

'What?' Elsie said.

'The music of the drips, Else.' He played his card and the game continued. 'It reminds me of Collingwood,' he said. 'Of playing cards in Collingwood. We used to have a wireless.'

Harry never spoke of his home. He'd talk about the news, the town, the truck, anything other than his family, but he'd opened the door so Gertrude asked her question.

'Are your folk still down there, Harry?'

'Dead,' he said and he played his card.

'Your mum and dad both?'

'And two little brothers. Your turn, Else.'

Elsie wasn't playing. She was staring at him. 'How?'

'Flu,' he said. 'Or that's what killed my little brothers. One was seven, one nine. I was going on twelve. We all got it. Five or six years back.'

He looked at the musical saucepans, looked up at the ceiling, expecting it to start leaking. The rain was thundering on the old tin roof, muffling their voices. Joey had placed his cards face down and gone to the window, expecting the power of the rain to smash through the glass.

'How did your mother die?' Gertrude said.

Harry lifted his eyes to the ceiling, and for an instant she though he wasn't going to reply.

'Killed herself, Mrs Foote. Blamed herself, Dad reckoned, for my little brothers dying — about six months after they died. It's still your turn, Else,' he said.

They were waiting for more. Joey returned to the table, waiting for more. Harry shrugged knowing he'd already let out too much of his private business, but the noise of that rain cancelled his words as they came out, so he set a few more free.

'Dad's eyes had started going wonky on him before Mum died. They got worse afterwards. He reckoned it was the shock of her doing what she'd done that made them worse. We thought they'd get better. He died a year after Mum. It turned out that he

315

had a growth in his head, pressing on his eye nerve. They found out after he was dead.'

He glanced around at the listeners, and Elsie played a card — chose the wrong card. Joey took the trick.

'I've gone and put you off the game,' he said. 'Don't mind me. It's just the rain. It washes off my outer layers, sort of gets under my skin a bit. I'll get going home then.'

'You're not going out in this weather,' Elsie said, as she may have said to Joey.

Harry slept the night on the kitchen floor, and the following morning, between showers, he fixed the leaking chimney. The lead moulded around it where it joined the roof had moved away. He hammered it back where it ought to be, and when skies opened up again, not a drip hissed onto the stove.

'You're a godsend, Harry Hall,' Gertrude said.

'Cut that out now or you'll make me go all coy, Mrs Foote.'

That boy needed a family and she needed that boy. Her shed was dry. Its back corner, currently used as a bathroom, was partially partitioned. A bit of work could make that corner into comfortable enough quarters, or more comfortable than McPherson's hut, and she could see that Harry ate regularly.

She told him he'd be doing her a favour, that he could work for his keep; told him that Joey needed a big brother to teach him things women couldn't teach him. Harry didn't put up much of an argument.

An odd relationship theirs, one of mutual need, mutual respect. Two independent people, a boy who looked sixteen but swore he was going on eighteen, and a woman past sixty, both more accustomed to giving than to receiving. He moved in that day, and a month later had added to the old partition and hammered down a rough floor. There was room enough in the corner of that shed to squeeze in two single beds. They moved Joey's bed out of the kitchen.

An equally odd relationship was developing over Norman's side fence. Jenny hadn't told Mr Foster about Amber's embroidery needle, but somehow he knew. On a Friday night in July, Jenny ran again from Amber, ran out the back door and tumbled over his back fence in the dark — and almost landed on him. He must have been out there listening, but he didn't ask why she was there so she didn't ask why he was standing outside in the dark.

She'd started visiting him on Saturday mornings, and he put her to work stamping Woody Creek's postmark on the envelopes; she stood on a chair behind his counter sorting mail into the alphabetically marked pigeonholes.

The XYZ pigeonhole never received a letter. She watched it for months, then one day played a trick on the little postmaster. She wrote a letter to *Mr Zebra*, signed it *Cara Jeanette Paris*, and sneaked it into the XYZ pigeonhole while Mr Foster wasn't looking. She popped in after school on Monday and the XYZ pigeonhole was empty again. Then, on Saturday morning, while she was filing new mail, she came on a rough-made brown-paper envelope, the stamp cancelled with a horseshoe footprint and the letter addressed to *Miss Cara Jeanette Paris* — in very clumsy Zebra print.

Give an imaginative child an imaginative friend and she'll push it to the limit. Cara and Mr Zebra corresponded weekly for a time.

Give a shy little man a pseudonym to hide behind and he can become a hero. While glancing at an issue of *Methodist Mission's Magazine*, he read of a woman's sorry plight and Mr Bob Zebra was moved to post off a small donation which he asked might be directed to that particular woman. He could afford it. He had few needs and a steady wage.

A week before Christmas, a card arrived from Melbourne addressed to *Mr Bob Zebra*. Had his little assistant not seen it, had her big blue eyes not been stretched to capacity by this magic she'd raised within a pokey little post office, he would have ended the game there. He could not deny those eyes. They opened the envelope together. It was a beautiful card with angels on it, a sheet of writing paper tucked inside.

Dear Mr Zebra,

Thanks to your kindness to a stranger, I am back on my feet once more, and this week I found a position as a copy typist. It is only for three days a week but this could increase if things continue to pick up. My disability restricts many activities, but I enjoy reading, writing letters and making new friends. If you should again find time to put pen to paper, I would be pleased to hear from you.
Best regards, Mary Jolly

Jenny wrote a two-page reply to Mary Jolly, about a brown elf who lived in a house built of letters. *His house smelled like a papery bouquet of all the world* . . . She signed it, *Cara Jeanette Paris.*

That child had magic in her soul and it was rubbing off on the little postmaster. And what harm could be done in posting off her little story? He could see no harm in it at all. He supplied the envelope and stamp; Jenny postmarked it and dropped it into the mail sack to ride the train to Melbourne. Perhaps that was the end of it.

But it wasn't. A week later a letter arrived addressed to *Cara Jeanette Paris.*

My dear Cara,

What a pretty name you have. And how delighted I was to hear that my letter ended up keeping the cruel winds away from that little brown elf. I do hope that he has found a new door for his house . . .

Jenny, now eleven, was finally growing, and far too old to believe in fairies, but still desperate to believe that a few might survive at the bottom of some people's gardens if not in Norman's. A clothes line lived down the bottom of Norman's garden and a lavatory and a few trees that didn't care if they grew or not. Stinging wasps hunted in Norman's garden for soft green spiders to lock in their umbrella-nest jails so their maggots could eat them alive. Fairies would never live there, but they might next door.

The elf's garden is a dark forest of trees and vines all growing happily together, so that purple trumpet flowers bloom on gum trees and orange roses bloom on grape vines and flowers pop up from the weeds wherever they like, though they have never been planted there. It is the safest place in all of the world because a good spell has been cast over it which keeps all evil witches out...

Norman's house smelled safe, smelled of polish and clean and cooking, but it wasn't safe and Amber wasn't safe sometimes. A lot of places that seemed safe weren't. Like Granny's forest wasn't safe, and even the swimming bend. Nelly had thought her big brothers could keep her safe from everything, everyone, but people had to learn to keep themselves safe.

Mr Foster was safe. Mary Jolly was safe. She was like a forever book, a paper friend, and she'd stay safe while she stayed a secret. Whenever a letter came for Cara Jeanette, she read it to Mr Foster then folded it back into its envelope and he put it in a box beneath his counter.

Waiting for Mary's letters could make a week go slowly. Writing back to her could make a Sunday be gone in a wink. Jenny could even write letters to her in her head, in bed at night, and at times make Sissy disappear from that bed.

Once upon a time, to a land called Creaky Woods where fairies once danced and played by moonlight, there came a wicked witch who was jealous of the fairies so she cast a spell over all of the land. No grass grew there, no flowers, and any tree where a fairy might find a hole to live in was quickly eaten by the witch's sharp-toothed monsters who howled and growled all day of hunger . . .

Some nights Sissy refused to disappear.
'Will you stay over your side, Sissy.'
'Shut up your moaning. I'm trying to sleep!'
'Then move over to your side and sleep!'
'I am over my side!'
'You're not. I'm on the edge.'
'Fall off then and go to hell.'

With her hair in rags, the only way Sissy could sleep was face down, sprawled on her stomach like a starfish, arms and legs spread. Jenny was half her size. She didn't need as much bed.

'You take up enough space without your arm and leg taking up my space. Move.'

'It's my bed! I'll sleep how I like in it. Now shut up, or he'll be in here again.'

'I'll yell out louder if you don't move.'

Norman still threatened that Amber would have to leave if their fighting in bed continued. Jenny wanted her to leave. Sissy didn't. She placed her arms beneath her pillow and gave up an inch or two of bed. There was peace for minutes, but her arms weren't comfortable under the pillow. One fell across Jenny's back. She picked it up, threw it back.

'I told you not to touch me!' Sissy snarled.

'You touched me first!'

'As if I'd ever touch you!'

'Well, you did!'

'You're a liar. It's you who is always touching me and waking me up.'

'If I was shipwrecked and you were the only thing floating, I'd sink before I touched you and got your BO all over me,' Jenny said.

That was below the belt. Sissy grabbed a handful of her hair and tried to rip it out, so Jenny grabbed two rag sausages and clung on until one of the rags pulled out.

'You rotten evil little stray dog. Now look what you've done. Mum! Mum!'

She could call all night and Amber wouldn't come. Once she went to bed, she stayed there.

Norman came. He did the old sausage blanket trick, which, once he'd closed the door, lasted for about five seconds. He came back and did the old 'Apologise to your sister'. He always made them apologise.

'She started it,' Sissy said.

'I did not. She pulled my hair first.'

'You didn't have to pull my curl out.'

'You didn't have to pull my hair out by the roots.'

'Apologise to each other,' Norman said.

They had their apologising down to a fine art. They did it together, on the count of three. It meant nothing, but pleased Norman.

'That bit will be straight in the morning, Dad,' Sissy whined.

'If you can stand me touching you, I'll put it back in,' Jenny said.

Sissy could stand anything in the cause of beauty.

Norman turned on the light, though Jenny may have managed in the dark. She'd watched it done a hundred times. He stood at the door watching the operation, watching those deft hands, that mass of dark gold hair, wild after its fight with the pillow. Childhood had started its withdrawal from Jenny's features; the woman stirring within was already showing brief glimpses of her face — though not yet of her shape. Still his skinny, nightgown-clad child, kneeling on the bed behind Sissy, rolling the hair around the rag, then the rag around the hair, tying a bow.

'Now, no more of your squabbling,' he said, plunging the room again into darkness. 'You are sisters. Treat each other with respect.'

He'd always said that. Before Amber had come home, he'd said that, and they'd tried to treat each other with respect. But respect wasn't easy when you shared a bed, when you shared a wardrobe, when every pretty frock in it belonged to Sissy.

Until Amber had come home, Sissy's frocks had looked much the same as Jenny's, and the worst part about that, which Jenny had learnt since she'd started growing, was that Norman had saved all of Sissy's outgrown dresses in a cardboard carton he kept in his bedroom. All of those faded greens, those washed-out navy blues, years and years of them waiting there like a threat for her to grow into.

Until Amber came home, Jenny had believed she had a mother somewhere, that her mother was like Dora Palmer's and Gloria's mother. This year, the year of her growing, was also the year of her knowing. Her mother wasn't like Mrs Palmer or Mrs Bull — and her father wasn't like their fathers either.

Dora Palmer's father called his wife 'love'. She called him 'darl', and when he got his pay, they sat together at the kitchen table putting money into different jars so they could pay the bills.

Norman called Amber 'Mrs Morrison' and she didn't call him anything. Every Friday, he gave her seven and sixpence — which she spent on or gave to Sissy. On Saturday mornings, Norman walked around town paying his weekly bills.

And the bedrooms too. Mr and Mrs Palmer slept in the same room in the same bed. Amber slept alone in the biggest bed in the biggest room. Norman slept in the smallest bed in the junk room, with the relief bag and his carton of Sissy's old clothes and his piles of old newspapers, and the preserving pan, and old vases, and even the chest of drawers where the clean linen lived.

Amber went to church now with Norman, but only since Sissy had joined the choir, which she'd only joined because Margaret Hooper liked to sing and Lorna wouldn't allow her to join the Methodists' choir. Amber sat beside Norman in church and that was as close as she ever got to him.

Mr Palmer crept up on Mrs Palmer sometimes and put his arms around her while she was cooking, kissed her neck sometimes, flicked her with the tea towel, laughed with her. Norman never went into his kitchen if Amber was in there.

At times, Jenny tried to remember what home had been like before Amber had got sick and gone away. She tried to remember seeing Norman ever putting his arms around Amber. Couldn't remember seeing her until that first night at Maisy's house — except for the wedding photograph. She'd always known that bride was her mother, though when she was small, she hadn't noticed how the bride wouldn't look at her. It was weird. Whichever place Jenny stood, Norman's photograph eyes were looking at her but Amber's never did. No matter what angle she stood on, she couldn't make Amber's photograph eyes look directly at her. She wondered if they looked at Sissy.

A third relationship of mutual need had evolved this past year.

During the Hoopers' two-week stay in Frankston, Lorna as snarly as a Tasmanian devil with fleas, Margaret had done as her father had instructed and kept an eye on Sissy Morrison. They'd gone to a local dance on the second Saturday, Jim delighted to accompany them if it meant escaping Lorna for a few hours. He'd sat for most of the evening at Sissy's side. Margaret sat out very few dances, and danced three times with Arthur Hogan, who, it turned out, was a builder from Willama. He and his father took work where they could get it. They'd taken jobs in Frankston. He'd spoken of the Willama Catholic Ball, held the first week in July, had suggested he may be there. She'd said she may see him there.

In June of 1935, Margaret saw an advertisement for the Willama Ball and she wanted to go. Perhaps Arthur Hogan might be there. When they were girls in Melbourne, Lorna had, on rare occasions, been coerced into accompanying her to balls. Not this year. Margaret walked around to Norman's house and asked Sissy to accompany her.

Sissy received few invitations. She said yes.

Norman said no. He told her she was too young to be attending balls, that she was not travelling to Willama by night. He told her that ballgowns cost money, that the railway department did not pay their stationmasters sufficient to supply ballgowns for sixteen-year-old girls. For two days he said no, but Sissy won. She always won.

She and Margaret chose the fabric, the style. Miss Blunt took her measurements. She and Margaret chose the shoes, with heels, and Sissy needed high heels like a rooster needs a pond. She was Gertrude's height, which in combination with the Duckworth hips, legs and ankles wasn't good. But Margaret wore high heels so Sissy wanted heels.

The entire house revolved around Sissy on the day of her first ball. Amber spent an hour on her hair. She powdered her freckles, painted her lips. Her eyebrows, plucked fine, were shaped with an eyebrow pencil, her eyes made larger with the same pencil. Then the gown was on, a green taffeta with a frill around the shoulders and a waist that would barely do up — and when it was done up, the gathered skirt made Sissy's backside look the size of a barn door.

Margaret Hooper arrived at seven, flushed and clad in frilly pink. Her backside wasn't as broad as Sissy's, but stuck out like an old-fashioned bustle.

Jim was driving them to Willama. He'd been driving since he was twelve. Half-boy, half-man, too tall and skinny, his front teeth rotting. Tonight, fashion or Margaret had decreed that his normally wiry hair should be parted in the centre and slicked down with grease. Nature knew best. His ears stuck out like car doors.

'G'day,' Jenny said.

'G'day,' he said.

'Have you got a licence for driving now?'

'No, but Margaret has.'

'Is she driving?'

'She can't — much.'

Jenny watched them walk out to the car, already planning her next letter to Mary Jolly. It was about a stick insect clad in a brand new dinner suit, who was escorting a plump little ladybird and a well-fed caterpillar to the ball. That poor green caterpillar attempting to walk upright on its back legs in high heels. It didn't look comfortable.

BIRTHS AND MARRIAGES

Lorna Hooper's mother had been the tight-laced daughter of an Englishman who had renounced her spinsterhood at twenty-nine and died of marriage before her fortieth birthday. Her blood ran true in Lorna.

Margaret's mother, the nineteen-year-old scatterbrained daughter of an illiterate farm labourer had enjoyed her first roll in the hay on her twelfth birthday. Her blood, somewhat diluted by an unknown party, a good Methodist education and being joined at the elbow to Lorna for twenty-six years, had modified Margaret's behaviour, but by July's end the sisters had come to a sad impasse.

Blame Arthur Hogan, the young carpenter from Willama who Vern was now encouraging. He'd given him and his father the job of converting one of the back bedrooms into a modern bathroom.

Lorna did not tolerate fools gladly and her sister was making a fool of herself over a roughshod navvy. She gave her the silent treatment, which on previous occasions had concerned Margaret dreadfully. Not this time.

Arthur Hogan had some talent as a pianist. He wanted Margaret to sing at the adults' concert in August. She agreed to, if he played the accompaniment.

Vern booked three seats and told Lorna she was attending. She, more or less, told him where he could stick one of his tickets. He asked her if she'd like to spend the rest of the winter out at the farm where they were cracking ice on washbasins before they could wash their faces in the morning.

August was starting out to be a cold month at Vern Hooper's house.

Fog covered Gertrude's land. She was looking out across her goat paddock, looking for her kids who had walked off into that fog over an hour ago to check their rabbit traps, when she saw a bulky shape moving slowly towards her. It looked too bulky to be one of her own, unless one was carrying the other. She walked out to the fence to meet them, and recognised Mini, a middle-aged, near full-blood black, one of Wadi's women. The bulk was not all her own. She had a baby clinging to her back like a monkey and another one, hessian bag-wrapped, in her arms.

'Them dyin' soon, missus,' she said, offering the baby, sliding a yellow-haired boy to the ground. He was naked from the waist down, and on a morning that would freeze the extremities off a marble statue. 'You give 'em Elsie, missus.'

'You give 'em to the mission feller, Mini.'

'Lucy bin comin' wid some white fella, missus. She say she comin' back soon and she not comin'. They bin dyin' tamorra.'

Gertrude looked down at what she held. The baby's eyes were glued shut by infection, its face encrusted, and if it weighed six pound, she'd eat her hat. It would be dying tomorrow if something wasn't done fast. She turned to the boy, shuddering so hard to keep warm, his little teeth were rattling.

'Pick him up before his feet freeze off.'

Mini had done what she'd come to do. She was backing away. 'Them you fellers, missus. White fellers. Wadi done like them white fellers.'

'That one's a blue feller,' Gertrude said. The boy was blue from the ears down. 'Pick him up. You bring him to my house.'

Mini wanted to be gone. She pushed him towards Gertrude, but, too cold to move, he sat and shuddered.

'Bring him to the house and get some tucker for Wadi,' Gertrude said, turning away and walking fast back to the house.

Inside, she opened her oven door and placed the bundle on the floor before the stove where the heat might start the thaw.

She'd left a blanket on her cane couch last night. She snatched it and went out to retrieve the other one.

Mini wanted that tucker for Wadi. She'd brought the boy. Gertrude got the blanket around him, then led Mini around the side to her chimney. It got as hot as hell at times, and even this morning was offering good warmth.

'Wait,' she said.

She found an unopened bag of oatmeal, poured a cup of sugar into a brown paper bag, a few cups of flour into another. She reached for a cane basket she could live without, tossed in a few potatoes, a few oranges, a dozen eggs, then exchanged the basket for the boy. Mini took off, with the blanket, walking faster without her load, no shoes on her feet.

'How the hell do they survive?' Gertrude said.

The boy felt like ice in her arms. She carried him into the warmth of her kitchen, closed her door, then set him down. He danced on blue feet, until he saw the baby. Knew they belonged together, and ran to it, squatted beside it, his mouth open in a scream but no scream coming out.

She had to get them clean. She had to get them warm. Wished those kids hadn't gone out rabbiting.

There was a small tin tub in her shed. She ran for it, set it on her table, poured in a bucket of cold water, added enough hot from her kettle to warm it, found soap, a piece of sheeting for a washcloth, a towel, then tackled the baby. She removed the sack it was wrapped in, removed a jacket that might have once been white, and got it into the warm water, got it soaped, washed its poor little face, its fluff of yellow hair, shook her head over its emaciated limbs as she wrapped it in a towel and placed it back on the floor.

The boy she'd last seen taking off into her bedroom. He'd gone under the bed. She got hold of a leg, got him out, fought the few rags off him, added a dash more hot water, then lifted him into the tub. His eyes were damn near glued shut, but there was nothing wrong with his vocal cords.

'I'm not murdering you, darlin'. I'm being cruel to be kind,' she soothed.

He didn't believe her and she couldn't blame him. Water went everywhere, and a fighting two year old, slippery with soap, is hard to hold. He turned the tub over, and went overboard with the water, but she caught him and, clean or not, called him clean enough and immobilised him in the straitjacket of a sheet while checking his head for lice.

'I think you're too cold for them to live on, darlin',' she said, finding no sign of lice.

Holding him then with one arm, working with the other, she poured milk into a saucepan, stirred in a good measure of sugar, warmed it, then poured half a mug full, offering it to the boy while his arms were imprisoned.

He spilled a bit before he got the taste, then he stopped screaming, stopped fighting and spilled no more. She offered a biscuit. His eyes told her he wanted it. She sat him on her cane couch, released his arms and handed him two biscuits, needing him occupied while she had a good look at that baby. He watched her every move, but knew what to do with biscuits.

Warmth may have anaesthetised the baby. She tried spooning milk into it, with little success. It was the weight of a newborn but the length of a four month old, a girl. She pinned a square of sheeting onto her scrawny little backside, wrapped her in one of Elsie's old sweaters and made her a bed in a cardboard carton she placed close to the stove.

Two more biscuits offered, and she went in search of something she might use to clothe the boy. Found one of Joey's outgrown sweaters. It would have to do. The boy looked to be around two years old. He liked her biscuits, but he wasn't having her handling him. She gave up on clothing and offered the last of the warmed milk. He downed it fast and looked for more. She was pouring more into the saucepan when the kids came in.

'We got six pair,' Joey greeted her.

'And a wild cat, Mum, and you should have seen —' Elsie silenced as she sighted Gertrude's catch. 'What?'

'Mini brought them in an hour back. She says they're Lucy's.'

'Mini seen her? Where?'

'From what I could gather, she left them at the camp a while ago and said she'd be back. I don't know how long they were out there, but long enough to get into a state. We'll get them out to the mission tomorrow.'

'She'll come back, Mum.'

'She might.'

The babies stole that day. Maybe Elsie looked like her sister — the boy didn't mind her getting that sweater on him. He let her roll the sleeves back and find his little hands. He needed those hands for biscuits. The sweater reached his knees, which was as well. They had no pants small enough to stay up on him. They tried him with a pair of socks, which he studied for a time before pulling them off.

Elsie found an old teat. It was perished, but they eased it over the neck of a bottle, and here was one baby who wasn't fussy. She sucked, watching Elsie with one blue eye while Gertrude attempted to bathe the other eye open.

'Did Mini say where she been, Mum? Lucy.'

'With some white chap, she said.'

Harry and Joey had been attending to their catch. They came in with two pairs of dressed rabbits. They'd sell the rest.

'You've got a sister, Else?' Harry said.

'A long time back, I did. She'll come back for 'em, Mum.'

'She might too, darlin', and if she does, she might leave these poor little mites someplace worse next time. I'll get Vern to take them out to the mission in the morning. They'll be safe there.'

The babies slept with Elsie that night, and the following morning Harry drove her out to Wadi's camp where they learned little other than the babies' names. The boy was Lenny, the girl may have been a Jeany, Joany or Janey. Elsie settled for Joany and they slept a second night in her bed.

The following morning, a not so foggy morning, Gertrude was milking her goats when Harry came out to lean on a fencepost.

'Me and Elsie are thinking about getting married, Mrs Foote. I hope you'd be all right with that.'

'I would not be all right with it, my lad, and you're doing no such damn fool thing.'

'Any good reason why not?'

He'd chosen his time well, while she was occupied. 'Because you're only a boy! That's why not!'

'Folk have been telling me that for what seems like half a lifetime. I've been pretty much ignoring them lately. Have you got something else?'

'You don't know what marriage is about, now stop your nonsense. You're upsetting the goat.'

Accustomed to more gentle hands, the nanny decided she'd given enough. Gertrude steadied her, steadied her hands, put her head down and squirted.

'Else wants to raise her sister's babies.'

'There's more to raising babies than wanting to. Go away, Harry. I'm trying to milk.'

'What's going to happen to them?'

'I'll speak to Vern when I go into town. He'll take them out to the mission.'

'Else doesn't like the idea of that.'

'A boy of eighteen doesn't suddenly decide to get married so he can raise his friend's niece and nephew.'

'I know what I'm doing, Mrs Foote.'

'It's an impulse, Harry. Things are picking up in the city. You'll want to go back there one of these days and that little girl has had enough hurt in her life.'

'I can't promise she won't ever get hurt, but you've got my word on it that I won't be doing the hurting — and as for going back to the city, as far as I'm concerned, that's the place that took my family. Here, this place, this land, is where I got them back — and I don't plan on losing any one of you, or on Else losing those little nippers either.'

'You'll have your own kids if you wed —'

'So we get a head start.'

'What if Lucy comes back wanting them?'

'She won't get a second chance at killing them,' he said.

'Where are you going to live?'

'There's empty houses in town.'

'Harry, Harry, Harry, don't force me to say this —'

'I know what you're going to say. There'll be a few who won't rent to us, a few more who won't want us living next door.'

'Her colour will hold you back all of your life!' She passed the bucket over the fence. 'Those two little mites might look white to you and me, but they won't be white to folk in town — and nor will your own if you wed Elsie.'

'You're talking to the wrong bloke about colouring, Mrs Foote. I never did see a lot of good in red hair and freckles.' He looked at the depth of milk in the bucket. 'Reckon you've got enough in here to fill up those little tykes?'

'How are you going to feed them?'

'Things are picking up. I had four days' driving last week.'

'Will George keep you on?'

'Else's colour shouldn't affect my driving —'

'You know what I mean, Harry!'

'I was making a joke.' He grinned. 'So, do you reckon you might drive in with me this arvo and have a chat to the Metho parson? He's more approachable than that other bloke.'

'You're eighteen. You'll need someone's permission to wed.'

'That's restricted information you wheedled out of me, Mrs Foote, which I'll ask you to keep under your hat. I told George I was eighteen a few years back.'

Elsie Gertrude Foote wed Harold Thomas Hall in the Methodist church on Saturday, 7 September 1935. Harry was decked out in one of Vern's old wedding suits. Elsie wore a gold crepe frock.

The stranger had worn that frock during the latter stages of her pregnancy. Elsie was a tiny slip of a girl, but the altering of it to fit her was a simple matter. It had no waist and no real shape, its only interest, its colour and the thousands of amber, gold and brown beads forming intricate swirls all over the yoke. She looked radiant, as all brides do.

Vern recognised the frock. He drove Elsie, Joey, Gertrude and the two infants into town and stayed on to hear the vows.

Maisy, George and a few of their daughters were there. They looked after the babies. Clarry Dobson worked with Harry; he'd brought his wife along. Dora Palmer and Jenny were there, Jenny clinging to a cheque for five pounds, a wedding gift from Norman who didn't attend. Maisy and George gave the newly-weds a ten-pound note. Vern gave them his old bed and a pair of new sheets and blankets to put on it. The Dobsons gave them a pretty china bowl.

John McPherson's camera trapped the bride and groom posed beneath a tree in front of the church. It would never be his best work, only another page in his pictorial history of Woody Creek, but an integral page: long, skinny, freckle-faced Harry looking as if his white collar was about to choke him, and pretty little Elsie, eyes down, embarrassed by the camera's attention.

By midday that gold crepe frock was back in Gertrude's trunk, Vern's old bed was set up in the partitioned-off corner of the shed, Joey moved back into the lean-to bed, and once again a single bed was set up down the bottom end of the kitchen for the babies.

Vern had assisted with the lifting. He stayed on to nag.

'You'll be overrun by them in a few years' time.'

'I always wanted a big family.'

'What about your family in town?'

'I never see any of them.'

'Then move in and see them. Your granddaughter spends half her life at my place.'

'And you're hoping that by me being there you'll get rid of her?' Gertrude said. Sissy didn't speak to her grandmother. 'If you'd stop attempting to control the world, life might work out more the way you want it to.' She'd been considering making the move. Mealtimes were bedlam in her kitchen.

Vern had harboured hopes of marrying Margaret off, but the bathroom now completed, Arthur Hogan's ardour seemed to have cooled. Vern did the wrong thing and decided to invite him to Margaret's birthday party. She didn't want him there. She'd be turning twenty-seven and she'd told Arthur she was twenty-two. Vern invited him anyway, invited Gertrude, and Sissy, two women from the church choir and their husbands, Denham and his wife, two of the Macdonald girls — which was his biggest mistake. They were man-hungry, and younger than Margaret.

All was going quite well until ten o'clock, when Margaret scuttled off to the kitchen, her eyes blue fish grown too large for their fish bowls spilling water. The Macdonald girls had Arthur Hogan bailed up in a corner, and he didn't look unhappy to be there.

Gertrude moved in to separate them — and ended up discussing house extensions. Vern had to move in to separate them.

'With timber costing what it does these days, it's usually cheaper to start from scratch,' Hogan said. Then he gave her a rough figure on a two-bedroomed house he and his father were building in Willama. 'It's nothing fancy,' he said.

Gertrude had received close to five hundred pounds from Archie's estate, and to date had spent a little over a hundred.

'Seventy?'

'Give or take,' he said. 'It's just a house. And I'd have to see the site.'

Sissy sat watching her grandmother, eyeing her blouse and wanting it. Wanting her black suit too, wanting her figure, her legs, shoes, wanting to be able to talk to people like her grandmother could talk to them.

She wasn't enjoying the party. No one was talking to her. The only good thing about it was watching Irene Palmer in her maid's uniform, bringing food in and carrying empty plates out, which was hilarious. She brought in a plate of cream-filled pastries with chocolate icing on top and strawberry jam in the middle. Sissy took one and wanted another, but the rest disappeared in seconds. Irene brought out a plate of jam tarts and they all went before she could get one.

Wanted to go home, but couldn't walk in her high heels. Vern had told Norman he'd drive her home before twelve, which was hours away. Watched her grandmother's glass filled with wine. It wasn't fair, everyone laughing and drinking wine while she drank cordial.

Margaret hadn't come back. Sissy didn't know if she liked Margaret or not, but she was handy, so she went off to find her. Saw her in the kitchen with Irene and the housekeeper, Sissy wasn't going in there, so she walked down to have a look at their bathroom, which she'd seen in its various stages though not since it was finished and the mess cleaned up. It took her breath away. It was tiled and had two dainty taps feeding into a shining white handbasin and two more over a matching bath. She tried the two taps over the basin and hot water came out of one like at the hotel they'd stayed at in Sydney. And there was a door where there had previously been no door. She opened it, expecting a cupboard but finding an indoor lavatory.

'Oh, you lucky dogs,' she breathed, wanting it, wanting that china bowl, the contoured wooden seat, the tiled walls and floor — and wanting Irene Palmer to keep it clean too. She ran her hand over the seat, down the tiles.

It wasn't fair how the Hoopers could have exactly what they wanted when Sissy had to crawl for a pair of shoes. A stationmaster's daughter had to learn to trim her sails to the available cloth, her father said every time she needed something. And she didn't want to trim her sails. She wanted to stay in Sydney hotels, wanted to go to balls, shop in Melbourne for ballgowns like Margaret shopped in Melbourne for ballgowns.

Couldn't have anything. Couldn't even have her own room, her own bed, or not since her mother had come home . . . though until she'd come home, she'd had nothing at all.

She'd been to two balls with Margaret Hooper, who had four ballgowns. Sissy had one. Nothing was fair. Margaret Hooper bathed in that bath, washed her face at that basin, peed into porcelain.

'You lucky dog.'

Sissy lifted her floral skirt and did what Margaret did, then reached to pull the chain. Loved watching that rush of water. It made a noise, though. She hoped they wouldn't hear it in the sitting room. The pipes hummed while refilling the cistern. She stood listening to the hum, dreaming of Irene Palmer scrubbing the seat she'd sat on, her hands deep down in that bowl, scrubbing off all of the . . .

'Missed a spot there, Palmer,' she whispered.

She never could stand Irene Palmer, who was less than a year older than Sissy but had been three grades ahead at school.

'And look at her now. She's the maid and I'm the guest.'

She checked her face, her lipstick, looked at her frock and her stocking seams, which would never stay straight. Wished she had slim legs like her grandmother, wished she had that black suit and striped blouse. Amber said she could get slim if she watched what she ate; the only trouble with that was she liked eating.

She applied more lipstick, washed her hands and dried them on a small hand towel folded on a shelf beside the basin. Amber's rule was to put things back where you found them. Lorna and Margaret left things for the maids to pick up.

'Pick it up, Palmer,' she said, dropping the towel to the floor.

With a final glance in the mirror, she walked down the passage and back to the party — though she didn't get that far. Lorna, Vern and Gertrude had escaped to the small sitting room. The wireless was in there. She walked in and stood a while listening, until she saw Jimmy hiding in the room next door. She went in to hide a while with him.

Two walls were lined with books, the other walls had new wallpaper. It looked so rich, and the carpet looked rich and the fancy light fitting. Jimmy, sitting on a big leather chair, reading, ruined the picture.

But he was a part of that picture too, and everyone said he'd get everything when Vern died, even this house, which had belonged to his mother's first husband anyway.

Girls had to marry someone. Look what Margaret Hooper wanted to marry — a common navvy. Two of Maisy's daughters were already married. Even Gertrude's darkie had got married.

She eyed him, held his eyes when he looked back.

'What's up?' he said.

'Nothing,' she said, perching on the arm of his chair. 'What are you reading, Jimmy?'

Everyone had to marry someone, so why not marry someone who was going to be rich one day.

OF CABBAGES AND KINGS

A crazy year 1936, a year of royal upheaval. On 20 January, old King George died, and it seemed to Jenny that no sooner had the new stamps and coins been issued displaying young King Edward's profile than they were gone, the year was gone and King Edward was gone. For love of a divorced woman who couldn't ever be a queen, he'd handed the throne of England down to his younger brother, George.

And how would a king feel about getting a hand-me-down throne? Jenny felt sorry for him. She lived in Sissy's hand-me-down dresses, baggy, faded, loathed.

'*Hark the herald angels sing, Mrs Simpson stole our king,*' the Macdonald twins sang in church the week before Christmas. '*Peace on earth and heavens bright, I'd like to be a fly on their wall at night . . .*'

Heads turned, the aged scowling, the young grinning. Jenny didn't need to turn her head to see. She sat in the back row of the choir box, to the right of the pulpit, like the minister, looking down on the congregation; on Margaret Hooper's silver blonde hair and tiny hat perched on top of it, and Sissy's hat and her tan suit, ordered from a city catalogue, with her tan and white striped shirt. The prices were in that catalogue. Jenny knew exactly how much they'd cost.

The second-worst part about growing up was seeing things you knew were wrong and not being able to change them. Sissy made a fool of Norman. Every time she wanted something she crawled around him, called him Daddy, kissed him goodnight, made him cups of tea, then as soon as he wrote his cheque, she ignored him. It was sickening, but more sickening because Norman looked so happy when Sissy was up to her tricks.

The depression had split Woody Creek down the middle, people said, cut it clean into the haves and have-nots. There had always been a rift between Jenny and Sissy, but Amber's return, the needle and the Alice Blue Gown, had turned that rift into a yawning gulch. Jenny stood alone on the far side, in baggy hand-me-downs, Sissy on the other, in nice clothes and with Amber clinging to her back, while Norman attempted to balance one foot on either side of that gulch. And he was splitting himself in half trying.

Jenny glanced at her sister's hair. Amber had done it this morning in an ear-to-ear roll copied from a photograph of a film star. They'd practised for days to get it right. It looked modern. She looked nice from the back. Jenny's hair was tied back in a frizzy weighty bunch. It looked as if she didn't care, and she didn't. Maybe she wanted Norman to see that she didn't care, but he didn't see much of anything now. Maybe he never had. Maybe she'd just thought he had.

She'd shown him the sweat stains under the armpits of Sissy's faded pink frock the first day he'd pulled it out of his carton, and all he'd said was that it had plenty of wear left in it. He'd bought it for Sissy in 1932 after the Sydney Harbour Bridge was opened, after she'd gone up to Sydney with the Hoopers. Sissy was thirteen in 1932, just beginning her Margaret Hooper period. She'd stamped her feet for that pink. It had been the beginning of her sweating period too. Every dress she'd worn around that time was stained and faded under the armpits.

And it wasn't just the stained armpits, which weren't armpits on Jenny. The shoulder seams hung halfway to her elbows, the sleeves flapped around her arms like wings, the waist was a foot too wide and the hem on speaking terms with her socks. She'd never forgive her father for keeping that dress, and she'd never forgive Sissy for the shape she'd been at thirteen, nor for shrinking since Amber had come home, which meant she would never grow out of any of her decent frocks.

Dora had grown early and stopped early. Jenny had caught up to her. She was as tall as Amber, and starting to round out in places, which was the worst part of growing up because it meant that she had to be covered up. That pink dress did the job.

'*Hark the herald angels sing, Mrs Simpson stole our king . . .*' The twins were at it again. They didn't come to church often and were only here today because their nephew was being baptised and there was a party afterwards. Jenny couldn't tell them apart. No one, other than Maisy and their sisters, could, not unless they called one of them Cecil. If it was Bernie, he ignored them; if it was Cecil, he hit them so hard it wasn't a worthwhile exercise finding out which was which. Their sisters used to torment hell out of Cecil, but he'd grown too big now so they called him Macka. George still couldn't tell them apart. He called both of them wild little bastards.

Jenny's mind always wandered in church. It wasn't supposed to. She liked the singing, liked studying the people while they sat heads bowed, liked wondering if their minds wandered and where they wandered to. Sissy was going out to the farm with the Hoopers this afternoon. She didn't like the farm but she liked Hooper picnics.

Once upon a time, Sundays had been Granny days. Norman never went down there now, and since Nelly had been murdered, Jenny didn't want to go there. Even going for a swim gave her knives down her back.

Sundays were bad. There were no trains, so no excuse to go to the station. Norman spent his Sundays trying to stay out of Amber's way. She didn't like newspapers leaving their print on her kitchen table, didn't like newspapers left in her parlour. The verandahs were safe, unless she found him sitting out there with Jenny.

In January of 1937, the train began a daily train service to Melbourne. From Monday to Saturday it passed through Woody Creek at noon and returned at seven in the evening, which meant different working hours for Norman and for the men who connected the flat-bed trucks of timber. Jenny spent her evenings with Norman at the station. He was more himself there, more like he used to be.

Some nights when he came home from playing poker, he was unlike himself, brave — brave enough to cook a midnight supper for two while Amber and Sissy slept. He smelled different on those nights, smelled of bravery and cigarettes and beer. And he was full of words again. He told her about Germany's funny little leader who was doing much for his people, and about a terrible war fought when he was a young man. He told her his eyes had not been strong enough for him to go to war, and had they been strong, he could not have fired a gun at another man.

He became too brave in August, the month of the adults' concert. Last August Sissy had recited in her daffodil yellow frock with two paper daffodils pinned over her ear — she'd recited 'Daffodils'. Amber prompting her from the wings.

And she wanted to recite that poem again this year!

'No,' Norman said.

'Why not?' Sissy said.

'Learn another poem if you wish to take part.' A safe suggestion. She still got stuck on the third verse of 'Daffodils'.

'I like doing "Daffodils".'

'You've had my last word on it, Cecelia.'

'Old Mister Murphy sings the same song every year and no one ever tells him he can't be in the concert.'

'Mr Murphy is an old man who once could sing. The audience is tolerant of his age. Now enough about it.'

'You don't tell Jenny she's not allowed to sing in the school concert, do you?'

'Your sister has a beautiful voice,' he said.

Shouldn't have said that. He knew it, as Jenny knew it, as soon as the words were out of his mouth. He stood, walked away from his meal, Jenny behind him. They went to the station and made a cup of tea there, ate station biscuits.

But Sissy won. She always won.

Her daffodil dress was starched and pressed. Miss Blunt made a new bunch of paper daffodils. Amber stood for hours putting Sissy's hair up in rags. They practised that poem for hours, Sissy came to bed to do her starfish.

'Get over your own side of the bed.'
'I'll do what I like in my own bed.'
'Get over, or I'm yelling out for Dad.'
'Go to hell, you evil-smelling stray bitch!'
'Daddy!'

Jenny walked across to the town hall with Norman. She sat with him. Mr Cox put off the inevitable as long as he could, but eventually Sissy came on stage in her yellow frock with her daffodils. Her hair looked nice. The overall picture was nice enough. Then the nice ended and Jenny and Norman, seated well back, looked at their shoes while Sissy *wandered lonely as a cloud*, and pranced like a cat on a hot tin roof when she sighted *a host of golden daffodils*.

And got no further.

The twins entered from the supper room side, waving bunches of gum leaves.

'*Beside the creek, beneath the trees,*
Sissy is quivering at the knees.
Please, Jim, kiss my drooling mouth,
before you venture way down south . . .'

The audience erupted into giggles and tut-tutting, while Mr Cox, master of ceremonies, pulled the curtains, but the twins stepped through the gap and continued their recitation.

'*Struth, said Jimmy, give me more.*
Open up your golden door . . .'

Constable Denham, sitting with his sourpuss wife and not so starched kids, took off for the stage. A twin went left, one went right, and ten minutes later old Dan Murphy came on stage to sing 'Danny Boy'.

Norman sold the twins one-way tickets to Melbourne on Monday night, pleased to see the back of them. Most in town were pleased to see that pair gone. Most agreed they'd end up hanging before they were much older, but two weeks later they returned and they'd brought some city disease home with them. Maisy put them to bed, fearful of polio. She nursed them for a week, and a week after that wondered why she'd bothered. They got into a fight on the hotel corner and one of the windows was broken.

All mouth, teeth and jaw, the Macdonald twins, no-necked, heavy-shouldered, barrel-chested, no hips, short bandy legs. Built like bulls, some said, but with less between their close-set ears than a bull and a double quota between their legs — so some said. A lot was said about Maisy's boys. One of the Duffy girls told Denham her baby belonged to them. Hard to tell. All babies were born with bandy legs. Maybe its eyes would turn purple, but until they did, there was no way of knowing if it was a Macdonald or not.

ALL HIS WORLDLY GOODS

The last time Gertrude had harnessed her old horse into the cart was the night she'd delivered Sophie Duffy's baby. Nugget, grown old, had grown lame. His age brought her own age home to her. As did Charlie White's son-in-law. She'd delivered Alfred Timms, had watched him march off to war with the other boys. He was a balding middle-aged man now. With her horse lame, Alfred drove down each week to pick up the eggs and deliver her staples. Harry collected any mail she might have, not that many wrote to her. She had no real need to go into town.

In some dark pocket of her heart, she still felt love for her daughter; on a few dark nights, she worried about her, but never during daylight hours. She'd done her best, and her best was all that could be done.

Vern spent his Saturdays with Gertrude — now that her house was again her own. He ate the evening meal with her, sat with her in the moonlight — and went home at dawn.

He gave advice too readily — perhaps a Hooper failing.

'I told you you'd be overrun by them,' he said, eyeing the new house in the goat paddock, a small house, on tall stilts. Elsie had produced a son ten months after the wedding. She was pregnant again.

'I told you I always wanted a big family.'

'Your family is in town, where you ought to be — and your flamin' granddaughter is making sheep's eyes at my fool of a boy.'

'She's built to bear Hoopers,' Gertrude said.

'He hasn't worked out what women are for yet.'

'I've never worked that out myself,' she said. 'What men are for.'

'I'm not having it.'

'I could see a lot worse for both of them.'

'She's got nothing between her ears.'

'Is that the first place men look?'

'I've sent him out to the farm for a month or two.'

'Did he want to go?'

'I don't know what he wants and never did.'

'Talk to him and find out then.'

'I saw her trying to kiss him a few nights back.'

'Are you sure he wasn't trying to kiss her?'

'She was going at him.'

'Unless he was fighting her off, putting a few miles between them won't stop her kissing him — as I seem to recall. Leave them alone, Vern.'

'I'm not having it.'

'Maybe this is the way it was meant to work out, you and me a generation on, our blood mixed in our grandkids.'

'Duckworth and Nicholas blood. She's not you, and he's not me. Lorna is more me. She should have had my grandkids.'

He'd developed a smidgen of respect for Lorna these past months. She was the one who had suggested sending Jim out to the farm. And she couldn't stand Sissy Morrison; they had that in common.

'You need to spend a week or two out at the farm with him and knock a bit of that weight off,' Gertrude said patting his expanding waistline. 'You used to cut a fine figure on horseback.'

'I haven't been on a horse in fifteen years.'

'And look what it's done to you. Your belly is keeping pace with the size of your cars.'

'You're an insulting bugger of a woman tonight, Trude.'

'I'm just speaking the truth. Look at Charlie White. He's still riding that bike like a madman, and not a skerrick of arthritis in him and no sign of a belly.'

'Been giving him the eye, have you?'

Charlie had been at the house when Vern arrived. Since his accident he'd taken to riding down occasionally on fine Saturdays. Gertrude might have preferred his company on rainy Saturdays, but she offered him tea and let him talk about Jean. Charlie had aged ten years in the days after he'd lost his wife, though most would admit he hadn't aged much since.

Age was on Gertrude's mind tonight, her horse's, her own. She needed a bottle of hair dye and had meant to ask Charlie to order some in. He used to say that she and Jean had discovered the fountain of youth in those little bottles. They'd never called it dye. It was their forever-young juice — and Gertrude was overdue for a dose of it. And her eyesight was letting her down lately. Years ago she'd bought herself a pair of glasses for close work. They were next door to useless now. She'd need to get into town the next time the eye chap came up. Vern would drive her in if she asked. He liked her asking. She liked her independence, and for independence sake, she needed a new horse.

'He was a four year old when I bought him. I worked it out the other night that I've had him for twenty years.'

'You've had me longer.'

'True.'

'That's what he used to call you — Tru. I can't hear that word without thinking about that bastard.'

'He called me worse. You might keep your eye out for a horse for me, Vern. I hate being stuck down here, reliant on people.'

'You've had Murph take a look at him?'

'He says there's swelling in his fetlock, that he's too old for it to improve much.'

'I've got swelling in my fetlock.'

'Charlie is fine in the fetlock.'

He kissed her when he left, told her he'd speak to Paul Jenner who might be interested in selling his carthorse. He'd bought Vern's old car.

She watched him drive off, his headlights washing over her land, and she thought of his first car, which he'd refused to drive after dark. A lot had changed in the last ten or so years — cars,

345

her horse. The world had changed. During the twenties she'd delivered most babies born in Woody Creek. Women gave birth in Willama now, or the bulk of them did. The blokes on susso had done a lot of work on that road, built it up where it was low, graded and gravelled it, and, bad times or not, there were more cars around to get those women to Willama. She'd never asked for the job of midwife, didn't miss being called out in the middle of the night. And dyed hair or not, she knew she was getting too old for the job. Her seventieth birthday was only two years away.

Seventy. It sounded ridiculous. Her father had died at seventy-two. Her mother had died a week before she'd turned seventy. At the time, Gertrude had considered them old. It could put fear into her if she thought about it. Not the dying part. The dead were dead and not worrying about much, but the dependence on others before the dying, that's what concerned her. She needed to get on a horse's back again, needed her bottle of forever-young juice to keep old age on the run.

'The best years of my life, these last years,' she told the night as she looked across the paddock to Elsie's house. 'The best — barring Amber.'

She still had three hundred pounds in the post office bank. She had a bunch of kids growing up in her top paddock. She had her accidental daughter, who loved her, and her accidental son too, and she had Joey, her boy, the love of her life.

She'd drawn that boy into the world, raised him as a boy should be raised, and she'd see him to maturity too and be around to meet his sons. Old Grandpa Hooper had sat a horse into his nineties, then dropped dead one day after a good meal. That was the way to live life, take off after dinner, the mind intact.

'I don't need Jenner's old carthorse,' she told the night. 'I'll get myself a young one with a bit of fire in his blood.'

BABY BREASTS

For Jenny's generation there was no shame in hand-me-downs and bare feet, patched trousers and sweaters with more darning in the sleeves than sleeve. There was no shame in borrowing your neighbour's best frock to wear to your daughter's wedding, or in cutting cardboard to slip inside your shoes. So long as you kept your feet on the ground, no one saw that the soles had worn through. This was a depression. People made do.

A few weddings were delayed by the depression. No job, no house, no money for a wedding party. A few were delayed too long. Several Woody Creek brides walked down the aisle with bellies protruding, while their mothers hung their heads in shame.

Not Irene Palmer. She'd been working at Hoopers' for years and her father was in work. Her wedding was an anachronism from the good old days. She wore her mother's wedding gown which transformed Hooper's apron-clad maid into a princess. Her groom's transformation wasn't as complete. Suited or not, Weasel Lewis still looked like a weasel.

Then in October, Emma Fulton married Wally Davis and, not to be outdone by the Palmers, Mrs Fulton had made her the most beautiful bridal gown from a worn-out linen sheet and mosquito netting. She pintucked and embroidered the bodice and sleeves, then embroidered the netting with a silk thread and tiny beads until that bridal veil looked like fairytale lace.

'That woman has learnt to make nothing go a long way,' Gertrude said.

'What some will do for love of a child,' Nancy Bryant said.

The two women turned from the bride to Jenny, clad in washed-out navy and heavy lace-up shoes.

For Jenny's generation, a white wedding was from the storybooks of *Cinderella* and *Snow White*. The last generation had expected white weddings, as might the children now being born, but not this one. The last generation of girls had not been expected to work. They worked now. A business could employ two female workers for near the wage of one male.

Emma Fulton had worked for Charlie White since her fourteenth birthday. Now Sally, her sister, had the job. She was less than a year older than Jenny. Dora could have taken Irene's place as Hoopers' maid. She'd wanted to take it, but her father told her that no more of his daughters would go out slushing for two grown women capable of doing for themselves. Nelly Dobson got the job.

In the years to come, when people spoke of those terrible years of the Great Depression, Vern's daughters would raise their eyebrows in question. Had there been a depression? They were above it, protected from it. No paint peeled from their roof, no pickets fell from their fence, no chook, no cow, defiled their lawn. They sat on their backsides and rang their bell.

In the years to come, when people spoke of the Great Depression, Jenny would speak of Emma Fulton's wedding dress, and Vern's roses that just didn't understand that they should have controlled their blooming. She'd speak of how the town had seemed to lose its raw, red timber stink for a time, and of the swagmen wandering the roads, and of Nelly Abbot too who had probably been murdered by one of those swagmen.

There were men on the move all over Australia, men who'd walked away from wife and family, all they possessed on their backs. City men walked to the country, hoping things might be better up there; country men walked to the city for the same reason. Just changing places, just waiting for the waiting to be over. Depression: a dip; a sinking; a despondency, the dictionary said. Whatever the depression meant to the older generation, those of Jenny's generation knew no other life. They left school at fourteen and got a job if they could. The newspapers might report that unemployment was down to twelve per cent in the city, that the economy was picking up, but the Woody Creek kids saw little evidence of it. A few came to school barefoot, many came shod in cheap canvas shoes you could buy at Blunt's for two bob a pair. They were fashionable and Jenny wanted a pair. Norman said they advertised a family's poverty so she wore leather shoes and wore them out fast. She walked too much, walked each school day between three thirty when school came out, and six each night when Norman went home. Never, never, ever went home until Norman was there. Some afternoons she went to Dora's house, but Dora had jobs to do, and if Jenny went there too often, they'd grow tired of seeing her. She went to Maisy's some days, but not if the twins were home. She went to Blunt's shop to look at the materials, to the post office to talk a while, but no more than once a week. Mrs Palmer had put her off visiting Mr Foster.

'He's an unmarried man, pet. I don't think it's a good idea for you to spent too much time there,' she said.

Since Nelly had died, there'd been a lot of talk about dangerous men who did terrible things to girls. Jenny didn't know what terrible things, didn't know how kids were supposed to tell a dangerous man from one who was safe, or why a married man was safe and an unmarried man wasn't. She knew Mr Foster wasn't dangerous, knew that he was the least dangerous man in Woody Creek. Grown-ups thought they knew things, but they didn't know much. Mothers weren't dangerous — that was what they thought. Jenny stayed away from her mother, and on Friday nights when Norman played poker and Sissy went out somewhere with the Hoopers, Jenny still went over that paling fence to listen to Mr Foster's wireless.

Her daily wandering always ended in the memorial park, on the swings. She loved swinging, eyes closed, listening to the shocked world-ending silence which seemed to enclose Woody Creek once those mill saws stopped screaming. She could think herself into other places on that swing. And when she opened her eyes and swung high enough, she could see the world, or her world. See right into Maisy's backyard, see the station, and Norman as he walked across the station yard to the side gate.

She was looking for Norman when she saw the old swagman, the one who had found that pearl-in-a-cage pendant. She could tell him by his white beard — and he was still wearing his big black coat. He looked like Noah from the Bible. She watched him cross the road, wondering which way he'd walk. And he kept on coming. He was going to walk through the park. Didn't want him to recognise her. He wouldn't, she was only ten when he was last here, but she tucked her chin down, closed her eyes and swung higher, visualising his footsteps and counting them, counting a hundred slow steps before she had a quick peep, then a glance over her shoulder.

He was standing near the bandstand looking at Maisy's house, maybe smelling her dinner cooking. Jenny could smell onions frying. Wondered what the old swaggie would eat tonight, or if he'd eat.

He walked on and she swung, backwards and forwards, the rhythmic motion, the whoosh of air, and nothingness of being nowhere, so peaceful. She let her mind roam where it would on that swing, dreamed of pretty frocks and Melbourne and aeroplanes, while the sun disappeared down behind Charlie's shop to set over the slaughteryards.

She wrote mind letters to Mary Jolly on that swing, and sometimes poems, which were easy with the squeaking song of metal on metal to make the rhyme.

> *Pretty frock hanging, that hands worked hard to make,*
> *Dead cow hanging for tomorrow's steak,*
> *Old swaggie hanging in the showground shed,*
> *Knowing that in Woody Creek he may as well be dead.*

Old Woe-is-me, an ancient swaggie who had wandered the area for months, had been found swinging from a rafter in the showgrounds shed. No one knew his name. No one knew if he'd hanged himself or if someone else had hanged him. Moe Kelly buried him, and Joss Palmer, one of the boys who found him, made a cross for his grave and painted his initials and the date of his death on the crossbeam: *W.I.M. R.I.P. 27-8-37.*

He'd become *Wim Rip* now. Poor old Wim Rip, just another part of Woody Creek folklore, like *J.C. LEFT THIS LIFE 31-12-23.* Just nameless strangers who came to Woody Creek and stayed.

> *Summer has come now, the creek is very low,*
> *Spring birds have gone to wherever they may go,*
> *The tomorrow I dream of, flies so far, so high,*
> *Like it knows that in Woody Creek, it's pie in the sky.*

She swung higher, repeating the words of her poem, memorising it. Backwards and forwards, higher and higher, her eyes closed, and when she whooshed down, it didn't feel like coming down, but going higher still, higher and higher until she was flying.

The old swaggie looked like Noah, but his thoughts weren't biblical. He was watching her from behind the shrubbery at the southernmost section of the park. He'd recognised her. Had recognised that hair. He stood, hands cupped to his mouth, taking the evening air from between the cage of his fingers, taking it in and releasing it in time to the squeak of that swing, his eyes following her arc, watching the push of air meld the light cotton shirt to her breasts.

'Baby breasts,' he said, his words little more than a purr in his throat, then he turned towards the showground. Last night he'd slept in a farm shed. The night before he'd camped down by the creek. Tonight . . . tonight was still a few hours away.

Shadows lengthening though, corellas screeching, a cloud of white flying overhead, protesting the loss of their day and too dumb to know there was always another one, that the sun would rise again tomorrow. He knew. He was like the sun, up and down, but even at his lowest ebb knowing he'd rise again.

He followed the arc of her swing, his head turning from side to side, his tongue creeping from between his lips, almost tasting the scent of pre-woman. She was perfection in rags, her skirt billowing high as her legs flexed and straightened. Backwards and forwards. Heavy chains couldn't hold her to those complaining posts.

'Kick,' he purred. 'Kick yourself free, my beauty.'

A glance over his shoulder. Not a soul moving about. No one to hear him. He glanced left to the town hall, tall and silent tonight. The house to his right was a blaze of lighted windows, and he sighed for watching eyes at windows and for sweet temptations that should have been locked safe indoors at twilight.

A step to his left took him deeper into the shrubbery, then, carefully, he worked his way through half-grown trees, and dense shrubs until he had closed the space between him and his lovely. And when he lifted a branch, just a little, he had his reward. On her downward arc that rag of skirt lifted and he glimpsed the full length of colt-slim legs. It took his breath away.

He moved a little to his right, his breath short, taken in sips of air between his teeth, a whistle of air, but enough. He ought not to be here. Self-control was necessary in this place — but control was so . . . so controlling.

Eyes alert, he stepped around the shrubs. Barely three yards between them now, but his vision blocked by some flowering thing, with thorns, which he discovered when he made a viewing space with his hand. But so close, close enough to see her pretty face. Her cloud of hair swept back by the push of air.

'Flawless.' The word breathed into his hand. 'A bud, waiting to burst open.'

'Jennifer!'

A male voice broke the spell. It jarred him. He had been watching his back, his sides. She was before him, the road before her. He had not been watching the road. A reflex step back almost undid him. Should have gone to the side. Caught his foot on a root and grasped a branch to save his fall. No thorns on that one, but the shrubbery moved, exposing him, and at the top of her arc she saw him.

He had come too close. Her pretty mouth opened.

But what had she seen? An old, old man, old as time, a weary old chap looking for a place to sleep.

At full extension of her swing, she jumped, landed on her feet and ran from him. And he felt her loss.

He stood in the shrubbery watching the swing's disturbed momentum. With no child to guide it, it twisted, barely missing its supporting posts. It would right itself. That was the nature of swings, the nature of all things — just a matter of time and they righted themselves. He watched it slow, watched it steady, watched her join her father on the road, and when they were gone, he walked to the swing to place his palm on the wooden seat where she had sat, seeking the warmth of her left on wood.

'What a pretty thing,' he said. 'What a pretty, pretty thing.'

LIKE WHITE SILK

If not for old Noah, Jenny would never have gone down to Granny's place that Saturday. Since Nelly had been killed, she saw every big tree as a threat, but she'd been down to the bridge to look at the birds, and as she was walking back, she saw Noah limping towards her. One of the Duffy kids had told someone at school that he was her grandmother's old boyfriend, that he stayed out there sometimes. To Jenny he didn't look the type of friend the Duffys might have. He looked too clean.

She knew she shouldn't stare at him, but he intrigued her, or his beard did. It wasn't like most old men's beards. It looked biblical, or elfin, like combed white silk. His hair was as white and silky, and almost as long as his beard. He never took his coat off. It was too big for him, it brushed his boot tops, and today he must have been hot wearing it, but he didn't look as if he felt the heat. Most swaggies looked as if they hadn't washed in years. He looked as if he had a hot bath every morning. Maybe that was where he was going, down to the creek for a wash. Maybe he carried a bar of soap in his coat pocket.

She nicked in behind a tree, determined to watch where he went and to maybe see him take that coat off. She was opposite McPherson's gate, near to where Granny's road forked off from Three Pines. The trees were tall down here, tall and wide. He wouldn't see her. Except he must have seen her nick in behind the tree, because when she popped her head out to see if he'd gone down to the creek, he was standing there spying on her, and only about four yards away.

'Hiding from me, Jennifer?' he said.

Didn't like him knowing her name. It made cold knives run up and down her spine.

'I'm going down to visit my grandmother,' she said.

'Didn't Goldilocks visit with the three bears?' he said.

She took off like a startled cat, cutting a diagonal course through the trees to Granny's road, and when she got to it, she kept on running, straight down its centre, running as fast as her legs would carry her — until a stitch in her side slowed her pace. She didn't stop though, didn't glance back either, just in case he was running behind.

And of course he wasn't; he was as old as Methuselah. He couldn't run if he tried, and now she'd got herself locked onto this road by trees with murderers hiding behind every one of them.

'Stupid.'

Hated this place, hated those trees lined up like prison bars on both sides of the road. Hadn't hated them when she was small. She'd loved them when she'd ridden down here behind Norman. Hadn't hated walking down this road on Christmas mornings either, Sissy lagging behind, complaining that her shoes hurt. Just hated them now, because of Nelly.

Dora knew everything — almost everything. She'd heard her father telling her mother that the murderer had done terrible things to Nelly with a knife, and that she'd been placed in her coffin with a cloth covering her face because if Mrs Abbot had seen what was done to her, she would have lost her mind. She'd lost it anyway, or she had for a little while, so Dora said. Which wasn't a good thing to be thinking about down here. Jenny walked faster, holding her side, hearing her own footsteps on the gravel and hoping they were her own, her eyes darting from one side of the road to the other, seeing movement where there was none.

Everyone said that some wandering stranger had killed Nelly. Noah could have been wandering around Woody Creek back then, and even if he couldn't run, couldn't catch someone who did run, he could be waiting behind a tree to pounce out when she was walking home.

It was her fault. She'd tried to spy on him when she should have walked straight back to town, down the centre of the road, and if he'd said, 'Good afternoon, Jennifer', she should have said, 'Good afternoon'. That was what she should have done. Too late now.

Things had a way of shrinking as people grew. She'd noticed it with the merry-go-round at the park, which had been huge the first time she'd spun on it. Now it wasn't worth riding. Granny's road must have shrunk because it wasn't nearly as far as she remembered. She could already see the track leading down to the boundary gate. A minute later, she was scrambling over it, and safe.

Granny's house looked shrunken, which may have been because there was a second house in her goat paddock, standing too tall, too high off the ground, which was because the creek had flooded in the olden days and floodwaters had covered all of Granny's land. Years and years ago, Granny had told her that.

It was good to be down here now that she was down here, to see those clucking chooks pecking, to see the walnut tree. It was even better seeing Granny.

'Well, my goodness. I knew it was going to be a good day when I woke up this morning,' Gertrude said.

'It's not as far as I remember, Granny.'

A pint-sized boy popped his head from behind Granny. 'Why's her say Granny?'

'That's Jenny, and I'm her granny too,' Gertrude said. 'I was just about to pick a few sticks of rhubarb, darlin'. I won't be a minute.'

They saw Lenny off across the paddock with a bunch of rhubarb larger than he, then they went inside, and it was a fine thing having Granny all to herself, crunching oatmeal biscuits, drinking tea that tasted of goat's milk, which wasn't good, but it was the way Granny's tea had always tasted.

'How is your mum?' Gertrude said.

Jenny didn't feel like answering that one so replied with a question. 'How come you didn't move into the new house and let them live over here?'

'Six of them and one of me, darlin', and if I moved anything, I'd never find it again.'

They laughed, but no doubt it was true. Nothing was ever moved in Gertrude's house. Her frying pan still hung on the same nail, her clock had grown roots in the centre of her mantelpiece, her couch was still beside her washstand, her preserving pan still hanging over the Coolgardie safe, and when she opened that heavy old safe door, that same old stone bottle of water was inside.

The microscope on the table stuck out like a sore toe.

'When did you get that, Granny?'

'It came with your grandfather's things,' Gertrude said.

'It doesn't look that old.'

'I doubt it is, darlin'. I doubt it had been out of its box until Joey started taking it out.'

Jenny stood and moved to the end of the table to place her eye to the glass. Just a blur.

'You need to turn it around so the mirror gets the light.'

'You were sort of divorced from Itchy-foot, weren't you, so how come you still got all of his things?'

Gertrude smiled at Jenny's use of her childish name for Archie Foote. 'I was his legal wife when he died, darlin'.'

'Did you get anything else interesting?'

'Books in the main.'

'She tells Sissy —'

Jenny closed her mouth and fiddled again with the contraption, fiddled until Gertrude took control and got it focused.

'There,' she said. 'Feast your eye on that.'

There was something gruesome in it, something weirdly gruesome. 'It's moving,' she said, springing back. 'What is it?'

'Joey said it was a fly's flea.'

They took turns then, Gertrude adjusting the mirror just a little to bring it into clearer focus.

'It's like some sort of awful beast creeping through a forest.'

'Flies have hairy legs.'

'Are we all crawling with those things?'

'The book that came with the microscope says we are. It's got coloured drawings of all the germs we live with, all different shapes and sizes for different diseases.'

Jenny looked at her hands, expecting to see them crawling with beasts, but that microscope and its captive was addictive. She was drawn back for another look.

'Did Itchy-foot have this to study germs?'

'I suppose he did, darlin'.'

'Did he work in other countries?'

'He spent a lot of time in other countries.'

'She says that you got five hundred pounds from his will. He must have made a lot of money.'

'It was his father's money.'

'Was his father rich?'

'He was a doctor, and comfortable enough.'

'Was Itchy-foot comfortable?'

That wasn't a word Gertrude might have used to describe him. She turned away, hoping to evade more or the same questions.

'Dad does that,' Jenny said. 'When he thinks I shouldn't ask, he walks off to do something important, which isn't important at all. How come you didn't live with . . . with our grandfather?'

Gertrude had never lied to her and didn't want to start. She'd made the mistake of allowing Amber to grow up believing her father was a wonderful man — a big mistake. Maybe she could get away with a mild watering-down of the truth.

'He wasn't a healthy man, darlin',' she said.

'What was wrong with him?'

You name it, Gertrude thought, brushing the soot from her stove and seeking a truth she might tell that was not too severe. Couldn't find one in time.

'He was sick in the head like her, wasn't he?' Jenny said, turning her eye again to the microscope. 'And you're not game to say it, like Dad's not game to say it about her. He pretends to people that she's normal, but she isn't.'

'She's better than she was, darlin'.'

'She must have been pretty bad then.'

'Your dad seems to think —'

'He . . . makes allowances. We must make allowances for those who are less fortunate than we,' Jenny said, in near perfect mimicry of Norman. 'The trouble is, Granny, if you keep on making allowances, one day there's nothing left to allow. Like with sharing your bed. You allow the person you sleep with two-thirds, then sooner or later she wants three-quarters, and one night you roll over and fall out. She's got the lot.'

Gertrude laughed, but learned something. She'd wondered at the sleeping arrangements in that house, had wondered if Norman put up with Amber because of the bed. Apparently not. More could be learned at times by not asking questions. She opened the firebox, poked in a few sticks of wood, then went to her bedroom to fetch the book that had come with the microscope.

'Do germs make people stink of BO?'

'The questions you ask!'

'But do they?'

'I don't know.'

Gertrude was on her knees sorting through Archie's books and not finding the one she was looking for when she heard Jenny's chuckle. Loved that sound. It had never changed.

'What are you giggling about?'

'Nothing. Just the flea on the fly.'

'What's it doing?'

'Nothing.' She giggled again. 'It just . . . it just reminded me of Amber shaving Sissy's hairy legs.'

'That's not nice.'

'She's like Sissy's flea, Granny, always crawling over her, shaving her legs, or plucking her eyebrows, doing her hair — living off her, like a parasite. Sissy doesn't mind most of the time, and when she does, she flicks her off and goes over to the Hoopers'.'

'A beautiful girl deserves a beautiful mind, and those sorts of thoughts don't do yours justice,' Gertrude said, placing a slim book on the table.

'They've got worse thoughts — worse words and actions too. Want to see the parasite's last action?' She didn't wait to see if Gertrude would like it or not, but hitched up her skirt to display a fading blue and yellow inch-wide stripe across the back of her upper thigh. 'She got me with the poker.'

'Your mother?'

'Mrs Morrison.'

'She didn't do that to you!'

'She did so. I didn't know she had the poker or I would have dodged.'

'Did you show your dad?'

'He doesn't know I've got legs yet. And it doesn't matter anyway. I just showed you so you'd know why my mind isn't very beautiful.'

She opened the book. It changed the subject. They removed the fly and flea later and pulled hairs from their heads to stretch side by side on the glass. They shook pollen from a rose and studied that; they watched a smear of blood race like a river.

'This is the only true magic,' Jenny said. 'This is the real fairies at the bottom of the garden, Granny. I think I might be a nurse or a scientist or something when I grow up. Girls can even be doctors now.'

'You'd need a lot of schooling for that.'

'In Melbourne. Which would be good. Gloria Bull goes to school in Melbourne.'

'Since when?'

'Since most of this year. It's sort of strange without her. Like . . . like there used to be four of us. We all started school on the same day, and now there're only two of us left. I'd love to go to school in Melbourne. It's safe down there.'

'Worse things happen in Melbourne than up here, and happen more often,' Gertrude said.

'Yeah, but it's not the same. There are so many people down there so you don't know the ones it happens to. Like, you read about it in the papers and you say, Oh, my goodness, isn't that dreadful. Then you forget about it and look at the cricket score. Up here, it's different. Nelly's photos are in Miss Rose's concert book. There's one of her and me, one of all four of us. Me and Dora and Gloria grew up and Nelly didn't, and it's horrible. I hate coming down here now. Your trees give me shivers up the spine.'

'We can't allow the terrible things that happen to dictate the terms of our lives, darlin'.'

'I know, but I'm still going to live in Melbourne when I'm old enough. I've got a penfriend who lives down there. She tells me heaps of things about it.' She glanced at her grandmother, aware she'd given up her secret. 'You're not allowed to tell anyone about her.'

'How did you meet her?'

'I didn't, not yet. She's a bit crippled like Mr Foster and she lives in a place called Surrey Hills. I got her address sort of by accident and we just keep on writing. I don't know what she looks like even, but she's got the most beautiful mind with nothing at all that's bad in it.' She didn't tell her that Mary Jolly was a woman in her forties. She hadn't meant to tell anything.

At five, Gertrude packed the microscope back into its box, back into the trunk, the space waiting for it between stacked books.

'There's a pretty jewellery case in here you might like to look at,' she said, removing books enough to expose a polished box, its lid inlaid with mother-of-pearl.

'It must have been like a lucky dip when you first opened that trunk.'

'I felt like a pirate searching for buried treasure.'

Jenny took the box to the table and the better light, more interested in its contents than its fancy wood. She flipped through a small notebook, dug deeper for the photographs.

'Who is she?'

It was a shot of a bride and groom, or a bride and her father. Gertrude shook her head. She shook her head again when Jenny showed her a shot of two children dressed in their Sunday best.

'They must be people he knew after my time. I don't know any of them,' she said.

'Are these his diaries?'

'I doubt it. They're written in some foreign language.'

Jenny opened one with a black cover. 'It's not foreign. It's just mirror writing. Mr Curry showed us how some ancient old bloke kept his journals so no one else could read what he'd written.'

Gertrude was frowning.

'You know, you write things backwards then hold them up to the mirror to read.' She took the diary to Gertrude's washstand mirror and reversed it. 'That's what it is, Granny,' she said, eyes squinting to read the minute script. 'It says, *Dec 17th, '22. Old trull like a meat grinder tonight — gold-plated though. I'll let her grind my beef until new year. Leave for Spain on 2nd. Might find her a bullfighter.*'

Gertrude helped herself to the notebook. Maybe she'd get those new reading glasses — or burn the filthy thing. She tucked it back into the box.

'The day is done, m'darlin'. My chooks want their dinner.'

Jenny didn't take the hint.

'It's weird how when people die some parts of them stay behind in photographs.' She picked up the photograph of the children. 'They're truly dead because no one remembers them, but Nelly's not because heaps of people remember her. One day she will be, though. One day in the far distant future, someone will pick up Miss Rose's album and they'll point to Nelly, and someone else will say, Oh, I don't know who she was. She must have been before my time. And they'll burn it. Then she'll be dead, Granny.'

Gertrude gathered her into her arms, held her tight for a moment, kissed both cheeks, then walked outside to call for Joey.

He came from around the side of the new house, came across to the fence.

'Will you walk back in with Jenny? She doesn't like walking through the bush alone.'

He did better than that. Harry had an old bike with an extra seat on the rear. Jenny straddled it, held on tight and they took off with a wobble. Gertrude watched them to where the road rounded a bend, and in the distance she heard that giggle.

'She's getting to be a pretty girl, Mum,' Elsie said.

'She's out of the top drawer, that one,' Gertrude said.

THE LIMELIGHT

Two days after Sissy's hurried exit from the stage, Norman had found the daffodil yellow frock stuffed into the bag of old clothing saved for the relief ladies. He abhorred waste. When Miss Rose chose Jenny's song for the school concert, he went to his carton of Sissy's hand-me-downs and removed that yellow frock.

'Infinitely suitable for your item,' he said. Jenny was singing 'Painting The Clouds With Sunshine'.

She tried it on, and apart from its length and width, it was perfect. Its sleeves were the best part. They were barely sleeves at all, just small caps, so it didn't matter if the shoulder seams hung low.

Maisy cut three inches off the hem and, not satisfied with the narrow belt that bunched the fabric at the waist, made a new and wider belt from the piece of excess hem. She bought stiffening and a brass buckle for the belt. The frock, almost new, had looked good before. With the wide belt hiding the bunching at the waist, it looked perfect.

On the Sunday before the concert, Jenny brought it home, already starched and pressed. For safety's sake, she hung it in Norman's wardrobe. It was there on Wednesday when she came in from final practice. It was there on Thursday, but when she opened Norman's wardrobe on Friday, the afternoon of the concert, that flash of yellow was gone.

She ran to Sissy's wardrobe, knowing Norman must have moved the frock. He hadn't. Maybe Amber had stuffed it back in the relief bag. She hadn't.

Down to the lavatory then, knowing, knowing Sissy had got rid of her daffodil dress the same way she'd got rid of the Alice Blue Gown. Held her nose, held her breath, looked down. No yellow, or not that she could see.

Back to the house, slowly, though her heart wasn't beating slowly. It was racing so fast she couldn't get a breath in deep enough. Inside, sucking air in through her mouth, and too fast, standing in the doorway watching Amber toss perfect cubes of meat in seasoned flour.

'What happened to that yellow dress?'

Amber didn't turn from her task.

'It was hanging in Dad's wardrobe.'

No reply.

'Where is Sissy?'

Might as well talk to the man in the moon as Amber.

'Maisy fixed that dress up for me to wear tonight.'

Maisy was Amber's friend — her only friend.

'Where is it?'

A large blackened pan waited on the stove, a lump of lard sliding as it melted into smoking fat. Amber took her plate of seasoned meat to the stove and stood placing each cube into hot fat. And the blood pumping through Jenny, rushing to her head, made her know what was heating that frying pan. The yellow dress was in the stove. She could almost smell the scorch of cotton, almost see those pretty yellow buttons glowing in the coals, the belt buckle buckling. Her heartbeat went wild, preparing her for flight. She stepped back. Or was her heart preparing her for fight?

Steak sizzling, fat spitting, Amber's fork turning the cubes, just going about the business of cooking dinner. It would be a tasty stew. She could cook very well. She could clean very well. She could shop, smile at church, serve tea in her good cups if Mrs Bryant or the minister and his wife came to call.

Breathing, breathing hard, hurting breaths but feeling breathless, Jenny stepped forward again. 'You burned it, didn't you?'

That received a response. Amber swung around, loathing in her eyes, her fork raised to gouge out Jenny's eyes, a cube of bloody meat impaled on its tines.

'Were you scared that dress might look better on me than it did on Sissy?'

The fork flew; it hit the doorframe, the meat leaving its fatty, bloody mark behind but still impaled. It fell to the floor where the fork spun in a half-circle, painting a curved bloody smear on Amber's clean floor.

The steak in the pan sending up smoke signals, Amber turned to lift it from the heat. Jenny stepped back, expecting the rest of the meat to follow the cube on the fork. But that would mean no meal ready at six. She always made a meal. She took another fork from the table drawer, placed the pan back on the stove and began turning the cubes, one at a time.

Jenny walked out to the verandah, thinking to walk over and tell Norman. He didn't like waste. And what would he do about it? Nothing. He didn't like disagreements and he did like her tasty stews. And what was the use of starting a war that would resolve nothing?

She stood at the window watching Amber wipe the smear from the doorframe, chase it across the floor. She didn't like dirt, couldn't stand mess. Interesting watching her work, like watching the fly's flea under glass at Granny's, and tonight Jenny felt a similar abhorrence, but a similar compulsion to watch that parasite move around.

When her Alice Blue Gown had disappeared, Jenny had grown years older. Today she could feel a hundred years of age swelling her head, a hundred tons of disappointment attempting to make her cry. She'd have to wear that pink dress. Have to keep her arms down. Cover up Sissy's faded sweat circles.

So stop covering everything up. Just stop it.

Can't. Norman likes to keep things covered up.

Cover up.

They covered it up.

He kept it covered up . . .

Maybe her pounding heart was pumping too much blood to her brain. Maybe her brain had exploded, because for an instant, for less than an instant, she saw Amber from before. Saw a white-clad monster, huge, bigger than the world. And a brown elf with his clunking boot who had saved her from the monster. Mr Foster. She knew why she'd always known he was safe. She knew.

Stared at the steamy glass.

The specimen beneath the glass looks like a mother. It wears an apron and stands at the stove for hours like a mother. The steamy glass between the specimen and the viewer helps with the illusion . . .

Not so big now. Like Granny's forest road, the monster has shrunk, Jenny thought, and I'm not letting her win any more.

Ignoring Amber, she went to Sissy's wardrobe, snatched that pink dress from its hanger and ran with it over to Maisy. She wasn't home. Jessie was there. Jenny borrowed Maisy's scissors and hacked two inches from the hem, hacked those flapping sleeves off to almost nothing, then Maisy arrived to take the scissors from her hand.

'Her mother has done something with the yellow,' Jessie said.

'Tell your father,' Maisy said.

'He never does anything,' Jenny said.

They stitched. Maisy did what she could with what was left of the sleeves. She made a decent belt from fabric cut from the hem. Norman called to Jenny at six. She didn't go home.

He ate stew, with potatoes and pumpkin. He asked after his missing daughter. Amber said she hadn't seen her. Sissy didn't reply. He ate rhubarb with custard, drank his tea, then returned to the station. He hoped the train would be on time.

It came in at seven ten; he was back at the house by seven twenty, where he changed quickly from stationmaster's uniform to suit.

'Has she been home?'

No reply, but the yellow frock hanging with his suit these past few days was not there. She had gone early to the hall.

He was seated before seven thirty, in the third row. Gertrude and Vern arrived early. They took the seats beside him. For years he'd been attending these school concerts. He came to see one performance. And was finally rewarded. The senior girls came on to sing two numbers. He was expecting to see a flash of yellow. He saw pink, then forgot pink as he relaxed and listened. Jenny's voice carried the group. He was watching her intently when the pink frock ripped from armhole to mid bodice. He drew breath, half-rose from his seat. Thankfully, she noticed, and stepped back to the second row. The item continued, her hand over her heart.

Clothing was necessary to cover the naked body. Clothing went in and out of fashion, but if one was not a slave to fashion then clothing might serve its owner for years, never quite in but also never quite out of fashion. His purchases for the girls, when their sole carer, had been made with that thought in mind. That pink frock was memorable only because he had not wished to purchase it. He preferred to see his daughters clad in more functional shades. The last time he'd seen Jennifer wearing it, it had covered more. He dared a glance, noticed the swell of breast, the developing shape of woman.

Mrs Fulton was waiting to grab Jenny as she came off stage. Miss Rose joined them to pull and prod at a faded armpit.

'I could put a stich in it, but I doubt it will hold. That fabric is rotten.'

'Leave it,' Miss Rose said, removing her own plum jacket.

Jenny stood, her hand still covering the gap. She had to go back on the next item bar one, and she'd have no one to hide behind.

'Slip it on, quickly,' Miss Rose said.

Jenny released the rip and did as she was told. It was a tailored jacket, nipped in at the waist. They got her buttoned up, turned her around.

'Get those shoes and socks off,' Miss Rose said. 'Dora, may we borrow your sandals, please? Quickly.'

They got Jenny's clodhoppers off, her socks off, got her shod in Dora's sandals. They fitted well enough. Then Miss Rose dragged the ribbon from Jenny's bunched-up hair.

'Leave it free tonight, Jennifer. You're painting the clouds with sunshine, so show the audience a little of that sunshine. A comb, please, Mrs Fulton.'

Mrs Fulton had put her comb down somewhere. They found it and dragged it through the frizz of Jenny's waist-length curls, and continued dragging until each hair was free to fly.

'It looks like spun gold,' Mrs Fulton said.

'I look top heavy,' Jenny said.

'You look like a sun goddess, now go out there and sing like one,' Miss Rose said.

She was as tall as she'd ever be, a smidgen under five foot five; Miss Rose's fitted jacket moulded her breasts, flared at her hips. Her hair, wild and beautiful tonight, took many a breath away.

Old Noah was at the hall, though not in the hall. He stood at an open window, listening and if he moved during her performance, he was unaware of it.

He moved while the audience applauded, found the unlocked door leading to the lavatories and, while the foot-stamping, the whistling, the calls for more continued, he let himself in.

The headmaster was on stage, calling for silence, and ignored. Not until Jennifer was drawn back to the stage by the infants' mistress did the clapping ease, though it didn't silence until the mistress sat at the piano to play the introduction to 'The Last Rose of Summer'.

He stood mouthing the words into his hand.

'No flower of her kindred,
No rosebud is nigh,
To reflect back her blushes,
Or give sigh for sigh . . .
So soon, may I follow,
When friendships decay . . .'

There were times when Norman forgot Jenny was not his own, or chose not to recall that nameless infant he'd taken into his house out of Christian charity. In the days following the concert, he strived to forget.

He had never courted the limelight. He was plain man, lacking in confidence, a man without friend, without home — until Jenny came into his life. This town had taken her into its heart, and with her it had opened its doors to him. Now, when the limelight shone on her golden head, it radiated out, showering warmth onto his own bald head, his own rounded shoulders. It raised them up.

He stood much taller when the bank manager congratulated him on Jenny's behalf. He glowed when her name was mentioned at town hall meetings, and his jowls lifted in pride when the church ladies praised her.

Perhaps he was too prideful. Perhaps he should have seen that Jenny's limelight was getting up Amber's nose, that his older daughter suffered agony for Jenny's success. He didn't notice. Norman didn't notice much. He was a happy man that December.

He should have noticed the missing yellow frock, should have recognised the remains of the brass belt buckle when he cleaned the ash from the stove. He didn't. The buckle had been blackened and deformed by fire. He tossed it with the ash to a pile already heaped beside the back fence, behind the lavatory. A shovel of ash in the lavatory pan helped kill the smell, some said.

Jenny didn't go looking for the buckle. She was loading a shovel with ash when she found it and, like a gold digger faced with a giant nugget, for a moment she couldn't believe what she had found. Sadness then, overwhelming sadness for a pretty dress; sadness too when she washed the ash and the black from the buckle. Then sadness was replaced by a need to avenge that dress. She strung the remains of the buckle on a length of twine and hung it like a long pendant around her neck.

Amber was making pastry on the marble pastry board. She didn't look at Jenny standing twirling that string in the doorway.

Sissy looked at her. 'What do you think that looks like?' she said.

'A cooked belt buckle from my yellow dress,' Jenny said. 'Maisy bought it from Miss Blunt.'

Amber folded the pastry, wrapped it around a large lump of butter, belted it flat with the rolling pin. Her hands were covered with flour.

Jenny twirled the pendant as she walked by her to fill a glass with water at the tap.

The trouble with Amber was she never gave a hint of what was in her mind. She snatched at the string with her floury hands, spraying flour to her polished floor. The twine burned the back of Jenny neck, became entangled in her hair, but she got away, with her pendant.

She wore it all day, wore it at the dinner table, put Amber off her meal with it. Norman didn't notice.

PEARLS IN GOLDEN CAGES

Family wars are fought on many fronts. Pretty frocks become casualties; beds become the battlefields; Christmas Day — on Christmas Day even the soldiers took time off in the trenches.

Norman gave his daughters slim books of poetry, their names and the date written on the flyleaves. What did Sissy want with a poetry book? She wanted that green dress in the new catalogue, wanted her own bedroom, wanted to go to Frankston with the Hoopers. She knew they were leaving sometime between Christmas and New Year. She'd expected an invitation before Christmas but all she'd got from them was a lousy box of hankies.

The war recommenced on Christmas night, in bed, and during that gap between Christmas and New Year, Jenny spent her days donating her services behind the post office counter.

It came in the mailbag, a tiny parcel, so small there was barely room on it for the stamps and address. *Miss Jennifer Morrison. The Stationmaster's Daughter. Co Woody Creek Post Office.* And whatever was inside it, rattled.

She should have opened it at the post office, as she opened her Cara Paris letters, but this was different. This was from someone in Geelong, and who in Geelong could possibly know her name? One of the many Duckworths? But why? She carried it home intact. Norman cut the string. He lifted the lid and poured the contents into his palm.

It was a pair of earrings, small pearls inside golden cages, an exact match for the pendant old Noah had found in the park and thrown to her when she was ten.

Jenny reached for one of the precious things. Sissy reached for the other, while Norman studied the box.

'What did you do with that necklace, Daddy? It's exactly the same as these.'

He wasn't so certain. He went to his room and returned with the pendant, and it was the same, though its tiny cage and pearl were larger.

'Who would send such a thing to a child?'

There was no accompanying card, no name of sender. Norman dropped the pendant into the box and reached out a hand to claim the earrings.

Jenny knew who had sent them, and the knowing sent a shiver down her spine. She knew too that she should have told Norman and Mr Denham about old Noah finding that necklace. She hadn't — only because she hadn't wanted to get into trouble for talking to strangers. And she hadn't spoken to him anyway, and most of those swagmen walked on over the bridge and never came back. But old Noah kept on coming back. He'd been back here at least three times. And he knew her name, knew Norman was her father.

She handed her earring back more willingly than Sissy.

'Where did you find the necklace?' Norman said.

'It was in the park. Near the swing.'

'A mystery,' Norman said.

He closed the box, took it to his room, then the meal proceeded. Only one topic of conversation, though; it continued until the tea was poured, when Sissy took her cup and flounced into her bedroom. Sissy didn't give a damn who had sent those earrings. She wanted them. Margaret Hooper had pierced ears and a dozen pairs of earrings.

Then the Hoopers left for Frankston without her, and their leaving coincided with Sissy's week of menstruation. She was a big girl. Perhaps she suffered more than most, and while suffering she craved toffee, which Amber wouldn't allow her to make. They argued, or Sissy snarled until she drove Amber from the house. Then she made her toffee.

Jealousy, boredom, too much sugar brought out Sissy's ill humour and her pustules. By the second week of January, her face was a riot of pimples. Amber's sugar canister was empty and would remain empty. As was her butter dish. You can't make toffee without sugar and butter.

Boredom can turn the mind to odd pursuits. Sissy spent a day removing the flyleaf from her book of poetry so she could return it to Mr Cox and get the money back. She was capable enough when the desire was there to be capable. The flyleaf was removed cleanly. Amber said she couldn't see where it had been. Amber would have said black was white if it saved her from Sissy's tantrum. Mr Cox wouldn't take it back. He told her he'd placed a special order for that book.

'I don't have a lot of call for poetry books up here, dear,' he said.

He was still apologising when Sissy caught sight of a large sign his wife was propping in the shop window. A radio talent quest was to be held on 19 February, in Willama. If there was a time, a date, an instant, when the fates conspired against Jenny Morrison, it was then.

'You might tell your father about that quest, dear. Your sister could have a good chance of taking the prize money,' Mrs Cox said.

Sissy burned. At that instant, she hated, loathed, despised, detested her sister. She'd come down here to get the money for that book so she could add it to Amber's money so they could get a postal order to send away for that green dress, which her father wouldn't pay for, and all she'd got was someone else singing Jenny's praises. She was sick of it. Sick, sick, sick of it. Wanted to haul off and hit Mrs Cox. Wanted to throw that book at her head, push her through that window.

And those bloody Hoopers could have invited her down to Frankston. And Jim could have given her a friendship ring or something halfway decent. Bloody handkerchiefs. She had a drawer full of handkerchiefs. She wanted those gold earrings, wanted to get away from Amber's nagging her about her pimples, nagging her to slim down.

She wasn't fat, just solid. She had nice hair, thick, near black, mid-shoulder length. Her face was as flat as a flounder; her chin too heavy; her eyes not quite green and not quite brown. She had her paternal grandmother's parrot nose, though not as large, and when in an amiable mood, when her pimples were controlled, her face painted, she was definitely not the plainest girl in Woody Creek.

But her sister was the prettiest, and she could sing, and some secret admirer had sent her a pair of gorgeous earrings, and this morning Sissy wanted to scratch her eyes out.

She stood before the poster reading it, then with relief turned to Mr Cox. 'It says no child performers.'

'Fourteen and over, it says, dear. Down near the bottom.'

Sissy hadn't got that far. She saw it now. Jenny was fourteen.

'You can put my name and Margaret Hooper's down. We'll go,' she said.

'It will be a little different to our own concerts,' Mr Cox said. 'They've got judges coming up from Melbourne.'

Sissy raised her eyebrows, so what? He turned to his wife who was better with words than he. She explained that each contestant had to fill in a form and sign it.

'If Miss Hooper wants to take part, she'll need to get a form, Cecelia.'

'You can give me one then.'

They gave her two, one for Jenny. She filled in one and pitched the other into the kitchen stove.

Then, three days later, Norman came home with his little hair cut to the bone and an entry form for the quest — and an offer from John McPherson to drive him and Jenny to Willama for the evening.

'I tried to give my entry form to Mr Cox yesterday and he told me that he couldn't take any more,' Sissy said.

Norman nodded. He also couldn't take any more. He filled his mouth.

Jenny was studying the entry form. 'It says there's prize money.'

It said too that the concert would be held in the Willama theatre where the finalists would be chosen to take part in a radio broadcast, after which the winners would be announced.

First prize was twenty pounds, second, ten, third place was five.

'If he gave you that entry form today, then he's a rotten old liar,' Sissy said, staring at Norman across the table. Norman again filled his mouth. 'If she's going, then I'm going. The Hoopers will drive me down.'

Norman swallowed. 'No.'

'Why not?'

His knife and fork placed down, he glanced at the three watching faces, aware there was no way of avoiding this confrontation, the thought of which raised acid in his stomach. His feet moved on the lino, urging him to walk away. He coughed, aware he must remain.

'We have heard enough of "Daffodils", Cecelia. Now the subject is closed.'

'No one has heard her in Willama,' Amber said.

'Good God, woman! Are you . . .' Mad? Deaf? Blind? He flinched, shook himself, looked at the ceiling for support, then back to his daughter. 'Your recitations are an embarrassment to me — as I believe your last experience was an embarrassment to you. There will be no repetition.'

'*She* doesn't embarrass you,' Amber said, flicking her fork towards Jenny.

Norman did not look at his housekeeper often. Tonight he looked at her.

'No,' he said. 'Her voice delights me and many, Mrs Morrison.'

Jenny stared at the entry form. She'd known about the talent quest. Miss Rose had spoken to her about it. She hadn't known there was prize money.

Sissy sitting opposite had buttered a slice of bread, celebrating butter's return to the ice chest. She wasn't a fast mover, not usually. Tonight, like a magician's sleight of hand, the bread left her plate and was slapped butter side down on Jenny's head.

'Well, I can tell you straight, she doesn't delight me. I'm sick of her,' she howled and ran to her room.

Norman went after her.

Jenny removed the bread but left most of the butter behind. She sat, her fingers pinching out the grease, while Amber went after Norman.

'Return to the kitchen and apologise to your sister!' Norman commanded.

'You always take her side,' Sissy wailed.

'She is the one with butter in her hair, for which you will apologise!'

'Leave her alone,' Amber said.

'This does not concern you, Mrs Morrison.'

'It concerns me. The way you put that little bitch before your own daughter concerns me.'

'You are here under sufferance. Recall the terms of our agreement and remove yourself.'

'If she wants to be in that concert, she can be in that concert.'

'Do you want to subject this girl to the ridicule of strangers?'

'You cruel bastard —'

'You have not yet seen my bastardry, Mrs Morrison. I suggest you may if you do not remove yourself from this room. Now!'

Sissy was starfished across the bed, attempting to kill the mattress with thumping fists. Amber attempted to get to her. Norman kept her at bay. He was a pacifist. She'd fight to the death. He had the bulk. She may have weighed seven stone. He wanted Sissy to apologise. Amber wanted to comfort her.

Jenny stood in the passage wiping at her head with a tea towel. And for the first time in her life, she saw Norman put his arms around Amber — to pick her up. He carried her to the kitchen where he reached for his key. He carried her to his room, tossed her to his bed and locked his door, while Jenny stood near the back door ready to make a quick getaway.

'Go to Maisy. Wash that butter from your hair. Stay there.'

She didn't need to be told twice.

She slept the night in a single bed in Jessie's room and didn't want to go home in the morning, so she didn't go. She stayed at

Maisy's until lunchtime, then went around to the Palmers' where she remained until six, watching Mrs Palmer and Dora dye faded green bedspreads maroon. Had to go home then. Afraid of what she might find when she got there, but she had to go.

And it was over. Amber was serving a steak and kidney pie. Sissy was reciting at the quest, Jenny was singing. Life was back to normal, or to as normal as it got in Norman's house, where nothing was ever normal but everyone pretended it was.

It became totally abnormal two days later.

'You will see Miss Blunt this week and be fitted with . . . the necessary.'

Norman had always waved away any mention of undergarment. Jenny knew what he meant. Maisy had told her a dozen times that she needed to wear a bra. She must have told him.

Then he said the magic words. 'Your mother has suggested you should have a suitable frock for the quest.'

Something had happened the night of her buttered hair. Even Amber was being abnormal.

Jenny went to see Miss Blunt the next morning, and once that bra was fitted, she didn't want to take it off. Miss Blunt let her wear it, even if it wouldn't be paid for until Friday. She allowed her to try on a blue print frock and it fitted perfectly. The colour was functional enough to suit Norman, the fabric light, but Miss Blunt said it was of a good quality. She said it was very suitable for a girl of Jenny's age.

'Mum is coming in on Friday, Miss Blunt. Can you . . . can you put this one somewhere else . . . in case it's sold before she comes?'

Miss Blunt hung it in her back room and Jenny ran over to Maisy's house to show off her bra, ran around to the Palmers' to show Dora.

Sissy's green dress came in the mail on Thursday. The material was as soft as spider's web, beautiful but not functional.

On Friday, Jenny and Dora were on the park swing when they saw Amber walking home from Blunt's. Back to the Palmers' to get Dora's sandals — Jenny wanted to try them with her dress —

then home to Norman's house. The parcel was on Cecelia's bed and already opened. Her second bra was in it, a pair of stockings, the garters — and a dirty brown replica of the pink thing she'd inherited from Sissy.

Couldn't believe what her eyes were telling her. Stared at it expecting it to turn blue, willing it to turn blue, while her head, her heart, her blood turned to ice. Dora picked the 'thing' up, held it before her. Jenny stared at her, then snatched the frock and took it out to the kitchen. 'Miss Blunt hung the one I wanted in her back room.'

Amber always did her mother act when Dora was around. She stretched her mouth in a smile. 'The blue was more suitable for a twenty-year-old woman. Hang it up.'

Jenny dropped it on the floor, wiped her hands on her hips, cleansing them of that gruesome thing as she turned to go.

'Pick up your frock and hang it.'

'It's not mine.'

Amber picked it up and threw it at her. Jenny evaded it. Dora had more respect for new frocks. She caught it and followed Jenny to the station. Norman knew she'd tried on a dress. He knew that Miss Blunt had said it was suitable.

'She bought the wrong one, Daddy. I'm taking it back.'

He looked at the brown rag Dora had placed on his office counter. He'd had a bad few weeks, and could see nothing wrong with the frock. The colour was functional, the fabric was of a good quality.

'Be grateful that you have a new frock to wear, Jennifer. There are children in town who have never seen a new frock.'

'That's like telling me to be grateful I've got smallpox instead of leprosy!'

'Watch your lip.'

'I want that blue print dress, Daddy.'

'A frock is a frock,' he said. 'Take it back to the house.'

'You may as well take it back to Mr Blunt and get your money, because I'm never, ever going to wear it.'

'Your mother chose it for you!'

'And you know why she chose it.' She turned away, stepped away, then turned back to face him. 'You know, Daddy. You have to know.'

He looked at Dora who was listening to every word. He was not one to air soiled family linen in public — nor did he like the airing of it by others.

'I am not impressed with your attitude, Jennifer. Say goodbye to your friend, then go back to the house.'

She walked away from him, walked east down the platform. He followed her. 'Go back to the house.'

An obedient girl, easy to handle, always an agreeable child. Not today. She ran from him.

'Jennifer! Jennifer!'

Wasn't going to let him see her crying over a dress. Ran fast, across the railway yard, Dora behind her, ran all the way to the Palmers' house. They served tea in big mugs like Granny's mugs, and they served up sympathy by the bucketful. They served plum jam sandwiches too. She stayed late at the Palmers' house, too scared to go home. She'd never disobeyed her father. Three times Mrs Palmer told her she should go home, but she didn't make her go.

People were normal at the Palmers'; they talked and laughed like human people, and they were everywhere, nine of them, plus Weasel Lewis and Irene tonight. The house was full of chatter and the smell of sausages frying up for dinner. Jenny and Dora had peeled a huge saucepan full of potatoes while Joss took to the skin of a tough pumpkin with a tommyhawk. Loved that house, loved the cooking and everyone under Mrs Palmer's feet in the kitchen, wished she was one of Mrs Palmer's kids, or wished she was a little kid again and she had no mother and Norman was at home cooking sausages and she was sitting on the kitchen table watching him cook.

Maybe her mouth was watering for sausages when the clock told her it was six thirty. Maybe Mrs Palmer saw her mouth — or her eyes still watering. She buttered a slice of bread, popped a sausage onto it, added a dollop of tomato sauce and handed it to her.

'You have to go home, pet. Your dad will be out looking for you. Try to look on the bright side. Not a soul is going to see what dress you're wearing when you're singing over the wireless.'

Jenny licked tomato sauce from her hand. 'I'll see me, Mrs Palmer.'

She left them to their feast and took a bite of bread and sausage, but her mouth was too scared to swallow it, and when she got it down, her stomach agreed with her mouth. She was walking past the park when she heard him.

'Good evening, Jennifer,' he said.

He was back. She didn't run from him tonight. Wished she could ask him about those earrings, or just say, How was Geelong? Couldn't. 'Good evening,' she said.

A warm night, not hot, but he was still wearing his black overcoat. He had a newspaper, had a pair of glasses perched on his nose so he could read it. He took them off, placed them into his coat pocket.

'You're late about,' he said.

She caught a drip of tomato sauce and licked it from her finger. He was a weird old man, but hardly a stranger. And he was related to the Duffys in some way, because she'd seen mail addressed to him sent care of Mrs Duffy.

'Your father has been calling.'

She turned to Norman's house, knowing she'd be in huge trouble when she got home — which was why she couldn't eat that sausage, even though the smell of it was urging her to eat.

'Have you had any dinner?' she said. She'd only taken one small bite.

'I smell hot sausage,' he said.

'You can have it if you like.'

'I like.'

He didn't rise to get it. She walked close enough to pass it with an outstretched arm. Wanted, wanted so badly to ask him about those earrings. She didn't. She stepped back and watched him take a bite, chew with relish, tomato sauce dripping red to his beard.

'God will provide,' he said, mouth full. 'If too little, and a little too late.'

'He doesn't provide much,' she said as she turned to walk the diagonal across the road, tucking her blouse into her skirt as she went, pulling up her socks, pushed escaping hair from her eyes.

They were eating. That brown dress hung over the back of her chair.

'Hang up your frock before you eat, Jennifer.'

She eyed the muddy brown thing, knowing this was the moment her stomach had been scared of for hours. This was when she'd win or forever lose.

'She must have bought it for Sissy. It's not mine, Daddy.'

He paled, reached for his key from the top of the dresser, but she wasn't backing down tonight. She didn't need to be told to go to his room. She led the way there and sat on his bed while he turned the key.

GALLERY OF FOOLS

The junk room had once been Jenny's room. She could remember her green iron cot being in this room. It smelled different now, smelled of Norman's cigarettes and his shoes and trains and newspapers. She reached for a bundle of newspapers, flipped the pages, glancing at old news while plates rattled in the kitchen. She wasn't hungry. Tonight, eating would have been more punishment than being locked in here.

She read about girls who were too selfish to marry.

Women once wed to gain their freedom. Now a ring on the finger means the loss of freedom. Every year we see more and more girls joining the workforce, girls loath to relinquish that newfound independence . . .

Jenny closed her eyes and wished she could join the workforce, buy her own frock, her own shoes. Sissy didn't want to work. Her one ambition in life was to be a Hooper. Only one way she could do that — and God help Jim.

The room was airless with that door closed. She kneeled on the bed and tried to open the window, knowing it was wasted effort. She'd tried when this room had been her own. It had never opened. Sissy's window opened. Amber's window opened. The parlour window opened.

Loved this room. It was too crowded for Amber's clean to get in and rip its heart out. She polished its little floor space, but Norman's ashtray, on its fancy stand, killed the smell of her polish. His shoes strung out in a row along the wall had their own smell, so did his shirt tossed over the end of the bed. A homely room, like home used to be, like Granny's home, where you could put things down and they stayed put down.

The light was fading. She reached to turn on the light globe, then decided against it, and instead lay on his bed, her own dear single bed, to watch old shadows creep across the ceiling – and to wonder at the cleverness of Amber. She'd chosen the exact frock Norman would have chosen. She was too clever to be really mad.

Better not to think about her. She concentrated on the ceiling, wondering if she kept on staring until it was pitch dark whether her eyes would keep on adjusting to that dark, or if there would be an instant between near dark and the total dark that she might catch.

Norman ruined her experiment. He opened the door and let the kitchen light in, then asked her if she was ready to hang up her frock.

'Tell her to burn it like she burned Sissy's daffodil dress, Daddy.' He was closing the door. 'Tell her to throw it down the lav like one of them threw my Alice Blue Gown dress down the lav.'

In a war, even when soldiers are taken prisoner, they don't bow and scrape to their captors. They find a way to fight on — or to escape.

The key turned.

Sissy and Amber would be enjoying this. They'd be sitting in the parlour listening to every word. Sissy had spent a lot of hours locked in this room before Amber came home, and a few since. Amber had been locked in here. Now it was Jenny's turn, but no real punishment. She had her own room back, her own bed, and she could hear everything. She heard Sissy walk by on her way to the lav.

'Don't forget to take that dress with you, Sissy,' she yelled. That was what a prisoner would do, torment from behind bars.

She heard the legs of Norman's chair squeal, heard his newspaper pages turning faster.

It was interesting to lie on your back in the dark listening to the sound of life, forcing the ears to compensate for the eyes.

She could see better if she closed her eyes, see him so plainly, see his face turning to the locked door, see him glance towards the clock, towards that brown frock, which, as the hours passed, grew bigger, wider, more brown, a monster frock swallowing up the back of her chair.

It would swallow her if she let it. And she wouldn't. Never. If she lived to be ninety-nine, she would never wear that rotten thing. And she wouldn't hang it up either. It could hang over the back of that chair until it rotted, until the chair rotted. She almost giggled at the image of her chair turning to powder and that dress falling to the floor.

> *The world had long ended, the houses had turned to dust, but one chair remained, protected by that gruesome gown . . .*

It tickled her funny bone. She got the giggles. Sissy's voice stopped them, and gave her the hiccups.

> '*Ten thousand saw I at a glance,*
> *Tossing their heads in sprightly dance . . .*'

Only a wall between this room and Sissy's, a thin wall. Norman must have heard every word when she and Sissy had been exchanging insults.

> '*The waves beside them danced, but they*
> *Out-did the sparkling waves . . . in glee.*'

Jenny rapped with her knuckles on the dividing wall, beating time with her knuckles.

> '*A poet could not but be gay*
> *In such jocund . . .*
> *In such a jocund company . . .*'

The rapping became louder, faster, until Norman's chair squealed again and he added his own thump to two doors. 'Desist,' he commanded. 'Both of you.'

Jenny desisted, as did Sissy for a minute or two, then she began again, so Jenny practised her song, loudly and off-key.

Norman thumped. 'Enough, I said. I will have quiet in this house!'

'I have to learn it. Mum isn't going with me,' Sissy whined.

'Then learn the thing in silence!'

A whisper can irritate when it continues too long.

'*For oft . . . for oft . . .*'

'*When on my couch I lie,*' Jenny sang to the tune of the twenty-third psalm. '*In vacant or in pensive mood.*'

'Shut up!'

'Shut up yourself,' Jenny yelled, then continued with her psalm while Sissy stopped reciting to hammer on the wall.

Norman threatened dire consequences, but that locked room was about as dire as it could get, and it was his fault she was in there anyway. He should have let her choose her own dress.

She heard him leave the kitchen. Heard him outside her door, then the back door opened and his footsteps hurried east along the verandah and out the squealing side gate. He was vacating the premises. She wished he'd let her out to go to the lav before he'd gone, but with him gone, she upped the ante, began that poem at the beginning and sang it right to the end, which brought Amber into the war.

It was delicious being locked in. It was freedom. Amber could belt against that locked door until she wore her fist down to the elbow, but she couldn't stop Jenny's singing. She sang the Macdonald twins' version of the poem, or the parts of it she could remember, sang it soprano and off-key. It was surprising how well the words fitted with the tune.

'*Oh, Jim, please kiss my drooling mouth,
Before you venture way down south.*'

'I hate you, you evil, filthy-mouthed stray dog,' Sissy screeched, which was preferable to her recitations.

The war might have continued for hours had Jenny not been desperate to go to the lav. No chamber-pot under Norman's bed, but the big blue-green vase was on top of his wardrobe. It matched the parlour curtains. It used to be in the parlour, holding a bunch of peacock feathers. She'd need light though, to lift it down.

Hard to find the light cord in the dark. Norman had tied it in a knot so his head wouldn't keep hitting it. She had to reach high, but she got it, got the light on, got the curtains pulled, then lifted the vase down. It wasn't an ideally shaped vessel for the task required of it, but desperate people couldn't afford to be choosy. She'd barely avoided a catastrophe when she heard someone at her window. Thought it must have been Norman. Pulled her pants up and her skirt down, moved the vase in against the wall and lifted the curtain.

It wasn't Norman.

It's a shock to the mind when you see what you're not expecting, when you're looking from light into dark. She could barely see her features, just the monster's anger, and seeing it up so close was scary. Jenny let the curtain fall and stepped back. It was all very well to say she wasn't afraid of Amber, but a part of her was. What if she got the axe and broke that window? It was a good three foot off the ground. She'd have to climb on something to get in, but she'd get in if she wanted to. She was strong. She walked for miles some nights.

Wished Norman would come home.

Turned the light off then and sat on the bed. In a war, someone had to stop the killing first. She wasn't surrendering though, just regrouping her troops. She lay down, her eyes turned to the window, for a time expecting an axe to fly through. Eyes grow weary, they stop watching, close just for a moment —

She was asleep when he opened the door. She sprang from bed, ready to dodge an axe. Saw his bulk in the doorway, smelled his smell, which was the same as he smelled when he came home brave from his poker nights. She'd forgotten it was Friday.

'What's the time?' she said.

'Late,' he said. 'Go to your room.'

'I want to stay here.'

'You will learn as you grow older that life is not about what we want. Go to your own room.'

'This was my room until she took yours.'

'The hour is late. No arguing.'

'Can I please change that dress, Daddy?'

He sighed, stepped into the room, closing the door behind him. His hand knew were to find the light cord. The room flooded with white light, blinding her for an instant. Then she remembered the vase and what it contained and she moved to pick it up, and with two hands hold it to her breast.

He reached to claim it, to place it back where it belonged. She shook her head and he frowned, confused by her attachment to it.

'Does a beautiful rose require a colourful vase, or does it show a truer beauty when placed alone in clear glass?'

She knew what he meant. 'You wouldn't poke it into a rusty old jam tin, though.'

His hand reached to brush back her bed-tumbled hair. 'You will look well enough in your rusty jam tin. Now please depart. I require my bed.'

'I'm not wearing it, Daddy. Never. I promise you.'

'You have the world at your feet, Jennifer. What more do you require?'

'The blue dress I asked Miss Blunt to put away.'

'Go to your bed.'

'It's Sissy's bed, and she hates me.'

She moved towards the door, the vase still cradled in her arms. 'Why do they hate me, Daddy?'

He sighed, waved her to be gone.

'You know they do.'

'You are a colourful singing bird, Jenny-wren, hatched into a nest of grey sparrows; a classical picture framed in gold and hung in a gallery of fools, and I the greatest fool of all. What is your attraction to that vase?'

'I have to empty it.'

'Empty . . .' he began, then waved his hand again for her to go.

But he followed her out to the rear verandah where he sat on the old cane chair and lit a final cigarette. She emptied the vase on the garden, rinsed it at the garden tap and returned to stand before him.

'May I please sleep on the couch tonight?'

'If man could foresee his future, little Jenny-wren, he may well choose to die in the womb. Use my room,' he said.

He was feeling his way to the couch when he saw Amber's open door. It was rarely left open at night — or not while she was sleeping. She walked on moonlit nights. No moon tonight. He peered into the dark of her bedroom, renewing his acquaintance with his beloved wide bed. And perhaps she was in it, her door left open tonight to gain a breath of air. On stockinged feet, he stepped closer to listen, and he heard her breathing. He backed away. But she was deeply, heavily asleep. For minutes he stood looking at the slight shape of her, barely enough to lift that sheet. So little woman, he thought. So much bed.

During his manhandling of her on the night of the argument, her lack of weight had surprised him. Her heavy sleep did not surprise him. She swallowed pills each night, pills he now procured for her, paid for and controlled, supplying her each day with three, placed each morning in a medicine glass on the top shelf in the bathroom.

He had promised himself nil involvement with her when she'd returned. Involvement had been forced on him when he'd caught her feeding her pills to Cecelia. That girl had problems enough — and a wide bed. He stood recalling a dawn of years ago when he'd come upon mother and daughter in that bed. He recalled the taking of Amber on this bedroom floor, between the bed and dressing table. She had fought that day to return to her daughter's bed. Perhaps she may learn to like it again.

She offered only a drugged murmur of protest as he lifted her, flung an arm at her disturber as he carried her into Sissy's room. No sheet covering the large hump of his daughter spread across that bed. Perhaps she thought Jennifer had come. She moaned, but made enough space. His burden down, he dusted his hands and walked to his reclaimed bed where he bounced a little, enjoying the firmness of the springs. He removed his winnings from his pocket. They played for small silver coins. He'd won a handful. And had drunk three glasses of ale — or was it four. Had followed them with a small brandy, then a second. He smiled, stripped off his shirt and flung it merrily over his shoulder, blessing the ale and the brandy and the child who had wanted her room. If not for child, ale and brandy, he would not have found the courage to reclaim his wide bed.

But he had. And he was in it, and could feel the heat of where she'd lain. How many years since he'd slept in this bed? How many years since she'd shared this bed with him?

Fingers counting on his pillow, but too weary tonight for mental arithmetic, he closed his eyes and slept, slept very well.

GOLD CREPE AND BEADS

Vern's car would carry six in comfort. Jim was picking the Morrisons up at six o'clock. Contestants in the talent quest had been told to present themselves at the Willama theatre by six forty-five, that the concert would begin at seven sharp. Sissy's item was listed at number nine, so they couldn't afford to get there late. Jenny was on at number twenty-two. Margaret, who was having second thoughts, was number thirty.

Sissy slept badly the night before the quest. Her hair in rags didn't encourage a good night's sleep, and she couldn't blame her bedmate for keeping her awake either. Once her mother's head was down, she didn't move. Her deep sleep annoyed Sissy, or the pills she took to get that sleep, pills denied to Sissy, annoyed her. She'd pleaded for one last night, Norman had ignored her plea. She'd been pleading with her mother to go with her to Willama, just in case she stumbled on the third verse. She knew the first and second, knew the last, but that third verse always sent her mind blank.

Norman and Jenny, pleased with the new sleeping arrangements, had slept soundly. Amber hadn't complained; she'd won the war of the dress. At breakfast on the morning after the epic battle, Norman had asked Jenny to hang up the frock and she'd hung it in Sissy's wardrobe, which didn't count as hanging it up now that Norman's wardrobe was once again her own. Winning that bedroom back was a huge victory.

She'd be wearing her pink dress to the quest, which Maisy had repaired. She'd taken the side seams in, which had got rid of a part of the rip and a portion of the sweat-faded circles, then she'd reinforced both armpits with the material cut from the sleeves. It was a nice pink, and with her stockings and Dora's sandals it looked good enough. She didn't take it home, had no intention of taking it home.

Sissy was in a foul mood. She'd gone beyond demanding Amber go with her to Willama to sulking and throwing things because she wouldn't. Around midday, Amber capitulated and went in search of her beige suit, unworn in years. She sponged it, hung it on the line to air, polished her best shoes. She was ironing when Jenny came home at three to bathe and wash her hair. Sissy's green frock had miles of fabric in the skirt, fabric, Amber was attempting to explain to her, that would not travel well.

'Wear your floral. It doesn't crush, and if it is a little creased, it won't be so obvious.'

'I told you, I'm wearing the green,' Sissy said.

They were still arguing when Jenny emerged half an hour later, her hair dripping. The iron had been put away. Cecelia was now seated between sink and table, Amber working around her, untying strips of sheeting, freeing thirty corkscrew curls and not doing it gently. Jenny stood in the doorway combing her hair and watching them, listening to a pair of cats snarling.

'Stop pulling it!'

'The rag is knotted. Sit still.'

'Cut it then.'

'If you sit still, I'll get it undone.'

'Get her the scissors,' Sissy said.

Jenny got them; didn't offer them but placed them on the table. No 'thank you', not from Sissy nor Amber, but they were used, the knot cut, the rag removed and the process continued. One after the other those curls were released. Amber would brush them later, let them fall just a little, then fiddle them into whatever style Sissy demanded.

How many times have I watched this? Once, twice a week since I was ten, Jenny thought. Maybe a hundred times a year for four years. How many times have I stood watching her powder Sissy's freckles, shape her eyebrows, paint her mouth, dress her, pin on her hat? She's like a kid dressing her doll, Jenny thought, but maybe she's growing out of dolls, or maybe it's just today. Her hands were shaking.

She had small hands. Granny's hands were as big as a man's and looked as hard-working as a man's. Jenny looked at her own hand. Maisy had always said that she resembled Amber. Her hand didn't. Jenny's hand was larger; her fingertips were square, as were her fingernails.

Sissy's fingers came to a point. Jenny had big hands, like Granny's, but her fingernails were small, like Norman's. She had Granny's hair. Studying people up close was as interesting as studying fleas under the microscope.

She bit at a ragged fingernail. Biting it only made it more ragged. They weren't using the scissors. She reached for them, snipped and watched a nail fly.

'Pick that up,' Amber snapped.

'Where did it land?'

'Probably in my hair,' Sissy said, shaking her head as Amber untied another rag.

'Sit still!'

'You're pulling it on purpose,' Sissy said.

'Get your hair permed and it will stay curly,' Jenny said.

'And end up like Mrs Bull with a head of wire,' Sissy said.

'Will you hold your head still, Cecelia!'

'I'm holding it still.'

'If my hair was straight I wouldn't want it curled,' Jenny said.

'You say that because it's not straight!'

Jenny snipped another fingernail, watching where it fell, wondering if it had landed beside its mate. Somewhere near the hearth. She walked around the table to find it, reached down to retrieve it, and Amber grabbed a handful of her hair.

'You told me to pick it up!'

'You bitch of a girl. I don't need your agitation today!'

'I don't need you pulling my hair either. Let me go.'

She tried to pull her hair free. It was wet, it might have slipped free had Amber not wound a hank around her hand.

If Amber hadn't whacked her across the head, Jenny might not have done it, but the scissors were still in her hand and it seemed that she had three choices: drop them, stab Amber's hand with them — or use them to free herself.

They were sharp. Close to her ear, they made a grinding noise — and Amber was left holding a hank of hair, more hair than Jenny had thought. She stood staring at it. Amber stared at it. Sissy's eyes almost looked big.

You can't take back the bite of scissors — like the sleeves she'd cut from that pink frock. You might like to take it back, but you can't.

She tossed the scissors down and ran. Halfway across to the station, she found the bunch of blunt ends behind her left ear. She wheeled around, looked at the house, wanting to run back. Couldn't go back and get that hair. Couldn't even hide there. Looked at the station, pulled her remaining hair forward. She'd have enough to cover the gap when it dried. Could never tie it back again though.

'Hell,' she swore. 'Hell and double hell and damn too,' and she ran down the fence and across the railway lines, hoping Norman wouldn't see her. In beneath the peppercorn tree to feel the damage. Should have run to Maisy — except the twins would kill themselves laughing if they were at home. Couldn't go to the Palmers'. They were too sensible to ever do anything without thinking about it for two weeks. Over the road, running then, running down past the hotel. There was only one place she could go. Past old Noah, busy raking the dirt beneath the hotel verandah. They'd pay him with a meal, or maybe a drink. She didn't speak to him, just kept running.

Norman would hate her. She'd never had her hair cut in her life. And she couldn't go to the talent quest. And she couldn't win the twenty pounds and buy that blue dress for herself. She'd done a stupid thing. She'd done the most stupid thing she'd ever done in her life.

Down past Hooper's corner, past Macdonald's mill, then out along the bush road to Granny. She'd have to hide down there until her hair grew back, that's all.

Hide down there until her hair grew back. Cover up. Cover it up.

Her feet slowed. She glanced at the trees hugging each side of the road. There was something about haircuts and staying at Granny's, something long, long ago. She'd . . . she'd cut her hair before. Once before.

Before what?

Before Amber went away.

Amber in her big white dress. Amber the monster. Mr Foster's clunking boot.

'Charlie's jar of humbugs . . .'

Forgot the trees. Forgot their trunks were hiding murderers, their prison bars were locking her into the road, forgot everything except . . . hiding . . . hiding at Granny's at the end of the road.

Gertrude saw her coming. She walked up the track to meet her, and Jenny was over the gate, howling now that she was safe, now that Gertrude's big safe hard-working hands were holding her, patting her shoulder, smoothing back that tangle of drying curls — and finding those blunt ends and not believing the evidence of her eyes.

'Did she do that to you?'

Jenny's hand reached to cover what Gertrude had exposed. 'I did it.'

'Whatever would possess you to go and do a thing like that?'

'I didn't know I was cutting so much.'

'You're singing tonight.'

'I can't now,' she howled.

Gertrude led her inside. She poured her a mug of water, offered a damp cloth to cool her face, while Jenny sobbed out the whole sorry tale of Amber not wanting to go tonight and Sissy snarly because she wouldn't go. She bawled harder when she reached the chapter on Sissy's green dress that was made of spider's web.

'And she bought me a brown prison dress, which no one would make the worst murderer in the world wear — even if she was being hanged. And he let her do it, Granny. And I told him Miss Blunt let me try on the blue dress. I told him she'd hung it in the back room for me, and he let her get away with buying me a brown thing that . . . that Mrs Duffy wouldn't wear to a funeral.'

'Shush, now,' Gertrude soothed. 'You'll put my chooks off the lay for a week with all that noise.'

'But it's not fair, Granny. And you know Sissy's daffodil dress — Dad gave it to me when they threw it out, and she burned it. She's evil, and I remembered that she was always the same, even before, even when I lived down here. Why does everyone . . . why do you all cover up for her?'

Jenny rarely told tales. She was making up for lost time today, spilling the lot, shedding her every hurt, along with buckets of tears. Her eyes were swollen, her nose blocked by tears, her voice full of tears.

'You have to stop crying, darlin'. You won't be able to sing tonight.'

'I can't sing! I'm never singing again. I'm staying down here with you and Elsie and Joey and I'm never seeing anyone ever again.'

'Vern gave me his old wireless so Elsie and Joey can hear you tonight. You're not going to disappoint them, are you? And who is going to know if you're wearing a prison dress or your nightie if you're singing on the wireless?'

'We have to sing at the concert first, and Maisy said they could only get tickets right up in the back row because they've all sold out, so thousands of people will know what I'm wearing it, Granny, and I wouldn't wear that brown thing if I was ninety-nine and dying of leprosy — and I'm not wearing anything anyway, because I'm not going anywhere until my hair grows.'

'It took fourteen years to get this long. Can you live down here until you're twenty-eight?'

'Yes.'

'Or will we just cut the rest of it off to match it?'

Jenny sniffed, wiped her eyes with the cloth and looked at her grandmother. 'Can you?'

'Elsie and Joey trust me with a pair of scissors.'

'Will I look stupid?'

'No more so than you do now.'

Jenny's hand reached for short tufts, shorter now than when they'd been wet. Given their freedom from the dragging length, they'd dried into tight curls.

'Would it all go like those bits?'

'It would.'

They took a chair out to the sunlight later and Gertrude found her scissors. She was afraid to begin, unsure of where to begin.

'It's going to be like harvesting a hundred-acre wheat paddock with a kitchen knife, darlin'. I hate making that first cut.'

'I made it, Granny. Just . . . just finish it.'

She cut, and bunches of gold fell to the dirt. She snipped until she found a shape she could work with, then her scissors became more selective, while Jenny sat eyes closed, soothed by the sun and her grandmother's touch, calmed by the snip of the scissors shaping her hair. Shaping it in at the nape of her neck, leaving it full at the crown, Gertrude's fingers measuring, matching the mutilated side to the other, her hands very certain.

They'd learnt their skills from a hard taskmaster and she was back with him, standing beneath an earlier sun, snipping enough but not too much. He'd been a vain man. Cut his hair too short and when he washed his curls, they coiled like springs back to his scalp. There were two weeks between a good haircut and a bad. She'd suffered through a couple of bad weeks.

Such familiar hair, the feel of it, the smell of it. She wet her hands, wet the curls, knowing exactly how that hair would behave when given water. She combed it up from the nape of the neck, watched the stubble become tight springs.

A breath held too long, released in a sigh, she stepped back — like a sleepwalker suddenly awakened, and surprised to find herself in her own yard, outside her own front door, Jenny seated on a battered kitchen chair, a cloud of gold spread at her feet. She was surprised too at what she had created.

'Have a look at yourself,' she said.

Lengths of hair clinging to her skirt, her shoes, Jenny stood, brushing them, kicking them off, while Gertrude brushed more from her back. Inside to the washstand mirror then, and shocked at what she saw.

'I look like a boy.'

'But a beautiful boy,' Gertrude said.

'I feel light-headed.'

Gertrude's own head felt light. Too long standing in the sun, or that was her excuse.

'Dad will hate me.'

'It will fluff up when it dries. It will look a lot more. Clean up the mess for me, darlin', while I make us a cup of tea.'

Needed her outside, just for a moment, just until she gathered her wits. She walked to her table to lean a while, her eyes not leaving that girl's head, bobbing about outside as she gathered that fallen hair. The sun had bleached the longer lengths, but close into the scalp the colour was a rich, burnished gold.

'Do I look that terrible?' Jenny said.

'You look beautiful.'

'You're looking at me funny.'

'I was thinking about Harry working for days on Vern's old wireless, getting a truck battery to connect up to it so we can hear you sing tonight,' she lied.

'I got nits once. Dad wouldn't let Maisy cut my hair. I can't . . . I can't let him see me like this.'

'You did what you did, darlin'. You should have thought of that before you did it.'

'She was pulling my hair. I wanted to get away.'

'Tell your dad. He'll understand.'

'You can't tell him things he doesn't want to know! He's like a horse wearing blinkers. He can't look left or right — and anyway, only the finalists will be on the wireless. I won't get into the finals.'

'You've got a darn good chance, and I'm not the only one in town who's saying so. Mr Cox was talking to me the other day. His son is driving him and his wife down, just to hear you. Vern reckons you've already got it won.'

397

'Why does a mother buy a gorgeous dress for one daughter and a prisoner's uniform for the other?'

'You're fourteen years old, darlin'. Sissy is a grown woman.'

'That doesn't wash any more, Granny. She came home when Sissy was fourteen. She's been buying her pretty things since. I love pretty things too.'

'You'll have them when you're older.'

'I thought I had that blue dress. I tried it on and it was perfect. And she took it back. It's like . . . it's like if someone gave you a whole bar of chocolate and you took one tiny little taste, then they snatched it away and handed you a huge bowl of raw liver. And I can't swallow it, Granny. I just can't.'

'Don't start crying again. You've done enough of that to last you for twelve months.'

'You tell me then why she hates me.'

'She doesn't hate you.'

'Oh, Granny, you know she does. You know she hates you too.'

'That's enough now.'

'You're wearing blinkers too. Every time you see me, you say, "How is your mother?" As if one day when you ask, I'll say, "Oh, we had the priest around last night and he exorcised her devil out of her."'

'I don't like that sort of talk.'

'Then you're lucky you don't hear her talking about you to Sissy. She says worse.'

Gertrude took her teapot outside to empty around the roots of her rose. Jenny picked up the damp rag and blew her nose on it. She was lifting the hot plate to burn it when Gertrude came back.

'You walk away because you don't want to know anything that's true.'

Gertrude placed the teapot down. 'I walk away because it's easier on the heart, darlin', easier if I pretend that something isn't what it is. I gave your mother life, and when she was a little girl she loved me.'

'I love you, Granny, and I always will.'

'I know that, darlin'.'

'Do you want to know why?'

'You tell me why.'

'Because you're the only other normal person in the family.'

They laughed then, and Gertrude looked at the clock. 'What time are you leaving?'

'I'm still not ever leaving, but they're leaving at six. Sissy will have more room to spread her skirt. It's got miles and miles of material in it.'

She stood before the washstand mirror, combing her hair and watching it settle back to where it wanted to settle. 'Do I look like her with my hair short?'

'You look like yourself.'

'I remind myself of someone I've seen.'

'What are you going to wear tonight if you don't wear your brown dress?'

'You don't believe me, do you? I'm not going. I'm never even going home. You've got a spare bed now.'

'Tonight is your big opportunity to show what you can do to more than Woody Creek and you're not missing out on it.'

'My big opportunity to watch my sister make a fool of herself and to watch Dad cringe. If I don't go, he won't go — more and more room for Sissy's skirt.'

'If you had a pretty dress to wear, you'd go.'

'If pigs had wings, we could saddle them and ride up to take tea with the man in the moon.'

Gertrude glanced at her clock. There was a good hour to six — if her clock was right. She glanced towards her bedroom, then back to Jenny, who couldn't get enough of pulling that comb through her short hair, or of the stranger in the mirror. Maybe it was the wrong thing to do, but Gertrude went to her bedroom and took the stranger's gold crepe from her trunk.

'Try that on.'

'Elsie's wedding dress?'

'It should fit you.'

The comb and mirror lost their allure. 'It's . . . it's too beautiful.'

'Quickly then. It's almost five, and that clock could be slow.'

'God, Granny.'

'Young ladies don't blaspheme.'

Jenny stripped to her petticoat, tossed her faded navy dress over the back of a chair and slid into golden riches. Her petticoat was too long. The dress came off. Her petticoat came off. She didn't need it anyway; that frock had its own built-in petticoat of gold silk.

'It's too —'

Lost for words then. It was too everything — the silk against skin accustomed to cotton, the weight of it, and the skirt, almost clinging to her hips but not quite. It was short. It barely reached to mid-knee. It had been longer on Elsie. There was very little of it, but what there was was far too much.

'It's so pure, unadulterated gorgeous, Granny. Who made it?'

'It was bought a long way from Woody Creek, many years ago,' Gertrude said, turning her around, needing to see the all-over picture. Its square-cut neckline was wide but not low. It had sleeves, small sleeves, no waist, a lot of beading. It was a woman's frock, but modest enough for a girl.

'Your neck looks bare.'

'You just didn't know I had one, that's all.'

'It hasn't seen much daylight, darlin',' Gertrude said, and she returned to her bedroom.

This time Jenny followed her, stood over her eager to see what else she might whip up with her magic wand or dig out of her trunk. Old garments were lifted out to the floor, most stiff with age, her wedding photograph was placed face down. Jenny pounced on that. She remembered it, remembered its fancy frame.

'Leave it!'

Too late.

'It used to hang on your wall with your fly swatter.'

'A long, long time ago.'

Gertrude removed a large embroidered tablecloth, a wedding present she'd never used. She offered it in exchange for the photograph, but Jenny had returned to the kitchen to stand in the doorway staring at that photograph, or at her grandfather . . . a curly-headed boy!

'Why didn't you tell me when I asked?'

'Tell you what?'

Head down in that near empty trunk and Gertrude couldn't find what she knew was in there. A fancy vase, another wedding present came out. Her father's family Bible. A shoe with a turned-up toe.

'That I'm the image of Itchy-foot.'

Gertrude pounced on a grey leather pouch. 'I knew it was in here.'

Stepping over old frocks, old shawls, tablecloth, her fingers working hard to untie a leather thong stiffened by age. She lifted back her bedroom curtain and saw Jenny holding that photograph, but staring at her.

'That's why she hates me. Because I'm the image of her father.'

'You're nothing like him. You couldn't —'

The gathering of the pouch neck demanded Gertrude's full attention; it didn't want to release its prize, but she got it open and poured a string of amber beads to her palm.

'I am like him,' Jenny said, uninterested in beads. 'And why couldn't I be like him?'

'Because you're a beautiful young girl and all you're looking at is his hair, and the only reason it looks the same is because I used to cut his in the same style. Now turn around.'

The amber beads filled the space nicely, and matched the beadwork of the dress, as she knew they would. Those school shoes and socks didn't match anything. The stranger's shoes were somewhere, and she may as well be hung for a sheep as a lamb. She looked in the bottom of her wardrobe, found them in the lean-to wardrobe, and Jenny more than willing to swap the photograph for the shoes.

Things like this didn't happen to her. The shoes had high heels. She craved heels. They were a size too large, though.

'Elsie's sandals will fit you. Get them off,' Gertrude said, again glancing at her clock.

'Who did they belong to?'

'Someone left them here, with the dress.'

They were a light tan, more sandal than shoe, the leather straps stiffened by fourteen years, the toes a mote misshapen by the newspaper Gertrude had stuffed into them.

'They're not that much too big.' She tried walking in them. They made her tall, made her walk tall. 'We could cut something up and put it in them. Miss Rose is always doing that with shoes at the concerts.'

Gertrude looked at what she'd done, at the shape of her granddaughter's legs. Everything about that girl was class. She was long in the calf, her ankles were slim. She'd done the wrong thing in putting that dress on her, had got more than she expected. Elsie had lent it little shape; it had been longer on her. Jenny was doing something else to it — as her mother may have done something else to it.

'Can I cut this up?'

There was a cardboard carton down the bottom end of the kitchen, overloaded with newspapers. Jenny had the scissors. They cut and trimmed cardboard innersoles and the shoes were back on.

'Can you walk in them? And it's no use saying you can if you can't.'

'I can fly in them, Granny.'

'You'll need to. Joey will take you in on Harry's bike.'

The skirt rose up to her thighs when she straddled the rear seat of Harry's bike, one of her shoes fell off. Harry picked it up, ran it up to them while Jenny removed the second shoe. She carried them the rest of the way, carried them to the King Street corner, where she decided she wasn't going home to wait for the Hoopers and probably get murdered while she waited. She wasn't riding by Hooper's with her shoes off either. She'd walk the rest of the way like a lady.

They stopped at King's corner. She leaned on Joey while she brushed her feet and got those shoes on. She straightened her skirt, then, because the world was a different place tonight and she a different person, she kissed her finger and touched it to his cheek.

'Ta very muchly, Joey.'

'I'll be listening, so you'd better win,' he said.

'Cross your fingers for me.'

Jenny walked the block to Hooper's corner, taking care where she put her feet. Heels were all very well, but not if you wanted to walk. And the cardboard innersoles were slippery. Her toes had to cling on like fingers.

But the car was in the side street, Jim cleaning dead insects from its windscreen.

'Gord's struth,' he said. 'What have you done to yourself, Jen?'

'Haircut.'

Margaret joined them, clad in floral frills. 'Oh, my, but don't you look the smart one tonight,' she said, her fishbowl eyes wide.

Lorna grunted a greeting and got into the car. Jenny thought to get in beside her, but Lorna had other ideas. She liked a window seat. 'Other side,' she said.

Safe then, jammed in the back seat between the Hooper sisters, not safe enough to stop her heart beating like a drum, to stop her throat from drying out, but pretty safe when they drove around to collect the rest of the party.

Norman had walked down to the station yard to look for her. Amber and Sissy were waiting on the verandah.

'We've got Jen with us, Mr Morrison,' Jim called.

Sissy saw her hair. She stared bug-eyed but made no comment. Amber didn't look at her. The car would hold six in comfort. It didn't like taking the seventh, but it did; Amber in the back seat beside Margaret, Norman and Sissy in front.

If Norman saw Jenny's hair, her frock, he chose not to, and once in, there was no room for him to turn around. Like Cinderella, she was safe until midnight.

MEMORIES

The chooks were fed, the goats milked, the lamp lit, the stove stoked and a pot of tea made before Gertrude sat down. She ate bread, cheese and pickled cucumber. She drank two mugs of tea before reaching for her wedding photograph. Didn't look at it, carried it to her bedroom to bury him once more.

Junk everywhere in there, still lying where she'd left it. She'd emptied that trunk before putting her hand on that necklace. Knew it was in there, though. It had to be. She hadn't taken it out since she'd packed it in India. So proud of it once. She'd worn it often. He'd bought her forgiveness with those beads back when she'd been a buyable, pliable twenty. Remembered that night clearly, remembered his lovemaking. She'd been so sure a baby would come of it, she'd chosen her name: Amber Rose.

God alone knew why she'd stuck with that name. Everything else had gone by the time Amber was born. All of those years of waiting for her baby girl, all of those years of hoping, and when she'd come, she'd looked like Amber Rose.

'Fool.'

Couldn't shake him out of her head tonight. It was the trunks. It was the junk on her floor. It was his photograph.

And why in the name of hell she'd saved any of that junk, she didn't know. She kicked a pile from her pathway. What use were old shoes, their toes curling up?

'Fool,' she repeated, reaching for a silk shawl, a pretty thing, or the embroidery on it had once been pretty. He'd bought that for her too. He'd bought her forgiveness a few times before she'd grown up enough to know that some sins were not forgivable.

She used the shawl to wrap the photograph, a burial shroud. He'd go down deep this time, down at the bottom of her trunk, so deep he couldn't get out to haunt her. But the silk shawl split in two and she dropped him. He landed on his feet, still laughing at her. He'd always landed on his feet.

'You're dead and buried in some hellhole in Egypt, and I've got your money to prove it, you conscienceless sod,' she said, finally looking him in the eye.

He'd had beautiful eyes, the clearest, the purest of blues. Chameleon eyes, altering to match his surroundings — or his moods. She'd learnt to read his eyes.

The photograph was black and white but tonight memory added colour. He looked like the angel Gabriel, complete with golden halo.

She'd thought he was the angel Gabriel the first time she'd set eyes on him.

It was at one of Monk's parties. She'd gone out there with Vern, had worn her new apple-green frock. They'd put on some wonderful parties back in those days. Vern and his family, being neighbours, had always been invited, and where Vern had gone, she'd gone. Eighteen at the time. Just a pair of kids, alike in so many ways. A perfect match, her and Vern. Always were.

Archie had been older, twenty-two at a time when twenty-two had sounded old. He'd been so city, so sophisticated. He was sitting at Monk's piano, singing, charming all of the girls, but she was the one who had caught his eye. A handsome man, a charming man, accustomed to getting what he wanted, he'd set his net for her, had ridden down here and charmed her mother. His occupation impressed her father.

And Gertrude had been flattered. There was no denying that. She hadn't known then that she was courting the devil, that he collected lovers like another man might collect butterflies — crippled them, pinned them to his display board, then ran off to chase the next one.

'I should have poisoned you with a cocktail of your own potions in Africa,' she said. 'I should have cut your throat in Argentina. I was too young,' she said. 'I was a stupid innocent fool . . .

'And I shouldn't have sent that little girl off dressed up like that tonight, not with her hair cut like that. She looked eighteen.'

She stood staring at the mess on her floor, her house so silent she could hear the clock ticking in the kitchen. Would have to get the right time from the wireless tonight. Vern always carried a watch. He used to set that clock for her. Never bothered now. Didn't want to admit that his eyes struggled to see the hands on his watch. She'd driven him mad in the city asking him the time. Always a train to catch, a solicitor to see, a doctor's office to get to, and no sun, no chooks and goats, to tell her the time.

She'd told the solicitor she had no use for Archie's trunk, that she needed no more junk, but Archie's sister hadn't wanted it, and in the end Vern made the decision to bring the thing home. He'd been more interested in its contents than she — and annoyed when he'd found it locked and the key missing. He'd tried to pick the lock the night it was delivered to their hotel. He'd asked the chap on the reception desk if he had a key that might fit. They'd tried a dozen.

They'd forced it open three days after they'd got it home. And the first time they lifted that lid, Gertrude had expected a spitting cobra to spring out and strike at her throat, a poisonous dart to fly into her eye, certain that somehow, some way, Archie would get in the last hit from the grave.

No booby traps. Not much of anything other than his books. His poison had died with him . . . or migrated into Amber.

'Change your thinking,' she demanded. 'Go over to Elsie's.'

She'd come in here to bury him and bury him she would tonight. Thinking about him and the past never did her a scrap of good, and she knew it. Hard though to stop digging at the past once you allowed your mind to wander back there.

If Amber's babies had lived, she would have been different. Maybe it took terrible pain, terrible disappointment, to activate

Archie's type of poison, though she'd never worked out what had activated his.

He'd been addicted to opium when she'd met him, not that she'd known that, or not then. Amber was now swallowing a derivative of that same drug, had been swallowing it since that operation which was supposed to cure her. She wasn't cured and that little girl suffering for Gertrude's interference.

I should have left her in that hellhole. I should have walked away like Vern warned me to walk away.

How does any mother walk away from her child?

Should have walked away from Archie long before she had. Some folk require a crutch in order to get through life, be it God, drug or bottle. She'd tried to be Archie's prop, had believed she could save him from his drugs — had believed until he'd used his drugs on her one night and taken her baby boy before he was even showing in her belly.

That was the day she'd learnt to hate Archie Foote.

She could see him now, see him standing over her bed in his doctor's coat, smiling down at her. 'All fixed, Tru,' he'd said. And that little boy lying in a basin, his minute mouth moving in an unborn scream. And that bastard had left him there so she could watch him die.

The photograph flew from her hand. It hit the curtained doorway, caught, landed easy, landed intact.

'You're unbreakable, you bastard.'

Almost heard him. *Don't fight me, Tru. You can't beat me, Tru.*

She'd tried to leave him after he took her son. She was twenty-three, had no money, couldn't speak the language, was half-crazed with grief, hadn't known a soul.

He'd spoken the language. He'd alerted the local authorities. They'd found her wandering in a daze. They'd taken her home to him. He was a doctor. He'd been working at the time in one of their hospitals. He told them she'd lost an infant, was crazed by grief; and when they were gone, he told her that the only way she'd ever leave him would be in a coffin.

Should have written to Vern. He would have come for her. Too proud to admit she'd made a mistake. She hadn't written.

A smart boy Vern; at eighteen, he'd seen through handsome Doctor Archibald Foote. 'Watch out for him, Trude,' he'd said. 'There's something not quite right about the pretty-faced little mongrel.'

She hadn't listened. She'd listened to her grandfather, her parents.

'Archie is a good man, with an honourable profession,' her father said. 'You'll want for nothing.'

'You make such a handsome pair, Gertie,' her mother had said. 'You'll have a fine-looking bunch of children.'

Barely nineteen when she'd wed, and a fine wedding it was too, and a fine wedding party at Monk's. Shy with Archie's family, they were so city, but good people.

'We're delighted Archie found himself such a pretty country girl,' his mother said.

They'd spent the night at Monk's. Maybe she'd believed she was in love. They'd travelled by train to Melbourne, her first trip on a train. She'd been nowhere, had seen nothing. For a month they'd lived in his father's house, Archie working with his doctor father and uncle, working long hours. She'd been homesick, had little to do. She'd tried to make a friend of Archie's fourteen-year-old sister. Gertrude had always wanted a sister. Then his sister was sent away to a sanatorium, and a week later, passage was booked for the newlyweds on a boat bound for South Africa, where Archie was to redeem himself by working with a group of missionaries.

She'd heard the raised voices, had seen his mother weeping, watched the uncle and aunt arrive, heard the doors close, watched them leave. She was the outsider, as was Archie. He'd clung to her during those weeks. It was a wife's place to support her husband, to not ask questions, to follow where he led. She'd been pleased to follow him from that house, relieved to board the boat bound for Africa.

They'd had a fine cabin on a ship of the line. There were parties every night. She wasn't seasick, wasn't afraid, loved those weeks, looked on them as the beginning of a huge adventure.

Archie, her handsome doctor, said he was feeling a little sick one night, that he needed to go to the cabin and lie down. She'd gone looking for him later, had opened the door and glimpsed a sight she hadn't understood — hadn't known then of the man's perverted desire for one of his own gender; had seen the naked limbs and closed that door faster than she'd opened it.

They'd joined a group of missionaries in Africa intent on leading the black heathens to God with prayer and medicine. Accustomed to hard labour, she'd been pleased to labour at her clever husband's side. Fell in love with the babies of Africa. Wanted one of her own.

She'd gone looking for Archie again one night, and found him at the little hospital hut, found his white body joined to black limbs. Knew what was happening this time. Reached for a bucket of water and tossed it. That broke them up.

She met her devil doctor that night. She was in bed when he came, had rolled herself into a sheet so he couldn't touch her flesh. He straddled her and the sheet became her straitjacket. A clever devil, Archie, he could punish without leaving a mark, or no visible mark when she was clothed. He told her many things while he abused her. Told her his sister didn't have tuberculosis, that he hadn't been sent to Africa to study the disease. Told her he'd been having his sister since she was nine years old, that she'd grown too old for their games and he'd got her with child. Told her that a female over twelve turned his stomach, that she turned his stomach, that her woman stink needed to be washed from his nostrils regularly by the clean sweat of man, that she could like it or lump it because that was the way it was.

'I want to go home.'

'Can't do that, Tru. You're my meal ticket.'

They'd left Africa soon after. He'd wanted to see Germany. A clever man, Archie Foote, he could make his needs known in the German tongue. She'd spent that year dependent on him. He spoke Spanish too. They were in Spain when she'd stitched up a gash in his head. He was appreciative. Her son was conceived in Spain and murdered in Argentina.

She hadn't got away from him in Argentina, but she'd grown up, woken up. In New Guinea, she'd grown strong. In India, she'd grown smart — and no longer dependent on his language skills. Plenty of English in India. Watched him closely, watched his eyes. She could read those eyes as her father could read the skies for rain. Watched the ports too. Getting ready, waiting, knowing she'd need to snatch that chance when it came, that she'd need to move fast. Amber was growing inside her and he hadn't known. She got herself home from India, worked her passage home on a boat full of diphtheria, and left him to rot.

His photograph was lying face up where it had fallen. She kicked it. It slid along the floor to rest against the leg of her table. She picked it up, held it close to her lamp and looked him in the eye.

'You're done with haunting me,' she said, and she smashed the frame down on the edge of her table. He left a dent in the wood. A strong frame; her parents had paid good money for it. She took it to the stove where she slammed it hard on cast iron. And the glass shattered, tinkling as it fell into the metal hearth tray.

'Now you're dead,' she said, and she walked away from him, walked out the door and into the clean air of night.

The fancy frame had come apart, the photograph fallen free to settle against the bucket Gertrude used for her kindling, to settle upright.

He was still smiling.

THE RADIO QUEST

Horses had had their day. Like it or not, a man was forced to move with the times. George Macdonald had moved with the times. He'd bought himself a 1935 Chrysler and a nice-looking car it was too, but he could no more control the bastard of a thing than he could his truck.

A man needed to get control of motors when he was young enough to learn new tricks. He needed to breed his sons when he was young enough to learn their tricks too. George was fifty the year those boys were born, and he had less control over them than he had over his Chrysler. He let them drive him around town for a week or two, taking turns behind the wheel, until the little bastards took off in his car one night and he had to put the copper onto them. They were picked up on the Willama bridge. He'd got his car back, little the worse for wear, but thereafter he'd kept it padlocked in his shed — until Maisy decided she wanted to go down to the talent quest.

She was twenty-odd years George's junior. It took Harry Hall seven days to put her in control of that car. It took Denham half an hour to give her a licence to drive it. She hadn't been out of the driver's seat since.

Maisy had never gained control over the boys, but she knew how to thwart them. On the night of the quest, she filled up the rear seat of the Chrysler with daughters, which left no room for their sons. They watched her back out, watched her get the thing pointed in the right direction, then the little bastards jumped on the running boards and clung on. George did his best to knock one of them off. He tried to wind up his window. The girls did the same on their side while Maisy did her best to keep that car on the road.

'I only booked seven seats,' she yelled. 'You won't get into the hall. It was booked out three days ago.'

'Watch the road,' they warned, in unison, from either side of the car.

They rode the running boards all the way to Willama, but were shaken off when she braked hard to miss a dray at the first crossroads. They were last seen still a good mile from the theatre, one carrying a half-full wheat bag over his shoulder. George hoped they were leaving home again.

The Macdonald party arrived late at the hall. The usher guided them up two sets of stairs to the back row of the dress circle while the master of ceremonies introduced the Melbourne judges. One had sung with Melba — before she was Melba. The pianist who would be accompanying the singers this evening had played professionally in London.

The Hooper party, having booked early, had secured seating on the left side of the hall, three rows back from the stage. They'd booked for four, on the off chance that Margaret might get cold feet. There should have been a seat for Amber, but Margaret, shaking from head to foot, required that seat. Lorna, as was her habit, claimed her aisle seat, Margaret sat beside her. Norman offered his seat to Amber, but Jim had no desire to sit beside her. He said he'd sit down the back where seats were being saved for the contestants who wouldn't be using them for a time. The contestants, on their arrival, had been ushered through a door to the right.

Twice Amber left her seat to find her daughter. She stood on Lorna's foot the first time, was near tripped by it on the second occasion, but when she returned, Lorna was in her seat, Margaret in Norman's and the aisle seat vacant. Amber sat, her head turning, eyes searching the exits for Cecelia, who she had to do something about. Norman had sat on those yards of green skirt and crushed the life out of it. The night was hot, the car crowded; they'd driven those thirty-nine miles with the car windows wide open. Cecelia's hair had suffered. Amber's attempt to remain with her daughter had been thwarted by a black-suited organiser. They had a possible thirty contestants to get through tonight, he'd said, and if one parent was allowed into the waiting area, the rest would want to be in there.

Amber's skirt was crushed, as was Margaret's. And that pretty little bitch standing in the foyer in her narrow skirt, fresh as a daisy, the lights glowing on her hair, glinting on the beads. Amber knew the tale of those beads, knew why she'd been named Amber. Knew her father had bought those beads. They belonged to Cecelia, not to that stray bitch. She'd wanted to snatch them from her throat.

And that great dumb beast of a man standing staring at her knees — couldn't force his eyes higher. Hated him for what he'd done to Cecelia. Hated him. Couldn't stand to sit at his side. Couldn't breathe for the smell of him. And the crowd. She shouldn't have come. Hadn't wanted to come.

She'd taken a tablet before leaving home, and had brought one for Cecelia, wrapped in her handkerchief. Her own need was greater. Handbag opened silently, hand inside it, feeling out the lump of pill, easing it free of its folds. Sat a while then, her bag closed, her eyes fixed on the stage while the first contestant was introduced. She'd have to dry-swallow it. Couldn't walk out now. Got it in her mouth, comfortingly bitter. Held it there while raising saliva enough to swallow. It stuck, and the taste was vile. Swallowed, swallowed again, while on stage a woman screeched.

Hours of this. Hours of sitting at his side. Hours and hours.

Amber swallowed and closed her eyes.

Number two was missing. The contestants had been given numbers when they'd arrived; they'd been offered glasses of cordial and told to sit along the sides of the room. A few sat. Most walked, smoked, talked. The room was thick with smoke and tension.

'Number two, Wilma Saunders. Is Wilma Saunders here?'

Many eyes searched for Wilma Saunders, wanting her to be there, but Wilma must have suffered a bout of second thoughts and remained at home, so Barry Andrews, number three, would now go on at number two.

'Grace Jones. Is Grace Jones here?'

Grace Jones was supposed to be number seven. Her number, with its yellow ribbon and small brass pin, waited unclaimed, along with number two, number nineteen, number twenty-six and number thirty — Margaret Hooper's number.

Sissy's frock had a belt. She'd slid the loop of her number over her belt. Jenny had no belt and no intention of poking pins into her borrowed frock. She wore the ribbon around her wrist. Sissy was sitting, Jenny standing beside her. She had to stand somewhere.

'You should have seen the way Dad was looking at the length of that dress,' Sissy said.

'You should have seen the way Amber was looking at yours. Go and do something about it — and your hair. There are mirrors in the ladies' room.'

'Have you got a comb?'

Jenny displayed empty hands. 'Someone in there will lend you one. You shouldn't be sitting down either. Your skirt looks like you slept in it.'

'At least I didn't borrow it from a blackfella,' Sissy said.

'At least it's not brown.'

'It's years out of fashion.'

They bickered. They always bickered now. The red-headed sisters Jenny had met in the bathroom weren't bickering. They were standing in the corner practising, or at least mouthing the words in practice.

'Is that her necklace?' Sissy said.

Unaccustomed to adornment, Jenny's hand kept fiddling with the beads at her throat. 'It's Granny's,' she said, dropping her hand to her side, then turning again to watch the red-headed sisters who had more in common than their red hair. They were the same size, they had similar faces, one older than the other, but dressed tonight in the same green, darker than Sissy's green but uncrushed. They had a comb. They'd combed each other's hair in the bathroom.

'Do you want me to borrow their comb?'

'It will probably have fleas in it.'

'Fleas will look better than it looks now.'

'Mum put one in her purse. She should have given it to me.'

Audience clapping, number four, now number three, waiting at the door to go on, number five being rounded up.

'They'll be calling you soon,' Jenny said.

'I can't do anything, can I!' Fact. She was useless without Amber, paralysed by her parasite.

'You can at least comb it!'

Jenny walked over to the red-headed girls. They lent her their comb and walked back with her, wanting to keep an eye on it.

'Turn around — if you can stand me touching you,' Jenny said.

Sissy turned around and Jenny did what she could, not out of sisterly love but face-saving and a form of pity — a bare smidgen — about as much as she might feel for a snarling dog, spoilt rotten by its owner then dumped out at the Duffys' to fend for itself.

Amber's fault. Up until yesterday, Norman had tried to talk Sissy out of reciting. He'd said that many concert performances were tolerated in Woody Creek because the performers were known to the community, but the Willama audience, having paid to be there, may not be as tolerant. He'd wasted his breath.

'You ought to get it cut,' she said, crossing two pins behind Sissy's ear, holding the wind-straightened hair up, back. The other side wasn't bad. She smoothed it with the comb, combed stray curls around her finger as she'd seen Amber do a hundred times. 'Now stand up and slap your skirt down.' They were clapping again, and calling for number six. 'And wash that grease off your stocking.'

'It's from his stupid gearstick,' Sissy said. 'I was supposed to sit in the back with Margaret but you were there.'

They called for Sissy while she was washing the grease from her stocking. She came, looking more bored than nervous. Jenny watched her walk to the black-suited man, watched her take her place in line. The organisers were wasting no time. Someone now playing the piano on stage. It sounded good. The audience liked it.

Then Sissy disappeared from the doorway and Jenny stepped back, got her back to the wall, stood head down, playing with Granny's beads and studying the toes of her borrowed shoes, knowing Norman would be sitting in the audience studying his own. Wished her name was Jenny Smith, Jenny Jones, Jenny anything. Didn't want it to be Jenny Morrison. Cringed internally and closed her eyes when she heard Sissy begin, but that was worse. Her internal eye saw too clearly, saw her sister wandering the stage *lonely as a cloud*, saw her floating *on high o'er vales and hills*. Saw her shading of her eyes so she might not be blinded by *a host of golden daffodils*.

*'Beside the lake, beneath the trees
Fluttering and dancing in the breeze . . .'*

Saw them breeze in through the waiting area, the contestants making way for the two chunky little men, one wearing an ancient army uniform and cap, one wearing an enamel basin on his head and a khaki overcoat. They scattered the contestants grouped around the door as they ran on stage, one of the black-suited men disappearing with them. Then no more of 'Daffodils'. The twins were singing of their aversion to daffodils to the tune of 'The Bold Gendarmes'.

Jenny pushed her way to the stage door, caught a bare glimpse of Sissy's crushed green, a twin holding an arm each, marching her backwards and forwards — or they were marching. She was struggling to get away.

*'We'll run her in. We'll run her in.
We'll run her in. We'll run her in.
We've had enough of daffodils.
We don't like flowers, we'll take no more, we'll show her out the bloody door, we'll show her what we do to dills.'*

Sissy kicked one, got an arm free and swung at the head of the one wearing the basin. It flew, rolled off stage. The other twin dodged her swinging arm, improvising now, playing to the audience.

'She's dangerous and that's no lie, but folk, we're here to do or die, and rid the earth of daffodils.'

They were performers. They'd always been performers. They could hold a tune too. The audience was a roar of laughter.

Sissy should have gone while the going was good, but the contestants had been told to exit from the other side, where they'd be met and shown to seats at the rear of the hall. She made her escape towards the waiting room door, where the organiser in black stood with the master of ceremonies and the pianist, all three laughing. She wailed, turned and ran back across the stage. The twins were taking their bows. The roar of applause became thunder, a few wits cheering her escape from custody, a few more yelling encouragement to the twins.

It took time to silence the laughter. A few were still tittering when the next contestant was introduced.

The twins came back to the waiting room, lit cigarettes and helped themselves to cordial. Jenny kept her distance, remaining with the group near the stage door, her back to them. They didn't recognise her until a fifteen-year-old boy went on stage, until the listeners were cringing at his awful rendition of 'Ramona'.

They grabbed her. 'You're under arrest for flaunting your kiddy tits,' one said.

'Do something worthwhile — arrest him,' one of the red-headed sisters said, nodding towards the stage door.

'You were so funny,' the other one said. 'We didn't realise it was a comedy act when she walked on.'

'Which was what made it so hilarious,' they said in unison.

Jenny left them to their four-way chat. She found a seat between a woman who looked fifty and a man who looked eighty, safe from the twins there.

A tenor went on next. He was a big man with a big voice and as soon as he opened his mouth, everyone knew who would win the prize money. He was better than Caruso. He was followed by a soprano, then another piano player, who was followed by a tap dancer, then a boy soprano who wasn't bad. The red-headed sisters went on after him, and the twins, having lost their first fans, left the waiting room.

The crowd of contestants had thinned and continued to thin. The fifty-year-old woman went on and a clarinet player gravitated to Jenny's side. He offered her a cigarette. She considered accepting it. People said they were good for nerves. She was nervous.

'My throat is too dry already,' she said, and he went over to the table and poured her a glass of cordial. Maybe he thought she was older. He looked about thirty.

A mixed bunch, the tail-enders: a woman in her thirties; a boy who might have been eighteen, who played the trombone; a woman of Amber's age; the old bloke, who looked eighty and was going deaf; the clarinet player; and a few who kept to themselves. The trombone player stopped and started twice. The audience gave him a clap for trying. The old bloke recited from 'The Sentimental Bloke'. Jenny had never heard of it, it wasn't Norman's style of poetry, but she loved it and wanted more. Strange how three minutes can alter in length, she thought, and wondered if Sissy was sitting at the back of the hall, wondered if Amber was listening to how a recitation should sound.

Amber had never heard Jenny sing, or not on stage. The thought of her sitting out there was scary, like she could will her to freeze, will her voice to seize. But Miss Rose was somewhere out there. She'd come down with John McPherson and Miss Blunt. And Maisy and George and five of their girls were out there, and Mr and Mrs Cox and their son and daughter-in-law. Anyway, Amber was probably outside comforting Sissy.

Wouldn't it be funny if Sissy and the twins got into the finals, she thought. The audience had loved them. What would Sissy do if she heard her name called?

But the judges wouldn't pick a comedy act, not for the wireless. Singers or musicians would make up the finalists; that's what most of the contestants said.

She drew a deep breath, held it long and wished those shoes would stop hurting. The right one felt as if it was cutting the ball of her foot in half, due to the cardboard innersole having split. She'd be pleased to get them off.

Her turn next. She stood, straightened her skirt. It felt as if it was sliding. Probably only its slippery lining that was sliding. Loved that dress, loved the colour and the beading. Another deep breath, straightened her shoulders, touched the amber necklace one more time for luck, then the black-suited man beckoned her forward as the applause died. And she walked on, in her borrowed dress, in her borrowed shoes, walked on, her head high. Easy to do. It felt so much lighter tonight.

'Miss Jennifer Morrison, the golden girl with the golden voice,' the master of ceremonies said, and the pianist, who had worked in London, played the introduction, which sounded much as Miss Rose played the introduction, if a bit more fancy.

Judges with their notepads in the front row. Amber sitting in the aisle seat, a couple of rows behind the judges. Jenny opened her mouth and sang.

THE AFTERMATH

The tenor won, the red-headed harmonising sisters came second and Jenny came third. She won five pounds, in an envelope with her name on it, which she held to her breast while the cameras flashed. When asked to hold it lower, she folded it, tucked it beneath her bra strap. It was her own money to spend on what she liked. And she liked that blue print dress, and she was going to buy it and leave it at Maisy's, and she'd buy a pair of sandals that fitted, with heels, but smaller heels.

The clarinet player, who had also made the finals, shook her hand outside the hall. Jim shook her hand and told her she should have won. Margaret Hooper kissed her cheek, Miss Rose hugged her, Miss Blunt gave her a peck, and Maisy and Jessie Macdonald danced her up and down the footpath. Norman kept his distance, kept his silence. He agreed with Lorna that they should start for home.

They'd found Sissy leaning against the car bawling her eyes out. Amber knew she'd been crying since she'd run off stage. Jim and Jenny knew she'd been sitting at the rear of the hall with the other contestants, that she'd been sitting there when the finalists' names were called. Jenny didn't know what had happened after that, but Jim knew. She'd taken off from the hall.

There was little conversation on the way home, only Jim's apology when he bumped Jenny's exposed knee while reaching for the gearstick. Only Norman's brief comments on the road, only Lorna's yawn from the rear seat, Sissy's blubbering, Margaret's and Amber's soothing.

The radio broadcast, timed for nine thirty, had started on time but ended late. Then the newspaper photographer had to line up the winners for a photograph, and not one either, but a dozen. It was after eleven when they got away.

There were car lights on the road ahead. One would be Maisy, one John McPherson. Jenny wished she was in Mr McPherson's car, or wished the road much longer. Didn't want to go home. Wanted to stay out there, bobbing along a dark road in the middle of no-man's-land. They were approaching the town when she broke the silence with words she'd practised for the last fifteen miles.

'I promised to take the necklace and Elsie's things back tonight. Can we drive down there first, please?' She'd made no promise. Her throat knew it was telling a lie. It choked the words out.

'That fine with everyone?' Jim said.

Not fine with some. 'Cecelia is distraught,' Amber said. 'Take them back tomorrow.'

Six hours of multiple Morrisons was five and a half hours too long for Lorna. 'Stop here,' she said. Jim stopped the car on Blunt's corner. Lorna got out to walk the last block home.

'Which way, folks?' he said.

'Home,' Amber said, so Jim turned left, over the railway lines, then right into Norman's street, Jenny's heart pounding like a hard-punching fist in her stomach, afraid now of Norman's lack of response.

Sissy was eased from the car, supported by Amber until Norman took his share of the load.

'Out,' Amber's demand was directed at Jenny who had remained in the car.

'I'll run straight in and straight out, Daddy. I promise.'

Promises going left, right and centre tonight, but she had to put off the inevitable, had to stay away from Norman's eyes, get to tomorrow and to daylight before she had to look at his hangdog eyes. Had to get that necklace and dress back safe to Granny too, get her prize money safe down there or it would end up in the stove.

'Off you go,' he said.

Margaret, happy to continue her outing, drove with them out along the forest road where the car's headlights lit their narrow way between those trees, showing a strange green world never noticed by day, showing the colours of the great trunks, glinting in the eyes of wild things, that light like a moving pool, erasing the black for an instant, but only an instant.

Jenny opened the gate, then slid back into the car to ride the last track. The balls of both feet were screaming, her toes so tired of clinging on. She couldn't bear to put those shoes on the ground when she stepped from the car, but she forced them to carry her just a few yards more.

'Granny,' she called, but not too loud, just in case she was sleeping. A light was showing beneath the door. Jenny opened it, took the shoes off and crept in. She peered into Gertrude's bedroom, expecting to see a shape in the bed. It was empty.

The table lamp burning low, its flickering light playing with her shadow, she unhooked the necklace, placed it on the table, removed the folded envelope from her bra, placed it beneath the beads, took Elsie's wedding frock off and hung it over a chair, pulled her own frock on, found her shoes where she'd left them. That was the beauty of Granny's house. Things stayed where they were put.

She was tying her shoelaces when she saw broken glass on the floor, saw the photograph propped against a bucket, its ruined frame fallen into the hearth tray. She reached for the photograph, took it to the lamp and turned the wick a little higher. They were like a film-star bride and groom, Granny's hair done in much the same style as she did it today, his hair cut in the same style as Jenny's.

'I love your haircut,' she told Itchy-foot. 'And I'm glad I look like someone, even if Granny doesn't want me to.'

She placed the photograph face up on the table, beside the beads and prize money, and was out the door. They were coming through the goat paddock gate in single file, Gertrude, Elsie, Harry, Joey and little Lenny. She walked through the dark to meet them.

'We thought you had it won, darlin'. We couldn't believe how beautiful you sounded over the air.'

'I said to Mum it was like hearing some singer on a record,' Elsie said.

They talked as they walked her to the car, but Jim was in no hurry. He joined the group, then Margaret came high-stepping around the car.

A minute can be ten minutes long or ten minutes can become one. Time is stretchable. It's shrinkable.

Those same minutes in Norman's house were agonisingly long, loud, and painful.

Cecelia had collapsed in the passage and his attempt to lift her had moved something in his back. He couldn't straighten.

'Give her one of my pills,' Amber demanded.

'Walk away from her, Mrs Morrison. She enjoys an audience.'

Certainly a poor choice of words. They increased the volume of Cecelia's wail, and offended her mother.

He stood in the passage supporting his back with a hand and considering that pill bottle he'd taken charge of. Tonight he was tempted, sorely tempted, and tempted too to help himself to a handful.

'You loved it, didn't you? You loved them making a fool of her, didn't you?'

He attempted to walk away, but pain shot from his back down his buttocks to thigh. He groaned and was forced to stay.

'You wanted to laugh at her with the rest of them, but you didn't have the guts.'

In any argument, there must be two participants. He tried once more to move and almost joined his daughter on the floor. Gathered himself, sighed.

'Let us not forget it was your decision that she should recite, Mrs Morrison. Let us not forget that it was you who chose to allow that girl to make a fool of herself. Go to your room. I will deal with my daughter.'

'Give her a pill and she'll settle down.'

'If you remove yourself, she will settle down.'

'Remove myself to where? I have to sleep in her bed?'

'No doubt you have shared worse beds.' His mouth was working independently of his head, but his back was killing him. He needed to sit down, lie down. He made a conciliatory gesture. 'Use my room if you wish.'

'I'll sleep in the gutter first.'

'As you no doubt have.'

He was not a cruel man. He knew himself to be soft-hearted. He had never raised a hand in anger, rarely raised his voice in anger. He was in pain. He wasn't himself. He heard his voice rising, then heard his words silence Sissy's wail. He saw Amber step back, then back again as his mouth sprayed her with the venom of his tongue, whipped her, then brutalised her with the bludgeon of Cousin Reginald.

Cowed by his bastardry, she backed into Cecelia's room, closed the door. And he saw Cecelia rise green from her collapse, her eyes staring at a monster. She got away from it. She followed her mother, slammed the door as car lights played across the parlour window.

That car shocked him back from the place where his mouth had been, jarred him, sending new pain screaming down his buttock, down his leg. God's punishment. He punished evil tongues.

Got himself out to the gate, where he took Jenny's arm and walked her away from the house, walked her through the railway yard to the station, moaned as he eased himself down to the station bench where he sat in silence, waiting for the pain to abate.

'I'm sorry, Daddy,' she said.

He offered his station keys. 'Tea,' he said. 'Tea and silence.'

He had thought to discuss the desecration of her hair, the borrowed frock. Now? What did it matter? What did anything matter? He had sworn never to use Amber's adultery against her, and he'd flung it in her face, and in front of Cecelia. What breed of man was he?

He sat staring at the water tower and at the moon perched on its rim, looking like a child's lost balloon caught up there by its string. Watched it for minutes, willing it to fly free, while she brought him tea, brought him biscuits, then sat with him, in silence, or silent for a time.

'She was pulling my hair, Daddy. I had the scissors, so I cut it.'

'Silence!'

He sipped his tea, refused the biscuits. She ate four, emptied her mug and stood, waiting for his, and looking at the moon. Hated standing there and no words. Wanted him to lecture her, lock her in her room, tell her she couldn't sing any more, anything.

'I was sorry I did it — as soon as I did it.'

'God forgive me,' he said. 'God forgive me.'

She placed her mug on the platform, and reached out to hold his face between her hands. 'You didn't do anything to forgive, Daddy.'

'Then God forgive me for that.'

He reached out with his free hand and touched her exposed ear. She was clad now in her old school dress, her school shoes, but the child was gone. The audience had applauded a woman. He'd watched a woman walk on stage, heard a woman's voice.

'I borrowed you for such a short time,' he said. 'The child has been lost with that beautiful hair.'

'I'm sorry, Daddy.'

He lifted a hand for silence.

The lights were turned off in the railway yard once the train went through. The streetlights were turned off at midnight; no lights showing at Norman's house. Dark now, only the moon now — disappearing behind the water tower.

'I remember things, Daddy — from before. I can't pretend any more. I know things from Jessie Macdonald too. I know my mother was in jail in Melbourne.'

Shock moved him, sent a jolt of white-hot pain radiating through his back to his bowel. 'You . . .'

Too hard to find the words. He'd flung all he had at that slut, that diseased whore. Only the ache remained where those words had been festering for years. Only a gaping hole in his gut now. Her infection had eaten through. So he watched the moon, going, going, gone.

'You're making me scared, Daddy. Talk to me.'

She stood before him, reached again to touch his face, and he grasped her hand, held it to his heavy cheek and he wept.

'My pride,' he whispered. 'My only pride.'

She held his head against her, patted his back, kissed his face, like Granny had patted her, had kissed her. She was the grown-up now, holding her crying child. 'I love you, Daddy. I love you best in the whole world. You know that. You know that.'

He stood later, much later, and he couldn't straighten. She helped him back to the house, supporting him up the steps, taking it slowly. She walked him down the passage, helped him off with his jacket. Took off his tie, removed the studs from his collar, held his arms while he sat down on the bed then lifted his feet up.

'You'll be better in the morning,' she said. 'Everything will be better in the morning.'

Deep, undisturbed sleep is the privilege of youth. Jenny had left her door open so she might listen for her father, but her day both physically and emotionally draining, she did not listen long.

Norman lay immobile, his back having found a nominal peace, though not his mind. It abused him, inflicting its barefisted blows. A man on his back cannot evade his own punishing mind; he cannot shield himself from self-inflicted pain. Imprisoned with self, by self, he lay, tears trickling, filling the cups of his ears, which overflowed and ran down the creases of his neck to his pillow. He thought of the brandy flask in his kitchen cupboard and for an hour or more willed himself to rise, to fetch that flask and kill his pain, still his mind.

The house was still, the town was still, when, in the early hours of morning, he rolled from his bed. Pulverised by pain, his feet on the floor, he knew the brandy was too far away so he reached for his underwear drawer and the bottle buried deep.

The pressure required to unscrew the cap ripped him apart, but he got it off and poured a mound of her poison to his palm, and from his palm took one pill with his tongue. She'd swallowed one dry tonight, he'd seen her do it. The taste was brutal. His tongue wanted to reject it. Cruel tongue, it deserved the punishment. He placed a second pill with the first, then stood, fingering what remained in his palm while his stomach threatened to vomit out her poison. Moved too fast. Excruciating pain overrode his stomach's need and, with a shaking hand, he attempted to pour the pills back into the bottle. Spilled them, to bed, to floor. The bottle top? His hand feeling for it found her pills, then found the cap. He replaced it and made his slow way to the kitchen to spit the vile paste. Or wash it down. Kill his pain as she killed her pain . . . killed her . . . humanity.

Did she feel pain? Did she feel anything other than what a rabid bitch might feel for her pup?

He swallowed the paste as he reached for his brandy flask, placed high in the kitchen cabinet. One sip to cleanse his tongue. He took it with him to the window, where he stood supporting his weight, his hands on the kitchen sink, while staring out into black. Silent house. Silent world. A second sip from the flask, a third, then, its comfort in his hand, he started back to his room. His feet stilled before Cecelia's closed door. He'd lost his fight for that girl when her mother came home — or perhaps before.

The door squeaked as he opened it, only opened it an inch or two, enough to see two heads on two pillows. How many pills had the whore horded in her handbag? How had she settled that girl tonight? Did he care tonight?

He should care.

Forgive us our trespasses as we forgive those who trespass against . . .

Forgive her betrayal? He could not. It was a dagger driven deep into his heart and worn there daily since she had attempted to decapitate him with the garden shovel. He could not remove that dagger, could not forget its presence, only ignore it, only bury it deep in the darkest pit of his mind and stay far away from its entrance.

He'd entered there tonight. Now he couldn't find his way out.

How many beds had she shared in the years she'd been gone? How many diseased dogs had she lain with? How many fools had she diseased? How many in this town looked at him and saw the dupe, the fat fool who had taken his whore back into his home?

Jessie Macdonald knew, a girl, a mere slip of a girl, eighteen, nineteen. There were eight Macdonald girls, and if each of the eight had told eight more . . . Eights began to multiply in Norman's mind, became sixteen, became thirty-two and sixty-four and one hundred and twenty-eight, and two hundred and fifty-six, and five hundred and twelve and . . .

The town would take no more of his multiplication. It escaped Woody Creek's boundaries to multiply in Melbourne.

Ogden had found that spitting shrew. Ogden's wife had seven sons, one wed to a Macdonald girl. Multiplication doing well in Melbourne.

And Charles knew, so every Duckworth knew. How many Duckworths were laughing at him tonight? He closed the door, slid the metal flask into his trouser pocket to clink against her bottle of poison, while he deducted Duckworth deaths, tried to recall family births. He could not, but certainly each flat-faced, newborn Duckworth looked north tonight and named him fool.

Born a fool, fatherless, friendless. His mother's fool, his wife's fool, his daughter's fool.

Until he'd chanced upon his Jenny-wren, his fairy child with her pink shell ears, content for so long to perch upon his shoulder, to lift him high on her fragile wings.

Not so fragile tonight. He'd seen those wings flexing, had heard her pure, sweet voice filling that large hall, reaching out, reaching out over all of the land, calling to others of her kind.

He was not of her kind. He was a fat fool, fit only to keep food in the mouth of a diseased whore who'd traded her body for bread — but offered no such trade with him. Ate his bread. Spent his money.

A man with a dagger buried in his heart could know these things but keep his distance from that knowledge while that knowledge was his alone to know.

'He cannot hide from the multitudes,' he said, patting his pocket. Flask and bottle clinked, comfortingly, companionably, bitterly.

The taste of her pills still on his tongue, he washed his mouth once more, then opened the front door and stepped out to the night.

At that point, the man who was not himself felt whoever he had become entering into the muddy wallow of an unknown place.

THE WINDOW

Jenny may have slept until midday had her window not caught the full force of the morning sun. Her sleep had been heavy, but her body and mind rested, she began emerging slowly from dream and her sheet — a butterfly shedding its clinging cocoon. As the sun crept higher, her bed, placed alongside the window, absorbed every ray. Not willing yet to awaken, she rolled to her right, turning her back on the glare.

The stirring of air opened one eye. Amber was at the chest of drawers removing sheets. The eye closed and Jenny feigned sleep until Amber walked out, until the door closed.

And the key scratched in the lock.

Norman was in charge of that key. What was she doing with it? And what was she doing getting out clean sheets on Sunday morning? Clean sheets were for Mondays.

Had Norman locked that door last night? Then she remembered last night, remembered putting him to bed, or getting him onto the bed.

She sat looking at the chest of six deep drawers, all bar one containing linen. A junk room, favourite dumping ground for anything that didn't have a home. Two vases and the big preserving pan lived on top of her wardrobe. A calico laundry bag hung by its drawstring on a hook behind her door — not for her dirty washing but for old clothing saved for the relief committee ladies. The wardrobe was against the wall between her room and Sissy's, and in the corner, at the foot of her bed, a carton of old newspapers sat on a whatnot that had once lived

431

in the passage where Norman could knock it from its three legs on dark nights. Nowhere else for that whatnot to go but in the corner of her room.

She stripped off her nightgown, dressed in the clothing she'd worn yesterday and walked to the door, aware that it was locked but trying it anyway. She was being punished for last night, for the haircut. She'd expected that, but had expected it to happen last night, not this morning. She shrugged and returned to her bed to squeeze out a few more winks of sleep.

Except she couldn't. Her mind was awake now. And she knew why Amber had come in after clean sheets too. Sissy had wet her bed.

She crept across to the strip of wall between wardrobe and whatnot, placed her ear to the wall. No talking, but activity on the other side, brisk footsteps, sheets flipped. Then Sissy's whine. She'd whine for a week about what those twins had done, and if it took a wet bed to convince Norman that she was suffering, then that's what she'd do.

Jenny returned to her own dear, narrow bed to spread herself in celebration of having it to herself, while listening for sounds of Norman, his voice, his footsteps, his chair scraping in the kitchen. Couldn't hear him. He must have gone to church. Then she was up again and lifting her curtain, attempting to judge the time. It could still be church time.

Why hadn't he woken her? Why hadn't he taken her to church to ask God's forgiveness for her sin of pride or something?

Fast footsteps walking by her door and across the verandah. Fast footsteps crunching on gravel. Amber would soak those sheets until tomorrow. Monday was washing day.

'Daddy!' Jenny knocked on her door. 'Daddy. I need to go to the lav.'

He didn't come. Amber came back and Jenny stopped knocking.

The relief bag had something in it. Knowing Sissy, her green dress was probably stuffed in there, as the yellow had been. Too many bad memories attached to that green dress to ever wear it again. And it crushed like a rag. Jenny lifted the bag down, drew its gathered mouth wide and peered in. No green, but something beige, something embroidered. She retrieved Amber's old blouse. It was coming apart at the sleeve seam but it had an embroidered collar and matching embroidery halfway down the front. That seam could be fixed, or made bigger. A needle and thread could fix a lot of things. She stuffed it into her bottom drawer, then dug for more buried treasure. Only Norman's old work trousers and one of Sissy's nightdresses. Jenny had plenty of raggy, baggy hand-me-down nightdresses. She stuffed it back in. Someone would wear it. Someone would wear Norman's old trousers.

Back on the bed, on her knees, her head beneath the curtain, she looked out on what could have been a midday sun. There were no shadows. She hadn't gone to bed until one o'clock. Norman had let her sleep in, had gone to church alone, was probably talking to someone there. Wished he'd come home. She'd drunk too much cordial last night. She looked at the preserving pan. Her bladder felt as if she might need that, but she lifted down the blue-green vase. It had served her well enough before and would serve her again if he didn't open that door soon.

Half an hour more she waited for him, until the last of the sun left her window to beat down on the roof. Church was over by eleven thirty. Where was he? Had he forgotten she was locked in? Had he left the key in the door so Amber could let her out?

He wouldn't do that.

Sleep is the best way to pass time in an airless room. She dozed a while and woke with a dry mouth. The way to stop moisture evaporating was to breath through the nose. She lay on her back, mouth firmly closed, staring at the ceiling and wondering how long it took a person to die of thirst, wondering if the body decided to hang on to any moisture it had trapped in the bladder. She thought of Vern and Jimmy Hooper and the day they'd picked her up when she'd gone for a walk along the railway lines, thought of the taste of cool water from Vern's water bag, and the mirage she'd believed was magic, the butterflies she'd chased. Butterflies were more beautiful then, larger then — or they'd seemed larger.

433

'Dad.' She rapped at the window. 'Daddy, are you out there?' Her window was only feet from the back verandah. He sat out there some Sundays. She knocked harder on the glass. Sometimes he chipped at weeds down the back on Sundays. 'Daddy.'

Yelling dried her mouth. Had to raise spit so she could swallow. Glanced around her prison, not scared but concerned. He'd been strange last night. He'd been worse than strange.

'Daddy.'

Sissy was only a wall away. She knocked on it. 'Sissy. Tell someone to open this door. I need to go to the lav.' Not that that would concern Sissy. 'I'm dying of thirst.'

Not a sound from Sissy's room. She pounded on the wall. 'Sissy, open this door.'

Swallowed, and for half an instant almost panicked, because for half an instant she couldn't swallow, which was mad. People didn't die of thirst in a day, and certainly not if they'd drunk about six glasses of cordial the night before, and they were not out in the sun, and they had full bladders. Anyway, she wouldn't die of thirst. She'd break the window.

Thought about bladders for a while, about having something like a football full of fluid inside, somewhere below the navel. Thought about the other bits that were down there. Dora knew heaps more about things than she. She knew that babies grew underneath their mother's navels, and how, when the baby was ready to be born, the navel opened up and out they popped, which was the only logical reason for anyone to have a navel. Except boys had them too. Maybe all babies started out the same and they only grew their extra bits in the last weeks so God gave them all navels, just in case.

She knew Amber and Norman had four babies die, which was what sent Amber mad in the first place. Jessie had told her that, and she'd told her how Granny had paid a city doctor to operate on her so she couldn't have any more babies. Not that she was likely to, because Dora said that women had babies because they slept in double beds with their husbands and being that close to a man got a baby started somehow, except the Duffy girls didn't have husbands and they still had babies.

She turned to the window, tried to lift it, aware it was wasted effort. Norman had tried a dozen times to open it. He'd written letters to the railway department about his window that wouldn't open. They'd come to paint the house once but they hadn't fixed the window.

'Daddy,' she yelled, her fist pounding against the frame. 'I need to go to the lav.'

The house sounded empty. She had to get out of here. And the shadows were lengthening now, the sun moving across the roof. It had to be after one, maybe even going on for two o'clock. And she was sweating. She'd sweat out all of her moisture.

There were small hooks on the top and bottom sashes, and a lock glued open by paint. She stood on her bed and tried heaving down on the top sash. She hammered at the frame at the sides, the bottom, the middle where the two sashes joined, and when her fist would take no more, she used the heel of her shoe.

'If someone doesn't open this door, I'm going to break the window,' she yelled.

Not a sound. They'd all gone out and left her to die. And if they'd all gone out, then no one would hear her hammering, so she belted harder at the frame, belting upwards, downwards.

They hadn't gone out. She raised Sissy.

'Shut up,' she whined.

'Open my door, Sissy.'

It was a relief knowing she was in the house. She jumped from the bed and went to the door, waited for Sissy's footsteps.

'Sissy. Open this door.'

Amber was in there too. Jenny heard the mutter of voices.

'I'll break the window in a minute.'

Nothing.

So she'd break it. On the bed again, head beneath the curtain, one last heave down. And it rattled. That window never rattled.

She got rid of the curtains, tossed them and their rod over her shoulder, then stood on the sill and hammered like hell along the top of the window frame, hammered again where the sashes joined. Then her fingers curling over hooks, her knees as a fulcrum, she bore down. And it moved. She could feel the air, hot air, but moving fresh air. It was coming through a slim slit at the top. She repeated her action and this time was able to get her fingers into the gap.

Key scratching in the lock. She swung around, picked up the curtain rod, thinking to get it back up, but Amber was standing in the doorway, a broom in her hand, her eyes like dead swamps.

'Hit me with that and I'll hit you back,' Jenny warned, spreading her feet.

The broom was long. The curtain rod was longer. Jenny was younger, more nimble and the bed offered her its springs. She feinted left, went right, copped a whack on the upper arm but she was out of that room, out the back door, out the side gate and over to the station tap, where the water was as hot as hell for a minute, but cooled as she soaked her head, doused her frock, then drank. The ground was hot underfoot. Wished she'd put her shoes on. She hadn't, and she sure as hell wasn't going back for them.

She used Maisy's lav. Maisy hadn't gone to church this morning. She hadn't sighted Norman since last night.

Two of the Dobson boys were at the café. They stared at her hair, told her they hadn't seen her father but they'd heard her singing on the wireless last night — which seemed like a week ago to Jenny, and unimportant today. She popped her head inside the café, took a look around.

'In or out,' Mrs Crone snapped.

'Has Dad been in this morning, Mrs Crone?'

Mrs Crone hadn't seen him, but she saw Jenny's bare feet. 'How the mighty have fallen,' she said. Didn't comment on her haircut.

No one could stand Mrs Crone. Her husband couldn't even stand her so he spent his life next door, drunk. Had there been another café in town, no one would have gone near Crone's.

Norman didn't like bare feet and Jenny's were not accustomed to being bare, so she ran around to the Palmers', attempting to keep to the shade, or walk where there was grass. It was surprising how dirt, which was miles deep, could heat up enough to burn bare feet.

'Was Dad in church today, Mrs Palmer?'

'I didn't see him, love. We noticed you weren't there.'

'I slept in,' Jenny said.

Dora lent her a pair of canvas shoes. She'd always wanted a pair, but canvas shoes were for those who couldn't afford leather, Norman said. They felt good on her feet, like bare feet with soles. She stayed a while at the Palmers' house, had a cup of tea and a slice of bread and jam while she told them all about the concert.

Norman was down at the creek, midway between the bridge and the town, on someone's land, McPherson's or Dobson's. Hatless, his head was burning; be the burn external or internal, he neither knew nor cared. He was alive. The burning told him so. He had not expected to find himself alive this morning — or was it now afternoon?

He didn't know what had brought him to this place or how long he'd been there, or why he'd come here, why he carried his brandy flask, now filled with water. He couldn't recall filling it with water, didn't know where he'd filled it.

He could recall wandering around Denham's backyard, which at one stage had seemed the most logical place to die. At some time during the night he had delivered himself to Moe Kelly. He could recall sitting on his verandah, or recall the dog sharing that verandah. Perhaps the dog had suggested he cut out the middle man and go direct to the cemetery. He seemed to recall baptising the son he'd placed nameless into his mother's grave. Simon, he had named him. Simon the Sensible.

A disjointed night. He'd slept on the river bank, had woken with twigs in his hair, leaf litter on his back. And he was not the only one who'd chosen the river bank that night. A swagman had used the opposite bank. He was cooking a meal — breakfast, lunch, dinner, or all three. Norman envied him his freedom, envied his blackened billy and dented pan, his lack of fear that allowed him to walk away from the untenable and take to the roads.

Norman knew himself for a coward, a beast who had coveted beauty, so certain she could transform him, breed from him a

437

race of beautiful children. Instead, the beast had transformed her. She had no heart. She had no soul.

And he had her bottle of pills in his pocket.

Perhaps he had unwittingly chosen the perfect place to empty that bottle; the creek before him might carry his worthless carcass away. The banks were high. The water deep enough at this point. He might roll down and float away from life. He sat tossing the bottle in his hand, staring across the water at the swagman now breaking an egg into his frying pan.

Had he bought that egg, begged it, stolen it? Would an egg taste better eaten in freedom with only the birds and Norman looking on from a distance? He watched the stranger pinch salt from a pouch, place that pouch carefully back into his pocket, watched him hack a thick slice of bread from a loaf, then eat from the pan. A forkful of egg, a bite of bread, then time to chew and to savour each mouthful. No rush to be done, no kitchen to vacate, to leave tidy.

Afraid of her tight-mouthed anger. Afraid of her dull, drugged eyes.

And he'd forced them on his daughters.

Vision in his left eye blurred, he closed it to watch the swagman take a light from his campfire, light a cigarette, to watch him dip, then pour a billy of water over the embers, watch the ash fly, watch him kick evidence of his campfire into the creek, roll up his swag, and, with a salute to his watcher, walk on his way downstream.

'Wait for me,' Norman sighed. 'Wait for me.'

How far might I walk, he thought. Two miles? Five? I am a creature of comfort, a weak, pompous dupe, dependent on my spectacles.

He placed the bottle down and removed his spectacles, and found one lens cracked through the centre. How? When? He had no answer. He sat polishing them on his shirt-tail, seeing his future more clearly without them. He could not, would not, live with her. He would take Jennifer and leave this town.

Go where? Crawl home to the relatives? Spend the late afternoon of his life relative-hopping, as he had relative-hopped through its long morning? Seeing their pleased faces when they carried his trunk to the station, their relief when they raised an arm to wave him on his way.

He sighed, replaced his spectacles, and watched the swagman disappear around the bend in the creek.

Alone then, he removed the lid from the pill bottle and, for the second time, poured a mound to his palm. No one to see him. Someone would find him.

Old ibis watching him, its head to one side. He had brought his Jenny-wren down here to watch the birds. How many times? They had been happy together, he and his Jenny. Cecelia too. He had shown her the dab chicks ducking their silly heads for a meal. He'd had a good life with his daughters. Against his better judgment, against the advice of his uncle, he had taken the adulteress, the addict, the whore, back into his house.

Why?

'Am I worthy of better?' he asked the ibis.

It shook its head and stalked off on long legs to find more worthy company. A family of dab chicks glanced at him then vacated his side of the creek.

Her pills were melting in the sweat of his palm. He stood and walked down to the water, tossed them far, watched them scatter, imagined fish below swimming for this new-food source — saw their muddy eyes, their fins flapping, wanting more, so he poured the last of the pills to his hand. Small miracles of modern science, they had killed the pain in his back, or perhaps the protesting nerve had died. He threw the bottle far, removing his option to retreat. And the dab chicks returned to ride the ripples of the bottle, to dive. He frowned. Poisoning the fish did not concern him, but small dab chicks?

He was standing at the water's edge, his hand full of pills, when he heard the children's voices. He turned, saw the Dobson boys running towards him, bathing-suit clad. And he flung the pills, watched them fall like hail, picked up a small branch to throw after them should the dab chicks approach. They knew better than he. They had no desire to lose the day.

'Jenny was looking for you, Mr Morrison,' a blond-headed boy said.

'The time,' he said. 'Would you know the time, lad?'

'It's after two.'

He looked like his father, blond-headed, blue-eyed. All five of them looked like their father. Some men bred beautiful children who lived, he thought, turning to the girl, a pretty child, clad in a too large swimming costume. She reminded him of a younger Jenny — a much younger Jenny. She stood chin up watching him, and, uncomfortable beneath her gaze, he brushed the dust from the seat of his trousers, adjusted his spectacles.

'We heard Jenny singing on Grandpa's wireless,' she said.

At his best, Norman was not good at conversing with children. He was not at his best. He nodded, adjusted his spectacles.

'She's nearly like a famous singer now, isn't she?'

He could find no words. He felt the sting of tears and adjusted his spectacles again.

'The glass is broken in one eye,' she said.

'Yes,' he said.

'It might cut your eye.'

'Yes.'

She gave up on him and ran down to join her brothers in the shallows.

He could stay here no longer. He walked upstream, through George McPherson's land and beneath the bridge, following the creek bank until the forest came down to the bank to block his way with fallen branches and rotting logs. He cut back through the trees to the forest road. He could go to Gertrude. But she would offer tea, offer sympathy, which may break him.

He turned back to town, walking through the heat until the shade of the hotel drew him, the lane behind the hotel drew him in. The rear door was unlocked. He entered into cool.

'We heard young Jenny last night,' Mrs Bull said. 'She ought to have won it.'

Norman nodded, waited for more, but she returned to her sweeping and he walked down the long passage to the dining room. Too late for lunch, too early for dinner, he sat, elbows on the table, head in his hands. Horrie brought him a pint of ale and didn't stay to talk. He'd been around pubs long enough to know there was no place for a man to go at times but into a pot of beer.

He'd poured more pots before Jenny found her father, and later returned with Jim Hooper. They poured Norman into one of Horrie's beds in the back sleep-out.

PILLS, PAIN AND NEWSPAPER

He'd left three pills in her medicine glass, but by Monday morning they were gone and he'd brought no more. She knew where he was. There were few in town unaware that Norman Morrison had taken a room at the hotel, that Jennifer was staying with Maisy Macdonald. Amber went to Charlie's to buy a pound of butter and four of sugar, and all eyes stared at her.

Tuesday was hell. She'd walked most of Tuesday night, fell into bed near dawn and was awakened a few hours later by the stink of ammonia and damp, clinging sheets. Rose from that bed and left Cecelia snoring in her pool of urine.

Swallowed the last of the aspirin tablets, burned newspapers enough to heat her bathwater, was attempting to wash the shaking aching crawl from her scalp when Maisy called to her at the front door. Rinsed out the soap, determined not to answer that call. And where did she get the nerve to come here anyway? She'd caused that wet bed. She'd taken those boys down there knowing what they'd had in mind.

'Amber. I know you're home. I need to talk to you.'

Amber stepped from the bath, towelled herself, slid her arms into a washed-out purple and blue floral dressing gown, opened the front door.

'You've got a nerve.' Mouth aching, mouth shaking around those words.

'What did I do?'

'You knew what they'd do.'

'I did not! We told them they weren't coming, but the idiots jumped on the running boards —'

'She's distraught!' A word used to excess loses its meaning. This morning, the meaning of life was lost. 'She's distraught.' It had less impact the second time, or her mouth couldn't give it impact.

'I'm sorry —'

'I heard you laugh.'

'I did not laugh. Jessie sounds just like me.' Amber tried to close the door but Maisy was halfway in. She was little taller than her neighbour, but weightier. 'And she wasn't laughing at Sissy anyway. She was laughing at the way they were dressed — and my new basin too. They chipped it. I promise you, Amber, none of us knew what they had in mind. I'll swear that on my life.'

'You're not fit to raise dogs.'

Maisy gave up attempting to keep the peace. 'I don't know about dogs, but by the smell of this house, you haven't made much of a show of raising kids.'

'Get out.'

'Who stood by you when everyone else in town kept their distance, Amb?'

Always a fighter, Amber was wiry and stronger than she looked. Not as strong as Maisy, who pushed the door wide and stepped into the passage.

'Who gave you a bed when your husband wouldn't take you in?'

Amber was looking for a weapon. Only the vase, the Queen Victoria vase. She'd wed him for that vase.

'Get out of my house, you no-name bitch.'

'People who live in glass houses can't afford to throw stones, Amber. What were you getting up to the day I spent trying to calm Sissy when she woke up thinking she was bleeding to death? You weren't home fussing with her then, were you?'

Amber went for Maisy's hair. It was too short to offer a grip. They were unequal opponents. Maisy had quelled a thousand arguments and, with the finesse of a wrestler, she got her opponent in a half-nelson and walked her out to the kitchen, where she sat her down and held her down.

Dry skin, yellowing complexion, straw-grey hair dripping water — as pretty as a picture at thirteen, the best-looking girl in town at twenty, Amber Morrison was ugly this morning, and ten years older than her years, a snarling straw shrew held against her will. Maisy hadn't come here to fight with her, but to sort things out. She was attempting to reason with the unreasonable when the stink of urine announced Sissy's presence. And her whine.

'You leave her alone, Maisy.'

'Clean yourself. You stink of wee, you selfish, whining bitch of a girl. Between you and your mother, you've driven your father out of his house and half out of his mind. What did he ever do but his best for both of you?'

What did he ever do, Amber thought, eyeing her daughter. What he'd done was standing in the doorway and it smelled of the asylum, of the stale urine stink of madness.

They'd bound her to a chair in the asylum. They'd let her wet herself, let her sit in it all day. They'd strapped her to her bed where she'd swum in pools of urine, paralysed by their pills.

'You've got no right even coming into our house after what you let those twins do to me.'

Maisy released Amber's wrists to face the girl. 'You couldn't recite the Lord's Prayer without putting Jesus Christ himself to sleep, Sissy, and it's time someone told you. All those boys did was get the audience laughing with you instead of at you. And that's the truth. You ought to be thanking them for saving you face. Now get into the bathroom and clean yourself up.'

Amber's back was to the stove, unlit this morning.

'Something has to be done, Amber,' Maisy said. 'Norman's not at work, and young Danny Lewis doesn't know his arse from his elbow.'

The kitchen was full of ammunition. The frying pan on a triangular pot stand beside the stove, a heavy pan. It flew.

Dented a dresser drawer. The hearth brush hit the door. A chair flew.

There is a commonly told tale of the man who could lift a full-grown bull above his head. It's said that one day he picked up a newborn bull calf and lifted it high, then every morning thereafter he repeated the exercise until the bull was fully grown. Maisy had been hauling her sons out of mischief for years, daily manhandling them. She could still throw them out of her kitchen. With little effort, she took control of Amber, half-dragging, half-walking her to Norman's room where she flung her down to the bed then slammed the door.

Amber turned to fight on — and stepped on a pill, crushed it beneath her shoe. Sacrilege.

She stooped, pinched up what she could and licked the powder from her finger, then with that moistened finger got the rest of it, and some dust.

Found three more caught up in the folds of his coverlet. Found two more when she moved his pillow, another on the floor, two beneath his bed. Forgot about Sissy and her wet bed; crawled around the floor on a pill hunt, dropping each find into the pocket of her gown.

Maisy changed Sissy's bed linen, heated water for her bath, opened windows to air the house, opened doors, then carried the soiled sheets down to the washhouse and got them soaking. An hour or two later when she looked into Norman's room, Amber was sleeping.

'You should be looking after her, not the other way around,' Maisy said. 'She's my age, Sissy, and she looks sixty.'

'So do you,' Sissy said. 'And you've got no right —'

'Jesus, you're a bitch of a girl,' Maisy said and she left her to it, walked over the railway lines to the hotel to see if she might get some sense out of Norman.

Found him sitting on his sleep-out bed crying over the *Willama Gazette*. It had a photograph of the quest's prize-winner on the front page, but Norman's paper was open at page two, at a head-and-shoulders study of a beautiful woman — with an inset of her in her Alice Blue Gown costume.

> *Woody Creek songbird's early promise was realised on Saturday evening when Jennifer Morrison, fourteen-year-old daughter of Woody Creek stationmaster, brought the audience to their feet . . .*

Maisy sat with him on the bed, reading around his teardrops. She read of the stationmaster's second daughter: '*a hilarious comedy sketch, which caught the audience off guard . . .*'

The Duffy family rarely wasted money on newspapers, and when they did, they liked weight for money. The *Willama Gazette* didn't offer weight for money, but nine-year-old Maryanne Duffy paid over her coins for a copy then started the long walk home.

In 1938 there was a veritable colony of Duffys living on a barren acre a mile out past the cemetery. Theirs was a matriarchal society, ruled by old Betty, now old enough to get the old-age pension. It was the first regular money she'd seen since she'd worked as a kitchen maid out at old man Monk's back when she was fourteen. She'd had her first at fifteen, a son she'd raised to eighteen months then lost to the measles. Male offspring didn't do as well as the females on Duffy land. Her father had owned a house of sorts, built close to the road. The huts had come later. Lots of huts. Her house was near ringed by crumbling sheds and huts.

Young Maryanne ran with the newspaper into a lean-to tacked onto the side of her mother's hut, and well off to the left of Nan Betty's house. She offered the paper to old Noah who, from time to time, lodged in that lean-to. Maryanne's mother liked him lodging there. He bought things sometimes, and he bought a lot of newspapers. Maryanne's mother used them to paper the walls.

'Thank you, Maryanne,' he said, his hand held out for his change. Sometimes he forgot to ask for it.

Hoping to sidetrack him Maryanne pointed to the front page. 'That girl goes to our school.'

'Why aren't you at school?' he said.

'Don't have to. Say what the words say.'

'*Woody Creek songbird's early promise was realised on Saturday evening when Jennifer Morrison, fourteen-year-old daughter of Woody Creek stationmaster,*' he read aloud.

'There's more bits than that.'

'Go to school and learn to read it for yourself,' he said. 'My change, please.'

'Want to play ice-cream for a penny?'

'Where is your mother?' he said.

'At Nan Betty's.'

The sun comes up each day, seen or not, and the sun goes down. Time passes; newspapers crisp with news on Monday grow stale by Friday. Time curls their corners, yellows their pages, turns them to dust. Time can alter history — or cleanse it of unacceptable fact. Time can turn myth into religion, turn saint to sinner, sinner to hero, while that sun keeps on coming up and keeps on going down and all men do what they must.

Hot as hell, the sun of late February, blistering, burning. Sissy sweltered while her mother searched for more than those thirteen pills, and didn't know if it was Monday or Sunday, didn't know if it was March yet or still February, didn't know it was her birthday, if she was forty-one or forty-three. No Norman, no newspapers to tell her the day, the month, the year.

Maisy remembered her birthday. She came when that evil sun had gone down, came with a bottle of rosewater and a bar of perfumed soap.

'Happy birthday, Amber.'

'Get out, you fat bitch.'

And Sissy bawled, bawled because she was hot and she'd forgotten what day it was, and because Maisy offering soap and perfume was as good as telling her mother that she stank, bawled too because Maisy was the only one who'd come to the house in days. The Hoopers hadn't come. She bawled because her mother had probably done what Norman had said she had done — and because she'd stopped cooking meals.

'What does he think he's doing?' Sissy bawled.

'He's suffering, love,' Maisy said.

The forest was suffering, the wood cutters said, and how can a forest suffer?

'I've never seen so many leaves falling.'

'We need a decent flood.'

'The creek is down to a trickle. You can walk across it down behind the slaughteryards.'

The swamp behind the slaughteryards had dried up long ago, leaving a new crazy-paved playground for the kids. They found the skeletons of fish and fox, and for a week carried around a skull they swore was Ray King's.

'Aboriginal,' the old chaps said. 'Used to be thousands of them around here. It's washed out of the sandhills in the last flood.'

'What's a flood?' the little children said.

The sun comes up and the sun goes down. Clocks on mantelpiece and dresser, their hands jerking around and around in eternal circles, keep moving time along.

'What's going on with Morrison? Has he left her?'

'Something happened the night that girlie sang on the wireless.'

'She's living with the Macdonalds, they say.'

'The mother has gone off her head again.'

'Then why the hell doesn't he put her away?'

Trains too hot to ride pulled into Norman's station, trains too hot to touch. The railway lines buckled out past Monk's siding. They could have caused a catastrophe but it was not meant to be that night.

'Ask him what he did with her pills,' Sissy wailed. 'She walks around the house all night keeping me awake.'

'She's been on them for too long,' Maisy said. 'They weren't curing her, love.'

'I need her to sleep. I need her to cook something.'

'It's too hot to cook,' Maisy said. She brought over a loaf of bread, a few slices of cold meat, two tomatoes.

Too hot to eat. Too hot to sleep. Too hot to drive while that sun beat down.

Jim Hooper had taken a liking to the farm—or to Monk's old house. He'd spent three nights, sleeping cool in its root cellar. At sundown on the Friday night he left for home and was halfway there when a cow stepped out from behind a clump of scraggy scrub. He hit her, lost control of the car, ran off the road, hit a tree and lay trapped in the wreckage until the sun rose once more.

Vern's farm manager had watched him leave. Vern thought he must have decided to spend the night in the cellar. No one worried.

There was little traffic on that road after dark. A drover found his injured cow at first light. He butchered her, skinned and dissected the carcass, tossed it into his wagon, then he saw the car and Jim, more dead than alive.

They got him out of the wreck. The garage mechanic drove him and Vern to the hospital, where Jim's injuries were deemed too serious for Willama. They patched up what they could and sent him via ambulance to Melbourne.

Norman heard about the accident. He liked that gangling Hooper youth, and though he could recall little of the Sunday he'd lost in a fog of alcohol and self-pity, he knew Jim had been there, knew it was Jim who had brought him a change of clothing.

Norman hadn't been back to the house, refused to look at it, turned his eyes to the earth when forced to look west. Maisy was caring for Jenny and keeping an eye on Cecelia, whom he saw at the station from time to time, always with some complaint.

She came to the station on the Saturday. 'I'm going down to Melbourne and I need money,' she said.

'Your mother will be alone,' he said.

'That's not my fault, is it? I don't know what you think you're doing. Everyone is talking about you.'

He had not seen Amber. He had fed her pills to the fish, had dreamt terrible dreams of befuddled fish, had swum with them, awakened gasping for air.

'The Hoopers are going down?'

'Margaret is. Her father passed out in Willama. He was supposed to stay in hospital, but he came home and passed out again, so he can't go, so Lorna won't go.'

'His heart?' Norman said.

'How would I know? Margaret just said he passed out. Twice. I'll need at least ten pounds.'

He wrote her a cheque for ten pounds, sent her to the post office to cash it, then walked across to speak to Vern. He found him sitting in the shade of a large oak, sitting looking into space.

'Bad news,' Norman said, offering his hand.

Vern took it, shook it. 'I've got to think he's in the best hands, Norm. I'm pleased they took him down there. It's too far away, but they've got all the knowledge down there.'

'He's a fine boy, Vern. God will not take him so soon.'

Vern didn't reply for a second. 'We've got tough heads,' he said. 'I've got a lot of faith in the Hooper skull. That's what I'm clinging to right now, Norm, and to the doctors. He's with the best. He's in the best hands.'

'He's a fine boy,' Norman repeated for lack of anything better to say.

'I could have done a lot worse,' Vern said. 'I could have done a whole lot worse.'

'Your own health?'

'I'm all right. They're panicking about nothing. It was just the shock of seeing him like that, that's all. It took us an hour to drag him out of it. That bloody car fell apart. We couldn't see what was up and what was down. I'm glad your girl can go along with Margaret. She'll need company down there.

'I've never seen anything like it. Never in my born days did I expect to see anything like it. We wouldn't have got him out if not for the garage chap and Denham. Say what they like about that pig of a man, but he's the chap to have around when you're in a tight hole. He got him out. And the garage chap —'

Telephone ringing. Vern up and running.

'Don't run, Father. It's not the hospital.'

Norman left them and returned to his station. Once, twice, he glanced towards his house.

She'd be alone.

AMBER ROSE

Amber had searched the floors, had moved his chest of drawers, moved his wardrobe, knowing there was just one more pill. Found one yesterday, or the day before, in one of his shoes. She'd stripped the bed, shaken his pillows, crawled the floor beneath his bed, certain there would be just one more pill. No more. And her every scar offering pain; every one of life's bruises a throbbing open sore.

She rose from her crouch and stood before the dressing table, seeing her bruises in the mirrors. Black and blue with bruises. Slid her dressing gown from her shoulders, watched it collapse like a purple and blue floral bruise at her feet. Naked beneath that gown, naked and bruised and scarred by them. Finger tracing the wide white scar down her belly where they'd tried to cut them out of her.

Take you in the dirt, fill you with their filth, then leave you. One after the other after the other.

Skin scrubbed raw and still she crawled with them. Needed her pills to kill that crawling, aching, twisting pain.

She'd kept her bargain. She'd kept her bargain. She'd cleaned his house.

You needed to see the dirt when it fell. Hard to see, those first fine grains, but if you missed those, let them settle for a day, there were more. She ran her hand over the wood of his mother's dressing table, traced her scar on the winged dressing table mirror. Three mirrors. Traced all sides of the scars of Amber Rose.

And those mirrors showed too much, showed the filth pulsing through her veins.

'It's in your blood,' he'd said. He was a doctor. He knew everything. 'Amber is dug from the dirt,' he'd said. 'Petrified sap. Insects crawling the earth millions of years ago became trapped in it. What is trapped within your core, pretty Amber?'

Stared at the winged mirrors, and three pale ghosts stared back, angry ghosts, wild-eyed, wild-haired.

Afraid of them. Too old, they knew too much. She reached to move the wings, to kill the ghosts of Amber Rose, but born of that move was a long corridor of ghosts, marching back, and back, and back, whispering about her, hissing at her. A chorus of hisses.

Two-bob whore.
Sold herself for the price of a loaf of bread.
How many thought their two bob well spent?

'Bastards,' she wailed. 'Bastards.' Slammed the wings of the mirror, but they swung back to show a different angle.

Sold herself once for a pair of pretty shoes.
And a frock with buttons down the front.
And a promise.
Men and their broken promises.
Norman kept his promises.
Paid more than two bob for her too.
Didn't get his money's worth.
None of them did.
Daddy did.

'Die, you bitches. Die and leave me alone!'

Look at her, still searching for a pill.
Wants to block out what we know.
Doesn't know the half of what we know.
Mad as a hatter, that one.
It's in her blood.

Slammed the wings against the central mirror, one and the other, again, again, slammed them until the central mirror cracked, then shattered, and the line of ghosts scattered. Only one then. One silent ghost left standing, staring at the scattered shards of her reflection.

Sky darkening, thunder rolling.

Now?

Then?

When?

Had to go home. She'd get wet. Had to get her pretty dress off. He'd bought it for her. She'd never had a white dress, never had pretty shoes, just boots. Boots were stronger, her mother said.

She'd met him under the bridge. That was where she'd always met him, because she wasn't allowed to meet him. She'd put that dress on under the bridge, taken her boots off.

'My pretty bud,' he'd said that last day. 'Almost ripe for the plucking,' and he'd kissed her, on the cheek but close to her mouth.

She'd told him she had to go home before the storm came, and he knew she couldn't wear that dress home or her mother would know.

It had tiny buttons right down the front of the bodice. He'd wanted to help undo them. He slid it down from her shoulders, then his hands measured her breasts. Maisy's breasts were much bigger, but she was fourteen. Amber's breasts were just baby breasts. He said so, and said he ought to look at them.

He was a doctor. He wouldn't do anything that was wrong.

'So sweet,' he said. 'A man's ultimate delight must be in the moulding of female perfection from a child of his own flesh, my pretty one.'

She didn't understand his fancy words, didn't know what to do except stand there while her beautiful dress slid down to the dirt. She didn't want it to get dirty.

Wanted to get dressed in her school dress, but he was holding her, his hands over her hips. She could get away if she wanted to. Half of her had wanted to, half of her wanted to stay.

Kissed her then on the mouth.

'You're not . . . Why?'

'You were panting for it, sweet thing.'

'I have to go home now.'

But the rain didn't want her to go home. It came heavy, came down on an angle, reaching in to where they stood. They had to move away from it, crawl up the bank beneath the bridge supports where the rain couldn't reach. He took off his jacket and placed it on the clay, and she sat on it. The jacket wasn't very big so he had to sit close, place his arm around her, right around her and beneath her arm so it touched her breast.

Like being inside their own house. Like the sheets of rain were their walls. Sitting close and listening to him telling about his house and his maids who polished his silver — his fingers moving against her, kept on moving, making that achy sweetness down low.

'Have you seen the city, my pretty Amber?'

She hadn't, but she couldn't talk. Didn't want to talk. Didn't want to move.

'You're begging for it,' he said. 'In a year or two, you'll be at the mercy of every lout in town.'

He lifted her chin and kissed her mouth. Laid her down, and his tongue was a cat's cleaning its kitten, cleaning her all over, sliding her petticoat up, off, cat tongue licking her baby breasts.

'It should be a father's unquestionable right to spread the legs of his ripe little buds,' he said. 'Want to go home to Mummy or stay with me, my pretty?'

'She thinks I'm at school.'

'I won't tell on you, if you don't on me.'

Left her pretty dress and shoes hidden behind one of the bridge pylons. Walked home in the late afternoon in her school dress and boots when the rain stopped. Told her mother she'd waited at Julia's house for the rain to stop.

Waited for him to come back and take her to his house in the city so she could always wear pretty dresses and fancy shoes and go to theatres and have maids and drive in his fine carriages with two white horses. He'd promised her.

Watched for him at the schoolyard fence.

Searched the streets for him.

Waited beneath the bridge for him, clad in her pretty dress, her shoes.

He didn't come.

The frock and shoes remained for a month beneath the bridge. Then Mr Blunt told her mother about a frock not yet paid for.

'Did he do anything to you? Did he hurt you, Amber? You were told to stay away from him, darlin'.'

Knew all about what the billygoat did to the nanny goats. Knew how her mother hated that billygoat getting at the young female goats. Knew it was wrong, that she'd done wrong.

'You ran away with another man and I hate you.'

Waited for her father to come back. Waited amid the chook dung and the goat dung and the dust of her mother's land, waited until its stink seeped into her skin, until it went in too deep to scrub out.

Knew things now that Maisy didn't know. Knew things Julia may never know. Stood at her mother's fence one day watching the billygoat going at one of the half-grown kids, and hated her mother anew when she whacked him with her garden rake, chained him up in the back paddock. Blamed her. She'd made him go away.

Waited for years for him. He'd never returned.

And there was fat, big-breasted Maisy living in George Macdonald's new house, having a baby every year; and there was Julia, an old maid in her twenties.

And there was Norman.

Gave up waiting for her father and sold herself to Norman for his railway house and his mother's furniture and her gold-rimmed tea set and Queen Victoria vase.

Then sold herself to Reginald to get away from Norman.

Sold herself for a lot less since.

FORGIVE US OUR TRESPASSES

Two babies were born the weekend of Jim Hooper's accident. Heat always brought the babies hurrying into life. Clarry Dobson's wife had a second daughter on Sunday morning, and at six that night, Sophie Duffy came down to get Gertrude. Milly was in labour, and a black storm brewing in the western sky. Gertrude didn't like the look of it, didn't want to take her horse out in it — and she was too weary to go. She went. She always went when she was called. And the shack she found that girl lying in was an insult to humanity.

'Get those dogs out of here. Get this place cleaned up,' she demanded. Outside then for a breath of purer air while dogs yelped and scattered. 'Get some lamps from somewhere. Beg them, borrow them, but get them.'

Seven o'clock when she arrived and by nine that baby was clinging in there, maybe knowing it was safer there. Gertrude took a break and went out to check on her horse. He didn't like the fireworks or the thunder.

In the thirty years she'd been delivering Duffy offspring, the accommodation had deteriorated. Old man Duffy had at least done a few running repairs and kept the dogs down to a minimum. There were more dogs than kids out here now, six or eight women and grown girls, and, as far as she could tell, two males: simple-minded Henry, a thirty-year-old child, and a bearded old bloke she'd sighted when she'd driven in.

'Easy boy,' she soothed, missing old Nugget tonight. He'd stood between those shafts through many a thunderstorm and never turned a hair. Time might teach his replacement patience, though she doubted it. She'd wanted a young horse, one who might see her out. He might, but the way he was behaving, he'd see her cart out tonight.

'Easy boy. I'll get you out of it. We're going to have a long night. Easy now.'

Dark out here, feeling out each buckle, each clasp, but she released him and hoped he didn't find a gap in Duffy's fence.

'Any rain in it?' the old bloke said. He was standing behind her.

'We need a decent downpour.'

'It's taking its time coming,' he said.

Maybe he meant the baby, maybe the storm, threatening now since late Saturday.

'They'll probably get it three hundred miles south,' she said. 'Like the last one.'

'A nice-looking horse.'

'He's got a soft mouth for riding. Doesn't like the cart much. You might tell those rampaging kids to give him space. He's inclined to kick first and ask questions later.'

'A prerogative of youth,' he said.

'True,' she replied, and someone walked over her grave.

The boy arrived an hour before midnight. He was a good size and healthy. Duffy infants did well in the womb, though not so well on dry land. She wondered who'd fathered him, wondered if he'd be alive twelve months from now, wondered who he might turn out to be if given half a chance. Some things you had to walk away from. Sometimes you had no choice but to walk away.

She found her horse in a back corner of Duffy's acre. He seemed pleased to see her. She was backing him in between the shafts when a flash of lightning near blinded her, and her horse took off, the harness dragging behind him. She followed its rattle, vowing she wouldn't be coming back to this place. She was past this foolishness.

The next clap of thunder rattled every sheet of corrugated iron on Duffy land, and there were plenty to rattle. The lightning a constant now, one flash coming on top of the last. And the old bloke standing out in it watching the show, and looking for all the world like Moses, sent down by God on a lightning bolt with a new set of commandments for the Duffy family — or maybe to issue a refresher course on the old.

She got her horse and was bringing him back when two heavy drops fell on her face and bare arm. A few more hit her while she was backing him in, and maybe he was calmer with the weight of that cart holding him down, or with her nearby, talking softly, telling him they were going home. She led him to the road before climbing up to her seat, not wanting anyone to see how dog tired she was, to see her struggling to make that climb, but she made it and flicked the reins.

'Home, boy,' she said. 'Take me home.'

He needed no urging. He needed urging to slow, but they got home and before the clouds burst open.

Her beautiful boys were waiting for her in the yard. They took charge of cart and horse while Elsie took charge of Gertrude. She carried water for her to wash, then sat her down to a fine supper and a strong mug of tea.

'It's too much for you, Mum. It's time you stopped doing this.'

'It's too much for me on a stormy night with a ratbag horse, darlin', and the worst part of it is knowing that poor mite doesn't stand a chance.'

Tea was a drug. It could lift you up when you felt down.

'Any news of Jim Hooper?' she asked.

'Nothing we've heard.'

That boy should have died in infancy and half a dozen times since. He'd been cut too soon from his mother's womb. She'd had no milk to feed him; he'd weighed less at two months than he had at birth, had damn near died when he'd taken the measles badly as a three year old; at five, when he'd gone down with influenza, he was running temperatures Gertrude had rarely seen.

'He's tougher than he looks,' she said. 'Give him half a chance and he'll make it.'

Daily, the town expected to hear Jim Hooper was dead. A few weren't too certain his father wouldn't go with him. Vern was an energetic man, always on the go. He'd spent his days since the accident sitting by the telephone, or sitting on the verandah, the window between him and that telephone, waiting for the call.

Margaret called. Jim was unconscious. They wouldn't let her see him.

Then Moe Kelly, cabinet-maker-cum-undertaker, fifty-nine years old, fit as a mallee bull, dropped dead in his shed halfway through building a new sink cupboard for Maisy's remodelled kitchen.

'His wife went out to call him in for morning tea, and there he was, on the floor, a plane in his hand,' Maisy said.

'A good way to go if you've got to go,' George said.

'If you're old enough to go! He was younger than you, George. It's like with Jean White. If I'd heard that Vern or Jim was dead, I might have been expecting it, but you don't expect someone like Moe Kelly to drop dead.'

Expected or not, he was gone, and who was going to bury him?

Through the good times and the bad, Moe had been planting Woody Creek's loved ones in pine box or fancy coffin. Through the good times and the bad, he'd taken folk on their last drive to the cemetery in his fancy black funeral van, and he'd never charged more than he knew a man could pay. It wasn't right that a stranger should be brought in from Willama to bury Moe. It wasn't right that Moe's last ride would be in a motor car. He'd never taken to cars.

The Willama undertaker got more than he'd bargained for on the day of his first Woody Creek funeral. He thought they were having some sort of fair. The shops were shut, the mill saws were silent, schoolkids were lining the road outside the church when he pulled in.

A mob came to meet him, led by an old chap with verandah eyebrows and purple eyes.

'You can get the coffin out and go on your way,' he said.

The undertaker didn't argue. He hung around through a brief service, saw Moe loaded into an ancient funeral van, then led on his final ride through town by an old bloke clad out in full kilt, and on a muggy day when a shirt was too much to have on your back.

'Moe had no more Scot in him than I've got,' people said.

'Who cares what he had in him? He would have loved this.'

He would have framed John McPherson's photographs. John took three shots of Moe's rig: one as it passed over Charlie White's crossing, one with the hotel as a backdrop, and one of the procession, old Jim McGee flashing his knobbly knees while squeezing hell out of aged bagpipes.

'I've heard a few get better music out of squeezing a bloody cat.'

'Be decent, Horrie.'

'Be decent nothing. I've heard Moe say the same thing himself.'

'Hooroo, mate.'

'Hooroo.'

'I always thought you'd bury me, Moe. Have a good journey.'

Down and around Blunt's corner, over Blunt's crossing and back to Cemetery Road, Moe riding proud in his old funeral van, his two sons driving his elderly black horses, resplendent for the last time in their finery. A memorable day. In fifty years' time, the kids lined up in the street would talk about the day Moe Kelly was planted.

The Willama undertaker would speak for thirty years of his first Woody Creek funeral. It started a rush of business. Before Moe was in the ground, he'd got his second customer. Old Jim McGee, eighty if he was a day, sat down to catch his breath for the final bagpipe salute and he never drew it. They thought he'd nodded off, but when his son nudged him into action, the bagpipes fell to the earth and old Jim toppled with them.

'A good way to go if you've got to go.'

'He had a good run did old Jim.'

'We'll miss his bagpipes at the concerts.'

'And by the living Christ, I'll be thankful to miss them too.'

There was a second storm the day old Jim was buried. A tree out on the Willama Road was struck by lightning. It took a power pole down with it and the power wires. Woody Creek residents, grown accustomed to light at the flick of a switch, were lighting candles again, attempting to read by the pale yellow glow of kerosene lamps. The power wasn't back come morning either. Charlie White and the local garage bloke did a roaring trade filling beer bottles with kerosene, just enough to tide folk over. Wirelesses were silent. Wind-up gramophones were dusted off, new needles found and near forgotten records played once more. Folk had become accustomed to eating their meals to the accompaniment of the wireless. Mr Cox sold out of newspapers before midday. Folk missed hearing the nightly news.

'Bloody refrigerators. Why did a man go and pitch out that old ice chest?'

'How long are they going to be fixing those wires? Has anyone heard anything?'

'They say they're down all over the place, that it could take days.'

'How the hell did we manage before electricity?'

They'd managed, and most had managed not to burn down their houses. Man becomes lax. He forgets. His wife grows old.

Anyone who'd had recent dealings with old Mrs Miller from the boot shop knew she was losing her memory. The boot shop went up in smoke with Miller and his wife asleep in the rear residence. If not for the Macdonald twins, the Willama undertaker would have got himself two more customers. Those boys dragged the old couple out through a rear window.

Constable Denham was inclined to believe that if the twins had stayed in Melbourne, the boot shop wouldn't have gone up in smoke, but no one was dead, the shops to the right and left were saved, so for a day or so the twins were heroes — tormenting, drunken, brawling, whoring little bastards, but heroes nonetheless.

Not so to Jenny. She'd loved living with Maisy, had learnt so much about cooking and sewing and knitting, and now she couldn't even have a bath in peace, couldn't go to the lav without the twins throwing things at the door, the roof.

'Just ignore them, love. Their sisters learned to ignore them,' Maisy said.

Hard to ignore those who don't wish to be ignored. Hard to ignore that blackened gaping gash of ash and blackened timber, of twisted corrugated iron, propped up by Mr Miller's blackened sewing machine. Hard to ignore the burnt boots.

And the sheets of rain washing rivers of black ash across the footpath where the boot shop's verandah had once stood, filling the overflowing gutters with ash, running down, and down, and down, to drain into the creek and leave its stain there.

Mill men couldn't work in the rain. Tree fellers couldn't cut down trees in the rain.

The forest rejoiced. Washed clean by the downpour, washed green, it drank its fill, and in the mud at its feet, a million seeds stirred.

Then Vern Hooper took the phone call he'd been waiting for, and finally he left his verandah to give his roses some attention.

'It's going to take a while, but he's awake and he spoke to the girls today,' Vern said to one, to all. 'He's knocked out most of his front teeth, but the doc said they'd needed to come out anyway.'

He worked on his roses until the sun went down, and for the first time in over a week was able to see the beauty of this land, most of it in the sky, red as fire tonight. He dead-headed roses until that red sky faded to salmon, faded to purple, then to grey. Lack of light sent him back to his verandah. He was sipping tea when he heard a lad calling at his fence, one of Clarry Dobson's lads, his maid's nephew.

'Your aunt went home an hour ago, lad.'

'It's Barbie, Mr Hooper. She's wandered off somewhere. Dad says can you get the constable? It's getting dark.'

Dobson owned a couple of acres down behind Macdonald's mill, half of it cleared, half of it heavily timbered.

'I've got no car, lad,' Vern said, returning to the fence. 'You'll run faster than me.'

'Sorry. I didn't think. How's Jim?'

'He's coming good. Now run, lad.'

Too dark to see anything much. Vern went inside for his flashlight, and walked off towards the creek to lend what light he could to the search.

Denham had a motorbike. He was down there with a handful of Dobson's neighbours. Barbie Dobson was eight years old, a pretty little blue-eyed blonde, and not the type to go wandering around at night. She'd been playing hidey with her brothers in their creek paddock and had hidden too well. The boys gave up looking. They'd spent the last hour working on their billycart. Their mother had a new baby. Their father had come home late. No one noticed that Barbie wasn't around until their father told them to get inside and clean themselves up for bed.

'I've told her not to go near the creek unless her brothers are with her,' Clarry said. 'I've told all of those kids that those banks are treacherous since the rain.'

Within fifteen minutes, fifty men, women and boys were down at the creek, calling to Barbie, scouring the forest alongside the creek, searching McPherson's land, Macdonald's mill, slipping, sliding in mud, walking the creek's shallows, feeling for her around snags, while the dark soaked up the little light from lantern and flashlight.

'Barbie! Barbie! You answer Daddy when you're called. Barbie!'

Only the frogs and night birds answered.

'We'll find nothing in the dark,' Denham said. 'If she's lying hurt somewhere, we could be walking right by her.'

'Barbie! You answer me. Barbie!'

Clarry Dobson and a few more stayed on, but Vern's flashlight batteries had given up. He gave up too and went home, but was back at daybreak, working his way downstream. A few kids had drowned in that creek. They hadn't found one of them for five days. They'd never found Ray King's body. It was a treacherous bastard, coming in too close to town before it started its curve to the west. Full of snags, silt feet thick in places, more water in it since the rain and moving faster, and the gutters from town pouring more in. A little dot like Barbie could have been carried for miles.

By late afternoon the next day, over a hundred men were searching both sides of that creek. A truckload had come up from Willama with a police sergeant and two constables. Out-of-town farmers had come in to lend a hand. Anyone with a boat had it on the creek, prodding now for that little body, dragging chains with cruel hooks attached, the town certain there had been another drowning.

Joey Hall found her, just before sundown, when he took the horses down to the creek for a drink.

He saw a small bare foot. A step closer and he recognised a leg. Blonde hair. And no face — like the last time. Same girl. Same place. Beneath the water-pumping log.

Then the young horse smelled the blood and took off downstream, and Joey took off for home.

Old Nugget limped closer to the dead child to stand guard until Gertrude came.

FORGIVENESS

Only a stranger can dissect a town, pare it down to the core and feel no pain. Only a stranger can ask the multiplicity of questions that turn every man's eye on his own neighbour. For days the town was overrun by strangers, strange policemen driving strange cars, big black cars.

The hotel was overrun by police; and Norman, queuing to use the limited facilities, was embarrassed by his situation, by the questions, by the cracked lens of his spectacles he was learning to look around. The older Dobson children had told the city men they'd seen him down at the creek one day, that he'd had a stick in his hand, that Barbie had spoken to him. He wasn't the only one they'd seen. Folk cut across Dobson's land on their way to the bridge, always had. Dobson's timber paddock was treated like crown land, as was McPherson's.

Having those city police in town had got Denham's loyalties a mote confused. He was a city man who might well have been one of those strangers had he not taken the move to the country when he had. He hadn't planned to stay more than a year or two, but his wife had had two more kids, and Simon, his oldest, had a good job in the council office, and somehow, somewhere along the years, that house and his back garden had become home. He still considered himself a city man, still named a few of the locals yokels, but as the days passed he began to dissociate himself from the city men who knocked too hard on folks' front doors at inconvenient hours, who saw evil in innocent endeavour.

Like them or not, small towns have a way of getting under your skin, as do a few of the folk living in them. Denham found himself defending a few. John McPherson, for one.

He'd gone with the city blokes to do a thorough search of McPherson's land, but he stood with the lanky photographer while the others went over the property with a small-toothed comb, raked over his rubbish heap, kicked in one wall of the makeshift hut Harry Hall and a few wanderers had called home for a time. They found blood splatters on a log out front of it.

'Rabbit blood more than likely. Old rabbit blood. There's a lot of trapping done along the creek,' Denham said.

They found a sardine tin near the hut. It smelled fishy.

'Have you seen anyone camping down here lately, John?' Denham asked.

'A few see it from the bridge and think it's on crown land. If they're looking for shade, it's shady.'

'Names?' a city cop asked.

McPherson and Denham eyed the man and wondered where he'd been.

'I don't trouble them, they don't trouble me,' McPherson said. 'They're usually gone the next day.'

He'd photographed a few of the wanderers. Years ago he'd caught old Noah sitting on a log, the bridge behind him. It was one of his best. McPherson felt he had trapped the essence of the depression in that one: an old chap sitting reading a book, his flowing hair and beard gleaming white in the sun, the bridge to nowhere just a blur amid the trees. He'd captured Harry Hall's cheeky grin that same year. A kid, clad in rags, squatting over a campfire, using a stick to stir some evil-smelling concoction.

'Anyone down here when the girl was taken?' a city bloke asked.

'There was a chap on his way up to a fencing job who camped here for a couple of days. I think he pushed on west when the rain cleared.'

'When did it clear?'

'The day Barbie went missing,' Denham said.

'Where was his fencing job?'

'West,' he said.

'Where west?' Another city cop asked, and Denham and John McPherson pointed over the bridge.

'What were you doing the day Barbie went missing, Mr McPherson?'

McPherson, an unmarried man in his early thirties living with his mother on a few acres of river land, was a natural suspect. Their property was only a gutter and a partial fence away from where that little girl was last seen. The city men knew McPherson spent a lot of time hanging around the school, that he liked photographing kids.

'My mother and I were listening to the wireless when we heard Clarry calling to her. I went down to help with the search,' John said.

Back in the car, Denham put them right on a few points. 'He hangs around the schoolmistress more than the school,' he said. 'He and Amy Rose have had some sort of an understanding for years. He's a decent chap.'

Water off a duck's back to the city men. He didn't attempt to turn their suspicions away from the Macdonald twins.

'Born bastards, those two. Any trouble in town has their names written all over it, though they were only kids when the Abbot girl was killed.'

'What aged kids?'

'Eleven, twelve, I'd guess offhand.'

'Means nothing,' one cop said.

'One egging on the other,' another said.

'They were away at school for a time. Curry, the headmaster, will know when.'

'What do you know about Henry Duffy?'

'If he found his way down to the creek, we'd be dragging it for him,' Denham said. 'He's harmless.'

'The stationmaster?'

'No violence in him.'

'His wife?'

'She cleared out with another chap a few years back — before my time. Morrison took her back for his kids' sake, so the story goes. They've grown up. Maybe he's had enough.'

'Where's this farm that chap was supposed to be fencing at?'

'Between here and the next place. There are farms all along that creek. The road out there will be a quagmire. Hooper's land is out that way. He might know who's likely to be putting up new fences.'

'Same Hooper as that big old bloke on the corner?'

'Same Hooper.'

It took half a day and a lot of mud-running to track the fencing bloke down, and before they'd tracked him down, rain was falling again. They found him sheltering in a shearers' hut and knew they had their man. He was a ferret-faced little bastard with close-set shifty eyes, who tried to make a run for it across a paddock the rain had turned into a lake. They got him. They dragged him back to shelter.

'I've done nothing,' the fencer said.

'What made you take off then?'

'Your ugly bloody faces.'

They asked him when he'd taken off from Woody Creek and he asked them why they wanted to know.

'Because an eight-year-old girl was murdered, mutilated and shoved under a log to rot, that's why.'

'You're stark raving mad if you think I'd do something like that. I've got five kids of my own —'

'I don't see them around.'

'I don't drag them around. When are you talking about?'

They told him when, and he stood counting on his fingers. 'I wasn't bloody there. I packed up near dawn that day and was four or five mile from the place by breakfast time. A farm dame cooked me some breakfast.'

'Out of the kindness of her heart.'

'For half a bloody ton of cut and stacked wood. Eggs. Three eggs she cooked me.'

'Is that right.'

'Ask her if you don't believe me.'

'We will.'

'Your wife and kids eating three eggs for breakfast?' they asked then.

'They're doing all right.'

'Why take off in the middle of the night?'

'I felt like it,' the fencer said, eyeing the farmer who stood smoking and enjoying the entertainment. Not a lot happened fifteen mile from town, or not in the wet.

'Same reasons you took off from your wife and kids?'

The rain wasn't letting up. The three cops lit smokes. The fencer held out his hand for one. It remained empty.

'Same as you felt like taking off on your kids and missus, I said.'

'I lost me job and had to move in with the wife's mother. She hates me guts and I hate hers. Anything else you want to know?'

'Yeah. Why you took off in the rain from Woody Creek.'

'Me hotel had a leak in its roof.'

'You're in big trouble, feller,' Denham said. 'As far as we can see, you were in the wrong place at the right time. You'd be well advised to cut the smart-arsing around and answer the man's questions.'

'The hut was leaking. I'd packed up and went down under the bridge. Some dame was down there waiting for her boyfriend. She thought I was him. I couldn't convince her otherwise, so I told her to go to buggery and I took off in the rain.'

'Young? Old? Middle-aged?'

'Christ almighty. It's raining cats and dogs, dark as pitch —'

'You must have got an idea.'

'I'm telling you, I don't know! All I know is she was waiting for someone and she sounded drunk or crazy — which was why I took off. I'm a returned soldier, for Christ's sake. I don't kill babies and I've never been in trouble with the cops and you drive me back along that road and I'll find that farmer dame with the eggs. And I can show you where I camped that night too. It's a big old empty place six or so mile west of where I ate breakfast. And a bloke seen my smoke there too. He come over to see what I was doing there. A bunch of monks used to own the place, he said.'

469

Denham knew Monk's old place. He took out his smokes and offered them to the fencer. 'The crazy dame went after you, eh?'

'You could say that.'

'You would have got an idea of her size then, I reckon. Tall, short, fat, skinny?'

'Christ knows.' He drew on his smoke, leaned against a wide bench. 'Skinny.'

'Black? White?'

'One of the two.'

They ran him to the car when the rain eased and they took off through the mud, one behind the wheel, two pushing, keeping those wheels spinning until they hit more solid ground. They were approaching Vern's property when the fencer pointed.

'That's it,' he said. 'I camped on its verandah.'

Maybe he had. Maybe he'd noticed it as he walked by too. Monk's old house wasn't easy to miss. He pointed to Lonnie Bryant's property a few miles on, so they drove down to the house and spoke to Nancy. She told them he was the chap who had cut and stacked a pile of wood for her, and yes, she'd fried him three eggs for his breakfast. She said he'd seemed a respectful sort of young chap, but then most of the men who came by looking for work were respectful. They checked the days with her. She wasn't young, they were hoping she'd got her days confused, but Nancy's mind was as sharp as a tack, and her daughter, still living with her, backed her up. The fencer was clean — though he no longer had a job to go to.

Clarry Dobson was waiting for them to bring him in. Most in town knew they'd gone after him. Clarry wanted to get his hands on the murdering mongrel and there was no gain in telling him they'd made a mistake. Denham locked the fencer in a cell. Clarry wasn't the only drunk in town, and there'd be more tomorrow. Little Barbie was being buried in the morning.

The train came through at seven. The community box paid for a one-way ticket to Melbourne. Denham saw the fencer on board.

'Kiss your mother-in-law's backside if you have to, and thank your lucky stars every morning that you're free to kiss it. If you'd been holed up at McPherson's the night that girl was taken, you'd be a dead man now,' he said. He saw the train on its way.

It's a terrible day when a child is buried. The new Dobson infant screamed for the sister she'd never known; her mother, out of bed too soon after the birth, fainted; the Dobson boys, big and small, howled; and their father was drunk. He'd been drunk since they'd found Barbie's body.

Gertrude was there with Joey. Vern had gone down to Melbourne. Jenny stood with them, only there because Mrs Dobson had wanted her to sing at the service. Barbie had been so excited to know someone who'd sung on the wireless.

The Melbourne police were there, unmoved by the burial, but watching, listening, moving through the crowd and keeping their eye on the stationmaster. They'd bumped into him at the hotel on their way to and from the bathroom. They'd seen him in the dining room. They watched him join Gertrude. The city men knew her; they'd spoken to her twice.

They recognised the stationmaster's wife. She'd told them she had been unwell for some time, had lost touch with what went on in town. They asked what the situation was between her and her husband. She told them he'd grown impatient with her illness.

'Is he a violent man, Mrs Morrison?'

The question had appeared to confuse her. She'd considered it, and for a brief moment they'd been sure she'd give them their murderer. Then she'd smiled. 'He'd call his mother in to kill a cockroach. Couldn't stand the crunch,' she'd said, and she'd asked if they had time for a cup of tea. A cup of tea when you're away from home always goes down well. She'd served it in gold-rimmed cups, in the parlour.

At the funeral, they watched her speak to the father of the dead girl, before approaching the man who had called his mother to kill cockroaches, watched her speak to him. And saw him step away, turn away. She gave up on him and spoke to Gertrude, then reached out her arms to her. They kissed. Perhaps Gertrude held her too long. They saw Norman's concern, watched him step from foot to foot, a man walking on burning embers.

After days in this town, they were getting the hang of things. Like tram tracks in Melbourne, each resident was connected up to the other.

They knew Maisy Macdonald and watched her leave her group and approach the stationmaster's wife. Maisy was a talker who had a voice that carried. The city police moved in near enough to eavesdrop.

'What a terrible funeral,' she said, filling the gap between Norman and Amber.

'A child's funeral is always unbearable,' Gertrude said.

'I'm pleased to see you here, Amber.'

'I had nothing dark to wear,' Amber said. She was wearing her beige suit and a brown felt hat, a wide-brimmed hat.

'I'd like to see me try to get into a ten-year-old suit. You look good too, Mrs Foote.' Gertrude was dressed for a funeral, in her black suit. 'I notice the Abbots aren't here,' Maisy said.

'It would have been too hard on the pour souls,' Gertrude said.

'Did you see the pictures in the *Willama Gazette*? I said to George that they had no right to go dredging up little Nelly's photograph. It must be like reliving it all over again for the Abbots.'

'She used to remind me of Nelly,' Jenny said.

'They were related, love. Mrs Abbot is an aunty to Barbie's mother.'

'Is it someone in the family who's doing it?' Amber said.

'God, no! They thought they had him yesterday. They brought this bloke in from one of the farms out past Three Pines, but it wasn't him.'

They walked off as a group, but split into pairs once outside the cemetery gates, Joey and Jenny, Norman and Gertrude, Maisy and Amber, mourners before them, mourners behind, strung out in twos and threes along the crown of the road like a herd of cows at milking time. The rain had stopped for little Barbie, but step off the crown of that road and you'd sink into foot-deep mud.

Maisy turned right at the town hall corner, Amber crossed over the road. The city police turned left into Denham's yard.

Gertrude's horse and cart was parked up near the church. Jenny turned to walk with them, but Norman held her back.

'Your mother spoke to you?' he said.

'Yes.'

'There is relief in forgiveness, Jennifer.'

'She's being nice because she wants something, like Sissy's nice when she wants something.'

'Cynicism is for the old and jaded, and not attractive in a child,' he said.

She shrugged and ran to catch up to Gertrude.

UNIFICATION

In the *Sun News–Pictorial* on 14 March, they printed a large photograph of Herr Hitler and another one of his goose-stepping troops as they crossed the frontier into Austria.

That was the day Charlie White started forecasting a war. 'You mark my words. Twelve months, two years at the most and there'll be war.'

'Old warmonger,' they said. 'As if things aren't bad enough, he's got to make them worse.'

'Germany doesn't want another war any more than we do,' they said.

Then, on 17 March, Norman did his own goose-stepping through his side gate; and though Jenny watched for him to come out, he didn't.

Samson had lost his strength when Delilah gave him a haircut. Jenny had lost her blindfold since Gertrude had cut her hair. She saw the world much more clearly now. Or maybe it had nothing to do with haircuts. Maybe it was due to the month she'd spent in Maisy's house where few subjects were taboo. She'd learnt to see Norman much more clearly in Maisy's house. Always the giant-killer of her infancy, he'd grown smaller as she'd grown taller. She loved him, but even that love had undergone a change. He'd left her alone in that house, left that key in the door — or where Amber could get it. Trust in her father had taken a blow on the day after the quest. During the four weeks since, she'd come to see him as less the giant and more the goose — or perhaps a great pelican, hatched and raised in a parrot's cage. There was nothing wrong with his wings, but no matter how hard she might try to teach him to fly, all he'd ever do was flap around in the same circles.

She'd been proud of him when he'd taken a room at the hotel. She cringed with embarrassment on the Saturday when she saw him carrying his case back home; almost died of embarrassment, for him, when he walked into church on Sunday, Amber at his side. Dodged him after church, knowing he'd expect her to go home. She looked for him to walk over the road on Sunday afternoon to take her home. And she wasn't going home. He didn't come.

Then, three days before Sissy's birthday, Vern Hooper arrived home in a brand new car, Margaret sitting beside him in the front seat, Jim sitting in the rear, with Sissy. Never had Jenny seen Jim sitting in the back seat, nor had anyone else in town. Stories were passed around during the next days about Jim Hooper — as if there wasn't enough drama in broken ribs and bruised lungs, people seemed to need the more dramatic impact of injuries to the brain.

The Macdonald girls heard all of the town gossip. Only Jessie and Dawn were living at home. Four were married, two were nurses in Willama. Jessie had a boyfriend, but Dawn, one of the middle girls, wasn't interested in men. She told anyone who asked that living with her brothers was enough to put her off the opposite sex for life. Maisy's girls came in a variety of shapes and sizes, all with similar pale blonde hair and varying shades of George's purplish eyes, apart from Dawn. She had Maisy's hazel eyes. Most of the girls were lucky to make five foot in height. Dawn was five foot two. She couldn't handle those twins like Maisy, but she managed quite well with a broom. Jenny didn't manage.

Fate was attempting to force her home.

She spent a lot of time at Blunt's shop, unpacking crates of goods from Melbourne. Loved burying her nose in the pure essence of the city. The post office was too close to Norman's front gate, but she always helped Mr Foster sort the mail when it came from the train on Saturday mornings, and Norman being home wasn't going to change that.

That Saturday, Sissy was standing out the front of the post office talking to Peggy Fulton. Like the Macdonalds, the Fulton girls enjoyed a gossip, and Sissy, having spent the best part of a month in Melbourne, was a fount of information.

'Happy birthday,' Jenny said.

'Thanks,' Sissy said.

And that was all they said, but maybe, just maybe, that month away from Amber hadn't done her any harm. And maybe she hadn't eaten as well during that month. She'd lost weight, had four inches cut from her hair. She looked better.

The fates kept conspiring. Near midday when Mr Foster locked his door, Jenny saw Norman and Danny struggling to heave a loaded trolley up the front step to the verandah, a large crate balanced on it. She stood at the gate watching until they got it up to the verandah, then Norman saw her, or saw her red print dress, one of Dawn's old dresses too short and fitting too well.

'It is past time that you were home,' he said. 'The door please.'

She opened it, held it wide, and the smell of home hit her like a punch in the pit of her stomach. The shine of it, and the parlour, not a cushion, not a curtain, out of place, no book on the table, no newspaper tossed down on a chair. Maisy's house was where people lived. No one lived in this place.

But they did today. The trolley wheels left gritty lines across the polished floor and on the parlour carpet, and Danny's boots left their own marks. She looked down at her shoes. She hadn't wiped them. And Amber wasn't dancing, wasn't snarling, going for her hair — not that she had much left to go for.

'Close the door, please, Jennifer. It's cool out today,' she said.

Didn't want to close that door, be closed in by it, but wanted to see what Norman had in his crate. She stepped inside. Danny closed the door on his way out.

The crate took some ripping open. She watched bits of it fall, watched packing paper spread over floor and couch. Then she saw it. It was a wireless and its wood matched the crystal cabinet.

Norman had the leaflet of directions. He liked instructions.

'Did you know it was going to match the cabinet, Norman?' Amber said.

'I ordered the mahogany,' he said.

'It's nicer than Hoopers',' Sissy said.

They moved it in against the couch, its back to the window, and Norman connected the aerial wire, which he fed up beneath the curtain and out through the top of the upper window sash to dangle down to the verandah.

'Stand back,' he said, pushing the power plug into a socket. Jenny hadn't known was there — or maybe it wasn't there before.

The thing made a loud pop, then screamed: *'British leaders believe there is little likelihood that the British Empire will be dragged into . . .'*

'Who turned it on?'

It howled until Norman found the knob to reduce the volume. The static was bad. Jenny knew all about static from Maisy's house. She went out to the verandah to hold the aerial wire high.

'You'll get electrocuted!' Norman yelled.

'It's much better, though,' Amber said. 'What are you doing to it?'

'Just holding it up,' Jenny called back.

And she'd gone and done it. She'd spoken to Amber . . . just by accident, though.

'Perhaps we could take turns holding it up,' Norman said.

He didn't make jokes. He used to once, a long, long time ago.

He brought out a chair and Jenny stood on it; they looped the aerial up and over a verandah rafter, then across another and another to the side of the house, where they allowed it to drop down to a water tap. A few twists around the galvanised pipe and —

'That's perfect, Norman,' Amber yelled.

She sounded so human. Jenny went back inside to investigate her mother, while Norman investigated the wireless knobs until he found the station they played at the hotel. Music in a house unaccustomed to music, mess in a parlour unaccustomed to mess, unaccustomed beep-beep-beeping and an announcer who told them the time.

'Good Lord,' Amber said, just like Mrs Palmer might have said it, 'is that the time? What happened to the morning?'

She made sandwiches for lunch and set four places at the table. So Jenny sat, and hoped her sandwich wasn't poisoned. It was so weird. Amber was weird — or so un-weird she was scary. And Norman calling her 'my dear' instead of 'Mrs Morrison'. Something had changed radically in Norman's house. Sissy was even human, or so full up with what she'd done in Melbourne, she had to let it out.

'We stayed in Jim's uncle's house in Balwyn, and Ian, Margaret's cousin, drove us everywhere. There's thousands of cars down there, thousands of people. Everywhere you go there's a crowd of people and cars. They have to have stoplights on some streets to stop cars and trams from running into each other. We went down to the beach three times, and every beach we went to there were thousands of people swimming. And the theatres. They're huge. We went to the pictures three times. He took us out to visit Uncle Charles and Aunty Jane . . .'

The doctors had taken out Jim's tonsils, which they said had been causing his septic throats. Vern had bought a Ford V8.

'Coming home in it was so much more convenient than the train,' Sissy said, and she almost sounded like Margaret. 'We could stop whenever we wanted to. We had lunch at a restaurant in a little town . . .'

Strange, eating in this kitchen. It was home. It had always been home. Good being able to go down to the lav after lunch where no one would dare to throw broken bricks at the roof. Even good walking up the passage and not having to dodge one or both of Maisy's twins — and how could you dodge two? It would be easier just dodging Amber.

And maybe Amber had turned into a mind-reader.

'Your room is made up for you, Jenny,' she said.

Had she ever called her Jenny before that day? Had she ever spoken to her in a normal voice? Maybe she was finally well. Gertrude said she was well. Maisy said she was well.

It would be nice to have her own wireless, to be able to turn it on and listen to what she liked, instead of what the twins or George liked.

They moved things around after lunch, moved the wireless into the corner beside the fireplace. They took the crate out to the woodheap — it would make good kindling. They cleaned up the packing paper, Amber swept her floor and still Jenny didn't leave. She stood in the doorway watching her place a figurine on the wireless. It looked too small. Amber must have thought so. She put it back in its place on the crystal cabinet, and Jenny dodged out of her way as she came for the doily and the vase of flowers from the hall table.

That looked right on the wireless, but Norman had the leaflet of instructions in his hand. 'It says here . . . *water and electricity do not mix.*'

'It needs something big,' Jenny said.

And she knew exactly what it needed. She ran down to the washhouse where she'd last seen those peacock feathers wrapped in an old sheet. Still there, and dusty. She unwrapped the parcel, gave the feathers a shake, gave them a good whack against the verandah post on the way back in, a final whack or two against the relief bag in her room. Her room, her bed, her whatnot and wardrobe and her pillow. Loved that pillow. It fitted her neck. She drew in a breath of it, held it for a moment, then turned to the wardrobe and reached for the blue-green vase. She gave the feathers a last whack on the relief bag, then stuffed them into the vase and carried it into the parlour.

'Oh, my word,' Norman said. 'Mother's feathers. I thought they had long gone to their rest.'

'Peacock feathers inside the house are unlucky,' Amber said.

'We make our own luck in life, my dear.'

Amber wasn't so sure. She stood back while Jenny placed the vase on the wireless. And they looked so right there. They matched the curtains, matched the cushions.

'They fill that corner nicely,' Amber admitted, moving in to take charge, to arrange them better to her liking, while Norman sat smiling his Cheshire cat smile, delighted his mother's feathers were back where they belonged, delighted to see his wife and daughter standing side by side, so oddly similar in height and build, in calf and ankle.

Jenny stayed an hour with them in the parlour, listening to music and advertisements for pills that could cure every ill, listening to the beeping of the hour and to news from overseas.

'Charlie White says Herr Hitler is going to start another war,' she said. 'If he did, would Australia have to fight in it again, Dad?'

'The German people were so soundly defeated last time, you can rest assured their leaders will not subject them to another war, Jennifer.'

'Why do they call them Nazis? It sounds . . . so sort of evil.'

'The National Socialists is a political party,' Norman said. 'Their aim, I believe, is to unite the many small countries bordering Germany.'

Australia and America were huge countries. Germany wasn't as big as Victoria, and Austria was even smaller. Uniting them sounded logical to Jenny. In 1938, it sounded logical to many.

Unification. It would be so easy to give in and come home. So . . . so logical.

'I'll see you later then,' she said, fast, before she did something stupid.

'Your sister is having a small gathering this evening,' Norman said.

'At eight,' Sissy said.

'I'll come back.'

Jim was there, with Margaret, and for one terrible instant Jenny thought the rumours about his brain damage were fact.

'No' foo' for me, fanks. Aw I gan ea is broff an yelly. Free momfs o' ut.'

He looked brain damaged. His time at death's door had stripped away the little meat he'd had covering his bones, and Mr Cox had given him a Woody Creek haircut, near clipped to the scalp with a tuft on top. He looked like a startled cockatoo with big ears. Then Jenny saw his mouth. Like the burnt-out boot shop, a dark waste of ash, a hole where no hole should have been, his speech, a toothless slurry of words, a mush of hollow vowels and swallowed consonants.

He was . . . had been her big brother, but he was sitting at Sissy's side now — as Robert Fulton's fiancée sat at his side, as Jessie Macdonald sat at her boyfriend's side. Jenny had eaten her first ice-cream at Jim's side, had learnt about mirages from him and in turn had taught him the joys of watching bull ants. She'd gone to him on that Sunday after the talent quest and they'd found Norman blind, howling drunk at the hotel. He'd helped her tuck him into the hotel bed, then gone with her to the house to get him a change of clothes. For years, forever, he'd been her big brother.

Saw him too clearly tonight. Saw the folded skeletal length of him, his bony wrists supporting hands too large for those wrists to hold. They sagged to his knees, where his kneebones threatened to cut through the fabric of his trousers, like his jaw and cheekbones threatening to cut through the pale skin stretched tight over his face.

Saw his fate too. He'd end up married to Sissy. She always got what she wanted, had always coveted Vern Hooper's house and indoor lavatory.

Wanted to warn him.

Wanted to warn Norman who seemed to be enjoying the party, sitting on the couch well fed and smiling — a grain-fed steer at the slaughteryards, unaware the butcher was sharpening his killing knife, waiting to turn him into next week's steak.

No use. Some people got what they wanted. Maybe others got what they needed. Jenny wanted . . . wanted to go.

DUFFY'S DOGS

The city police had squeezed that town for information and come up with no answer as to who had murdered, mutilated, little Barbie, or why. A lot of strangers passed through Woody Creek, a lot of forest surrounded it, a lot of roads led into and out of it. Eight-year-old Barbara Jean Dobson had been murdered by person or persons unknown.

There was more distrust in the town now, or distrust of strangers. Denham moved them on, hunted those swagmen from his town. He went to the school to speak about the danger of strangers; he kept a closer eye on his own kids.

They were playing in the backyard the day old Betty, the Duffy matriarch, walked into town. She came in once a week for a few supplies but usually kept her distance from the police station. Not today. She went directly to Denham's door, and the five or six mangy dogs that followed her everywhere proceeded to leave their calling cards on doorstep and wall — and dance back smartly to water Denham's verandah posts when he opened the door.

'Are them city coppers still hanging around here somewhere?'

Denham stepped back. The Duffy family washed less often than their dogs. From the safety of his doorway, he studied the woman. Betty didn't waste money on corset or underwear but she ate well. Her rag of a dress stretched across sagging breasts, moulded her gross stomach, leaving little to the imagination. Her hair, whitened by the years, yellowed by nicotine, trimmed twelve months back with a carving knife, hung around her neck, stuck to her sweat-beaded face, caught up in facial crevices. The day wasn't hot but her walk into town had raised a sweat, which at close range was a chargeable offence.

He stepped outside, closed his door, skirted around her and her dogs, and walked down the end of his verandah to the kid-trodden earth between his house and lockup, a natural wind tunnel. Betty followed him, her dogs followed her, peeing as they came. It never failed to amaze him how Mrs Duffy's dogs could keep finding more pee. They didn't look as if they had enough liquid in them to wet a match head.

'What's your trouble, Mrs Duffy?'

'I just caught old Albert at Maryanne and I brained him with the backside of me shovel. He could be dead.'

As far as Denham could tell, someone was always getting at one of the Duffy girls. He stood upwind of her, took his cigarettes from his pocket. He knew Albert, known to most in town as old Noah, who was over seventy.

'He's a bit old for it, isn't he?'

'His type are never too old for it. I been letting him stay on me land, for his pension like, and the old bastard turns around and bites the hand that feeds him.'

Her hand was out for a smoke. Denham wasn't having her touching his packet; he removed a second cigarette, tossed it, lit his own smoke, then tossed his box of matches.

'Is he dead?'

'Bleeding like a stuck pig.' She tapped the cigarette on the matchbox, placed it between toothless gums, lit up, slid the matches into a pocket and spat a tobacco thread. 'I see the dogs sniffing around Sophie's place and I think the old bastard might have croaked, so I walk down to have a look and I catch him red-handed.' She spat a second tobacco thread. 'I roll me own,' she said. 'More horse dung than tobacco in these ready-rolled. Any rate, the kid's got her pants off and she's somersaulting and he's bloody applauding her, so I pick up the nearest thing and give him the back end of me shovel.'

Denham stayed away from the Duffys when he could. There were six or eight women and near-adult girls out there, and the mental image of any one of them turning somersaults with her bloomers off wasn't pretty. He turned away, turned to her dogs, one of them getting down to some serious foreplay with the wheel of his motorbike.

'Clear off, you mongrel.' He aimed a kick. It leered at him but kept pumping. 'What's he doing now?'

'Me dog?'

'Your lodger, Mrs Duffy.'

'He's Sophie's, not mine. She reckons I killed him.' She sucked more smoke, blew it at the gathering flies. 'As soon as I saw that bastard sitting there smiling, I knew who done young Barbie and that Abbot girl. She's nine year old.'

'Who?'

'Maryanne.'

That changed Denham's outlook. He turned to his backyard where his kids had suddenly gone quiet. The little buggers would be standing around the corner listening in to this.

'One of the children?'

'Sophie's girl.'

Denham wanted her away from his kids. He started towards his front gate, hoping she'd follow. The dogs followed. And it was a bad move. John McPherson's car was parked out front of Charlie's, his brown kelpie stepping sedately down from the front passenger seat. The Duffy dogs didn't like toffs who rode in cars. As one, they took off across the road to rough him up.

'Come back here, you mob of mongrels,' Betty bellowed. They didn't come back. 'Dogs will be dogs,' she said, spitting another tobacco thread. 'He was the bastard that ruint me, you know.'

Denham was watching McPherson. 'How did he do that, Mrs Duffy?'

'How do you bloody well think he did it? I was a fourteen-year-old girl at the time.'

'Right.'

Charlie White, armed with a heavy broom, was out and attempting to break a few backs. Betty stood sucking her fag, sucking it down to the bone, sucking it until it burned her fingers, until she was forced to drop it.

'Where?' Denham said.

'Where what?'

'Where did you know old Albert from — when you were fourteen, Mrs Duffy?'

'Out at Three Pines. Monk's place. Me old man did a bit of work out there and he got me work in the kitchen. That old bastard used to come up there with a mob from the city.'

The dogs came back, one shaking its head, one licking its backside. 'Mongrels,' she said. 'They all need a dose of lead but they're not worth the bullets. Give us another smoke to go on with, will you? I'm shook up about this.'

He took two more from his packet. She had the matches. He accepted a light.

'Your girl all right?'

'Her mother took care of her with a broomstick. You're not locking me up for it. He deserved what he got.'

Denham had too much respect for his cell. 'I'll follow you back out, Mrs Duffy.'

He stood on for a time, allowing her to get a head start. He'd signed the papers to get old Albert on the aged pension. Before he'd taken lodgings out at Duffy's, he'd camped from time to time in McPherson's hut. Denham knew him as a harmless old chap, an interesting old chap too if you got him talking. He liked hanging around the park, though. Always kids in that park. He spent time down by the creek. Kids liked hanging around down there too. He was in town when Barbie died. He could have been around when Nelly Abbot was murdered.

He pitched his smoke and walked to his motorbike. It stank of Duffy's dogs. It would stink more before it was much older.

Six o'clock and the city police were on their way back to town. Old Noah, known to Denham as Albert Forester, transported in Vern's new car to Denham's jail, had left his blood on the upholstery. Leather washed down smelled of wet cow. Gertrude noticed it when she got in.

'Old Betty brained her lodger,' Vern explained. 'She told Denham she caught him at one of her daughter's, or granddaughter's, kids. She's made a decent hole in his head.'

'I wish she'd done it earlier,' Gertrude said, eyeing the evening sky.

'Old Betty reckons he did the same to her out at Monk's, back when she was working in the kitchen out there. Do you remember an Albert Forester ever being out there?'

'There used to be a Forester working for someone out the Willama Road. He married one of the Dobson girls.'

'It would have been before his time. Betty's damn near our age.'

'If she says she knew him, she did. She's never bothered to lie.'

Denham's jail was a green ten-by-ten box with a barred window and a solid door. Electricity had been connected but the first globe had blown the second time he'd turned the switch. He hadn't bothered to replace it. There was little light left in the day and not much of it getting through the east-facing door.

They'd placed the old bloke on one of the bunks, on a bare mattress, and wrapped his head in a towel, now bloody.

'You look like a wounded Arab,' Gertrude said. 'Can you lift your head?'

He was conscious when she'd walked in. She'd seen one hand moving. His eyes were closed now and he didn't lift his head, so she lifted it and got the towel off. The gash was two inches across, the bone exposed.

'Has he been talking?' she asked.

'The women said he'd come around. He's said nothing to me,' Denham said.

She held a clean pad against the wound. His blood was still running. 'I can put a stitch in it, which might stop him bleeding, but you need to get him down to the hospital. She's probably cracked his skull.'

'The city chaps want me to hold him until they get here.'

'He could be bleeding into the brain.'

'Stitch him,' Denham said.

'You'll need to turn him around so I can get at him, and get me some light.'

There were two bunks in the cell and little room between them. They got him turned around. With his overcoat off, there wasn't much of him to turn. Denham went inside to steal a light globe from his kitchen. Gertrude put her glasses on, then sat on the edge of the bunk to peer at the wound and the patient.

'He looks bloodless.'

'He's always looked bloodless,' Denham said.

That globe was next door to useless. Wherever she moved, her shadow was in the way. Denham went for his flashlight and, with its beam directed on the scalp, she had a good look at Betty's handiwork. If his skull was cracked, she couldn't feel it.

Denham got her stitching thread through the eye of her curved needle. She took it and turned to her patient.

'This is going to hurt,' she told him. 'I hope you're not playing possum.' She slapped his face, and maybe his eyelid flickered. 'You might come over here, Vern, and hold him down.'

Then she lifted an eyelid and a blue, blue eye looked into her own, blue as the sky, blue as the ocean. The mind attempts to hang on to what it's been told, to override what it knows, but reflexes respond. She stepped back onto Vern's foot, dropped her needle and near fell on her face. Vern caught her, steadied her, and caught the look in her eye.

'He's dead,' she said.

'He's breathing, Mrs Foote,' Denham said.

Vern knew what she'd seen, and he stepped in to see for himself, to lift that same eyelid. A veiny white eyeball stared back. 'It's not him, Trude.'

'Not who?' Denham said, searching for, finding and picking up the needle, wiping it clean on his shirtsleeve.

'It's him,' she said.

'He's dead,' Vern said. Died in Egypt, and she had his money to prove it, had his microscope.

'Who?' Denham asked.

Gertrude picked up a hand, old hand, age spotted, fingernails still neatly trimmed, though not so clean. A bump on the bridge of his nose. That wasn't there forty years ago. There was one way to prove it. Over his left ear. She forgot the blood, forgot the new gash, and felt for the old, separating that long blood-caked hair, separating it until she found what she knew would be there. And she found it. She hadn't done much of a job on stitching that one.

Only a girl then, twenty-one or two. Blood everywhere that night — trying to pinch the sides of that gaping wound together, struggling to force the needle through his flesh, so much tougher than she'd expected. And his hair in the way. And unable to see for tears, washing that wound with her great dripping tears. Long, long before she'd forgotten how to cry for Archie Foote.

Like a magnet, that man, he'd drawn folk to him; then, like a magnet reversed, repelled them. He repelled her now. Her hands drew back from him, but his blood was dripping. She had to stop it. She had to touch him.

Took up her scissors with a shaking hand, rinsed them in her jar of methylated spirits, and told that hand it had work to do. Hacked off a hank of blood-matted hair and dropped it, hacked through another, and another, clearing the area of hair. She reached for the needle, sank it and its thread in metho.

'You know him?' Denham said.

'A relative of Monk's,' she said. 'I thought he was dead.' And she drove that needle through his flesh and he opened his eyes. 'Hold his head still, Vern.'

Maybe she put in more stitches than necessary. Maybe Vern took more pleasure than he ought in holding him down, but they got him stitched, they got that bleeding stopped, got wound and stitches doused with iodine, and hoped it stung.

Denham's wife brought out a basin of water for Gertrude to wash in. She left it with soap and towel on the verandah. Gertrude stood soaping too long, her hands shaking hard now that their work was done. She soaped and allowed them their time to shake. Her legs shook in sympathy. She let them sit her down on the front steps while Vern soaped his own hands. She was no leaner, but tonight, when Vern sat beside her, she leaned.

He slid an arm around her and they sat in silence, sat listening to Denham's kids playing a wall away.

'Are you going to tell Denham?'

'What would that do to Amber? She's just coming back to herself.'

'Stop letting that girl dictate your life, Trude.'

'He's Albert Forester, Vern,' she said. 'That's what I'm saying. The name is even starting to sound familiar.'

They charged Albert Forester with the murder of Barbara Dobson and Nelly Abbot, and with the lesser charge of molestation of a minor. The city police took him back to the city and Woody Creek breathed a sigh of relief. They'd got him.

Old Betty and one of her granddaughters got an all-expenses-paid trip to Melbourne, accommodation supplied by the Salvation Army, along with new outfits and haircuts. But you can't make a kid glove out of well-worn buffalo hide. They looked what they were, and when they opened their mouths, the jurors knew what they were.

The newspapers liked Betty. She livened up the proceedings, determined to tell how that bastard had 'ruint' her as a fourteen-year-old girl. She wanted him hanged. She said so several times.

The defence appreciated Sophie, who admitted she wasn't too certain of her lodger's movements on the day Barbie Dobson died, that he could have been out at the time, though she couldn't say for sure that he wasn't napping in his room, which wasn't really attached to her house, which was why she hadn't seen what he was getting up to with young Maryanne.

Maryanne, the victim, who had made a lucky escape, wasn't called on to give evidence. The examining doctor was. He stated that the child was intact, that she'd admitted getting pennies from old Noah if she played rude games with him.

Denham stated that Albert Forester had been in town at the time Nelly Abbot was murdered, that he was sharing a hut fifty yards from where she had last been seen swimming with her brothers. He had photographic evidence to prove it — John

McPherson dated every photograph he developed. Denham stated that the hut was situated seventy-five yards from Dobson's wood paddock, where Barbie had last been seen. He said too that in his opinion, Albert Forester was capable of carrying a finely built eight-year-old child a mile through heavily timbered country, that he'd seen him lifting crates around in the grocer's yard where he did a few hours' work from time to time. He said that Albert Forester had spent much of his time down by the creek or in the park, places where the town children congregated.

'Since the defendant's arrest, I have spoken to Maryanne Duffy and to two of her female cousins, Teresa and Cristobel. All three mentioned playing ice-cream games with the defendant for pennies. To use the girls' own words: "Like, I don't scream and then I get a penny for an ice-cream."'

Denham was a good witness. The jury believed him.

Albert Forester took the stand late on the second day, making hard work of his climb up to it, requiring a supporting arm until he was seated. His right arm had been weakened by stroke, he said. He used his walking cane with his left hand. The defence council made much of his weakened state, of his great age, covering and re-covering the same ground until Betty took offence and was threatened with removal from the courtroom.

The jury listened intently to Albert Forester when he said the girls came to him asking for money, that he had not put a hand on any one of them, that Maryanne had wanted to show him a game, taught to her by her mother's boyfriend, that she had named it the ice-cream game.

Betty was removed from the courtroom at that point, and the timing was perfect. Place a well-dressed, courtly old gentleman beside a foul-mouthed old slut and see who the jury wants to believe.

They deliberated for two hours, between lunch and afternoon tea on the Friday.

Saturday's edition of Melbourne's favourite newspaper, which now claimed to sell 240,000 copies each day, carried the verdict and a photograph of Betty Duffy. 'FORESTER INNOCENT ON MURDER CHARGE. FOUND GUILTY ON LESSER CHARGE OF CORRUPTION OF A MINOR.'

Betty and her granddaughter arrived home on the train that brought those papers to Woody Creek. Betty took her city shoes off for the long walk home. Two hours later, minus her city underwear, her feet comfortably shod in old boots, she was back and belting on Denham's door.

'What have you done with me bloody dogs?'

Denham and Tom Vevers had shot her bloody dogs, every last diseased mongrel. He told her what he'd done with them, then stood back and waited for her to ask what he'd done with her grandkids. He wasn't guilty on that charge. The state had stepped in and removed eight Duffy kids ranging in age from two months to twelve years. The city orphanages left a lot to be desired but a few of those kids might learn something more useful than how to drop their pants for a penny.

'Those dogs kept an eye on my Henry. He's wandered off somewhere.'

'He needs to be in a home, Mrs Duffy.'

'You keep your bloody hands off that boy. He never done no harm to no one. Now you get out there and find him before he does himself a harm.'

THE WOODEN SPOON

Gertrude didn't get her hands on that newspaper until Sunday, when she read every word of the report. Vern sat with her, sharing her paper and the afternoon sun.

'I thought they'd hang him,' Vern said.

'They probably got it right,' Gertrude said. 'There's not much I'd say for him, but I never believed he'd killed those little girls.'

'He'll get a few years for the other.'

'I'll guarantee the jury got that right,' she said. 'He'd charm the pants off a nun and have the choirboys' off for seconds.'

'Who knows what he's progressed to since you knew him.'

'You didn't see what I saw, Vern. Those little girls' faces were cut to shreds, their little bodies mutilated. Rape of a child, I'd believe that, murder maybe, if he was pushed into a corner, but the mutilation of a pretty little girl's face? That wasn't in the man. It wasn't in him. Some things you know.'

Some things you know and you face them, like it or not. Some things you damn near know and you turn your back on them, close your mind to them, shake your head so hard it damn near flies off whenever those thoughts attempt to rise. There's certain things you have to deny or you'd lose your mind.

Norman's Aunty Lizzie had lost her mind these past twelve months. Thankfully, she died in June. Norman hadn't seen her since 1932, but he caught the train down to Melbourne for the funeral, caught up with his relatives and arrived home smiling. Aunty Lizzie had left him four hundred pounds.

The money came through in July, a week before Jim was to pick up his new false teeth. Norman, on the Church of England ball committee for the past ten years, always attended, and this year Amber had agreed to accompany him. She hadn't worn a ballgown in fifteen years, and the only one she owned was mouldy and moth-eaten. Sissy owned three ballgowns, but Margaret Hooper owned a dozen and she was buying a new one in Willama, so Sissy and Amber were going with her to buy gowns.

Jenny had gone to the ball with Norman last year and the year before. A lot of kids went with their parents. They danced in the supper room or ran wild in the park. Last year, Jenny and Dora had run wild in the park. This year, she was fourteen and a half, and Dora, who had already turned fifteen, was allowed to wear Irene's lemon ballgown. No chance of Jenny wearing one of Sissy's old gowns. No mention either of her getting a new dress from Norman's inheritance. If she'd moved back home, she might have. Norman said from time to time that he wanted her home, but not for a new dress, not for a king's ransom, was she living with Sissy and Amber again. Maisy's house was paradise again and would stay paradise while the twins remained in Melbourne.

On the night before the Willama trip, Jenny was visiting in Norman's parlour, listening to a radio play George Macdonald couldn't stand but Norman enjoyed, when the broadcaster cut into the play to praise the merits of Pears Soap.

'Would you care to accompany your mother and sister tomorrow, Jennifer?'

'She's got school,' said Amber.

'I've finished all of my leaflets. I could miss one day.'

'Jennifer has an unworn frock in her wardrobe,' Amber said, and said it so nicely.

She looked . . . looked almost nice these days, looked almost motherly, sitting at her embroidery, the light shining on her hair. Jenny watched the embroidery needle drawing the silk thread through, watched it for minutes. That needle was as sharp as it had ever been.

'Mr Curry has suggested you sit for the bursary this year,' Norman said.

'When the leaflets are done . . .' Jenny started, but what was the use of explaining. She left before the play was over. It didn't matter. What mattered was getting out of that house.

The following morning, she waved as they drove by, waved to Jim. Sissy in the front seat with him, Margaret and Amber in the back seat. Norman's house would be empty all day.

The few students who continued on at school after grade six were allowed to work at their own pace. Jenny liked finishing things. If she went to school she'd spend the day helping Miss Rose with the little kids, and today she didn't feel like listening to five year olds lisping through their first primers. She felt like having Norman and his house to herself, having the wireless to herself.

Someone had hung that brown rag in her wardrobe, and it looked no better than the last time she'd seen it. If it had been a darker brown or a lighter brown, something might have been done with it, but it was muddy. And the style was an old lady's. It had square floppy sleeves, a floppy collar and a boring gored skirt, which was half a mile too long. It looked worse than she remembered it, because of Dawn's hand-me-downs, which fitted — with the hems let down.

Jenny spread the brown frock on her bed, considering trims, considering embroidering it all over with white daisies, considering the sleeves, making a decent belt for it. Cancelled that out. She couldn't make a belt out of the hem of a gored skirt that had been cut from eight pieces. Wished she was brave enough to burn it, or stuff it into the relief bag so some desperate old lady could wear it.

At nine o'clock, she went over to the station. 'I've got nothing to do at school, Daddy.'

'It's a great pity you have no access to a secondary education,' he said.

'Gloria Bull stays with her aunty and uncle in Melbourne . . .'

'Had your Aunt Lizzie been alive . . .'

Had Aunty Lizzie been alive, Sissy and Amber wouldn't have been spending her money on new ballgowns.

'I'll make you some dinner,' she said.

Loved owning that house for a day, loved being able to try on Sissy's green ballgown . . . which looked ridiculous. Six inches of skirt drooped around her feet, and Dora could have got into it with her.

Amber's moth-eaten cream was in the relief bag. She dug it out and tried it on. It fitted her. It must have been nice years ago. It had big puffy sleeves and a pintucked bodice, but it was stained and the moths had been picnicking on the skirt. She stuffed it back, found an old book and took it out to the kitchen, where she stoked up the stove then sat before it reading. Good to sit on that familiar chair. Good light for reading in Norman's kitchen. Good too, when Norman came home for lunch. She fried cheese sandwiches while he spoke of many things — or it was good until he progressed to the brown dress.

'Your mother chose it for you,' he said.

She buttered bread and bit her tongue.

'That frock has become a stumbling block between you. It would please her to see you wearing it.'

'I'd rather wear the stumbling block, Daddy.'

'That is a reply worthy of the Macdonald girls.'

Maybe it was. Live with people long enough and their ways rub off — better ways.

'It's past time you came home.'

'Maisy doesn't mind me living there.'

'This antagonism between you and your mother must end. She has your best interests at heart, Jennifer.'

'She didn't want me to go with them today.'

He wasn't good at arguing. 'You will bring your belongings home today and be here when she returns,' he said, and he emptied his teacup, rose from the table and left the room.

'I'd rather wear that brown dress to the ball,' she told a sandwich as she placed it into the pan. That's what Jessie would have said.

And he heard her. He came back to the doorway. 'Then wear it you will,' he said. And he left her frying her sandwich.

She ate it in Maisy's kitchen. She was poking around Maisy's washhouse later when she found the dye, two bottles, both half-full, very old bottles, most of their labels were missing, but one had surely held green. Some had dripped onto what was left of the label. The lids were rusted on. She ran with them across the road to get Norman's pliers. One lid came off and took a part of the bottle's neck with it; it contained an evil blackish-green liquid. The second one screwed off. It was blue, blue-bag blue, gruesome blue. But not as gruesome as that brown frock, which supposedly was a good-quality cotton. You could dye cotton. Mrs Palmer did it all the time. She'd dyed a bedspread and two faded frocks one day and when they were dry they'd looked almost new.

What if I ruin it? she thought.

How can you ruin something that was born ruined?

She took her bottles to Amber's kitchen, looked at the clock, added more wood to the stove, considered Amber's biggest saucepan — or maybe her preserving pan. The preserving pan would be better. Got it down from the top of her wardrobe, emptied the boiling water from the kettle into it. Judged it insufficient and added cold water until it looked enough, then stood over it urging that pot to boil while the hands of the clock ticked away fifteen minutes.

At steaming point, she poured in a dash of blue dye, watched it pool then slowly disperse. It wasn't a nice blue so she added a dash of green, which made the water look more green than blue. Emptied in the last of the blue, gave it a stir with Amber's long wooden spoon — and before her eyes that spoon turned bright blue.

'Oh, hell!'

She emptied in the last of the green, stirred again and watched the spoon darken.

'Oh, hell's bells in Scotland!' Jessie said that.

Her brew wasn't even boiling, and Jim's appointment was for one thirty, and it was almost that already. They could be home in less than an hour.

Skirt first, she fed the prison brown into the pan, sinking it with the spoon. It sank, apart from a sleeve which blew up and reached for help. She held it under until it stopped blowing bubbles attempting to get out. Noticed she was steaming up Amber's kitchen. Opened the back door, then the west window, allowing cold air to blow through. Her face was wet, be it from steam, fear or heat from that red-hot stove she was uncertain, but she added more wood and opened the north window.

Pink-faced witch's apprentice, stirring her cauldron, gazing through the steam at her uncertain brew, unsure if she was performing magic or conjuring up a monster.

Ten minutes later there was little doubt.

She fished the frock out, flopped it into a bucket, attempted to lift the preserving pan, two-thirds full of lying bubbling liquid, which had promised much but offered her a gruesome grisly grey. And why should it turn grey when the wooden spoon was now a very interesting shade of deep blue-green?

'Something light would have gone blue,' she told that gruesome grey. 'Something light.'

Glanced at Amber's tea towel, then ran for the relief bag and for Amber's moth-eaten ballgown. Bodice first, she fed it into the now bubbling brew. And in the blink of an eye it turned, at least in part, the most gorgeous bluey-green she'd ever seen in her life.

Forced it down, stirred it, turned it, splashing blue water. Forgot to watch the clock, mesmerised now by the colour. She'd done this. She shouldn't have done it, but she'd done it now. She'd put water in that pan, added dye and heat and created something that had not been before.

She'd also created a mess Amber's kitchen had not seen before. A glance around, her glance ending at the clock, suggested she had done enough stirring of that dress. She had to get it over to Maisy's and clean up.

Time can limp along on crutches, barely making any ground when you want it to run fast. In all of her life, Jenny had never known a day to fly so fast. The rinsing, the hanging, the running backwards and forwards over the road with her bucket. She wasted time on Amber's wooden spoon, before giving it a fast funeral underneath the oleander tree. It dug its own grave, and serve it right. She'd copped a whack or two from it when she was smaller. Lost the half-hour between three thirty and four, but Amber's stove was clean, the preserving pan shining and back on her wardrobe. She was closing the windows when she heard the car. Considered taking off out the back door, but saw a splash of blue on the lino . . . then two more drips near the door.

Got them with her hanky as Jim carried the shopping inside. He greeted her with a blinding flash of white china-cup teeth — he'd looked better toothless. She did the right thing, remained a while to admire Amber's pinkish beige, to be amazed by Sissy's rainbow taffeta, then off she ran to admire her own ballgown, if the wind hadn't blown it to shreds.

It hadn't, and Maisy had hung both frocks properly. They were flapping merrily or the bluey-green looked merry; the brown, now grey, still looked gruesome.

THE BALL

The ballgown was moth-eaten, but it had yards and more yards in its skirt that the moths hadn't yet sampled. The dying was not perfect, they found a few streaks where the colour hadn't taken so well, or had taken too well. But the skirt was full enough to hide the faults and the colour even more gorgeous beneath electric light. It was blue, but when the light caught a different angle, it looked almost greenish. And the pintucks had gone a darker shade, which disguised the shadow of stain.

'You've got your mother's shape,' Maisy said. 'Or the shape she had when she was eighteen or nineteen.'

There was no doubting that. The ballgown might have been made to Jenny's measurements. The skirt was a smidgen long, but Amber had worn heels with it, and Maisy had enough daughters to fix that.

'Get those old sandals Rachael wore to Maureen's wedding, Dawn. They could fit.'

They were black, had inch heels. They lifted the skirt off the floor.

'Get that petticoat you wore under that green voile, Jessie.'

The twins came home on a motorbike, like two hairy bears, one clinging on behind the other; came home on the Thursday before the ball. It could have been worse; they could have come home sooner.

Maisy was always pleased to see them, though not so pleased about their ginger beards. She couldn't see which one had the chickenpox scar on his jaw.

'Shave yourselves and have a bath before you come into my kitchen,' she said. 'You smell like a pair of polecats.'

They didn't shave or have a bath, but she fed them in her kitchen. It was the end of paradise, the end of long chats, of peaceful meals. Jessie screamed at them, pitched water at them. Dawn chased one of them with the hair broom and didn't hold back when she cornered him. George threatened to take to their bike with the wood axe.

Jenny got out, went over the road. She could stand Sissy and Amber easier than she could stand the twins.

She sat in Norman's parlour listening to the wireless, until the twins started using their bike as a weapon against the town. It howled up one street and down the next, and every dog in town howled at it, chased it, barked at it, or did all three, but with them on the street, it was safe to go back to Maisy's and have a bath, wash her hair.

They were in bed when she left for school on Friday morning. They were eating breakfast when she came home at three thirty. She escaped to the Palmers' and stayed until it was Dora's turn for the bathroom. A nomad, Jenny, a swaggie without a swag, now the twins were home. She went to the station, but Norman wasn't there so she went to the house. He was bathing, shaving for the ball. Sissy was resting. Amber was ironing.

Jenny stood at the kitchen door, watching that rainbow taffeta skirt spread, watching the iron run up and down the colourful fabric, magical fabric. That gown had cost eighteen pounds.

'What do they think they're doing?' Amber moaned as the bike screamed by.

'Acting like maniacs,' Jenny said.

'Why doesn't Denham do something?'

'He's told the garage not to sell them any more petrol.'

They were having a normal conversation — or almost.

'Your father said you were wearing the brown. Bring it out and I'll give it a quick run over,' she said.

She sounded like a mother, looked like a mother, and Jenny felt her face flush with guilt.

'It's over at Maisy's.'

It was, but it wasn't brown, and if she could ever forget it had once been brown, she might even wear it. They'd cut two inches off the hem and about six off the sleeves. Jessie had found a photograph of a frock in a Myer's catalogue, a black frock trimmed with white, and she'd bought three yards of narrow white braid at Blunt's, which they'd hand-stitched around the collar, on the shoulders and sleeves, doing their best to copy the trim on the frock in the catalogue. Jessie said it looked quite smart.

She stood watching Amber fold up her ironing blanket, dodged as she placed it on the chest of drawers in the junk room, wished she could tell her about that old ballgown, how it fitted her perfectly. Wished . . . just wished.

She ate at Amber's table that night, ate early. Amber needed the kitchen to do Sissy's hair. Norman went back to the station and Jenny went with him. She watched the train coming into town, its one large light like a great all-seeing eye. She stared at the faces of the travellers, faces just wanting to get where they were going, and that train shunting around while the timber trucks were connected. Then off it went, off into the dark, the one-eyed night monster carrying its load away. One day, one fine day, she'd ride it.

Tonight, she followed Norman home, home to Sissy and Amber who had now taken over the main bedroom with its newly repaired winged mirror. Norman dressed in Jenny's discarded room. His suit, his dancing shoes, were in that front bedroom. She wondered why, wondered why he called Amber 'my dear' instead of 'Mrs Morrison'.

'Can you put these confounded collar studs in for me, Jennifer?'

'Bring that comb from the table, Jennifer.'

'My spectacles. Did anyone see where I put my spectacles when I came in?'

Jenny found his spectacles. She took Amber's comb to the front bedroom. She fixed Norman's collar studs, held his suit coat while he slid his arms into the sleeves, dodged Sissy as she swished by in the passage, dodged Amber when she came to the kitchen for a Bex powder.

Maybe she shouldn't go tonight. Maisy wasn't going. The twins weren't going. They had no suits to wear.

'A glass of water, if you please, Jennifer.'

'Have you seen that little purse I bought in Melbourne, Mum?'

'It's in that left-hand side drawer.'

'Answer the door, please, Jennifer.'

Like Cinderella, homeless, but handy. She opened the door. No prince come to take her to the ball, only Sissy's intended — whether he knew it or not, and his ugly sister.

'Not going tonight, Jen?' Jim said.

'My fairy godmother is running late,' she said.

He flashed those blinding teeth and she stepped back from their glare. Maybe he'd grow into them.

'Ready, folks?' he said.

She watched them cross the road. Sissy's backside broader, or broader in taffeta, but she was clinging possessively to Jim's arm. Poor slim Jim, slim-legged tonight in his new suit. Poor Norman, all pomp and ceremony in tails, holding Amber's arm. Margaret, frilly little hen, fast stepping, head pecking from side to side, trying to keep up.

Mr Cox had hired a five-piece band from Willama and for the past half-hour intermittent bursts of music had been floating over the road. Everyone said it was the best band around. Everyone said this would be the best ball Woody Creek had ever seen, and by the look of the cars in that street, they might be right.

Another carful arrived. It parked outside Norman's gate as the twins howled by on their bike, pursued now by Denham's bike, and two were worse than one. But it was safe to go back to Maisy's house. She closed the door and was crossing the road when she saw Dora walking with her brothers, and Irene and her husband.

'You're not dressed,' Dora said.

'I've been waiting for the twins to get out of the house,' Jenny said.

'They're out,' Joss said as they heard those bikes coming back, and the Palmer party laughed.

Maisy had a long mirror in her bedroom, and there was a stranger in that mirror tonight, a stranger in a frock that may have been that Alice Blue Gown all grown up. Jenny hardly dared to touch it.

'You look beautiful, love,' Maisy said. 'Now go and enjoy yourself.'

Jenny had believed in fairytales once. Tonight, she tried to believe that Amber and Norman wouldn't mind her wearing that dress, that they'd be interested to see how well it fitted. Fairytales were for kids.

Bobby Vevers and half a dozen boys stood outside the hall smoking. They looked at her.

'Baby's growing up,' one said.

'Five foot two, eyes of blue,' another said.

She swished by them, her skirt whispering old secrets to her stockings.

Mrs Cox was at the ticket table. She and Mr Cox were on the ball committee with Norman. She didn't expect Jenny to pay.

'My, but don't you look the grown-up girl tonight,' she said.

Inside the hall then, inside and lost in a kaleidoscope of coloured gowns and dark suits. She stood just inside the door, seeking Dora, catching a glimpse of Sissy's rainbow as she danced by with Jim. Their height, or his height, made them visible. Keeping close to the wall, she made her way towards the stage end, down to the supper room door.

At most of the town's dances, old Mr Dobson played the piano, Horrie Bull played the accordion and Wally Lewis beat out his crazy rhythms on an old drum. Not many kids here tonight, and the few who had come with their parents were being supervised in the supper room by two women. She'd thought Norman might have been in the supper room. He wasn't, but Mr Cox was.

'Have you seen Dad?' she said.

'I believe he's dancing, Jennifer.'

She was standing half-in, half-out of the supper room when Bobby Vevers tapped her on the shoulder.

'Like to dance?' he said.

He was Sissy's age, too old for her to dance with.

'I'm looking for Dora,' she said.

'You'll find her easier if you're dancing.' And he took her hand and led her out to the floor.

He was right. They found Dora dancing with Joss. Everything was better then. Everything was perfect. Dora said her dress was beautiful, and Irene said it matched her eyes. Jenny danced with Joss Palmer later, she danced with Mr Cox because his wife refused to dance with him.

'Who did you borrow that from?' Sissy said when they met in the middle.

'Mum.'

Danced away from her, which was the beauty of a hall crammed full. It offered fast separation.

'It's a huge crowd, Mr Cox.'

'And early days yet. We could get more.'

For every face Jenny recognised, there were two she didn't know. She danced with a farmer's son who told her his father had a place twenty-five miles west. Several groups had driven up from Willama. Jenny was dancing with a Willama boy when Amber saw her, and there was no more reaction than a slight widening of the eyes. Norman even offered his tight little smile. Weird seeing him with his arms around his Mrs Morrison. So weird. Something strange had happened to them.

A magical night though, the best of Jenny's life. Miss Rose and John McPherson were there. They were talking to Jenny and Dora when Mr Cox and the clarinet player from the talent quest joined them. He was in the Willama band and he'd recognised her. He asked if she'd like to sing a few songs with them during supper. She didn't mind. She'd been standing on that stage singing since she was five years old, and she had her beautiful blue dress back, and everything in the entire world was perfect.

Until the twins ran out of petrol, or realised there were more people to annoy in the hall than outside. They got in via a side door, unshaven, unwashed, still wearing the clothes they'd come home in, and they made a beeline for Jenny and Dora.

'As if we'd dance with you,' Jenny said.

'Buzz off,' Dora said.

Maisy had told them they smelled like polecats, which may have been insulting to the polecat, but they were determined to dance, their chosen partners agreeable or not. One grabbed Jenny, the other one made a grab for Dora. She kicked him. He shoved her. The floor was slippery. Dora's foot went from beneath her and down she went, petticoats flying, long legs flashing their garters. Which brought Joss and Geoff Palmer running. They took on a twin each. Joss lost his collar, a twin wouldn't be seeing out of one of his eyes for a week, two band members jumped down from the stage, half a dozen men left their partners stranded, and after a five-minute scuffle the twins were thrown out the same door they'd come in.

'Trust you to be in the thick of it,' Sissy said.

'Buzz off, Sissy,' Jenny said, more concerned about Dora's ankle and Joss's collar. She should have been concerned about Amber standing behind that rainbow taffeta, behind long slim Jim.

'Home,' Amber said.

'What have I done?'

'Made a spectacle of yourself by flirting around with those larrikins.'

'I didn't. I wouldn't. I hate the sight of them. We told them to leave us alone.'

'You come over here dressed up like a little tart in your borrowed finery and what do you expect?' Amber hissed.

'It's your old dress. I dyed it.'

Mrs Cox came to look at Dora's ankle, so Amber had to look at it too. Broken ankle or not, Dora wanted to go to the lav and pull her stocking up. One garter had slid down to her knee. Jenny went with her. Her brothers came out to stand at the side door while they ran down the back. They took their time, and when they returned, Amber and Norman had gone into supper and the clarinet player was looking for her.

Jenny sang for half an hour, sang her lungs out, and perhaps glimpsed her future. She wanted to sing when she was older. A lot of people said she had a good voice.

Not many dancing now, more were watching, tapping their feet. Norman came from the supper room, his spectacles flashing, she hoped with pride. Amber wasn't with him.

Jenny was singing 'You're The Cream In My Coffee' when she caught sight of Amber's pinkish beige in the stage wings, where she'd stood to prompt Sissy through her first recitation. She wasn't waiting to prompt Jenny. And her face didn't look like a mother's face. Tonight wasn't over yet. Jenny hadn't got away with wearing that dress. Heart beating like a small drum inside her, but not sticking to the band's rhythm, she forgot the words, until one of the men in the band joined in.

There are two sides to a stage. Amber was at the supper room side door. Jenny didn't wait to tell anyone she'd done enough singing. She went west, out through the dressing room-cum-committee room where Mr Lewis manned the side door, keeping the twins out while letting dancers in and out to the lavatories.

She ran down the back and used the lav this time. Amber's eyes gave her nerves in the bladder. Hitched up her stockings, adjusted her garters, washed her hands and opened the door.

And the twins were there, blocking her way.

'I'm sick of you. Get away from this door or I'll scream out to Mr Lewis.'

'Scream,' one said.

'I've had enough of you to last me ten years. Let me get past!'

'We wouldn't mind having a bit more of you,' one said.

She wasn't dumb, mainly because Dora wasn't dumb. She knew that everything those twins said had a dirty second meaning.

'Mr Lewis,' she yelled. 'Mr Lewis!'

Someone was coming, because the twins glanced over their shoulders then skulked off down towards the men's lavatories.

Amber took their place. 'This time you've gone too far.'

'They wouldn't let me out,' Jenny said, attempting to get by her.

Amber pushed her and Jenny stepped back.

'One not enough for you, you little slut?' A hiss of words; Norman must have been nearby. 'Out here in the dark with the two of them.' Hissing like a snake, full up with venom.

'Daddy? Are you there?'

'Jennifer?' He was out there.

He changed Amber from snake to mother. 'You were asked tonight to wear your brown, Jennifer, and you come over here dressed up like a twenty-year-old tart.'

'Did you look like a tart when you wore it?'

Got past her. Got out. Norman was standing halfway between the lavatory and the hall's side door.

Too much material in that old skirt. Amber caught a handful of it. Fabric, abused by dye, moth-eaten, silverfish-nibbled, mouldy, of course it ripped. Jenny heard that rip, saw the gash of white petticoat, and it may as well have been a gash in her heart.

'Destroyer,' she said, snatching the material, hearing it rip again as she pulled free, backed away. 'Evil, jealous destroyer of everything good. Does Sissy look better now? Have you made her look better now?'

Norman approached and Jenny ran from him too, darted between trees and out to Cemetery Road, the train of blue skirt dragging behind her, feeling the chill of the night cutting through the thin fabric of her petticoat.

Walked to the corner and glanced back, glanced towards Maisy's house. Couldn't walk past the hall with her skirt dragging, couldn't go to Maisy anyway. Those mongrels could be there. Gathered up what she could of her skirt and looked at the post office, thought about knocking on Mr Foster's door. Couldn't go there late at night, her dress hanging half off her. Nowhere to go. Stood on the corner panting with anger, panting to hold back her tears, panting with frustration and hurt for that dress, panting out her hatred of those twins who were the cause of her being on this corner — and hatred of Amber. Hated her. Hated her, and hated Norman for being so blind he couldn't see who she really was.

Nowhere to go. Nowhere. She was a swaggie with nowhere to sleep and freezing cold. Only Granny, and Granny two miles away, down a dark road, in the middle of the night. She couldn't go down there.

Nowhere.

Shivering, shivering and crying, because there was only one place to go — over the road and through Norman's gate, down the side of the house. The doors were never locked. She went inside, went into her room to strip a blanket from her bed. Cocooned in wool, she returned to the verandah, where she sat in the old cane chair, head down, bawling her heart out, bawling so loud she didn't hear him coming until he stepped up to the verandah.

'You'll catch your death of cold. Go to your bed.'

'I didn't do anything wrong. I sang. I went to the lav. I didn't do anything wrong and she ripped that dress off me, Daddy.'

'You're a fourteen-year-old child, will dress as a child and behave as a child. If you had done so tonight, as you were instructed to do, you would not have caught the eye of those louts and been found by your mother in a compromising situation. Tonight your wilful behaviour ends. Now go to your bed!'

'She's a liar. I wasn't in any situation. I was trying to get out. And I hate her as much as I hate them.'

'You are beyond me,' he said, and he walked back the way he'd come.

She stood, shed her blanket, heard that skirt rip. 'Don't you run away from me, Daddy. You know she's lying. You know I didn't do anything.'

'There is a hall full of dancers over the road. Do you want them to hear you?'

'It's all right to say she's a liar if no one hears me say it. It's all right for her to be the devil himself so long as no one knows.'

He came back. 'Inside,' he said.

'It's all right for her to half-kill me out here one day, so long as no one remembers it. But I remember it, Daddy,' she yelled. 'I remember every single thing she's ever done to me. She's a destroyer of . . . of everything. She's destroyed our house, and now she's destroying you.'

He took her arm, to move her inside; she grasped the chair, determined that if he wanted her inside, he'd take the chair too.

'I'm never living in that house, never until I die. I hate your house.'

'Lower your voice!'

He shook the chair off. He had her halfway through that door, but she clung to the frame, hand and foot, and her frock ripped again, its skirt still attempting to cling to the raggedy cane of the old chair.

'She stuck a needle halfway through my leg when I was ten. She threw my Alice Blue Gown costume down the lav because Sissy wasn't allowed to recite "Daffodils". She burned that yellow dress so I couldn't wear it. I'm not lying to you, Daddy.'

'Daughters and their dresses,' he said.

'I'm talking about lies, not dresses! Why can't you hear me!'

He'd got that back door shut. He was panting, but he got her into her bedroom, dumped her on the bed and went for his key. Had to turn the kitchen light on to find it. And she was out of that room, the blue-green dress hanging off her, only her knee-length petticoat offering a minimum of modesty.

'Cover yourself,' he demanded.

'Cover *your*self,' she said. 'If that scar on your shoulder is covered up you can't even remember she tried to cut your head off with the shovel, can you?'

'You go too far!'

'And you don't go anywhere. You're acting in a radio play called *Happy Families*, and there has to be a wife in it, and you know she's the devil, but it doesn't matter because she's in the play now and everyone will be shocked if she goes missing — except you're the one who's going missing. I love you, Daddy! I want you to be who you used to be!'

Saw his eyes then, and they looked like the Palmers' dog's eyes the day Mr Palmer took her pups away, just too old and sad, knowing she should snarl and bite and save her pups, but didn't have the teeth to do it. She moaned, looked down at her petticoat, at the shredded blue-green skirt, looked at its very fine colour.

'What makes Sissy worth an eighteen-pound dress and me worth nothing, Daddy? Who says she's worth more than me?'

'We'll speak in the morning.' He closed the door.

'No, you won't, because I won't be here.'

He didn't believe her. His key was in the lock. It turned. He walked down the passage and out the front door, walked back to the ball to dance with the devil, back to smile his Cheshire cat smile.

She felt the tears coming, but killed them with light; glaring white light she blinked from, turned her back on. She'd said she wouldn't be here in the morning and she wouldn't. She'd got that top window sash open once, or got it started. She could do it again.

Up on the bed then, head beneath the curtain and she reached for the twin hooks and heaved — and felt a trickle of colder air immediately. She heaved again, using her knees to gain leverage. Only an inch, but an inch was a start. She'd get out of this town too. She'd go down to Granny's, get her talent quest money, get the train to Melbourne and live with Mary Jolly.

That window refused to budge further. She wasn't going anywhere. And Norman wouldn't sell her a train ticket. And five pounds wouldn't last long, and she wanted to finish school this year because Mr Curry had put her name down to sit for a bursary, which was worth a lot more than five pounds.

Wanted to howl. Instead, she reached for the curtain rod and pulled it down, pitched it and the curtains at the door. Saw an angry stranger reflected in the dark window glass. Like a black and white photograph of . . . of someone . . . somewhere. Couldn't see the ripped skirt, could only see the puffy sleeves and fitted bodice, see her hair.

But she wasn't on this bed to look at herself. She reached high, putting her weight on that sash and gaining nothing. Sighed, pressed her hot face to cold glass, her brow, both cheeks, thought about giving in and going to bed.

And letting him find her in bed when he unlocked the door? That was losing. That was losing forever. She'd been a singer tonight with a band. She could get a job in Melbourne singing with a band. She could . . .

Up again, standing feet spread, her fingers through the space she'd opened up. Free fingers, chilled fingers. And she swung on that window. And it slid past the jamb and kept on going. She gained eight inches, then gained another inch before it jammed again. It needed soap on the runners. Maisy used soap when her windows jammed. No soap available, she tried saliva, and thought of Dora who had once told her that if a mouse could get his head through a hole, the rest of him would fit. She considered trying to get her head through, imagined Norman opening that door in the morning and finding her hanging, head out, frozen stiff.

She could hear the band well with the window open. They'd been hired to play until one, which was why the ball was on a Friday night instead of Saturday. Saturday entertainment had to end at midnight — dancing was a sin on Sundays. Loved dancing. It would have been all right if the twins had stayed in Melbourne, if they'd left her alone.

'Mongrel polecats,' she said.

Icy air was coming with the music through that gap; she climbed down and opened drawers, opened her wardrobe. Most of what she owned was at Maisy's, but Norman's carton of Sissy's hand-me-downs was still underneath the bed. She found an old cardigan, an old winter skirt, a long-sleeved sweater; hoped no one was looking in the window as she stripped off the remains of the ballgown and pulled the sweater over her head. The skirt was too long, but warm. The cardigan, hand-knitted for a larger frame, reached her thighs. Almost smiled at her new reflection in the window glass, almost laughed. It must have been past midnight: Cinderella had returned to her fairytale and Jenny in hand-me-downs was back. Warm hand-me-downs, though.

Warmth gave energy, and those rotten old baggy clothes renewed her determination. She belted the window with the heel of her sandal, belted it top and sides, and on her next heave when it moved a good four inches she called it enough.

The cardigan was too bulky. She took it off and dropped it through to the ground, dropped the sandals too, wished she had her school shoes and socks, but she didn't.

Up onto the window ledge then, one toe gripping the top of the lower sash, and she got a leg out. Easier then. She had to flatten her body, she had to wriggle, but she got through, got both feet on the outside sill, then jumped to the ground. The sandals had chilled. They chilled her feet. The cardigan was still warm. Blessing whoever had knitted that thing, she buttoned it as she ran out the side gate and along the fence to the road.

The ball must have been winding down. They were playing a slow waltz. Still a few couples standing out the front of the hall, but they were more interested in each other than in a shapeless old woman hurrying diagonally across the road towards the park.

She had no plan other than making it to the bandstand, which didn't offer much shelter but had a roof. A couple had already claimed it. They were kissing. They didn't see her. The sports oval had a shelter shed. She'd stay there until daylight.

Through the park then, head down, over the road to the oval. Its fence, a low, white-painted post-and-rail, encouraged her to sit a while. There was no light in the street. No one would see her sitting there swinging frozen feet in time to the music.

Wondered what time daylight came, wondered what Granny would say when she turned up at her place for breakfast. Wondered what Norman would say when he unlocked that door and found the bed empty, the window that wouldn't open left wide open.

The chill creeps into your bones when you're sitting on a timber fence in the middle of winter, no overcoat on, no beret to keep your ears warm. Pretty little Jenny Morrison, swinging borrowed sandals above the frosty ground, hugging her old cardigan close. Pretty little fourteen-year-old girl on a collision course with her future.

They crept up on her like a pair of mongrel dogs rounding up a runaway lamb. She didn't even have the good sense to bleat.

EXPECTING THE UNEXPECTED

Few recognise evil when it comes in a familiar shape. Adolf Hitler had been around for years, his goose-stepping troops were running amok in Europe, but on the night of the ball few recognised him as a real threat to world peace.

'There is no likelihood that the British Empire will be dragged into the European turmoil,' Chamberlain, the British prime minister said. 'A communiqué protesting Germany's actions in the strongest terms will be sent to Herr Hitler,' he said. His protest was about as effective as a teacup of water thrown on an out-of-control forest fire. It didn't raise a splutter.

Norman's protest to Gertrude when, on the Sunday after the ball, he rode down to bring home his absconding daughter caused more than a splutter.

'I have been remiss in my handling of the girl, and it ends today,' he said. 'Given her . . . her known family history, when added to the difficulties of . . . of pubescence, the girl requires a mother's firm hand.'

'I've seen the marks of your wife's firm hand, Norman, so don't come down here spouting about her firm hands to me. She's got no love for that little girl and never has — and if you can't see that by now, then you're more fool than I gave you credit for.'

'You forget yourself —'

'I've forgotten a lot — and forgiven more. I wanted to raise that little girl ten years ago and made the mistake of sending her home. She's old enough now to decide where she wants to live, and she wants to live with me.'

She hadn't invited him to enter. Now she invited him to leave by closing the door, but she changed her mind and opened it again.

'I carried Amber home from India under my heart and in my heart, Norman. I saved her from the crazy swine I'd wed, and for what? No mother should live long enough to wish her child unborn, but I've lived that long. Your wife has got her father's bad blood in her, and I'm past denying it. Now go home. You've upset me enough.'

'I . . . the girl has school to go to. She is being primed for a bursary.'

'I'll get her to school.'

'I'll speak to her . . .'

'You won't. She saw you coming. She's gone.'

Gertrude closed the door.

Norman stood a moment, then walked away, his stomach burning. He walked to his bicycle and stood staring down at the machine he had purchased with so much happiness, remembering other days, that bike leaning against the walnut tree. The child who had ridden behind him was gone. The child's seat had long been removed. He turned, looked back at the house. His mother-in-law was not a harsh woman. She had never been a harsh woman. He shuddered, picked up his bike and mounted.

The forest road had been built up in recent years. There was a steep rise to negotiate where Gertrude's track joined the road. He dismounted and walked his bike up the rise. He did little riding these days; his calf muscles were protesting.

The mind at times is an evil tool. It can choose to replay one's worst hours over, over and over again. Once a gate to the dark sections of the mind is opened, there is no locking of it. It swings on screaming hinges.

No mother should live long enough to wish her child unborn . . .

For weeks after the talent quest, Norman had kept his distance from his house, but at its best a hotel is not a home, and Horrie

Bull's hotel was far from the best. It had worsened once taken over by the city police, worsened to such an extent Norman had spent his days staring at his house, craving his own bathtub where he might spend more than five minutes without someone hammering at the door to get in. He had made wild plans, had considered throwing that woman bodily out of his house. He'd come up with the idea of offering her a hundred pounds for vacant possession. Then the little Dobson girl's funeral, and a letter from Cecelia, followed by an invitation to dinner.

'We need to talk, Norman,' his wife had said.

Certainly they needed to talk. She'd asked him to come by at six. He'd agreed. She'd served him a fine meal: her braised lamb shanks with mashed potatoes, one of his favourites, followed by an apple pie. He had praised her skill in the kitchen, sipped tea from his own large cup while waiting for her to raise her concerns. She had not.

Having moved to the parlour, he'd sat leafing through an old newspaper, his mind wandering over the road to Jennifer, wandering to the city to Cecelia, his eyes glancing from the pages of the newspaper to his housekeeper, willing her to get to whatever was on her mind.

He had fed her pills to the fishes. Perhaps she intended asking him to procure more. He would not. Or had she heard again from Cecelia? The girl required more money, no doubt. No doubt.

'You have heard again from Cecelia,' he said.

She had not. She said she had seen Jennifer at the post office, said she saw her walking by from time to time. He said that Jennifer was well, that he spoke to her daily, that he had been proud of her maturity at the Dobson funeral.

'A sad day,' Amber said.

He'd asked after Gertrude. She said she had been to the house twice. Their conversation deteriorated to the weather. Then came the silence, long, longer.

'A woman of my age still has needs, Norman.'

'Yes,' he said. The seven shillings and sixpence housekeeping wage he had been paying her had, since the talent quest, gone towards paying for his own accommodation — and rightly so. But no doubt she had some womanly need and had invited him to the house to speak of her missing wages. Relieved, he'd folded his newspaper.

'I have been considering a small sum, Mrs Morrison, enough to give you a little security. As you know I am not a rich man, but perhaps fifty pounds could be found —'

He had misunderstood her womanly needs. She had surprised him, made advances towards him in his mother's parlour, in a room bright with electricity. His position in the deep chair made evasion difficult, though he had fought valiantly to evade her. He'd hit her with his folded newspaper, hit her until the thing had fallen apart — as had his resolve.

His experience of women began and ended with Amber; began late, ended early. Show me the middle-aged fool who will refuse a willing woman and I will show you a man who is not a man. Norman was a man. He had taken her on his mother's velvet carpet — or she had taken him. Thankfully, his mother's heavy drapes had been drawn.

He'd escaped. Had returned at a loping run to his hotel bed, though not to sleep.

A long night, followed by a longer day, his face burning for much of it as he recalled intimate details. He would remove her. He would go to Denham and have her removed. Instead, he returned to that house of carnality — only to pay her for services rendered, seven shillings and sixpence, which he placed on the kitchen table.

She hadn't wished him to leave. Again she had her way with him — or he with her. The following afternoon he'd given up his room at the hotel.

Certainly his wife was not the girl he had wed. From the earliest days of their marriage she had never been a willing partner in the bedroom and had considered his Saturday evening requests for relief as excessive. In the days between his return to the house and Cecelia's return from the city, Amber had encouraged him in excesses. Her knowledge of things carnal appalled him — after the event. His knowledge of where she had gained her vast experience of the male body appalled him — and excited him. Others had paid for her sinful service. He could partake of the service without the sin. She was his wife — and this knowledge appalled him.

He was on the slipway to hell — but for a time it had been a very fine ride.

Cecelia again installed in his house, had offered some respite from fornication, though not from the bitching of his bitches.

'You should have seen her today, Mum. She was wearing that red dress of Dawn Macdonald's and it hardly came down to her knees.'

'She's heading for big trouble.'

And in bed at night — after servicing. 'We made a mistake by taking her in, Norman. You can't make a silk purse out of a sow's ear.'

'Indeed you cannot, my dear.'

Cecelia was his proof of that. Hours and a small fortune had been spent in attempting to shape that girl into that which she was not. A sow's ear is a sow's ear — as a Duckworth is a Duckworth, and that rainbow taffeta ballgown, purchased at an exorbitant price, only adding to her Duckworthness. And his Jenny-wren standing on stage in moth-eaten blue, singing like an angel.

I didn't do anything wrong, Daddy.

He had locked the door that night and thought little more about it. They'd come home late and heard no sound from the locked room. He had not felt the chill from that open window, not then. His whore had required his assistance in getting herself from her gown.

A heavy frost covered the earth by morning. He'd risen late, had felt the icy draught coming from beneath Jennifer's door. The window that refused to open was open. In his rush to close it, he'd tripped over the curtain rail. The noise of his landing brought the whore from his bed.

'Her mother was an unwed harlot, Norman. What else can you expect?'

What makes Sissy worth an eighteen-pound dress and me worth nothing, Daddy?

'It's in the blood, Norman. That girl will lie until she's blue in the face. She'll tell you that black is white and look you in the eye while she's lying.'

She stuck a needle halfway through my leg when I was ten, Daddy.

'We did our Christian duty by her, Norman. We gave her a good home, fed her, clothed her, gave her our name — now she's intent on dragging it through the dirt.'

I've never lied to you, Daddy.

'I saw what she was doing with those twins, Norman. And I can tell you straight, it disgusted me.'

What makes Sissy worth an eighteen-pound dress and me worth nothing, Daddy?

Your mother, the whore. Your father, the fool, my pretty songbird.

'It's in the blood, Norman.'

See what treasures we find when we discount blood, Mother Foote . . .

Your wife has got her father's bad blood in her, and I'm past denying it . . .

Norman didn't go home that Sunday. He walked his bicycle into town where he leaned it against the fence in the hotel's back lane. It spent the remainder of Sunday afternoon there, also the evening, his bike quite at home against the fence, Norman at home in the dining room. He drank quickly to forget, and by eight that evening he'd been so successful, he'd forgotten what it was he had wished to forget.

The share market was making up lost ground. Unemployment was down to eight per cent. There was room for optimism, the newspapers reported.

Little optimism for the farmers. Wool prices were down to eleven pence a pound, well below the last five-year average; wheat was bringing in two and six a bushel.

September came with its scent of almond blossom and milking cows and crushed grass, but little hope.

The situation in Europe was becoming critical, the newspapers reported.

"I propose to come over at once to see you, with a view to trying to find a peaceful solution," Chamberlain wrote to Hitler. *"I propose to come by air and am ready to make a start tomorrow. Please indicate the earliest time that you can see me and suggest a place of meeting."*

'Give him six months, twelve at the most,' Charlie White told anyone who would listen.

'The Germans don't want another war,' many argued.

'They're ready for this one. You mark my words. We'll see a war like the world has never known,' Charlie said.

Woody Creek was at its best in spring, but winter was coming in Europe.

By November, Norman had dropped two stone in weight. He looked ragged. His knees felt ragged. He spent too much time on them, prayed each night beside his junk room bed.

'Forgive us our trespasses as we forgive those who trespass against us. And lead us not into temptation . . .'

'For God's sake, Norman, will you shut up your praying and get into bed? You'll catch your death of cold, and give it to me and Cecelia again.'

He had given them everything else. Why not a cold?

December, and the green of Woody Creek surrendered to brown, the bush road surrendered to dust, and Norman surrendered to depression. He forgot where he was going, forgot the time, forgot to wake in the morning — or wished not to. He forgot to bathe, to shave. Forgot to forget.

In December, Miss Rose finally surrendered to John McPherson. She wed him in the Catholic church on the Sunday after the school concert.

'She's years older than him. What does she think she's doing getting married at her time of life?'

'Such a pretty wedding,' Margaret Hooper said, still unready to surrender to spinsterhood.

A magical wedding, trapped by the groom's own camera, Joss Palmer behind it that day, given instruction on what to press and when to press it, while John took his proud place, for once on the wrong side of the lens.

On the final evening of December 1938, half of Woody Creek said goodbye to the old year at the Town Hall Party. Gertrude had spent the evening preparing fruit for her apricot jam. Now she sat reading, catching up on her newspapers.

> *Looking back over 1938, which for the world was a year of tremendous shocks and difficulties, Australia could be grateful for coming through it so well. Although there was a decline in the volume of international trade, a heavy fall in the prices of some of our major exports, and the effects of the drought were felt on our agriculture, as the year draws to a close Australia finds herself in a better position generally than most other countries.*
>
> *There have been wonderful advances in our manufacturing industry. The number of hands employed in these industries increased by twenty-two thousand. An aircraft-manufacturing plant is now at work in Victoria on the first large order of modern planes for the Royal Australian Air Force. Australia is a step nearer to manufacturing cars. A company with fifty thousand in capital to invest is now setting up a factory which will produce radiator assemblies.*

She turned the page and glanced towards the green curtain. Jenny had been in bed since nine. Hard to believe that fifteen years ago tonight, Nancy Bryant had carried that tiny mite into her house. Fifteen years? 'The older I grow, the faster a year goes,' she murmured.

Her mind far away, she sensed rather than heard movement behind her.

'I hope that's you and not a burglar, darlin'.'

'Hold me, Granny?'

Gertrude held her, held her closer when she felt that slim nightgown-clad frame trembling.

'What is it, pet?'

'Can you put the light out?'

It came out in the dark, came out shredded like the skirt of that blue-green gown, came out at times like a cat dragged backwards through a hole, fighting and clawing all the way, but it came out.

'I was so stupid. I was so stupid. I wasn't even scared. I was mad because Dad had locked me in, I was madder at them because it was all their fault. I called them names, Granny, and told them to go to hell. I thought it was just another one of their tormenting games.'

Perhaps it had started out as a game, one twin egging on the other. When they'd taken her arms and run her across the oval, when they'd pushed and pulled her through the hole in the cemetery fence, it had seemed like the sort of stupid childish thing they'd always done. Perhaps it had still been a game when they'd held her down on Cecelia Morrison's fancy tombstone and told her they were sacrificing her for some decent weather.

'Whoops, we forgot to bring the sacrificial dagger,' one said.

'Have you got something that would do the job? Because, by the Jesus, I have,' the other one said.

'I dare you.'

'Don't you dare me, you ugly bastard.'

That's when she'd known it wasn't a game. That's when she'd got scared. That's when she'd known that climbing out the window didn't matter; when she'd known it didn't matter if everyone at the town hall came running across the oval, if Amber called her a common little trollop in front of the whole town. She'd screamed, until one of them had shoved his filthy hand into her mouth and she'd gagged.

You can't scream when you're gagging. Tried to fight them — like a choking rabbit fighting off two rabid dogs.

'They took turns, Granny. They swapped places and took turns on me.'

VINDICATION

Gertrude held her all night in her bed. She didn't close her eyes and was out at the break of day, her stove lit, her pan of apricots placed over the central hotplate to start their long boil. Jenny was still sleeping, Gertrude bottling jam when Vern drove down at nine with a few bags of wheat she'd asked him to pick up for her chooks. She didn't invite him in, didn't want him inside and waking up that little girl who hadn't slept until dawn.

He expected tea. She had to tell him. Leaned against his car and talked, blamed herself for not knowing, blamed herself for not asking.

'I should have seen it, Vern.'

He wanted to drive her in to speak to Denham. He wanted to hang that pair of raping runty little bastards.

'I'll speak to her father first. I'll get you to drive me in tonight. I can't do it yet.'

She spoke to Elsie at midday, spoke to Harry at five, and, like steam forced through a pinhole in a boiler, Jenny's trouble leaking out into other ears released some of the pressure in Gertrude's head.

Jenny didn't want her to tell Norman, but he had to be told.

'He won't blame you, darlin'. No one will blame you.'

Vern came down after the seven o'clock news broadcast. Jenny left in Elsie's care, they drove into town. Norman wasn't at the station and Gertrude wasn't going to the house. She sent Vern in to bring him out.

He came, with the smell of drink on his breath. They spoke to him on the street, the car between them and the house.

'What's going on, Norman?' Amber called from the front door. Norman signalled her back, but she came to the gate. 'What's going on out here?'

'Your daughter is in trouble,' Vern said. 'The Macdonald twins raped her.'

'The twins went back to Melbourne on Christmas Day,' Amber scoffed.

'The night of the ball,' he said.

'I knew it,' she said. 'What did I tell you, Norman?' She sounded jubilant, and Gertrude who had vowed she wouldn't speak to her, broke her vow.

'Get inside Amber.'

'I caught her in the lavatories with those boys, and I'll bet you a pound to a penny it wasn't rape —'

'Get out of my sight or I won't be responsible —' Gertrude said. Norman stepping from foot to foot, wanting to be anywhere but on this street. Knees too weak to carry him away. Vern standing back smoking, wondering how far he should let this go.

'She's been seen riding around with your darkie. It's probably his,' Amber said.

She was close, her face was in Gertrude's face. She looked like her father, and Gertrude had been suffering from the internal shakes since they'd brought her into town that night to stitch up that bastard's head. Her hands weren't shaking. They were large and work-hardened. It was more reflex than violence, a backhand, saved forty years for Archie Foote. His daughter felt the sting of it in her jaw. She backed off but didn't back down.

'For all I know, she's been on with half the town louts for years.'

'You're transferring your own sins onto the innocent. You've got less conscience than your father — and that's saying a mouthful.'

'You grabbed his money fast enough when he was dead, you old trollop —'

Vern had hoped for this confrontation thirty years ago. Too late now. He tossed his cigarette down.

'She wasted a lot of it in buying you out of your madhouse, you snake-eyed bitch of a girl,' he said. 'And got poor value for money spent.'

A big man, Vern, accustomed to lumping bags of wheat around. He tossed her over his shoulder as he might a bag of chaff and carried her in through the gate.

'You take your filthy hands off me, you ugly old bastard!'

'You've had plenty worse on you from all accounts,' he said, dumping her in the passage and slamming the door on his way out.

Denham was drawn out onto his verandah by the action. He stood staring, his wife staring as hard from behind a lifted curtain. Norman saw his neighbour and turned to follow his whore indoors.

'We have to talk,' Gertrude said. 'That little girl is going to need you.'

'In the morning,' he said. 'I will . . . I will discuss it . . . in the morning.'

Gertrude looked for him before train time. She looked for him after train time. He didn't come. He hadn't come by noon, by evening, when Jenny walked Gertrude's track looking for him. And the night came down and still he didn't come.

For two days Jenny waited for Norman, then she gave up.

Vern drove down each day. On the evening of the third day, he brought news from town.

'He's telling everyone she's in Melbourne, that she's taking singing lessons. Margaret came home from the post office with the story at two, then just before dinner Jim came home with it, got straight from the horse's mouth . . . or from your other granddaughter's . . .'

Jenny lay in the sag of that old lean-to's bed, her eyes staring up at the corrugated-iron roof. It had nail holes in it, and when the sun was in exactly the right place those nail holes turned into flashing stars. Only dark up there tonight, only the little light from Granny's table lamp peering around the green

525

curtain, painting eerie patterns in the corrugations. No ceiling ever placed in Gertrude's lean-to, no door, only that old curtain to offer the illusion of privacy. It didn't block out sound. She could hear Vern's voice clearly, hear his every word. Gertrude's replies were not so clear.

'Maybe it's time you took a step back, Trude. For all legal intents and purposes, he's her father.'

'Then where is he?'

'He looks like death warmed up. I saw him leaving the hotel around five and he was weaving.'

'Have you told your family anything?'

'They know nothing.'

'I need a cigarette.'

'They don't suit you.'

'I need something, Vern.'

'I've been trying to look at this thing from another angle since tea, and maybe I can see where Norman is coming from. He could be doing the best thing for her — in the long term.'

'She's a schoolgirl. She was a fourteen-year-old schoolgirl when that pair of bastards held her down and took what they wanted from her. They can't be allowed to get away with it.'

'I hear what you're saying. I hear you. Now look at it from her angle.'

'I can't see past watching them hang!'

'And what good is that going to do her? What good can come out of dragging her name through the mud while you're getting them hanged? I'm not saying that what he's doing is the right thing, but sullying her name won't do her one skerrick of good in the long term. That's all I'm saying.'

'They'll do it again.'

'And no doubt they've done it before, but forget them for a minute and think about her. Isn't it better for folk to believe she's down in the city with her parson uncle, having singing lessons, than to know she's down here hiding a swollen belly? She can come home from her singing lessons in a few months' time, her head held high, and no one any the wiser.'

'What about the baby!'

'The town doesn't need another bloody Macdonald. It's overrun by purple-eyed Macdonalds!'

'Girls don't come through something like this unscathed.'

'I'm not saying they do, but she's not the first it's happened to and won't be the last. There's places in the city set up to handle this situation. They take the infants at birth and find homes for them.'

'And two rapists get off scott-free?'

'What's the alternative?'

'I don't know.'

'It's days of sitting at her side in a courtroom, that's what it is. Days of every newspaper in the state reporting it word for word. It's that girl up against a pair of bastards who couldn't lie straight in bed, and your own bitch of a daughter throwing more mud at her. Innocent or not, you toss enough mud around and some of it sticks. Where's her future then, Trude?'

'She had the world at her feet.'

Jenny looked at the bare boards beneath her feet. She hadn't thought about court cases and newspapers. She hadn't thought about anything except what they'd left inside her. But singing lessons. Singing lessons in Melbourne. That had been her dream a while back, and singing with a band in pretty dresses and high-heeled shoes.

She lifted the green curtain and walked to the kitchen door. They were standing beside Vern's car. He was smoking, Gertrude was rubbing her brow.

'Given half a chance, she'll buy and sell this town before she's done. And to tell you straight, the way I'm seeing it tonight, her father is trying to give her that half-chance.'

'Where is the useless sod?'

'Drunk,' Vern said. Then he saw Jenny, or saw her shadow.

'I'm having singing lessons in Melbourne, Granny. Let him cover it up,' she said.

Time is slow in passing once you can no longer deny that your belly is full of rapists' leavings, when you can feel their leavings seething inside you, feeding on you like maggots feeding on the carcass of a dead rabbit.

Jenny felt dead, spent her days lying on the bed like the dead.

The New Year came in hot. The temperature on 12 January 1939 was the highest on record. The state was burning. Towns were burning, people dying, while Jenny lay on that sagging bed.

Gertrude spoke to her of the baby, that dear little baby which had no more say in its beginning than she.

'It's not to blame, darlin', like you're not to blame.'

'Stop!'

'It's a part of you. Your blood is feeding it.'

'If I could stop my blood from getting to it, I would!'

Caged now, caged by that swelling belly, denied the cool of the creek by that belly, denied Joey's company and playing cards. She hid from Joey, hid from Harry. Didn't want them to see her shame.

Didn't want to see herself. Couldn't stand to think of her flesh mixing with their flesh. Couldn't stand to think of Norman's mixing with Amber's, to think of herself swelling up Amber's belly. Couldn't stand to think of how she'd got out of Amber's belly. Wanted to vomit. Wanted to vomit out what they'd put inside her. Stuck her fingers down her throat some nights, and thought of them and their filthy hands down her throat. Vomited her heart out, vomited until there was nothing left inside her — except their maggots.

The nights were longer than the days. Her head went crazy at night with telling her things she didn't want to know. Knew too much now. She knew why Amber had moved back into Norman's bed. Couldn't block those thoughts. Tried to write mind letters to Mary and ended up thinking of Dora telling her that babies got started by married people rubbing bellybuttons together. Thought about Sally Fulton telling her you got babies by kissing a boy with your mouth open.

Now she knew. Knew everything. Knew they got out the same way they got in. Granny had told her. She'd run away from that. She'd hidden from that.

Recognised every sound in Granny's house, every board that creaked. The boards warned her when someone was coming to lift that green curtain.

'You have to eat to live, darlin'. Come out and have some tea with me.'

'I'm not hungry.'

If she couldn't stop her blood from feeding it, maybe if she stopped feeding herself, it would starve to death.

Birds ate to live. They pecked insects from the roof of the lean-to. She could hear their peck-pecking, hear the scraping dance of their feet as they ran for their next morsel. Hear their happy chirping before daylight, their different calls at sundown.

She knew Elsie's soft canvas-shoed tread. Knew the way she lifted that green curtain just enough to pop her head through, lower down than where Granny's head popped through.

'How are you feeling today, lovey?'

How was she feeling today? Worse than yesterday. Worse than the day before yesterday. And the day before that. And the day before that.

She hadn't known that what they'd done to her could make a baby. When she'd come down here the morning after they'd done it, come while it was still dark, come shivering through that frosty pre-dawn with that borrowed sandal rubbing a huge blister, she hadn't known. She'd seen dogs doing it, but hadn't known that's what made pups. Just felt dirty, filthy, like a dog, and hurting, hurting everywhere.

The water in Granny's tank had felt warm. It was so strange. She'd half-filled a bucket so she could wash them off her and that water had felt . . . felt almost warm. Got herself clean before Granny got up. Got her hair combed. She should have told her. Didn't. Just told her she'd had a fight with Amber, told her about dyeing that old dress, and about Amber ripping it half off her outside the hall, and about her father taking Amber's side and locking her in. Told her enough, but not the worst part. Too ashamed of the worst part.

Harry had picked up her clothes from Maisy's on the Saturday morning. He'd said that Maisy was hopping mad — not about him wanting her to pack up Jenny's clothes, but about the twins. They'd drained the petrol out of her car and gone back to Melbourne.

And thank God, Jenny had thought. Thank God that no one need ever know anything about it. She had her clothes. She had Granny. She had Joey and Elsie. It was over, and Granny had said she could live with her, and Joey said she could ride his bike to school.

She hadn't worried when something went missing that month, just celebrated because it had gone missing. Hadn't known why it had gone missing.

Now she knew. Now she knew everything.

Time is slow in passing when there's nothing to see but timber walls, nothing to do but think, nothing to think about other than a belly that keeps blowing up even when you starve it.

In February, Elsie came in her canvas sneakers with the green wraparound dress she'd worn when she was carrying Teddy. It was too short but nothing else fitted. Jenny had to wear it. It had a belt that tied at the back and she looked like a green spider, all belly and skinny limbs. Felt like a spider, paralysed by a hornet's venom, fresh food for the hornet's maggot when it hatched, just lying there, just waiting to be eaten alive.

Recognised Vern's heavy footsteps on bare boards. He knocked before he lifted that curtain and he spoke about a place he'd found, full of good Christian people who would look after her and find a good home for her infant.

Her infant. They kept on saying it. Your infant. Your dear little baby. They kept on at her, on, and on, and on, and on. As if she cared about it. She hated it. Hated them. Hated Amber.

Dear Mary . . . my dear Mary, it has been so long since . . .

Dear Mary, I have not written in recent weeks because . . . because . . .

The ink of her mind wouldn't stick to her mental page. It was disappearing ink, or maybe her brain was disappearing. Everything was gone, every dream she'd had was gone from her head, like it had been sucked out by Maisy's electric cleaner, like someone had put the hose to her ear and sucked everything good out.

She'd always had Mary Jolly when she'd been lonely. Whenever she'd felt sad, she'd been able to write in her head to Mary.

Up until Christmas, she'd written to her on paper, and called into the post office after school to read Cara Jeanette's mail. She'd written about the ball, or about Cinderella's ball, and about what really happened to those glass slippers. Hadn't been into the post office since a week before Christmas . . .

My dear Mary, thank you for the beautiful . . . for the delightful Christmas card . . .

She roamed in the early morning while the maggots in her belly were asleep, before the birds began their chirping. She borrowed Gertrude's writing tablet on a February morning.

My dear Mary,

I am so sorry I haven't written for so long, but since my mother was arrested for murder and my father's fatal heart attack, I have been forced to seek employment, under an assumed name. I am now delighted to tell you that I have found work as a governess on a large property many miles from town . . .

She wrote three pages, was still writing when Gertrude came out to light the stove. She offered an envelope, so Jenny addressed it. Harry posted it the following day.

THE SPIDER AND THE HORNET

Mr Foster's side fence was a bare five feet from Norman's house. For years he had spent more time than he should hiding behind that fence, listening. He'd seen and heard more than he should, which of course had encouraged him to return, again and again. A single man, now approaching fifty, he was aware that he had no right to spy on his neighbour, that he'd had no right to befriend his neighbour's daughter, nor to encourage her in a deception. He was nobody's hero, had not been built to perform heroic acts, but he believed, rightfully or wrongfully, that he had saved her infant life, and daily since her mother's return, he'd kept an eye and an ear to that fence.

He'd read Jenny's first letters to Mary Jolly. They had been handed to him to fold, to slide into envelopes. He'd supplied the writing paper, the stamps. Through the years, he'd watched a child's handwriting evolve into a young lady's. He knew it well, knew her curled Js, her fancy Ms, as he did Mary Jolly's perfect copperplate script. He'd kept her every reply in a shoebox in his post office cupboard. He saw that script in late February, on a letter addressed to *The Governess, c/o Mrs Foote, Forest Road, Woody Creek*. He took his spectacles off, polished them, placed the envelope on his counter, then reached for the box of her old letters. A random selection set beside the new and he studied both envelopes closely. There was no question. It was Mary Jolly's handwriting.

He'd been told by the stationmaster that Jennifer was studying music in the city, and he'd celebrated for her. When the last letter addressed to Cara Paris had arrived, he'd held it for weeks while weighing up the breaking of a confidence against the getting of that item of mail to its owner. In the end he'd returned it to Mary with a brief note, stating that Cara was in the city studying music.

Now he knew that Jennifer was not in the city. Jennifer was with her grandmother. They had hidden her down there once before. He'd heard the scuffle on his neighbour's verandah on the night of the ball. He'd heard Jennifer's voice. Then silence.

'What has been done to that child?'

He worried about her, and the letter, thinking to confront Norman Morrison. Did he have the right? He had no rights.

Perhaps he should speak to Mrs Foote when she came next to collect her mail — or offer her the letter and ask if Jennifer was well. No harm in that. But Friday passed, and if she came to town, she did not come by for her mail.

Mid-week, Harry Hall came to the post office. 'Anything for Mrs Foote?' he said.

And what else could he do but pass that letter across the counter?

Gone.

But his concern grew. He sat at his bedroom window on Saturday afternoon, sat for most of that Sunday, watching the comings and goings from his neighbour's house. All seemed well enough.

Then on the Tuesday, he recognised the Js, the Ms, on an outgoing envelope, a stamp already attached. All was not well next door. Something was very wrong next door.

He spied more often on his neighbours, his eye to a knothole in his fence, an eye to a convenient rip in the sitting room blind. He watched the wife walk by the post office window on her way to the grocer, watched her hang washing in her backyard.

'Any news of young Jennifer?' he asked on the Friday when Norman came for his mail.

'Doing well,' the stationmaster lied, his eyes fastened on two envelopes. 'Very well,' he said, and he left.

Old images began to haunt Mr Foster's lonely nights. Midway through reading a newspaper, halfway through a meal, in the dark of his bedroom, in the grey light of pre-dawn, he saw that battered, bruised little face . . . hidden from the town at her grandmother's house.

Pretty little blue-eyed blonde. Battered. Smashed. Broken.

Pretty little blue-eyed blonde, face smashed, slashed —

Imagination is an evil thing when you live alone, but he had seen his neighbour's wife wandering at dusk. And had he not personally witnessed her brutality?

'You carry this thing too far,' he warned himself.

Then in late March another letter arrived for *The Governess, c/o Mrs Foote*; and on the first day of April, the fool's day, he sat down and penned his own letter to Mary Jolly, uncaring if he were fool or not.

> *My dear Miss Jolly,*
>
> *I am penning this line in the hope that you are still in touch with our mutual young friend, Cara.* (The first time he'd written that line he'd written 'Jennifer'. He would not break that child's confidence.) *I have not seen nor had word of Cara in several months, and am concerned for her wellbeing.*
>
> *Please find enclosed stamped, self-addressed envelope for your swift reply.*
>
> *Yours faithfully, Bob Foster*

He did not wait long for his envelope's return. It arrived on 7 April, the day Joe Lyons, prime minister of Australia, died. Prime ministers didn't die, they were voted out; and Joe, a popular man, would not have been voted out. The nation in shock, Mr Foster ripped that envelope open.

> *Dear Bob,*
>
> *Like you, I am feeling more than a little concern for Cara. Her father died late last year, and it seems that she has tutoring work with the grandchildren of a local property owner, a Mrs Foote, which, she says, is well out of town.*
>
> *As you may or may not be aware, her letters are often fanciful tales of incredible happenings or odd little poems about her town. One I received recently concerns me deeply.*

> *I am forwarding a copy to you. Your kindness to a stranger in her hour of need tells me you have a good and kind heart, and that your concern for Cara is as great as mine.*
> *My best regards, Mary Jolly*

Mr Foster was still reading when he limped from the post office and crossed over the road to the Denham residence.

The two men stood together at the police station counter, Denham a good six foot and solid, Mr Foster a bare inch over five foot and thin. His spine was twisted, Denham's was straight, but they shared a common bond; a deep-seated loathing of the Macdonald twins; and there was no doubt in either mind they were reading about them.

> *Foolish green spider, non-venomous thing from a web of imperfect creation,*
> *Was seen by two hornets, out seeking fun and with appetites above their station.*
> *Untutored in living, the spider spun on, threading her web with moonbeams,*
> *While the hornets, they buzzed and flitted around, uncaring of green spider dreams.*
>
> *They trap prey with laughter, with strong nets of lies, hook prey with their ugly deceit,*
> *For hornets must feed their repulsive greed, and green spiders the rarest of treat.*
> *They flit ever nearer, their need growing large as they settle for closer inspection.*
> *A gossamer web of inferior style, it offers so little protection.*
>
> *Silly green spider, stung once and again, then sealed in a nest of cold clay,*
> *Paralysed by their venom, unable to run, so slowly she rots clean away.*
> *And so dies the spider, not born to combat, just a spinner of imperfect thread,*

> *While maggots once hatched from the cruel hornet eggs
> suck the last dreams from her head.*

Denham rode a BSA motorbike. It was well known around town but had never negotiated Gertrude's track. He came in the late afternoon. She stood at her wire gate, determined to keep him out. He didn't attempt to force entrance.

'I have information leading me to believe that your granddaughter is staying out here with you, Mrs Foote.'

'You need to speak to her father,' Gertrude said.

'I'll speak to him when I know I've got my facts straight. Your granddaughter has a penfriend who writes to her at your address. I've got a few ideas about what might be going on, but what I'm down here for today is the facts.'

'Her father will tell you she's having singing lessons in the city.'

'I'm asking you, Mrs Foote. I know we started off on the wrong . . . that we got off to a bad start, but you've got the reputation of being a straight-talking woman.' He leaned against her fence, took out a cigarette and lit it, telling her by his actions that he wasn't planning to leave. 'What if I tell you what I know, and you put me right if I've got it wrong? She's in the family way.'

Her reaction told him he and Foster had hit the nail on the head.

'You've been talking to Vern,' she said.

'The girl more or less told her city penfriend.'

She glanced towards the house, then opened the gate, stepped out to the yard and walked him back to his bike, where, head down, she told him all she knew, told him she'd wanted to go to him the night she'd found out, but Norman had decided to keep it quiet, which was what Jenny wanted them to do.

'I need to talk to her.'

'She's barely holding on as it is.'

'This can't be covered up.'

She looked up from his bike to his face. He was no Ernie Ogden. He didn't have the soul of that man. She could have spoken to Ernie, explained how that little girl spent her life hiding behind that green curtain, existing in some form of dreamworld. She would have spoken to Ernie at the start, had his support these past months. She'd never liked Denham. Had he demanded to go inside, she might have given him a taste of the back of her hand.

'The Macdonald twins,' he said.

'Bastards,' she said.

'There's a topic we agree on, Mrs Foote. It's a start.'

And he patted her shoulder and got on his bike.

Jenny heard the bike arrive. She heard it leave. She was waiting, just inside the door. Gertrude couldn't tell a lie.

Norman wasn't good at it either. He heard that bike coming. He watched it raise more than the usual dust as those wheels spun to a halt in the station yard, and he knew what Denham wanted. His burning gut knew, his aching shoulder knew, and he willed a train to come thundering down the tracks so he might throw himself beneath its wheels; willed God to send a bolt of lightning down to wipe him from this earth. No train, no lightning, and the constable walking up the platform. Norman scuttled for his ticket office.

Little room in there for two men, and no back door. Norman shuffled papers.

'Covering up a crime is as bad as doing that crime, Mr Morrison.'

'We had hoped . . . only to protect . . .'

'Your daughter, or your neighbour's sons?'

'My daughter. The shame —'

'The shame is yours, Mr Morrison.'

'In May she can return —'

'Your girl was pack-raped, Mr Morrison. Those two bastards held her down and took turns.'

Norman cringed, turned his face to the wall.

'And I'm going to see to it personally that those no-necked little bastards will have necks before they die.'

Gertrude, tired for weeks, worried sick for months, had spent the night in Jenny's bed promising she wouldn't let Amber bury her in one of Sissy's hand-me-downs, promising she'd cut that seething mass out of her belly before they buried her, promising anything that might give that little girl sleep. It was no use telling her that she wasn't going to die of it, no use telling her she'd delivered hundreds of babies. Jenny didn't believe in that baby. She knew what they'd left inside her.

She also knew Mr Denham; he'd been her neighbour for most of her life. She knew his daughters; and if he knew about her swollen belly, his daughters knew too. She wanted to die.

Gertrude could no longer handle what was going on in Jenny's head. She was afraid for her. They had to get her down to the hospital, whether she wanted to go or not.

CHOICES

On 15 April, the twins arrived home on their motorbike. Maisy told them to get back on it, to get back to where they'd come from if they valued their lives.

'The old man didn't send our money,' they chorused.

You couldn't drink in Melbourne without money. You could drink without it in Woody Creek, or some could.

The mill hooters were playing their off-key notes when the twins walked into the hotel. Horrie Bull served them. He'd filled their glasses a second time before Denham walked in.

'It's still ten minutes off six!' Horrie said.

Denham wasn't interested in the time. He approached the laughing duo. They didn't laugh long. 'Bernard and Cecil Macdonald, I'm arresting you for the carnal knowledge of a minor,' he said.

One tossed his beer in Denham's face and went south. The other tossed his beer and went north, over the counter and out through the rear of the bar. They'd perfected the art of escape before they'd learnt to walk, having realised early that their mother was one and they were two.

Denham followed the one who'd gone over the bar, followed him through the rabbit warren of dining room and passage. His legs were a good foot longer than the twins', his reach was longer. He caught his quarry in the lane at the back of the hotel, brought him down with a tackle, and once he had him down, he sat on him and rammed his bullet head into hard-packed clay, which did the clay more harm than the head, but he did it anyway because he'd been wanting to do it for years.

Fifteen or twenty men watched him get the cuffs on, watched him drag that twin up the lane by the cuffs, drag his trousers off his bum, then drag that bum another twenty feet before the twin yelled 'barley'. He stood and walked across the railway yards, walked like a tame lamb, eight or ten kids now following behind. They saw Denham leave his boot print on that gravel-rashed bum, saw the twin sprawl into the cell.

Maybe they expected Denham to go after the other one. He didn't. He went inside to have his tea, aware that getting one of those little bastards was as good as getting two. There was something missing in their heads, something they needed to get from the other for their survival. He'd have both by sundown. He ate with his family, listened to the six o'clock news, and was standing on his verandah by seven, waiting for the second twin to show up. They'd been separated for over an hour. They'd be starting to feel the pinch right about . . .

'Now,' he said, sighting a trio walking up past the town hall: the missing twin, his father, and a taller man, a suit-clad stranger, who turned out to be a solicitor from Willama.

The Church of England ball and that escapade long forgotten, Bernie, the twin who'd got away, had gone home to his father swearing that he was innocent of carnal knowledge of any minor, that neither he nor his brother had ever put as much as a finger on any under-aged girl — unless they'd paid for it in Melbourne, and they wouldn't have paid for it anyway if they'd known she was under-age.

April in Woody Creek was usually a pleasant month; that evening's warmth brought many out to rake up the autumn leaves and put a match to them. Smoke in the air that night. Raised voices carry on warm still nights, and a front verandah, built eight or ten feet from the main street, is not the best place to raise your voice, not when your neighbours are keen gardeners, not when there's a council meeting at the town hall. Several councillors saw the group on Denham's verandah. A few heard the Morrison name mentioned.

Let a cat get one whisker out from a bag and you'll never get it back in. A snarling, fighting, biting tiger was released that night in Woody Creek, and come morning, the bag was in shreds, bits of it blowing all over town.

The hotel bar had been full when Denham had charged the Macdonald boys, drinkers had gone home with news of the what, but not of the who. Come morning, those who knew the who got together with those who knew the what and the few who also knew the when, and before the sun set on that day, only the few in town who were hard of hearing and the kids too young to understand remained in the dark about what had happened to Woody Creek's songbird. She wasn't taking singing lessons in Melbourne.

George Macdonald had more men in his employ than Vern Hooper. He was a respected man. All right, his boys were drunken little bastards, and there was no doubting that they'd done what they'd done, but they were eighteen-year-old drunken little bastards who could spend the next twenty years in jail — if they escaped the noose — and he had to do something.

Maisy, substitute mother to Jenny for most of her life, told him that his mongrel-bred sons deserved to hang. George and Maisy who never argued now tongue-lashed each other in bed and kept it up at the breakfast table.

On the second morning, the solicitor spoke to the twins, separately and together, and, true or false, they told the same story.

'She came after us,' one said. 'She was having a fight with her mother and she came to us looking for a bit of sympathy,' the other added. 'One thing led to another.' 'And it wasn't the first time either.' 'No, it wasn't either,' the other agreed. 'While she was living with Mum and Dad, every time we come home, it was on,' one said. 'We thought she was older,' they chorused. 'We thought she was sixteen or so.'

The solicitor believed them, or didn't believe them; it didn't matter one way or the other to him.

It mattered to Denham. He wanted to stretch their necks.

Once again, that bike roared down Gertrude's track. Once again, she barred that gate with her body.

'I need to hear the girl's side, Mrs Foote.'

'I just got her to sleep. That cursed bike will have woken her up again.'

'Her mother's telling the same story as those Macdonalds. If I'm charging those boys with a capital crime, I need the facts, from your granddaughter's mouth.'

'Leave her be.'

'What's going on between her and her mother?'

Gertrude turned to walk inside.

'The postmaster is in contact with that city woman. Your granddaughter is an imaginative girl, Mrs Foote. She told that woman her mother had been arrested for murder. Does she know what's real from what's not?'

Gertrude felt a jolt in her heart and she closed her eyes, remembering Amber's kiss at Barbie's funeral, remembering the cups of tea, those pleasant chats with her daughter. Turned off like a tap. Cut off like power to the light globe. On the Friday after she'd stitched up that scalp wound. After they'd arrested Albert Forester for murder . . .

She'd seen Amber's eyes that day. Seen the smile of the victor. No cup of tea for Gertrude that day. No pleasant chat in Norman's kitchen. That's when Gertrude had stopped ignoring her gut feeling that Barbie Dobson's and Nelly Abbot's resemblance to Jenny hadn't been coincidental.

And how could any mother live with thinking something like that? How could she keep it down inside her? Her head spun with it, her heart ached with it, her bones howled with it. Her mouth opened now to let it out to Denham. Then closed, swallowed those words —

And found others.

'Speak to Charlie White about what's between that little girl and her mother. He saw what she was capable of doing to a three-year-old baby. Mr Foster saw it. Talk to him. And Vern. Ask Vern about the asylum. And the chap who used to be up here before you came — Ogden. He's still in Mitcham. One of the Macdonald girls is married to his son. If he's got a phone number, Maisy will know it. Talk to him.'

Maisy was bawling and moving her clothing into the back bedroom. George wasn't accustomed to her tears. He wasn't accustomed to having his dinner thrown at him either, or to having jailbird sons. He was paying his solicitor to fix this, and he wasn't fixing it.

Norman no longer played poker with him on Friday nights, but the two men had a history of friendship. He had to talk to him, see if they could fix this man to man. At seven that night, he walked over the road and knocked on Norman's door.

'We've been friends for years, Norm,' he opened the conversation. 'Our wives have been friends for forty. There's got to be a way we can work this out between us.'

Norman stood in the doorway, head down. He had nothing to say.

'I'm not denying that they should have known Jenny was under-age, but they swear black and blue that they didn't. I'm not saying that what they're saying is fact either. Those little bastards will tell the same story blindfolded and twenty mile apart, but they are telling the same story and the solicitor says she won't have a leg to stand on in court.'

Norman flinched.

'Court's not what you want for that girlie. It's not what any of us want for her.'

Norman shook his head. He had no words left.

George, uncertain if the shake of the head meant Norm did or didn't want to go to court, continued. 'I'm not for ten seconds saying that this is fact, but they swear that Jenny came looking for them, hopping mad at her mother, and asked for their cigarettes. You know her mother told our solicitor chap what she saw — that she caught her with them earlier in the night.'

These days there was less of Norman to cringe, but he cringed more. His jowls hung like rags over his collar, his jacket hung from his rounded shoulders, his trousers sagged, bagged, around backside and knee. His hair, gone grey overnight, they said, looked more grey because there was more of it. He hadn't sat in the barber's chair since a week prior to Christmas. Tufts jutted above his ears. Too much of his life spent now in leaning head in hands.

'The thought came from the boys when I spoke to them this afternoon. Maisy will back me up on this, but both of them have had eyes for Jenny since she was a twelve year old. They're talking about a wedding, Norm, a fast wedding before the infant comes.'

Norman's jowls lifted off his collar, the hairs on the back of his neck quivered. His wife the whore was behind him.

She stepped around him and out to the verandah. He stood staring at the dark green paint peeling from his front door. He picked off a flake, which jammed beneath his fingernail, and while his whore and neighbour spoke of weddings, he stared at that green flake. He'd kept this thing covered up. In a month or so it would have been over and Jennifer could have come home. His lower lids, drawn down by sagging cheeks, were red half-moons, his hangdog eyes constantly wet, his spectacles continually fogged. His shoulder ached, his gut burned . . .

Cecelia, her hair half up in rag curls, half hanging wet to her shoulder stood beside him.

'Mum?'

'Go back inside. And either come out or stay in, Norman.'

He came out. His whore closed the door.

'It's a terrible time for all concerned,' George said. 'Maisy is over there bawling her brains out. Your girl has been like one of her own.'

Sissy placed an ear to the door. She could hear the mumble of voices, hear their footsteps as they left the verandah, but little more.

The wireless was on in the parlour. She turned it off, then went to see where they'd gone. They were at the gate, George and Amber on the street side, Norman on the path leading out.

Until the twins were arrested, Sissy, like everyone else, had believed the singing lesson lie. And she'd resented the money

Norman was spending on Jenny when he complained about every pair of stockings Sissy bought. She knew of a few girls who had got themselves in the family way and been rushed to the altar. She knew of one boy who had got out of town, and the bride's father and brother had gone after him and dragged him back to do the right thing.

The window was open at the top where the wireless aerial had been fed through. She stood on the couch, placed one foot on the arm and got her ear close to the half-inch gap.

'It's a mess all round, but locking those boys up for twenty years won't do your girl's name a skerrick of good in the long term, Norm. A fast wedding will. That's all I'm saying,' George said, and clearly.

Wedding? Sissy wanted a wedding, her wedding.

She was a bottom-heavy girl, most of her weight in her backside and legs, which should have offered stability, but the arm of the leather couch was rounded and covered by one of Amber's antimacassars. Her foot slipped; she grasped what she could, the curtain. The rod slid from its hooks, one end brushing the peacock feathers, which overbalanced the blue-green vase. It fell, then Sissy fell, landing hard on her well-padded backside and her not so well-padded funny bone — which is never funny. In other circumstances, she would have bellowed. Not tonight. She sprang to her feet and, through the now undraped window, saw the three walking out to the road.

Then she saw why. Maisy was coming. Still rubbing her elbow, Sissy opened the front door and crept out, crept down to the side fence, where she crouched low.

'Get home now, George, or by God, I'll get in that bloody car and go out to Patricia's and I'll stay there.'

'They're eighteen-year-old boys. I'm the first to admit that they've got some growing up to do, but they're not going to do it with their necks stretched, are they?'

'She's fifteen years old, and she loathes your bloody sons and so do I,' Maisy howled.

'They're not all bad. Look how they saved old Miller and his missus from the fire. One eggs the other one on, that's all.

You know as well as me that they're different boys when we get them separated.'

'Then shoot one of the little mongrels and separate them, George!'

'Who's going to marry her if not one of those boys?'

'She's a child,' Norman wailed. 'A child!'

'Maisy wasn't much more when we wed. It did her no harm.'

'It didn't do me much good either,' Maisy yelled.

'You're the only bloody woman in town who drives around in her own car.'

'And the only fool in town who walked around pregnant for ten years too.'

'All I was going to say, before you put in your tuppence worth, was we have a fast wedding, pack both of those little bastards back to Melbourne and Jenny moves in with us. She liked living with us. You liked her living with us. You can help her look after the infant. It's got a name, and there's no court case. Do you want a nameless grandchild, Norm?'

Grandchild? Norman cringed. He'd given no thought to the infant, had spent the months since New Year almost believing his own singing lesson lie.

Maisy had thought about it, had thought about raising it. She had two grandchildren in Melbourne, but rarely saw them. She had three in Willama, saw them once a month, if she was lucky. She had one on a farm twenty miles out of town.

'All I'm saying is that we need to talk to her — or you need to talk to her, Norm. For all any of us knows, she might be more than willing to get a ring on her finger before the infant comes.'

'What choice has she got?' Amber said.

SORTING THINGS OUT

It had been a bad, bad day. Elsie came over at seven with the newspaper. She stood at the curtained door, looking at the girl lying unmoving on the bed.

'Do you want Harry to ride in and get Vern, Mum?'

'She seems to be sleeping. Let her sleep. He'll be down in the morning, and if he's not, Joey can ride in for him.'

Wednesday, 19 April 1939: the front page of the newspaper was full of Bob Menzies' defeat of Billy Hughes in a battle for the leadership of the United Australia Party. Gertrude knew nothing about it, knew nothing about Bob Menzies. She hadn't looked at a paper in weeks.

Harry liked the look of Bob Menzies, so Elsie liked the look of him. If there was ever a match made in heaven, it was Elsie and Harry. Why it worked, Gertrude didn't know, but it did.

At seven fifty, Elsie went home, and Gertrude sat on alone, staring at the photograph of the chap who'd no doubt end up prime minister. He looked like a round-faced boy and he made her feel old — as the half-inch of white showing at her hair partings made her feel old — as did her bones. They were moaning about their age tonight.

'Exercise. That's what I need.'

She'd had little exercise these past weeks. More often than not, Joey milked the goats. He cut greens, fed her chooks, carried water, collected her eggs. Charlie's son-in-law still picked up the bulk of them. Harry took the rest into Mrs Crone and to a few

547

regular buyers. Harry carried Gertrude's shopping home. They'd kill her with kindness before she was much older.

At eight thirty, she checked on Jenny. She was tossing and turning but sleeping.

A strange little girl with a strange little mind, always full of life and questions. Who would have believed it could come to this? Who would have believed Amber could become what she'd become? Life played out its cruel games and there was no way to dodge its barbs.

She walked to her door, opened it and looked out at the moon. Amber had loved moonlit nights when she was small, loved to go walking in the moonlight. They'd had some good years.

She sighed, and walked out into the moonlight, out her gate and up her track to the road. She'd feel better for some exercise. What was she always telling Vern? 'Walk,' she said. 'Get out of that car and walk. Legs were meant to be walked on.'

Tonight she took her own advice and walked. One moonlit night she'd walked Amber out to Macdonald's bush mill, near on three mile further out her road — and she'd carried her girl home on her back. Only in her thirties then. A lifetime ago in years, but in living time it seemed like yesterday.

She walked too far, determined to prove she could still do it, and when she turned back, she wished she hadn't been such a dogmatic woman, wished someone was with her to carry her home. She'd cut through her eastern paddock and was walking by her shed, eager for her bed, when she heard it and, like Nancy Bryant on a darker night fifteen years ago, recognised it.

She looked towards Elsie's house. Elsie's Teddy was eleven months old. What she'd heard was the cry of a newborn. She ran, or raised something faster than a walk, swung her door open, knocked a chair over on her way to the lean-to where she saw what she hadn't expected to see for two or three weeks more. It was on the floor, Jenny standing, her back to the wall.

'I'm sorry, darlin'. I'm sorry —'

'Is it all out?'

'Hop into bed. You're bleeding.' Gertrude stepped over the infant and tried to lead her to her bed.

'Is it all out?' Wild-eyed, staring at the wailing bloody thing on the floor, shuddering. 'Is it all out?'

'Elsie! Elsie! Harry!' Gertrude called. 'Elsie! Harry!'

'Is it all out?'

'Yes,' Gertrude said. 'Yes. It's all out, darlin'.' She was holding her up, Jenny's shuddering shaking her. 'You have to lie down for me, darlin'. We have to get your head down flat before you fall down.'

'Get it out of here!'

'I will. You get into bed, and I will.'

She got her on the bed, grabbed a towel and wrapped the baby, and was placing it on her kitchen table when Elsie came through the door, barefoot and nightgown clad, Harry behind her, still doing up his trousers.

They took it away. Teddy was still at Elsie's breast. She fed the baby its first meal.

SEPARATION

The town learned of the birth the following morning. Harry told Vern, who told Norman, who told Amber. She told Maisy, who told her daughters. They told the rest.

The twins learned of the birth when Maisy pitched clean shirts and two bananas between the bars. Like apes, they allowed the shirts to fall to the floor but snatched the bananas, and, like apes, ate them.

The cell was ten by ten. Two narrow bunks fixed to the walls left little room to move. They had a tin dish for washing, a bucket for squatting, spent too little time at the dish, too much time at the bucket, and their cell smelled rancid.

'Have a wash. You smell like Duffy's dogs.'

'It's our shit-can, not us,' Bernie said.

'When's he letting us out?' Cecil said.

'When they fix a date for the hanging,' Maisy said. 'And I hope it's soon.'

They weren't overly worried about their predicament. Their father would fix it. He always did. Their stink had got them down for the first few days. They'd grown accustomed to it now, though not to the bars and lack of space.

Too much togetherness when the togetherness is not of your own choosing, when you're locked in together isn't good. After five days of it, had they found the space to do it, one may have killed the other. Lack of space saved them.

Their one serious attempt at mutual murder had knocked over their mutual bucket, which, after hours of complaints, gagging and high-stepping, they'd been forced to clean up with newspaper. Their wars were now largely verbal, somewhat repetitious, and reserved for the safe end of the cell, well away from that bucket.

'You shouldn't have dared me, you ugly bastard.'

'You bloody wanted me to dare you, you ugly bastard.'

Denham listened in. He made notes, and at times looked on his catch as a big-game hunter might look on something yet unnamed that he'd found in his trap. Sooner or later he'd be forced to pass them on to a larger zoo or release them back into the wild, but for years he'd been tracking them, studying their habits from a distance. Now he had them.

Each morning he woke with a delicious lurch of sweet recall, knowing he had a focus to his day: the feeding of his beasts, the giving of them fresh water, the hosing down of their cage — and them. He was a happy man that April, or he was until that infant was born, until George's solicitor got the Willama sergeant involved.

There was more traffic than usual down the forest road during the final week of April. Maisy came to spend an hour or two with Elsie and her new granddaughter. Brand new babies are addictive to some. Once that scent seeps into the nostrils, they can't get enough.

Vern, always a regular down that road, didn't share that addiction. He could take babies or leave them, and until they learned to talk back, he preferred to leave them.

The Willama sergeant drove down in a sleek black car, Denham at his side. They had spoken to Norman and to Amber.

'We need to speak to Jennifer, Mrs Foote,' Denham said.

She didn't argue today. She led them into her kitchen, where Jenny sat knitting beside the stove, knitting green, not white. She kept her eyes on her knitting, kept her mouth closed, but she listened, and at times shook her head.

They left, and Norman came, on his bike.

Jenny wasn't knitting. She was seated at the kitchen table, setting out worn playing cards. She glanced up when he filled the doorway.

'Come to take me home already?' Her eyes derided him. They were not a child's eyes.

'A decision,' he said. 'It must be made.' He stepped inside, glancing around for the crib, the infant. It was not there. 'Sergeant Thompson . . . He spoke to you?'

Jenny shrugged and placed a card.

'They were here yesterday,' Gertrude said. 'Vern is taking the baby down to the hospital in the morning.'

'Ill?'

'It's sturdy enough.'

They stood side by side, Gertrude and her son-in-law, watching the cards fall, watching an ace placed down, listening to the rhythmic slap of cards, three, then three more. Nothing was as Norman had expected. Perhaps he had visualised the young mother seated, the child at her breast.

'I had expected —'

'Elsie has been caring for her. I'll fetch her over.'

'Don't bother, Granny,' Jenny said, but Gertrude was out the door.

Norman stood watching the six of hearts placed down, then the jack of diamonds, a black five on the red six.

She looked up and caught his eye. 'Want me to get married, Daddy? Is that why you're here?'

He shook his head and stared at the cards.

'Maisy said you think I should marry one of them — for my good name's sake. Is that what you want?'

'Forgive me,' he said.

'I can't,' she said. 'I won't. Ever.'

She placed a card, flipped three more, then three more, concentrating on those cards, not wanting to see his face, to see the weight of his spectacles drawing his lower lids down, forming pouches beneath his bloodhound eyes. She'd warned him. He wouldn't listen. It was too late now.

Black ten on the red jack. She'd almost missed that one. You needed to concentrate when you played Patience. And moving that ten gave her a space for a king — if she could still get that red king from the pack. Once more through, but the king was buried. 'Damn.' Once more those cards were slapped down. Three, and three more, and three more, until there were no more.

'When there are no more moves, the game is over,' she said, sweeping up the cards, shuffling the pack. Sooner or later she'd win. It just took patience, that's all. That was the name of the game.

'If I said I'd marry one of them, would you say it was for the best, Daddy?'

'I would never advise —'

'It would make her happy, wouldn't it?'

He didn't deny that. His jowl rags folded in on themselves.

'Maisy said it would be a marriage in name only. I'd live with her, not them.'

He couldn't advise. He couldn't think. The Willama sergeant had told him to speak to her. He'd ridden down here to speak to her, but could find no words to say. What did he think? What did he want?

The peace of death.

She read his mind, or his eyes, and looked away. 'Constable Denham and that old policeman told me what it would be like in a courtroom. Do you want to sit at my side in a courtroom?'

'If that is your decision.'

'She wouldn't let you.' She set out the cards for another game. 'Anyway, I'm not doing it. *Jennifer Morrison, Woody Creek songbird, sings in court* — do you want to see those headlines in Mr Cox's shop?'

'No,' he admitted.

'Me either.'

She flipped the cards. This was a bad deal. There were too many black cards turned up. She needed a red jack, a knight in shining armour who would come through that door to fight off all the infidels, but Gertrude came through the door with that whimpering white worm in her arms.

Norman turned to look at the featureless being, bald, its ears crumpled. His index finger reaching out to touch was withdrawn and he turned back to the child he'd fallen in love

553

with. Her head was down, her concentration on her game of cards. She didn't acknowledge the infant's presence and Gertrude took her away.

'A nameless child has no future,' he said.

'Fair is fair. It stole mine.' She placed a red eight on a black nine. 'Sit down,' she said.

He sat, sat in silence, watching her flip through the cards. She got the ace of clubs. That was better. She placed it, moved the two of clubs, and turned up the ace of spades.

'Looking better,' he said when the silence grew too long.

'Better and better.'

The king of diamonds made it better still. The queen of clubs to the red king and suddenly she had a game.

'They made me filthy,' she said. 'I've had three baths and I can't feel clean. Their lawyer will make me filthier still. So will your very dear Mrs Morrison.'

She got a red four, which meant she could move the black three. And she turned up the jack of diamonds. She was going to win this game.

'Do you know if she's still got her wedding gown?'

'Your mother?'

'Mrs Morrison,' she said. 'It would fit me.'

'I . . . I believe . . . so.'

'Saved for Sissy?' She smiled. 'That's a joke, Daddy. Smile.' He tried to smile and it looked like a death mask. Looked away, looked away fast. 'Tell them I'll get married if I can wear her dress — and my pearl in a cage pendant and earrings.'

'It wouldn't be . . . be . . .'

'Fitting? Am I too soiled to get married in white?'

No reply. She turned the king of hearts, showed it to him before placing it in the space, which meant she could move the queen of spades, which meant turning up her last hidden card.

And she had it. She smiled, pleased with herself, almost his Jenny-wren's smile. Older, though. The child was gone from her face. That sweet innocence was gone from her eyes.

'You never know what is going to happen next, do you? Maybe a toad will turn into a prince when I kiss him at the altar.'

If the news of Jenny Morrison's baby had gone through the town like a dose of Epsom salts, news of her wedding sent the town's collective bowel into spasm.

Margaret Hooper learned about it at Blunt's when she went in to buy two more skeins of maroon wool for a sweater she was knitting for Vern; he needed more room in his sweaters these days.

'Amber and Maisy were in there with what looked like an old wedding gown,' she reported back at the house.

'Hmph,' Lorna said.

The twins were released from their cell on 26 April, the day Bob Menzies was voted into the top parliamentary job. Maisy wouldn't let them into the house until they'd bathed and shaved. They considered taking off for Melbourne, but Denham had their bike chained to a tree in his backyard. Not that the idea of a wedding wasn't appealing, not that the gaining of legal right to Jenny Morrison wasn't very appealing, except they couldn't both have her.

They bathed but didn't shave. They put on the clothing Maisy had laid out on their beds, helped themselves to a few bob from her purse and headed over the road to the hotel.

Denham cut them off at the pass. 'If you want another dose of your cell, keep heading the way you're heading.'

They didn't want the cell. They went home.

By April's end, they were fighting over which one should get her, but too well matched in height, weight and reach, knowing the other one's move before he made it, left both of them bruised but no closer to a decision. Bernie was the oldest by five minutes. He argued that it was his right to wed first. Cecil, still known as Macka, said he was the first on her that night, that the kid had to be his, so he ought to be the one wedding her.

The date had been set. The wedding was to take place at eleven thirty on Saturday 24 May. The sooner the better, Maisy said. The baby, still unnamed, unregistered, could be registered late and who was to know the difference. She drove

555

her sons to Willama to be fitted out for wedding suits. Neither twin had owned a suit since they'd grown out of their boarding school suits.

George tossed a coin that night. It came up tails for Cecil, but Bernie refused to accept one toss, so they made it two out of three. The coin came up heads on the next two tosses, so Cecil wanted three out of five. George could have stood all night tossing that coin. They wouldn't have agreed.

A week before the wedding, Gertrude watched Maisy's car pull up in front of Elsie's house, a common enough occurrence. Then she saw George and those raping little bastards step from it.

'You can't mean to go through with it, darlin'.'

'Stop worrying, Granny. It's turning your hair grey.'

Grey hair was the last of her worries.

'You don't want to raise that baby. You loathe those boys and you can't do it. It doesn't matter what Maisy says she'll do — or what those boys won't do, so soon as you're wed to one of them, you're giving him the right to take what he wants from you, whenever he wants, any way he wants.'

Jenny smiled and played with the knotted threads keeping open the holes pierced in her lobes. Gertrude had used a red-hot needle, which brought back memories of Amber's needle but hurt more. They'd almost healed. Norman had brought down the pendant and earrings. She couldn't wait to try them.

'You're throwing your life away.'

'You know, in one of Itchy-foot's books, they write about the old people sacrificing virgins to the gods so the tribe stays healthy. They mated virgins with horses, it could have been worse, Granny.'

'Don't talk like that. You sound like your grandfather.'

'I look like him too — even if you won't admit it.'

Gertrude had cut her hair short again, short like a boy's. She'd wanted it short to show off her earrings. Her face was thinner than it had been a year ago; she was thinner, still a beautiful girl, but damaged, and vengeful.

Jenny glanced out the door. The Macdonalds were talking to Elsie, or Maisy was talking to her. George and the twins were looking across at Gertrude's house. She shrugged, walked to the dresser drawer and removed her playing cards, drew out a chair and sat shuffling them.

She had no fear of them. Maybe they'd stolen her fear along with her innocence. She walked that bush road now and didn't flinch, walked it alone by night. We all need a little fear, Gertrude thought.

The light from the window behind the card player turned her hair into a glowing halo of gold. He was in that hair. He was in the lift of her chin, the shape of her brow. He'd had no fear. He'd dragged Gertrude into places few white women had seen. She'd feared. For a time she'd lived in fear.

Shook him from her head and turned back to Jenny, saw him in her eyes and again turned away.

'God help you, darlin'.'

'He's already helped me. He got it out of me before I even knew it was coming out. Now I'm helping myself, Granny.'

Someone had been watching over that little girl while Gertrude had been walking in the moonlight — and had been helping her since. She'd been up eating pancakes the next morning and outside reading for the sunny part of the day, making up for lost time, she'd said, or taking back lost time.

They were coming, Maisy leading the way, George behind her, their duo walking side by side behind him. Strange how features are passed down through a family, Gertrude thought. Those raping little bastards were the image of their father. Strange too how the eye seeks out family resemblances. Man's instinctive need to find a continuity of life. That baby's eyes were a slaty grey, as were all babies' eyes at birth; they'd end up the Macdonald purple. There was little of Jenny in her.

'You're a beautiful girl, and cutting off your nose to spite your face will only make you ugly. Go to court like Denham and that Sergeant Thompson want you to, and let the judge punish them. I'll stay by your side all the way.'

'I know you would.' She picked up the battered old queen of diamonds and turned it front and back. 'It's filthy, Granny, and you can't make it clean again. Too many hands have been

557

on it. That's what I feel like — as if nothing will ever make me clean again. Going to court would be like letting more hands touch me. And the newspapers too. They've got photographs of me when I was clean and new. I'm not letting everyone make them dirty.'

'It wasn't your fault.'

'Who cares, if it's on the news?'

The twins were in her yard and Gertrude couldn't stand to look at them, couldn't keep her mouth shut if she was in the same room as them. She went to her bedroom, leaned against her dressing table.

'Are you there, Mrs Foote?' Maisy called.

'The door is open,' Jenny said.

Maisy came in, followed by her men. 'Is your grandma about, love?'

'Try the orchard,' Jenny said.

'We're here to see you, girlie. We had a talk to the minister this morning,' George said.

She eyed him and slapped three cards down, then three more. Her game wasn't progressing.

'The problem here is we've got two very willing grooms. We need you to make the decision.'

'There are legal papers the minister needs filled in, love,' Maisy explained.

'He says we can't both have you,' one of the mongrels said.

'Why not? You did last time,' Jenny said, sweeping the cards together, collecting and shuffling them while Maisy coloured and George looked out the door.

She dealt the cards then, in two piles, one in front of each twin. She dealt the pack, slapping the final card down hard. 'Whoopie. You win.'

Bernie won her.

Cecil, the losing twin, won a drive out to his brother-in-law's property, where he was told to remain until he cooled down. He left for home when they left, and by sundown Bernie couldn't sit still. At seven that night he set off to meet his twin.

At the same time, Jenny, the third point of this ill-shaped triangle, left on her evening walk. She went the same way each night, through the bush, up to where the road forked, then back again. That road, always her demon, had kept her from Granny's house. All of those wasted years of fearing strangers hiding behind trees. Danger didn't come from trees and strangers. It came from mothers and boys you'd known all your life.

Loved the bush now, loved the sound of the bush by night, the night things, the whispering of the trees. Loved the walking too, and feeling the strength returning to her legs.

She'd let herself get sick because of them. Every day now she ate like a horse and every bite she ate made her stronger. She'd be strong enough when the time came.

Gertrude had timed her walk last night. She was back in twenty-three minutes. Tonight she watched her to the gate, looked at her clock, then went to the lean-to where she reached for the old shoebox placed on top of that wardrobe the night Ernie Ogden had given the stranger's few belongings into her keeping.

Back in the kitchen, the purse emptied to her table, she looked again at the handkerchief and the brooch pinned to it. It was a beautiful thing and valuable. She turned it this way and that, watching those stones flare. But that wasn't what she'd gone looking for; nor the old luggage label, that bleeding ink no clearer tonight than it had been fifteen years ago. Less clear. She set her reading glasses on her nose, got the light at the best angle. The T and the V were clear — clearer now that she knew what had been written there.

The sheet of paper Ernie Ogden had placed into the purse resented giving up its folds, but she flattened it and held it close to the light. And it was there. *Albert Forester*, Ernie Ogden's handwriting still black and clear. *Albert Forester. No fixed address. Inquired after identifying jewellery.*

It was no real surprise. Gertrude had known it since she'd cut Jenny's hair, had known it when she'd seen her silhouetted against the window, when she'd seen her smile as she'd watched the Macdonalds walking back across the goat paddock.

She had his eye colouring, and, like his, Jenny's could change in an instant from the clearest, purest of blue to the chill of the ocean floor. He'd been in her from the beginning. She should have seen it earlier.

And she had his voice.

The first time Gertrude had set eyes on Archie Foote, he'd been at Monk's piano, looking at her and singing 'Greensleeves'. She'd been wearing green that day. She'd known he was singing it to her. He'd charmed her with his voice.

'He looks like the angel Gabriel but they say he's a prize mongrel,' Vern had said. He'd known. As an eighteen-year-old boy, he'd known.

Always something biblical about Archie Foote's looks. The angel Gabriel had aged into old Noah or maybe Moses.

Man's mind is a mystery, she thought, how it works, what disturbs it, how it sorts and sifts information until the dross is shaken off and only a pure hard lump of knowledge sits waiting to be viewed beneath a magnifying glass — which was the way she'd come to realise what had once been written on that old luggage label. The V had once been attached to Via, the T was attached to Three. Whoever had used that label had been travelling to *Three Pines Via Woody Creek*.

Max Monk's city guests had used that siding, as had others living out that way. Monk had last seen his mad cousin at Three Pines, a few months before Archie's father passed away. Gertrude knew the date of her father-in-law's death. He'd passed on in early March of '24. Jenny would have been a bare two months old.

Had Archie taken his lady love up there in December of 1923 — or deserted her and she'd followed him, carrying that old label so she'd know where to get off the train? Got off at that old mill siding maybe, and found nothing there but acres of wheat stubble. Had she tried to follow the train lines back into town? Had she fallen — or been pushed? Had Archie drugged her, tried to take the baby, and she'd got away?

A fiction writer would have found an answer. Gertrude was just a woman with an enquiring mind.

She sighed, glanced at the clock, removed her glasses and slid them into their case. She folded the paper, tucked it with the handkerchief and brooch into the purse, placed the purse into the shoebox, the shoebox back on top of the lean-to's wardrobe. Some things were better off left buried. Someone would find that brooch when she was gone. She wouldn't be looking at it again.

THE MIRAGE

Sissy was the older daughter. She was supposed to be getting married first. The fact that Jim hadn't asked her, the fact that she hadn't seen him in ten days, didn't enter into the argument. She was five years older than Jenny and it was ridiculous, and ridiculous that they were letting her have a white wedding. Not that Amber's wedding gown was worth wearing, not that it was even white, but they shouldn't have been letting her wear it anyway. Jenny wanted photographs too, and they were giving her anything she asked for. And it was ridiculous her wanting it. Anyone else would be hiding their head in shame, and a lot of people were saying the same thing too, not just Sissy. It was worse than ridiculous. It was disgusting, and if anyone thought that she'd be showing her face at that church, then they had another think coming to them.

She prayed for a cloudburst, timed to drop its load on Woody Creek at eleven thirty on Saturday morning. Perhaps that was being too specific, so she prayed for it to arrive any time between Friday midnight and Saturday at eleven thirty. Jim was coming in on Friday to take her and Margaret to a dance. She didn't want rain on Friday. Didn't want a pea soup fog either, but she'd raised one by Friday morning and it hung around all day.

By four thirty, Woody Creek was a white-out. Jim telephoned his father asking him to pass on to Sissy that he wouldn't be attempting to drive in through this fog. Vern rang Norman at the station, who forgot to tell Sissy until Amber had started on her hair at six thirty.

'He can go to hell,' she said. 'And so can she. She's a slut, and if you think I'm embarrassing myself by going within a mile of her wedding, then you've got another think coming.'

By six thirty, visibility was down to nil. Gertrude told Jenny that she wasn't going out in that fog, told her it would be like feeling her way through a bag of cottonwool. Jenny walked every night. She knew that road. Tonight, she didn't turn back when she reached the fork but continued on into town.

Vern was peering out his living-room window when he saw a dark-clad shape walk by. He couldn't tell if it was man or woman.

She was wearing the black overcoat Gertrude had taken from the stranger. It reached her ankles, near wrapped her twice, but it kept her warm. She'd crocheted a beret from wool leftover from a pale green sweater she and Gertrude had spent a week in knitting. She wore it pulled low, her hair tucked beneath it — though not so low it hid her pearl in a cage earrings. She was wearing her pendant too.

Her walking shoes were new and comfortable, though she resented the seventeen and sixpence Gertrude had paid for them. Norman had given her ten pounds for shoes and the necessary. Nothing else was necessary, or not as necessary as the eight pounds of change she'd tied into the corner of a handkerchief and pinned to her bra. Touched it for luck as she walked by the hotel and crossed over the road to the big old peppercorn tree leaning low over the railway yard fence. The night was clammy cold, the fog clinging to her face like damp sheeting, but it was hiding her, as was that black coat.

She wasn't scared. Not one bit. Nothing could hurt her now, not the monsters and murderers hiding in Granny's forest, not the cold, not the fog, not Amber. Nothing and no one would ever hurt her again.

Sometimes the train was late. She'd thought it could be late tonight because of the fog, thought she might have to stand around shivering for an hour, but right on time, she heard it hoot-hooting up beyond Charlie's crossing. With a glance behind her, she ran through the cottonwool fog to the western end of the station platform where she flattened herself against the wall, her eyes seeking Norman. Couldn't see him; and if she couldn't see him, he couldn't see her.

On a clear night if she looked west down those lines, she would have seen the train light coming long before it got to Charlie's crossing. Only the foggy dark up there tonight. Nothing to see in any direction. Norman's house had been wiped from the earth by that fog. There was no fence, no road, only the station, which seemed right somehow. So much of her life had been spent at that station, watching the trains come in, watching them go out. Her first memories were all joined to Norman's station. So many years she'd spent watching all of those people travelling on by to a better place.

An eerie night; the sound of the approaching train wheels down that line was eerie, like a ghost train that wasn't really there, a ghost train come to get one ghostly passenger. She felt like the ghost of Jenny, or the dust of Jenny, all of her juices sucked away by that thing feeding on her, only Granny's coat was holding her together.

It came then, out of the dark, came with the strangest light she'd ever seen. A white light, not penetrating, but flattening against the fog, turning it into a glowing swirling wall.

Or a window, a misty, ripply window like the one she'd seen on the day of the mirage.

She'd run so far that day, trying to get through that window to where the trees and the fences could fly, but no matter how far she'd run, she couldn't get there, not then. Tonight, that window had come to get her and take her away to a land where she could fly.

And she would. One day, when she felt clean again, she would fly.

No passengers boarding. None stepping down. Who'd be crazy enough to end his journey in Woody Creek? This town had nothing to offer, other than its timber. Loaded flatbed trucks waiting for that train.

She sighted Norman, an indistinct figure going about his business down the eastern end of the platform. He wasn't always so indistinct. He'd been big enough to kill giants when she was small. He'd just . . . he'd just shrunk, just grown ragged in the wash of life, that's all.

Loved him still, just didn't like him any more.

She watched him, her back to the wall, watched him until the door of the goods van opened, until the guard walked down to speak to him.

Then she ran across the platform and stepped on board.

MORE BESTSELLING FICTION AVAILABLE FROM PAN MACMILLAN

Liz Byrski
Bad Behaviour

One mistake can change a life forever.

Zoë is living a conventional suburban life in Fremantle. She works, she gardens and she loves her supportive husband Archie and their three children. But the arrival of a new woman into her son Daniel's life unsettles Zoë. Suddenly she is feeling angry and hurt, and is lashing out at those closest to her.

In Sussex, England, Julia is feeling nostalgic as she nurses her best friend through the last painful stages of cancer. Her enthusiastic but dithering husband Tom is trying to convince Julia to slow down. Although she knows Tom means well, Julia cannot help but feel frustrated that he is pushing her into old age before she is ready. But she knows she is lucky to have him. She so nearly didn't ...

These two women's lives have been shaped by the decisions they made back in 1968 – when they were young, idealistic and naïve. In a world that was a whirl of politics and protest, consciousness raising and sexual liberation, Zoë and Julia were looking for love, truth and their own happy endings. They soon discover that life is rarely that simple, as their bad behaviour leads them down paths that they can never turn back from.

Liane Moriarty
What Alice Forgot

When Alice Love surfaces from a strange, beautiful dream to find she's been injured in a gym, she knows that something is very wrong – she *hates* exercise. Alice's first concern is for her unborn baby, and she's desperate to see her husband, Nick, who she knows will be worried about her.

But Alice isn't pregnant. And Nick isn't worried – he is in the process of divorcing her. Alice has lost ten years of her life.

When Alice returns 'home', it is totally unrecognisable, as is the rest of her life. Why is her sister, Elisabeth, being so cold? Who is this 'Gina' that everyone is carefully trying not to mention? And what's all this talk about a giant lemon meringue pie?

Over the days that follow, small bubbles of the past slowly rise to the surface, and Alice is forced to confront uncomfortable truths. It turns out forgetting might be the most memorable thing that's ever happened to her.

Shireen Lolesi
Wives and Girlfriends

Angel Blakely leads the perfect life. With a handsome husband in the form of a famous rugby league star, a million-dollar apartment in Sydney's sought-after Eastern Suburbs, and a gorgeous baby son, she seems to have it all.

But her glamorous life is not what it seems. Beneath the money and the status that go with football at its highest level lies a dark world of alcohol and drug abuse and sexual misbehaviour. As Angel begins to understand the man and the life she's married into, her world starts to unravel around her. And soon she finds herself on the verge of breaking the ultimate football taboo – an affair with one of her husband's teammates.

Shireen Lolesi, the former wife of a high-profile rugby league player, has written a compulsively readable novel set in a high-testosterone world that pulsates with cocaine, binge drinking, groupies and sex. But just how much is fiction, and how much is fact . . .

Ilsa Evans
The Family Tree

Everybody has a book in them, or so the saying goes. For Kate – wife, mother, freelance editor and aspiring writer – it's just a matter of finding a spare five minutes, a little peace and quiet ... and something to write about.

When her cousin Angie announces she has a room to let, Kate's spur of the moment decision to move temporarily out of the family home and in with Angie takes everyone, not the least her husband and teenage children, by complete surprise. Yet Kate's sure that in this room of her own, she'll finally be able to write the novel she's always wanted to.

But writer's block, dirty laundry and emergency babysitting duties all conspire against her. Amid the endless distractions, Kate is drawn into exploring the story of her family: her unconventional childhood with Angie on the family farm, her father's recent death, and the mystery behind Angie's enigmatic, absent mother.

As the months pass, Kate writes her novel. And while it will probably never be the bestseller she had envisioned, it's the story Kate weaves for herself and her family that is the ultimate triumph.